Praise for Fredrik Backman

'About strength and tribal loyalty and what we unwittingly do when trying to show our boys how to be men. I utterly believed in the residents of Beartown, and felt ripped apart by the events in the book'
Jojo Moyes

'A brilliant and comforting read'
Matt Haig

'Funny, compassionate and wise. An absolute joy'
A. J. Pearce

'A stunning read that plunges you into another world. Backman writes with incredible sensitivity and insight. Every one of the characters is real and multi-faceted, having you breathlessly turning the pages, following their fears and hopes, fretting for their futures. This is storytelling at its best: emotional, vivid, wise and utterly brilliant'
Hazel Prior

'It's the most enchanting, beautiful tale'
Ben Fogle

'Funny, sad, clever, insightful, surprising and hopeful. Brilliant in every way'
Sarah Morgan

'A surefooted insight into the absurdity, beauty and ache of life'
Guardian

'A mature, compassionate novel'
Sunday Times

'Warm, funny, and almost unbearably moving'
Daily Mail

'[A] dramatic and highly satisfying novel . . . If this really is the last Beartown novel, it's a hell of a conclusion to an outstanding series'
Booklist

'In his dark but warmhearted way, Backman is a psychologist . . . he creates an astute emotional world much bigger than a small Swedish town. It's a novel you can sink into'
Chicago Tribune

'Backman is a masterful writer, his characters familiar yet distinct, flawed yet heroic . . . A thoroughly empathetic examination of the fragile human spirit, Backman's latest will resonate a long time'
Kirkus Reviews

'Backman's excellent novel has an atmosphere of both Scandinavian folktale and Greek tragedy. Darkness and grit exist alongside tenderness and levity, creating a blunt realism that brings the setting's small-town atmosphere to vivid life'
Publishers Weekly

'Fredrik Backman is known for his engrossing page-turners, and his latest novel follows suit . . . A story of revenge, loss and forgiveness'
Woman's World

'Backman leaves no emotion unturned, sweeping up the reader in riveting family dramas that jump the boundaries of hockey-town rivalries. Another winner'
Library Journal

'Fredrik Backman writes wonderfully about men, with a love and understanding for the ones who would rather solve conflicts with their fists. It's hard not to love it'
Dagens Nyheter

Also by Fredrik Backman

Fiction

A Man Called Ove

My Grandmother Asked Me to Tell You She's Sorry

Britt-Marie Was Here

And Every Morning the Way Home Gets Longer and Longer

Beartown

The Deal of a Lifetime

Us Against You

Anxious People

Nonfiction

Things My Son Needs to Know About the World

THE WINNERS

FREDRIK BACKMAN

Translated by Neil Smith

SIMON &
SCHUSTER

London · New York · Sydney · Toronto · New Delhi

Originally published in Sweden as *Vinnarna* by Forum, 2021
First published in the United States by Atria Books,
an imprint of Simon & Schuster, Inc., 2022
First published in Great Britain by Simon & Schuster UK Ltd, 2022
This paperback edition first published 2023

1 3 5 7 9 10 8 6 4 2

Simon & Schuster UK Ltd
1st Floor
222 Gray's Inn Road
London WC1X 8HB

Simon & Schuster Australia, Sydney
Simon & Schuster India, New Delhi

www.simonandschuster.co.uk
www.simonandschuster.com.au
www.simonandschuster.co.in

A CIP catalogue record for this book
is available from the British Library

Paperback ISBN: 978-1-3985-1638-0
eBook ISBN: 978-1-3985-1636-6
Audio ISBN: 978-1-3985-1637-3

Interior design by Erika R. Genova

Printed and bound in the UK using 100% Renewable Electricity at CPI Group (UK) Ltd

MIX
Paper | Supporting
responsible forestry
FSC
www.fsc.org   FSC® C171272

*To you who talk too much and sing too loud
and cry too often and love something in life more
than you should.*

THE
WINNERS

1

Stories

Everyone who knew Benjamin Ovich, particularly those of us who knew him well enough to call him Benji, probably knew deep down that he was never the sort of person who would get a happy ending.

Obviously we still hoped. Dear God, how we hoped. Naive dreams are love's last line of defense, so somehow we always convince ourselves that no terrible tragedies will ever afflict those we love, and that our people will succeed in escaping fate. For their sakes we dream of eternal life, we wish for superpowers and try to build time machines. We hope. Dear God, how we hope.

But the truth is that stories about boys like Benji hardly ever end with them as old men. They don't get long stories, and they don't die peacefully in old people's homes with their heads resting on soft pillows.

Boys like Benji die young. They die violently.

2

Storms

"Keep it simple." That's a common piece of advice in hockey, as it is in life. Never make things more complicated than they need to be, don't think too much, and ideally not at all. Perhaps that ought to apply to stories like this as well, because it shouldn't take long to tell, it starts right here and ends in less than two weeks, and how much can happen in two hockey towns during that time? Not much, obviously.

Only everything.

The problem with both hockey and life is that simple moments are rare. All the others are a struggle. This story doesn't start today, it's been going on for two years, because that was when Maya Andersson moved away from here. She left Beartown and traveled through Hed on her way south. The two forest communities lie so close to each other and so far from everywhere else that it felt like emigrating. One day Maya will sing that the people who grow up this close to wilderness maybe find it easier to access the wilderness within them, that will probably be both an exaggeration and an understatement, almost everything that's said about us is. But if you take a trip here and get lost and find yourself in the Bearskin pub, and don't get slapped for being stupid enough to ask how old she is, or asking for a slice of lemon in your drink, maybe Ramona behind the bar will tell you something important: "Here in the forest, people are more dependent on each other than in the big cities. People are stuck together here, whether we like it or not, so stuck together that if one bugger rolls over too quickly in his sleep, some other bugger loses his shirt on the other side of the district."

You want to understand this place? Then you need to understand its connections, the way everything and everyone is tied to everything and everyone else by invisible threads of relationships and loyalties and debts: the ice rink and the factory, the hockey team and the politicians, league position and money, sports and employment opportunities, childhood friends and teammates, neighbors and colleagues and families. That's made people stick together and survive out here, but it's also made us commit terrible crimes against each other. Ramona won't tell you everything, no one will do that, but do you want to understand? Truly understand? Then you need to know what led us to this point.

One winter, two and a half years ago, Maya was raped at a party by Kevin Erdahl. The best hockey player anyone had ever seen in these parts up till then. No one uses the word "rape" these days, of course, they speak of "the scandal" or "that thing that happened" or "well, you know . . ." Everyone is ashamed, no one can forget. The sequence of events that started at that party eventually affected political decisions, and money was moved from one town to another. That in turn led to a spring and summer of terrible betrayals, then to an autumn and winter of violence. It started with a fight in the ice rink and almost ended with war on the streets, the men in black jackets who the police call "hooligans" but who everyone in Beartown knows only as "the Pack" attacked their enemies over in Hed, and the men from Hed responded by setting fire to the Bearskin pub. In their hunt for revenge the Pack lost one young man whom they loved above everything else, Vidar, in a car accident. That was the culmination of everything, the final consequence of years of aggression, after that no one could bear it any longer. Vidar was laid to rest, two men from Hed ended up in prison, and a truce was declared among the hooligans, but also between the towns. The truce has largely held since then, but is feeling more and more fragile with each passing day now.

Kevin and his family moved away from here, they'll never come back, no one would allow that. The whole of Beartown has done its best to erase all memory of Kevin, and even if no one here would admit it, that was much easier to do after Maya had also packed her bags. She moved all the way to the capital, started studying at the College of Music and almost became a different person, meaning that everyone who was left could talk less and less about "the scandal" until it was almost like it had never happened.

Benji Ovich, who was once best friends with Kevin, also packed his bag. It was much smaller than Maya's—she left to go somewhere whereas he just left. She sought answers in the light and he in the darkness, she in art and he at the bottom of bottles. Neither of them probably really succeeded.

In the place they left behind, Beartown Hockey was on the brink of collapse. In a town that had always dreamed impossible dreams, hardly anyone dared to dream at all anymore. Peter Andersson, Maya's dad, resigned as general manager and gave up hockey altogether. The sponsors fled and the council even discussed shutting down the entire club and letting Hed Hockey take over all the resources and grants. In fact it was only at the very last minute that Beartown was saved by new money and stubborn local businessmen. The factory's new owners saw the club as a way of being accepted by the local community, and an optimistic politician named Richard Theo saw an opportunity to win votes, and between them just enough capital was conjured up in time to prevent the club's demise. At the same time the old committee members were replaced, meetings about the club's "brand" took place, and soon they were able to proudly present an entirely new "values system." Brochures were sent out with the wheedling message: "It isn't just easy to sponsor Beartown Hockey, it's also the right thing to do!" And against all odds things did actually turn around, first on the ice, then outside the rink. Beartown's coach, Elisabeth Zackell, applied for a job with a larger club but didn't get it—the job went to Hed's coach instead, so he left the forest and took several of Hed's best players with him. Suddenly Hed was without a coach, and was soon digging in the same trench of plots and power struggles that all clubs in that situation seem to end up in. In the meantime Zackell put together a new team in Beartown, appointed a young man named Bobo assistant coach, and gathered a ragtag band of players with a sixteen-year-old called Amat at their head. Amat is now eighteen and easily the biggest star in the whole district, such a serious talent that there were rumors last winter that he was going to be drafted to the NHL and turn professional in North America. He dominated every game throughout the whole of last season until he got injured in the spring, and if that hadn't happened the whole town was convinced that Beartown would have won the league and been promoted to a higher division. And if Hed hadn't managed to gain a few miraculous points from their final matches they would have come in at the bottom and been relegated to a lower division.

So everything that seemed so utterly improbable when Maya and Benji left now feels, two years later, like merely a question of time: the green town is on the way up and the red town is on the way down. Every month Beartown seems to gain new sponsors and Hed has fewer, Beartown's rink has been renovated while the roof of Hed's is close to collapse. The biggest employers in Beartown, the factory and the supermarket, are advertising for staff again. The largest employer in Hed, the hospital, has to make cutbacks every year. Now it's Beartown that has the money, this is where the jobs are, we're the winners.

Do you want to understand? Then you need to understand that this is about more than maps. From above we probably look just like two ordinary forest towns, hardly more than villages in some people's eyes. The only thing that actually separates Beartown and Hed is a winding road through the trees. It doesn't even look that long, but you'll soon learn that it's a serious walk if you turn up and try it when the temperature's below freezing and there's a headwind—and there aren't any other sort of temperatures and winds here. We hate Hed and Hed hates us. If we win every other hockey game throughout the entire season but lose just one game against them, it feels like a failed season. It isn't enough for things to go well for us, things also need to go to hell for them, only then can we be properly happy. Beartown plays in green jerseys with a bear on them, and Hed plays in red with a bull, which sounds simple, but the colors make it impossible to say where hockey problems end and all the other problems start. There isn't a single picket fence in Beartown that's painted red, and not one in Hed that's painted green, regardless of whether the home owner is interested in hockey or not, so no one knows if the hockey clubs took their colors from the fences or vice versa. If the hate gave rise to the clubs, or if the clubs gave rise to the hate. You want to understand hockey towns? Then you need to understand that here, sport is about much more than sport.

But do you want to understand the people? Really understand them? Then you also need to understand that very soon a terrible natural disaster is going to destroy things we love. Because while we may live in a hockey town, first and foremost we are forest folk. We are surrounded by trees and rocks and land that has seen species arise and be wiped out over thousands of years, we may pretend that we're big and strong, but we can't fight the environment. One day the wind starts blowing here, and during the night that follows it feels like it's never going to stop.

Soon Maya will sing songs about us, we who are close to wilderness, inside and out. She will sing that the place where she grew up is defined by tragedies, the ones that hit us, and the ones we were guilty of instigating. She will sing about this autumn, when the forest turns against us with full force. She will sing that all communities are the sum of their choices and that all that holds us together in the end are our stories. She will sing:

It started with a storm

It's the worst storm in a generation in these parts. Maybe we say that about every storm, but this one was beyond compare. It's been said that the snow might be late this year, but that the winds are early, August ends with sultry, ominous heat before autumn kicks the door in at the end of the month and the temperature tumbles in free fall. The natural world around us becomes erratic and aggressive, the dogs and hunters feel it first, but soon everyone else does too. We notice the warnings, yet still the storm arrives with such force that it knocks the breath out of us. It devastates the forest and blocks out the sky, it attacks our homes and our towns like a grown man beating a child. Ancient tree trunks collapse, trees that have stood as immovable as rocks are suddenly no stronger than blades of grass beneath someone's foot, the wind roars so loudly in our ears that the people nearby just see the trees fall without even hearing them crack. In among the houses, roof panels and tiles are torn off and thrown heavily through the air, razor-sharp projectiles hunting out anyone who is simply trying to get home. The forest falls across roads until it is as impossible to get here as it is to leave, the power cuts that follow leave the towns blind at night, and cell phones only work intermittently. Anybody who manages to get hold of anyone they love yells the same thing into their phone: stay indoors, stay indoors!

But one young man from Beartown is driving, panic-stricken, in a small car along narrow roads to reach the hospital in Hed. He doesn't dare really leave home, but he doesn't dare stay either, his pregnant wife is sitting beside him and it's time now, storm or no storm. He prays to God the way atheists in the trenches do, she screams as the tree crashes mercilessly onto the hood and the metal crumples so violently that she's thrown against the windshield. No one hears them.

3

Firemen

Do you want to understand the people who live in two hockey towns? Really understand them? Then you need to know the worst that they are capable of.

The wind isn't whistling across the building on the outskirts of Hed, it's howling. The walls are sucked outward, the floor is vibrating, making the red Hed Hockey jerseys and pennants hanging all around the walls swing. In hindsight, the four children in the house will say that it felt like the universe was trying to kill them. Tess is the oldest, seventeen, followed by fifteen-year-old Tobias, thirteen-year-old Ted, and seven-year-old Ture. They're scared, like all children, but they're awake and prepared, because they aren't altogether like other children. Their mother is a midwife, their dad's a fireman, and sometimes it feels like crises are the only occasions in which this family truly functions. As soon as they realized what was happening the children were out in the yard gathering together the patio furniture and swings and climbing frame so that they wouldn't be thrown through the windows when the wind caught hold of them. Their dad, Johnny, ran off to help in a yard down the street. Their mother, Hannah, called everyone they knew to ask if they wanted anything. That was a lot of calls, because they seem to know everyone, both of them were born and raised in Hed, and seeing as one works at the fire station and the other at the hospital, there isn't really anyone who doesn't know who they are. This is their community, their children learned to ride their bikes in the same cul-de-sac where they themselves learned, and are being brought up according to simple principles: love your family, work hard, be happy when Hed Hockey wins a game, and even happier when Beartown Hockey take a thrashing. Help people who need help, be a good neighbor, and never forget where you come from.

The parents don't teach this last point to their children by saying it, but by doing it. They teach them that you can argue about everything, but when it really matters you stick together, because no one stands a chance if they're alone.

The storm outside the window interrupted a different sort of storm inside, the parents were having another one of their fights, one of the worst. Hannah is a small, slight woman and she's standing by the kitchen window biting her cheeks now, rubbing her bruises. She's married to an idiot. Johnny is tall and broad-shouldered, with a thick beard and heavy fists. As a hockey player he was known for being the first to drop his gloves and start fighting, the mad bull in Hed Hockey's badge could easily have been a caricature of him. He's fiery and stubborn, old-fashioned and prejudiced, one of those stereotypically mouthy high school guys who never really grew up. He played hockey as long as they let him, then he became a fireman, swapped one locker room for another, and carried on competing in everything: who can bench-press the most, run faster through the forest, drink the most beer at the barbeque. She knew from the very first day with him that what made him charming could turn dangerous one day, sore losers can become aggressive, a passionate temperament can turn to violence. "A long fuse but a lot of powder, they're the worst," as her father-in-law used to say. There's a vase in the hall that was once smashed into a hundred pieces, then carefully glued back together again, so that Hannah wouldn't forget.

Johnny comes in from the yard. He glances at her to see if she's still upset. Their fights always end like this, because she's married to an idiot and he never listens, so something always gets broken.

She often thinks about how he tries to persuade everyone how tough he is, but how incredibly sensitive and thin-skinned he can actually be. When Hed Hockey gets beaten it's as if he gets beaten too. Back in the spring, when the local paper said "Beartown Hockey represents the future, while Hed Hockey stands for everything old-fashioned and obsolete," he took it personally, as if they had simultaneously said that his entire life and all his values were wrong. The club is the town, and the town is his family—that's how unshakably loyal he is, and it always brings out the most extreme in him. He always tries to act tough, never show any fear, always the first to run toward disaster.

A few years ago the country suffered terrible forest fires, neither Hed nor Beartown was directly affected, but things were really bad just a couple of hours away. Johnny, Hannah, and the children were on holiday for the first time in ages, they were on their way to a water park down south when they heard the news on the radio. The argument started before his phone even rang, because Hannah knew the moment it rang that he'd turn the car around. The children huddled in their seats in the back of the van because they'd seen this before: the same argument, the same yelling, the same clenched fists. Married to an idiot.

Each day Johnny was away at the forest fires the images on the television news got worse and worse, and every evening Hannah had to pretend she wasn't at all worried as the children cried themselves to sleep, and every night she went to pieces alone by the kitchen window. Then, at last, he came home, after what might have been one week but which felt like a hundred, emaciated and so filthy that some of it never quite seemed to wash off his skin. She stood in the kitchen and watched as he got out of a car down by the junction and staggered the last bit of the way on his own, looking like he might crumble into a heap of dust at any moment. Hannah ran to the kitchen door but the children had already seen him, they flew downstairs and pushed past her, tripping over each other on the way out. Hannah stayed by the window and watched as they threw themselves into Johnny's arms until all four of them were clinging to his huge frame like monkeys: Tobias and Ted around his neck, Tess on his back and little Ture clinging to one arm. Their dad was filthy, sweaty, and exhausted, but he still picked all four of them up and carried them into the house as if they didn't weigh anything. That night he slept on a mattress in Ture's room, and all the other kids ended up dragging their own mattresses in there too, and it took four nights before Hannah got him back. Before she even felt his arms around her, breathing through his sweater once more. The last morning she was so jealous of her own children and so angry with herself and so tired of holding all her feelings in that she threw that damn vase on the floor.

She glued it back together again, and no one in the family dared speak to her until she was finished. Then her husband sat down beside her on the floor, as usual, and whispered: "Don't be cross with me, I can't bear it when you're cross with me." Her voice felt like it was breaking when she managed to reply: "It wasn't even your fire, darling, it wasn't even HERE!" He leaned forward cautiously, she felt his breath on the palms of her hands as he kissed them, then he said: "Any fire is my fire." How she hated and worshipped the idiot for that. "Your job is to come home. Your only job is to come home," she reminded him, and he smiled: "I'm here, aren't I?" She hit him as hard as she could on his shoulder. She's met so many idiotic men who tell themselves that they're the sort who would be first into a burning building to rescue other people, but her idiot is the sort of idiot who actually does that. So they have the same argument every time he goes, because every time she gets just as angry with herself for getting so scared. It always ends with her breaking something. It was a vase that time, and today it was her own knuckles. When the storm began and he immediately went to charge his phone so he was ready, she slammed her fist down onto the sink. Now she's rubbing the bruises and swearing. She wants him to go, but she hates it at the same time, and this is how it comes out.

He comes into the kitchen, she feels his beard against the back of her neck. He thinks he's so tough and hard, but really he's more sensitive than anyone, that's why he never yells back at her. The storm beats against the window and they both know that the phone will soon ring and he'll have to leave and then she'll get angry again. "You need to get worried the day she stops being angry with you, because that will mean she doesn't love you anymore," Johnny's dad told him when they got married. "A long fuse but a lot of powder in that woman, so watch out!" his dad had said with a laugh.

Hannah may be married to an idiot, but she's hardly that much better herself, her moods can drive Johnny to the brink of exhaustion, and her chaotic behavior drives him mad. He panics when things aren't in the right place so he knows where everything is, that goes for the fire engine and his wardrobe and the kitchen drawer, and he married someone who doesn't even think you need to have fixed sides in bed. Hannah went and lay down on one side one night, then on the other side the next night, and he didn't even know where to start with his frustration. Who doesn't have fixed sides in *bed*? And she walks into the house with her shoes on, and doesn't rinse the sink after her, and swaps the butter knives and cheese slicers around so that every damn breakfast turns into a treasure hunt. She's worse than the kids.

But now, as she reaches up with her hand and runs her fingers through his beard and his hands clasp together on her stomach, none of that matters. They've gotten used to each other. She's accepted that life with a fireman has a rhythm that other people can never understand. For instance, she's learned to pee in the dark, because the first few times after they moved in together when she turned the light on in the middle of the night, he woke with a start, thinking it was the light at the station alerting them to a call out. He flew out of bed and got dressed and made it all the way out to the car before she caught up with him wearing just her underwear, wondering what the hell he was doing. It took several more confused nights before she accepted that he wasn't able to stop behaving like that, and realized that deep down she didn't really want him to either.

He's the sort of person who runs toward a fire. No hesitation, no questions, he just runs. People like that are rare, but you know who they are when you see them.

———

Ana is eighteen years old. She peers out of the window of her dad's house on the outskirts of Beartown. She's limping slightly because she recently injured her knee at martial arts training after a boy the same age said something about girls not being able to kick properly. She cracked his ribs with a kick, then kneed him in the head, and even if his head was empty it was still hard, so now she's limping. She's always had a lightning-fast body but slow judgment, she's bad at reading people but good at reading nature. She can see the trees moving outside the window now, she noticed them this morning and knew that the storm was on its way long before most other people. Children of dads who are good hunters eventually learn to feel that sort of thing, and there's no better hunter around here than her dad. That man has spent so much time in the forest that he often forgets the difference between a hunting radio and a telephone, and says "over" at the end of each sentence when the phone rings at home. So Ana learned to crawl and walk in that forest, it was the only way she could be with him. The forest was her playground and her school, he taught her everything about wild creatures and the invisible forces of the earth and the air. That was his gift of love to her. When she was little he showed her how to track prey, how to shoot, and when she got older he took her along on searches when the council called him after accidents involving game animals, when wounded animals needed to be found and put down. If you live surrounded by forest you learn to protect it, but also how it can protect you. In the end you look forward to the same things as the plants, like spring and warmth, but you also fear the same things: fire, of course, but now, almost even more, the wind. Because the wind can't be stopped or extinguished, tree trunks and skin don't stop it, the wind crushes and snaps and kills whatever it wants.

So Ana could hear the storm in the treetops and sense it in her chest when everything was still calm and quiet out there. She filled all the tubs and buckets with water, fetched the paraffin stove from the cellar and put new batteries in the headlamps, dug out candles and matches. And finally she chopped wood, mechanically and determinedly for several hours, and hauled it into the main room. Now, as the storm reaches Beartown, she closes the windows and doors, noisily does the dishes in the kitchen, and plays her best friend Maya's songs on the stereo, because her voice calms Ana, and because the sound of Ana doing everyday things calms the dogs. When she was little they used to protect her, but now it's the other way around. If you ask Maya who Ana is, she'll reply: "A fighter." But she doesn't just say that because Ana can beat the shit out of anyone, but because life has tried to beat the shit out of Ana since she was born, only it never stood a chance. Ana is unbreakable.

She's in the last year of high school in Beartown, but she's been an adult for a long time, the daughters of parents who take refuge in the bottom of bottles grow up faster. When Ana was little her dad taught her to watch the fire in the open hearth, to put more wood on at just the right time, to make sure it never burned out completely. When he has one of his episodes, sometimes for days, sometimes for months, he watches over his drinking in the same way. He never gets mean, never even gets loud, he's just never properly sober. He'll sleep through the whole of this storm, snoring in his chair in the living room surrounded by Ana's martial arts trophies that he's so proud of, and all the photographs of her as a child, which she has so carefully cut her mother out of. He's too drunk to hear the phone ring. Ana is washing up, and turns up the volume of the stereo, the dogs are lying at her feet, they don't hear it either. The telephone rings and rings and rings.

Eventually the doorbell rings instead.

―――――

"It's nothing to worry about, just a bit of wind," Johnny whispers. Hannah tries to believe that. He's not going off to fight a fire this time, he and the other firemen are setting out with chain saws to clear a path through the fallen trees so that the other emergency vehicles and responders can get through. He often complains that being a fireman means being a lumberjack ninety percent of the time, but she knows he still takes pride in that. He belongs to this forest.

She turns around and stretches up on tiptoe and nips him on the cheek with her teeth, and his knees buckle. He's biggest and strongest pretty much everywhere he goes, but no matter what other people might think, he knows that if the children were on the other side of a fire, she'd be quicker than him. She's complicated and unruly and argumentative and really not very easy to please, but he loves her most of all for her brutally uncompromising protective instinct. "We help those we can," she always whispers in his ear after the very worst days, when he's lost someone at work, or when she has. As a fireman he has to be prepared to see death in every stage of life, but as a midwife she sees it in the very worst moments: the first seconds of life. When she says those words they are both a consolation and a way of reminding them both of their duty. We help if we can, when we can, to the extent that we can. It's a particular sort of job, but also a particular sort of person.

Slowly he lets go of her, he never gets used to the fact that a messy troublemaker like her can still turn him upside down. He goes and checks that his phone is charging and she watches him for a long time, she never gets used to the fact that a nagging pedant like him can still, after twenty years, be the sort of person she wants to rip the clothes off of if he so much as looks at her.

She hears the phone out in the hall. It's time. She closes her eyes and curses to herself, promises herself that she's not going to fight with him. He never promises to come home safely, because that would be bad luck. Instead he always says that he loves her, over and over again, and she replies: "Good thing too." The phone goes on ringing, she thinks he must be in the bathroom seeing as he hasn't answered it, so she yells his name because the windows are already rattling loudly from the wind. The children are lined up on the stairs to give him a good-bye hug. Tess has her arms around her three younger brothers: Tobias, Ted, Ture. Their dad thinks it's ridiculous that they all have names that start with the same letter, but when he and their mother first fell in love, he agreed that she could name the children if he could name the dogs. They never got a dog. She's always been a better negotiator.

Ture is crying into Tess's sweater, none of his siblings tell him to stop. They used to cry too when they were little, because you don't just have one member of the family who's a fireman, it doesn't work like that, the whole family is in the fire service. They don't have the luxury of thinking "it doesn't happen to us," they have to know better. So the parents' agreement is simple: never put themselves in danger at the same time. The children must always have one parent left if the worst were to happen.

Johnny is standing in the hall, raising his voice to speak into the phone, in the end he's shouting, but there's no one there. He thinks he must have pressed the wrong button by mistake so he checks the call log, but no one has called since he rang his mother ten minutes ago. It takes several rings before he realizes that it isn't his phone ringing, it's hers. Hannah picks it up, slightly confused, stares at the number, hears her boss's voice at the other end of the line. Thirty seconds later she starts running.

Do you want to understand people? Really understand them? Then you need to know all the best that we are capable of.

4

Fighters

Benji will be woken up by a bang. He won't know where he is when he sits up, his hangover will mess up all sense of scale and he'll feel too big for the room, as if he's woken up in a doll's house. That's nothing unusual, it's been going on for a long time, every morning these days he seems to open his eyes surprised that he's still alive.

It will be the day after the storm, but he won't know that yet, he won't know if he's forgotten what he was dreaming, or if he's still dreaming. His long hair will hang down in front of his eyes, every limb, every muscle will be aching, his body still has the hard musculature of a life in and around hockey, but he's twenty now and hasn't worn a pair of skates for almost two years. He smokes too much and eats too little. He will try to get out of bed but will stumble onto one knee, the empty bottles of alcohol will roll across the floor among the cigarette papers and lighters and scraps of tinfoil, and his headache will hit him so hard that even with his palms clamped to his ears he won't be able to tell if the noise is coming from outside or within himself. Then there will be another bang, the walls will shake so hard that he crouches down, afraid that the window above the bed is going to shatter and bury him beneath splinters of glass. And in the corner of the room his phone will be ringing and ringing and ringing.

Two years ago he left Beartown, and ever since then he has been traveling. He left the place where he had lived his whole life, and took trains and boats and hitchhiked for lifts in trucks until the towns along the way no longer had hockey teams. He has gotten lost on purpose, and has destroyed himself in every way imaginable, but he has also found things he didn't know he had been longing for. Glances and hands and breath on his neck. Dance floors with no questions. It took chaos to set him free, loneliness to stop him being alone. He hasn't had a single thought about turning back, going home, home could just as well be a different planet now.

Is he happy? If you're asking that, perhaps you don't understand him at all. Happiness was never what he hoped for.

He will stand at the window of the small hotel room, hungover and barely awake, looking down on the world outside without being a part of it. Two cars will have collided in the street below, that was the bang that woke him. People screaming. Benji's ears will ring. Ring, ring, ring, until he eventually realizes that it's his phone.

"Hello?" he will manage to say, his voice hoarse from not having been used for many hours, and used far too much before that.

"It's me," his eldest sister will say at the other end, heavy and tired.

"Adri? What's happened?"

She'll choose her words carefully, he's too far away for her to be able to hold him the way a sister wants to hold her little brother when she has to say this. He'll listen in silence, he's spent his whole life training not to let on whenever something dies inside him.

"Dead?" he will finally manage to say, and his sister will have to repeat herself, as if he has forgotten parts of the language.

In the end he will simply whisper "okay," and the crackle on the line as he breathes out will be the only indication of the little pressure wave as his heart breaks.

He will end the call and pack his bag. It won't take long, he's been traveling light, always ready to leave everything behind.

"What's going on? What time is it?" another voice will whisper, from the bed.

"I have to go," Benji says, already on his way out through the door, his chest still bare. The large tattoo of a bear on his arm seems paler after months in the sun, and his many scars glow pink against his suntanned skin. More on his knuckles than on his face, because he's better at being a fighter than most other people.

"Go where?"

"Home."

The voice will yell something after him, but Benji will already be halfway down the stairs. He could call back and promise to call the man upstairs, but if there's one thing Benji learned where he grew up, it's that he can't be bothered to lie to anyone anymore.

5

Midwives

A storm sweeps in across two hockey towns tonight, felling trees and people. Tomorrow a young man and a young woman, he with a bear tattooed on his arm, she with a guitar and a rifle tattooed on hers, will turn homeward to attend a funeral. That's how everything starts this time. In communities surrounded by wilderness people are connected by invisible threads, but also by sharp hooks, so when one turns too suddenly, it isn't always just their shirt that someone else loses. Sometimes it rips the heart out of all of us.

Johnny runs through the house in Hed with his wife, up the stairs and into the bedroom, and she tells him the basics as she packs her work bag: a young couple from a farm north of Beartown is expecting their first child, and when her water broke they set off from home for the hospital in Hed, unaware of how violent the storm was going to be. They tried cutting through the small roads over to the east instead of taking the main road, and were in the middle of the forest between the two towns when they swerved to avoid a fallen tree. They didn't see the next tree fall, and now the car is pinned down somewhere out there. They managed to call the hospital, but there were no ambulances nearby and no one knows if they'd even be able to get through the chaos now that the forest roads are impassable. The best hope for the woman and baby in the car is if a midwife who isn't on duty tonight and who lives close enough can get herself there, even if she has to walk the last part of the way on foot.

Johnny stands by the bedroom door, wanting to ask his wife if she's completely mad, but after twenty years he knows what the answer would be. She turns around so abruptly that her forehead hits his chest, and his arms fold tenderly around her and she disappears into him.

"I love you, I love you so damn much, you stupid idiot," she whispers.

"Good thing too," he replies.

"There are extra blankets in the loft, and the flashlights are . . ."

"I know, don't worry about us, but you really need to . . . I mean, you can't . . . ," he begins, and when she buries her head in his sweater she can feel that he's shaking.

"Don't be angry with me, darling. I'm the angry one, you need to be the sensible one," she mutters into his rib cage.

"You have to take someone with you. Someone who knows the forest, darling, it's going to be dark and . . ."

"You can't come with me. You know that. Never both on the same plane, never out in a storm together, the children need . . ."

"I know, I KNOW," he whispers disconsolately, he's never felt so powerless, and that's a terrible thing for a fireman to experience.

His silly superstitions always stop her saying "come back safe" when he goes out on a call, so she usually thinks of something banal that he needs to do the next day, so that he has to promise to be home for that: "Don't forget that you're going to the dump tomorrow" or "We're having lunch at your mom's at twelve o'clock." It's become their secret little ritual.

So he doesn't say "come home safe" now. He doesn't even tell her not to go, because he knows what he would have replied to that. He may be strong, but not even he can stop the wind blowing. She can deliver babies, she's the one who's needed now. We help if we can, when we can, to the extent that we can. As they leave the bedroom he just takes hold of her arm, he wants to say something banal and everyday, so that she remembers that there's a tomorrow, and all he can think of is:

"I'm going to have sex with you tomorrow!"

She bursts out laughing, in his face, right at him.

"There's something seriously wrong with you."

"Just be absolutely clear about the fact that I'm going to have sex with you tomorrow!"

He has tears in his eyes, she does too, they hear the force of the wind outside and know better than to imagine that they're immortal.

"Do you know anyone who can help me find my way in that part of the forest?" she asks, trying to control her voice.

"Yes, I know someone, I'll call and say you're on your way," he replies, and writes down the address even though his hand is shaking.

She takes the van and sets out, into the night and into a storm that's snapping tree trunks and killing people at will. She doesn't promise to come home safe. He stands at the kitchen window with the children.

———

It's the dogs that eventually react to the fact there's someone at the front door, maybe it's more instinct than the doorbell that makes them start to bark. Ana goes warily out into the hall and peers through the window. Who the hell is out in this weather? There's a lone woman standing on the steps, the hood of her raincoat pulled up, her thin frame bent double by the wind.

"IS YOUR DAD HOME?" the woman yells when Ana forces the door open, the whole forest is roaring, as if they were standing inside a jar being kicked around by giants.

The woman's van is parked on the grass a few yards away, rocking in the wind. What a stupid vehicle to set out in during a storm, if you absolutely have to set out anywhere during a storm, Ana thinks. And the woman is wearing a red coat, has she driven all the way from *Hed*? Maybe she isn't actually real? Ana is so busy thinking that she barely reacts when the woman steps closer and yells once more:

"A car's got stuck in the forest, and my husband says that if there's anyone who can get me to it in this weather, it's your dad!"

She spits the words out, Ana just blinks, still confused.

"Look . . . what? I mean, you know, why is a car even out in the forest at a time like this?"

"The woman in the car is having a BABY! Is your dad home or NOT?" the woman snaps impatiently, taking a step into the hall.

Ana tries to stop her, but the woman doesn't have time to see the panic in her eyes. The empty beer cans and vodka bottles are lined up on the draining board, the daughter has carefully rinsed them so they won't smell in the recycling bin and she won't have to feel ashamed in front of the neighbors. Her dad's arms are hanging listlessly by the sides of the armchair in the living room, but his abused lungs are making his chest rise and fall with the breaths of an addict. The midwife is stressed and her heart is in her throat, so when it plummets to the pit of her stomach the drop is more extreme than she was prepared for.

"I . . . I understand. Sorry . . . sorry for disturbing you," she mutters to Ana in embarrassment and turns sharply toward the door, then hurries out to the yard and back into the van.

Ana doesn't hesitate for a moment before she rushes after her. She bangs on the window. The woman opens it warily.

"Where are you going?" Ana cries.

"I need to get to the woman in the forest!" the woman shouts as she tries to start the engine, but the damn rust bucket merely splutters.

"Are you mad or something? Do you know how dangerous that is in this weather?"

"SHE'S HAVING A BABY AND I'M A MIDWIFE!" the woman yells back in a sudden flash of rage, slamming her hands down on the stone-dead dashboard of the van.

In hindsight Ana won't be able to pinpoint exactly what happens inside her at that moment. Maybe it was something poetic, the sort of thing people say in films, that they felt themselves "called by a higher purpose." But it's probably mostly the fact that the woman looks crazy in exactly the same way that everyone always says Ana looks crazy.

She runs into the house, feeds the dogs, and turns up the volume of their favorite song by Maya, then comes back with the keys to a rusty pickup in her hand, and a jacket that's far too big flapping behind her like a cape in the wind.

"WE CAN TAKE DAD'S TRUCK!"

"I CAN'T TAKE YOU WITH ME!" the woman shouts.

"YOUR CAR IS SHIT!"

"YOU THINK I DON'T KNOW THAT?" the woman yells.

"YOU'LL BE A HELL OF A LOT SAFER IF I'M WITH YOU!"

The woman stares at the crazy eighteen-year-old. This isn't the sort of situation they teach you about when you're training to be a midwife. In the end she sighs resignedly, grabs her bag, and follows the girl to her dad's pickup.

"MY NAME IS HANNAH!" she yells.

"ANA!" Ana bellows.

It's kind of fitting that their names are so similar, because Hannah will have plenty of occasions when she alternately swears and laughs at how much this crazy teenager reminds her of herself. They clamber into the front seats and struggle to close the doors properly as the wind peppers the chassis like hailstones. Then Ana sees the rifle on the back-seat. She turns beetroot-red with shame, snatches it up, and runs back inside the house. When she comes back she says, without making eye contact:

"He sometimes leaves the rifle in the pickup when he's . . . you know. I must have yelled at him a million times about that."

The midwife nods uncomfortably.

"Your dad and my husband met during the forest fires a few years ago. I think they called your dad because he knows the forest. They've been hunting together a few times since then. I think your dad might be the only person from Beartown my husband respects."

It's a pathetic attempt to lighten the mood, she feels that her-self.

"Dad's easy to like, he just doesn't always like himself that much," Ana says with a bluntness that makes the midwife's stomach clench.

"Maybe you should stay at home with him, Ana?"

"What for? He's drunk. He won't even notice I'm gone."

"My husband told me I should only trust your dad if I have to go out into the forest, no one else, and I'm not comfortable with the idea of you . . ."

Ana snorts.

"Your husband's stupid if he thinks that old men are the only people who know their way around the forest!"

The midwife smiles resignedly.

"If you think that's the only reason my husband is stupid, you don't know many men . . ."

She's been telling Johnny all year to take the van to a proper garage, but he just keeps muttering that all firemen can mend their own cars. She's tried pointing out that in actual fact, all firemen THINK they can mend their own cars. Being married is easy, she usually thinks. You just pick an argument you're really good at, then repeat it at least once a week for all eternity.

"So where's this woman who's having a baby?" Ana asks impatiently.

The midwife hesitates, sighs, then pulls out a map. She took the main road from Hed to Beartown, but hers was the last vehicle that got through, she saw trees fall across the roadway behind her. She ought to have felt scared, but adrenaline stopped her. She points at the map:

"They're out here somewhere. See? They didn't take the main road, they tried to take a shortcut along the old forest roads, but most of those are probably blocked now. Is it even possible to get out there?"

"Let's find out," Ana replies.

Hannah clears her throat.

"Sorry to ask, but are you even old enough to have a driver's license?"

"Yes! I mean, yes, I'm *old* enough!" Ana says evasively, and puts her foot down.

"But you . . . you have got a driver's license?" the midwife asks, slightly anxiously, as Ana skids out onto the road.

"Well, no, not exactly. But Dad's taught me to drive. He's often a bit drunk, so he needs someone to drive him around."

That doesn't exactly calm the midwife's nerves. It really doesn't.

6

Superheroes

Matteo is only fourteen years old. He isn't important to this story, not yet. He's just the sort of character who passes by in the background, one of the many thousands of faces that make up the inhabitants of a community. No one pays him any attention as he cycles around Beartown at the start of the storm, not just because everyone is busy trying to get indoors, but because Matteo simply isn't the sort of person anyone notices. If invisibility is a superpower, it was never the one he dreamed of. He would have preferred superhuman strength instead, so he could protect his family. Or the ability to change the past, to save his big sister. But he isn't a superhero, he's just as powerless in the face of his existence as the town he lives in is in the face of nature.

He's on his own at home when the wind starts whipping the trees and the electricity goes off in the small house his parents rent right on the boundary between the last buildings and the start of the forest. They've gone abroad to bring his sister home. Matteo is good at being alone, but he can't bear to be in a house with no lights, so he gets on his bicycle and sets off. The defiant teenager inside his head doesn't want to ask for help, at the same time the scared child in his chest hopes that someone will see that he needs looking after. But no one has the time.

A tall, fat man in a suit rushes past him in the other direction. Matteo doesn't know his real name, only that everyone calls him "Tails," and that he owns the big supermarket and is one of the richest men in the whole town. The man doesn't even notice the boy he rushes past, he's on his way down to the flagpoles outside the ice rink in a panicked attempt to take down the green flags with the bear on them so that they don't get torn to shreds. That's the man's first instinct at a time of danger: save the flags, not people.

As Matteo carries on through Beartown he sees neighbors helping one another empty their yards of loose items, carrying in the sticks and nets that had been standing in every cul-de-sac. The kids around here play with tennis balls on pavement at this time of year, but as soon as the snow comes every other dad will spray water on their yard to make a hockey rink. Matteo has heard plenty of neighbors boast: "in this town we have good friends and bad yards," because down south people boast about perfect lawns and neat flower beds, whereas here you gain status from having grit-strewn patches of ground and pucks littering the soil when the snow melts. That shows that you've used the frozen months for the right things.

Matteo often wonders if he'd be as odd and alone in other places as he is here. If anyone would have talked to him, if he'd have friends, be visible. Where you're born and who you become there is a lottery, what's right in one place and wrong in another. In almost all of the world, being obsessed with hockey would make you an outsider, a weirdo, but not here. Here it's like the weather, all small talk in every social situation is about one or the other. And you can't escape storms or sport in Beartown.

It gets dark and cold quickly, the snow hasn't arrived yet but the wind is already eating through flesh and sinew, the boy has no gloves and is losing the feeling in his fingers. He pedals without really knowing where he's going, takes one hand off the handlebars to get the circulation going again, and he loses concentration for a moment, sees the vehicle too late. It comes so fast and its lights dazzle him. He brakes so hard that his bike skids sideways. The headlights blind him and he waits for the impact, and when it doesn't come at first he thinks he's already dead, but at the last moment he somehow manages to shift his weight and throw both himself and his bicycle out of the way. He rolls over, scraping his hands and arms, and lets out a yell, but no one hears him over the wind.

Neither the young woman driving the vehicle nor the midwife sitting beside her see him in the darkness. It's such a small event, everything happens so fast, but if the bumper had so much as grazed the fourteen-year-old he would have been tossed into the trees with horrific force. If he had ended up unconscious there in the middle of the storm, his lifeless body would probably not have been found for several days, by which time the invisible threads between him and everything that is on its way to happening would have been severed. But now he staggers to his feet, bruised but alive.

This is how small the margins are, between us never having heard of Matteo, and us soon never being able to forget his name.

1

Children

Beartown and Hed are old towns in an even older forest. People say that age brings wisdom, but for most of us that really isn't true, when we get old we've just accumulated more experiences, good and bad. The result is more likely to be cynicism than wisdom. When we're young we know nothing about all the very worst that can hit us, which is just as well, because otherwise we'd never leave the house.

And we would definitely never let go of those we love.

"Do you know . . . where you're going?" Hannah wonders anxiously.

As a midwife, she wants them to get there quickly, but as a human being who wants to carry on being one, she can't help wishing that Ana wasn't driving like someone who'd just stolen the pickup.

The girl doesn't reply. She's wearing her dad's jacket, bright orange and covered with reflectors, with the words "Game accident" on the back. He wears it when he's tracking animals that have been hit by vehicles, the whole pickup is full of equipment to help you move through the forest in the dark, half of Ana's childhood has consisted of running after him and the dogs out here. She has always thought she could find her way in a blindfold, and this storm is evidently planning on testing her.

"So . . . .you know where you're going?" Hannah asks again, and gets no response this time either.

Two tennis balls are rolling around on the floor by the midwife's feet. She picks one up and smiles tentatively.

"So . . . how many dogs have you got?"

Still no answer, so she clears her throat and goes on:

"I mean, nobody really plays tennis around here, the only uses I can think of for tennis balls in Hed and Beartown are if you have dogs, if you play land hockey, or if you're tumble-drying a duvet . . ."

Ana just peers silently over the steering wheel and drives even faster.

"What sort of dogs are they?" the midwife persists, and then the girl finally sighs:

"You're the sort who talks when you're nervous, aren't you?"

"Yes . . . ," the midwife admits.

"Me too," Ana says.

Then she says nothing at all for several minutes. The midwife closes her eyes and holds on tight. She does her best not to speak, but as her heartbeat increases her mouth stops obeying her:

"My husband wants to have dogs! He's been going on about it ever since we first met. To be honest, I don't really like animals, but I was thinking that I might surprise him for his birthday and let him buy one he can go hunting with! I've even spoken to a breeder! Apparently, you want a good hunting dog to have a clear 'on and off button,' so it's really keen when it's hunting, but can wind down as soon as it gets home? Is that right? I laughed when I heard that, because I wish the same thing applied to firemen and kids who play hockey . . ."

The pickup speeds up. Ana glances at her and mutters:

"For someone who doesn't like dogs, you know a lot about them."

"Thanks!" the midwife exclaims, and raises her arms in front of her face because she's convinced they're going to hit a fallen tree that Ana swerves around at the last moment.

Then the girl grunts:

"That's one hell of a brave jacket to wear if you're coming to Beartown. I'm wearing mine so we don't get run over if we're standing in the road, and you pick one that's going to make people aim right at us . . ."

"What?" the midwife all but shouts before realizing that she's wearing her eldest son's jacket, the red one with the Hed Hockey logo on the chest, she grabbed it without thinking when she was on her way out of the house.

Tobias has grown out of it now, but it's still too big for her. Life goes so quickly.

"Piece of shit team," Ana declares so firmly that Hannah suddenly flares up:

"Watch what you say! That's my kids' team!"

"It's not your kids' fault you let them play on a piece of shit team," Ana replies, completely nonplussed.

The midwife stares at her. Then she smiles reluctantly.

"So you like hockey?"

"I hate hockey, but I hate Hed more," Ana replies.

"Our A-team's probably going to beat yours this season," the midwife says hopefully, grateful to have something to talk about to distract herself.

Ana snorts and slows down for a few seconds as she tries to get her bearings in the darkness.

"Your team couldn't even beat a carpet. You'd need a calendar to measure the time it takes your backs to move from zone to zone . . . ," she mutters, squinting through the windshield.

The midwife rolls her eyes.

"My husband was right, there really isn't anything as smug as Beartown smugness. It's not that long since the whole club was on the brink of bankruptcy, but now you're suddenly full of it? And you were only good last season because you found that guy Amat? Without him you probably won't find winning so easy . . ."

"We've still got Amat," Ana snorts, and lets the pickup roll forward slowly.

"He's in the USA, isn't he? Playing in the NHL? It felt like the local paper didn't write about anything else all spring. How superior Beartown's youth setup is, the talented players you're producing, saying that you're the new style of hockey and we're the old . . ."

The midwife can hear her husband's bitterness in her own voice, which surprises her, but that's what life in Hed is like these days: you take everything personally. Every success for Beartown is a defeat on the other side of the town boundary.

"Amat never got drafted. He's home again. I think he's just

injured . . . ," Ana begins, but falls silent when she spots what she's been looking for: a narrow track through the trees, possibly not quite wide enough for a truck.

"For someone who doesn't like hockey, you seem to know a lot about it." The midwife smiles.

Ana brings the pickup to a halt, measures the gap with her eyes, then takes a deep breath. Then she says:

"It doesn't matter if Amat plays or not, we're still going to beat you. You know why?"

"No?"

Ana bites her bottom lip and slowly releases the clutch.

"Because you're a shit team. HOLD TIGHT!"

Then she leaves the road fast enough not to get stuck in the ditch, and veers in among the trees. The gap is wide enough, but only just, and she can hear the trunks scrape the paintwork. The midwife loses her breath and stops babbling as they jolt over the uneven ground. She hits her head on the windshield, and it seems to go on and on for hours until Ana stops abruptly. She winds down the window and sticks her head out, then reverses a few yards so that they're reasonably safe if a tree should happen to fall.

"Here!" she declares, nodding toward the midwife's map, then out of the window.

The midwife can't see her hand in front of her when they get out of the pickup, but Ana gestures with her jacket and the midwife grabs hold of it, and the girl leads her the last bit of the way through the forest, huddled up against the wind. It's astonishing that she knows where she is, it's as if she's sniffing her way, then suddenly they reach the car and hear the woman inside screaming, then the man calling:

"THERE'S SOMEONE COMING NOW, DARLING! THE AMBULANCE IS HERE!"

He's furious when he realizes that there isn't an ambulance, fear turns some people into heroes but most of us only reveal our worst sides when we're caught in its shadow. The midwife can't help getting the distinct impression that the man probably isn't just irritated by the nature of the vehicle they arrived in, but would above all have preferred male paramedics.

"Are you sure you know what you're doing?" he demands as Hannah climbs into the backseat and starts whispering to the woman.

"What's your job?" the midwife asks in a controlled voice.

"Painter," he replies, clearing his throat.

"How about I decide how we help your wife give birth, then you can make the decisions next time we paint a wall?" she says, nudging him gently out of the way.

Ana gets in the front seat, her eyes flitting about manically.

"What can I do?" she pants.

"Talk to her," the midwife says.

"About what?"

"Anything."

Ana nods, confused, then peers over the seat at the woman in labor and says:

"Hi!"

The woman manages to smile between contractions.

"H-hello . . . are you a midwife as well?"

The man interrupts in exasperation.

"Are you kidding darling? She's, like, twelve years old!"

"So go and paint something, idiot!" Ana snaps back, and the midwife laughs out loud.

For a moment the man is so insulted that he gets out of the car and tries to slam the door behind him, but the wind spoils his dramatic gesture. He can barely manage to stand upright out there, but with the wind in his eyes it's probably easier to persuade himself that the tears in his eyes are tears of fear.

"What's your name?" the woman in the backseat pants.

"Ana."

"Thanks . . . thanks for coming, Ana. I'm sorry my husband . . ."

"He's just angry because he loves you and he thinks you and the baby are going to die and he can't do anything about it," Ana blurts out.

The midwife glares at her disapprovingly, so Ana mutters defensively: "You told me to talk!"

The woman in the backseat smiles wearily.

"You know a lot about men for someone so young."

"They just think we want them to protect us the whole goddamn time, as if we need their fucking protection," Ana snorts.

The midwife and woman in the backseat both laugh quietly at this.

"Do you have a boyfriend?" the woman asks.

"No. Well, sort of. But he died!"

The woman stares at her. Ana lets out a regretful cough and adds:

"But look, I'm sure you're not going to die!"

Then the midwife says, in a friendly but firm way, that perhaps a bit of silence wouldn't be such a bad idea after all. Then the woman screams and her husband races back into the car and takes hold of her hand, and then he starts screaming too when she almost breaks his fingers.

Johnny spends all night sitting by the kitchen window. It's an unbearable position for a fireman to be in. All four children are asleep on mattresses on the floor around him. Ture, the youngest, in the arms of Tess, the eldest. Tobias and Ted, the two middle boys, start off farther away, but soon end up as close to the others as they can get. In a crisis we instinctively seek out the only thing that really matters, even in our sleep: the breath of others, a pulse for our own to keep time with. Every now and then their dad gently puts one hand on his sons' and daughter's backs, one at a time, to make sure they're still breathing. There's no good reason to suspect that they aren't, but there's nothing reasonable about being a parent. The only thing everyone said when he was about to become a father was: "Don't worry." What a meaningless thing to say. There's an immensity of love that bursts from your chest the first time you hear your child cry, every emotion you've ever felt is amplified to the point of absurdity, children open floodgates inside us, upward as well as down. You've never felt so happy, and never felt so scared. Don't say "don't worry" to someone in that position. You can't love someone like this without worrying about everything, forever. It hurts your chest at times, a real, physical pain that makes Johnny bend over and gasp for breath. His skeleton creaks, his body aches, love never has enough space. He should have known better than to have four children, he should have thought about it, but everyone said "don't worry," and he's always been an easily persuaded idiot. Thank goodness. We fool ourselves that we can protect the people we love, because if we accepted the truth we'd never let them out of our sight.

Johnny spends the whole night by the kitchen window, and this is the first time he truly experiences what his wife has felt every hour of every night without him since they first fell in love: What am I going to do if you don't come home again?

———

Hannah knows when something is wrong. It's the result of training and experience, sure, but after enough years it's also something else. If the midwife didn't know better, she'd say it's almost spiritual. It can be such tiny things, the slightest change in skin color, or a fragile little rib cage that's rising and falling a fraction too slowly. She knows when it's happening before it happens. Giving birth to a child ought to be impossible, the ocean is so vast and our vessel so fragile, none of us ought to stand a chance.

Even Ana is frightened now. When the wind snaps a tree a yard behind them it sounds like a pistol shot inside the car, and when it falls and misses the car by just a handsbreadth, the branches scrape the chassis with such a shriek that the sound echoes in her head for several minutes. The ground shakes and when the worst gusts of wind come they think plenty of times that more trees have fallen on them, then something comes flying and hits the windshield, it's a miracle it doesn't break, it was probably just a stone or a large stick, but the force is so great that it sounds like hitting an elk at a hundred miles an hour.

But through the chaos and noise the midwife's voice is still calm, intimate, promising that everything's going to be fine. The man is sitting ashen-faced in the front seat beside Ana now. Then the baby cries for the first time and the world stops turning. The midwife smiles warmly to the mom and dad, and it isn't until she glances at Ana that the girl realizes that something is wrong. The midwife leans forward from the backseat and whispers:

"How close can you get your dad's truck?"

"Close!" Ana promises.

"What's going on? Why are you whispering?" the man exclaims, panic-stricken, he grabs the midwife's arm and the midwife lets out a cry, and Ana reacts instinctively and hits him in the jaw.

He tumbles back against the side window. The midwife stares at him, then at Ana. The girl is blinking in embarrassment.

"Sorry. I didn't mean to hit him so hard. I'll get the truck."

The man is huddled up in pain, half on the seat and half on the floor, blood trickling from his lip. The midwife's voice is gentle, her words all the harsher:

"Your baby and your wife need to get to the hospital. Right away. I'm pretty sure you can't paint us there. That kid out there is pretty crazy, sure, but she's all we've got right now. Do you understand what I'm saying?"

The man nods in despair.

"Will it . . . please, will the baby, will it . . . ?"

"We need to get to the hospital," the midwife whispers, looking him in the eye until his heart stops beating.

Ana rushes through the trees with her arms stretched out, so that her fingertips can memorize where they stand. Then she reverses her dad's pickup blindly back between the trunks. Gently, gently the midwife and the new dad move the newborn baby and the new mother from one vehicle to the other. Then Ana drives on instinct through the darkness, she can only see a few yards in front of her, but that's all she needs, a few yards at a time, then a few yards more. They don't see the biggest tree sway and bend before it falls with terrible force over the car they have just left behind them in the darkness. Perhaps that's just as well. It isn't always a blessing to know how close to death you have been.

The mother in the backseat tries to whisper something, feeble and terrified, the midwife has to lean close to her mouth to hear.

"She wants you to know that she's sorry about your boyfriend," the midwife says, placing a gentle hand on Ana's shoulder.

The man in the passenger seat has blood on his collar, and is beside himself with shame.

"What . . . happened to your boyfriend?"

"Well, he died, but it was two years ago so it's okay, I mean, I loved him, but he was a right pain in the backside at times!" Ana blurts out.

She swerves between two tree trunks, and for a few seconds it feels as if all four wheels have left the ground, the man sees nothing but black outside the windshield, but suddenly Ana turns in to what seems to be a path.

"WHAT WAS HIS NAME? YOUR BOYFRIEND?" the man yells, mostly just so he could yell something.

"VIDAR!" Ana shouts, then accelerates, the others all grab hold of the doors in panic, so perhaps this isn't the best moment for her to say:

"HE DIED IN A CAR ACCIDENT!"

8

"LOOK OUT! FOR GOD'S . . ."

The car stops abruptly, the tires clutch desperately at the pavement, the man yells through the wound-down window and blows the horn hard. But the young woman in front of him calmly carries on crossing the street as if nothing has happened. It's evening down here in the capital, almost no wind, no one knows anything about storms in the forests up to the north. Not even Maya Andersson. Do you want to understand Beartown? Then you need to understand her, the girl who moved away from there.

The driver of the car blows his horn again, more resigned than angry now, and at first Maya doesn't even notice that it's aimed at her. She crosses the road even though the light is red and skips up onto the pavement on the other side, weaving between the tower blocks and the roadworks. It took two years to become a different person. A big city person.

The driver of the car yells something at her, she doesn't hear what, but she turns and notices the first half of the license plate.

SDS.

It feels like a whole lifetime since Maya thought about those letters, she's changed so much. The driver of the car gives up and accelerates demonstratively away and she realizes several seconds later that she's standing in the middle of the pavement daydreaming, and people are having to elbow their way past. She doesn't know what's got into her today, she's been in such a good mood all evening that she feels . . . light. She's on her way to a party with her classmates at the College of Music, carried along on a gentle rush of anticipation, it feels like she's only just learned not to feel guilty about that. She's allowed to feel happy, she's kept telling herself over and over again during the last few months, she's allowed to have fun. She'll hate herself for that a few hours from now. She's always wondered how far her musical talent might be able to carry her, and this is the answer: far enough that she doesn't even know that the whole of Beartown is on the brink of being blown to pieces while she goes to a party.

She has one missed call on her phone, from Ana, but she can call her later. They live so far apart these days that she doesn't call her back at once. They're no longer so closely connected.

She sets off again, quicker, when she first moved here she couldn't understand why everyone walked so quickly, and now it drives her crazy when she goes back to Beartown and the whole world is so slow there. She's already forgotten the man in the car, she's become so good at living in a big city: you have to forget everyone you meet in an instant here, our brains don't have room for so many impressions otherwise, no one is allowed to mean anything.

In the forests to the north where she grew up there's a storm, but here she hasn't even buttoned her thin coat, so blissfully unaware of winds tearing through houses and people. She gets a text from her classmates at the party, and realizes from the punctuation that everyone there is already drunk. She laughs, because every so often it strikes her how remarkable it is: in less than four college terms she has constructed a whole new life. The last time she was in Beartown she accidently said she was going "home" when she came back here. She saw how much that hurt her dad, and now there's a sort of silence between them. He wasn't ready to let go of her, parents never are, they just have no choice.

Maya knows that everyone thinks she moved here because she wanted to grow up, but it's actually the reverse. Kevin took so much from her, far more than she can explain, for him the rape lasted a few minutes but for her it never stopped. He took all the bright summer mornings, all the crisp autumn air, the snow under her feet, laughter that makes your chest hurt, everything that was simple. Most people can't pinpoint the exact moment when they stop being little children, but Maya can, Kevin took her childhood and when she moved here she tore and ripped and scratched out a little bit of it and reclaimed it. She taught herself to be naive again, because she doesn't want to be grown-up yet, doesn't want to live a life with no illusions. Doesn't want to learn that one day she won't be able to protect her own children. That all girls can be victims and all boys perpetrators.

In the end it felt as if only her mother really understood why she left. "I'm so angry with you for leaving me, but I'll be even more angry if you stay," Kira whispered in her daughter's ear that last morning in Beartown. "Promise me that you'll be careful, always, but also that you . . . oh . . . that you *won't* be sometimes. But not too much!" Maya laughed and cried and hugged her second to last, and her dad last, because he didn't let go until just before the train started to move. She jumped on board and the forest closed around the windows and then Beartown was no longer home.

She soon got used to the crowds and rush-hour traffic and the freedom offered by anonymity down here. It felt like the answer to everything. "If no one knows who you are, you can be whoever you want," she told Ana over the phone that first spring. "I don't give a shit, I like you the way you are already, what do you want to change for?" Ana snapped. Not such a small compliment from a girl who looked at Maya the first time she started to light a fire when they were little and said: "Several million sperm, and YOU managed to win? Unbelievable!!!" Ana will never leave the forest, her roots are deeper than the trees', Maya finds that both incomprehensible and enviable. Truth be told, she probably doesn't know where "home" is anymore, she's even started using quotation marks when she thinks about it. She's tried explaining to Ana that she feels more like a nomad now, but Ana can't understand that, a nomad wouldn't survive a winter in Beartown, if you can't find a home there you'll freeze to death before morning. In the end Maya told her: "Here I can be something that I've done, but in Beartown I'm just something that happened to me." Ana understood that.

Another text message from her classmates at the party. Maya crosses another street so she can cut through the big park, thinking that it would be quicker, not about what might be hiding in there. That's how much she's changed.

SDS.

She walks along the narrow gritted pavement and is halfway into the park when the letters on the license plate crash back into her consciousness. Her memories fight over which emotions to summon up, she thinks about Ana and almost starts to laugh, almost starts to cry. It feels like she hasn't thought about her for ages, but they spoke on the phone just the other day, didn't they? Or was it a week ago?

The distance between the lights in the park gets longer, the sound of traffic and humanity thins out, and she walks slower without reflecting upon it. She forgets to look around, doesn't notice the man a little way behind her slow down too. When she speeds up again, so does he.

She really ought to be missing Ana less and less the longer they are apart, but the reverse seems to be happening. She remembers every detail of the look on her face the time she exclaimed: "You know? *Shoot . . . dig . . . silence?* SDS!"

"What?" Maya said, and Ana, never able to hide her astonishment at all the things Maya didn't know about the world, exclaimed: "Have you seriously NEVER heard that? That Toronto where you used to live is still on the planet EARTH, isn't it? Sometimes it feels like you were made in a laboratory, that's why you're so pretty, but there are some seriously loose connections in there!" She grinned, tapping the top of Maya's head.

Maya felt like an alien. She remembers feeling confused and scared for the whole of her first year in Beartown, as much of the wilderness as of the people, as much because this new place seemed to have grief in its heart as the fact that there always seemed to be violence in the air. She couldn't for the life of her understand how anyone would choose to live there voluntarily, in a little cluster of houses besieged by darkness and cold and trees, trees, trees, nothing but millions of trees in all directions. The narrow road through the forest that you drove along to get there seemed to go on forever, into a world with no horizon, so long and deep that in the end it seemed to curve downward and disappear into the abyss. Maya was only a child, and in all the stories she had read only witches lived in places like this. She thought she would never get used to it, but children get used to almost everything.

During the years she grew up and became a teenager she never really realized how much Beartown had changed her. She didn't even know she had the local accent until she moved away. There in the forest Ana teased her for pronouncing her vowels wrong, but whenever Maya's new classmates at the College of Music wanted to tease her, they made fun of her grammar, the way she never conjugated verbs. She pretended it was funny, even though they were mimicking a dialect from hundreds of miles away in Beartown.

So she tried to sing the way the teachers wanted, smoothing off her rough edges until she sounded like everyone else. Most of her classmates had attended music schools and had had expensive private tuition since they were young, they knew all the secret codes, knew exactly what was expected of them. Maya had gotten there on raw talent alone. She cried a lot at night during those first months, at first from insecurity, then out of anger. It felt as if all the other kids had to do to get into the college was to have rich parents and be able to sing adequately, whereas all Maya had to do to get there was to be the best. Best of all.

When one of the teachers talked about the music industry during her first term, he said you needed to bear in mind that "we live in a small country." Maya thought that something like that could only be said by someone who had never noticed two-thirds of the map. She was astonished to realize that some of her classmates thought they lived in the middle of the country when they actually lived pretty close to the bottom. She thought about Ana's father, and how he would sometimes bump into tourists from the south in the forest who were surprised how far you could walk without seeing a house, and how when he got home he always muttered: "They think they own this country, and they don't even know that seventy percent of it is trees? Only three percent of the entire country has been built on! Three percent!!!" One time he roared: "There's less agricultural land than bog in this country, but they probably don't even know what a bog is!" at Maya, then Ana had to whisper to Maya what a bog was, so she could nod in agreement. And now she herself was surrounded by people who didn't have a clue. In the end she realized that it was her classmates, with their expensive clothes and complacent smiles, who were the real uneducated ones, not her. That was when she stopped crying at night. Stopped waiting and started to make a space for herself, stopped imitating other people's voices and started singing with her own. Everything changed.

Last winter she found a small, artificial skating rink in the middle of the apartment blocks and rush hour traffic, and the next day she took some of her classmates there, and remembers how shocked she was that so many of them couldn't even skate. Every child in Beartown can skate, probably more of them than can ride a bike. After all, how could anyone *not* know how to skate? When the autumn came, her new friends complained about the cold, and said the darkness made them depressed. Maya felt ashamed of herself when she realized how quick she was to judge them for their weakness. Depressed by the darkness in a city where the lights are always lit? Cold? This wasn't *cold*!

She can remember how the breath was knocked out of her when she fell through the ice at the age of six when she was skating alone in Beartown. That was just after they had moved there, no one even knew she was down at the lake, she would have died if that hand hadn't suddenly appeared out of nowhere and pulled her out. Ana, as scrawny as if she was never fed at home, but already incredibly strong, sat wide-eyed on the ice beside her, wondering what on earth she was doing. Couldn't she see the variation in the color of the ice? Didn't she understand anything? Ana thought Maya was stupid, and Maya thought Ana was an idiot, and they became best friends instantly. Ana taught Maya to use a rifle, and Ana's dad muttered that the pair of them were "the smallest hunting team in the area, and probably the most dangerous." Sometimes, if only for a moment, Maya managed to convince herself that she belonged in Beartown. That never lasted long.

Once when they were little, she had a sleepover at Ana's, almost every other time during their childhoods it was the other way around, but this time they were going to sleep out in the forest, only the weather turned bad and they set off for the nearest house: Ana's. Later that evening they heard Ana's dad answer the phone. Someone had seen a wolf. Ana's dad asked tersely: "You haven't called it in yet, have you?"

Maya didn't understand what that meant, so Ana explained in a low voice: "You're supposed to report wolf sightings to the authorities, but if you do that, it means the wolf exists. Get it?" Maya really didn't, so Ana sighed: "If the wolf exists, the authorities will miss it if it disappears. But something that doesn't exist can't disappear. So . . . SDS."

Then a man came and collected Ana's dad, he had a rifle on the front seat of his pickup, and shovels in the back. When they returned at dawn the next day they had soil and blood on their boots. Shoot, dig, silence. That was how Maya learned about that.

When Kira came to collect her a few hours later Maya pretended nothing had happened, and it wasn't until several years later that she realized that her mother was also pretending. She knew perfectly well what had happened to the wolf, everyone in Beartown knew. Maya wondered if her mother still thinks about that, the way that silence reflected all the other silences that Beartown taught its children?

The only person who didn't keep quiet was Ramona. Maya only remembered that recently, it was the sort of memory her brain had archived, only for it to pop up suddenly one day when she was at the other end of the country. A few days after Maya learned what SDS meant, she had to go with Ana to the Bearskin pub to pick up Ana's dad's car keys, because sometimes he got drunk enough to sell his car for a couple of last beers, and Ramona always let him do it because it was better for him to walk home after two more beers than drive home without them. Unfortunately Ana's rucksack was in the car and she needed her math book the following morning, so the girls had no choice but to trudge to the pub. Naturally, Maya's parents would have gone crazy if they'd known she'd been to the pub, it was full of the men in black jackets who fought with the opposing team's supporters on hockey nights, and with each other pretty much every other night. Ramona handed Ana the keys across the bar counter, and told her not to forget to take the rifle home as well, because her dad had left it in the pickup as usual. Ana promised. Then Ramona looked down at Maya, the old woman looked far too much like a witch for the girl to be able to look her in the eye.

"I heard you saw the shovels. Those stupid old men could have spared you that. But I guess sooner or later you have to learn that predators need to be dealt with. Maybe it isn't like that everywhere, but that's what it's like here," Ramona hissed, then gave them both a chocolate cookie, coughing so much she almost couldn't carry on smoking. But only almost.

Then a fight broke out right next to the bar between two men and sixteen beers, Ramona swore and swung her broom and Maya pulled Ana away, terrified. Ana, of course, was so unconcerned by the violence that all she was annoyed about was dropping part of her chocolate cookie on the way out. The girls had different types of parents, they were used to expecting completely different things from adults. Maya learned more slowly, but she did learn.

Shoot. Dig.

Ramona was wrong, Maya thinks now. It wasn't predators that people in Beartown got rid of, it was problems. Because when Maya came running out of Kevin's bedroom several years later, it wasn't the predator that most people wanted to attack, it was her. Because it would have been much easier for everyone if she had just disappeared rather than Kevin. She was the problem.

Silence.

She slows down. The park is so quiet she can hear the movement of every piece of grit beneath her shoes. She glances over her shoulder. No, it isn't her imagination, that man is following her. Damn. She suddenly feels so stupid that for a moment it stops her feeling scared. How could she let her brain lose itself in memories and not notice the danger. "Pull yourself together, Maya! Think!" she snarls to herself. One of the streetlights in the park isn't working, she's been moving between circles of light, but now she's swallowed up by the shadows. "What the hell am I doing? Why did I take the shortcut through the park? If anyone should know better, it's me!" she yells inside her head. That's how much she's changed, how well she's taught herself to be naive again. Out of the corner of her eye she sees the man a short way behind her, a bit closer now than before, black jacket, hood pulled up.

Damn damn damn.

She has time to think of her mother. Has time to wish she was home.

9

Mothers

"Home."

There really ought to be several different words for that, one for the place and one for the people, because after enough years a person's relationship to their town becomes more and more like a marriage. Both are held together by stories of what we have in common, the little things no one else knows about, the private jokes that only we think are funny, and that very particular laugh that you only laugh for me. Falling in love with a place and falling in love with a person are related adventures. At first we run around street corners giggling and explore every inch of each other's skin, over the years we get to know every cobblestone and strand of hair and snore, and the waters of time soften our passion into unfailing love, and in the end the eyes we wake up next to and the horizon outside our window are the same thing: home.

So there ought to be two words for that, one for the home which can carry you through your darkest moments, and one for the home which binds you. Because sometimes we stay in towns and marriages simply because we would otherwise have no story. We have too much in common. We think no one else would be able to understand us.

———

Kira Andersson is alone in her office over in Hed when the storm gets going for real. She sent all her employees home when the radio first started reporting that trees had fallen on the roads. In the end even Kira's best friend and colleague, the woman she owns the business with, set off for home. She refused at first, of course, declaring that "those old men on the radio get incontinent the minute we get a puff of wind," but Kira pointed out that when there's a storm people usually stockpile important groceries, and that maybe all the wine would run out, and that's when her colleague panicked and left.

Kira's husband, Peter, wanted to stay too, of course, but Kira insisted he go home to their house in Beartown so that Leo wasn't on his own. Not that it would really make that much difference, the teenage boy will just sit at his computer hidden under his earphones, and as long as there's electricity the storm could have been an alien invasion and he still wouldn't notice anything. They live in the same house but his parents barely see him, he's fourteen now, meaning that they no longer have a child but a lodger.

Peter gave up and set off before it even turned into a discussion, Kira isn't sure if it was disappointment or relief she saw in his eyes. Two years ago he stepped down as general manager of Beartown Hockey to work with Kira instead, drawing a line under a whole life that had been about nothing but sport, and now he's married to her when they're at home but employed by her when they're here. Sometimes they both forget the difference. From time to time she asks him if he's okay and he smiles and nods. But she can see that he's unhappy. She's so angry with herself for being so angry with him about that.

Today she promised him that she was just going to do a few last things before she went home, but she hasn't actually turned her computer on since the door closed behind him. Nature is tearing itself to pieces outside the window and she's sitting on the other side of the glass with the tips of her fingers on a framed photograph of her children.

Her psychologist told her, not that long ago, that she often returns to the idea that she's a bad mother. Not that she *feels* bad, but that she *is* bad. She replied that it was true, because she could have had just a job, but chose to have a career. You have a job for your family's sake and a career for your own. She's selfish with her time. She could have lived for them, but that isn't enough for her.

"We've talked about your extreme need to control things before . . ."

"It isn't extreme!"

She's only been seeing this psychologist for a couple of months. She hasn't mentioned it to anyone because it's nothing serious, she's just been having panic attacks again. She pays the psychologist in cash so Peter won't find any invoices in the mail and think she's got problems. She hasn't got problems.

"Okay. But both your children are older now. Leo is . . . fourteen, is that right? And Maya's eighteen? She's even left home now, hasn't she?" the psychologist said.

"She hasn't left home! She's studying at music college, she lives in a student residence, that's not the same thing!" Kira snapped, close to tears, she felt like yelling at him that she doesn't have two children, she has three: Isak, Maya, Leo. One in Heaven and two who barely answer the phone. But instead she mumbled:

"Please, can we just focus on the reason why I'm here?"

"Your panic attacks? I'm inclined to think they're linked to the fact that you're . . ."

"What? A mom? Am I supposed to stop being that because I have a business to run?"

The psychologist smiled.

"Do you think your children would describe you as overprotective?"

Kira sulked in silence. She felt like yelling, asking if the psychologist knew what the worst thing about being an overprotective mother is. Sometimes being RIGHT! But she kept quiet, because she hasn't told the psychologist about what happened to Isak, nor about what happened to Maya. She doesn't want to talk about that, she just wants to sort out the panic attacks, get some medication or whatever it's going to take. Even with psychologists she wants to be efficient and show how clever she is.

But he's right. The children are small in all the photographs on the desk in the office, to help her forget how big they are now. Leo is a teenager, and soon Maya won't even be that anymore. It's been two years since she moved away to the big city to study at her beloved College of Music. Two YEARS, it's almost as incomprehensible that her daughter has been gone so long as it is that Kira has started using the phrase "big city." She used to chuckle at how provincial it sounded when the people around here said that sort of thing when she and Peter and the children moved here. Now she's become one of them. Forest folk. The sort of person who mutters that "even the elk are lazy down south," and is only half-joking when she says: "There's nothing wrong with the big city, it's just so damn hard to get to."

"All teenagers think their moms are overprotective. I could be in prison and they'd still think they saw too much of me," she eventually muttered to the psychologist.

He clasped his hands together in his lap, because by now he had learned that if he made any notes, Kira would immediately demand to know exactly what he was writing. Not that she needed to be in control, obviously. No, not at all.

"You sound like my own mother," he said gently.

Kira's eyelashes quivered.

"That's because you don't get it. We're your mothers. We loved you first. Maybe everyone else loves you now, but we loved you first."

"Doesn't feeling like that make you a good mother?"

"It just makes me a mother."

The psychologist chuckled.

"Well, you're right about that, of course. I'm almost sixty and my mom still worries that I'm not eating properly."

Kira raised her chin but lowered her voice.

"We're your mothers. You can't stop us."

The psychologist really wished he could have written that down.

"What about your husband, Peter? You gave up an awful lot for his career for many years, and now he's given up his career for you for a while. Do you still feel guilty about that?"

Her breath whistled in her nostrils.

"I don't see why we have to talk about that. I've told you that I . . . well . . . yes, I feel guilty! Because I don't know how to make him happy. That's the only thing I never needed to do for him in all the years he devoted to hockey, I did everything at home and I fitted the whole of my life around his career, but I never needed to make him *happy*. Hockey did that. And now I don't know if I can."

The psychologist asked, the way psychologists do:

"Is it really your responsibility to make him happy, then?"

Kira's voice may have wavered, but her answer was firm:

"He's my husband. He can't stop me."

She meant it, she still means it, yet she's still sitting in her office on her own right now. She still has time to get home, but she doesn't leave. She just looks out of the window and sees the storm approaching, not frightened even though she knows she should be.

———

You can learn everything you need to know about Ana from her way of driving tonight. She's driving as if it's her fault if they don't all make it, her fault if everyone isn't happy, her fault if something goes wrong. Anything at all. The midwife sees it, recognizes it, she reaches forward and touches the girl's shoulder and brushes her hair aside so it isn't hanging in front of her eyes. Ana probably doesn't even notice, she's peering through the windshield with white knuckles clutching the steering wheel and her feet dancing across the pedals, and the pickup surges through the darkness. Afterward the others will barely remember how they got out of the forest, but all of a sudden the vehicle is on a road, and soon they see the lights outside the hospital.

Ana stops right in front of the entrance and then everything happens incredibly fast: hospital staff seem to rush out from every direction to help them. All the pickup's doors are opened, the wind is roaring outside, nurses shout at one another and Ana sits in the middle of the chaos, feeling so much in the way that she daren't move at all. Hannah, the dad, the mom, and the baby disappear in the tide of people and the truck doors close behind them and suddenly everything is silent. So unbearably silent.

Ana takes out her phone and calls Maya. She wants to tell someone about all this, but how on earth can she even start? She doesn't have to. Maya doesn't answer. Ana slips her phone into the compartment in the door and leans her head on the steering wheel.

It takes an hour before the mother and baby are stabilized to the point where it occurs to Hannah that Ana is probably still sitting outside in the parking lot. When she goes out, the girl is still sitting with her forehead on the wheel, her eyes wide open. The midwife gets into the passenger seat, it takes all her strength to close the door and stop the wind breaking the hinges and tossing it away like a glove. The pickup is rocking, the rain arrives, and they sit in silence beneath the clatter on the roof for a long time before Hannah says:

"You did really well, Ana."

Ana blinks hard.

"Is the kid okay?"

"Yes, everything's going to be fine. Thanks to you. Are *you* okay?"

"Yeah . . . Yeah. That was . . . I mean, when you delivered that baby there in the car, and when he cried for the first time, I don't know how to describe it . . . it was like being high! Do you get what I mean? I mean, I'm not saying I do drugs! But you know? I mean . . . you do know?"

"I think so."

"Is it like that every time?"

"Not every time."

"Because you get used to it?"

The little lines in the skin around the midwife's lips are the scars of relief rather than laughter lines when she replies:

"Because not everyone always makes it. You have to make the most of the happy endings whenever you get the chance."

The silence that follows presses them deep into their seats.

"I need to get home to Dad," Ana whispers.

"Is your mother home?"

"She doesn't live with us."

The girl says this so matter-of-factly that the midwife doesn't ask anything more. There's no mother. There was a woman who gave birth to Ana once upon a time, she lives somewhere else now and has a new life, but there's no longer a mom. When the midwife carefully touches her fingers to the girl's cheek, her shock eases and tears trickle over Hannah's hand.

"You promise the kid's going to be okay?"

"I promise, Ana."

"I'm sorry I hit that stupid painter. And I'm sorry I drove so fast. And I'm . . ."

The midwife hushes her gently.

"You saved a baby's life tonight, Ana. You're a bit daft, sure, I'm not going to pretend otherwise. I wouldn't even let you use my sewing machine if there hadn't been a storm, I can tell you that much. But you're also really, really brave. You're the sort of person who runs toward fire. Believe me, I recognize the type."

Ana tries to nod like she believes that. Her dad is still asleep in his chair when she gets home, a bottle still in his hand, he hasn't even noticed that the world is falling apart outside the windows. Ana finishes the dishes, then checks the batteries in the flashlights before lying down under a blanket on the floor in front of the open fire with the dogs huddled closely around her. She's left her phone in the truck, where it lies, ringing and ringing and ringing.

The next day Ana doesn't tell anyone what she did the previous night, not even Maya.

———

In the hospital a woman is lying in a bed. No one told her how it would really feel to be someone's mom. Which is just as well. She's going to be scared forever now.

"Vidar is a good name," she whispers.

"It's a brilliant name," the dad sniffs.

And it is. A name for a boy born far out in the forest between two towns that hate each other, on a wild night during the worst storm anyone can remember. A child of the wind, saved by a hunter's daughter. If that boy ever starts to play hockey, it will be one of our very, very best fairy tales.

We're going to need them. Fairy tales are what help us cope with funerals.

———

Hannah goes back inside the hospital, into the locker room, where she gets changed and leans her forehead against the door. Then she allows herself to have a minor breakdown, just a small one, only for a moment. She lets all that is brightest and darkest sing inside her without struggling against it. Then she closes all the dampers and hatches inside herself and opens her eyes, so that she doesn't take all those feelings home. No one can bear to feel everything all the time. She's only a few miles from home, but as she walks toward the parking lot she realizes that the van is still parked outside Ana's house in Beartown. It's far too dangerous to walk home in the storm now, especially when she's so exhausted, so she calls her husband, hardly able to speak: "It all went fine, darling, but I haven't got the car here so I'm going to stay until the storm . . ." But Johnny has already hung up, he carries all four sleeping children to the neighbors' and borrows their car to drive to the hospital and collect his wife. Not even a natural disaster can stop her idiot from doing that.

———

Kira is sitting on her own at her desk in the office, she can see nothing but herself in the window, the other side is pitch black, the sky has swallowed the earth. She thinks a hundred times that she's going to phone her daughter, but it's so late and she's probably at some party with her classmates, Kira doesn't want to worry her. But most of all she doesn't want Maya to hear in her voice how frightened she is. How lost.

The storm is going to be worse than they said on the news, much, much worse. But Kira doesn't go home. She ought to, but she doesn't.

Towns and marriages consist of stories. Where one starts, another one ends.

10

Migrating birds

Maya has heard many times back home in Beartown that "in a crisis you find out who you really are." People love their damn aphorisms in hockey towns. "When your back's against the wall you find out what you're really capable of," they declare, without ever questioning what that really means. After all, the vast majority of people never find out what they're capable of, most of them don't even know if they're the sort of animal that runs, or the sort of animal that hunts. Maya envies them. She envies them so much.

She walks a little faster through the park but without starting to run, she knows that the man behind her would catch up with her in a matter of seconds if she did that. She's trying to buy some time, get as close to the exit of the park as possible before making a break for it, hopefully get him to underestimate her.

Idiot.

Maya used to watch the migrating birds as they passed over the forest between Hed and Beartown in the spring, and wonder why they did that. "I mean, I understand why they leave but not why they come back," she said to Ana, but Ana just shrugged her shoulders and said: "They're gone for the whole of the hockey season. Smart!" She always used to laugh off anything painful, but when Maya left to attend music college she whispered: "You're like those birds now. Flying away." Maya dearly wished it could have been so easy.

They spent their first night on opposite sides of the country talking on the phone until the sun came up, Maya was making a huge effort to pretend that she was normal to her classmates, but everything crumbled when she was on the phone. She admitted in a low voice to Ana that she wondered if she was a psychopath who no longer even regretted holding that rifle to Kevin's head. Ana groaned at the other end: "God, you were a psychopath WAY before that!" Maya smiled. It always ended with a joke from one or other of them, so that they wouldn't dig too deep. Maya hated herself for having been in that room with Kevin, Ana hated herself for not being there. Maya spared him out on that jogging trail, but Ana would never have done that. "All animals fight for their own survival first, they hunt if it's in their nature, and they die if they have to," Ana said, and Maya thought for a while before she replied: "But not all animals want revenge, we're the only ones who do that, waiting in the darkness all night so we can get back at someone for something. Only we do that." Ana snorted and told her about how her mom had hit one of her dad's hunting dogs on the nose, then a few weeks later the dog crept out and pulled down all the white laundry Ana's mom had hung on the clothesline. "It was getting its revenge," Ana grinned.

They continued talking on the phone, but less and less frequently, and less and less about animals. Maya really did try to forget everything. Her new classmates knew nothing about her, so she decided to become someone else, someone nothing had happened to. It almost worked.

Idiot idiot.

"You never tell us anything about yourself, we've known you for two years but it feels like we hardly know anything about you!" one of her classmates exclaimed recently when they were studying in the library. Maya was shocked when she saw that all the others around the table agreed. There was no malice in the remark, just curiosity, they had no idea what doors they were trying to open. She tried to laugh it off and said she was really a contract killer for the mafia, adopting her strongest Beartown dialect because she knew that always made them laugh. What else was she supposed to say? Where could she start? Their world was far too small for them to understand, they were still children, they got drunk at every party because they weren't worried about not being in control, because nothing had ever happened to them. They've never hated themselves so much that they wanted to kill themselves simply because they went to a party when they were fifteen in a town where afterward everyone wished that they had never existed, because someone who doesn't exist can't be raped. They've never wondered what would have happened if they simply hadn't gone to the police, hadn't said anything, had just let life go on without turning the entire world upside down for the people they loved. They've never dreamed of a rifle against a forehead and woken up as relieved as Maya does, because she'd rather dream about what she did to him than about what he did to her. They've never wondered if perhaps they should actually have followed the advice the town had given her: Shoot. Dig. Silence.

At a party a few months ago one guy asked Maya why she never drank more than one or two glasses of wine, and what could she say? Because of guys like you. Because you're everywhere.

But she *almost* succeeded in becoming a different person in this city. She *almost* succeeded in changing. She succeeded to the extent that one evening she decided to take a shortcut across the park in the dark without thinking about it.

Idiot idiot idiot.

She quickens her pace on the gravel path, just a little, and the man behind her speeds up too. Perhaps she's wrong? Perhaps it's her imagination? So she slows down, and he almost stops then. When she starts to move again she is no longer in any doubt about what he wants, and by then it is already too late. Her hand fumbles in her bag but her fingers feel clumsy and her phone slips from her grasp and lands on the path. He's approaching so quickly. She hears his breathing and the next second she feels his breath against her cheek.

She has time to get so angry with herself, so furious with everything and everyone, but most of all herself. Because she already has the knife in her hand. That was what she was looking for in her bag when her phone fell out, she knows she wouldn't have time to call anyone anyway, only defend herself. The blade is thin and not particularly long, she tells herself that she'll aim at the man's hands, he isn't wearing gloves, so if she cuts him there the pain might be bad enough to give her a head start when she starts running. They're so small, his hands, she finds herself thinking. The last thing that flits through her mind is the wish that she had tied her sneakers tighter. That's how much she's changed: she's become the sort of person who doesn't tie her shoes properly when she goes out. As if the world weren't full of men.

He moves. She lashes out.

She hears herself scream, not with fear but rage. Two years. She almost succeeded in becoming another person here. But in a crisis she finds out the truth about herself, and then she remembers Kevin's breath, his hard grip, her pounding heart. But she also remembers his gasps, his trembling fingertips when he saw the rifle, the smell of urine when he pissed himself with fear. Is he still out there on the jogging track at night, the way she's still in the room where he raped her? Did he ever come home from the forest? Is he still scared of the dark? She hopes so.

The man in front of her in the park screams, a pathetic little whimper. Did she get him with the knife? God, she hopes so.

It was Ramona who gave her the knife, on the morning of Maya's last day in Beartown before she left. "Take this and keep it in your handbag. Down there in the capital people are so damn touchy that they probably don't even let you take a shotgun with you if you're going into town. But for God's sake don't mention this to . . . ," she began, and Maya misunderstood and hurried to promise: "Don't worry, I won't say anything to Dad!" Whereupon Ramona snorted so hard that the candles went out on the other side of the bar: "Why the hell would you think I'm scared of your FATHER? Now, your mother, on the other hand . . . if she hears I gave you a knife, I'll probably get it in the ass. Literally."

Ramona wasn't good at hugs, so Maya did most of the work, but it was at least a hug. Maya has thought of getting rid of the knife a thousand times, but it's stayed in her handbag. "I daresay everyone has already asked you what the point of moving away from here is," were Ramona's parting words, "so all I'll say is that you need to be damn clear that the only people who move away from Beartown are smug bastards who think they're really something. And that's good. I want you to think you're something, girl."

"Wait. WAIT!"

Maya doesn't realize it's the man yelling at first, the voice is too young, too thin. He's leapt backward and Maya stays the knife at the last moment. He's standing with one hand in the air, the other is holding out her phone, trembling so much that it almost falls to the ground again. Shame washes through Maya when she realizes that it isn't even a man, it's a girl, about thirteen years old or so. A little kid. She stares at the knife in Maya's hand with tears streaming down her face.

"Sorry! I'm sorry!!!"

"What the HELL?" Maya yells, dropping the knife into her bag in panic, she's shaking uncontrollably now and the girl stammers nervously:

"Can I . . . can I walk with you? They took my phone and I didn't want to tell them the code, so they chased me and I saw you and thought . . ."

Only then does Maya see the other three girls, the same age, farther away in the park. Maya's heart is beating so hard that her ears are buzzing, and all she can think is what her mother said about the difference between moving to little Beartown from Toronto with its several million inhabitants: "In Beartown you only need to worry about wild animals if you go out at night, Maya, but in a big city you have to be afraid of everything." She was wrong, and she probably knew it even back then, it was as much a lie for her own sake as her daughter's. There are predators everywhere, just different sorts.

"Here . . . your phone . . . ," the girl in front of her whispers.

Maya sees the red marks on her wrists and knows how you get those: you tear yourself free, you fight for your life. She takes the phone, the girls farther away see the screen light up her face, maybe they think she's calling the police, because they turn as quickly as they appeared and vanish.

"Come on. Hurry!" Maya whispers, pulling the girl with her in the other direction.

The girl runs close beside her until they reach the end of the park.

"Where . . . where can you get a knife like that?" she asks when she eventually dares to speak.

Maya is leaning over breathlessly, hands on her knees, and wishes Ana was here to make fun of how out of shape she is. She avoids the girl's gaze and mumbles:

"A witch in the forest gave it to me."

"What?"

"Never mind. You shouldn't get a knife."

"Why not?"

"Because you should only have one if you're prepared to use it," Maya whispers, and hopes the girl is never as prepared as she is.

She hands the girl her phone and tells her to call her parents, and the girl does as she says. Maya hears her explain what happened, and swear over and over again that she's fine, Maya can see she's trying not to cry, not for her sake but her parents'. Most people don't know when their childhood ends, but this girl will always know exactly.

Maya remembers the hospital, after the rape, when her own mom wanted to murder the whole town and her dad whispered: "What can I do?" and all Maya could manage to say was: "Love me." It's a terrible moment for all kids when we realize that our parents can't protect us. That we won't be able to protect our own. That the whole world can come and take us whenever it likes.

The girl hands the phone back, says her mom wants to talk to Maya, and she hears a woman sobbing at the other end of the line:

"Thank you, oh, THANK YOU, I'm so happy my daughter was lucky enough to find you! We've taught her that if anything happens, she should run to an adult!"

This is the first time anyone has called Maya that. She waits with the girl until they see her parents' car come around the corner, the girl looks away from Maya for a moment, and when she looks back Maya has disappeared. Disappeared into the city where no one knows who you are and you can be who you want to be.

But who do you want to be?

A couple of blocks away Maya sits down warily on an ice-cold bench and goes to pieces. She sobs so hard she can't breathe. Everything she has spent all these months trying to forget is suddenly back: the sound of the buttons of her blouse bouncing across the floor, the posters on the walls of Kevin's room, the weight of his body, and the panic, the panic, the panic. The smell of him on her skin afterward, which she tried to scrub away until she was bleeding.

People say that our worst moments reveal who our real friends are, but of course most of all we reveal ourselves. Maya pulls out her phone. She could call any of her classmates, but what could she say? They don't have knives in their bags. They wouldn't understand.

Most of all she just wants to call her mom, she wants to hear her ask: "Is everything okay, darling?" and whisper back: "No, Mom, no, I'm not okay I'm not okay I'm not okay." She wants to yell into the phone that her mom should drive the whole way across the country and pick her up, the way she did so many times as a child when she went camping in the forest with Ana and got scared of the dark. Her mom was always in the car before Maya had time to finish the question, she always slept with her clothes on when the children weren't home. That's the only thing that stops Maya calling now. Her mom would have set off at once, driving all night, all the way, without any hesitation, but Maya has just been called an adult. So that's what she tries to be.

So instead she calls the only person she's got, the only person she's always had, because that's the question a crisis asks us: Who's your person? She calls Ana.

No reply. She calls again and again, and in the end she sends a text: `Pick up! I need you!` She'll feel so ashamed of that a few hours from now. She's going to hate herself so much when she finds out what's been going on at home.

11

Flagpoles

Home. It's never felt like home for Matteo. This town has never been interested in him.

He's sitting crouched in the ditch, when he flew off his bike he landed on his arm and now it's hurting so badly that for a few seconds he wonders if he was actually run over. He lets out a whimper as he stands up, the car is already long gone in the darkness. Ana, who was driving it, and Hannah, sitting beside her, didn't even see him. The trees shriek in the wind like metal scraping against porcelain. It's the space of a blink in an entire life, but perhaps it's there and then that Matteo finally decides he's had enough of being powerless. Enough of being weak. He decides to give as good as he gets, to anyone, any way he can.

He hauls himself up onto the road again, leaning into the wind and dragging his bicycle behind him. He loses his bearings. When he looks up he realizes he's gone in completely the wrong direction. He's up in the Heights, where the most expensive houses in town are, he can walk here from his own street in less than half an hour, but it's like a different country. The houses here are so large that two people could probably shout at each other from either end and still not hear each other, the windows so high that Matteo can't imagine how anyone cleans them. There are two cars parked in each drive, and a trampoline in each yard. This town is incredibly good at telling you what you can't afford to have.

He stops on the jogging track where there's a view across the whole lake, if you follow the shore with your eyes you can see all the way to the ice rink. Outside it there are twelve flagpoles arranged in two neat lines, green flags with the bear on them are always fluttering at the top of the poles, but someone is taking them down now, one by one, so they don't get torn to shreds in the storm. As carefully and tenderly as if each one of them were incredibly valuable.

The chain on Matteo's bicycle has come off, he tries to put it back on but his frozen fingers are shaking too much. He drags his bike most of the way into the center of Beartown, but in the end he gives up and abandons it.

No one who is out sees him, no one offers to help, all they care about is flags.

12

Roofs

Everything and everyone is connected in this forest, we're connected to the extent that when the roof collapses at an ice rink in Hed, a man automatically starts running in Beartown. One of the man's former coaches once said: "You get success by having extremely high integrity but absolutely zero prestige. Because integrity is about who you are, whereas prestige is only about what other people think of you." The man often thinks that this might be true in sports, but when you're talking about the survival of a town the opposite is true: prestige is everything. That's why he's running.

At some point during the past two years, hardly anyone knows exactly when because it wasn't even reported in the local paper, a few men and women gathered in a small room in the council building and made a political decision that seemed like a formality at the time: it has been proposed that the renovation of the ice rink in Hed should be postponed and renovation of the rink in Beartown brought forward instead. Afterward no one can remember on which grounds the decision was made, exactly, but it's the usual story, politics isn't always decided by politicians around here.

What actually happened was that a small but vocal "interested party" in Beartown had spent months cultivating the people in power, in conference rooms and in hunting lodges and in the supermarket, while the committee over at Hed Hockey was too busy trying to recruit a new coach to have time to object. Naturally not all the politicians were convinced that Beartown's ice rink was more important than Hed's, but enough of them buckled out of fear of losing allies. Political reality is harsh: the gaps between elections seem to get shorter and shorter, and election campaigns longer and longer.

The interested party managed to produce a survey which concluded that the risk of a collapse at Beartown ice rink was suddenly "imminent," which was obviously of additional concern given the club's extensive youth program. Surely they had to think about the children? The fact that the survey was conducted by the brother of a committee member at Beartown Hockey was never discussed. When someone asked to look at the report a couple of weeks later, no one could find it. But by then the decision had already been made and one ice rink had been prioritized over another.

The biggest item of expenditure in the renovation was the new roof for Beartown's ice rink. Right after the work was finished one single sponsor funded twelve flagpoles in the parking lot, with huge Beartown flags fluttering at the top as if in celebration. The same sponsor happened to have been the leader of the "interested party," which naturally hadn't contributed a penny toward the cost of the roof, because of course roofs aren't as much fun as flags. People see flags every time they go to a game, but no one pays any attention to a roof until it gets blown off.

Hardly anyone took any notice of the political decisions at the time, but now the storm has arrived, and the first thing to collapse over in Hed is the roof of the ice rink. At the same time a man is running through Beartown to save twelve flagpoles. That seems ridiculous, of course, until we see the consequences. A storm strikes a forest, one ice rink collapses and another remains standing, this will soon drive the inhabitants of two towns into a new battle for resources, and it will finish the way everything seems to finish around here: with violence. So much will have happened by then that we'll have forgotten how it all started, but it starts here. Now.

The man running toward the flagpoles is six feet tall, and he needs three digits to count his weight in pounds and his coat flaps behind him in the wind. He tries to untie the knots to get the flags down, but the knots are tight and his fingers are cold, and he ends up screaming out loud in frustration. Anyone who doesn't know him might think he's gone mad, but if you were to ask anyone who does, they'd exclaim: "*Gone* mad?"

He's known as Tails but has another, real name, of course. Many grown men in this town have two names: the one their parents gave them, and the one hockey gave them. As a young man he always tried to stick out from the crowd by wearing a suit when everyone else was wearing jeans and T-shirts, but on one occasion the whole team attended a funeral and all wore suits, so to stand out there he wore a tailcoat. Ever since then, he hasn't been called anything else.

His loafers are sliding on the ground and he keeps having to hoist his trousers up, but he struggles on with the knots regardless. He rushed past a boy on his way here, he doesn't know his name is Matteo, he didn't even see him. All he could think about were the scraps of green fabric fluttering at the top of some poles. For God's sake, they're only flags, people from other places might think, it's only a damn hockey club. But not for Tails.

His whole life he has been underestimated and dismissed, declared stupid and laughed at. His grocery store has come close to collapse, he's been on the brink of bankruptcy several times, but his enemies say he's like a garden weed: you can't get rid of him. He's been chased by the Tax Office, he's so notorious for financial graft and cooking the books that "he could find a shortcut on a straight line" is actually one of the kinder things that is said of him these days. But Tails keeps going, he just keeps going. Always with a smile and clenched fists, and the constant battle cry: "Let's do this!" He's survived every battle and in recent years has accumulated a small fortune. If you ask him, he'll say it's because he always looks a bit further ahead than everyone else, and if you don't ask him he'll tell you anyway. After the hospital in Hed and the factory in Beartown, his supermarket is the largest employer in the whole district. He's also one of the biggest sponsors of Beartown Hockey, and one of the town's worst kept secrets is that he personally handpicked several of the committee members. If you want to control this town, first you have to control the jobs, and secondly you have to control hockey, and if you want to have anything to do with either of those, these days you have to go through Tails. No one has any real idea precisely when the hell he has time to run his supermarket, because he seems to spend more time at the rink than the players, and more time in the council offices than the politicians. Everyone has an opinion about him, but no one can ignore him. They tried that around two years ago, and he won't let them forget him again.

That was after what he calls "the scandal," because he can't quite bring himself to say "the rape." He never says "Maya" either, even though he's known her father practically his whole life, he just says "the young woman." It was obviously a terrible year for everyone, but as usual no one seems to appreciate who the real victim was: a middle-aged man with large financial interests. Tails came close to losing everything.

Very few people around here probably realize just how close the politicians came to closing down Beartown Hockey and letting Hed Hockey take over everything. Beartown was only saved at the very last minute, by its supporters and new committee members and new sponsorship money from the factory, but everyone knows that Tails worked tirelessly in the background. Just in case anyone didn't know before, he was interviewed in the local paper last spring and he told the reporter: "I work BEHIND THE SCENES, you see, without being seen!" Then he offered some very useful advice on how the reporter ought to photograph him, and how large the picture ought to be, and then he showed him the brochure he had had printed for all the local businesses: "It isn't just *easy* to sponsor Beartown Hockey, it's also the *right* thing to do," the brochure said. Because when Beartown was facing the worst crisis in its history after "the scandal," Tails raised his eyes to the horizon and looked farther ahead.

Beartown had been just a club like all the others, he claimed, but now it was going to be a club like no other. Suddenly he embraced everything he had previously snorted at as politically correct innovations, so wholeheartedly that hardly anyone managed to keep up with him. He told the local paper proudly: "There are plenty of clubs that don't acknowledge their social responsibilities, but Beartown Hockey is different! Have I mentioned our huge investment in girls' hockey? Unique!"

Some people might call his actions shameless opportunism, but Tails would take that as a compliment: being an opportunist means seeing a chance and grabbing it. During his time as a hockey player he learned that every tactical decision is seen as either an act of genius or idiocy in hindsight, depending entirely upon the end result.

Naturally Tails also held up Amat, who came from the poorest part of Beartown but had gone on to become the club's biggest star, as proof that hockey "is open to everyone." Obviously he doesn't have precise figures for how many other players from the Hollow have ever played on the A-team, but didn't Benjamin Ovich's mom ALMOST live in the Hollow, so surely he should count? Admittedly, Benjamin moved abroad two years ago and no longer plays hockey, but he was actually HOMOSEXUAL, did the reporter know that? "Not that it makes any difference to us, of course, in this club we treat everyone the same!" Tails declared, without really explaining why he didn't feel the need to identify all of the other players on the team by their sexual orientation.

Of course Tails doesn't want to talk about "the scandal" with the reporter, "out of respect for those involved," because respect was very important to Tails. But in the brochure Tails had made sure that a photograph of Peter Andersson was displayed prominently, even though he no longer worked at the club, and next to Peter, Tails had added a picture of a little girl from the kids' team. You couldn't see her face, but you could see her long hair, the same color as Maya's, a subtle reminder that the sponsors should remember whose club Beartown was. Not Kevin's, but Maya's. Well, it was "subtle" for Tails, anyway. And it was "the *right* thing to do."

He paid for the twelve flagpoles outside the rink out of his own pocket, so that everyone on the way to a game now passed through a majestic avenue lined with huge green flags with the bear in their center, and because the local paper wrote about it and because people in general like flags far more than they like roofs, plenty of people got the idea that it was Tails who had funded the entire renovation. Not the council.

Tails himself was obviously too modest to boast about that, so he just said it in confidence to a couple of hundred people as well as the reporter. Shameless opportunism? Only if you regard that as something bad.

Of course Ramona over at the Bearskin pub always takes every chance to tell Tails how stupid he is. But behind his back, because that's the only time she *doesn't* make fun of him, she even admitted once: "Damn easy to tease men like Tails, but do you know what he is? He's the right sort of passionate. This town is his life's work. You might laugh at that, but what the hell have you ever created? What have you built in this town? And what's the state ever built? Do you think the government's going to come here and organize jobs and homes? They don't even know we exist!" Then she drank her supplementary breakfast and added: "Tails might be a massive idiot, but without massive idiots like him places like this don't survive."

That may have been an exaggeration, but it certainly wasn't untrue. Tails knows that everything is connected, the flags are a symbol of the club, if they get torn to shreds in the storm, tomorrow people will think hockey is weak. But if they're flying as proudly as ever, as if Beartown was immortal, people will feel instead that that's the truth. That's why Tails ran, because he sees a little farther ahead than everyone else.

And because he's a massive idiot.

The storm is so loud in his ears that he doesn't even know if he screams or not when his fingertip gets caught in the knot of one of the ropes and his fingernail gets torn right off. The pain is so immediate and so unbearable that he sinks to his knees and feels both his hand and his cheeks get wet.

He drags himself to his feet and hammers on the door of the ice rink. When no one opens up he kicks at the metal in despair.

Bangbangbang.

13

Kings

Matteo cuts through a smart residential area in the hope that the wind isn't blowing quite as hard between the houses. He holds on to walls and fences whenever he can, keeping his eyes closed, but the wind cuts through the gap between his eyelids anyway, as if it wants to force him to see the destruction. He walks past a house with a wooden sign on the door, written a long time ago by a small child who's a teenager now: "LEO AND MAYA AND PETER AND KIRA ANDERSSON LIVE HERE." Matteo walks a little too close to the driveway and a motion detector switches a light on. The electricity hasn't been cut off in this part of town yet, only on the outskirts at the edge of the forest where Matteo lives. The man inside the house jumps up in the living room and peers out through the window. Matteo knows who he is, everyone knows, his name is Peter Andersson and he used to be general manager of Beartown Hockey. He was once a professional player in the NHL. All hockey towns are monarchies and Peter used to be king around here. But he looks older now than he used to, more alone, more unhappy. That makes Matteo happy. The boy hopes that all the hockey men in this town, every single one, lose everything they love so that they can find out how it feels too.

Peter peers through the window and tries to see what made the light come on in the driveway, as if he's hoping to see a car there meaning that someone has come home. But he sees nothing, Matteo has already run off, into the wind. Peter will never know that he was there, he doesn't actually even know who the boy is. Not yet.

14

Chocolate balls

*B*ang bang bang.

Bangbangbangbangbang.

For a moment it sounds like hockey pucks against the wall of the house, but it's only the wind knocking a branch from the garden hedge against a fallen bin. Peter Andersson looks out at it in disappointment through the window, the storm is sweeping the whole town out there but he's dry and safe inside, he doesn't have to go out to rescue anyone, because no one needs his help. He feels sorry for himself about that, he feels sorry for himself a lot of the time these days, but mostly he feels sorry for himself for feeling sorry for himself. It's a form of internalized hatred that he can't see an end to.

It's only been two years since he resigned as general manager of Beartown Hockey, but he looks ten years older. It takes less and less time to comb his hair in the morning, longer and longer to pee. He's cleaned and cooked and baked bread today, he's started to get good at it, the way you do if you have too much time to practice. Maya is at her music college on the other side of the country and Leo, although he may be in his room, feels just as far away. Kira is still at the office over in Hed, and Peter is keeping her meal warm even though he knows there's no point. Small rituals in the war against loneliness, fleeting illusions of being needed.

"Dad, have you . . . I mean, maybe you should talk to someone? You seem so low!" Maya said when she was home during the summer.

That was the time she accidentally let slip that she was going "home" when she left Beartown, and saw how sad it made him. He lied, of course, and said he was just tired, because who would he talk to? A psychologist? That would be like paying someone to complain about the weather. Because how could he possibly explain? In Canada he had a coach who used to like repeating that it's "speed that kills" on the ice, it isn't the size of the player you get tackled by that's dangerous but the speed at which he approaches, and Peter didn't realize that was a lie until the day he left the rink for the last time. It's silence that kills. Not being part of anything anymore. He stepped down from his position as general manager of Beartown Hockey of his own accord, started working with his wife because he wanted to be a better husband and a better dad, and he's fairly sure he succeeded. He's better now. So how can he explain that he doesn't actually regret it, but regrets it nonetheless? That he just wasn't prepared to be forgotten so quickly?

The club is in better shape than it has been for a long time. They have new sponsors, the support of local politicians, stronger finances than they had for years, and a good team. A really, really good team. Last season they thrashed Hed Hockey each time they played by such a margin that it was almost humiliating, the towns are no longer equal, Beartown almost won the whole league and Hed almost got relegated. The clubs will meet each other again this year, but it feels as if this will be the last time that will happen, Hed seems to be set on an inexorable downward trajectory through the leagues, and Beartown is heading upward. One club is getting poorer and the other richer, it all changed so fast, just a few years ago their positions were reversed.

So how can Peter admit that the success everyone has been dreaming of cuts him like a knife? That it feels as if he was the problem? He lived an entire life in Beartown Hockey, but when he left it was like lifting a boot out of a bucket of water, he left no trace, it was as if he had never even been there. To an outsider hockey might be a ridiculous game, but never for someone who has been involved in it. It's as impossible to explain how the ice feels as it would be to explain what flying is like to someone who has lived their whole life on the ground. What does the sky matter if you've never seen it?

So what would he say to a psychologist? That he wishes someone needed him? That his life isn't enough? No. It's enough. It has to be enough.

The storm rattles the windows and gutters in its hunt for something that's hanging loose and can be torn off. Peter peers through the window when the light on the driveway comes on, hoping that Kira has come home. But there's nothing but shadows and senseless wind out there.

He looks at his phone and thinks about calling her, but he doesn't want to nag. He thinks about calling Maya too, but he doesn't want to be a nuisance.

So he just stands at the window, hating himself for feeling so sorry for himself.

———

Bang bang bang.

Maya is still out of breath, and her heart is beating so hard it's making her feel sick. She walks toward the apartment where her classmates are having a party, but stops in the street outside the building, alone, and can't bring herself to go in, far too terrified that her classmates will ask questions and that they'll be able to see what she's done in her eyes. They would never understand, they've never thought about animals that hunt and animals that take flight, the only animals they know anything about are in the zoo or in the refrigerator. They're sweet, naive children. Unlike Maya.

She looks around. There's a small pub on the other side of the street, a broken neon sign outside and a row of drunks on stools in front of a bartender who's tired of life. She's still so unused to being eighteen that she often forgets she's allowed to go to bars, she's fought so hard not to grow up that she missed when it happened, but now she crosses the street and opens the door and lets the gloom swallow her up instead of going up to her friends' party. She's met by the smell of spilled beer, but no raised glances, the clientele just stare into their glasses even when they speak to one another, it's the sort of place where it's an act of mercy that there are no mirrors in the bathrooms.

Bang bang bang. She takes a seat in the far corner, orders a glass of wine, downs it. The bartender asks to see some ID, but when Maya starts searching through her bag he just sighs and waves her away.

"Just wanted to know that you've got ID," he grunts.

Maya downs the next glass too. Her heart is still beating hard, partly because she had to run, and now because she realizes how close she came to stabbing that girl in the park. Now she knows what she's capable of. She's never felt more lonely than she does with that realization.

Bang. Bang. Bang. It slowly dawns on her that it isn't her heart making the noise, it's coming from the television on the wall. She knows what it is before she even looks up, she could recognize that sound anywhere, hockey is a sport of sounds more than anything else. The blades on the ice, one heavy body being slammed into the Plexiglas screen by another, the echo of the rink, the puck shooting like a bullet against the side of the rink: *bangbangbangbangbang.* She looks up and sees the game on the screen above the bar, the same sort of men as always, even if they look younger with each passing year. She hears the commentator say that it's a training match, the real season hasn't started yet, Maya thinks back to when her dad tried to explain that to her when she was little, and she exclaimed: "You want us to watch a TRAINING MATCH? That's like watching someone's PE lesson, Dad!" She'll never forget the way her mom laughed at that.

She drinks another glass of wine, slower this time. Her heart is thudding and thudding and she thinks about the psychologist her parents took her to two years ago, who said that sometimes it's hard for the human body to understand the difference between mental and physical exertion, between being out of breath because you've been running, and because you're having a panic attack. "That might be why some sportsmen play as if their lives depend on it, because that's what it feels like for them," the psychologist smiled without thinking, because where Maya grew up even the psychologists use hockey in their analogies. Even after what happened to her.

Bangbangbang.

The hockey doesn't make Maya angry, for the first time in ages. Maybe it's the wine, or the adrenaline, or the loneliness. But she's sitting in a pub in a city on the other side of the country and hockey sounds like . . . home. *Bang. Bang. Bang.* It sounds like being eight years old and holding her dad's hand.

———

Knock. Knock. Knock.

Peter taps gently on the door to Leo's room. When there's no answer he sticks his head in anyway and asks if his teenage son wants anything to eat. Children never understand that's the easiest way for us to feel useful: when we eat. But of course his son just swears when his dad distracts him and he loses his game. It used to be easier to be a dad, Peter thinks, it used to be possible to put a sandwich down without someone on the internet shooting your child in the head. No one tells you before you procreate that the hardest thing about being a good parent is that you never feel like one. If you're absent you're committing one big mistake, but if you're present the whole time you commit a million tiny ones, and teenagers keep a count. Oh, how they keep a count.

"Close the DOOR Dad!" Leo yells angrily.

Peter obeys and goes and sinks onto the sofa. The framed photographs on the wall next to the window rattle from time to time, the storm is really getting going outside now, the house is in the middle of town but they won't be safe even here. He eats the sandwich he made for his son, thinks once again about texting Kira or Maya, but doesn't. There's hockey on television, he raises the volume, but it doesn't feel as good as it used to. Sports used to remind him of who he was, but now it just reminds him of who he no longer is. He even changes channels for a while, but soon clicks back, forcing himself to concentrate on the game so he can't worry so much about everything else.

The game is between teams from the big city down south, down where there's no wind, so they don't give a damn about the fact that the forest up here is falling, he thinks. "As long as there are no trees on the motorways the national media doesn't care about the countryside being destroyed, but if they get two inches of snow the trains are canceled and the newspapers report it like the country's been invaded," Ramona used to say, and there's a lot of truth in that.

The photographs on the wall rattle again, so he gets up and takes them down. Almost all of them are of the children, of course. They had three, buried one. Maya and Leo don't even have any memories of their older brother, Isak, he was so young when he died, but his dad is still almost knocked flat every time he sees his firstborn son's smile. There are fingerprints on the glass of the frames because Peter leans against them at night sometimes when he feels like he has no identity. He may not be a hockey player or the general manager of a hockey club anymore, but he belongs to them.

He holds one photograph in his hands longer than the others, taken when Maya and Leo were little, skating down at the lake. Peter remembers it as if they used to do that every weekend, even though they probably only did it a few times each winter. He didn't have time more often than that during the hockey season, but everything that happens in childhood is a postcard that parents send to themselves. Things are never quite the way we remember them.

Once when Maya was little, she was still in primary school, she had new skates and started complaining that she had blisters after ten minutes.

Peter shouted at her for giving up so easily, so harshly that she started to cry and he started to hate himself. She tried to carry on skating, but fell and hit herself, and then he was the one who almost cried instead. "It wasn't your fault, Daddy," she whispered as he hugged her and said he was sorry, and he whispered back: "Everything that happens is my fault, Pumpkin." Then they sat on a jetty and ate chocolate balls and she put her hand in his and he can't remember any moment in his life being better than that.

———

The door of the bar opens, Maya doesn't have to look up to hear the young men stumble in, they're the sort who always make themselves heard everywhere, they keep their scarves on even though they're inside and they ask the bartender to recite the whole range of beers on offer. One of them looks up hopefully at the television and sighs dramatically when he sees it's hockey.

"Damn, I thought it was soccer! What the hell are you watching HOCKEY for?"

Maya empties her wineglass and contemplates throwing it at him. When she moved here she thought she'd find a thousand different types of men, but they're all the same here as well, only they're the same in a different way to where she comes from. They like soccer instead of hockey, they vote for different political parties, but they're just as convinced that their own worldview is the only one that exists, they think they're worldly when they actually live in the same narrow-minded little village as everyone else.

She remembers a story the neighbors always told her when she was a child, about when her dad was team captain of Beartown Hockey and they were playing a crucial match down here in the capital, and the way the newspapers derisively called the club from the small town in the forest "the call of the wild." Maya's dad, who hardly ever raised his voice, heard about that and yelled at his teammates in the locker room: "They might have the money, but hockey? Hockey is OURS!"

She thought it was a silly story when she was young, but now she's sitting in a bar and feels like yelling the same thing at strangers. The young man at the bar asks the bartender to change channels, and the bartender raises the volume instead. Maya decides to tip him double just for that.

Her dad gave everything he had out on the ice in that game twenty years ago, they still lost. He never really recovered, it was as if Beartown as a community never did either. That was probably one of the reasons he persuaded Maya's mother to move back home from Canada all those years later, to try to regain that, to make up for what he couldn't quite manage the first time around.

Maya stares down into the wineglass and tries to slow her heart rate by force of will. *Bang bang bang* comes from the television. It sounds like childhood. She used to love eating pumpkin, seeds and all, but when she was nine she made her dad stop calling her that, and secretly missed it from then on. She liked the lake in winter because he was so happy on skates, so calm, they were to him what her guitar is for her.

"Christ, what a retarded sport this is, go out and screw a lynx or something instead, stupid rednecks!" one of the young men slurs at the television, and his friends laugh in a dialect that isn't even a dialect, just a big, anxious nothing.

Maya feels the alcohol burning her synapses like fireworks in her brain. She thinks about one winter when she was a child, one of those perfect, still days when the whole family was skating down on the lake and her mother said: "What an incredible place this is, though." Her dad replied: "The most incredible thing is that it's still here. That there are still people here." He sounded so sad, Maya didn't understand it at the time, but she does now: everything gets shut down in the forest, everyone moves to the big cities, even your own daughters. It's incredible that there's anything left. "They don't feel enough shame," people in Beartown say about the people down here, Maya never used to agree, but now she does.

"Hello? Earth calling girl! Do you want a drink or not?"

The young men sitting a short distance away are waving at her. She shakes her head.

"What the hell? Don't be so miserable! Smile a little!" one of them leers.

She looks away, he says something else but she doesn't hear it because the bartender has already taken his tip from the bar and puts the television remote in front of her with a friendly wink. She raises the volume: *BANG BANG BANG BANG BANG BANG.*

She remembers the chocolate ball that was so frozen after lying in her bag that she had to take her glove off and thaw it out in her hand, and then her hand was so cold that she had to warm it up by sticking it in her dad's much larger glove and holding his hand. She remembers the boys, a few years older, playing hockey a bit farther away on the ice. Always hockey, everywhere, always. *Bangbangbang.* When one of the boys scored a goal and cheered, she asked her dad: "Who scored?" Not because she cared, but because she knew that he did. He replied so quickly that he turned bright red with shame: "Isak! No . . . I mean . . ." He fell silent. "You said Isak," Maya said quietly. "Sorry, sometimes . . . sometimes that boy is so like Isak somehow . . . ," he confessed.

Maya chewed the rest of her chocolate ball slowly for a long time before she dared ask: "Do you miss Isak every day?" Peter kissed her hair. "Yes, all the time," he admitted. "I want to miss him too, but I don't really even remember him," Maya replied unhappily. "I think you can miss him just as much anyway," her dad assured her. "How does it feel?" she asked. "Like having blisters in your heart," he said.

She thawed a chocolate ball between her fingers and ate it slowly, then she put her cold hand inside her dad's glove, and she had no idea how long he would remember that. When half of the boys over on the ice raised their sticks and cheered again, she asked: "Who scored this time?"

Her dad smiled and answered, and he had no idea how long she would remember that: "His name is Kevin."

The first time Maya can remember hearing that name, it was her dad who said it, with admiration in his voice.

Bang bang bang.

The young men in the bar have moved closer.

15

Weapons

Matteo stops outside the Bearskin pub. An old woman is collecting beer glasses on her own inside. The lights are on and when Matteo stands really close to the door he can smell fried food and cigarette smoke. He's only fourteen years old, but he wonders if the landlady might make an exception to the rules today, he just wants somewhere to sit out the storm, anywhere that isn't home. He tries the handle but the door is locked. He bangs on it, but the old woman doesn't hear him.

Then the power goes off there too. The woman goes upstairs, and the noise of the wind against the roof drowns out all the boy's cries. Maybe things would have turned out differently if she had opened up. We'll never know.

Shivering, Matteo sets off for home. All the buildings on the street where he lives have no electricity now, but he can see circles of light from flashlights bouncing around upstairs in the neighboring house. An elderly couple lives there, but he daren't knock on their door. He knows they don't like his family, for the same reason a lot of other people don't like his family: they're regarded as odd. Not dangerous or unpleasant, just odd. If you spend too many years being odd, people start to find you unsettling, and if you're unsettling enough, no one wants to let you inside even when there's a storm.

So Matteo digs out an iron bar in his neighbors' toolshed and pries open their basement window. It's as dark in there as it is in his own house, but here he can hear the old couple's voices and then at least he knows that he isn't dead. The little room is a mixture of guest room and office, and even if it looks like it hasn't been used as either of those for a long time, he still finds a small bag of tea lights and some matches in a drawer. Old couples like this, who lived in Beartown long before the modern electricity grid, are always prepared for power cuts, and have matches in almost every room.

In the flickering glow of the tea lights Matteo spends the night like a thief. The voices from the floor above have fallen silent, or perhaps are just being drowned out by the roar of the storm, when the boy finds the gun cabinet.

He doesn't manage to open it. Not tonight.

16

Violence

Night falls outside the living room window of the house while Peter leaves fingerprints on the glass of the framed photographs. Life has gone so damn fast, but he really should have been prepared for that, because hockey warned him, after all. One of the first things you learn as a young player is to shoot the moment you see an opening, because otherwise a thousand other things can happen and the chance on goal is gone in the blink of an eye. You have to be an opportunist.

On the bookcase in the living room he catches sight of two drumsticks, he doesn't know why he left them there, but he knows exactly when it was: the day Maya left home, the last time they played together. Peter wasn't much of a drummer, sadly, he managed to fool her for a few years when she was little, but she was soon so good on the guitar that he struggled even to keep up with her. That's the lot of being a parent: at first all activities are done for their sake, and in the end for ours. Eventually we realize that everything is about us wanting to be wherever they are, as much as possible, for as long as they let us. Peter weighs the drumsticks in his hand. Maya hated hockey and he was so desperate for music to bring them closer together, then she grew up and music took her away from here.

That's the problem, really: everything is about him, even when it's about her. It's a terrible thing for a grown man to have to admit to himself that not everything he did was actually for his child's sake. Very little of it was, in actual fact.

He was so proud of himself when he resigned from the club and started working for Kira. Before that, so many years had passed when the whole house would be asleep when he got home at night that it actually felt kind of cool now that Kira was the one who stayed late at the office and felt bad about it. Peter was the one who went home first, took Leo to his various activities and left a note on the kitchen table saying "your dinner's in the fridge, love you" when he went to bed. He was the one who drove right across the country to Maya's dorm room at her new college and helped her drill holes in the wall for bookshelves. They ended up a bit wonky, admittedly, but still. He was the one who was there, not her mother, and he was so pleased with himself when his daughter whispered: "Thanks Dad, what would I do without you?"

The next time Peter visited, the shelves were straight. Maya had bought a drill and fixed them herself. Naturally she never told him because she didn't want to hurt his feelings, and he coughed to clear the lump in his throat and pretended he hadn't noticed. Our children never warn us that they're thinking of growing up, one day they're just too big to want to hold our hand, it's just as well we never know when the last time is going to be or we'd never let go. They drive you mad when they're little, yelling every time you leave the room, because you don't realize at the time that whenever someone yells "Daddy!" that means you're important. It's hard to get used to not being important.

Peter sacrificed hockey to become a better dad. But now his children no longer need a dad. He is no longer anything for anyone. The worst thing about leaving hockey was that it was only then that he realized that he'd never been anywhere near as good at anything else. He gave the game the best years of his life, and became one of the best in the world. He only played four NHL games and injured his foot in the fifth, the doctors might as well have ripped the lungs out of his body when they said he wouldn't be able to play again, because he couldn't breathe for several years, but he was *there*. Out of all the millions of hockey playing kids out there, *he* was the one who got to play with the best in the world. How many people get that far in anything?

Then he came home and became general manager of his hometown club, he built up the whole youth program, turned the young guys' achievements into his own. Now no one even calls and asks him for his opinion anymore. Nothing is as good at showing you what's now in your past as hockey and children, they make you an old man so quickly.

So what would he say to a psychologist? That he misses the emotions, even the disappointments, because no one stands up and cries out in either delight or frustration in an office? That now every day is like any other, the job is just a job, but hockey was an obsession for him, and a life without obsessions feels like sitting in a waiting room without any doors. No one's going to call your name. You're waiting for nothing.

He gave that game his life, that was his mistake, he doesn't need a psychologist to tell him that. He was looking the wrong way. He made the wrong children's successes his own. By the time he resigned his job and left hockey, it was already too late, Maya and Leo could manage without him. Childhood goes so fast, if you get the opportunity and don't take it, a thousand things can happen and then the chance is gone in the blink of an eye.

One time he said, heavy with bitterness: "What can the sport give us? We devote our lives to it, and what's the best we can hope for? A few moments . . . a few victories, a few seconds when we feel bigger than we really are." He received this reply: "So what the hell is life, Peter, other than moments?" Obviously he was talking to Ramona. The old crone doesn't offer discounts on either beer or scolding.

Sometimes he calls in at the Bearskin pub on the way home from work, the way his dad always did, but without getting as drunk as him. "That's the way it is with the sons of dads who liked whiskey too much: you either drink all the time or not at all," Ramona usually snorts as she pours scorched coffee into a beer glass for him. But on one occasion, when she had drunk twice as much breakfast as normal and happened to get a bit bogged down in emotions, she prodded him and grunted: "That's the way it is with sons who had bad dads: you either become bad dads as well, or you end up really good. But the fact that your dad, who was such an unbelievably terrible dad, didn't manage to turn you the slightest bit bad, that's a total fucking mystery to me."

Peter just stared so hard at the counter that he could have drilled holes in it. She thought that was because he was thinking of all the times his dad came home from that very bar and tried to find reasons to beat his wife and child, so she shut up. Peter drank his coffee and felt more of a fraud than ever, because he wasn't thinking about his dad at all, just about himself. And the sound of hockey pucks.

One winter, when the family had only just moved back here, Maya hadn't even started school at the time, a child, only a few years older, went missing in the forest when the temperature was way below freezing. It was a boy who had been playing in a kids' game, and missed a shot in the final seconds. Like every other hockey player in Beartown he had already learned that nothing but perfection was good enough, so he was inconsolable and furious and that night he ran away from home. Everyone knew how quickly a small body can freeze to death in the darkness here, so the whole of Beartown was out looking for him. They found him down on the lake. He had dragged a goal and some pucks and all the flashlights he could find, and was standing out there shooting from the same angle from which he had missed the final shot of the game. He was sobbing with rage, and fought like a wounded animal with anyone who tried to get close, it wasn't until Peter went over and grabbed his hands and hugged him that he calmed down. In those days everyone in the town looked up to the general manager who had been an NHL pro so much that he was like royalty to the boy. "I know you want to be the best, and I promise to do all I can to help you get there, but training's finished for tonight," Peter whispered in the boy's ear. He was still sobbing when Peter picked him up and carried him home. In the years that followed Peter kept his promise: he led the club that helped Kevin Erdahl become the best player the town had ever seen, taught him that he was invincible, that he should never tolerate defeat. Or the word no. It was Peter who lifted him up into his arms down on the lake. It was Peter who *carried* the boy home.

Ten years later Peter was sitting in a hospital with his fifteen-year-old daughter, whispering: "What can I do?" and she replied: "Love me."

So what could a psychologist say to him now? Nothing. He already knows that everything that happens to his children is his fault.

Everything.

———

"Maya?"

Maya doesn't hear, she's busy with wine and hockey and the banging, from both the television and inside her. "We are the bears," she grins to herself with intoxication's inability to distinguish between what she's thinking and what she's actually singing out loud: "The Beeeears from Beeeartooown . . ." She thinks of how her mother used to say that "this damn place is a hockey town with alcohol problems for six months of the year, and an alcoholic town with hockey problems for the other six." She misses them both, her mother and home. At least the way she remembers them, both of them. Things are different now.

She thinks back to when she returned to Beartown in the summer and by chance happened to see one of those brochures that Tails, her dad's childhood friend, had printed to attract new sponsors to the club. It was on the floor of the supermarket, dropped accidentally or discarded, she read the main heading several times: "It isn't just easy to sponsor Beartown Hockey, it's also the right thing to do!" Inside was a picture of Maya's dad, and beside him a picture of a little girl from the kids' program. Maya never told her dad she'd seen the brochure, but she understood exactly what the club was trying to achieve with it: now suddenly Beartown was *her* club, now that she was of some use to them. Now that there was money to be gained, suddenly they were the most enlightened and equal sports club in the whole country. She was actually supposed to have stayed in Beartown a couple more days back in the summer, but she threw away the brochure, changed her ticket, and left the following morning.

"Maya?" the voice in the bar says again, followed immediately by another voice:

"It IS you! Why haven't you come up to the apartment? Why are you sitting here like some . . . alcoholic?"

Surprised, Maya tears her eyes away from the hockey and stares at two of her classmates. They're giggling nervously as if they've just looked at her computer and found some porn. Their hair is perfect even though they're drunk, and she really hates them for that, they've just left the party to come and ask the bartender if they can buy some ice. Paying for *ice*, Maya thinks. What sort of planet has she actually moved to?

"Are you . . . okay?" one of the classmates with perfect hair asks.

"Yes, yes, I'm just tired, I needed to be on my own and think for a bit . . . ," Maya mumbles.

"Think?" the other girl with even more perfect hair smiles, as if the word was incredibly exotic.

The young men in the bar notice what's going on, and one of them immediately blurts out in delight:

"Girls! Do you know each other? Now we can have a party! And can you cheer up Grumpy over there?"

Maya's classmates roll their eyes at them but Maya doesn't even hear them. She's turned the volume of the television up again.

"Maya, come back to the party with us now, we . . . ," the girls start to say, but Maya hushes them.

"Just wait . . . I said WAIT!"

The commentator on television is talking about which training matches due to be played tonight have been postponed. "Because of the storm," he says, then lists club after club in towns up in the north, and Maya taps her forehead in an effort to make sense of the geographic refer-ences. Beartown lies at the center of all the places he mentions. She pulls out her phone and checks the newsfeed and her fingers start to shake when she sees the weather report: "Storm warning!" That was why Ana didn't answer. Maya's been sitting here feeling sorry for herself and back home the whole world is being blown apart?

"Look, are you coming or what? To the party?" one of her classmates asks impatiently.

"I don't get it, you're sitting here watching . . . hockey? I mean . . . is that ironic? I didn't think you liked stuff like that!" the other girl says.

One of the young men cheers when he hears that, and jumps down from his barstool. His scarf gets caught and almost strangles him, but in the middle of an involuntary full-body spin he manages to say:

"Exactly what I said! What sort of girl even likes hockey? Huh? It's not a sport, it's just VIOLENCE!"

"It really is!" Maya's classmate agrees.

Maya hears what they say this time but doesn't respond, she just stares at her phone. "*Storm could be the region's worst natural disaster since the forest fires,*" she reads on the website of her hometown's local newspaper and it feels like she's in a different country. The wine sloshes around in her head like a broken spirit level when she tries to stand up, far too quickly, she takes two swaying steps and almost loses her balance. The young man snatches up his scarf and holds out his hand to catch her, but she manages to find her footing and bats him away with such force that he jumps back, sadly not fast enough. Because she's already so furious that she instinctively takes a step forward and shoves him in the chest, sending him flying into the stools behind him. Her classmates stammer her name, they make tentative moves to touch her, but when they see the black look in her eyes they shrink back and retreat.

"Violence? What the hell do you know about violence?" Maya hisses, then marches past them all, out into the street.

They're too shocked even to call after her. For two years they've wanted to know more about her, and now they know everything. Now she's shown them what sort of animal she is.

———

Peter rests his elbows on the coffee table and his forehead on the palms of his hands and hopes desperately that he's going to see light on the drive. He got his friend Hog to install a motion sensor that turns the light on when Kira turns in to the drive. Peter says it's for her benefit, so she can see better, but really it's for him. So he can count the minutes she remains in the car before she comes indoors. The number keeps growing and growing. Often he pretends to be asleep when he hears the key in the lock because he knows that's what she's hoping.

He sends her a text message. She replies in brief, that's how they communicate these days, two or three words at a time.

```
On your way?


                                        Yes. You?


Yes. Home.


                                        Leo ok?


All ok. You?


                                              Ok.
```

But she never sets off. Peter closes his eyes and rubs his eyelids as hard as he can, and when he opens them again it's still dark. He blinks, at first surprised, then horrified, he fumbles around in the darkness and stumbles away from the coffee table. Then a single source of light dazzles him and he hears Leo's voice:

"What the hell are you doing, Dad?"

He's shining his cell phone toward Peter.

"Nothing. Why did you turn all the lights off?" Peter gasps.

Leo snorts.

"It's a power cut! Have you had a stroke or something?"

Peter blinks away everything inside him. He reaches for Leo and leads him to the garage to fetch flashlights. Leo takes one and at first goes back into his room, then comes back out. He's fourteen years old, so obviously he isn't scared of the dark, of course not, but maybe he'll sit on the sofa next to his dad anyway?

He plays games on his phone until the battery dies, then he plays with Peter's until that dies too. The last thing Peter sees is a text from Kira: About to leave. He replies with a simple Ok, and as soon as the screen dies he regrets not writing "Love you."

———

At home in her student room Maya is sitting on the floor beneath her bookshelves refreshing news websites and weather forecasts over and over again to get news about the storm. She cries and calls Ana in turn, until in the end she's just crying. She spends ages thinking about calling her parents, but they'll hear that she's drunk and her mother will be angry and her dad disappointed. In the end she calls her little brother, but his phone is switched off.

"Shit, Leo, please answer . . . ," she whispers into the darkness, but he won't even see that she's called until the power comes back on the following morning and he can charge his phone again. That's how he ends up being the one who calls and wakes his sister and tells her what's happened.

"Dead? Wha-what do you mean, dead?" Maya will slur, half-asleep and hungover.

Then she'll book a train ticket, pack a bag, and head north. She'll think about her dad the whole way home.

17

Dead

"Home." There really ought to be more words for that. One to cover the people we have there, another with room for those we have lost.

Kira stands in her office in Hed staring out into the night until the storm presses the building's windowpanes in so claustrophobically hard that she starts to panic. She turns toward her desk but suddenly that goes dark as well, the power goes off so abruptly that it feels like an assault. She starts and swears out loud as she hits her knee on a chair, then she sinks down onto the floor alone, overwhelmed by a feeling of impotence. The darkness seems to make the deserted office gigantic.

She and her colleague moved the company here last year when the business was expanding and they took on more staff, it was really far too big but Kira fell in love with the premises, in an old station building more than one hundred years old. She had started to love old things, even though she had always dreamed of fresh, modern interiors, perhaps that's a sign that she's more of a forest person than anything else now. I'm only missing the cross-country skis and refusal to conjugate verbs now, she thinks bitterly.

She lies on the floor with her eyes closed as the windows start to rattle worse and worse. She thinks that she should have gone home to Peter and she feels ashamed that she ought to *want* to go home more than she does. She knows something is wrong, somewhere inside her, if she would rather stay here.

Somewhere between dozing and almost being asleep she remembers how Peter took the car, not all that long ago, and drove down to Maya's new city, her new home, to help her put some shelves up in her student room. And how Kira sat here in her office in the meantime, and how her phone buzzed with a text message from him. He had sent a picture of the car, parked fairly close to a junction, with the question: `Can I park here without getting a ticket, do you think?` She starts to laugh in the darkness at how stupid it is. Their love story is so peculiar that he seriously thought she could judge thirty feet on a PHOTOGRAPH and determine if he was too close to the intersection or not. Perhaps that was why she dared to set up this business, because he genuinely believes she can do anything, and sometimes that can be infectious.

Maybe, she thinks to herself somewhere between thought and dream, it's actually no more complicated than that she simply won't tell him the extent of the company's financial problems at the moment. They've lost some big clients and are up to their eyes in unpaid invoices, but she just keeps quiet about it to him because she can't bear to disappoint him when he's sacrificed everything. When you're young and in love you think the difficult part of being in a relationship is admitting when you need help, but when you've been married for half your life you know that the hardest thing is admitting that you really don't: you don't need anyone's help to feel inadequate and a failure and worthless. Because no one is as good at making us feel all those things as we are ourselves. Kira can see it in Peter's eyes every time she happens to criticize him. "I don't need any help," he wants to yell at her, but all she gets is silence. She knows exactly how he feels, because she too is the best.

She loves this office, the only real problem with the old station building is that it's in Hed, not in Beartown. She has been obliged to live with Peter's unspoken fury about that, so much so that she has occasionally asked herself if that might have been the subconscious reason for her choosing it, to force him to distance himself even more from hockey, so that it couldn't drag him back. But for what? For whose benefit? It hasn't saved their marriage, possibly just prolonged it. She doesn't even go home when there's a storm coming, so when *would* you go home then? What is it, anyway, "home," when she spends more time in Hed than in Beartown these days? What does that make her?

These crappy towns, she thinks, perhaps mostly to feel that there's someone else to blame. These crappy towns and their childishly petty feelings of jealousy and hatred that always force everyone to pick a side in everything. Because of course Peter wasn't the only person who was annoyed that the office was in Hed, his childhood friend Tails turned up here only a couple of weeks ago with four other men, they were careful to explain that it wasn't an "official visit," and that they weren't "representing either the council or the club," but were just "a sort of interested party." Beartown and its bullshit interested parties, Kira thought as she heard them running on, that pathetic town and their pathetic game. Tails was, in line with his nickname, ridiculously overdressed, this time in a pin-striped suit over a waistcoat and tie, while the other four were in the usual uniform of the district's entrepreneurial cowboys: jeans, shirt, tight jacket, and delusions of grandeur. Kira thought about what her colleague said when they first started the company: "The only thing two women like us need to succeed in the world of business is ten years of combined study of the law, thirty years of combined professional experience, and the collected self-confidence of one really mediocre middle-aged man."

The five men were all successful businessmen from the area, sponsors of Beartown Hockey and regular "concerned residents" in the local paper's letters page. They gathered around Kira's desk as if it were an art installation, because of course it looked like a man's desk, only there was a woman sitting behind it, and that seemed to fascinate them. One of them thought that Kira's colleague was really her assistant, so he asked if he could have a cappuccino, to which her colleague replied that he'd get one in the face if he wasn't careful, and Kira had to grab hold of her arm to stop her demonstrating that this was no empty threat. One of the other men asked if Peter wasn't going to take part in the meeting, whereupon her colleague replied: "Sure, he makes a really good cappuccino!" Tails picked up the hint and threw his arms out grandly: "Ladies, we don't want to take up your valuable time." After which he promptly took up forty minutes of it.

"This really doesn't look good," he smiled, by which he meant the fact that Kira, in her capacity as Mrs. Andersson, wife of the former general manager of Beartown Hockey, had chosen to locate her successful business in Hed. "We need to stick together, don't we, us Beartown folk? Don't you think? In a small town everything is connected, Kira, businesses and politics and inhabitants . . . ," he declared, stopping himself from adding "and hockey!" seeing as he saw that Kira's colleague was weighing her coffee cup on her hand as if trying to determine how hard she could throw it. Instead Tails proudly pulled out, as if it were a Renaissance painting, a document that turned out to be a very advantageous rental contract for some newly renovated office premises in Beartown. They were owned by the council but that wasn't a problem, Tails assured them, because he had negotiated a reduction in the rent directly with the politicians. "And of course this is only TEMPORARY, because within the next couple of years you'll be able to move the company HERE!" More documents were produced and spread out across the desk. "Beartown Business Park!" Tails declared triumphantly.

These pompous men and their grandiose plans, Kira thought, there's always something. In recent years they have fantasized, successively, about an airport, an art gallery, hosting a skiing world championship, and now this. New office buildings right next to Tails's supermarket, a center for business life in the whole district, built with council money and with him at its center. And down by the ice rink a new training facility will be built at the same time, Tails explained, adding proudly: "We're investing in the children, Kira, all this is for the children!" None of it ever is really, of course. Children are always just the alibi. *Beartown Business Park*, even the name was perfect in its sparkling stupidity. She never ceases to be surprised at how they never cease to surprise her, these aging men. Tails took her silence as admiration and grinned the way only men who don't know the difference between dialogue and monologue can: "We have to stick together, Kira, don't we? What's good for the town is also good for us!"

Instinctively, Kira felt like throwing him out of the window without opening it first, of course, but sadly she noticed from the contract on the desk that the rent he was offering in Beartown was half what they were paying for the old station building here in Hed. Their finances could certainly do with the help. Not even her colleague knows how badly things are going, Kira has hidden everything from everyone, stubbornly thinking that she's going to find a way to solve everything herself. It's wrong, she knows that, but it's gone on for too long for her to be able to retreat now. So when her colleague squinted suspiciously at Kira when she saw that she was even considering the offer in the contract, Kira felt obliged to play hardball and ask: "What about you, Tails? What do you and the club want in return?"

Tails threw his arms out in a gesture so dramatic that he knocked over a stack of files. "What do we want? We HELP each other, surely, Kira? We're friends. Neighbors, almost!"

Only then did one of the other men lean forward and suggest, in good faith and to "add my thoughts," that Kira and her colleague might consider sponsoring Beartown Hockey for an amount that might, purely coincidentally, match the reduction Tails had negotiated on the rent with the council. "And of course as sponsorship that would be tax deductible, our accountants can sort that out. Win-win for you *and* us!"

So that was why. Of course. Always an ulterior motive, always a plan. Graft, graft, graft, it never ends. If Beartown is a family, the ice rink is the spoiled child who eats everyone out of house and home.

"Well . . . look . . . that's only a suggestion," Tails said, clearing his throat, and Kira could see that he wished the other man hadn't been quite so plainspoken.

Tails loved secrets, he understands that secrets are power, so when the man beside him opened his mouth it probably wasn't planned. The old man was just getting impatient and was doing what all old men do when they meet women like Kira and her colleague: underestimate them.

"Soon NO businesses are going to want to be left in Hed, you know, because soon there won't be anything here! Soon Hed won't even have a hockey team!"

Aghast, Tails nudged him hard with his elbow, but it was too late, Kira raised an eyebrow and put on her most naive smile and asked:

"Really?"

Naturally the old man couldn't resist:

"The council wants to close down Hed Hockey! They only want one club in the district, that was why they spent years trying to shut Beartown down, but now Beartown is the big brother and Hed the little brother. Do you see? We have the best team and the best finances and the biggest sponsors! So Hed Hockey will be the one that gets closed down, and soon everything else will follow! By the time we're done Beartown will be a big city and Hed a small backwater, so take the chance to move back while you can, because soon you might not be able to afford it!" The old man laughed so hard that his stomach bounced, like the wind on wet canvas. Tails had a strained smile on his face and avoided Kira's gaze as he mumbled, almost embarrassed:

"Well . . . obviously . . . that's not official. That business about the hockey clubs. No one knows that discussions are taking place, not even . . . your husband."

He couldn't even bring himself to say "Peter." Kira and her colleague stood up to indicate that the meeting was over. They nodded diplomatically, or at least Kira did, and shook hands and promised to think about the offer to change address.

As the jeans and jackets lumbered out of the office Tails raised one hand in mournful greeting to Peter, alone in his office behind a transparent door. Peter sat there in his glass box like a lion that had lost its mane, and Kira felt like a woman who had lost her man. Once upon a time Peter used to know all the secrets in this forest, but now Kira knew more about the hockey club than he did. Now she was more important than him.

The door closed behind Tails and the other middle-aged men. Kira sat at her desk staring at photographs. During the weeks that had passed since then, Peter has gone home earlier and earlier to pick up Leo and she gets home later and later and sits longer and longer in her car on the drive. It was his idea to start working here, but maybe he only did that because he thought that was what she wanted, and now she doesn't know what she wants anymore. The most impossible thing about a marriage is that even if you do everything right, you're never done with it.

It isn't Peter's fault that the job ended up like this, nor hers either, the company simply grew too big too quickly. When he started working here, Kira promised that he would work with "human resources" and "staff issues," which was fine when they didn't have many employees, but now there are too many and he's like the weakest player on a hockey team that has been promoted to a higher league. He's not cut out for this level. Everyone else has training and experience, he's merely married to the boss. Kira tries to hide his lack of serious tasks with paperwork, but it's just getting worse and worse. Peter hasn't shrunk with her success, but she's grown so much that he now looks smaller by her side.

"Soon you'll have to start a pretend company and hire in actors to do pretend jobs so he can think he's doing something important," her colleague teased her recently.

"It's not that bad!" Kira countered.

Her colleague shrugged. She teases Peter a lot, so much so that he thinks she hates him, which eventually made her feel sympathetic instead. When he started work here it was the first time in his life he had to wear a tie, which turned out to be a challenge in itself: it always seemed to end up either too short or too long when he knotted it. So he started using a ready-knotted version, until Kira's colleague caught sight of the Velcro strap sticking out from under his collar and exclaimed: "I didn't know they made those in your size!" Peter blushed and tried to defend himself, saying it wasn't a child's tie at all, but a "safety tie," the sort bodyguards wear so they don't get strangled if anyone pulls on it. Kira's colleague's face cracked into a delighted smile: "A bodyguard? Like Kevin Costner in that film?" Peter realized his mistake far too late, and now he had to put up with her singing "*I will always love youuuu*" every time she went past his office, which she found an improbable number of reasons to do each day seeing as her own office was at the other end of the building. Kira had pretended not to notice Peter practicing over and over every morning since then, but his tie still ends up being either too short or too long. He's never going to feel completely comfortable in her world.

So in the end Kira's colleague looked her in the eye the other day and said: "Listen, my experience of men is that most of them only want two things from a woman: that she bolsters his self-confidence and that she leaves him alone. When a man gets really stupid, it's usually because he has poor self-confidence or because he feels smothered. But in Peter's case? Hell, I think you've probably left him alone far too much . . ."

Kira snapped back at her, pointing out that a woman who can't maintain a relationship unless she glues herself to a man while he's asleep probably wasn't an expert on the subject. Her colleague calmly responded by saying that Kira had been married forever and that didn't seem to have helped much either. Then Kira closed her eyes and whispered through clenched teeth:

"Damn. Have things gone this far now?"

"What?" her colleague wondered.

"That even you're on Peter's side?"

Her colleague said nothing for a while, before replying honestly:

"I don't know anything about marriage. But I don't think you're supposed to have sides."

———

Damn, Kira thinks now, alone on the floor of the office. Damn. Damn. Damn!

She knows what everyone else thinks, of course: why doesn't she just let Peter go back to working at the club again? Give hockey back to him?

Because she knows how that would end up, because she's spent half her life living in Peter's world. You can't be a bit involved in that club, it's a monster, it consumes relationships like a jealous lover. Hockey will never be satisfied, no one is ever enough, and that goes for life outside the rink as well.

Two years ago, after all the horrors of the world had landed on Maya, for a few moments Kira and Peter forgot to keep an eye on Leo. So their son found new friends, the worst sort, the sort with black jackets who drew out all the darkness in him. Kira and Peter got a sneak preview of how Leo's life might turn out if they left him to his own devices, with his demons and lack of impulse control. After that they promised each other that one of them would have to be home more. To *see* him.

Is that not reasonable? Hasn't Kira done her bit, for all those years, isn't it her turn to be allowed to devote herself to her work now? She starts ten different text messages to Peter but deletes them all, in the end writing just: About to leave. She almost hopes he'll call back and yell at her because it's such a blatant lie, but he just replies: Ok.

Damn.

There's a flashlight in the desk drawer but she doesn't take it out. Rain is rumbling against the windows, the glow from her cell phone is all that lights her face as she scrolls through years of saved photographs of her children, birthday parties and snowball fights and Sundays spent skating on the frozen lake. They look like the perfect family, and, like so many times before, she wonders if they were ever really that.

She dozes off, curled up on the carpet, but never really falls asleep. Slowly her brain gets used to the banging and roaring outside, and her body stops twitching. She never hears Peter come in, he can walk so quietly, touch her with such gentleness. She feels his breath on the back of her neck, and his rough hands with the crooked fingers that got broken in all manner of different ice rinks reach around her waist. She smiles but keeps her eyes closed, tighter and tighter because she doesn't want to wake up and realize that she's only dreaming about him.

"Do we have to lie on the floor?" he eventually whispers in her ear.

"What?" she murmurs.

"Do we have to lie on the floor, darling?" he repeats.

She doesn't know whether to hug him or yell at him, so all she manages to say is:

"How did you even get here?"

"I walked."

"WALKED?"

"Yes. With a flashlight, through the forest."

"Oh darling, why?"

"Leo's with the neighbors' kids. I didn't want to be alone."

"You're crazy," she says, lacing her fingers hard through his.

"So I've been told," he says, and she can feel his smile against her shoulder blade.

They lie there listening to the wind and for the first time in a very long time she feels that it might not be too late to put everything right. She drifts off. Almost forgets.

She wakes up when her phone starts to ring. At first she just sits on the floor, confused and still half-asleep, and tries to take in the fact that dawn is breaking outside the windows. She's slept through a *storm*, how exhausted do you have to be to do that? Her phone rings and rings and her heart flutters and falls just as fast when she sees Peter's name on the screen. He was never here. She has ten thousand things she wants to say but when she answers she doesn't manage to say any of them. No one else had heard the sob in Peter's throat, if you get beaten as a child you learn to hold back your sobs, but not for her. Never for his wife.

"Dead . . . what do you mean, dead?" is all Kira can manage to say once he's told her, because surely there's no way she can be dead? Not *her*?

For several days after the storm Peter will stand in their bedroom trying to knot his tie the perfect length for a funeral. Kira will stand outside the door and never find a breath that's deep enough to break the silence. The forest lost so many of its most beautiful trees that night, and what makes it even more unbearable is that it also lost one of its best people.

18

Darkness

Less than an hour from now Fatima will be lying in a ditch, but right now she's cleaning the ice rink. She's approaching middle age, she looks much younger but feels considerably older as she straightens her back up in the stands. It hurts, but she hides it well, she's good at keeping secrets, others' as well as her own. Every day she cleans the whole of this ice rink, and the next day she starts again, following the same strict routine. She doesn't complain, she's grateful, always grateful, grateful, grateful. To the job, to the town, to the country that took her and her son in so many years ago when he was still small. Grateful, grateful, grateful for everything he has received here. Everything he has been able to become.

"Fatima!"

It's the caretaker, yelling again. He's been yelling all evening, he thinks she ought to go home before the storm gets worse and the buses to the Hollow stop running. But she's not going to leave things half-finished, the old fool knows that, he just doesn't have any other way of communicating his concern except by moaning. Once he grinned at her and said there were loads of good things one could be in a hockey club, but none of them was better than being taken for granted. It was a beautiful thought, of course, cleaners and caretakers never get their uniforms hung up in the roof of the rink at the end of their careers, but they stay longer than anyone who's accorded that honor. Coaches and players come and go, and the entire team can be replaced over the course of a couple of seasons, but the people in the background go to work as usual on Monday. If they do their jobs perfectly, no one will even notice how important they are until the day they disappear. And often not even then, sadly.

The day Fatima is buried she won't be remembered primarily for who she was, but for whose mother she was. She's Amat's mother, of course, the boy who went on to be the best. That's all that counts in hockey towns.

———

The wind bangs on the door but the caretaker takes no notice of it. It'll take more than a bit of wind to scare him into going home.

"You have to go home now, you silly woman! You can finish the cleaning tomorrow!" he yells up at Fatima from the boards.

"Some of us have real work to do here, we don't just pretend, old man!" she calls back from the stands.

"*Old man?* Go and jump in the lake!"

"Oh, just be quiet!"

There's only one person Fatima ever raises her voice to apart from her son, and that's the caretaker. That's how close they are now, woman and old man, he's worked here forever and she'll soon have been here for so long that no one can remember when she started, and over the years they've developed a confidential friendship based on few words and simple humor. Not long ago the caretaker brought in a photograph of a statue in a different part of the country, and beneath it was written: "Coarse from work, soft from love." And he thought of her.

"You missed a spot over there!" he calls.

"You only see spots because you've got cataracts!" she calls back.

He chuckles happily, there aren't many people who can make him do that. It's often said that "children and drunks tell you the truth," but if you go to a hockey town and want to know what's really going on, you should go to the ice rink and ask the caretaker. The only problem is that he won't tell you a damn thing, because hockey clubs need "high ceilings and thick walls," and the caretaker takes that saying seriously. He's seen coaches and committees come and go, he's seen the club when it was second best in the country and he saw it two years ago when it almost went bankrupt. He's good at closing storeroom doors and switching on the blade sharpener so he doesn't overhear sponsors and politicians concluding shady agreements in corridors, he didn't spend a day longer than necessary at school but he understands enough about numbers to know that no club in the country would have survived if they'd followed every accounting regulation, everyone does what it takes to survive here. Then you keep your mouth shut. The caretaker has experienced fairy tales and disasters in this ice rink, he's seen boys become men and men become stars, but often he has seen them fade just as quickly. He saw Peter Andersson turn up here from home with black eyes but never give one to anyone else, he saw him grow up to become captain of the A-team, he waved him off when he went to Canada to become a pro in the NHL, and was still here when he came back and became general manager. Up until just a couple of winters ago it would never have occurred to the caretaker to say any other name if he was asked who Beartown's best ever player was. But then came Amat. It is often said that a player is "an overnight success," or "came out of nowhere," but that's never true, of course, Amat has had to spend every day of his whole life fighting to be better than anyone else, because nothing less will be enough if you're a poor kid in the rich kids' ice rink. You have to be the best. The caretaker knows, because if you love a club for as long as he has, eventually it can't hide anything from you.

When Fatima arrived here all those years ago with her young son from somewhere on the other side of the planet, she had never even seen an ice rink, but she quickly learned that, regardless of what your mother tongue might be, "hockey" is the most important word in the local dialect here. The caretaker and Peter himself were the ones who made sure Amat was able to borrow skates, they agreed that would be better than language lessons if he was going to blend in. When the boy grew older the caretaker had to pay for the goodness of his heart when the boy did extra training before dawn or after sunset and the old man's working day became at least four hours longer between opening up and closing. He and Peter were almost as proud as Fatima when Amat made his debut on the A-team. "Quick as a cat out of a sack, that one," the caretaker chuckled, and Fatima exploded inside whenever her son scored a goal. Boys never understand that, the way their mothers see them, but how could they? They haven't had to divide their own hearts yet.

So they can't understand when their mothers go to pieces on their behalf either, that crushed dreams can hurt more for those who love us than they do for us ourselves. Fatima used to love the autumn, because the caretaker and Peter taught her that the Beartown year starts then, when the hockey season starts. But not this year, not for her son.

No one really knows what happened to him, not even the caretaker. He doesn't have the heart to ask Fatima straight out, because he can see in her eyes every day that she's broken. Back in the spring Amat was the most celebrated star in town, he was on his way to winning the entire league with Beartown, then he got injured and they had to play the last few games without him, and lost and missed out on promotion. There were rumors at the time that he wasn't really injured, that he just didn't want to risk getting hurt, that the NHL draft during the summer was more important to him than Beartown. The caretaker's blood starts to boil if he so much as thinks about that. No one—absolutely *no one*—has sacrificed more for Beartown than Amat! But this town really can be both the most beautiful and the most repulsive.

Amat took those rumors personally, as did Fatima, the caretaker could see it even if he didn't say anything. So now he doesn't know how to ask what everyone wants to know: What happened to Amat when he went for the NHL draft in the summer? He wasn't picked, everyone knows that, but why not? He came home, and there were rumors that he'd gotten injured again, other rumors that that was just an excuse, but an excuse for what? When Beartown Hockey's pre-season training started, he didn't show up, but he didn't sign a contract for any other club either. He just sits at home in the apartment in the Hollow. He was the town's most magical fairy tale, but now he's on his way to becoming its most impenetrable mystery, and in the middle of everything stands his mother, the woman who would die for him.

The caretaker looks at the empty ice and sighs with the sorrow of a man who has no grandchildren of his own. The wind bangs on the ice rink's door until he realizes that it isn't the wind. Someone is yelling outside.

"I'VE BEEN KNOCKING FOR FIFTEEN MINUTES!" Tails bellows when the door flies open and almost knocks him unconscious.

"BAMBI? WHAT ARE YOU DOING OUT IN THIS WEATHER YOU IDIOT?" the caretaker shouts back irritably.

He's the only person who calls Tails Bambi, because the caretaker has worked here so long that thirty years ago some joker carved a small wooden figure representing him, sitting on an ice machine with an angry speech bubble above its head, and placed it behind the nativity scene in the church so that it was yelling "GET OUT SO I CAN CLEAN THE ICE!" at Jesus's parents and the three wise men. Naturally, the caretaker found out who was responsible at once, because the caretaker finds out everything, but he never told anyone, not even the vicar. High ceilings, thick walls. But when the joker in question was about to play his next game, the caretaker went to a lot of trouble to sharpen the joker's skates unevenly, so he couldn't skate straight, and every time he fell over the caretaker yelled "Bambi!" from the stands. Of course he's known as "Tails" to everyone else these days, but the caretaker has never let him forget his first nickname. He grew up to be a fat, middle-aged grocer, but to the caretaker he'll never be anything but a downy junior.

"THE FLAGS! YOU HAVE TO HELP ME GET THE FLAGS DOWN!" Tails gasps.

"YOU CAME HERE IN THE MIDDLE OF A STORM BECAUSE OF . . . FLAGS?" the caretaker snorts.

Tails has always been a man with a peculiar sense of priorities, but surely this takes the cake?

"THEY'RE TOO BIG! THEY'LL CATCH THE WIND AND SNAP THE FLAGPOLES!"

Only then does the caretaker see that Tails's hand is bleeding. He pulls him in through the doorway and mutters:

"Anyone who's allergic to dust wouldn't be able to lobotomize you. What did I say to you when you bought those flags? Huh? I told you they were too big! I said . . ."

Tails yells, even though they're inside, as if the wind has made him deaf:

"YES, YES, YOU WERE RIGHT! JUST HELP ME!"

The caretaker is so shocked that Tails is prepared to admit he was wrong about something so quickly that he forgets to be mean.

"Well, then, let's see . . . ," he just mumbles, then goes and gets a bandage for Tails's hand and a knife for the ropes.

Then the two men go out into the storm. Not that it isn't a stupid idea, because it is, but sometimes stupidity is the only logical option. The flags need to be taken down so they can be raised again tomorrow. That might not be important in other places, but it's important here. As long as the flags are flying outside the ice rink, everyone knows that it's open, and as long as it's open, life goes on and there are no mornings when life needs to do that more than the morning after a storm. The caretaker may be stubborn, and Tails may be a pea-brain, but they both understand that. Tails lives for Beartown. He was a terrible skater even before his skates were sharpened unevenly, but he still fought hard enough to get onto the A-team, where Peter was the big star and Tails's only talent was provoking their opponents into fighting and incurring penalties. When one opposing team from the south came to Beartown one winter, when it was twenty degrees below zero, Tails persuaded the caretaker to switch off the heating in their locker room, and if he got the chance he would hide their equipment in storerooms and ruin their sticks, the dirtier the trick the better, both on and off the ice. If you were to ask Tails, he would say: "Don't you think I'd rather have been the star player and scored all the goals? Of course I would! But if you can't do what you want, you have to contribute in any way that you can. We're a small club in a small town, and if we play by the rules of the big cities we don't stand a chance!" Then he'd grin: "Cheating? It's only cheating if you get caught! Do you want to win or not?" That was how he and the caretaker embarked upon their long, dysfunctional friendship. Because the caretaker hates cheating, everyone in Beartown does, but they love winning even more.

When Tails's hockey career was over he became part of the district's "invisible power elite," as the local paper has called it. Of course it's hardly that invisible, and sadly it isn't particularly silent either, Tails has been thrown out of every hunting team in the entire district because he scares the animals away. He's at the ice rink every day even when he doesn't have official business there, mostly to argue about the schedule for time on the ice, which he always wants the caretaker to rearrange so that it favors one of the boys' teams where there's a wealthy parent Tails is trying to persuade to become a sponsor. And the caretaker snatches the pen from him when he counts the hours wrong and sighs: "It's hardly surprising that someone like you who can't count ends up a businessman when you couldn't skate but still tried to play hockey . . ."

But in the end they compromise, in spite of everything, because they want the same thing: what's best for the club. Always. Tails keeps promising the caretaker that "Beartown Business Park" will soon be built, including plans for a new, ultra-modern training facility next to the ice rink, and then there'll be enough time on the ice for everyone. He has a finger in every pie, the pea-brain, for good and ill. Officially it may have been Peter Andersson who got Ramona a place on the club's committee two years ago, but it was Tails who gave him the idea, and for that he has the caretaker's respect. Ramona's too, even if she'd never admit that. Once, after eleven or possibly twelve beers in the Bearskin, she told the caretaker in confidence: "People think Tails loves a TEAM. Bullshit—he doesn't love any team. He loves a CLUB. Anyone can love a team, that's a selfish sort of love, demanding and easily hurt and easy to give up . . . but loving a club, an entire club, the whole way from the little kids' team to the A-team and the rivets that keep the roof and the people together . . . that sort of love has no place for selfish-ness."

"YOU'D BETTER HOPE THIS WAS IMPORTANT, BAMBI!" the caretaker yells above the wind once they've taken down all the flags. His hands are bleeding as well now.

"I SWEAR!" Tails shouts back.

He isn't actually as certain as he sounds, but he'll end up being right, just not in the way he thinks.

Not one flagpole will be snapped by the storm. Tomorrow Tails and the caretaker will hoist the flags up all the poles once more. What they don't know now is that they'll be hoisting them at half-mast.

19

Screams

People say that bad news travels faster than good, that if someone dies
people in the town know about it sooner than if someone is born, but if you
ask Ramona down at the Bearskin pub of course she'll grunt: "Bullshit.
It just feels like that because plenty more people die than are born in this
town these days, more funerals than christenings." She should know, the
Bearskin is the district's watering hole but it's also its unofficial census
office, every change up or down is celebrated or mourned by someone
at her bar. Most of them have learned to celebrate twice as hard as they
grieve, to compensate, and that's probably why they've loved hockey
more than ever in recent years. They're a winning town again, they live
more than they die.

If you think that sounds like an exaggeration and ask Ramona straight
out if hockey is really that important, she'd probably reply: "No. But
what the hell is *important* in life, really?" She doesn't get to give many
speeches at funerals, it has to be said, but she probably has a point.

There's a story people often tell, about her and a tourist from the big
city who was passing through one summer and stopped his car outside
the Bearskin pub. He saw through the window that there was a television
inside, so he hurried in and asked: "Can I watch the soccer game here?"
The television was showing a grainy video recording of an old hockey
game, and a small group of elderly men were watching and telling each
other what was going to happen next, evidently not for the first time.
Ramona stood behind the bar glaring at the tourist, and muttered: "Soccer? What soccer?" The man exclaimed with equal amounts of surprise
and bemusement: "What . . . what soccer? It's the World Cup FINAL!"
Ramona shrugged her shoulders. "We only watch hockey in this town.
Are you going to order something? This isn't public transport, you can't
just stand there looking stupid for nothing."

It's only a story, it might not even be true, but that doesn't mean it's improbable. This is the sort of pub that one way or another says everything about a town and its inhabitants, about their place in the world and their view of the rest of it. The Bearskin is as close to the factory as it is to the ice rink, and most of the people who drink there live their lives between these three places. The suggestion that the Bearskin has been here longer than the town, and that houses were built around it the way they used to get built around a well is such an old lie that it almost feels true. Two years ago the whole building almost burned down, and now, after it's been rebuilt, people often joke that it smelled better immediately after the fire than it did before.

There are photographs of hockey players all over the walls. Some of them, like Benji and Vidar, probably spent more time in the Bearskin than the ice rink some seasons, and that says quite a lot about them. Others, like Amat, have never set foot here, and that says even more about them. Ramona has always had room in her heart for those who have succeeded in life, but the space she spares for those whose lives have gone to Hell will always be infinitely larger.

The Bearskin is in a basement, you can only see the sky through its small windows. But if you stand on the steps with the door open, where Ramona smokes when the weather is at its worst and you can't get your lighter to work out in the street, you can see all the way to the flagpoles outside the ice rink. She would never admit it to Tails, but she's started to like them, every time she goes to a committee meeting and passes beneath them she walks extra slowly, elated at the chance to cause trouble for the old men up in the conference room one more time.

But someone is taking the flags down now, and the storm stops even Ramona from lighting her cigarette outside, so tonight she smokes inside. The door would probably have been torn off its hinges if she opened it anyway. That's why she doesn't see Fatima leave the ice rink a short while from now and stand at the bus stop on the main road, before she gives up and starts walking to the Hollow on her own. Nor does Ramona see the fourteen-year-old boy, Matteo, who has been wandering around the town on his own all evening. She doesn't hear him yelling and banging on the door of the Bearskin, she'd almost certainly have opened up if she'd heard. She's let all manner of idiots inside over the years, even tourists who like soccer, so she'd probably have had room for a frozen and frightened fourteen-year-old. She just doesn't see him. But that isn't how Matteo will remember this moment, he'll just remember it in the simplest words possible.

"They only watch hockey in this town."

20

Cats

The last thing Fatima does is clean the upper floor in the rink, which used to be dominated by offices and the committee room, but they're squeezed into a smaller space at the back now. Most of the upstairs is now occupied by the new preschool. Some children around here learn to stand on skates before they can walk, which really says all you need to know about this town's relationship to hockey, the sport always forces life to move on. As terrible as that might be.

Fatima has started avoiding people in the supermarket recently, everyone wants to know what's happened to her son, and she can't answer. Back in the spring everything was like a dream, he was winning and everyone loved him, then he got injured and disappointed everyone. Then he went to North America to be selected for the NHL draft, which Fatima barely understands at all. He sat at the kitchen table and explained it as if she were a child and he the grown-up: "The NHL is the best league, Mom, where the pros play, in North America. Every summer the league has a draft, where the clubs take turns to choose two hundred young players who get the chance to become pros over there. That's what could happen to me now. Like Peter did!" Amat promised he would buy his mom a big house in the Heights, and a Mercedes, when he got his first professional contract. She laughed: "What would I want that for? If you want to give me something, get me a new dishwasher and a bit of peace and quiet."

Amat had such big dreams in the spring that there was hardly room for them in their cramped apartment. All that is left of them now is a broken dishwasher. He shut himself away in his room and has barely emerged for several months, and what sort of mother does that make her if she can't even tell people what's wrong? The caretaker has taught her that in hockey you never say exactly where a player is injured, because then opponents will seize the chance to hurt him there again, so you just say "lower body injury" or "upper body injury." But Fatima doesn't even know which of those Amat has. If it's his leg or his heart that's broken.

She turns the lights out and goes up into the stands and looks down at the center circle, fighting back tears. New players will triumph and lose there, long after Amat, the ice doesn't care. It's so easy for other people to think that if you want to know about youth sport, you should look at the smile on a teenage boy who has just managed to turn professional, because every year Fatima sees hundreds of parents devote thousands of hours to this ice rink, hoping for precisely that. They arrive stressed and leave exhausted, sweating in their cars and freezing at training sessions, paying a small fortune in membership fees and even more for all the equipment, but they still have to sell lottery tickets and work for nothing in the kiosk whenever the club asks them. They're expected to have all the time in the world, never complain, to dry wet skates and wipe tears and, most of all, do the laundry. Dear God, all the laundry. Naturally everyone is expected to be self-sacrificial in the pursuit of a dream for their children, but if you want to know anything about youth sports, really know, then it isn't enough to know the name of the child who made it all the way. You also need to know the ones who only almost made it.

Fatima lets her eyes roam across the ice, from one end to the other, trying to remember how quickly he could skate that distance. "Like a cat out of a sack," as the caretaker put it. "One day that boy could go all the way." That meant turn professional, Fatima learned. "All the way" meant earning money from a game. That's why it wasn't a game for anyone here, because it wasn't just Amat who would profit from that, everyone would. "Nothing comes for free in hockey, Mom, you have to give it all you've got!" Amat said when he was little, and he was right. He played in secondhand equipment all his childhood, they were always dependent on charity from people like Peter Andersson. "Don't call it charity, it's an investment," Peter said, he meant it in a friendly way but when Amat became the best she understood what it meant: they wanted payback.

She blinks away her tears, takes a deep breath with her eyes closed, and goes down to the main door of the rink. She meets the caretaker, he hesitates for a moment and glances out at the storm, and says tentatively:

"Look, Tails is here, I can ask him to get his car and give you a lift . . ."

"I don't need anything from that man, I'll take the bus," Fatima replies.

There's no hatred in her voice, but that tone is as close as she gets to it. The caretaker tries to persuade her, but there's no reasoning with her. So he sighs and lets her go.

Tails is standing outside, his hair is a mess, and he has blood on the cuffs of his shirt. They almost get blown into each other but Tails jumps out of the way and Fatima walks past him before he has time to open his mouth. She knows he wants to ask how Amat is, because everyone in town asks, but no one really cares. They don't care if he's happy. They just want to know if he can play, if he can win, if they can use him in their brochures. But not even his mom knows what he can do anymore.

She walks to the bus stop, hunched up against the wind, half a step back for every step forward. She waits for the bus but it never comes. The storm has emptied the community. She could have gone back to the ice rink and asked Tails for a lift, in spite of everything, but she can't help feeling that she'd rather die than ask that man for help.

So she sets out on the long walk home to the Hollow along the main road, alone. The wind tugs at her hair but she struggles on, a few steps at a time. Her legs ache the whole while but the pain in her back comes in bursts, without warning, sometimes so sharply that it makes her stagger.

The trees lean over the road, making the sky disappear, and she remembers how scared she was of nature here when she and Amat first arrived, all those years ago. The wind and the cold and the ice and the endless forest, everything seemed to be waiting for a chance to kill you, it was so cold that she didn't think she was even going to get through the first winter. Now she can't think of anything more beautiful. Sometimes nature still makes her giddy, when the snow is so white that her eyes can't look at it for more than a few seconds at a time, when the ice is so shiny that if you stand on the lake behind the ice rink the landscape goes on forever until it merges with the sky. The shapeless world can make you dizzy, the forest can be so silent that it makes your ears pop, as if the trees were sucking all the sound from the world. She used to like people and want to protect her child from nature, but now it's the other way around.

She stops at the side of the road. Deep down she knows she shouldn't, that it's dangerous, she needs to get home before the storm gets even worse. But her legs can't carry her any farther, her back aches, her lungs are shrinking. She's halfway between the ice rink and the Hollow, the worst part to be alone on, this section of road is nothing but pavement and loneliness. She stands with her hands on her knees, trying to catch her breath. Thinks about hockey. That isn't so strange, when you're scared you seek refuge in your happiest moments, and her happiest moments are her son's. Sons never understand that.

Amat is so like his dad, the same soft voice, the same determined look in his eyes. It's both a delight and a curse for Fatima that every proud moment also comes with a stab of grief. Amat's father died before they came here, and he never saw his son get this good at a sport his dad never even knew existed, the boy was born in a town close to the desert, but found a home in a place made of ice.

Everything is her fault, she thinks, because she was the one who taught him to be grateful for everything. It was this town that broke him, but it was her fault it was able to do that. "We need to be grateful," she repeated, until the words were invisible tattoos on the inside of his eyelids. He became the best, and she was happy, because finally he was treated as if he belonged here. As if this was his club, his town, his country too. She just didn't know that the only thing heavier than Beartown's prejudices were its expectations. Amat is still only a boy, this is only his eighteenth year on the planet, but hockey placed a burden on him that no adult man could bear.

Just a few years ago he seemed too small and weak for hockey at all. The latter of those was worst, of course, you're not allowed to be weak here. It was Peter who consoled Fatima back then, she'd heard the stories about him standing in a locker room ahead of the town's biggest match and yelling that the big cities might have the money, but "hockey is ours!," so she listened. Peter said that what the others saw as weakness was actually the boy's great strength: he was supple, when he skated it looked like he didn't have to make an effort, that's why everything happened faster for him than it did for anyone else. Fatima thought to herself that that might perhaps be true, but maybe he was also just trying to get away from all the boys who were twice his size and were trying to kill him. It's such a violent sport, and she never got used to that, either in the young bears on the ice or the big ones off it, because that was what all the dads of the other boys looked like as they hung around the side of the rink yelling during games: slow and heavy on the surface, and lightning-fast and brutal as soon as they got you in their sights. She learned that around here hockey was like nobility, that was how they wanted it, only someone born into the right family should have access to it. That was why they invented so many traditions and codes, an entire language with its own terminology, so that even the youngsters could tell the difference between those who belonged here and those who didn't. One time she heard one of the men joke that "there's too much sport in sports!" and she knew what he meant by that. They didn't want a pure sport, not really, they wanted a rigged game where they could buy a place for themselves and their kids.

It was Tails who said that, he had hardly said a word to Fatima in all the time she had worked here until Amat made it onto the A-team. Then, suddenly, he wanted to give Fatima advice about "the future," tell her what was "best for the boy," discuss the NHL and agents and contracts. Fatima may not have understood all the big words, but she understood that he thought Beartown owned her boy. Tails printed a brochure containing a picture of Amat with text saying that it wasn't just easy to sponsor Beartown, it was also the right thing to do, because suddenly the fact that he was from the Hollow was perfectly acceptable. Tails even wanted a picture of Fatima, showing her and Amat collecting empty drinks cans from the stands, because he'd heard that they did that to help with the money for the rent, but the caretaker yelled at him so hard that the windows of the rink rattled. Fatima herself said nothing, she tried to be grateful, but it was getting harder and harder.

She opens her eyes. Crouches down in the middle of the road between the ice rink and the Hollow. Slowly she digs her heels into the ground and stands up and starts walking again, but she hardly has the strength. The wind is coming from behind, like a kick in the small of her back, and she tries to fight against it but fails, stumbles and falls headlong into the ditch. She lies on the ground with the wind roaring in her ears. And drifts off.

Back in the spring Tails gave an interview to the local paper, and she read everything he said about Amat, how he was "a Cinderella story," and how he proved that "anyone can play hockey in Beartown." No, Fatima thought, that's precisely why it's a Cinderella story: because it hardly ever happens. She read Tails's boasts about the "investment in the girls' team" too, even though she knew that every week he tried to persuade the caretaker to give them the worst times on the ice and the rich dads' boys the best. They didn't want girls in the club any more than they wanted kids from the Hollow, they were all competitors for time on the ice. Because hockey belonged to them, just like Peter had said.

Fatima's thoughts drift off to her very first years here, she knew nothing about bears then but there were pictures of them all over the ice rink, so she borrowed a book from the library and started reading in the hope of understanding the town better by understanding the animal. And she did. One of the first things she learned was that up to forty percent of all young bears die during their first year of life, and that the most common cause of death was being killed by an adult male bear that wasn't their father. That was when Fatima realized that one day she would have to be a bear as well, when someone threatened her offspring. So she fought for his right to be a carefree bear, naive and untroubled, like all the others. For him to be able to play and have fun. Because, to be honest, not even she believed that Amat would become as good as he did, that he would make it "all the way," she just loved the fact that he didn't have to think on the ice. He had no pain there, he was free, that was enough. But gradually, the older he got, the more fair hockey actually seemed to become. When they were young the rich kids had an advantage, but by the time Amat was a teenager no one cared who his parents were anymore, they just cared about his talent. As long as the team was winning, everybody loved him. He soon got used to it. Fatima too, maybe. She feels ashamed of that now, she's worried she might have challenged God and the universe and has taken everything for granted, everything that is given can be taken away just as quickly. She was the first person to notice that something was wrong back in the spring, Amat was still scoring goals in every match but he was no longer as supple. He looked tense, because he was playing with the weight of the world on his shoulders, until his body couldn't take it anymore.

Shortly after that one of their neighbors in the Hollow told Fatima that the neighbors were upset by the "rumors," and that they were all on Amat's side. "What rumors?" Fatima wondered, and was told that people in the town were saying on the internet that they thought Amat was faking his injury. That he was only bothered about the NHL draft and wasn't "loyal." Loyal? To what? As if his body belonged to them.

So many men showed up at the rink and in the supermarket, all keen to give Fatima advice, until in the end she didn't listen to any of them, not even Peter. Amat went to North America and lost everything and came home empty.

She has no idea how long she lies there on the ground, but when she eventually gathers her strength one last time and crawls up, she feels so sore that the wind hurts her skin. For a moment she regrets being so proud when the bus didn't come, she should have gone back to the rink and asked Tails for a lift. The fact that she's thinking that reveals how frightened she is.

The storm is whistling in her ears so hard that she hardly hears Amat cry "Mom!" Sons never understand that that's the biggest word in the world. "Mom. Mom. MOM!" It takes such a long time for her to see that he's running along the road toward her. He doesn't really look like himself anymore. He's always been thin as a stick, but now he looks plump, and he hasn't shaved and smells of alcohol. But his hands are as strong as a man's as he lifts her up on her feet.

"What are you doing here?" she wonders anxiously.

"What are YOU doing here, Mom? Why are you WALKING home?" Amat roars over the wind.

The caretaker of the ice rink is the best thing you can be in a hockey club, so he's not stupid enough to take Fatima for granted. When she left the rink he called the bus company and asked to be put through to the bus driver, to make sure she had caught the bus. When they said they had canceled the bus because of the storm, the caretaker called Amat at once. The old man was about to set out himself to search, but Amat persuaded him not to, so that he wouldn't end up having to look for both of them. It was an awkward conversation, the caretaker used to see Amat in the rink every day, but the boy hasn't been there since he injured his foot back in the spring and missed the end of the season. He hasn't even left the Hollow since he got back from the NHL draft in the summer, has hardly been outside the apartment. This is actually the first time since he got injured that he's done any running at all.

But how he runs. Like a cat out of a sack.

From the Hollow, along the road, through the storm until he sees his mother. He tears his jacket off and wraps it around hers. Then they walk home, huddled against the forces of nature, she with her arm tucked under his.

"Are you hungry? Should we go and get some of that bread you like?" she yells above the wind.

"The supermarket's closed, Mom! Stop talking, we have to get home!" he yells back.

"You shouldn't have run here, you need to take care of your foot!" she cries.

"Stop worrying about me!" he says.

He can say that as much as he wants, of course, but she's his mother. Good luck trying to stop her.

21

Names

When the Bearskin was rebuilt after the fire two years ago, Ramona didn't bother putting a sign up again. It doesn't make any difference, after all, everyone knows where the Bearskin is, everyone knows where Ramona is.

No one could call her "pleasant," no one could call the pub "welcoming," that isn't what this sort of pub is for. Ramona swears at you if you take too long to order, because there isn't any damn choice anyway, and then she swears just as much if you try to rush her. You'll feel unwelcome, but you'll know where you are, because there are green scarves all over the walls that tell you that in this town we stick together. There's an envelope behind the bar with the words "the Fund" written on it, where anyone who has any money to spare at the end of the month puts a note or two so that Ramona can give it to someone who's on the ropes. There's a lot of gossip about the old bag behind the bar, but the worst lie anyone can say about her is that she's lost her marbles recently. She hasn't had any marbles for at least thirty years. Her heart, on the other hand, that's right where it should be.

She and Holger used to run the Bearskin together, they did everything together, they went to every hockey game together. "Lethal in the forest and useless everywhere else," she used to mutter about him when he put the beer glasses in the wrong place, and he would grin and reply "I love you," because nothing made her more angry than that when she was already angry. But he really did love her, the way only a thoroughly kind man could, quietly but beyond measure. The only thing he ever demanded of her was that she should stop smoking. "You have to live longer than me, because I couldn't bear to outlive you," he said, and she patted him tenderly on the cheek and whispered: "Shut up!"

One of the regulars at the Bearskin used to tell an old joke about a man who was sitting in a full-capacity crowd at a hockey game with an empty seat next to him, and the person on the other side asked why it was empty, and the man replied sadly: "It's my wife's, but she passed away recently." Visibly moved, the other man said: "I'm sorry to hear that. But isn't there someone in your family or a friend who could come to the game with you?" The man replied: "No, they're all at the funeral." The joke, of course, was that Holger would be that man the day Ramona was buried, so no one has told that joke since he died, years ago now. She was the one who smoked, he was the one who got cancer. She never says he died, she says he left her, and somehow that shows that she's the worst loser in a town full of them. She still hasn't forgiven the old bastard for going first. "Men go and lie down and women carry on working," she used to mutter if anyone mentioned the subject, and then it doesn't get mentioned again for a while.

She still smokes just as much, drinks even more, the only thing she stopped doing was going to watch the hockey, because her lungs couldn't take it. They wasted away without him. For a long, long time she couldn't even get to the supermarket when she couldn't feel his pulse in her hand, his nagging in her ear, so the young men in black jackets who regarded the Bearskin as their second home went shopping for her, keeping her going so she could keep everyone else going. They wrote the words for the announcement of Holger's death in the paper when she was crying too much to do so: "Damn, Holger, how are the players going to know when to shoot when you're not there to yell at them?," it said. She laughed quietly at that and poured more beer. The death notice was still hanging on the wall in the bar, between match jerseys and scarves from Holger's beloved, hated, worthless, wonderful Beartown Hockey when the fire took the building. It almost took Ramona too, and sometimes she wishes it had. People can bury so many of their loved ones during a lifetime and still get up the morning after, but something inside gets a bit heavier each time. She's had more than a few mornings when she's woken up and wondered if she can be bothered to get up once more.

Then suddenly, one day early last summer, she raised the price of the beer. Naturally that caused a huge fuss among the regulars in a bar where there isn't any other sort of customer, because the last time she raised the prices was fifteen years ago. All she ever does is raise the prices, the old bag.

The only people who didn't complain were actually the young men in black jackets. Because Teemu, the biggest idiot in a large gang of big idiots, hadn't looked so happy for a long time.

"What are you grinning about?" Ramona snapped at him, and Teemu confessed:

"If you're raising the prices, you're thinking of the future."

People like him and her need a future, otherwise they sink. The same night as the fire at the Bearskin they lost Teemu's younger brother, Vidar, in the car accident. The boy used to do his homework in the bar at the Bearskin when he was little, forced to do it by the older brother who had never done any homework in his life because no one made him do it. Their dads were long gone, and their mother was at home but disconnected by pills, Teemu and Vidar had seen so much violence and abuse before they even started school that the bar was their haven. They were safe at the Bearskin, they found all their friends there, Teemu found a new sense of belonging with the black jackets there who would always protect his little brother. Ramona never had kids of her own, but these boys were hers, when Vidar died she and Teemu were like old trees that have been torn out by the roots, they couldn't find any meaning to the next day at all. Apart from hockey. That moved life on, one game at a time, one noisy argument at the Bearskin afterward at a time, about which player ought to have tried which shot. There are no two people in this town who can argue like Ramona and Teemu, because most people don't have the energy to like each other enough as much as that demands. They rarely said the words to each other, they didn't need to, the old bag behind the bar raised the price of beer and the hooligan almost started to cry, and that was enough. They belonged to each other.

When the storm sweeps in over Beartown and darkness envelops the buildings, Ramona thinks of him. Of her boys. She probably thinks of Holger too, of course, because she always does that when evening turns to night. He used to like going to bed, Holger, the lazy bastard. When the wind starts to rattle the windows and all the lights go out, she puts the beer glasses in their place below the bar and fumbles for the flashlight in the dark. Behind a weak, fluttering beam of light she feels her way upstairs to her bedroom, slowly on old feet, passing pennants and scarves and the hundreds of photographs that people in the town collected for her after the fire. Silent greetings from an entire life lived in and around a hockey club.

She was one of the first sponsors. In recent years she has sat on the committee. Oh, how she has fought with the old men there, and oh, what fun she has had! Beartown Hockey is better than it has been for years, and Hed is completely useless, and you probably can't have more fun than that without being naked, if you ask Ramona. She goes to bed with Holger's photograph in her arms. The storm shakes the building until it rocks her to sleep.

A fair way into the forest the same storm, not long before, shook a small car on its way to the hospital in Hed. The pregnant woman inside had cried, "It's time, it's time, it's coming now!" to her husband, and they had set off. A falling tree hits the car in the forest and they get rescued by a midwife and a crazy eighteen-year-old called Ana. They'll end up naming the child after a boy both Ana and Ramona loved. Vidar. The end of life is as unstoppable as its beginning, we can't stop the first and last breaths we take any more than we can stop the wind.

Ramona doesn't change into her nightdress, she sleeps with her clothes on so no one will have to carry her out when she isn't decent.

And as little Vidar is born in the forest, she dies in the Bearskin. There's nothing untoward about it, it's time.

When she is buried, so many green scarves will be laid on the grave that the name on the stone can't be read. It doesn't matter, everyone knows who she is. All that holds us together in the forest is our stories, and we will never stop telling hers.

22

Losses

The most unbearable thing about death is that the world just goes on. Time doesn't care. The morning after the storm, the sun goes up as if it's mocking us, over a wrecked forest and a battered town. Two, in fact. If she were still with us, Ramona would no doubt have pointed out that there are always two of everything, "one that wins, and one that's all the other bastards." There are two towns and two clubs and always two hockey players: one who takes a place on the team, and one who takes a place at the bar in the Bearskin. "Two of everything, one we see and one we don't, an upside and a downside," she used to grunt, and it could possibly be claimed that she had often drunk a fair amount of breakfast by then, and that she sometimes added a few last drops so sneaky that they were almost embarrassing. But when she was focused she could reach out across the counter and pat someone tenderly on the cheek and say: "Everything and everyone is connected around here, whether they like it or not." She was right, invisible hooks and threads, that's why everything and everyone stopped when she died.

"Cheers for faithful women and reliable men, wherever they may be, but for you other ne'er-do-wells it's time to go home!" she used to shout when she rang the bell for last orders. The small oasis of alcohol between dusk and dawn was over, the second hand started ticking again and cell phones were reluctantly pulled out of pockets so that angry text messages could be read. Heading home through the darkness, the opposite of upsides and winners stumbled back to reality, secure in the knowledge that they could return tomorrow, but one tomorrow Ramona was no more, and it was incomprehensible that the sun still rose. That it could bear to. That it dared to.

———

So many phone calls are made the day after the storm to share what has happened, it's as much of a shock for everyone who picks up and gets the message, but the most unexpected phone call is probably the very first one.

It's Teemu who finds Ramona, because he's the first person who misses her. We will say that it was early in the morning after the storm, but the storm is actually still going on. Teemu was half a day's drive away, when the storm swept in he was engaged in the sort of buying and selling that Ramona wouldn't let him do in Beartown. She knew how he made his living, she knew better than to let him do it anywhere near her, because just like all kids he would only find something even worse to do when she wasn't looking. Teemu has never had a real parent, and there was no way in hell that Ramona was going to try to be one either, but insofar as she could express feelings and he could express them back, they did so by her laying down a few rules, and him sticking to them.

He called her when he saw the weather forecast, when she didn't answer he knew something was wrong, she'd never admit it but she always kept her phone close when he was out on the road. He turned his old Saab around and drove all night on barely passable roads, straight into the wind, as fast as it would go, and kicked in the door of the Bearskin. And in the dawn, when the storm finally lifted its hand from the shattered towns and all that remained was the rain against the windows, he sat by Ramona's bed and wept like a boy, and like a grown man. When we are little we grieve for the person we have lost, but when we're older we grieve even more for ourselves. He wept for her loneliness, but also his own.

"Everyone I know with any sense has two families, the one they were given and the one they chose. You can't do anything about the first, but you can damn well take responsibility for the second!" Ramona yelled at him every time anyone in the Pack caused trouble after a hockey game, stole a snow scooter from the wrong store, or punched the wrong person in the face and Teemu hadn't stopped them. She always held him personally responsible for all the idiots who followed him, and when he got angry and asked why, she roared:

"Because I think better of you!"

She never let him be less than he was capable of. Everyone else only saw a violent madman, a hooligan, and a criminal, but Ramona saw a leader. He loves the guys in his Pack, but he has to direct them. He loves his mother, but is always responsible for her. She likes pills that let her not feel anything at all, so he has to feel everything instead. When his little brother, Vidar, died, his mother said that sometimes she saw happy families down on the lake in winter, a mom and a dad and a child skating and laughing, the sort of family that functioned and lived in a house where everything was intact. "I pretend it's Vidar, that little kid, that he had a family like that," she whispered through her drugged fog to her eldest son. Not that she wished that for Teemu, just Vidar, she needed Teemu too much even to fantasize about a different life for him.

Ramona knew that, understood that constant responsibility for others weighs a young man down, it isn't visible on the outside, but he is slowly being filled with lead. Teemu is far too many people's first phone call whenever something goes to hell. It was only at the Bearskin, late in the evening just before the lights were turned out and the door locked, that he could relax and let his shoulders drop a few inches. Unclench his fists. He would get one last beer and a pat on the cheek and Ramona would ask how he was. No one else ever did that.

So, early in the morning when the storm finally sweeps past he sits on the edge of her bed and wishes he had told her that she was right. We have two families. She was the one he chose.

He takes a cigarette from the packet on the bedside table and smokes with her one last time. He suddenly starts laughing, because she looks so angry, even when she's dead. If she's in any sort of Heaven now, Vidar is also there, and his little brother will be getting one *hell* of a telling-off for daring to die before her, he thinks. Then he gently closes the old woman's eyes and pats her on the cheek, and whispers:

"Say hi to the little shit. And Holger."

Then Teemu just sits there, not knowing what to do with the body or who to call. Ramona was the nearest thing to a normal adult he had in his life, so he doesn't know what normal adults do when they lose other normal adults. In the end he calls Peter Andersson.

Perhaps that's as incomprehensible as it is obvious. They hated each other for years, when Peter was general manager of Beartown Hockey and the foremost symbol of everything the Pack hated: the privileged little elite of wealthy men who governed the club as if it belonged to them. Things went so far that the Pack placed an announcement of Peter's death in the paper, and arranged for his wife to get a call from a moving company about emptying their house.

It was in the bar at the Bearskin that Teemu and Peter finally stopped being enemies, under Ramona's watchful eye, after Peter had resigned from his job as general manager, but they never became friends. Even so, Teemu has no one else right now. He's half-expecting Peter to hang up instantly, but instead he replies softly:

"Hold on, hold on, what are you saying, Teemu?"

The words tumble out of Teemu once again.

"She's dead, for fuck's sake," he sobs.

"Dead?" Peter whispers.

"Mmm," Teemu manages to say, as if all he has left are consonants.

"Bloody hell. Bloody hell, Teemu. Are you okay?" Peter asks.

Teemu doesn't know what to say, because he's never been asked that by a grown man before.

"Mmm."

"Where are you now?" Peter asks, as if he's trying not to startle a deer in his garden.

"In the car with her," Teemu sobs, barely audibly.

"With . . . with who?" Peter asks.

"With Ramona!"

Peter just breathes into the phone, waiting to hear that this is a joke. It isn't.

"You've got her in the CAR, Teemu?"

"I didn't know what I was supposed to do, so I'm on my way to yours, but I didn't want to leave her alone!" Teemu sniffs, snapping defensively down the phone.

Peter sighs very, very, very deeply at the other end. Then he tells Teemu to stop at the side of the road. He isn't entirely sure what sort of crime driving a corpse around in an old Saab would be categorized as, but he's pretty sure there'll be something.

"Just stay there, I'll come and get you."

Teemu does as he says, which feels strange, not just because Ramona is sitting next to him and is dead, but because he has never in the whole of his life had anyone come and get him.

———

So many phone calls get made, first from one neighbor to another, then another, and another, until one reaches Adri Ovich up at the dog kennels. When she hears about Ramona, she has to make a call to as far away as is possible.

"Benji," she whispers, then tells him everything as gently as she can, and hears him break.

He gets up and packs and sets off, without hesitating, and now he's asleep on a bench in an airport on the other side of the planet. One of his eyes is a single, red-blue bruise, and his nostrils are black with dirt and dried blood. He's twenty years old, and has spent the past two years living drunk and free in a way that only a self-medicating liar can, young and immortal. Outside the windows in this part of the world the sun is on its way up toward another day warm enough to go topless on endless beaches, but Benji is on his way to the far north, toward hockey towns and temperatures below freezing.

The proof that time machines will never exist is that if one is ever invented at some point in the future, someone who loved Benji would use it at once to go back to this precise moment and stop him. Someone would stand here and take his arm and grin: "Oh, screw the flight! Come on, let's got to the beach, grab a beer! Let's buy a boat!" Because then everything that is going to happen would never have happened. If only someone had appeared now and stopped him from going home. That's why we know time machines don't exist. Because they're far more plentiful in Beartown than Benji believes, the people who love him.

———

Leo Andersson can't remember the last time he felt such pure, uncomplicated joy as when the electricity comes back on in the house in the center of Beartown the day after the storm and his computer starts up again. Life begins once more. His dad gets a call from someone and Leo doesn't care about the content of the call, but he hears his dad hang up, then call Leo's mother right away and tell her that someone's dead. Leo doesn't hear who. His mother drives home at once from her office in Hed, where she's spent the whole night, and as soon as she walks through the door Peter sets out. They look at each other very briefly, as if love could wait while they're busy, as if they imagine that all the time they need to say everything they're longing to say will just magically appear one fine day. Leo hasn't told anyone how often he has thought about how to solve all the practical problems when they get divorced, how they're going to live and how he can move his computer back and forth. Because it feels like a countdown.

The front door closes behind his dad and his mom goes to the kitchen to make more phone calls. Leo closes the door to his room and returns to his computer game, and breathes out like he's been given painkillers, free to stop thinking, the flicker of the screen and the gunfire in his headphones would be unbearable for other people, but for him they're a form of meditation. He takes his eyes off the screen for just one moment when the text message arrives. It's from his sister. I'm coming home, it begins. He smiles.

In another part of Beartown, in a much smaller house, Matteo is sitting in front of his computer. The boys are the same age, they're playing the same game, Matteo's sister is also on her way home. But he isn't smiling.

I'm coming home, Maya's text message begins. Her mom has just called and told her, and explained that she doesn't have to come home, that everything's fine. So Maya packs her bag and writes to her brother: Don't say anything to Mom and Dad or they'll just come and get me. I'll take the train. Be nice to Dad because he's sadder about Ramona than he seems, okay? Love you! Leo merely replies Ok, but he's smiling. He misses his sister. He got her room when she moved out, he's arranged it entirely around his computer: an ergonomic chair that he asked for at Christmas, new headphones, new screen. He's become good at the fact that even if his parents don't like the violence in his gaming world, they like it better than him being out all night in the real world.

Matteo is sitting on the floor in a small room on the other side of town, he's hooked up to the neighbors' Wi-Fi and his computer is a mishmash of parts he's rescued from discarded machines when the office department of the factory where his parents work tossed their old computers in a dumpster. Naturally his parents don't know he's got it, they'd never allow that. No one plays games in Matteo's family, they barely even watch television, not that Matteo has ever figured out exactly what God has got against that, but he's never questioned it. His family lives in silence and terror. Not that Matteo is afraid of his parents, they've never hit him, their control over their children is of a different sort. Shame and guilt and disappointment, the Devil's most effective tools.

On the other side of town Leo takes his eyes off the screen for a few seconds while he reads Maya's text message. The smile fades from his face when he turns back to the computer again and sees that someone's shot him in the head.

Matteo clenches his fist in front of his screen when the shot goes off. He goes to the same school as Leo but he's fairly sure Leo doesn't even know who he is, they're the same age but live in different realities. One gets sandwiches made for him without even having to ask for them, the other sits hungry in an empty house. One's parents are barely religious, yet he still got an expensive ergonomic chair for Christmas, the other's parents do nothing but talk about God and Jesus, but don't even celebrate Christmas. Leo has everything Matteo doesn't have, in every sense, so computer games are fair in a way that the real world never is. There a boy with a secondhand computer sitting on the floor can seek out a boy surrounded by the newest, most expensive technology, wait for him to lose concentration and shoot him in the head.

For a single second Matteo is able to clench his fist and feel like a winner. Then the power goes off again.

———

Peter comes hurrying along the side of the road, his hair a mess and dressed in tatty jeans and a dirty green hooded top with the bear on it. Teemu rolls the Saab's window down, as shamefaced as if he'd been caught speeding.

"You always think of safety first," Peter says with just a hint of irony when he sees that Teemu has fastened the safety belt around Ramona.

Teemu doesn't know how to interpret that, so he mumbles:

"I didn't know what to do. It felt wrong to put her in the trunk."

Ramona is sitting in the passenger seat, and looks like she might wake up any moment and yell at Teemu for driving like an old woman. Peter quickly closes his eyes, opens them slowly, and for a moment looks as if he'd like to rest his hand gently against her cheek, but resists.

"It's okay, Teemu. We're going to sort this out," he whispers instead.

Teemu spent his whole childhood practicing not crying in front of other people, as did Peter, and they both put that knowledge to good use today. Peter makes all the phone calls a normal adult would make, they carefully lay Ramona on the backseat and drive slowly toward the center of town. The undertakers don't have set opening hours, just a sign on the door with a telephone number, around here those who work with death only do so when required. They have to wait several hours before someone shows up, it's that hard to get through the forest roads.

Throughout the whole time they're waiting Peter hears a buzzing sound, at first far off, like an annoying insect trapped inside a glass dome, but it grows to a roar and he rubs his fingers over his ears in case it's his imagination. Only when he hears cries and sees a tree fall not far from the car does he realize what it is: chain saws. A whirring symphony that rises and falls in all directions around them. It's barely even daylight yet, the storm has only just abated, but the forest is already full of people clearing fallen trees and debris. Peter notes that many of them are firemen, but none of them needed to be ordered to go and help. The teams are always uneven, storms against humanity, but humanity's persistence wins in the end.

"I didn't know Ramona was ill, I wish I'd been there," Teemu suddenly says tentatively.

Peter gives a curt nod and wishes he knew what to say to comfort him.

"She was old, Teemu. It isn't anyone's fault. Ramona loved you," is the best he can manage.

The tip of Teemu's nose moves almost imperceptibly up and down.

"You too."

"Not like you and Vidar, Teemu. You were like sons to her."

Teemu's eyebrows bounce.

"Are you kidding? Do you know how much the old bag used to boast about you? Damn, I hated that. I thought you were an arrogant bastard who believed you were better than the rest of us just because you don't drink and stuff. But she . . . well, you know . . . until she explained what sort of dad you'd had. Then I got it. You had a really shit childhood and turned out well in spite of it. That was why she boasted."

"It was a long time ago, things were different then, dads were . . . different," Peter says quietly, even though he knows it isn't true, Teemu is half his age and his dad was just the same.

"It's okay to say your dad was an asshole," Teemu says, not surprised, but like a boy who, when he was a child, never met a grown man who wasn't violent.

Peter looks at him and is astonished, as he always is, at how thin Teemu is. He may be the most feared man in the forest, but from a distance he could pass as an upper-class kid at boarding school. His hair is neat, his posture relaxed, his eyes aren't labyrinths of darkness. On the contrary, he often looks almost cheerful, like a mischievous little kid. It's funny the way the potential for violence works, Peter thinks, you can't see it on someone, you just feel it in their presence.

The older generation of hockey fans in Beartown often talk about players who have "the dog in them." Peter knows what that is because of its absence from descriptions of him when he was young. "Peter Andersson? Sure, he's good with a stick, but he doesn't have the dog in him." Peter refused to fight, even when he was attacked on the ice, which meant that a fair number of men didn't trust him, and others challenged him, he learned to recognize the difference. Plenty of men can talk about being up for a fight, but when it comes to it everyone has a bridge they have to cross, from the peaceful creatures we've learned to be, to the animals we need to become to physically attack another person. The length of that bridge varies for different people, those with the shortest bridge behave like Peter's dad, but Teemu? Peter has never sat next to anyone like him. He has no bridge, the two different shores within him are just a stride apart. On the outside you couldn't tell the difference between him and a hundred other men, but on the inside he's nothing but dog.

So Peter rubs his stubble awkwardly and replies vaguely:

"Oh, there were worse dads. Now I've got kids, it often feels like I'm not so damn great at it myself . . ."

Teemu turns away and looks through the window, and perhaps he should have said what he was thinking: that he's seen a lot of bad dads, and Peter isn't one of them. Perhaps Peter should have said something to Teemu too, ask him how he's feeling. But neither of them can figure out how to formulate their thoughts, so in the end they just talk about hockey instead.

"So what do you think about the team this year?" Peter asks, almost as a polite formality, but partly out of genuine curiosity. There was a time when everyone forced their opinions on him, and now he can't help missing that a bit.

"Surely you should be telling me?" Teemu chuckles, before he realizes that Peter probably knows less about the team now than he does. He almost feels like apologizing.

Peter shakes his head slowly.

"You know how people always gossip in this town, Teemu, and when you ask 'How do you know that?' they just say, 'You know, people talk.' I never hear that anymore. It was never me people talked to, they just talked to the general manager."

Teemu nods with a degree of sympathy. Two years since Peter left, and the club still hasn't appointed a new general manager, they replaced his position with a "leadership committee" consisting of the coach and a handful of committee members, which ought to have been a disaster but instead has coincided with the club's best seasons for years. It's hard for someone like Peter not to feel that perhaps he was the problem. Teemu understands that, because he knows what it's like to love a club that would rather not have anything to do with you.

"Can I ask . . . what do . . . I mean, what do you *do* all day? Without hockey?" Teemu asks.

"I bake bread," Peter says.

"Br-bread?"

Peter nods. He looks at the time, then at the deserted road.

"And, to be brutally honest, I don't even like bread much. So if we're going to talk about anything, you might as well tell me what you think of the team, because with Ramona gone there's no one else I can ask."

For a moment Teemu looks like he thinks it's a trap.

"Okay . . . I think the team has two problems. The first is that Amat's a great player, but no one seems to know what's wrong with him. The second is that . . . oh, what the hell . . . you know, we almost won the whole league in the spring, but when it really mattered we buckled.

We need someone who doesn't back down. Someone who . . . someone with . . ."

He searches for the right words, like a parent trying to avoid the swear jar.

"Someone with the dog in him," Peter says helpfully.

Teemu laughs.

"You sound like Ramona."

Peter shakes his head.

"No. I just sound old."

Teemu grins.

"But you're right. That's who we're missing. Number sixteen."

He doesn't have to say the name, Peter knows. The whole town knows.

23

Sisters

"BENJAMIN OVICH," a tired voice calls over a crackling loudspeaker at the airport. "BENJAMIN OVICH TO GATE 74." Benji wakes up on a bench, half because of his name being called out and half because tears are stinging the wounds on his face. He doesn't know what time it is in Beartown, he can't remember if the time difference is six or eight hours, but he assumes that one advantage of drinking all night and sleeping all day for the past few months will mean he's immune to jet lag. He sits up, groaning from the pain in his body.

Ramona once told him that his biggest problem was that he had an unused brain and a worn-out heart, and that his feet only went in one damn direction. She was right, of course, people in the airport are taking detours around the bench, his nose and mouth are bloodier than his fists. On the way to the airport he got into a situation where he ought to have gone into reverse, and this is what happens when you never learn how to do that.

The departure board is flashing as he drags his body and bag up from the bench and limps toward his plane. There are many things that people have thought about him over the years that have been wrong, but if Ramona was still around she would probably have said that no lie has been bigger than the idea that this boy has the dog in him. If there was ever one there, if got frightened away a long time ago. Benjamin Ovich has nothing but demons left now.

———

It's almost lunchtime on the day after the storm when Ana calls her best friend. She doesn't answer, so Ana does the only reasonable thing. She calls again, and again, and again. In the end Maya answers, sounding irritated. She's on the train, which obviously wouldn't have been a problem, only she was sitting on the toilet in the train, which again wouldn't have been a problem if Ana didn't always insist on video calls.

"Can't you take the hint if people reject your calls or what?" Maya snaps, trying to balance the phone on the sink.

"Are you doing a poo?" Ana asks, unconcerned, her mouth full of chips.

"Well if I was, and you're eating chips at the same time, I'd still be the only person who was disgusted."

"Why should I be disgusted? I can't even see the poo!" Ana wonders, shoveling in some more chips.

"There's something wrong with you."

"With me? You're the one talking about poo. Is there something wrong with your poo? Are you ill?"

"Stop it!"

"Is it sticky? It's not supposed to be sticky."

"What do you WANT, Ana?"

"Hello? Sorry I exist, then—I just wanted to ask if you'd like me to pick you up from the train."

"You haven't got a driver's license."

"And?"

"I don't have the energy to have this discussion with you. Don't worry. I'll get the bus."

"Why don't you call your parents?"

"Because then they'd pick me up."

"Yes?"

"Yes!"

"Isn't that the point?"

"The point is that I don't want to bother them. They've got enough crap to think . . . what are you doing? Are you okay?"

"I just got some chips stuck in my throat. Now I've got stuff on the screen. Hang on, I'll just wipe it off."

"Charming, Ana. Really."

"Is that your guitar next to you? You take your guitar with you when you're doing a poo?"

"I'm on the train, you idiot, I don't want anyone to steal it!"

"No one wants your useless guitar, loser!"

"It's great to be going home, it really is."

"Mmm. Don't talk crap, you miss me loads."

Maya smiles.

"I miss my best friend."

Ana softens and whispers to the screen:

"I miss you too."

Whereupon Maya obviously can't resist adding:

"You really should meet my best friend, she's way funnier than you are!"

It's fortunate for her that this is a video call, because now Ana can only slap the screen, but Maya still flinches. The first time Maya went home Ana accidentally hit her for real when she meant it as a joke, and then Maya couldn't sleep on that shoulder for a week.

"Play something for me," Ana mutters, nodding to the guitar case.

"I only play for my best friend," Maya grins.

"Ha! If I had a heart, I'd have been really hurt by that," she fires back, and they both laugh.

Then Maya opens the case and pulls out her guitar, and plays for her best friend, sitting in a cramped bathroom on a jolting train. Ana loves her for that. The song is new, the words old:

Me and you, you and me
Let the whole world come and see
They don't know who I can be
They've never seen the real me
They're status symbols, careless trifles
Your defiant eyes, loaded rifles
Let them talk, they've got nothing for me
Let them hate, we're a two-woman army
Let them scream, let them fight
Let them leave, step out of sight

None of them knew me, just my name, anyway
I never needed anyone else, come what may
Whatever must fall can fall
It's you and me against it all
When it's tough, when it's not
Always, always, no matter what,
Me and you, you and me
Let the whole damn world come and see
They don't know who we can be

The final notes of the guitar strings bounce between the screens until space swallows all the echoes. The train is rumbling against Maya's backside, the tumble-dryer against Ana's, she's washing her dad's sheets, Maya doesn't have to ask to know that he's had a relapse. Ana always calls when she's doing the laundry, to stop her having to be alone. They say nothing for what must be almost ten minutes before Ana says:

"Nice song. Your new best friend must like it a lot."

Maya laughs, making the guitar bounce on her stomach.

"You're such a dork."

"Mmm. Says the girl going to music college. If there was a world championship in being a dork, you wouldn't be allowed to take part because you're dork-doped. The jury would be like: No, sadly, everyone else has worked really hard to be a dork, but you obviously just fell into a vat of DORK JAM when you were little so it wouldn't be a fair contest if you took part!"

Maya laughs so loud she's pretty sure the whole train can hear. She doesn't care. She and Ana are half a country apart for months at a time, but a single phone call is enough, then it's as if they've never been apart. As if nothing terrible had ever happened.

"I'm sorry I didn't realize there was a storm at home, I should have...," Maya begins, but Ana interrupts:

"Shut up. How were you supposed to know?"

"I miss you," Maya whispers.

"Call me as soon as you get home," Ana whispers back.

Maya promises, and the incomprehensible idea that so many people who don't have Ana in their lives still manage to be people at all gives her a headache.

They end the call and Maya maneuvers the guitar case out of the train bathroom. The same case she had when she moved away from Beartown, she was sixteen then, is eighteen now, she left soon after Vidar's funeral and is going back to attend Ramona's. She doesn't know if she's sad because she's grieving or because she's feeling nostalgic. She hardly knew Ramona at all, not really, but when some people die it's like watching the string on a balloon snap. We don't miss what she was but what we lose when she isn't there.

Maya wonders who will be at the funeral. Most of all, if Benji will be there. Deep down in a pocket inside the battered guitar case are the lyrics to the last song she wrote before they both left.

> *Love that gets out of control*
> *The most intense adventures*
> *I hope you find your way out*
> *I hope you're the kind of person*
> *Who gets a happy ending*

She's thought so much about him. The wildest, loneliest person she knows.

———

Benji has done his best not to think about anyone at all, but the shield of drink and smoke gets more brittle as his heart beats against the plane ticket in the chest pocket of his shirt. He has a postcard in his hand, the last one he was going to send Ramona, there was always more silence than words between them, but he thought she'd like to stick it up on the wall in the bar anyway. He's long since given up hoping that anyone would be proud of him, but he hopes that at least Ramona didn't think he was an embarrassment.

On the way to the airport he found a bar that reminded him of the Bearskin. If you want to know how little he's changed, it's enough to know that it took him four drinks to get into a fight with two guys who were talking crap about his long hair and tattoos. If you want to know how much he's changed, it's enough to know that he lost the fight. He isn't as strong as he used to be, not as fast, perhaps not even as wild.

His eye is bruised and he has blood in his nostrils, but he doesn't mind the fact that it hurts. As least he can feel it, it's been a long time since he felt anything at all.

He wonders who his hometown will see him as when he returns. He was a hockey player and a 'fucking fag' when he left, and he doesn't know if they're going to tolerate the fact that he's still the latter but no longer the former. You are loved if you win in Beartown, he learned that at an early age, you can get away with almost anything as long as you win and win and win. But now? He's of no value to anyone now.

He's traveled so far, so long in the hope of finding all the answers, but no one ever manages that. You just find more bodies, more dance floors, more mornings of hangovers so heavy that it hurts to blink. There are no new lives, just different versions of the old one. People talk about "coming out" as if it's something you only do once, but obviously you never run out of new people, so you keep having to come out and come out until you snap. Night after night he dreams that he stayed with Kevin at that party. It's almost two and a half years ago now, but he still can't stop it happening over and over again every time he closes his eyes.

When they were little they did everything together, Benji never left Kevin's side. When some boys find their first best friend it's the first real love of their lives, they just don't know what falling in love is yet, so that's how they learn what love is: it feels like climbing trees, it feels like jumping in puddles, it feels like having one single person in your life who you don't even want to play hide-and-seek with because you can't bear being without him for a single minute. For most boys this infatuation obviously fades as the years pass, but for some it never does. Benji traveled right across the world but never found a single place where he could stop hating himself for still loving Kevin.

When they were young the boys were always having sleepovers, where they read superhero comics and talked about nightmares they'd never tell anyone else about. Sometimes Benji would wake from a really bad one with his arms flailing and Kevin would have to duck to avoid ending up with a broken nose. When they went off to tournaments and had to sleep with other guys in gym halls, Kevin would sneak out of bed at night and pull the zip of Benji's sleeping bag right up to his chin, so if anyone else woke him they wouldn't get a fist in the face before Kevin had time to intervene. In summer the boys would set off alone into the forest, swimming naked in lakes and spending weeks at a time sleeping on an island that only they knew existed. In winter Kevin was the whole town's hockey hero and Benji was the one the old men in the stands called the "insurance policy," because if anyone attacked Kevin, Benji went after them, pursuing them to the ends of the earth. Benji was Kevin's best friend, and Kevin was the love of Benji's life.

So it's Benji's fault, he knows that. It was his job to protect Kevin from everyone else, and everyone else from Kevin. If only Benji had stayed at the party, Kevin wouldn't have raped Maya, and then everything would just have carried on as normal. If only Benji hadn't gotten jealous when Maya arrived at the party and he saw the way Kevin looked at her, if only he had stayed when Kevin asked him to, then Maya's life would never have been shattered. She would have been happy. Kevin would almost certainly be playing in the NHL now. And maybe no one would have known the truth about Benji either, but he wouldn't have minded, he would have swapped being able to be himself for everything staying the way it used to be. He might still have been playing hockey now, and perhaps it would have been worth it. Because he misses how simple it was: just win. Then we'll love you. He misses fighting on other people's behalf, meaning something in a group, being the person their opponents fear will leap over the boards if they touch his teammates. He misses the locker room and shaving foam in shoes and sitting at the back of the bus throwing peanuts at the heads of Bobo and the other idiots. He misses feeling the coach's palm slap the top of his helmet the way a dog owner pats his dog's head, because then Benji knew he'd done something right. He misses having somewhere he belongs, even if it was a lie—sooner that than being lost in the truth.

We all have a hundred fake personalities depending upon who we're with. We pretend and dissemble and stifle ourselves just to fit in. The very last words Benji said to Kevin the last time they saw each other were: "I hope you find him: the Kevin you're looking for." He doesn't know if Kevin ever did. Benji has been looking for a Kevin he can put up with, but hasn't succeeded yet.

When he finally boards the plane he pulls his safety belt as tight as he can before slipping his hands under it, so he doesn't hit anyone if he gets woken up.

Then he sleeps and dreams about time machines. Those are his worst nightmares.

———

When the power goes off again Leo walks out into the kitchen and sits at the table with his mother for a while. On the chair next to her, not opposite. They eat sandwiches and drink chocolate milk, and even a fourteen-year-old has trouble denying how good it feels that something so simple can make anyone as happy as it makes her then.

Matteo crawls in through the basement window of his neighbors' house and lies on the floor in the darkness listening to the sound of their voices. He tries once more to open the gun cabinet, but fails again.

Leo says nothing to his mom about his sister being on her way home. It will be a surprise.

Matteo wishes he could call his sister and tell her to stay where she is, wherever that might be. He doesn't want her to come home. She can be anywhere in the world, as long as she doesn't come home. His joy at shooting Leo in the head in the game quickly leaves his body. Leo still has everything that Matteo has lost.

"Two of everything, one we see and one we don't," as Ramona used to say. Two funerals. Two fourteen-year-olds in two houses waiting for their big sisters. Two young women on their way home to the town they haven't quite managed to leave behind. One coming by train, the other in an urn.

24

Dreams

A common misconception about dangerous people is that they lack emotions. That they aren't sentimental. That's almost never true, often the most sentimental and sensitive people are the most dangerous, because they're not only capable of abuse, but can also justify it. Sensitive people never feel that they're doing the wrong thing because their feelings always convince them that they're on the right side.

"Star Wars guys," Ramona used to call them. "Show those films to a hundred men with a hundred different political opinions, and every damn one of them will think he's Luke Skywalker. No bastard ever thinks they're that Darth Vader." She wasn't really that bothered about films, but when Vidar was little she used to watch them with him, she didn't love them but she loved him. She loved being right too, but even she would probably have hated how right she is going to be proved over the next few days.

Tails is already up and about when he hears that she's dead. He goes to the ice rink and helps the caretaker hoist the flags at half-mast. Then he starts making calls. He has tears in his eyes, that makes it easy to underestimate him, because he's already started looking further ahead than anyone else. Ramona doesn't just leave an empty pub behind, but also an empty seat on the committee of Beartown Hockey.

When most of us look back on the storm in years to come, we won't be able to tell the stories in the right order. That's why psychologists get patients who have been through trauma to start by putting together a timeline, trying to find a chronological order made up of fragments, because terror muddles dates up. People too, sometimes. But the memory we share, the one everyone in Beartown and Hed remembers most clearly, is probably the silence. It comes as soon as the wind has moved on and the trees have stopped swaying, and is almost as harsh in our ears as the chaos that preceded it. The town centers of Beartown and Hed look like bombs have gone off there, but that isn't the worst of it: at kitchen tables on the outskirts of both towns, men and women who have owned forest for generations sit with pocket calculators and count the cost of survival, with their entire inheritance to their children and grandchildren erased outside their windows, the wind smashed their lives into the ground and left only the ruins of silent tragedies behind. Not everyone around here had their insurance in order, and of course the insurance companies will do all they can to avoid paying out even to those who did have insurance. In the weeks following the storm younger members of the family will take turns staying awake and sitting by their older relatives' side to make sure they're not thinking of taking their shotgun and going out into the forest. That's what the hunters call it around here. No one says "suicide" in these parts.

All the boundaries between Beartown and Hed become less defined directly after the storm, not only between plots of land but even between neighbors. Sometimes that's good, and sometimes it's terrible. We'll spend many years from now thinking about what hit us and what we ourselves were the cause of in the days that followed, what was coincidence and what was conspiracy. But it begins the way it always does: with politics.

It's Tails who makes sure all the council's most powerful men and women meet up at lunchtime on the day after the storm. "To come up with a crisis plan," he says repeatedly over the phone. Obviously the politicians will have loads of meetings with local business leaders in coming days, even in Hed, but the very first of them is held in the office of the supermarket in Beartown. In hindsight we'll know that this was a bad idea, and that people in Hed saw this as symbolic. All the strongest voices in the district come to the meeting, but the person who speaks most is Tails, he holds no elected office but he seems to direct everything anyway, and in time we'll understand that this too was a bad idea.

The first item on the agenda is how the clearance work should be prioritized. The fire brigade and volunteers are already out trying to make the roads passable, but someone has to decide which roads should be cleared first. Everyone expects Tails, with his customary lack of modesty, to suggest that the road to his supermarket be placed near the top of the list, but instead he gets to his feet and says:

"The important thing now, the *most* important thing of all, is that we think of the *children*! Don't you agree? For that reason, I think we should agree that all the teams at Hed Hockey, which has so tragically lost its ice rink, should be allowed to come and train in Beartown's rink. That's an obvious gesture of solidarity, isn't it, so can we agree on that?"

The moment he starts to get murmurs of agreement from the room, he adds:

"So obviously we need to clear all the roads to Beartown ice rink first! Agreed?"

The murmuring isn't quite as enthusiastic now, everyone knows that the roads to the ice rink just happen to be the same roads that lead to Tails's supermarket, but pointing that out now would look like you were anti-children. Or even worse: anti-hockey. To silence any potential critics before they've even opened their mouths, Tails gives a didactic speech in his own defense:

"Do you know what always runs out first in my supermarket whenever there's a crisis? Toilet paper! Do you know why? Because it gives us a feeling of being in control of the chaos. When the world doesn't feel safe, people go and do a big shop, because it makes them feel like they're DOING something. But they don't know what they should buy. Milk? You can't buy a hundred gallons of milk, it'll just go bad. Cans? Pasta? People rush around like headless chickens buying thousands of different things, but do you know what every single one of them buys? Toilet paper! Because that's the sort of thing you buy every time you go shopping, and the whole family uses it every day. Can we live without it? Of course we can! But it has been imprinted on us as an everyday item, as normality, so when we get scared we drag great bundles of the stuff home with us, not because we need it but because it feels like we're taking control of the situation. Do you get what I mean? People need normality in a crisis. And around here, for people like us, hockey is toilet paper. It has to be there. It mustn't run out. What we need in this district right now more than electricity and more than heat are symbols and dreams. There was a storm yesterday, but today life goes on. And life starts with hockey!"

No one there is really able to argue against that, so the decision about which roads should be cleared as a priority is passed, along with the decision to let Hed and Beartown share ice time at Beartown's ice rink.

We will remember that meeting in different ways, depending on which town we live in. As the years pass, some of those involved won't even remember if they were actually present at the meeting, or if they have had the story told to them so many times that it just *feels* like they were there.

The only thing we will agree on is that both decisions were a disaster. We kicked a hornet's nest. Maybe that was Tails's fault, maybe that was his intention.

But no one, absolutely no one, loved Star Wars more than he did as a child.

25

Clichés

Amat wakes up early the morning after the storm. He ties the laces of his running shoes as if he's forgotten how to do it, creeps out of the apartment, and scuttles through the shadows by the walls of the buildings like a rat, as if what he's about to do was a terrible sin. It's actually the opposite, but he doesn't want anyone to see him in case he fails.

Fatima sees him leave the apartment but pretends not to notice, singing inside but trying to stop herself dancing on the ceiling. When they got home the night before, after he came to get her on the road in the storm, he whispered: "I'm sorry I let you down, Mom." She replied the way she always does: "You'll never let me down as long as you don't give up."

So now he's running again. A few tentative, shameful steps at first, but soon at full speed. Anxiety and alcohol have piled on the pounds since summer, but his feet have been longing for this. They just need to learn everything afresh, become a machine again, so that his brain can switch off without his body stopping. Over the past few years he's heard so much about what a "talent" he is, but the people who use that word know nothing about hockey. They say "talent" as if it comes for free. As if Amat hadn't been the first person at the ice rink every morning and last to leave ever since he started junior high school, as if he hadn't trained harder than everyone else year after year, covering thousands of miles on his skates, running until he threw up, dribbling empty cans at home in the apartment until his hands were blistered and the neighbors furious. As if hockey hadn't cost him precisely what it costs everyone who wants to be any good: everything.

The one thing he has learned about talent is that the only sort of talent that's worth anything is to submit totally to training. To tough it out. He was already out of breath when he started running today, but as soon as he is away from the built-up area he runs at full speed away from the Hollow, up the hill toward the forest, into the jumble of fallen trees. A few times he has to leap sideways, terrified of torn roots and falling branches, because the forest can be even more dangerous after a storm than during it, but there's nowhere else for him to go. He couldn't bear the judgmental looks he would get if he were to run through the town, and he doesn't even know if he's welcome at the ice rink after everything that happened in the spring. He only has himself now. He stops in a clearing at the highest point on the hill, there was no clearing here before the storm, an invisible fist has punched right through the trees. From here he would have been able to see the whole town if his eyes weren't full of tears after he throws up from the exertion. He used to be able to run up and down here a hundred times without even getting out of breath, now he feels like an old alcoholic who can't cope with a flight of stairs without gasping his way to a heart attack.

But at least he's here. He's running again. All the way back to the person he used to be.

———

"What are you saying? You've got her in the CAR?" the man from the undertakers exclaims when he finally arrives.

It's the day after the storm, the town is in chaos but the man is still wearing a suit and smart shoes, a gray man who gives the impression of having been sixty years old ever since he was fifteen.

"The circumstances were rather unusual," Peter says.

"She was wearing a seat belt, for God's sake," Teemu mutters.

If he had been a different man in a different town, the man from the undertakers may well have said one or two ill-chosen words about this, but this is the notorious Teemu Rinnius and this is Beartown, so the man clears his throat and just says quietly to Peter:

"This isn't the way it usually happens. This really isn't the way it usually happens."

Peter nods sympathetically, and says that the storm and the power cut and the shock made him take an ill-considered decision. He doesn't blame Teemu, takes all the flak himself. In a vain attempt to find a comfortable topic of conversation, he asks the man:

"So what do you think about the hockey team this year?"

"I don't follow sports," the man replies curtly.

Teemu rolls his eyes so far that Peter thinks he's going to faint. The man goes into the building and Peter sighs and follows him. The man makes some calls about dealing with Ramona's body, and Peter and Teemu sit like two naughty schoolboys in the headmaster's office, passing the time by reading the framed extracts of poems that are popular in death notices that are hanging on the wall. "*Don't say there's nothing left of the most beautiful butterfly life bestowed,*" one says, and Teemu nudges Peter in the side and grins:

"She'd have hated that one, right? Let's have that on the gravestone!"

Peter bursts out laughing, then has to spend several minutes apologizing to the undertaker, who stares at them and mutters "hooligans" when he thinks they can't hear him, and then Teemu laughs so loudly that he loses his breath.

Peter reads the other poems on the wall: "*When a mother dies, you lose a point on the compass, you lose every other breath, you lose a glade in the forest. When a mother dies, weeds sprout up everywhere,*" one of them says.

"That doesn't even rhyme!" Teemu says.

"Tell me more about your great knowledge of poetry," Peter teases.

"Roses are red, violets are blue, give me a beer and I'll try not to hit you!" Teemu retorts with a grin.

Peter nods toward a quotation at the far end of the row and says:

"I think she'd have liked that one."

Teemu reads it and for once says nothing. "*One day you will be one of the people who lived long ago,*" it says. He nods. When one of the old men in the Bearskin was complaining as usual about her raising the price of beer, and she was drunk enough herself to come up with some completely new insults, she replied: "Yeah, yeah, we're all going to die and before we do, everything we love will be taken from us. Stop feeling sorry for yourself, you miserable old cunt!" That would have looked good framed.

The gray undertaker clears his throat, clearly as keen to get rid of his visitors as they are to leave, and asks when they'd like the funeral to take place. Peter hasn't even thought about that, but when he counts the days he says instinctively:

"It has to be this Sunday."

The gray man looks horrified.

"The day after tomorrow? Impossible! It's customary to wait at least . . ."

"It can't be the week after, because that's the start of elk hunting season," Peter says seriously.

"Nor the week after that, because that's when the hockey season starts," Teemu notes, even more seriously.

"So it has to be this Sunday," Peter declares.

The gray man stares down at his diary and manages to say:

"There's already one funeral booked for Sunday. Two the same day? In Beartown? This really isn't the way it usually happens!"

Teemu kicks Peter's shin excitedly and giggles:

"You know what we should put in the death notice? 'Ramona has left us. Now the beer in Heaven will be more expensive.'"

Peter glances at him, suddenly feeling mischievous in a way he hasn't for years, and says:

"Yes, well, death notices are something of a speciality for you. What was it you said in mine?"

"For Christ's sake, it wasn't ME who . . . ," Teemu snaps, insulted, and Peter laughs so loudly that the gray man from the undertakers looks like he really, really regrets answering his phone this morning.

———

Amat has played hockey his whole life, and every locker room is a cliché factory, you get so used to most of them that you don't even hear them, but one which Sune, the former A-team coach, used to shout has stuck: "The only day you can influence is today. You can't do a damn thing about yesterday and tomorrow, but you can do something about TODAY!" Amat repeats those words quietly and manically to himself as his throat burns and his legs buckle, and all he can think is how long the way back is. Today, only today.

He stands up in the clearing and looks at the Hollow, the cluster of apartment buildings way below him, it's survived the storm better than other parts of the town because it was built on the slopes leading down to the old gravel quarry. Things are worse for the Heights, the wealthiest area up on the hill on the far side of town, with its open view of the lake. When the wind arrived it didn't give a damn if you had money, it tore the roofs off the largest houses and tossed ridiculously expensive gas barbeques through newly cleaned picture windows. It's the first time Amat can remember that an injustice in Beartown has afflicted those at the top. Every time he feels schadenfreude course warmly though his body about that, he knows that's how everyone else must have felt this summer when everything went to hell for him.

He runs down from the hill, stops to breathe with his hands on his knees, then turns and staggers back up once more. "Sports always show us the truth," he used to be told by all the adult men in Beartown when he was a child. "There's nowhere to hide in a league table." They love their sayings, the men around here. "Pressure is a privilege," "Only losers have excuses," "Attitude beats class." The whistle at the end of a game is a simple liberation for them when other aspects of life are full of gray areas. In hockey we know who the winners are, because winners win. That made the sport an easy thing to live inside, even for Amat, until it eventually became unbearable.

This time last year he was seventeen, everyone knew he had promise but no one had said anything about the NHL, not yet. Beartown is a small club in one of the lower leagues, it takes something remarkable to drag agents and scouts all the way out here. Someone heard about him last autumn, then more during the winter, and all of them in January. He had grown several inches, had put on a few pounds of muscle, and suddenly everything was so simple. He could do whatever he wanted on the ice, as if time moved slower for him than everyone else, he felt immortal. Just three years ago, when he was fifteen, even playing on the junior team with Kevin, Benji, Bobo, and the others seemed like an impossible dream. Then suddenly he was there, and the A-team felt out of reach, and then suddenly he was THERE. Everything moves so fast in hockey, a change of line, a game, a whole season just rushes past. Last winter everything was spinning so fast that in the end he lost his footing.

It started with love, it always starts that way. He scored goals in every game and old men in the supermarket would stop him and his mother to shake his hand and tell him how proud the town was of him, the sort of men who used to feel the pocket holding their wallet if he got a bit too close to them suddenly started acting like they were family. Naturally they liked squeezing his upper arms and chuckling that he "needed more muscle," and occasionally they would tease him, saying that "in years gone by we always had five yards of thread ready for each Beartown game, and sometimes that wasn't enough, so they'd just stick a bit of duct tape over your eyebrow and then you could play again!" They didn't like the fact that he preferred to jump out of the way rather than get hit on the ice, he was regarded as being a bit weak, but they loved him when he won. They wrinkled their noses when his friends from the Hollow started coming to games, but he just kept on winning and winning and winning. First the kids in the Hollow started yelling "I'm Amat!" when they played out in the street, then the kids in the Heights started to do the same. Eventually the kids over in Hed started doing it as well, even if they didn't let their parents hear.

Suddenly everyone started talking about the NHL, life as a pro, all the millions. Amat tried not to listen. "Be grateful and humble," his mother said when he helped her clean the ice rink late in the evening, but when enough other people are sufficiently convinced that you can go all the way, in the end it's hard not to start believing in yourself. Then "can" turns into "will," and then "will" becomes "must." You *must* go all the way now. Hope becomes pressure, happiness becomes stress, the old men in the supermarket stopped praising him if he scored two goals because he should have scored three. When the season began they were happy if he could save Beartown Hockey from relegation, but by the time they were top of the league at New Year's suddenly that wasn't enough: they started talking about the chances of the club being promoted. In just a few months everyone went from talking about what Amat had given the town to what he owed it. So he bowed his head and trained even harder. Grateful, grateful, grateful. Humble, humble, humble.

He did everything they asked. He did everything right. And everything still went to hell.

———

Peter and Teemu leave the undertakers after the gray man asked "how payment was to be resolved" and Peter discovers how incredibly quickly and quietly Teemu can sneak out of a building when the question of payment is mentioned. He's standing by the car smoking when Peter comes out.

"Can you give me a lift home?" Peter asks.

Teemu nods down toward the pavement.

"Sure. Sure. But could you, I mean, can I, erm . . . all the paperwork at the Bearskin. The bank and . . . the grown-up stuff. Can you help me with that? And the funeral? Can you . . . do you know what to do?"

Peter clears his throat uncomfortably.

"Shouldn't you ask someone who was closer to Ramona about that?"

"Who the hell was closer to her?" Teemu asks bluntly.

It comes as something of a shock for Peter to realize how lost for words that leaves him. So he doesn't say no, he doesn't say anything at all, they just head off to the Bearskin and he texts Kira to say he's going to be gone a couple more hours, and she just replies: Ok. He fiddles with his phone for several minutes, but doesn't write anything else.

Ramona's accounts look like they're written in code, to conceal any clues that might lead to the buried treasure, but all they actually lead to are tax debts and missing VAT returns. Peter makes phone call after phone call to resolve one thing at a time, and is surprised by how good it feels: organizing something again. It briefly reminds him so much of what being general manager used to be like that he almost imagines that Ramona has died on purpose just to mess with him.

"Have you seen this? Obviously your photograph was going to hang in the best spot, Mr. Perfect!" Teemu says, pointing to the row of pictures of former Beartown players on the wall.

Peter glances at the photograph of himself as a young man, he's never liked it, it's from the season they were second best in the country. Only second best. It reminds him of how he never achieved what everyone demanded of him. "One day you will be one of the people who lived long ago," he thinks to himself, then asks absentmindedly:

"What did you mean by that? 'Mr. Perfect'?"

Teemu chuckles.

"The old boys in the bar call you that, because Ramona always used to go on about how good you were at everything. You're the reason why we dream impossible dreams in this town—God, the number of times she said that! Because you came from nothing and became the best!"

Peter blushes so hard he can feel it all the way down to his throat. He's never heard a less appropriate nickname for anyone in his entire life.

"Second best," he murmurs.

Teemu sees his shoulders slump, so doesn't say anything else. He finds a photograph near the bottom of one wall and takes it off its hook and places it carefully on the bar instead. It's of Ramona, she's standing next to Vidar, they're both laughing. Peter sees it, and he says nothing either. They clean the bar and sort paperwork for several hours, and when they eventually start to talk again, it's about hockey. It's autumn now, and that's when the new year starts here, a new season when everything is possible again. When you can forget everything that was and can discuss everything you hope for instead. Dream impossible dreams.

Teemu goes to the bathroom and leaves his phone on the bar. It buzzes as a text message arrives, Peter doesn't react, he doesn't even react when it buzzes ten more times. The rumors have begun, people have started talking, but not to Peter, not yet. So he doesn't know what was agreed at that meeting between Tails and the politicians today. He doesn't know that every time Teemu's phone moves a few inches across the bar, the whole community is shifting at the same time. In the wrong direction.

26

Rumors

In a corridor in Hed hospital stand a midwife and a fireman. Hannah feels exhausted mentally, Johnny feels exhausted physically. They're doing what they can not to take it out on each other, but that isn't really working. It's the day after the storm and he's been working in the forest nonstop, so she's had to work nonstop with everything else. The hospital staff who live over in Beartown can't get to work because the road is blocked by trees, so Hannah and the rest of the staff who live in Hed are having to work double shifts, but someone has to take care of the children at home, and that's an impossible equation: Hannah can't go home until the road is cleared, but Johnny can't go home because he's the one clearing the road. That pretty much sums up their relationship, both to each other and to their community. Hannah once heard a marriage guidance counselor on television say that "the important thing in a marriage is to have shared goals and to keep facing the same direction," but she often thinks that the problem with that is that if you're both facing the same direction, you never see each other.

"So what do you want me to do?" Johnny wonders now, grimy and sweaty.

Hannah just sighs in the absence of a good way to explain. He set out as soon as the wind began to die down, that's his job, but he's also offered to help another fireman's father clear his field tonight after work, and to help the hairdresser in Hed replace a large pane of glass. Hannah can see the obsession in her husband's eyes, he thinks he's got to save the world again now, that he can save it. She hates being the person who has to hold him back, but no one else will do that. Everyone thinks he's Superman.

"Take a break? Go home and see your children for an hour so they can see you're still alive? Maybe stop thinking you have to do everything yourself?" Hannah suggests, crumpled and desperate and in serious need of a bath, a glass of wine, and sixteen hours' sleep.

She can see how much that last remark hurts him, because she knows he's working twice as hard as all the others out there with the chain saw to make up for the fact that he wasn't there yesterday. He had to stay at home when Hannah went off with that crazy eighteen-year-old, Ana, out into the forest to deliver a baby, while his colleagues at the fire station were already out in the town trying to help people. A tree fell on one of them, Bengt, and broke his leg. That's why all the firemen are at the hospital, a fact that escapes no one because the sound of a dozen men laughing echoes from Bengt's room every ten seconds. He's a popular boss, always quick with a joke and slow to chastise, he's twenty years older than Johnny and was the person who helped get him his job as a fireman. That was in the days when fire stations had to do their own recruitment, not like now when they have to go through a complex application process. Johnny often mutters that the new system is "supposed to make everything so damn equal, so that we employ the same number of useless firemen as good ones, so that no single group in society feels left out." In his day you got recruited straight out of the hockey team, because then the men who had spent half their lives next to you in the locker room could vouch for the fact that you were the right sort of guy. You can learn to become a fireman, but you're either the right sort of guy or you aren't. Bengt knew that, and now Johnny feels he's let his mentor down. He should have been there last night. All trees that fall are his trees. All broken legs are his fault.

"I should have been there, I could . . . ," Johnny begins irritably.

"You couldn't have changed anything!" Hannah replies.

It was the meanest thing she could have said, she knows that, claiming that someone who has devoted his working life to making a difference is powerless.

"I should . . . ," he mutters.

"I know, I know, sorry," she replies, and they both feel ashamed.

When they first got together, a hundred years ago, Johnny once said: "I can't talk about how I feel the whole time, because I'm not an emotional person like you," and that might be the stupidest thing Hannah has ever heard him say. Not an emotional person? That's pretty much all he is! Maybe she talks a lot about her feelings, but he's entirely *governed* by his, that's the difference. But that's what makes him a good fireman, and a good dad too, and it was his emotions she fell in love with. And it's emotions that have made their sons good hockey players and their daughter a fantastic figure skater, because you can't get good at a sport if you're not sensitive enough for it to mean everything to you, if you don't take every setback personally, if every loss doesn't feel like dying. So don't try to talk to Hannah about "emotional people," because they're all she lives with.

"I'll be careful, there's no need to worry, we're mostly just going to be sawing trees and directing traffic . . . ," Johnny says tentatively.

"Don't tell me that! What is it you always tell the kids when there's a fire? That there's a greater statistical risk of you being run over attending an accident on the highway than of you dying in a fire!" she retorts.

"I'll be home for dinner. I promise. And I can drive the kids to hockey tomorrow," he says, his voice wavering with guilt.

"Drive them in what? We need to get the car . . . ," she sighs, angry at herself for sounding angry with him.

The van is still parked outside Ana's house, where she left it during the storm.

"I'll get it this evening, one of the guys can drive me over as soon as we've cleared the road," Johnny nods. He hadn't even thought about the damn van.

She nods slowly.

"Sorry, I'm just tired, it's been a stressful day. Everything's just so . . . crazy. Did you get the email from the coaching staff? All the kids are going to be training in . . ."

She bites her tongue. Too late. He explodes instantaneously.

"Over in BEARTOWN'S ice rink, yes! I heard that at the station! What colossal nerve! So now we're expected to be grateful for their kindness, letting us come and borrow their rink? Of course it withstood the storm, seeing as it was recently renovated at a cost of millions while ours was left to decay! The council should have renovated OUR rink before . . ."

He stops himself, he knows she can't bear it when he gets like this, but Beartown brings out the worst of him in every way.

"Yes, yes, I know, but it is what it is," she concludes sternly.

"It is what it is because we let it! Have you seen where we were sent to clear the roads first? To Beartown, the road to their ice rink and that bastard Tails's supermarket. As if there aren't any roads to clear in Hed! As if there's no one who lives here!"

He mutters at the start of the sentence, and he mutters at the end of it. The road that always gets prioritized first is actually the road here to the hospital, but she understands what he means. If the council keeps saying that one town is more important than the other, then eventually the inhabitants start to believe it. Especially emotional people. She leans forward, puts her hand on his cheek and whispers:

"We do what we can. Okay? We just have to ignore the things we can't control. Concentrate on the things you can actually do something about."

He nods, and the corners of his mouth twitch beneath his stubble.

"Okay, Dalai Lama."

She hits his arm and he kisses her a little longer than is probably suitable for a workplace. He whispers that he loves her, and she whispers various indecent things back that leave him so dumbfounded that she bursts out laughing.

"Okay, take your little playmates out into the forest again before they wreck the whole hospital," she says, nodding along the corridor where the sound of the firemen's voices are still echoing from Bengt's room.

Johnny obeys. But before he goes he bursts out eagerly:

"Do you want to hear a funny story? It's one of Bengt's!"

"I haven't got time, darling . . . ," she begins, but of course it's already too late.

"So, there's this hunter called Allan who dies in a fire. Have you heard this one? No? Well anyway: Allan's face is so badly burned that he can't be identified, so the hospital calls his two best hunting friends and asks them to come to the mortuary. They look at the body but can't tell from his face if it's him or not, so they ask the doctors to turn the body over. The doctors are surprised, but they do it, and when Allan's body is lying there on its front naked, one of his friends says: 'No, that's not Allan.' And the other friend says: 'No. Definitely not Allan!' The doctor scratches his head and wonders: 'How can you be so certain?' And the friends squirm a bit, then they say: 'Well, Allan had a particular physical . . . defect. He had two assholes, you see.' The doctor stares at the friends: 'Two assholes?' They nod: 'Mmm, two assholes.' The doctor shakes his head and says: 'Are you CERTAIN about that?' The friends look a bit hesitant now, but then they say: 'Well . . . we haven't actually SEEN them . . . but ever since we were children, people have always said: 'Look! Here comes Allan with the two assholes!'"

Hannah has heard it before, but she still laughs, not with Johnny but at him.

"Good, isn't it?" he giggles, so joyously that it's infectious.

"Just GO!" she sighs, and the air turns into laughter on its way out.

So at last he leaves, taking all the other firemen with him, and their laughter lingers long after they are gone. They're like brothers, it drives Hannah mad but also makes her jealous, the fact that they have a whole extra family. Most of them have been friends since they were kids, and if you have friends like that you never really need to grow up. They went to school together and played hockey together and now they fish and hunt and talk about cars they can't fix and women they don't understand and compete at bench press and are colleagues and dads and firemen together. A group.

"Are you coming out for a smoke?" a nurse asks as she hurries past, obviously a joke because she knows Hannah gave it up years ago.

"If I ever start again, I promise I'll come with you!" Hannah smiles.

She slips into the gossip swamp instead, or the "staffroom" as some people still call it. As usual, she just has time to get herself a cup of coffee but has no time to drink it before someone calls her out again, but she's there long enough to hear the others talking. About hockey, of course, but what else? There was a different tone to it today. This is a mixed workplace, half the staff live in Beartown, half in Hed, everyone has learned to skirt around sports, the way people presumably do with religion or politics in other places around the world. But today the Beartown half of the staff are missing, so today a lot of people are saying what they really feel.

It starts with a complaint about Hed's youth team having to train in Beartown. Then someone says there's a rumor that the council aren't going to rebuild Hed's ice rink at all. Then someone else says she's heard that the politicians have a secret plan to merge the two clubs, now that they have an opportunity to do it.

"Which one are they going to close down?" someone wonders.

"Which one do you think? The one with the least money!" someone else exclaims.

"So where does Beartown's money come from, then? Wasn't it the council that paid to have their rink renovated? Are we in Hed supposed to pay taxes to support THEIR club?"

Hannah waits silently by the coffee machine, she knows where this discussion is going, it's been going on forever but has gotten worse recently. Hannah wishes she didn't agree with them, that she could be the voice of reason here, but the truth is that she's merely silent. Because she gets it. The hospital is always weighed down by rumors of more cutbacks, maybe complete closure, so if the council even threatens to remove the hockey club it would probably be best for all concerned if they stop clearing the road to Beartown altogether. And maybe build a wall instead.

Hannah is a hypocrite, of course, she knows that. Wouldn't all the taxpayers' money that's been sunk into Hed Hockey over the years have done more good here at the hospital? Obviously. But when her own children are on the ice nothing else exists, the world fades away, and what would she sacrifice for that? Stupid question. What wouldn't she sacrifice? Besides, the taxpayers' money from ice hockey would never end up at the hospital instead, it never does, it would have gone to wind farms or some political inquiry into how to teach badgers to express their feelings through watercolors or some other nonsense. At least hockey gives some sort of return. Something for the whole town, old and young, to be passionate about and unite around: the fact that everyone hates Beartown. Naturally there are people in Hed who don't like hockey, but that's regarded almost as a sexual perversion here: what you do in the comfort of your own home is up to you, but please just keep it to yourself.

Someone in the staffroom has a brother-in-law who's talked about "Beartown Business Park," she hears.

"They're trying to keep it secret, but they're offering every business in Hed offices there now! And then what's going to be left here?"

"Did you see that the hockey association has changed the A-team's match schedule because of the storm? They're not sure if teams from the south will be able to get here, so guess who we're playing first? Beartown!"

"Bloody hell."

"What an opportunity, though! They can hardly close down a winning club, so if we WIN that one, then . . ."

"It won't be enough just to win against a shit club like that! We need to CRUSH them!"

"It'll be war!"

"Hope that asshole Amat doesn't play, then . . ."

"What if he managed to break his leg? Maybe he could have an accident?"

They laugh as if that was funny, and so it goes on. Hannah doesn't have time to listen to more, someone calls her name and she leaves her coffee untouched on the counter and runs out. She has time to hope that her idiot sons won't hear all the rumors before they're due to train over in Beartown tomorrow, because then there would no doubt be the usual trouble. Above all, she hopes that Johnny, the biggest idiot of them all, doesn't hear the rumors.

But of course it's already too late for that.

27

Dads

The train from the capital drills its way slowly northward, stopping at station after station after station in communities that could all have been Beartown or Hed, this country is full of them. Most of the names appear and are forgotten just as quickly, but a few have clung to the national consciousness thanks to some local speciality: a cake, a music festival, a water park, perhaps a prison. Or a hockey team. Anything that makes people say, "Ah, you're the ones who have . . ." when you tell them where you were born. Anything that puts a place on the map.

As the train moves north, the worse the damage from the storm is, and the denser the forest, the more obvious the destruction. At one station a few hours into the interior, whose name everyone has forgotten before the train has even rolled past the sign, an old man climbs aboard. No one pays him any attention apart from the eighteen-year-old girl in the seat opposite his, she immediately stands up politely and helps him lift his suitcase up into the luggage rack without him even having to ask.

"Thank you, young lady, thank you very much, very much indeed!" he says, like a relic from a black-and-white matinee.

Her smile makes her look younger than she is. The way he uses his umbrella as a walking stick does the opposite for him.

"Just say when you're getting off and I'll help you get it down," Maya smiles considerately.

"Thank you, that would be kind of you. The train probably won't be going all the way now after the storm, so I'll most likely have to get off at the same station as you and catch the bus from there . . ."

She stiffens and he sees that he's scared her, so he gives an explanatory nod toward her woolly hat:

"The bear from Beartown, I recognize that. I assume that's where you're going?"

Maya breathes out, a little too quickly, embarrassed at her paranoia.

"Yes, yes, of course . . . it's my dad's. I don't usually wear it. I just thought I would now that I'm going . . . home. Colder up there."

Her face breaks into an embarrassed smile. The man nods understandingly.

"One gets more patriotic about where one is from the farther away from home one is."

She runs her fingertips over the hat.

"Yes, I suppose that's true. I just didn't think it applied to me."

Years ago, her mom used to say that you should never trust anyone who doesn't have something in their life that they love beyond measure. She can relate to that more and more.

The man opposite leans forward and whispers, as if it was a great secret:

"I'm going to visit my daughter, she lives in Hed, but don't hold that against me."

Maya laughs out loud.

"God, I don't miss THAT when I'm away from home, at any rate. The idea that we have to hate Hed and they have to hate us. So bloody ridiculous."

"Yes, I've understood from my daughter that ice hockey influences a lot of things up there . . ."

She rolls her eyes.

"No, no, not that much. Only everything."

"To be honest, I think that people in Hed are a little jealous. Things seem to be going better for Beartown than Hed at the moment, don't they? And not just in hockey. The factory there has expanded and taken more people on, I read. And businesses are moving there rather than moving away. There aren't many towns of that size that can make that boast."

Maya nods in agreement, even though it's so unusual to hear someone talk about her hometown like that, as a place that's doing well. "Things turn quickly in hockey," her dad used to say to her when anything went badly for her when she was little, "things can turn quickly in life as well, you just have to keep moving forward!"

"People in Beartown are industrious, they work hard!" she finds herself telling the man opposite, and is surprised at how proud she sounds.

The man notes that her accent is getting broader. He glances out at the forest that's growing denser around the windows until it feels like they're traveling through a tunnel.

"Are you going home because of the storm? My daughter says it was pretty terrible."

"No . . . well, yes, in a way. I'm going home for a funeral."

"My condolences. Someone close?"

The whole of the year she turned sixteen has time to rattle through Maya before she replies. How her dad took her to the police station, how she told them everything and how he was almost fired from Beartown Hockey when Kevin couldn't play in the most important game of the year because of her. How there was a meeting where all the club's members had to decide about the future, and how it felt like it was Maya's family against the whole town. The first person who stood up to speak in their defense was Ramona. She had the Pack behind her, Maya knows how much that rankles for her dad, but neither he nor Maya will ever forget what Ramona did: she believed a fifteen-year-old girl when no one else did. Stood up for her when no one else dared. She smiles sadly at the man in the seat opposite her.

"Dad knew her better. They were . . . really old friends. She owned a pub, and Dad used to have to collect Grandpa there when he'd had too much to drink."

The man chuckles.

"Ah, that old story. But you never had to collect your dad?"

"My dad doesn't drink!"

She says it too quickly, always too eager to defend him. The man raises his hands apologetically.

"Sorry. I didn't mean to offend you."

She sighs.

"No . . . no, I understand. It's just that if you knew my dad . . . he's like the most regular man in the world. The sort who never breaks any rules at all."

"Is he as keen on hockey as everyone else in Beartown?"

She bursts into loud laughter.

"No kidding. He used to be general manager there, actually. But now he works in my mom's company."

"Ah, so it's your *mom* who's one of the 'industrious' people in Beartown you mentioned," the man teases.

Maya smiles.

"Her company's actually based in Hed. Dad's really mad about that."

"I can imagine. How did he come to stop being general manager?"

"He loves my mom."

She says it so instinctively that the man loses his thread for a moment. He smiles sadly and looks down at his hands, Maya can't see a wedding ring. He reaches for his briefcase and takes out a thick bundle of papers and puts them on his lap.

"Then they're very lucky, both of them," he says without looking up from the papers.

Maya nods. He says nothing for so long that she wonders if she's insulted him, so she asks:

"What are you reading?"

"Annual reports."

"Wow. That sounds . . . exciting."

"It can be, if you just know where to look," he assures her.

She doesn't believe him. That's a mistake.

———

There's an old American car parked in the street outside the Bearskin. Peter stands in the doorway looking at it, he doesn't know who it belongs to, and he has only a passing interest in cars, but he actually happens to know exactly what year's model this one is. When he got to the NHL he was driven to his first training sessions by a teammate who had bought one exactly like it. It was brand-new back then, but the one parked in the street now is rusty and ramshackle. Peter feels much the same.

Teemu has emerged from the bathroom and is reading all the messages on his phone down in the bar. Much later Peter will think how odd it is that a man like him doesn't flare up at bad news. The young man does not, in contrast to what people say about him, have a hot temper. It's more that what he reads on his phone lowers his body temperature, one degree at a time, he grows colder and more silent as Peter grows more uncomfortable. He's learned to judge which men he should be afraid of, not from their behavior in his vicinity, but his own in theirs.

"I need to go, can we carry on with this tomorrow?" Teemu asks, still staring at his phone.

Peter nods, not knowing what else he ought to say. As they turn the lights out and lock the door, his eyes fall on a photograph near the exit, a little girl standing on the ice with a green sweater and a dark expression, so small that she isn't wearing gloves the right size.

"She's going to be better than you," Teemu says behind him, and Peter is taken aback by the sudden love in his voice.

Teemu actually looks surprised himself, almost embarrassed. They avoid each other's gaze, clear their throats and step out onto the street. Peter has heard about the girl, of course. She's six or seven years old, her name is Alicia, and she spends a lot of time with Sune, an old man now, but once the coach of Beartown's A-team, where she does her best to fire holes in the wall of his house with pucks. She's the sort of child who has a terrible life, but not terrible enough to get any help, she's growing up in a home full of empty kitchen cupboards and clenched fists, but never empty or hard enough for the authorities to remove her. So Sune's yard is her refuge, her playground, and Ramona got Teemu to do the best they could a couple of years ago: some black-clad men went to Alicia's home one night when she was asleep, marched into the kitchen and put a hockey bag full of equipment on the table, and explained to the adults there that the girl was under the Pack's protection now. She's had considerably fewer black eyes from home since then, and considerably more bruises from the ice rink. And one day she's going to be the best.

Teemu walks toward the car, Peter follows and it strikes him how bad this would have looked not so very long ago, him getting into a car with the worst hooligan in the district. But now? No one cares what Peter does anymore, not even him. The forest wears down all illusions if it's given long enough, even his. Because he knows all about Teemu's violence, but he can also remember, just like everyone else, how the police didn't have time to show up when there was a spate of burglaries in the district a few years ago, but how the same police had the resources to send an armed response unit and helicopter every time there was so much as a *rumor* that someone was out hunting wolves illegally. It was the Pack that took care of the burglars, Peter doesn't want to know how, but at least he recognized where Teemu's authority came from. It isn't violence that sets him apart from the police, its dependability. Just ask Alicia.

The American car is still parked in the street when they walk past. Teemu's phone vibrates with more messages but he doesn't react, they all say the same thing.

"Popular today?" Peter asks.

"Just people talking," Teemu replies in a toneless voice.

"My kids also send text messages the whole time. They don't even write, just send a load of those little pictures. And isn't there anyone who actually calls anymore?"

Teemu laughs out loud.

"Shit, Peter, are you a hundred years old or what?"

"Sometimes it feels like it."

They get into Teemu's Saab and drive a little way in silence, and when it gets uncomfortable Teemu breaks it with hockey, of course:

"Do you think he'll play this year, then?" he asks.

"Who?" Peter wonders.

"Amat! They say he's been drinking a lot . . ."

"Who's said that?"

Teemu shrugs his shoulders.

"You know. People talk."

They certainly do, just not to Peter. Time waits for no man, boys become men and talents become has-beens and demons can catch up with anyone at all. Perhaps even the town's fastest ever skater. Sune once said that Peter's best characteristic as general manager was that he saw "all the kids in the club as his own kids," which was meant as a compliment, but when Kira said the same thing a few years later it was an accusation. Back in the spring Peter tried to talk to Amat and give him some advice about the NHL draft, but the boy had become a man by then, and the man an old man.

"I don't know," he has to confess.

Teemu sighs.

"He was savage last season. Properly savage. Better than Kevin. Better than . . . you."

"You never saw me play," Peter snorts, to hide his embarrassment, and Teemu splutters like a startled pony.

"Ramona showed me all your games on video! Even the NHL games!"

"There weren't many of those, so that wouldn't have taken long," Peter muttered.

"Shit! Did you think I hadn't seen them? A hundred times! You think I'm just some stupid hooligan, but I love hockey just as much as you, you bastard. That's the only reason I never punched you in the face when you were general manager and were doing all that crap like getting rid of the standing area in the stands. I knew you loved hockey the way I love hockey. I respected that. Even when you acted like a clown!"

It takes a few breaths for Peter to digest being called a "clown" by a guy who once broke into the visiting team's bus and set fire to thirty plastic bags full of dog shit. The planning and logistics required to get thirty bags of the stuff? Dear God. If that guy had dedicated his mental abilities to something sensible he could have taken over the world.

"You're wrong," Peter eventually says with a smile.

"I'm not wrong!"

"I only played four games. And got injured at the start of the fifth. And I don't think you're a stupid hooligan."

"Sure," Teemu mutters.

Peter laughs quietly.

"Well, I don't think you're only a stupid hooligan, anyway . . ."

Teemu bursts out laughing so hard that he almost drives off the road, and for a moment Peter understands what everyone sees in him. Why they all follow him. When he laughs you laugh along with him. Teemu casts a quick glance at him and says:

"You should have talked to Amat back in the spring, before the NHL draft. I think he had the wrong people giving him advice. He could have done with someone like you."

Peter looks down, doesn't want to admit that he tried because Teemu evidently has such a high opinion of him, and it's been a long time since that happened.

———

If people have to guess, they always think Maya is younger than eighteen, it often irritates her, but she isn't very good at guessing people's ages either. For instance, she thinks that the man sitting opposite her on the train has been retired for a while, but he's actually only just past sixty. Some men's bodies just have a tendency to punish their custodian for sinful living with all the afflictions of age in one go. The checkered shirt strains to cover the stomach, breathing comes in heavy gasps through the nostrils. He's wearing a brown hat, the hair beneath it has grown thin and his beard has turned gray, the features of his face are soft from too much drink and too little compromise. Pain in his joints forces him to walk with some sort of support, so he takes an umbrella with him regardless of the weather, because he sure as hell isn't old enough for a cane. But his gaze is steady and his mind still sharp, he's good at his job, possibly even better now that he looks so wretched. That makes it easier for people to underestimate him and he knows how to exploit that.

They make small talk for the whole of the journey, so casually that Maya never realizes how good at it the man is. One little innocent question leads to another, and soon she's told him a lot about herself and he's said very little about himself.

When she gets up to go to the bathroom again she makes a gesture toward taking her guitar case with her.

"I can probably manage to look after that," the man offers.

She smiles awkwardly, as if it's so dear to her that it isn't about it being stolen, but because she doesn't want to be parted from it. But she relents and sets off, and once she's out of sight the man immediately opens the guitar case. Inside the lid is taped a photograph of the girl with her family: younger brother, mom, dad. It looks fairly recent, although the dad's sweater looks old, a washed-out, pale green top with the hockey club's logo across the stomach. "After everything that happened to this family, they still wear clothes with the bear on them," the man thinks, and closes the case. He reaches for his briefcase and in a small notebook writes down what the girl said a short while ago: "*My dad's the sort of man who never breaks any rules at all.*" Maya has changed in the past two years, new hairstyle, more mature body, taller and stronger. The man hardly recognized her at first, even though he's gone to a lot of trouble, using favors owed by and promised to an old contact at the train company to find out which train she was taking today. The most recent pictures he has seen of her are from when she was fifteen, almost sixteen years old, then she became harder to research. After that year, after the rape, she stopped posting any pictures of herself on the internet.

The man knows his own daughter will say it was over the top to approach Maya this way. Possibly even unethical. But a whole life as a journalist has taught him that if you're going to uncover a big scandal, you need to tell a good story, otherwise the readers lose interest long before you get to the point, and a good story is like a set of annual accounts: it can be really boring if you don't know where to start looking. He's always tried to teach his daughter that, their relationship has been turbulent, but he's fairly sure he did a good job of teaching her journalism, otherwise she wouldn't have moved to Hed and become editor in chief of the local paper last year.

So when she called him recently and told him about the stories she'd uncovered about the hockey club, and asked for his help, he asked why she couldn't use her own reporters. "Please Dad, these aren't just any two towns, I've got reporters whose kids go to school in Beartown, the same school as the kids of the men who could end up in prison if we publish this. How are my reporters supposed to have the guts to write anything then?"

Her dad understood, of course, so now he's sitting on a train. For his daughter's sake, but also for his own. He drank away the whole of her childhood, yet she still wanted to do the same job as him. Never underestimate a dad who's trying to be forgiven, he's capable of anything.

The pile of papers in his lap are the annual accounts of Beartown Hockey from the past ten years. His daughter's instincts were right: the whole existence of the club is based upon financial criminality. The graft has been so systemic that it couldn't possibly have taken place without the knowledge of the committee, the sponsors, and the politicians. They've done their best to cover their tracks, the man notes, most journalists with less experience probably wouldn't have known where to start looking. "No one digs like you, Dad, you lunatic," his daughter said over the phone, and he could hear her smiling. So he's been digging. Beneath the annual accounts are contracts and bank transfers and documents, little pieces of the puzzle of a thoroughly corrupt sporting association. Many of the guilty men have obviously been too smart to put their names to anything, but one name keeps recurring, the same signature at the bottom of document after document: Peter Andersson.

In his notebook the man writes: "*Maya's hat is green, with a bear on it. It's a little too big for her.*"

28

Men of God

Matteo won't remember how he found out that the old woman who owned the pub had died. He doesn't talk to anyone, but maybe he reads about it somewhere online when the electricity comes back on, maybe he just hears the old couple talking about it upstairs while he lies curled up on the floor of their basement the morning after the storm. He wakes from a dream about his sister and for a few moments his heart feels like frozen hands when you hold them in front of a fire. At first you're numb, then it hurts a bit because you're so cold, then comes the real pain: when you start to get warm. It's only when the numbness of cold and sleep let go and your body knows it's safe and secure that it lets you feel just how bloody awful things are. Matteo finds a small bottle of moonshine in a basket next to the gun cabinet, possibly hidden there after the old man of the house went hunting, or possibly just hidden from his wife. Matteo drinks some slowly with his eyes closed, his head starts to feel warm and his heart cold again.

Matteo crawls out through the basement window and sneaks home. The house is empty. His parents haven't gotten back to Beartown with his sister yet, he assumes his mother has had to stop at every single church along the way. His big sister always used to argue with their mom about God, but Matteo never does. He has just as little faith in God as his sister, but he never wanted to hurt his mom, she was too brittle.

"You're the only good person I know," his sister used to say as she ruffled his hair.

She was the only person who talked to him. No one at school did, and his parents spent so much time talking to God that they didn't even speak to each other anymore. His sister and Matteo were their miracles, their mother had had four miscarriages and had prayed to God for a healthy child, and then she had her daughter. A few years later Matteo arrived.

Their mom was so frightened of losing them that she didn't even dare feel happy. Heaven had demonstrated its power to her, and after that she spent her whole life in irreconcilable fear that it might take everything back at any moment. She repeated the same thing time after time to her son:

"You must grow up to be a great man of God. Not a sinner! A man of God!"

Matteo never disagreed, but one night when they were alone his sister snapped:

"You know Mom's mentally ill, don't you?"

Matteo had never been angrier than he was then, but not really at his sister. Most of all he was angry with his dad, who did nothing to help his mother, and who was just silent. He went to work, came home, ate dinner, read books, went to bed. Silence, nothing but silence.

"You know I've got to get away from here, don't you? I need to live, Matteo!" his sister whispered the night she left Beartown.

She promised she was going to be rich one day, and would come back and fetch him. He waited. Now she's on her way home, but not to fetch him, and once again he's mostly angry with his dad. If his dad had just been a different sort of dad, everything would have been different. If he had been a powerful man, a rich man, a hockey man. Then Matteo's sister would also have gotten help, then people would have believed her, stood on her side. Then she would have been alive.

Men of God can't save anyone. Not here.

29

Hockey guys

Amat runs out into the forest, as far away as he can, but it doesn't make any difference. He never ends up alone.

In hockey everyone loves talking about players' heads: you need to have a "winning mind-set," a "strong head." If you play hockey as a child you will be told that you need to be "mentally strong," but very little about what that actually means. You will hear a lot about injuries and pain, but nothing about the sort of pain that doesn't show up in X-rays. You will learn all about how the different parts of the body function except the part that controls everything else.

Amat runs deeper and deeper into the forest, but he still can't escape the voices inside his head:

"Sure, he's good, but isn't he too small?"

"What about his frame of mind? You can never know about that. After all, he isn't . . . well, you know . . . he doesn't exactly come from a hockey family."

"But he's got good hands! And he's faster than Kevin!"

"Maybe, but Kevin's got a strong head. He's got a winning mind-set."

Amat heard them everywhere, at the ice rink and in the supermarket and at school, and he knew perfectly well what "hockey family" was code for. They liked it when he scored goals for their team, but they wished he looked like all the other hockey guys, lived in the same smart residential area, laughed at the same jokes. They wished he was Kevin, they only let him be Amat as long as he was winning. So that's what he did. Win, win, win.

By New Year's Beartown was top of the league and Hed was bottom. Throughout the whole of Amat's childhood Hed had been better, richer, bigger, and more powerful, but he became the embodiment of the change. His shoulders ached every morning, at first from the exertion of training, later from the weight of expectation. The caretaker let him into the rink every morning but Amat spent less and less time on the ice and more and more in the gym. He knew everyone said he was too small for the NHL, so he battled with the barbells until he could hardly walk home, thinking the whole time of all the other clichés he had heard from coaches and general managers and other old men: "We don't judge competitions at the start but at the finishing line! Attitude beats class! Desire beats talent!"

One night he was so exhausted when he left the rink that as he stepped through the snowdrifts he slipped and fell in the darkness. His wrist didn't hurt much at first, but the more he trained, the more it swelled up. He didn't say anything to anyone. No NHL club drafts an injured player. He has to play, has to win, he can't disappoint everyone now. Not just the old men in the supermarket, but all his friends in the Hollow, the ones who made him promise to buy them fancy watches when he turned pro. Without them he wouldn't be here. One summer a few years ago they took turns running up the hill behind the apartment blocks with him, so he wouldn't give up. His dreams became their dreams. He needs to repay that. Needs to repay his mom. His coach. The town. Everyone.

In one game he scored three goals but retreated from one tackle. In the locker room the other players joked:

"You know they tackle harder in the NHL, right, princess?"

When he came out of the shower there was a box of tampons by his locker. It was only a joke, of course, but that's how it always starts.

In the next match Amat took another blow to his wrist. The pain was so intense that it became claustrophobic, he took painkillers but they didn't even take the edge off it, so that evening he went to see a girl he knew in the Hollow whose brother sold strong liquor. When she came back with a bottle she said:

"If I tell my brother it's for you, you'll get it for nothing. He loves you! He keeps going on about how someone from the Hollow's going to the NHL!"

Amat shook his head. She added, more seriously:

"My brother says all the rich people in town are trying to exploit you. They only care about you because you can make money for them. Don't let anyone blow you out, okay?"

"Okay," Amat promised.

"Don't say okay if you don't mean it!" she snapped.

"Okay, okay, okay," Amat smiled sadly, and she smiled back sadly, and said something he hadn't been able to forget:

"You know all the little kids in the Hollow look at you and think that if you can be someone, then so can they? So don't fuck that up, okay? Be someone!"

She said it to pick him up, she couldn't know that it only weighed him down even more. It wasn't a pep talk, it was another rock in his backpack. Amat went home and drank away the pain in his wrist so he could sleep, and hid the half-empty bottle in the hockey bag in his wardrobe so his mother wouldn't find it, and within two weeks it was harder for him to hide the empty bottles than the full ones.

He doesn't remember exactly when the phone started ringing. At first it was just one or two agents, then suddenly it felt like there was a new voice every time. They told him he could get drafted. "Could" became "would," which soon became "must." Amat hadn't been to ice hockey academy, he hadn't been scouted by a bigger club, but he had the raw talent. They said he was a Cinderella story. "You came from nowhere, but you can go all the way!" Shall. Must. The agents told him to sign a contract with them, not to worry about anything, "just leave it all to us." Amat had met men like that before. When Kevin was the town's big star and Amat knew the truth about the rape, Kevin's dad showed up in his flashy car and tried to buy his silence. The men calling now sounded like him, a year ago they didn't even know who Amat was, but now he was suddenly a salable asset. He looked up their names on the internet and found hundreds of rumors about dodgy activities: agents signing contracts with kids before they were even teenagers, other agents who gave junior coaches in small clubs well-paid jobs out of the blue if they agreed to bring certain players to their agencies, parents being given paybacks in secret. All the men on the phone sounded the same when they assured him that all of that only applied to other agents, never them, so how was Amat supposed to know who was reliable and who was full of crap?

Soon he had to take his skates out of his hockey bag to make space for more empty bottles. His wrist hurt in the evening, his head hurt in the morning, and in the end he stopped answering the phone altogether.

The local paper wrote about his chances in the NHL draft, the locker room changed, the jokes became serious. If he lost the puck or missed a shot, there was mockery. It wasn't enough for him to be best in games anymore, he needed to be invincible. The voices in his head yelled: "You're a fake, you've just been lucky, you've just been up against bad defenders."

The ice became quicksand, and the harder he struggled the slower he became. Late one evening when he had been training alone in the gym and his top was black with sweat, the caretaker came in and apologized for having to lock up and go home. He *apologized*. "I'm proud of you," the old man said when they parted in the parking lot. To him it was just a kind thing to say, but to Amat it was another hundred tons of rock in his backpack.

Spring came, the snow melted, and every inch of pavement that appeared was a day closer to the draft in June. Amat had nightmares, sometimes he woke up to find himself having a nosebleed, he started to get migraines. What if they discovered he'd lied about his injury? He scored two goals in games when he should have scored three, one when he should have scored two, eventually none at all. Everyone felt qualified to give him advice, every bastard knew what he ought to do. In the newspaper Beartown Hockey was described as a "talent factory" and Amat as a "home-grown product." One day his mother came home from the supermarket and said that Tails, who owned it, had said to her, "You need to tell Amat that even if he gets drafted, he should demand to be allowed to play a couple more seasons for Beartown! That would be in his best interests! He can stay here, Fatima, so that he *develops*, tell him that!" She looked almost frightened when she passed on the message.

"He talked about you like you were a . . . a product in the shop . . . as if you had a barcode."

Amat lay in bed with his laptop that night and saw somewhere on the internet that someone had said that if he got drafted, Beartown would get three hundred thousand dollars from the NHL. Three hundred thousand DOLLARS. But he also read: "After the draft, the NHL club, in agreement with the player's agent, often lets the player have one or more seasons in a lower league so that he can develop before he gets taken across to North America." That was why Tails said that, Beartown wanted the money for Amat but they also wanted him to carry on winning for them. His mom was right. He was just a barcode.

———

The train stops and a group of boys aged around fifteen get on. Maya comes back from the bathroom and stares at them a little too long, and blushes when she realizes that. The man opposite raises an eyebrow over his annual reports when she sits down.

"Do you know them? I can move if you'd like to sit . . ."

"No, no, I don't know them. I just know thousands of guys exactly like them. You know, hockey guys . . ."

"How do you know they're hockey guys?"

"Are you kidding? The same sneakers, the same track suits, the same back-to-front caps. The same confused expression because they've all taken too many pucks to the head. You can recognize hockey guys anywhere . . ."

The man chuckles. Then he asks, as if he's just thinking out loud and there isn't a deeper meaning to the question:

"So is your dad like that as well? A hockey guy?"

He sees her eyelashes flutter, very briefly. Her smile becomes less genuine and more of a defense mechanism.

"He probably used to be. But he's old now."

"So now he's a . . . hockey old man?" The man smiles back.

She shakes her head, almost as if she feels guilty.

"No, no, he's finished with hockey. He just works with Mom now."

The man nods as he looks down at the annual accounts. He glances at the boys a little farther away. They're already so big, so loud, so used to being physically privileged: everywhere belongs to them.

"Can I ask a question that might sound stupid?"

"Sure," Maya nods.

"Do you think all hockey guys look the same to make it harder for someone who's different to break into the group? Or do you think they look the same because they're afraid of being different themselves?"

Maya says nothing for so long that the man starts to worry that he's gone too far, that she's seen through him. Perhaps it was too obviously a journalist's question. But just as he's about to dismiss it with a little joke she looks out through the window and replies:

"Everyone involved in hockey talks about 'fighting.' They learn it as children: 'Get in there and fight.' And that kind of sticks around in their brains, so when they get older they still behave as though they're under attack. They're still aggressive, as if they're trying . . . to overcompensate."

"Overcompensate for what?" the man asks.

Maya meets his gaze.

"Have you ever been to a hockey game? Have you sat close to the ice and seen how fast it moves? How hard the collisions are? The injuries they get? If the opponents can see that a player is afraid, they go for him ten times as hard. So they learn to look like they aren't afraid of anything. Like . . ."

She falls silent. The man fills in, tentatively:

"Warriors?"

"Yes. More or less."

"Perhaps that's why they want to look the same off the ice as well. To remind themselves and everyone else that they're an army?"

The girl lowers her gaze and smiles vaguely.

"Oh, I don't know. I'm just talking nonsense."

The man is worried he's pushed her too hard, so he changes focus by asking if she can help him get his suitcase down from the rack. He has his medication there, he says, breathing heavily to remind her that he's just a harmless old man. It works.

"Are you okay?" she asks.

"I've just been alive too long," the old man grunts.

"You sound like Ramona," she smiles sadly.

"Who's that?" he asks, as if he doesn't know.

"The person whose funeral it is."

"Oh, your dad's friend? Was she interested in hockey too?"

"Interested? Obsessed! She was even on the committee of the club at the end."

"Really? So she worked with your dad?"

"No. He stopped being general manager the same year she was elected onto the committee. But he probably saw her more after that than he did before, Mom says he used to stop off at the Bearskin most days on his way home from the office. He probably missed having someone to talk hockey with, no one in Mom's office cares about sports . . ."

Maya laughs. So does the man opposite her. He excuses himself and makes his way to the bathroom, limping more than he needs to. Once he's closed the door he writes in his notebook:

"*Through Ramona, Peter still had influence in the club, even after officially stepping down as general manager.*"

Further down he writes: "*When Maya talks about hockey guys as warriors, I think about the soldier I interviewed in Afghanistan, who said his greatest fear wasn't death, the worst thing would be not being allowed to be a soldier anymore. His worst fear was being excluded. What is a soldier without an army?*"

He taps his pen thoughtfully against the notebook for a long time before he writes at the bottom of the page:

"*What is a man in Beartown without his hockey club?*"

———

One day, early in the spring, the local paper wrote that the police had conducted drug raids on the other side of the yard that Amat and Fatima can see from their kitchen window. When Amat bought more drink from the girl that evening, she told him they'd taken her brother. "When the central heating doesn't work and we call the housing association, it takes six months before they send anyone, but if you sell two grams of hash the cops show up with dogs within five minutes," she says, quivering with equal measures of despair and rage.

The following evening Peter Andersson was sitting in the kitchen with his mom when Amat got home. He evidently hadn't come of his own volition, Amat realized that Tails and the other sponsors had sent him because they thought he could "talk some sense" into Amat. As if Amat owed him everything as well. Peter was "concerned," he said. Staring at the floor, Amat promised that there was no need for him to be. "Peter thinks you should talk to one of the agents who called, one he knows . . . ," his mother said, but what did she know? What had Peter said to her? Had he made her feel guilty because Peter used to get hold of equipment for Amat when he was younger? So was Amat expected to pay his debt now or something? "Okay, I'll think about it," Amat promised tersely, just to stop his mother feeling sad.

It could have stopped there, but when Peter was about to leave, he said quietly so Amat's mother wouldn't hear: "I can smell the alcohol on you, Amat, I only want to help . . ." It wasn't Peter's fault, everything just hit Amat all at once then. He looked Peter in the eye and snapped: "How many other people in the Hollow are you trying to help? Do you help anyone who isn't good at hockey? Stop lying! You just want to profit from me like all the others!" He stared into Peter's eyes when he ran out of air. The former general manager walked slowly out through the door and Amat slammed it behind him. That evening he asked the girl in the Hollow if she could get hold of anything apart from alcohol. She came back with pills. He slept the whole night through and had less pain in his wrist when he woke up.

———

The guys on the train are engaged in some sort of contest, showing each other things on their phones and howling at private jokes. Everything is a contest for them, Maya knows, because Beartown is full of men who used to be that sort of fifteen-year-old and never really stopped. As adults they just compete to see who has the biggest house, the newest car, the most expensive hunting and fishing equipment, or whose son is best on the boys' team. Ana used to say that all hockey guys really only play for their dad, to live up to his expectations or to prove that he was wrong, to make him proud or to tease the shit out of him. Perhaps she understood them because she had all those dads rolled into one and the same man at home herself.

Maya looks at the fifteen-year-olds and is amazed at how much older than them she feels, how much life has passed by. She can see from self-confident grins that their coach has already taught them how valuable that is, but she wonders if they know that that only applies as long as they're winning, if they've understood that they're commodities that can be discarded in an instant by agents and bigger clubs if they get injured or play badly or just stick out a bit from the group. If they're different. If they aren't machines.

She wonders if they still love the game the way they did when they were children, playing on the lake or on their driveways. If they still throw themselves against the Plexiglas in the ice rink in delight when they score a goal. Ana used to imitate them so well, she always swore that all hockey guys look exactly the same when they cum in bed as they do when they score a goal on the ice. Once when just she and Maya were on their own in the changing room at school after PE, she pressed herself against the wall of the shower and muttered desperately with her face contorted: "See me! Validate me! Tell me I'm a real man now, Daddy!" Maya remembers how much she laughed, they were children then, nothing was deadly serious yet.

The fifteen-year-olds on the train laugh, and she wonders what they're finding so funny. Which photographs they're looking at. If they use girls' names when they talk about them or if they use other words. She wonders if the best of those guys dare speak out when the worst cross the line. Because she can see a Benji and a Bobo and an Amat in this gang, she wonders if there's a Kevin among them as well. If there is, she hopes these boys know who he is, because the more other people can't see the difference between them as a group, the more important it is that they can see the difference in each other.

She looks out of the window and realizes that she recognizes where they are. The kids from the south would only see forest, but she knows exactly how close to home she is now. She shuts her eyes and all the things she can't forget grow clearer with each mile: the details of his room. The layout of the furniture. Every sound. All the breathing. The rape never ends, not for her. She wonders if he feels the same about the rifle and the jogging track. If he remembers how he wet himself, if he closes his eyes and can still feel the cold metal against his skin as she pressed the gun to his forehead. If the click when she pulled the trigger still echoes in his head. She wonders where he is now, and if he's still so frightened that he has to sleep with the light on.

She hopes so. Dear God, she hopes so.

30

Butterflies

Matteo's big sister had a butterfly tattoo on her shoulder, in secret, obviously, her parents would have gone mad. She chose it after reading that a butterfly flapping its wings can cause a storm on the other side of the planet. She felt so powerless that this was the most powerful thing she could dream of being: an insect.

It's visible on the photograph of her that Matteo keeps behind another picture on his wall, so that his parents won't see it if they come into his room. They would probably have hated the tattoo more than the drugs and alcohol, defiling your body was the Devil's work, so many things on earth are the Devil's work that when Matteo's sister really wanted to hurt her mother she would exclaim: "So, when does GOD actually do anything?" The only reason she wasn't even more unkind was that Matteo would also get sad when his mother was sad, and his sister never wanted to upset him. That was his only weapon, he defended his whole family from each other by using his heart as a shield. When his sister left Beartown she was smart, telling her parents that she was going to a church, she had even contacted the parish and talked her way into being allowed to stay there. They had taken "children with problems" before. Her parents thought their daughter had finally found the truth, her mother cried, and by the time the church phoned to say she had never arrived she had already left the country. That was two and a half years ago.

When the next call came, very recently, in the middle of the night, and a police officer pronounced her name in broken English, it was as if her parents couldn't even cry for her because they had already mourned her loss long before then. "The Devil took her" was all Matteo's mother whispered, and Matteo couldn't bear to hurt her by asking: "So why didn't God save her? Wasn't she worth fighting for?"

Now his parents are on their way home with her ashes, and Matteo is staring at the black screen of his computer. Where you are born and who you become is a cruel lottery. He wonders exactly what it was that divided him and his sister from happiness, and if it is even possible to measure all the "if only"s and "if that hadn't"s, because when it comes down to it, that's really all life is.

If only Beartown and Hed hadn't been such shitholes. If only people hadn't been so awful. If only their parents had believed the words their daughter said as much as they believed the word of God. If only Matteo and his sister had been born somewhere else where they were worth something. If they had been born into the Andersson family instead. If Matteo had been Leo and his sister had been Maya. If their mother had been a lawyer and their dad had been general manager of the hockey club.

Then someone would have fought for her too.

31

Dishwashers

One day back in the spring a lone man suddenly appeared in the stands at the ice rink during training. He was short and overweight, had thinning hair, and wore a heavy gold chain over a thick polo-neck sweater beneath a thin leather jacket. "Who's the taxi driver?" a few of the recent arrivals joked, but when none of the players who grew up there laughed, they quickly fell silent. The man in the stands kept his eyes on Amat for the whole of the training session, didn't say a word to anyone afterward, then came back again for the next session. And the next, and the next. Eventually one of the newer players asked again: "Seriously? Who's the old guy?" Amat pretended he didn't know, as did most of the others. But one of the players who grew up in the Heights, and who was therefore convinced of his own immortality, sniggered: "That's Lev! One of the trash bandits from over near Hed! Haven't you heard about those tramps?" He wasn't so tough out on the ice, Amat noted, but the locker room always feels like a safe place for small men. Naturally, Amat had heard all the rumors about Lev as well, but his mother taught him at an early age not to talk crap about anyone, seeing as they may well turn out to be not just anyone.

His teammate, on the other hand, was now happily explaining all about the trash bandits, so called because they had taken over the old scrapyard below the hill outside Hed a few years ago. No one really knew where they came from, at first there was just Lev and a few others, but now twenty or more people were said to be living in the trailers there. Some said that they sold stolen cars, some said they sold drugs, some said they did far worse things. The atmosphere in the locker room gradually became more jovial, because all muscles relax there, especially tongues. So one of the recent arrivals tried his taxi driver joke again, and this time a lot of them laughed. Encouraged by this, the first player told a joke about how things got a bit messy when the trash bandits took over the scrapyard because they didn't understand how they were supposed to have space for their camels under the car hoods, fewer of them laughed at that, but he had built up a head of steam and carried on: "All that scrap is probably the biggest family business in the area now, because all those foreigners must be related to each other, right?" Suddenly everyone fell silent and glanced anxiously at Amat, as if he might get annoyed. The other player's face turned bright red, and that probably said a lot about the sort of jokes he used to make when Amat wasn't in the room, but of course it also said even more about the other players seeing as they just sat there in silence. So Amat pretended he hadn't heard anything, packed his things, and went home, telling himself that he had more important things to worry about than crap like that.

Lev came back for the next training session, and the next, he never spoke to anyone and he kept his eyes on just one player. No one made any jokes about him anymore, at least not in front of Amat, but a sense of silent unease was growing in the building. The old guys who used to watch every training session moved farther away and the players glanced at the stands more often. No one said anything to Amat, pre-sumably they were waiting for him to say something himself, as if he ought to apologize to the whole team for the sort of people he attracted to the rink. He was usually very good at that, apologizing for things, but for some reason he didn't on this occasion. Perhaps he'd just had enough of the jokes, perhaps he'd just had enough of feeling respon-sible for everything.

So it went on for almost two more weeks, until one evening Amat met the girl in the Hollow to get pills and she shook her head. "Sorry, I'm not allowed to sell to you anymore." Amat exclaimed in surprise: "Says who?" Her reply was blunt: "Lev." Amat asked: "Is he the guy you get them from, then?" When she shook her head he snapped: "So what's he got to do with it, then?" She just shrugged her shoulders: "Does it mat-ter? Do you think I want to commit suicide or something? If Lev says no, no it is. I'm not going to fall out with the trash bandits. You'll have to talk to him yourself."

So the next day after training, to his teammates' great surprise, Amat marched up into the stands, stared at Lev, and roared: "DO YOU THINK YOU'RE MY DAD LIKE EVERYONE ELSE IN THIS TOWN, THEN?"

Lev was leaning back in his seat, he looked Amat straight in the eye and shook his head, adjusted his gold chain, and let Amat stand there long enough for him to hear his own pulse in his ears.

"I'm no one's dad. You don't need a dad. And you're your own man, yes? You don't need a dad," he eventually said. Amat said nothing for a long time, then asked, considerably more cautiously: "So what are you doing here, then?" Lev replied: "I want to help you, yes?" His grammar made it unclear if this was a question or not, so Amat muttered: "So does every other old guy in this town . . ." Lev's face cracked into a broad smile: "Do I look like all the other old guys in this town?" He said this in Amat's mother's language, even though he didn't look like he came from the same country as her. "Where are you from?" Amat asked in his mother's language, embarrassed at how badly he pronounced the words because she was the only person he ever spoke them to. "I am from no-where, I know many languages, you feel like this sometimes, yes? As if you come from nowhere?" Lev smiled.

It was a tentative relationship at first. Lev offered Amat a lift home from training, Amat hesitated for a long time before he said yes, mostly out of curiosity. "You're not to use those crap pills you can buy in the Hollow. If you're in pain, I'll sort out proper medication, yes?" Lev said seriously. Amat nodded. Lev looked him in the eye and asked: "So you're in pain?" Amat nodded again. This was the first time he had admitted it to anyone. Lev said no more about it, he started asking other questions instead, not about hockey like everyone else, but about Amat and his mother and what it was like to grow up in Beartown. Amat gave curt replies at first, but they gradually became longer monologues. He talked about how Hed and Beartown hated each other, and Lev replied that it was only hatred for people with money. "The difference between the inhabitants isn't the difference between Hed and Beartown. Just the difference between rich and poor, my friend. I live in Hed, yes? But aren't you more like me than a man from the Heights? Because we're the same in his eyes, you and I. We're poor. We're his slaves. Men like him demand that you feel grateful now, don't they, Amat? But grateful for what? Do you think those rich men would have cared about you if you weren't good at hockey? They're not like us, Amat. We'll never be part of their town."

That was the first time in a long time that Amat felt anyone understood him.

———

"Look out for that tree," Peter exclaims, pointing at one that's blocking half the road.

They're everywhere, a gigantic game of Pick-up Sticks, Teemu keeps having to slow down and comes close to driving into the ditch several times. His phone buzzes in his pocket again.

"Hold the wheel," Teemu says, then lets go of it, forcing Peter to lunge across the seats.

Teemu starts to reply to the text message as Peter tries to steer through the debris.

"Are you . . . can't you . . . TEEMU!" Peter eventually yells, and Teemu brakes at the last moment before they crash into what looks like half a fence and a bathtub that have escaped down someone's driveway.

Teemu stops the car, but carries on tapping his phone.

"People seem to be doing a lot of talking today," Peter mutters.

"They've changed the match schedule. Guess who we're playing in the first round? Hed!" Teemu snaps back.

"Oh," Peter says, for want of a better word.

"Hell of a lot of rumors right now, I need to . . . ," Teemu goes on, then seems to change his mind.

"Rumors about what?" Peter asks, even though he doesn't really want to know.

Teemu glances at him, apparently weighing up what he should say and what he shouldn't, then sighs and explains:

"The council had a meeting this morning with your friend, Tails. Hed's ice rink collapsed in the storm, so all their teams are going to be training in our rink."

Peter says nothing for a long time. The windows are closed but he still imagines he can feel the wind off the lake, from beyond the ice rink where the flags are flying at half-mast, his clothes feel too thin.

"I'm sure it's just a temporary measure, Teemu, you and your guys mustn't . . ."

"The council will use this as an excuse to try to merge the clubs, you know that!" Teemu interrupts.

Peter nods, hesitates, and shudders.

"They've tried to merge the clubs before, Teemu. I've sat in those meetings myself. It will never . . ."

"It's different this time."

"How?"

Teemu lowers his eyebrows.

"Because this time it's Beartown that's got the money. People like Tails have something to gain from a merger now."

As soon as the following words pass his lips, Peter regrets saying something so ridiculous:

"Would that really be so bad? All the council's resources devoted to one and the same club, maybe that would . . ."

Teemu's reply isn't aggressive, which somehow makes it worse:

"This club doesn't belong to Tails, it belongs to us. If they want to merge our club with those red bastards, it's going to happen over my dead body."

Peter looks down at his lap and nods, unable to reply because he knows that isn't true. It will happen over other people's dead bodies, anyone who happens to be standing in the way. That's what Teemu means by "it belongs to us," because either you are part of "us" or you aren't, and Peter knows all too well from experience that the most dangerous place in this forest is between men and power. They say no more until the car pulls up outside Peter's house. He thanks Teemu for the lift and Teemu merely nods, and Peter says without making eye contact:

"Teemu, I know this won't mean anything to you because I'm the one saying it, but there's been peace between your guys and the guys in Hed for a long time, hasn't there? Your guys follow you, whatever you do, so you can choose to . . . well . . . you can be a tool for the town now, or a weapon. That's going to make all the difference."

Teemu smiles, revealing all his teeth.

"You really do sound like her."

"Thanks," Peter says quietly.

"But you're wrong. There's never been peace. Only a truce," Teemu adds, almost sadly.

"What's the difference?"

"Truces are temporary."

He holds out his hand, Peter takes it. Then Teemu says something very unusual for him:

"Thanks."

"Don't mention it," Peter mumbles.

"I mean it. Thanks for everything today," Teemu says, looking at the steering wheel.

Peter doesn't move as the young man drives off, ashamed of how happy he feels. When he and Kira moved here from Canada all those years ago, he promised her that relationships in the town would feel less complicated with time. The opposite happened. Everything and everyone are even more tightly connected now, until finally people can hardly move at all.

———

One evening when Lev was driving him home, he asked Amat what he was planning to buy when he turned professional. "A Mercedes and a house for Mom," the boy replied. Lev smiled. "Is that what she wants?" Amat laughed and shook his head. "No, she just wants a dishwasher." Lev laughed so hard that his stomach bounced. "I promise, I'll help you get an NHL contract so you can employ staff for her. She'll never have to do the dishes again, okay?" He handed Amat a small box of prescription tablets for the pain in his wrist. Amat hesitated, then handed him his cell phone. Every time an agent called from then on, Lev took the call.

The next time they were sitting in the car he said: "They say hockey is a contact sport, yes? They say it's because of the violence on the ice. Rubbish! It's off the ice that it's violent! A contact sport? The entire sport is made up of contacts! How many NHL players look like you, Amat? Hardly any! Why? Because none of the coaches look like you. Because these wealthy men only want to give the jobs to each other. They stick together, yes? That's why they win. That's how they keep people like us away from power and money." Amat nodded. Lev has continued to attend every training session, and they had the same discussion time after time as they drove home to the Hollow afterward. The days grew longer, the daylight more generous, summer was on its way. From his balcony one night Amat saw a group of people lighting candles up on the hill. The next day he found out that the brother of the girl he bought drink from had been in another town and got into a fight, and ended up getting stabbed. He was in intensive care. The following day Beartown had an away game and at the back of the bus on the way to the game Amat's teammates, who had never set foot in the Hollow, were talking about it: "It was drugs," one said. "How do you know?" another wondered. "Do you think it was just a coincidence he got stabbed, or what? I mean, you know where he's from, you know what it's like there . . ." Amat said nothing, but heard everything.

Bobo, Amat's best friend on the team and these days assistant coach under Zackell, was sitting at the front of the bus and heard nothing. It wasn't his fault, he was no longer aware of what was said in the locker room, he was busy doing his job. He and Amat spent less and less time together off the ice, Amat didn't know if that was his fault or Bobo's, it just felt like they didn't have anything in common anymore. But just before the game Bobo asked Amat if he was okay, and perhaps Amat could have told him the truth then, but instead he said: "Yeah. Fine." Bobo smiled: "Okay . . . you just seemed angry. Tell me if there's something. We're counting on you today, superstar!" He didn't mean any harm. Even so, Amat was furious.

With one minute to go the teams were tied, and Beartown had a face-off in the offensive zone. Zackell called a time-out and gathered the team by the bench. Everyone was waiting for their coach's tactical instructions, but instead she just looked at Amat and said: "What do you think?"

He should have realized she was testing him, but he was too tired, too angry. So he said: "What do I think? About our tactics? Our tactics are that you give me the puck and get out of the way!"

He turned his back on them before anyone had time to reply. They gave him the puck, he scored, no one celebrated with him. Not even Bobo.

Zackell gathered the team after the game but Amat wasn't there, he had gone up into the stands to Lev and went home in his car rather than on the bus. That was how he came to win a game and lose a locker room.

The train finally stops, and Maya stands up and helps the old man get his suitcase down again." He slips his annual accounts into his briefcase, puts on his brown hat, and picks up his umbrella, then gives a slight bow. She laughs and bows back. They part on the platform and she doesn't spare him another thought, but he thinks all the more about her.

A woman in her early thirties is standing a short distance away in a thick jacket, with her woolly hat pulled down low over her forehead, the way only new arrivals do at this time of year. They wait until Maya is out of sight before hugging each other.

"Hi Dad," the woman says.

"Hi Editor in Chief," he chuckles, and bows.

But she can hear the pride behind the sarcastic tone. When she was a child she always said she wanted to be a journalist like him, and he always grunted that he hadn't spent his whole life working himself to death just so she could become something as uncivilized as that! But deep down obviously he loves the fact that she turned out like him rather than her mother.

"Good journey?" she asks.

"Why do you sound so worried?"

He's missed seeing that wrinkle on her forehead.

"You know, Dad! Did you talk to the girl? Maya?"

"The whole way," he grunts happily.

His daughter sighs deeply, two minutes together and she already has a dad-migraine.

"And you didn't tell her you were a journalist? You didn't say what you're doing up here?"

"That would have been rather counterproductive," he chuckles.

"It's not ethical, Dad, it could undermine the whole investigation . . ."

He waves his umbrella dismissively and starts walking along the platform.

"Ethical? Nonsense! She's Peter Andersson's daughter. You know what she said to me? 'My dad's the sort of man who never breaks any rules at all.' That's the perfect quote to start the entire series of articles with! What have I always told you, about how many thoughts people can have in their head at any one time?"

"Stop it, Dad . . . ," she groans, but can't help giggling.

"How many?"

"One. People can only have one thought in their head, Dad."

He nods so hard that his brown hat almost slips off his head. She bursts out laughing, because it's so typical of him, always some tiny, stupid detail that marks him out from the crowd. When she was little he always wore a bow tie when everyone else was wearing a normal tie, always a pocket watch instead of a wristwatch, always going against the current somehow. He fixes his eyes on her:

"Exactly. And the whole reason that Beartown Hockey has gotten away with financial crimes as long as it has is that people like Peter are regarded as above suspicion. Especially after what happened to his daughter! People can only follow one thought at a time, and right now

Beartown Hockey is on the good, decent, honest side. It's the Andersson family's club, the club that had an openly homosexual player, the club with the biggest star from the poorest part of town, only discovered by hockey because his mother cleaned the ice rink. Have you READ that brochure you sent me? 'It isn't just easy to sponsor Beartown Hockey, it's also the right thing to do!' Seriously, have you ever heard anything so arrogant?"

His daughter is taking deep, patient breaths.

"Dad, listen: I'm grateful that you're here. I really am. And I want the same thing you do, but we have to do this . . . well, you know . . . by the book. I have a source in the council who says that the politicians are seriously considering trying to merge Beartown and Hed Hockey now, and that would give them the chance to establish a whole new accounting process and bury all traces of embezzlement and corruption, but I need to do this *properly*, Dad. I don't want to make it . . . personal."

He throws his arms out, making his stomach wobble beneath his checkered shirt. He's at least twenty pounds heavier than when she last saw him. His beard is grayer, his smoker's cough worse.

"How can it *not* be personal? Beartown Hockey is using its politically correct image as a shield to guard against all scrutiny. After all, even your own reporters daren't cross them!"

The look in her eyes darkens, even after all these years it still surprises him how quickly that can happen.

"They're good journalists, Dad. But you don't live here. You don't know what it's like. We're not only going to be attacking the hockey club, but the whole of the local economy. People's livelihoods."

He raises his head, suddenly more accommodating, and nods.

"Okay, okay, you're right, sorry."

"You just need to be a bit careful. And if we're going to *start* by attacking Peter Andersson, you need to realize . . . and this is serious . . . that he isn't just anyone around here. He has powerful friends. And . . . violent friends."

Her dad waves his umbrella:

"There's no point me being here if I'm going to be afraid, is there? If we're going to uncover a scandal, we need a good story! And you know who's a good story? Peter Andersson!"

"Hmm, I've missed this, your lectures—" she says with a grin.

He interrupts sharply:

"Stop being ridiculous, you didn't call me because I'm your dad, you called because you want to ruin these bastards' lives, and no one's better at that than me!"

He looks so pleased with this last phrase that he forgets to put his umbrella on the ground as he walks and almost falls over. She catches him. Feels how old he is. Whispers:

"You've been longing for this, haven't you? Having an enemy again?"

He scratches his beard.

"Is it that obvious?"

He used to be the star reporter at his paper, the journalist who brought down celebrities and politicians, the journalist the rich and powerful used to fear finding out was digging into their affairs. But that was a while ago now, the newspaper gives the heavy jobs to younger talents, he's more of a mascot than a reporter these days.

"This is going to be seriously hard, Dad."

"That's how you know something's worth doing, kid."

She hates being called that, but she's missed hearing it.

32

Hatred

Johnny keeps his promise and is home in time for dinner, all Hannah and the children have to do is pretend that 10:30 is a normal time for dinner. They can see he is embarrassed, so they let him get away with it, because they can also see how hard he's been working in the forest and how exhausted he is. The road between the towns is still a mess of trees and debris, but it's finally clear enough for the hospital staff living in Beartown to get to work in Hed. Hannah stands on tiptoe in the kitchen and kisses her husband on the back of the neck.

"Did you get the van?" she asks, and all the color drains from his cheeks.

"I . . . damn . . . tomorrow! I'll ask one of the guys to drive me there first thing, then I'll come home and take the kids to training!"

She doesn't have the energy to fight about it.

"Okay, let's deal with that tomorrow. I'm just going to sort out the laundry, then I'll organize dinner . . . ," she says, with her eyelids starting to droop.

But Tess, the eldest child and super-big-sister, steps up and puts her arm around her mother and says:

"Stop it, Mom. Go and have a hot bath. I'll sort out the laundry, and Dad can do dinner."

Tess has already done the cleaning while her mom helped her brothers with their homework. Sometimes Hannah bursts out crying out of nowhere because she feels so guilty at how much responsibility their seventeen-year-old daughter has to take on. She suffers for being so organized—if you show you're capable, you get even more to do, that's the curse of being a smart girl.

"Thanks darling, but I . . . ," Hannah starts to say.

"This offer expires in five, four, three, two . . . ," Tess interrupts, and her mother laughs and kisses her hair.

"Okay, okay, thanks! I'll grab a quick shower!"

Johnny stands at the stove and fries schnitzels, the boys' favorite. Ture, seven years old, is delighted at being allowed to stay up so late after bedtime. Tess sets the table and puts herself at the end, not because she wants to sit there but because if Tobias and Ted get the chance to fight about who sits there, they will kill each other. Tobias might be fifteen and Ted only thirteen, but Ted is already almost as tall and as strong. He's already better at hockey too, even if no one in the family acts like he is so as not to hurt Tobias's feelings. That isn't because of genes or talent, it's just that Tobias isn't a fanatic, he likes other things as well: girls and parties and computer games. The only thing Ted thinks about, to the exclusion of everything else, is hockey. If he doesn't have a training session with the team, he either fires holes in the walls in the basement or practices his shots out on the driveway for hours at a time. Sometimes Tobias has to be forced to go to training, whereas it can be hard to drag Ted away. As soon as the lake freezes over he'll be there every morning shoveling snow so he can play with his friends before school starts.

"Is the road clear, Dad? Can we go to training tomorrow?" he asks eagerly now.

"Yes, it'll probably be okay," his dad nods, tired but proud.

Tobias can't help moaning:

"Do we really have to train in Beartown's crappy rink?"

Tess retorts:

"Are you stupid or something? Have you seen the state of our rink? The entire roof has collapsed!"

Johnny shoots her a grateful look, his daughter is taking on the role of sensible parent more often these days, letting him off the hook.

"Don't call your brother 'stupid,'" he whispers.

"Sorry. Toby, you're a real bright spark!" his daughter declares.

"What does that mean?" Tobias wonders suspiciously.

His father's laughter lasts until Ture suddenly exclaims from his chair:

"We have to use the rink in Beartown because Hed's rink is SHIT!"

Tess hushes him, Ture looks surprised and insists: "That's what Dad said!" Johnny rubs his receding hairline with his fingertips.

"That . . . that isn't what I meant. I was just a bit upset on the phone this morning."

That's an understatement, all the children think, but—unexpectedly—Ted is the one who speaks up:

"Our rink *is* actually shit. Beartown's is a hundred times better. Did you know they have a preschool there? Just think how much more time on the ice they get than we do in Hed."

Johnny directs all his frustration at the frying pan, turning the schnitzels so hard that the butter splashes and burns him on the wrist without him even reacting. That's all that counts in Ted's world: time on the ice. Every year his team has to fight harder and harder to get it, with the other teams and the figure skaters and then the sessions for the general public that the council insists on squeezing in every weekend. So what's going to happen now?

"Someone ought to drop a bomb on the whole of fucking Beartown," Tobias mutters in response.

He's two years older than Ted, old enough to meet guys from Beartown at parties now. Old enough to get into fights with them pretty often as well.

"TOBY!" Tess yells, so her dad doesn't have to.

"What? Everyone hates us in Beartown. And we hate them. There's no point lying."

"Stop it, Toby, we don't hate anyone," Johnny says halfheartedly.

"You've said that yourself, Dad!"

"Only when we . . . only in hockey . . . when the hockey teams play each other, it's just something people say . . . ," Johnny says tentatively.

"We PLAY on the hockey team, Dad!"

Johnny has no response to that. The little bastard's right.

"Do you think we'll see the A-team play tomorrow?" Ted interrupts, suddenly hopeful.

"I don't know if Hed's A-team is going to . . . ," Johnny says, misunderstanding.

"He means Beartown's A-team. He wants to see Amat," Tess clarifies cautiously.

"Amat? He plays for the wrong team!" Johnny blurts out instinctively.

"He's going to play in the NHL!!!" Ted points out with the absolute certainty that only a thirteen-year-old can muster.

Johnny ought to have kept quiet, he wishes Hannah wasn't taking so long in the shower, because she'd have slapped his thigh before he giggled and said:

"Amat? The NHL? He wasn't even drafted! There was a hell of a lot of talk over in Beartown all last spring, it was obvious Amat was going to be the best player in the whole world! And what happened? Nothing! He came back home again and now apparently he's 'injured.' Maybe he's a bit overrated, just like the rest of Beartown?"

He hates himself even as he says the words. Hannah says that hockey brings out the worst in him at times, but of course that isn't true. It's only *Beartown* Hockey that brings out the worst in him. Tobias chortles with laughter.

"Shit, Amat's just the worst!"

"He's going to play in the NHL! He's better than anyone in Hed!" Ted mutters back defiantly.

"Bloody hell, you're in love with him," Tobias grins, and a second later the fight is in full flow, right across the kitchen table, with Tess yelling and Ture cheering them on.

Johnny lets go of the frying pan and rushes over to grab someone, anyone at all, from the chaos. Hannah hears them all the way up in the shower and thinks to herself how reasonable it is of Johnny to call her the "sensitive" one in the family. Sure.

Downstairs in the kitchen Johnny yells:

"STOP FIGHTING! For God's sake, I'm trying to cook h—TOBY!!! Just stop it and apologize to your brother! Of course Ted isn't in love with Amat! For goodness' sake, he isn't even . . ."

Johnny stops himself and clears his throat when he feels his daughter's disapproving glare. So he corrects himself a little clumsily:

"I mean, IF he was, there wouldn't be anything wrong with that. But . . . he isn't. Are you?"

He looks at his daughter to see if he's said the right thing. She rolls her eyes. It isn't easy to say anything right these days, he thinks. So he takes a deep breath and says instead:

"If you keep fighting you can't play any computer games, Toby. And you won't be allowed to go to training tomorrow, Ted!"

That's the only thing that works, they both calm down at once, especially Ted. Tess rolls her eyes again. Johnny wonders about telling a joke to get Ture to start laughing, because he's the only person in the family who still appreciates Johnny's jokes, but he doesn't have time before Tess's phone buzzes as a message arrives. Then another one. Soon Tobias's is buzzing as well. In the end even Ted's is buzzing. Johnny leans over Tess's shoulder as she opens the picture that everyone in school is circulating online. It shows the Beartown town sign over on the forest road, right on the boundary with Hed, someone has been out and draped it with green scarves. Beneath it is a large sheet of tin with a spray-painted message: "OUR RINK IS OUR RINK!!! GO HOME, BITCHES!!!"

Tomorrow all of Hed's youth teams will have to pass that way, the youngest of them Ture's age, and those are the words that will welcome them. Tess deletes the picture. Johnny doesn't say a word, but he's thinking how much he'd like to call one of the reporters at the local paper who are always writing about lovely, cuddly Beartown Hockey and their lovely, cuddly "values system" these days, and ask them if this is what they mean. He dishes up dinner with his jaw clenched, then sits down at the table. They eat in silence until Tess tries to get Tobias to put his phone down with a series of pointed gestures. He obeys, but not without grunting:

"Do you believe me now, then? What did I say? They hate us!"

No one protests this time.

33

Returning home

"It's so easy to fool people. They're happy to believe so much crap that you can make them believe pretty much anything if you make enough effort."

That was what Adri Ovich told her little brother many years ago, after their father had taken his rifle and gone out into the forest, and some of the older kids on the street where they grew up were spreading rumors about why. Each rumor was more ridiculous than the last, of course, suggesting that Alain Ovich owed the mafia money, or that he was actually murdered because he was a war criminal in hiding here who had finally been found by his enemies. "People are stupid. Don't listen to them. Punch them in the face if you want to, but don't listen to them," Adri told her little brother, and he did as she said, and both suggestions turned out pretty well.

But people really are still stupid if you ask Adri, that's why she prefers animals. That's also why she lives a fair way out in the forest and not in town, which is usually a blessing, but not in the days after a storm. She's had help from her sisters Gaby and Katia, but even so they've barely made a start on clearing up the destruction. They've repaired the fence around the kennels and cleared all the debris littering the yard, but the barn that was converted into a martial arts gym took a severe battering and is going to need a lot of work. The electricity is still intermittent out here, and the roads are still impassable in many places. But Adri isn't complaining, telling herself that she's gotten through it better than most people, after all. The hunters who buy their dogs from her, and these days that means almost every hunter in both Beartown and Hed, know every tree out here. They told her in advance which ones she needed to saw down. They saved her, the house, and the dogs.

She can hear them barking now. They do that all the time, of course, but on this occasion she stops what she's doing and straightens her back, aware of what's happening before she sees him coming. If you devote your life to dogs, their barks are full of nuances, Adri can tell at once if they're barking at an animal or a person, and if they're doing it to mark their territory, for protection, or out of fear. Often it's the younger ones who need to assert themselves, but this time it's only the oldest dogs barking, the ones she never sold, the ones who have been in the family since they were puppies. They're barking because they're happy.

It's so easy to fool people, Adri thinks as she starts running. Benji is cycling along the gravel track, she knows it's him before she even sees his silhouette, she recognizes him from the happy, bubbling, euphoric barking and the eager scrabbling of paws against the fence. So many rumors have circulated about her little brother in the past two years, because it's so easy to fool people: that he's a disappointment, that he wasn't prepared to stand up for who he was, that he gave up hockey and moved away because he was a coward. That he's nothing but a drunk and a junkie these days, that he isn't worth anything. But you can never fool dogs.

They know all that's best in you.

———

Maya hasn't even thought about how she's going to get home to Beartown from the last station. She stands on the platform for a few seconds, confused, thinking how stupid it was not to let Ana pick her up after all, but then she hears someone calling from the road.

"Maya? Lovely to see you! Do you want a lift?"

It's one of their neighbors from the same street leaning out of his car, and Maya remembers what living here is like, there's always someone going the same way as you. It doesn't matter where you are, things always work out in the end, there's always someone willing to help. She hadn't known she was going to miss that.

She makes polite conversation with the neighbor during the drive, but the closer they get to Beartown, the less she says. By the time they're passing through Hed, she can barely breathe.

"Incredible, isn't it? It's looks like there's been a war here . . . ," the neighbor nods.

Maya has woken up on days after storms before, but none of them was ever like this. She can't see how everything is going to be repaired again, and can't begin to imagine how much it's going to cost.

———

Benji comes cycling along the little forest road, a couple of years older than when his sisters last saw him, and much thinner. His skin is browner and his long hair paler, but the grin is the same. Adri drops everything and runs, pulling him off the bicycle and kissing his hair and telling him he's a brain dead moron and that she worships him.

"How did you get here? Why didn't you call? Whose bike is that?" she wants to know.

He shrugs, without making it clear which of her questions this is a response to. The dogs force their way out of the fenced yard and throw themselves into his arms, quickly followed by Gaby and Katia. When their mother hears the commotion up at the house and comes outside, at first she can barely stand, then the next second she's rushing across the yard, already in the middle of a scolding, in the language of her homeland seeing as this country doesn't have anywhere near enough adjectives to describe the curses and threats her son deserves after drifting around the world like a tramp and not calling his mother often enough. Then she hugs him so hard that her spine creaks, and whispers that she'd die without his heartbeat, and that she's hardly dared breathe since he left because she didn't want to exhale the last of his air from her lungs. Benji grins like he's only been gone a couple of hours and whispers that he loves her, and then his sisters lay into him because he's so emaciated and if he'd died of starvation they'd never have heard the end of their mother's moaning about it and how could they have put up with that, so why does he only think of himself, the little brat? Then they sob into his hair, and then they eat.

Maya gets dropped off outside her house, and thanks the neighbor so effusively for the lift that he retorts: "It was hardly that much trouble, so you can drop all that big city nonsense." Maya thinks to herself that it's a good thing she didn't offer to pay for the gas or she'd probably have gotten a slap, and can't help smiling. She picks up some broken pieces of wood and other debris from the flower bed before opening the door of her childhood home. It's been left unlocked, as usual. She used to think that was completely natural, but now she can't help thinking it's the sort of crazy, eccentric thing that people only do in Beartown.

Everything in the house is the same as usual. The same furniture, the same wallpaper, the same everyday life. As if her parents thought they could fool time by refusing to admit that it was passing. Maya stops on the stairs, inhaling deep breaths of home, running her fingertips over the photographs that hang all over the walls of her and her brothers. The oldest picture is of Isak. Parents who lose a child never trust the universe again. Once Maya heard her dad admit that on the phone, she didn't know who he was talking to, saying that he sometimes thought all the blessings he himself had received were the reason why God or whoever needed to redress the balance, and took Isak from them. Peter Andersson had a wife who loved him and three beautiful children and a career as a professional hockey player in the NHL, then the job of general manager in the club that had raised him, and no one can have everything—presumably that was how he was thinking. It's simultaneously both remarkably unselfish and absurdly self-centered, Maya remembers thinking. As if children only live good lives or have a terrible time because their parents are in either debt or credit to some system of cosmic rules. But perhaps that's what having children is like, she doesn't know, perhaps you can't avoid going completely stupid.

She takes a deep, deep breath alone on the stairs. Sometimes the memories of everything that happened are like electric shocks, sometimes she wakes up screaming at night, but every time she comes home she gets a bit better at not thinking about Kevin. Every time she grows a little and gains stronger, thicker armor. She can still hear in her parents' voices every time she calls that the same thing isn't true of them. They're stuck in that moment, still believing that everything is their fault. When Maya's dad was sitting with her in the hospital after the rape, he asked what he could do for her, and the only thing she could whisper in her despair was: "Love me." And he did. The whole family did. Sometimes she feels that she dragged them with her into a black hole, and when she climbed out they were left at the bottom. It doesn't matter that she knows that isn't true. Guilt is always stronger than logic.

She walks silently up the stairs that only she and Leo can step on without making them creak. She goes into her parents' room. Her dad is standing in front of the mirror practicing knotting his tie, but fingers won't do what he wants and his face is heavy with grief.

"Hi, Dad."

His favorite word. "Dad." He doesn't even turn around, because he thinks he's imagining it. She has to say it again, louder. He looks at her in the mirror, blinking hard in confusion.

"Darling . . . ? DARLING! What . . . what are YOU doing here?"

"I want to go to Ramona's funeral on Sunday."

"But how . . . how did you get here?"

"I got the train. Well, as far as I could. Then I got a lift. It's chaos out there on the roads, it must have been completely unbearable during the storm. How are you doing, Dad?"

All the words pour out of her at once and he is still trying to comprehend that she is actually here.

"But . . . what about college?" he manages to say as he hugs her, ever the dad.

"College will be fine," she smiles.

"But how . . . how did you even know that we were having the funeral this weekend?"

Maya smiles condescendingly at his naiveté.

"The elk hunting season starts next week. Then hockey starts. When else were you going to bury her?"

He scratches his hair with the tie.

"But darling, you didn't have to come home for Ramona's funeral. She . . ."

"I'm here for your sake, Dad," she whispers.

She feels him almost collapse into a heap of dust.

"Thanks," he struggles to say.

"What can I do, Dad?"

He tries to smile and shrugs his shoulders, so slowly and listlessly that they look like badly hung barn doors on old hinges. When they hug again, she's the adult, he the child.

"Love me, Pumpkin."

"Always, Dad."

They hear the sound of the front door opening downstairs. Kira comes home, steps through the door and stops for just one breath when she sees her daughter's shoes on the hall floor, and her mother's heart skips a beat. Upstairs Maya lets go of her dad with a sympathetic little smile when she hears the thuds and cries, and stands with her back to the bed, because when her mother rushes up the stairs and flies into the bedroom and wraps her arms around her daughter's neck, Maya wants to have a soft landing.

––––––

That night, before anyone except his family even knows that he's back in town, Benji creeps out of his sister's house and cycles down to the ice rink. The roads are strewn with fallen trees and the parking lot is full of debris, but the rink looks almost entirely unscathed. As if God Himself had revealed who He supported. Benji forces open one of the bathroom windows at the back and climbs in, then drifts about, assaulted by childhood memories. How many hours has he spent here? Will he ever again be as happy as he was then? Will anything else ever feel as good as gliding out onto the ice with his best friend and playing against the whole world? How could it?

He feels his way in the dark and finds the switch for the lights down by the boards, he doesn't turn on the main lights in the roof because the caretaker would see them from home and rush down here and then there'd be a hell of a fuss. At the back of the storeroom Benji finds an old pair of skates his size, he laces them so tightly that they make his feet feel numb, then sets off toward the light. He knows exactly how many steps he can take before he has to lift his foot from the floor to step onto the ice, out of all the things he loved about hockey there probably isn't anything he ever loved more than this, a thousand games and a million training sessions, but his lungs and stomach still think he's stepping off a cliff every time. Everything else disappears with that first glide out onto the ice, out to where he was free his whole childhood. Only there. That was the only place in the entire world where he always knew exactly who he was and what was expected of him. No confusion, no fear.

He glides in slow, painful circles, wider and wilder. He stops by the penalty box, taps nostalgically at the glass. It was all so simple when he arrived at the rink for the first time as a child, so obvious, the sport was like a magical language that he had been specially selected to understand. He loved the rhythm of the other bodies, the collisions, the breathing, the cuts on the ice, the desperate cries of the crowd when the game suddenly turned. The frenetic banging of sticks, the roar in his ears as they flew forward together: unstoppable, inseparable, immortal. He doesn't know where that part of him has gone, when he lost himself so completely, but it was never the same without Kevin. Benji was never quite able to forgive himself for still feeling that way.

So two years ago he put a puck in his bag and kept on traveling, only stopping when he could put the puck down on the counter of a bar in a part of the world where no one knew what the hell it was. There were no tourists there. He left one place where he had always been different on the inside and found another where he was different on the outside. He doesn't know what he was hoping that would lead to. Nothing, maybe. Perhaps he was just hoping that the noise in his head would stop. The chaos in his chest. In some ways perhaps he even succeeded, because now, as he looks over at the huge picture of the angry bear painted around the center circle, he expects to feel something, anything at all, but nothing comes. No longing, no hatred, no belonging, no exclusion. He's just tired. So very, very tired.

He takes the skates off, puts them back in the storeroom, turns the lights out, and climbs out of the same window he came in through. Then he slowly wanders across the parking lot, away from the town and out into the forest. The ground is torn and churned up. He left the bicycle at the ice rink, it isn't his, nothing here is really his anymore. When the wind turns away from the town he is sitting at the top of a tree, the way he used to as a child.

———

Matteo spends all day looking for his bicycle in the part of town where he left it during the storm after the chain came off. He doesn't find it until the following morning, much farther away than even the wind could have carried it: neatly propped up against the wall down by the ice rink. Someone found it, fixed the chain, then rode off on it without even feeling guilty enough to try to hide it afterward. Matteo isn't surprised, not when he finds it precisely here, by the ice rink. Hockey guys are taught as children that everything belongs to them. That everyone belongs to them.

———

The first frost arrives in Beartown and Hed that night. The universe's silencer. It stupefies in a way that words can never encompass, if you ask anyone who's moved away from here what they miss most about the forest, they'd probably say that first foretaste of winter, the gentle sorrow of a summer gone by, autumn that seems to last no more than an instant here. The birds become wary, the lake freezes, soon we will see our breath in front of us and our footsteps behind us. The air gets fresher, everything crunches each morning, the snow doesn't really settle for a while yet, but you still have to brush the first thin white dusting from the stones in the cemetery to see whose graves they are. One headstone will soon read "Ramona," no surname because there's no need, everyone knows. Another, a little farther away, reads "Alain Ovich," in an almost forgotten corner up by the wall. His whole name, because considerably fewer people remember him. Sometimes weeks go by without him getting any visitors, but when the sun goes up this time his son is sitting there smoking.

Tales of boys and their fathers are the same in every age, in every place. We love each other, hate each other, miss each other, hold each other back, but we can never live unaffected by each other. We try to be men and never really know how. The tales about us who live here are the same sort of tales that are told about everyone, everywhere, we think we're in charge of the way they unfold but of course that happens unbearably seldom. They just carry us wherever they want to go. Some of them will have happy endings, and some of them will end exactly the way we were always afraid they would.

34

Competitive people

"Things happen fast in hockey." "Keep your head up." "Hubris always gets punished." Clichés may be clichés, but they often start out as truths. This is a sport that is constantly finding more and more imaginative ways to humble the most self-confident of us, but somehow we still manage to forget that every victory is merely part of the countdown to the next defeat.

When the season was approaching its end back in the spring, Beartown was top of the league, but Lev could see how swollen Amat's wrist was, it was just getting worse and worse. "You shouldn't be playing," he said. "I have to, we need to win our final games," Amat said. Lev put one hand on his shoulder and asked seriously: "If you damage it even more and don't get drafted to the NHL, who's going to buy your mom that dishwasher?" Amat had no reply to that. At that training session the same guy who had joked about Lev in the locker room hit Amat on the arm in a futile gesture of frustration. Perhaps it wasn't intentional, Amat was flying past him and was so much faster that the guy just lost his temper, fed up with being humiliated. Amat exploded and they fought like crazy, and if Bobo hadn't thrown his large frame between them it could have ended with something much worse than a few bruises and wounded egos. "What are you doing? It was hardly that hard, was it?" Bobo asked Amat tentatively when they were on their way off the ice, and because Amat didn't know what else to say, he replied with the very worst he had within him: "Do you think this is a game? Do you think this shit team would be anything without me? That no-hoper shouldn't touch me! I'm going to play in the NHL, what's he going to do? Get a job in the storeroom at the supermarket? Work at the factory? End up as some goddamn . . . some goddamn . . ."

He managed to stop himself before he blurted out "some goddamn car mechanic," because that was what Bobo's dad was, and what Bobo was going to be. Amat should have apologized at once, but he was too angry during those first few seconds, and then it was too late. Bobo turned and walked away, with his broad shoulders almost touching the floor, and Amat broke his stick. No one on the team so much as glanced at him as he gathered his things together in the locker room and stormed out of the rink.

He didn't play in the next game. Zackell merely informed the team that he was "injured." How seriously and for how long, no one knew. He sat up in the stands for that game, and the next, but he didn't turn up at all for the final games. Rumors began to circulate that he was faking it, that his mind was already on the NHL, that he didn't give a damn about the club that had given him everything.

"Am I supposed to go and show them my wrist or something?" Amat said to Lev, close to tears, as they sat in his car. Beartown had just lost their last game and failed to win the promotion to a higher league everyone had been dreaming about. They would never have been so high up the table without Amat, but now suddenly it was all his fault? "Doesn't matter. You can never do enough. This is their game, their rules, you'll never be one of them. People like you and me have to make our own rules, yes?" Lev replied.

Amat didn't go to the final training sessions, and he didn't show up at the end-of-season club dinner. Bobo called a few times to ask why but Amat didn't pick up, he knew Bobo wanted an apology but no longer felt he owed one to anybody. He had apologized enough, had been grateful enough. He trained on his own in the forest, but apart from that he barely left the area where he lived, and the only person he spoke to on the phone was Lev, and everything Lev said felt true: "Trust me, Amat, they don't care about you. If you got injured again, could never play hockey again, would they care about you then? Pay your mom's rent, yes? Not a chance! They just want to own you. You'll see! The rich men will tell you not to go for the draft. They'll try to get you to believe that you're bad, because then they'll have power over you, and you'll stay here and play for their shitty little club! They don't want you to turn professional because that would prove that everyone was wrong about you!"

Late in the spring he was proved right. Fatima opened the door of the apartment and Peter Andersson was standing there again. The former general manager looked pathetic as he said, weighing his words very carefully: "I don't want to get involved, Amat . . ." So Amat retorted at once: "So don't, then!" Peter glanced at Fatima, but she made no attempt to calm her son's fury, possibly because she knew there was no point, but possibly also because she thought he had a certain right to feel that way.

Peter took a deep breath and made one final attempt: "I don't know what other people have told you, Amat. What that guy . . . Lev . . . has promised you . . . but I've spoken to the agent I know over there, Amat. I think you should talk to him too. I've also spoken to a scout in one of the NHL clubs, a former player from when I was there, he's been doing this for a long time now, Amat and . . . you need to understand that I'm not saying this to be mean . . . but he says you'll be a long way down the draft. In the sixth or seventh round. The hundred-and-eightieth player, something like that."

Amat snorted: "Thanks for the vote of confidence!" Peter looked despairing. "I just mean . . . most people who are that low down in the draft don't even get interviewed in person by the clubs. I just don't want you to go all that way and end up disappointed. Maybe it would be better for you stay at home and recover from your injury and do some training, they'll still draft you if they think you're good enough, and you'd be able to follow the whole drafting process online, I really think that . . ."

Amat interrupted him with a dark look in his eyes: "The difference between the agents you know and Lev is that Lev believes in me enough to pay for flights and a hotel for me!" Peter blinked sadly and gave up. He turned to leave, then stopped and said: "Okay. You're a grown man now, Amat. Do what you want. But . . . can I give you some advice?" Amat shrugged his shoulders, so Peter said: "When you get to the hotel over there: go to the gym. And eat a proper breakfast. The scouts for the

teams check things like that. They notice who's eating doughnuts and
fizzy drinks and who takes their diet seriously. If they see you in the gym
the evening before the draft instead of playing video games or hanging
out in the bar, they'll know you're willing to do whatever it takes to be
the best."

Amat closed the door without a word. The next morning he woke up
when someone knocked on the door. He found a courier standing outside
with a new dishwasher and a note: "Not a gift! Tell your mom you're
buying it with your first NHL wages. LEV."

Naturally, his mother muttered that it was too much, because everything was always too much for her, but she accepted it because she could
see what it meant for Amat. "When I come home you're getting a castle,"
he promised, and she kissed him on the cheek and whispered: "Nonsense!
Don't worry about me!" But he was her son, and she couldn't stop him.

It wasn't until he got to the airport that Amat realized Lev wasn't
crossing the Atlantic with him. "They don't give people like me visas.
I've got a bit of a criminal record, and they love keeping tabs on people
like us, yes? Don't worry, I've got a friend over there, yes? We've organized everything! You're going to be interviewed by the best clubs. Do
you think they'd have interviewed you if they didn't want to draft you
higher than the sixth or seventh round? Don't listen to Peter! He doesn't
want you to be a bigger star than he was, because then you wouldn't have
to be grateful anymore, and people like him would have no power over
you! Yes?"

Amat met Lev's friend at the airport when he arrived, an irritable
middle-aged man holding a sign with Amat's name, spelled wrong. Amat
had to pay for the taxi, and the friend barely looked up from his phone
the whole way into town, and just said "See you tomorrow!" when they
parted at the hotel reception desk. That evening Amat sat in his room on
his own, so nervous that he contemplated emptying the minibar before
finally going to the gym instead. He lifted as many weights as he could,
and was inwardly delighted that his wrist didn't hurt. He had been there
for an hour when a very fit man in his sixties came in, ran for a while on a

running machine without paying any attention to anyone else, but when he left he suddenly nodded to Amat and said: "Good luck tomorrow, kid." Peter had been right about something after all.

The following morning Lev's friend knocked on the door and asked Amat for money to pay a chambermaid. When Amat asked why, the friend got annoyed: "Do you think we can get into the hotel where the big teams hold their interviews if we don't bribe someone?" Amat stammered: "Lev said you'd already arranged interviews for me . . ." The friend rolled his eyes. "Lev said you were a star, but you sound like a spoiled little kid! Are we doing this or not?" Somewhat reluctantly, Amat went with him to the larger hotel, the friend vanished, and Amat spent several hours sitting in the lobby waiting for him. The friend never reappeared. Amat sat there all day. The man from the gym turned up in the lobby dressed in an expensive suit, but he didn't even notice Amat. He was busy with other young players and their parents, all full of self-confidence and assurance, the sort who knew the world belonged to them. Late that afternoon the man in the suit came back alone, stopped in front of Amat, and fixed his eyes on him.

"Amat, right?" he said. Amat stared back in horror, assuming he was about to be thrown out of the hotel, but instead the man said: "Do you have time for an interview?" Amat nodded distractedly, so shocked that Lev had actually managed to arrange this that he was lost for words. The man ushered him along a corridor and into a conference room containing a number of men, all from one of the best teams in the league. Amat's head was spinning, his English was almost as shaky as his hands, but he replied to all their questions as best he could. It was less about hockey than he had expected, and he had no idea how they came to know so damn much about him: they asked him what it was like growing up with a single mother, about his relationship to his teammates in Beartown, why he hadn't played in the final games of the season. He was sweating, it felt like a police interrogation, and only when it was over did the man in the suit say: "Send my best regards to Peter Andersson, alright? We're old friends. He told me to keep an eye out for you." The other men had already starting looking through their papers and were talking about another player, they didn't even say good-bye. Amat blinked vacantly, stood up on unsteady legs, and left the room, crushed. So they had just done all this as a favor to Peter. Lev and his friend had tried to bribe half the hotel to get an interview, and all Peter needed to do was pick up the phone back home in Beartown. "Lev was right," he thought. "This is their game, their rules."

The friend reappeared the following morning and asked if Amat had any money, then he disappeared again. When the NHL draft actually began Amat sat alone in the stands for the whole of the first round and watched as every team picked its new superstar. Later that evening he stayed in the gym until he collapsed. The next day he sat in the stands again from ten in the morning until six in the evening, watching as more than two hundred other eighteen-year-olds hugged their parents when they got picked, but no one picked him. The ice rink emptied, he sat there, the friend never showed up.

Amat called Lev and cried down the phone, but Lev sounded untroubled. "Never mind, yes? Americans, they don't know how to do business! I have a friend in Russia! He can get you onto a team there, yes? We'll earn more money there than in . . ." He carried on talking, but all Amat could hear was a rushing sound. So that was it? He pretended the line was breaking up and ended the call, then he fell to pieces.

When he got back to the hotel the man in the suit was waiting in the lobby. He shook Amat by the hand and flashed him a genuine smile: "I'm sorry it didn't work out, kid. We really liked you, but we just don't do business the way your uncle wants, okay? Go home, work hard, ask Peter to get you a real agent, and come back next year. Alright?" Amat stammered: "What . . . what do you mean . . . uncle? What uncle? What business?" The man in the suit didn't reply, just patted him on the shoulder and left. Amat called Lev again and yelled: "WHAT THE FUCK HAVE YOU DONE?" Lev's voice darkened: "Who do you think you are, Amat? You're yelling at me after everything I have done, yes? Do you think I'd pay for your flight and hotel and not expect something in return? I don't get paid by you like the other agents, I get paid by the club that takes you instead! But those Americans think they're better than us, yes? They don't want to negotiate, they think they can have you for nothing! Listen to me now, my friends in Russia . . ."

Amat threw the phone on the floor, breaking it. He had to use the phone at the reception desk to call home and ask his mother to send money so he could buy a plane ticket. She had to borrow the money from a neighbor, and he hated himself. He drank and cried in his room all night. Drank, drank, drank. Early the next morning there was a knock on the door, he was still horribly drunk when he answered, the man in the suit was standing outside with his suitcases, and he jerked back from the alcohol fumes. Amat opened his mouth to explain but realized it was already too late. Peter had called the man again and had presumably pleaded with him, maybe Amat could get a final chance in one of the training camps that gathered together players who hadn't been drafted, but not now. Not like this. The man sighed: "Tell Peter I did what I could. I hope you get yourself together, kid. Peter says you're the best he's ever seen. Don't make him a liar."

The man left. Amat didn't move. It was all over, just like that. He caught a flight and then took a bus all the way home, and shut himself away in the apartment in the Hollow. He kicked the dishwasher so hard he thought he'd broken his foot. The next day it was horribly swollen, and he didn't run again for several months.

So now? What happens now?

When Beartown started their preseason training, Bobo called Amat several times a day. Amat didn't answer, just sent a text saying he was injured. After a week Bobo only called twice a day instead of three times, then once instead of twice, until eventually he stopped calling altogether. Silence settled on the apartment in the Hollow, Amat spent all day asleep and was out all night, the recycling bin for glass in the basement filled up quicker than ever, and the days flew by on the calendar until he had wasted the whole summer.

He didn't run again until the night his mother was out alone in the storm. His body coped, his foot coped. The morning after that he starts running again, out in the forest until he throws up. Early on Saturday morning he finally plucks up the courage to send Bobo a text. Just three words: I need help. Bobo replies with three words: Where are you?

When the twigs snap beneath his huge friend's size 14 sneakers in the clearing behind him, Amat has a thousand excuses ready, but he doesn't need a single one. Bobo's smile tells him that everything is already forgotten.

"Have you seen my friend Amat anywhere? He looks like you, only he's about thirty pounds lighter!"

Amat pinches his stomach in a self-mocking way.

"I was in America and learned to eat breakfast like you!"

"You've always been a short-ass, but now you're wider than you are tall," Bobo laughs.

"I'm fat, you're ugly—but at least I can lose weight!"

"You're quick, I'm strong—you might break your legs!"

"I could weigh four hundred pounds and you still wouldn't catch me, you stupid elephant!"

Bobo roars with laughter.

"We've missed you at training, mate."

Amat looks down at the ground.

"Sorry I haven't been answering my phone. I . . . you know . . . I was kind of an asshole for a while."

Bobo stretches his neck until it creaks.

"Screw all that, are we here to run or talk?"

That was all it took to get a friend like Bobo back again. The best sort of friend. They start running together, up and down, up and down. Amat throws up first, but soon Bobo joins him, he's in worse shape now that he's a coach than he was when he was a player, and he was never very fit then either. They carry on running up and down another ten times. As they stagger home afterward Bobo throws up one last time in the ditch beside the main road.

"Lupines," he gasps when he's finished.

"What?" Amat groans. He's lying on the ground a short distance away, too tired to stand up and wait.

Bobo repeats the word and jerks his head toward the purple flowers he's just vomited his breakfast over.

"Lupines. Mom used to like them. You're not supposed to really, because they're one of those 'invasive species.'"

Amat manages to find expression for all his feelings:

"W-what?"

Bobo sounds irritated, which doesn't happen often:

"Lupines, I just told you! Mom used to say they were beautiful, but one of the neighbors, an old bag who works for the council, said they're a weed. The council's trying to eradicate them, you know, because they're 'out-competing local plants,' something like that. But you can't eradicate them, because they just keep coming back. They're strong as anything."

Amat laughs wearily.

"Okay, what have you been sniffing?"

Bobo straightens up. He holds out one fist to his much shorter and half-as-heavy friend and pulls him to his feet with a single tug.

"They're like you."

Amat grins at him, not understanding.

"What are?"

Bobo shrugs his shoulders and starts walking.

"The lupines. They're like you. You grew up in a ditch, and nothing can stop you either."

They say nothing more until they part outside Amat's door. Amat is ashamed to realize that he's hoping Bobo is going to ask him to come to training with the A-team later today. Bobo is ashamed because he doesn't ask. There's nothing he wants more, but Zackell doesn't work like that, if Amat wants to play, he's going to have to go to the rink himself and ask her. Amat knows that too, deep down.

"Do you want to go running again tomorrow?" he asks instead.

"Definitely," Bobo nods.

They hug briefly, then Amat watches the big lummox as he lumbers away, exhausted. He can't help hoping that Bobo becomes a father, because he has all the best qualities for that: a big heart and a short memory.

Amat goes up to the apartment and sits there with his phone in his hand, Zackell's number on the screen. But he's too ashamed of his weight, scared of turning up and being slow and bad, so he doesn't make the call. He laces his shoes once more and heads out again instead, because that's another cliché he remembers from the locker room: "If you want to achieve what no one else can, you have to do what no one else wants to do." He used to snort at those words, but now he repeats them to himself in his head the whole stumbling way up the hill. When he stops retching in the clearing up at the top because there's nothing left in his stomach, he lifts his eyes and looks all the way to the ice rink. From there he can see exactly how far the way back is to everything he has dreamed of. Ten months until the next NHL draft, but he can only change one day before then.

This one.

35

Hiding places

Matteo cycles home and sits down at his computer. He starts a game and focuses so hard on every movement with the weapon on the screen, the way you do when you're trying to force yourself to forget. He can still hear his big sister's voice so clearly: "Just stay away from them, the hockey guys!" That was her most important piece of advice to him on his very first day at school when he was six years old. She knew they would pick on him, because he was small and weak and different. She knew he couldn't defend himself, there was nothing to be done about that, so she tried to teach him all she could to help him get through his time at school more or less intact: where the hiding places were, which teachers let you stay in classrooms during break, which route was safest to take coming home. "From now until your last year of high school, that's only thirteen years, then you and I can go out into the world!" she told him the night before his first day of school. "Just stay away from the hockey guys."

Matteo loved and trusted his big sister, so he obeyed. He stayed away from them. She was the one who didn't.

36

Muscles

Peter gets up early on Saturday morning, there was a frost overnight and the yard outside the window is covered by a thin and as yet undisturbed white blanket. It's two days since the storm, and one day before the funeral, his head feels heavy with grief for Ramona, but his chest feels so light now that Maya is home again that his feet almost trip over each other, unsure whether to walk or dance. He carries his record player into the kitchen and puts on a really old record, and bakes some really good bread alone at the counter while the rest of the family sleeps. For a fleeting moment he manages to resuscitate the charade of normality again.

But when he opens the front door to take the rubbish out, he is reminded of what the storm has left behind: broken windows in the next house, shattered fences, a storeroom door that's been ripped off its hinges like a sheet of paper, and everywhere rubbish, rubbish, rubbish. Peter finds his bin several hundred yards down the street, and only when he has dragged it all the way back does he notice the American car parked on the other side of the street. The same one as yesterday. The man behind the wheel is wearing a cap and sunglasses, and his shoulders are too broad for the seat. "He's not muscular, just full of muscle," as Peter's old coach used to say about the most dangerous madmen on opposing teams. "You don't get a body like that at the gym, you get it from carrying wood all summer and wading through snow to the outhouse all winter." The man is watching Peter but doesn't move. Instead the passenger door opens and a considerably older and fatter man gets out, dressed in a battered leather jacket with a heavy gold necklace outside a knitted polo sweater. Peter's body stiffens involuntarily, Lev can see that from a distance, he knows what effect he has on people. Peter may not hear all the rumors anymore, but even he has heard about this man. So Lev walks slowly, making Peter wait before establishing eye contact, smiling in a way that you can let yourself do when you have someone like the man in the car with you.

"Peter Andersson? My name is Lev, I——"

"I know who you are," Peter interrupts, more abruptly than he intended, and hopes that his thudding heartbeat isn't evident in his voice.

"Oh?" Lev smiles.

"Can I help you?" Peter hears himself say, unable to stop himself.

Lev smiles more broadly and moves closer to Peter than Peter is comfortable with.

"I want to thank you! You called your friends, yes? When Amat was at the NHL draft!" he says and holds out his hand. When Peter reluctantly shakes it, Lev holds it harder and longer than Peter can bear.

"Don't mention it," Peter mumbles, pulling his hand away quickly.

Lev stays where he is, far too close. There's gentle mockery in his voice:

"No, no, no need for modesty! The great Peter Andersson! Your name is important over there, yes? Everyone was impressed, my goodness, they were impressed that Amat knew you! Everyone was very, very impressed. A shame it didn't help, yes?"

Peter bites his cheek. He remembers the phone calls after the draft, with his old friends and contacts in the NHL wondering about the idiot "uncle" who called around introducing himself as Amat's "agent" and wanting unofficial payments from the clubs that were considering drafting him.

"Yes, a great shame," Peter nods sternly, and feels the man's breath. All he wants is to push him away, but he doesn't dare.

Lev looks him intently in the eye, then bursts into joyous laughter, then finally takes a step back and throws his arms out.

"Well! Enough of that, yes? Is that what people say? Yes? Enough about Amat. I want to talk to you. I saw you with Teemu yesterday, at the Bearskin. I have a . . . how do you say? A 'sensitive subject' to discuss? I can't discuss it with Teemu because he's . . . well . . . you know, yes?"

"No, no, I really don't understand at all," Peter manages to say, fairly irritably to hide the fact that he's scared.

Lev's eyebrows flick upward for a fraction of a second, almost amused.

"Teemu is a violent man. You're diplomatic. So I've come to you, yes?"

"And what sort of man are you?" Peter wonders, glancing at the man in the car.

Lev chuckles.

"I can be both, Peter, but I prefer to be like you, yes? We aren't young men, no? I get up in the middle of the night to pee, I'm too old to fight, you know. But Ramona owed me money. A lot of money."

He falls silent, as if Peter ought to offer some sort of response to that. It's such an obvious trap that Peter's mouth dries out until he can barely move his tongue:

"What's that got to do with me?"

Lev turns his palms up and shrugs his shoulders demonstratively.

"Debts need to be paid, yes?"

"How? She's dead!" Peter replies, then realizes that this is precisely what Lev is waiting for.

"But the Bearskin will be sold, yes?"

It's such a ridiculous idea that Peter can't help exclaiming:

"Sell the Bearskin? Are you cra— Sold to who, then?"

Lev smiles with exaggerated warmth.

"Me. I'll take it. No debt anymore. Everyone wins, yes?"

Peter's jaw falls open slightly, long enough for a single word to tumble out:

"So . . . rry?"

Lev smiles again, a little more impatiently.

"I get the Bearskin. No debt. No problems. I've had a pub before."

"Not in . . . Beartown, you haven't run a pub here, you don't know what you're . . . ," Peter begins.

"Drunks are the same everywhere, yes? You'll help me?"

It doesn't sound like a question. Peter is less scared now, more angry.

"Help you? With what? Can you even . . . how can I know . . . can you even prove that Ramona owed you money?"

Lev is still smiling, but his lips harden and his teeth curl around his words:

"We signed documents. But that doesn't matter to people like you, yes?"

"People like . . . me?"

"Laws, rules, contracts, they only apply to people like you, yes? Your game, your rules? Perhaps you didn't help Amat? Perhaps . . . the opposite? Perhaps he didn't get drafted because of you?"

Peter is so shocked by the sudden accusation that he forgets what they've been discussing, and above all forgets who he's talking to.

"You sent a . . . a . . . a GANGSTER to the draft to try to extort money from NHL clubs! Did you really think that was going to work?"

Lev's feet don't move but he leans his head a few inches closer to Peter.

"I want money from the club. You want money from Amat. That's the difference, yes?"

"I don't want anything from Amat!"

Lev sniggers.

"You have a figure of speech here that I learned when I arrived, I like it a lot. 'He always has his hand in his pocket,' is that right? Someone generous, always ready to help others, yes?"

"You don't have your hand in your own pocket, your hand is in Amat's," Peter hisses, simultaneously taking half a step back.

"And you, Peter? If you don't want the boy's money, what are you trying to find in that pocket?" Lev mocks.

"I was trying to help him!"

"Like you helped other boys in the Hollow? Yes? Because surely you don't just help boys who are good at ice hockey? That would be a strange coincidence, yes? That people like you always want to be charitable when poor boys can do something for you. But I'm not a boy, Peter. And I only want what I have a right to: I get the Bearskin and I forget Ramona's debt, yes? But perhaps I shouldn't be talking to you? Perhaps I should talk to your wife?"

Peter won't be able to explain exactly what happens inside him just then, he simply explodes:

"WHAT THE HELL ARE YOU SAYING?" he roars, and to both his own and Lev's surprise, he puts his hands on Lev's chest so hard that the fat man stumbles backward.

It only takes a second, but Peter could account for every hundredth part of it: the young man in the car flies out of the door, his hand is in his inside pocket, Peter has far too much time to imagine what he has in there. He raises his hands to his face, but there's no need, Lev has already regained his balance and raised two fingers and the man behind him stops abruptly midstride. Lev calmly adjusts his leather jacket as if nothing had happened, then he turns to Peter:

"She's a lawyer, yes? Your wife? I signed a contract with Ramona. I have, how do you say, the letter of the law on my side. Perhaps I should have a lawyer?"

"Get as many lawyers as you like, but don't ever come near my family, you hear that? And you'll never get the Bearskin, people around here will never . . . ," Peter says before biting his lip, the words fire out in a confusion of rage and his pulse is roaring in his ears.

Lev waits until he falls silent, then smiles again and concludes, apparently untroubled:

"Think about it, yes? I'll come back! Is that what you say? No! I'll get back to you, yes? I'll get back to you!"

He takes a long glance at Peter's house. A light has come on upstairs, Kira and the children are just waking up in there, Peter's whole body is shaking but he doesn't get a chance to formulate a reply. Lev is already getting into the American car, the man behind the wheel is in no hurry as he pulls away, but as soon as the car is out of sight Peter takes out his phone without knowing who to call. He stands there, his fists heavy, his head empty, until in the end he calls Teemu.

Not the police and not his friends. Teemu. That's how closely everything and everyone in Beartown are connected this autumn.

———

Maya rolls out of bed, pulls an old green hooded top over her head, and hurries sleepily out of her room. Her mother is sitting at a makeshift desk in the hall, she's only just up but already in the middle of a video call with some client or employee, the storm has turned her whole business upside down, and obviously that's exactly what she needed, Maya thinks: more stress. In the kitchen Leo has his head so far inside the fridge that he seems to think he'll find a witch and a lion on the other side. The whole house smells of freshly baked bread.

"Who's been baking?" Maya wonders in surprise.

"Dad," Leo says, as if it wasn't the weirdest thing he could possibly have said.

"Dad?" Maya repeats.

"Mmm. He bakes. He's like, obsessed," her little brother replies.

Maya glances out of the kitchen window and sees him. He's standing by the mailbox. A car stops in the street and out steps a man Maya recognizes, she just can't imagine him in the company of her dad.

"Is that . . . Teemu?" she exclaims.

"Mmm," Leo confirms with a quick look out of the window before he returns to the fridge.

"With . . . Dad?"

"Mmm. They're friends now, I think."

Maya stares at Leo, then out of the window, then at Leo again.

"Okay, sorry, but HOW long have I actually been asleep?"

———

Teemu gets out of the car and looks around, not as if he's looking for something but more like he's memorizing things.

"So Lev was here?" he says, getting straight to the point.

Peter is holding two mugs of coffee and hands one to Teemu, a mug that's been washed so often that the green bear is barely visible now. Teemu nods gratefully as he takes it.

"He says Ramona owed him money. I don't know how much, but we must be able to repay it if . . ."

Teemu shakes his head, not angry, just cold.

"He doesn't want money. He wants the Bearskin. He tried to buy it off her when she was alive. Lev does a lot of shit, shit you don't want to know anything about. He needs legal cover, and there's no better cover than a pub."

"So why did Ramona borrow money from HIM, then?" Peter says, and immediately regrets the accusatory tone.

Teemu sighs into his coffee.

"One of my guys ended up in prison last winter. His mom couldn't afford to pay the rent and the bills, so Ramona gave me everything that was in the Fund. I didn't know she . . ."

He drinks some coffee. Says no more. It's the first time Peter can ever remember seeing Teemu ashamed.

"She used her own money?"

"Yes."

"What was he in prison for? Your friend?" Peter asks.

"Aggravated assault," comes the reply.

Now Peter's the one who feels ashamed. Because this is evidently the company he keeps these days.

"What are we going to do about Lev?" he sighs.

"You're not going to do anything. The trash bandits aren't the sort of people you want to argue with, believe me."

Peter is surprised by the force of his response.

"So he can just come here and threaten my family? Take the Bearskin? Ramona would never . . ."

Teemu raises one hand to stop him.

"I'll take care of Lev."

"I thought you said . . ."

Teemu finishes his coffee and hands the mug back.

"I said they're not the sort of people YOU want to argue with."

Peter fumbles for something to say when he suddenly realizes what he's started:

"Okay. But be careful, don't start . . ."

"You want ME to be careful?" Teemu declares theatrically as if he's deeply insulted, and Peter groans and almost hits himself on his temples with the coffee mugs.

"Okay, okay. See you tomorrow at the funeral, then? An hour before, like we agreed with the priest?"

Teemu nods and promises, and Peter doesn't ask any more, he'll just have to live with that. When he turns to walk back to the house Teemu calls out curiously:

"What did Lev say that made you this angry?"

"What do you mean, angry?" Peter grunts.

Teemu grins.

"You're trying to act calm but your eyes are totally dark. You don't care that much about the Bearskin. What did he say?"

"He . . . mentioned Kira."

Teemu lets loose a low, triumphant laugh that goes on far longer than Peter would like. Then the hooligan says to the former general manager:

"People might not believe it of you, Mr. Perfect, but there's a bit of dog in you after all."

37

Mules

Johnny yawns and glances irritably at the time. He's standing outside the house swearing in the dawn light because the workmate who promised to drive him to Beartown to pick up the van is late. Ted has already packed all his things and is waiting in the hall, while his big brother, Tobias, hasn't even woken up yet, obviously. Tess is helping their youngest brother, Ture, to pack his skates, then she puts rice cakes and cartons of juice in the outside pocket and makes him promise not to open them until after training. He'll have to wait in the rink for several hours while his brothers train and Tess herself is coaching the youngest children from Hed how to figure skate. That's just what it's like being part of a family that spends more of its time on the ice than off it.

"Have you got everything? I got a call from work, I have to . . . ," their mother says behind her, and Tess looks at her anxiously.

"You look exhausted, Mom. Shouldn't you stay at home?"

"We've got so many people off sick, and others are having to stay at home to clear up after the storm, so I really have to . . ."

"You need to get some sleep tonight, Mom! Promise!"

Hannah whispers to her daughter:

"I promise, darling. Look after your brothers now . . . you know how things can get over in Beartown . . ."

"Don't worry, Mom. It's only hockey training."

"Sure. Sure. 'Only.' And sorry, it really isn't your job, darling, you should just . . . God, you should only have to worry about yourself. I haven't even asked how your math test went!"

"I got them alright."

"Of course you did. That's incredible. I don't think I've ever gotten everything right on a test in my entire life. Are you sure you're my daughter?"

It's an old joke but Tess's laughter feels new every time. She really is too good for this family, Hannah thinks. High grades in all subjects, never gets in any trouble, looks after her brothers. She never even used to get dirty when she was little, the only child who could go to school in white clothes and come home with them the same color. While other children climbed trees and had fights in muddy puddles, she sat at home and read books. Even her hair always looks freshly brushed, in contrast to her mom's, which always looks like someone has put a scouring pad through a document shredder.

"I love that you're growing up, but I hate you growing up," her mother whispers.

"Don't be silly." Her daughter smiles.

"You should . . . you know, you shouldn't have to take everything so seriously all the time. You should be going to parties, meeting boys . . ."

"Boys? In Hed? You have to spend three months investigating people's family trees before you dare go on a date with anyone here," Tess giggles.

"Now who's being silly?" Her mother smiles.

"Seriously? All the boys here are so immature!" Tess insists, and at that moment a shout from Tobias's bedroom fills the house because Ture and Ted have run upstairs and woken him up with water pistols. Tess shrugs her shoulders at her mother as if to say "prove me wrong!," but Hannah doesn't notice because she's staring out of the window.

"What the . . . ?" she begins.

"WHAT THE HELL???" Johnny fills in from the yard.

Out on the road their van is approaching, at speed. Hannah and Tess make it outside onto the steps just as it skids to a halt by the fence and a crazy eighteen-year-old jumps out.

"ANA!" Hannah exclaims with such delight that Tess is taken aback.

"What the hell?" Johnny wonders once more.

Hannah wraps her arms around the strange girl and introduces her.

"This is Ana! Who helped me in the forest during the storm!"

Johnny's face softens.

"Damn. I know your dad. How's he doing?"

Ana doesn't answer, just tosses the keys to the van to him.

"I thought I might as well drive this thing back here seeing as our yard isn't exactly a parking lot. I checked the engine this morning, and you should probably take it to a garage to get . . ."

"OKAY! THANKS!" Johnny interrupts, so affronted that Hannah bursts out laughing.

"Come inside, Ana! Would you like coffee?"

But Ana glances at Tess and sees the wariness in the daughter's eyes, that sort of girl doesn't like girls like Ana, so she replies curtly:

"No, I have to get home to the dogs."

"We can . . . drive you home. Wait here and I'll just get the boys," Johnny says, politely but still a little insulted.

"Don't worry. I'll run back," Ana says.

"Run?! To Beartown?" he repeats.

"It's hardly that far. Anyway, I need to exercise my knee, I injured it," she nods.

"What happened to your knee?" Hannah asks.

"I hit it."

"On what?"

"A boy's forehead."

"You did what?" Johnny exclaims.

"He was being a real dick, so he deserved it!" Ana says defensively.

Hannah laughs again and hugs her once more, and insists that she come back and have dinner with them one evening. Ana gives a half-hearted promise and glances at Tess again, she's a year younger and has white trousers and hair that looks like cartoon hair. Ana's wearing a pair of jeans so torn that they're barely pants anymore, and she hasn't showered in two days. She feels like a tramp visiting a castle. So she turns and runs away.

Hannah looks after her for a long time and Tess looks at her mother for a long time. That's the sort of daughter she should have had, Tess thinks.

Bobo knocks on the door of Zackell's house. The A-team coach opens the door in a cloud of cigar smoke wearing a dressing gown so filthy that it doesn't even sway when she moves. Three different screens in her kitchen are showing three different hockey games, and the table is covered with notepads. Bobo has never met anyone who knows more about this sport and less about the individuals who play it than her. When she appointed him her assistant coach she was completely open about why she needed him: "People stuff, talking to people, all that sort of thing." She's only interested in hockey stuff.

"Amat called me this morning. I went running with him in the forest. I think he wants to come and train again . . . ," Bobo begins.

"How much does he weigh?" Zackell asks unsentimentally.

"Too much," Bobo admits.

"Did he throw up?"

"Like a drain."

She nods, smokes her cigar, and suddenly looks surprised.

"And?"

"And . . . ?" Bobo wonders.

"Was there anything else?" she asks.

"No, no, I don't think so, I just . . ."

"Well, then! I heard that all the teams from Hed are going to be training in our rink, so I want you to reschedule our training session last this evening."

"Last? The guys on the team won't be happy about having to train so late . . . ," Bobo begins, but then he realizes that that's precisely what she wants. One of the first things she asks new players on the team is: "Do you want to have fun or do you want to win hockey games?"

"See you this evening!" Zackell says, and starts to close the door.

Bobo splutters:

"Maybe you could call Amat? He's ashamed! Maybe he's afraid to make the call himself, I . . ."

Zackell looks like the question makes no sense.

"Call him?"

"Look, I know that you don't believe in *motivating* players, you've explained that, that we all have to want to do it ourselves. What was that thing about mules? You can lead a mule to water but you can't force it to drink? I get that! But Amat is . . . I mean, he's *Amat*! All he needs is a bit of encouragement . . . so maybe you could . . . ?"

Zackell smokes in silence as if she's waiting for him to go on. Bobo's mouth is open but empty. So, with the stress on "we," Zackell explains as patiently as she can:

"WE don't train players. WE train a team. Amat doesn't have to prove that he can play hockey, he has to prove that he isn't stupid. Because we can win with mediocre intelligent players, but we can never win with brilliant stupid players. Because intelligent players sometimes do stupid things, but stupid players never do intelligent things."

"I . . . ," Bobo groans, because he gets a headache when she talks like this.

"Anyone can learn to be an idiot, but an idiot can never learn anything at all," Zackell summarizes in a rare attempt to be a bit pedagogical.

"Amat isn't an idiot," Bobo says, wounded.

Zackell taps the ash from the cigar into the pocket of her dressing gown, if it had been remotely clean it would have caught light but it's so stained and grimy that it's flameproof. So she says:

"That remains to be seen. First we need to find out what sort of mule he is."

Then she closes the door without saying good-bye. She probably doesn't even realize that that's impolite.

———

It takes Johnny twelve attempts to get the van started. He mutters that Ana must have done something to it. The children all put their bags inside, even Tobias is ready in the end, and they set off to Beartown. Johnny sulks all the way because his seat isn't set the way he likes it, and because Ana has changed the settings on the radio.

"Please, Dad, do we have to listen to this old man's music?" Tess asks when he finally finds the right station.

She's sitting in the front, of course, to stop Tobias and Ted fighting for the right to sit there.

"Don't you dare insult Springsteen, he's the only thing left in my life that doesn't moan at me," her dad grunts.

Tess sighs.

"You're such a drama queen."

Her dad turns the volume up.

"Bruce understands me."

Tess rolls her eyes and turns toward the backseat.

"Did you finish your essay for English, Ted?"

"Mmm," Ted mumbles.

"Can I read it, then?"

He digs the laptop out of his hockey bag. They share one laptop to do homework in the stands at the rink while they wait for each other's training sessions to end.

"Can you maybe . . . correct the grammar and all that?" he asks.

"You need to learn how to do that yourself," his big sister retorts, but of course she's going to correct his grammar.

As they approach the boundary to Beartown their dad clears his throat, and Ted and Tobias and Tess, like good elder siblings, all start laughing and joking and even singing to distract Ture, to stop him looking out of the window and wondering what's been written on the town sign.

Elisabeth Zackell lights another cigar in her kitchen, eats some boiled potatoes straight from the pan, and watches hockey on three screens. When people praise her abilities as a coach, they often talk about her strategic and analytical skills, but her greatest talent is actually that she is very rarely surprised. That's because she interprets information as it is, not as what she wants it to be. She's seen too many other coaches give a player too many chances, or not give a player any chances at all, based on what they think could happen. Those same coaches talk about "instinct" and "gut feeling," but the only gut feeling Zackell worries about is diarrhea. She keeps everything to do with hockey in her head. That's why she's able to drop players from the team even though they're fine individuals, she doesn't even have to consider whether they're good hockey players, the only thing that matters to her is whether they're the right hockey player.

People call her "cynical," but she doesn't understand how anyone could win hockey games any other way. Are you supposed to just wish for victory? Talk your way to victory with just and persuasive arguments? She's convinced that most seasons are decided before they even start, winning teams are based upon team selection, not by a coach standing at the bench yelling his way to a stroke. Back in the spring, when Beartown was at its very best, reporters suddenly started calling the club a "talent factory" and Zackell a "genius." She thinks they should make their minds up: Surely it's either the result of talent *or* her? Besides, what has she actually done? She didn't turn Amat into a star, she just let him play. She didn't teach him to be better, she just put him in situations where he made fewer mistakes. People in the town say she likes to "test" her players, that she subjects them to "psychological experiments," but obviously that isn't true. She just tries to find out what kind of mules she's dealing with so she knows which ones she can give up all hope on right away.

So after Bobo came to her house and told her about Amat, she's spent the day in her kitchen smoking and making notes in front of her screens. Maybe she doesn't have as many feelings as other people, but she doesn't lack empathy, she understands that Bobo's big heart wants the best for all the players, and especially Amat. But when it comes down to it, it isn't a coach's job to nurture individuals, no matter how many brochures and beautifully formulated "declarations of values" a club can present to the media. A coach's job is to win hockey games. Results aren't measured in feelings but in tables. So on one screen Zackell plays Amat's games from last season, and on the other two she runs other players' games for other teams, as a comparison. She used to do this to understand their opponents and try to work out which players might be a problem for Amat to play against. Now she's doing it because she's looking for someone who could replace him.

Perhaps that's cynical, perhaps even lacking in emotion, but she's just interpreting all the information she has available: Bobo is one of Amat's best friends, and no one believes in his friends as much as Bobo. If even he thinks Amat is so brittle that he needs an encouraging phone call from his coach in order to want to play hockey rather than sit at home and drink, then it's already too late. Zackell knows Bobo came here to give his friend a last chance, but instead he actually took it away from him.

———

No one ever tells you when you become a parent that it's a trap, a trick question, a cruel joke: you're never enough, and you can never win.

Johnny stops the van outside the ice rink in Beartown. His phone is ringing the whole time, his colleagues are waiting in the forest, yet he's still thinking about going inside with his children. His daughter notices.

"It's okay, Dad. It's just stupid kids who defaced that sign. We'll be fine. I'll keep an eye on Toby and make sure he doesn't get into any trouble."

"Are you sure? It doesn't feel . . . I mean, I could come in for a bit . . . ," her dad begins.

Tobias and Ted drag their bags out of the back of the van. They were born two years apart to the same parents, but they could easily be different species. Johnny is worried about demanding too much from one, and too little from the other. He was at one of Ted's games in the spring and as usual had to be told to sit down a hundred times. Ted didn't play his best, although he was still the best player on the ice, he just wasn't as good as he *could* be. "It's all the shouting," Tess eventually pointed out. As usual, Johnny misunderstood and glared at the opposing team's parents, and said: "Yes, I know, they shout a lot, but Ted needs to get used to that and perform well in spite of it!" Tess sighed quietly and then told the truth: "Dad, their shouting doesn't affect him at all. Yours does." Johnny couldn't look her in the eye, he just stood there in the stands with his hands pressed so hard into his pockets that he made holes in them, before he muttered: "I shout just as much at Toby, it's nothing to . . ." Tess shook her head honestly and replied in a low voice: "No. You know you don't."

Johnny remained seated for the rest of the game. It was true, after all. He shouts at Ted more because he can see the thirteen-year-old's potential, and he shouts less at Toby because he can see that he's already reached his.

"It's okay, Dad, I promise!" Tess repeats now.

She helps Ture out of his seat belt. The youngest boy laughs, excited at the prospect of seeing his friends. He looks cute and gentle, but he's a tornado. The last time Johnny lost his temper when Ture did something naughty and Hannah asked why he was so frustrated, Johnny just blurted out in despair: "Because he's our FOURTH kid and I ought to be GOOD at it by now!" Hannah couldn't stop laughing at that, then she kissed him and said: "Darling, the day you think you're a good dad is the day you're a terrible dad." Johnny gets cross whenever he thinks about that. What did that even mean? He wasn't prepared for Ture, he thought he was done, he still insists that they ought to have named him "Surprise." When he told Bengt at work, Bengt smiled the way only a man with adult children can smile and told Johnny not to worry, as long as the children were still alive and had relatively clean underwear on, he was a good enough dad. That's easy to say, harder to feel.

Tess lifts Ture out of the van, closes the door, then leans in through the driver's window and kisses her dad on the cheek.

"You can't watch us every second of our lives. We'll be fine. The boys' coach is here and there are loads of grown-ups in there. Just go, and be careful out in the forest!"

"Don't worry about me!" he says, affronted.

"Just be careful, Dad, okay? Bruce Springsteen needs you alive so SOMEONE listens to him."

He laughs. He feels guiltiest of all about her, he never feels good enough for any of the children, but most of all for his daughter. He hasn't been able to help with her homework since she was nine years old, and now she's in high school and dreaming of studying law at university, and that's an alien world for him. So when she tells him about cities she wants to move to and study in he defends himself with ridiculous feelings: Why does she want to move? Isn't Hed good enough? Has her childhood been so bloody awful that all she wants is to get away from here? What if she picks the wrong college? What if it's his fault? What if she'd had different parents? More like her? Would she have done better then? Gotten further? Been happier? What about Tobias and Ted and Ture? Has Johnny shouted too much? Has he shouted too little? Has he done all he can?

"Go now, Dad," Tess whispers.

Her dad pulls himself together.

"I'll pick you up as early as I can. Keep an eye on Tobias to make sure he isn't, you know, too much like . . . me."

His daughter smiles and promises. He doesn't care about the blaring horns behind him, he waits in the parking lot until his children have gone inside before driving off.

———

One simple, painful truth for all teenagers is that their lives are rarely defined by what they do, what really matters is what they almost do.

There's snow on the ground when Amat sets out from home. It's almost winter, almost dark, and he almost rings Zackell a thousand times. He almost manages to silence the voices in his head. He walks from the Hollow almost all the way to the ice rink, but stops a couple of hundred yards away from the parking lot. It's full of children being dropped off for training by their parents, bouncing out of their cars and laughing and joking with their friends. Amat recognizes a lot of them, he's seen them cheering with delight behind the Plexiglas every time he scored for the A-team. He knows that a lot of them still pretend to be him when they're playing outside in the street, because they only remember him the way he was when he was at his best, as the superstar, the idol. But now? If he goes onto the ice today and fails, who is he then? Just one more guy who almost became something, almost won the league with Beartown back in the spring, almost got drafted to the NHL. He almost calls Bobo. He almost walks across the parking lot. He almost goes in and asks Zackell if he can be on the team again. The majority of teenagers don't know that their lives are determined by that one small word, but it echoes inside Amat the whole way home. "Almost almost almost." He doesn't want anything but solitude, but the voices in his head never shut up: "You were overrated. A fraud. Everyone knows. You might as well go home and get drunk again. Then you won't have to feel any of this. Stop trying. Stop failing. Stop feeling pain."

Back in the apartment he finds one last bottle of drink, unopened, at the back of his wardrobe. He goes up into the forest, he doesn't run, he sits in the clearing with the view of the ice rink with the bottle in his lap. The rest of his life will begin with him almost opening it or almost not.

38

Radicalizations

The bags of recycling clink when Ana lifts them, even though she's tried to tuck milk cartons in between, but she can't get through enough milk to provide insulation to hide the evidence of her dad's drinking right now, not even if she poured the milk straight down the drain. She opens the front door and goes into the yard, Maya is coming along the road with her guitar case over her shoulder, and the childhood friends catch sight of each other at the same time. One of the very, very best things Maya likes about Ana is that she never bothers to say hello.

"Help me with the bags!" she just giggles, and passes one to Maya, as if mere hours rather than months had passed since they last met.

They walk toward the recycling bins.

"I've missed you." Maya smiles.

"What sort of shoes do you call those? Are you going to a ball or something?" Ana replies.

"What about you, then? Are you homeless or what?"

Ana raises her eyebrows:

"I've always dressed like this. You're the one who's turned into a snob."

"A snob? Because I don't look like an extra in a zombie film?"

"You look like you put your makeup on in the middle of an earthquake!"

They roar with laughter. Roar and roar. Two minutes, and everything is normal. The same jibes, the same laughter, the same tattoos on their arms: guitars and rifles. The musician and the hunter. Never have two girls with so little in common been so inseparable. They talk at the same time, sisterhood's capacity for simultaneity, neither of them ever has to shut up to hear what the other is saying. Maya is only lost for words when she opens the bag Ana gave her and sees all the bottles.

"He's sober today because the funeral is tomorrow and he doesn't want to miss the wake afterward," Ana says, because Maya is the only person she never has to apologize to.

Maya nods sternly and starts to feed the bottles into the recycling bin. The day before the funeral people are sober "out of respect," then as soon as Ramona is in the ground they'll be legless for the same reason.

"I thought your dad had gotten better," she says quietly.

"He was for a while. Then I won that competition and called home to tell him, and the only way he knows how to celebrate anything is to drink," Ana replies, as if it was her fault.

"I'm sorry . . . I . . . ," Maya begins, but Ana sighs:

"Stop it. It is what it is. Can we talk about something else?"

She's become harder, Maya thinks. Unless she's just grown up. Unless she's started closing doors and windows around all her feelings, because that's what adults do, only children can live in emotional cross-winds.

"I'm sorry I haven't phoned more. There's been so much going on with college, but I should still have come to visit more often."

"You're here now," Ana declares.

"Yeah, but you know what I mean."

Ana laughs out loud and suddenly wraps her arms around Maya's neck.

"I love you, you stupid donkey! You're the only person I know who apologizes for being here while you're here! Seriously? You can hardly be more here than HERE, can you?"

Maya holds her best friend so tightly that her lungs hurt.

"I miss you so damn much."

"You're actually HOLDING me, you donkey!"

"Shut up!"

How do other people bear it, Maya wonders, how do they live without an Ana? How the hell do people cope? They walk back along the road, arm in arm. There are still fallen trees here and there, the damage from the storm is still obvious in the yards, it's so easy for the wind to wreck our illusions that we're the ones making the decisions.

"How much do you suppose it's going to cost to fix all this?" Maya wonders out loud.

"You must be getting me confused with your new economics professor friends," Ana smiles.

Maya smiles too, but the corners of her mouth feel tight.

"Still not worst here. Have you seen what it's like in Hed?"

Ana becomes serious.

"Yes. I was there this morning. And I heard Dad talking to the old guys on his hunting team. Apparently the ice rink there was completely blown apart so all the teams from Hed are training in our rink instead. Everyone's really pissed off about it. Dad says it's only going to get worse."

Maya notes that she says "our rink." That's another thing that's changed with Ana, she started to hate Hed more when Vidar died.

"I saw my dad with Teemu this morning . . . ," Maya says, just to see if her friend reacts.

"They're probably planning Ramona's funeral," Ana replies, shrugging her shoulders as if it were nothing.

"Mmm," Maya says, as if trying to convince herself.

She doesn't know how to move the conversation on, because she gave up the right to judge Ana when she moved away. That left Ana with no one to talk to about Vidar, so she talked to the guys in the Pack instead, because they understood what she was going through. They go to Ana's competitions now, standing in the crowd in their black jackets while Maya is too busy with her new life.

"I can imagine Teemu wants to talk to your dad about the rumors about the clubs as well. My dad says the guys on his hunting team talk all the time about how the council wants to close Hed down and just have Beartown."

"What?"

"Well, you know, Hed has, like, no sponsors left, no money, the council's keeping them afloat. Are they going to use the money from our taxes to rebuild their rink? Come on! Makes much more sense to have just one club!"

These aren't her words, they come from her dad and the other guys, Maya can hear that. But she can't argue with them because this is no longer her town.

"It's not that long ago that Beartown didn't have any sponsors . . . ," she says quietly.

"Sure. But that was then and this is now," Ana says with another shrug.

"Mmm," Maya says, and then Ana suddenly shoots her a guilty look and says, to avoid an argument:

"Are you just going to drag that guitar around like an ornament or are you going to play something for me?"

So they go inside the house and into Ana's room and there Maya plays for her best friend and the dogs, as if everything was the same as normal. Afterward they lie side by side on Ana's bed and look up at the ceiling and Ana asks what she's thinking, and Maya can't think of anything to say except the truth:

"We studied religious sects in school. About radicalization. The same thing as with terrorists. The 'slippery slope' and all that. No one starts out crazy, no one is born violent, they just do one little thing, then another. Radicalization is when all the sick shit gets normalized, everyone gets a bit more dangerous, one step at a time. That's kind of what this town is like, everyone thinks they're fighting for the right things. Everyone thinks they're acting in . . . self-defense."

Ana lies there silent, staring up at the ceiling for a long time. Then she takes hold of Maya's hand without turning toward her, and whispers:

"What the hell can we do about it, then, if it's happening everywhere?"

"I don't know."

"So don't think about it then."

"You're better at not thinking than me."

"That's because I'm so damn smart that I'm done with thinking."

"Really? Really?! That seems incredibly likely!"

Ana giggles.

"I like your new songs, you idiot."

Maya giggles back.

"Thanks, you tramp."

They doze off there on the bed and sleep more soundly than either of them has slept for a long time. Back-to-back, as always.

39

Shot holes

The car workshop in Beartown is empty this morning, so the man who owns it is drinking coffee and reading the newspaper for longer than usual in the garage. He's called "Hog" because that was how he played hockey many years ago, like a wild hog, but when he mends things his pan-sized hands are unexpectedly gentle and delicate. So people don't just bring their cars here, they turn up with all sorts of things, snow scooters and lawn mowers and espresso machines and the occasional illicit still. Over the past two years they've been coming more regularly, after his wife died, that's how people let a man who isn't great at hearing that he needs looking after know that they care.

His son Bobo is down at the ice rink. He's the assistant coach of the A-team and sometimes his dad has to bend extra deep over a car engine so as not to let on how often he thinks about how proud his wife would have been of that. Bobo's younger brother and sister have dealt with the grief okay, under the circumstances, they're laughing again now and no longer asking as many questions. Today they're playing at some of their friends' houses.

Teemu already knows that, he has too much respect for Hog to let the children see him come, they deserve to be allowed to think that their dad has nothing to do with men like him.

"Are you on holiday or something?" he calls from the yard.

Hog looks up. They shake hands. Hog is a middle-aged man, he's never been part of Teemu's group, but he isn't ashamed of their friendship either. When his wife passed away, Peter, his childhood friend, was obviously the first to show up and offer his help, but right after him came the men in black jackets. They relaid Hog's roof, painted the house, and when things were at their most chaotic with the children they took turns coming over to work for him in the garage for several weeks, for free.

That sort of thing doesn't get forgotten. He smiles at Teemu and nods toward the half-empty parking lot.

"No one around here gets their motor repaired the week before the elk hunt, you know that. Half of them will still end up with shot holes in the roof afterward because they drive around the forest tracks drunk and forget they're holding their rifles . . ."

Teemu bursts out laughing.

"More birds get shot by accident than elk on purpose in these forests."

Hog joins in the laughter. That's the sort of joke hunters in the area like to tell each other, but would never tolerate from other people. Neither Hog nor Teemu would ever set off into the forest with anyone who couldn't handle their weapon. Hunters need to be able to trust blindly in the person beside them, but above all in the person behind them.

"Coffee?"

"Please."

They drink. Exchange small talk about snow scooters and hockey. Hog waits two cups before he says:

"So. What do you want?"

Teemu almost looks ashamed, but only almost.

"A favor. You don't have to do it if you'd rather not . . ."

"Is it your friends asking me to do something, or you?"

"It's me."

"Then you know that I'll do it."

Teemu nods appreciatively. Then he points at one of the few vehicles that are still parked outside the workshop.

"I need that."

40

Threats

Lev rents a small house a stone's throw from the high fence surrounding the scrapyard. The men who work for him live in trailers inside the fence. He's their boss so he can't be their friend, they need this slight distance so they can vent any discontent without him overhearing everything. The job he offers isn't simple, so simple men don't apply for it.

"Lev! LEV!" one of them calls from the yard.

He bangs on the door of the house, Lev opens it, irritated.

"Yes?"

"There's some suit here! Looks like a cop!" the man says in one of the many languages Lev understands the basics of.

He peers out through the gap in the door, over to the entrance to the scrapyard, and sure enough, a man in a suit is standing there. But he looks terrified.

"That isn't a cop," Lev mutters, then goes and fetches his jacket.

The man in the suit waits nervously as he approaches. Lev locks the house and takes his time.

"Yes?" he says, when he's really close.

"Yes . . . erm, I, I think my car is here? It was in for repair at the workshop in Beartown and when I called this morning to ask if it was ready, they said someone had already collected it and that it was going to be dropped off . . . here."

Lev looks around with a degree of wariness.

"Someone collected your car and dropped it off here?"

"Yes, yes, that's what he said."

"Who?"

"The man at the workshop."

"In Beartown?"

"Yes."

Lev doesn't take his eyes off the man in the suit.

"What sort of car is it?"

"It's . . . black," the man in the suit says, clearing his throat.

Lev nods expressionlessly.

"Okay. We'll go and look, yes?" he says, showing the man in through the gate.

"No . . . no, that's okay, I can come back, I . . . ," the man splutters, but Lev insists.

"Come on. Nothing to worry about. We're not murderers or thieves, even if that's what you've heard, yes?"

There's only one way in, the fence is high and crowned with security cameras, and there's a smell of burning inside. Lev trudges through the fresh snow, the man in the suit pads after him. They meet a large man with a thick beard and a thin T-shirt and Lev mutters instructions to him in a language the man in the suit can't place. The T-shirt disappears into a trailer and Lev leads the man in the suit around the edge of the scrapyard, it's bigger than you'd imagine from the outside but even so the man in the suit only sees a fraction of what's actually in there.

"Is it here?" Lev wonders when they've followed the fence all the way around, past rows of wrecked cars and unidentifiable piles of scrap metal.

The man in the suit shakes his head anxiously. Lev's eyes are narrower now, his neck stiffer. The man in the T-shirt comes back from the trailer.

"Has anyone been here overnight? Did the alarm go off?" Lev asks him.

The man in the T-shirt shakes his head grimly. Lev turns toward the man in the suit.

"What's your job?"

"Sorry?"

"Your job!"

The man swallows hard.

"I run the funeral parlor in Beartown."

Lev steps closer to him.

"Tell me what he said, yes? The man you spoke to on the phone. He said you had to pick the car up *here*?"

The man flinches at every syllable and shakes his head.

"No, no, he said . . . your name. He said: 'It's at Lev's.'"

Lev has already started to walk.

"Wait here, yes?"

The man in the suit does as he's told. Lev leaves the scrapyard and walks the short distance back to his house. The front door is open even though he's sure he locked it before he left. On the kitchen table is an empty beer glass from the Bearskin pub, and beside it some car keys. Lev looks out through the window at the small yard behind the house. One section of fencing has been removed, it must have taken several men, working extremely fast. This is how they let you know that they're everywhere, that they can reach you anywhere, that they can get you whenever they want. It isn't a subtle threat. Teemu isn't a subtle man.

He's left the hearse in the middle of Lev's yard.

41

Trouble

Afterward, naturally there are a hundred different versions of what happens now, depending on who you ask, and as usual most of the stories won't be about what actually happened, but about what people felt happened. It felt as if every conflict between the two towns over the past fifty years exploded at once. For that reason it isn't possible to determine how much was planned, how much was revenge, and how much was just a coincidence. The stories will eventually become so intertwined that if you tug at one tiny thread at one end, you tear open the stitches holding all our wounds together at the other end. But no matter who tells it, and regardless of which side you're on, everyone will agree on one thing: the truce between Beartown and Hed, if there has ever really been one, definitely comes to an end today.

The entrance is crowded when Tess and her brothers walk in, there's already a murmur of trouble, just as, deep down, she was worried there would be. But if she had told the truth, her dad would have insisted on coming in with them, and then chaos would have been *guaranteed*. So Tess thought she could deal with it herself. That was stupid.

She pulls her brothers with her toward the locker rooms. A boys' team from Beartown has just finished their training and are on their way off the ice down by the boards, another team from Hed are on their way in, and moms and dads from both sides are tugging and pushing their kids and equipment. Tess and her brothers have to elbow their way through, not because people are lining up for anything but because a whole load of people have decided to pick today to mark their territory. As usual, the youngsters aren't even the worst, that's their parents, they're standing in groups all over the place with their thermos flasks and bags of snacks, pretending not to understand that they're in the way of the children from Hed, even though they're obviously perfectly aware. "How can anyone behave like this against children when they have children themselves?" Tess thinks just as someone yells something and something hits Ture on the head and he starts to cry. A moment later a gang of players from Hed start singing something, then all the Beartown parents start shouting hysterically.

"What happened, Ture? What HAPPENED?" Tess shouts over all the noise, grabbing hold of Tobias and Ted so she doesn't lose them.

The crush suddenly gets worse, the parents get aggressive, Ture ends up terrified. Tess tries to pick him up, but can't when she's already carrying both his and her own bags, adults stumble over her and she cries out when her legs buckle, and in a matter of seconds she's in full-blown panic. That's when she sees a fist as large as snow shovel reach down into the pile of bodies and pick up Ture, the bags, and her.

"Come on!" the round, carefree face that belongs to the fist says, and pulls first the four siblings after him, then any other red-clad children he can see.

He parts the crowd of parents as if they were no more than curtains of flesh in front of him and shows them into one of the locker rooms. Once they're inside, Tess gasps from a mixture of breathlessness and fury and stares at him, and she draws two conclusions: 1. The boy is a giant. 2. He's wearing a *green* top.

"Are you okay?" she asks her brothers.

They nod. Ture is frightened, Tobias is angry, but Ted is just staring at the giant in admiration.

"I recognize you! Your name is Bobo, isn't it?"

The giant blushes because he probably thinks his achievements as a hockey player have made him famous all the way to Hed.

"Yes, erm . . ."

"You know Amat, don't you? Is he here?" Ted interrupts, so enthusiastic that he's bouncing up and down.

The giant squirms so uncomfortably that Tess feels sorry for him. He glances at her and says:

"No, well, I don't really know, I don't think Amat is coming today. And the A-team has changed their training time, so we won't be training until late this evening . . ."

"Can we stay and watch?" Ted wants to know.

"Are you stupid? Stay here till THIS EVENING to watch BEAR-TOWN?" Tobias exclaims.

Tess looks at Bobo apologetically.

"Thanks for your help out there. My brothers are grateful too, but sadly they're not intelligent enough to express it. But you . . . you rescued us."

The giant blushes so quickly and so deeply that he has to get down on his knees in front of Ture so he doesn't have to look Tess in the eye, because he's afraid his face might actually burn up then.

"Are you okay? There were a few stupid people out there, but I'm going to throw them out, okay? Not everyone in Beartown is like that, I promise we've got plenty of nice people in the rink who will look after you, so there's no need to be afraid, okay?" he asks the boy.

"The stupid ones can go to hell!" Ture replies instantly and gives Bobo a high five.

"TURE!" Tess exclaims, and Bobo can't stop laughing.

He gets to his feet and glances at her, then says:

"I've got a younger brother and sister."

"It shows," she says with equal measures of admiration and criti-cism.

He scratches his stubble absentmindedly. He's three years older than Tess but feels younger, he's never seen eyes like hers, she looks at him as if she could just as easily start to laugh or scold him. Bobo's voice fails him when he opens his mouth:

"If . . . look, if Amat shows up, I promise I'll fetch your brother so he can meet him. And if you, I mean, any of you, need anything, just shout for me, I won't be far away, unless I'm in the cafeteria or something, but I . . . well, I'll still be . . . ," he stammers.

"You're . . . quite easy to find? Seeing as you're five yards tall and seven yards wide?" Tobias suggests in a gently mocking tone which earns him a kick on the shin from his sister.

"Thanks again! Really!" she says.

Bobo smiles and nods, looking down at his shoes.

"I'm sorry some people are stupid here. But we . . . we're not all like that," he promises.

"Nor are we," she replies.

They both feel like liars.

There are still a lot of people out in the hall, but during the hours that follow, everyone calms down, first the youngsters and then their parents. The age groups from the respective clubs share time on the ice: Ted trains with his team in one half while Beartown's boys use the other half. Then Ture trains with the other seven-year-olds, and finally Tobias trains with the fifteen-year-olds. After them it's the turn of the figure skaters. The last thing Tess says to Tobias before she heads toward the ice is:

"Take Ted and Ture and wait in the locker room, and don't get into any trouble! We'll be going home as soon as my training session's over!"

A few minutes later Bobo is buying an ice cream in the cafeteria when someone comes in and yells:

"A massive fight's broken out down there, Bobo! It was that crazy bitch who started it!"

Everything happens so fast.

So many different stories will be told about what happened in the ice rink that day, and none of them will be the whole truth. In Beartown, for instance, a lot of people will leave out the bit about four siblings arriving at the rink and Ture getting a bottle top thrown at his head, and someone else yelling "HED BITCHES" at Tess. She grabbed hold of Ture to stop him getting trampled, and tried to grab Tobias to stop him fighting, and only just managed to get hold of them both, but it didn't help because the corridor was full of other teenagers from Hed. Some of them started to hum a tune, and soon all the others joined in. When this story is told in Hed, a striking number of people will omit the fact that the tune was the one Hed supporters used when they sang their "Beartown: Rapists!" song two years ago when the truth about Kevin had just come out and the hatred between the clubs was at its worst.

A lot of people in Hed will also "forget" to mention that there were candles in the corridor outside the locker rooms, beneath a photograph of Ramona, and that—a couple of hours after the first scuffle by the entrance—a boy from Hed kicked them over. In return, many people in Beartown skip over the bit where the mother of a boy on the Beartown's boys' team had already grabbed hold of a seventeen-year-old figure skater from Hed just as she was about to lead her little girls onto the ice, because the mother claimed it wasn't their turn. In Hed people will laugh and say she picked the wrong seventeen-year-old to act tough against, because her name is Tess and she's Johnny and Hannah's daughter, she may have a longer fuse than her brothers but there's still a hell of a lot of powder packed inside her. In Beartown people will pretend to be appalled and claim that this Tess shoved the mother. In Hed people will say the mother grabbed hold of her first, that Tess merely pulled herself free and the mother lost her balance and fell on her backside. In Beartown people will say that Tess's fifteen-year-old brother came storming out of the locker room at the same time and kicked over all the candles beneath Ramona's picture. In Hed people will claim that he had just heard that someone had attacked his sister and rushed out to defend her, and that he didn't even see the candles.

It is often said that history is written by the winners, but there are no winners here.

When Bobo hears what's happening he rushes down from the cafeteria and clears the corridor of wildly flailing fifteen-year-olds, trying as well as he can to throw the green ones one way and the red ones the other, but they aren't the people he's most worried about. After the first tussle in the rink today someone made a phone call and a short while later a handful of black jackets turned up and took up position in the stands at one end of the rink. Only the youngest members of the Pack have appeared so far, the runners, but Bobo knows the older and more dangerous members are only a text message away. If Teemu and his closest associates show up in the middle of all this, Bobo isn't confident that everyone in the ice rink will leave it on their feet.

"Come on, we'd better go," he says quickly to Tess, and she can see in his eyes that he isn't frightened for himself.

"Toby! Ted! Ture!" she calls at once to her brothers, and pulls them with her through the rink and out into the parking lot, and sends her dad a text at the same time: Training finished early. Can you pick us up right away?

She knows better than to say that there's been trouble, she did that once when she was at a birthday party when she was twelve, and he turned up with six other firemen and looked like he was going to kill any boy who so much as looked at her. Breathless, she turns to Bobo, he looks embarrassed, as if all this was his fault. She almost starts laughing.

"I . . . I like the fact that you broke things up. That you didn't hit anyone," she says.

"I'm not much good at fighting. I'm just big," Bobo smiles shyly.

"Good. I don't like people who are good at fighting," she says.

Bobo doesn't know where to look, so he spins almost all the way around to avoid having to look her in the eye. Instead he catches sight of Tobias, who has a serious black eye, so Bobo hands him his ice cream to hold against the swelling. It probably says quite a lot about Bobo that he was able to break up the fight in there without dropping his ice cream. It also says quite a lot about him that someone who likes ice cream as much as he does is prepared to give one away to Tess's younger brother.

"How's your eye?" he asks.

"Fine," Tobias mutters, still raging.

"What about your knuckles?" Bobo asks with a trace of a smile that vanishes instantly when Tess glares at him.

"They hurt like hell," Tobias grins weakly.

"I told you not to get into any trouble!" Tess hisses.

"YOU were the one who got into trouble, I just came out to help YOU!" Tobias snaps back.

Ted just stands there completely silent, glancing over at the entrance to the rink. All the other kids from Hed are streaming out into the parking lot. The entrance is full of green-clad kids shouting "HED BITCHES!" and worse. It's clear that they'd like to come over to Tobias and finish what they started, but not while Bobo is standing here.

"You should go back inside now," Tess says when she sees the van coming, Johnny is driving as if he'd just stolen it.

"Are you sure? I can . . . ," Bobo begins.

"Believe me: I'm not worried about anything happening to us when Dad arrives. I'm worried about what Dad would do inside the rink if we don't get him away from here right away," Tess replies.

She's right. It takes all her powers of persuasion and all Ture's frightened glances to stop her dad grabbing the first weapon he can find and taking on everyone who attacked his kids. He weighs three times as much as Tess but she still manages to hold him back.

She can see it so clearly in his eyes, that thing that some men have, that inability to see other people as people when he's angry, so she persuades him by summoning the only thing she knows is stronger than his violence. His instinct to protect.

"Dad! DAD! LISTEN!!! We need to get all the kids from Hed home, we need to get everyone away from here before anything else happens, do you hear me? You need to take care of ALL the kids here!"

Johnny's shoulders finally sink. He looks around at all the frightened, confused youngsters in red tops, standing in groups in the parking lot. There are a handful of adults there too, coaches and a few parents, but they look almost as frightened as the children. Johnny glances over at the entrance to the rink. A Beartown guy of around twenty is standing in the middle of it, he has a round, kind face and a build so solid that it looks as if he's single-handedly holding back all the green-clad idiots inside. Johnny takes out his phone and calls all his colleagues, and not long after that car after car from Hed comes screeching in from the forest.

Everything could have gotten completely out of hand from that point, but before any of the men in the cars had time to jump out and think about causing more trouble, Tess and Johnny have shepherded the kids from Hed into all the backseats and forced them to drive away again. They soon empty the parking lot. Johnny and his children wait until last before they follow the others. Tess puts Springsteen on the stereo and puts her hand on her dad's arm. In the rearview mirror she sees Bobo, still blocking the doorway to the rink, not a single person has managed to get out past him. But not even he can stop them making phone calls.

Johnny, Tess, and the boys are silent all the way to the boundary between Beartown and the forest. There was hardly time for it to get light today before it gets dark again, the days are shrinking fast now, yet still the figures are clearly visible in the gloom. Beside the signs on either side of the road stand a dozen men in black jackets, all masked apart from Teemu. He stares into the van as it passes. Johnny has never spoken to him, but of course he knows who he is, everyone in Hed knows, he's the person they warn their children about whenever there's a local sports match. And now Teemu knows who Johnny is too.

As the vehicle rolls into the forest one of the men next to Teemu throws a glass bottle, which shatters against the rear door, a final parting gift. The noise makes the other three siblings jump, and Ture starts to cry, but Tobias doesn't so much as raise an eyebrow.

"Didn't I say? Everyone there hates us!" he merely declares.

Then he leans his head back and closes his eyes. Two minutes later he's snoring. Their mother always says this is Tobias's real talent in life: that he can fall asleep anywhere, at any time. Just like his dad.

42

Goalkeepers

Tails is on the phone to the politicians on the council when he hears about the fight down at the ice rink. He hurries over there but by the time he arrives the rink is almost empty. Everyone from Hed has gone home and the trouble seemed to end as abruptly as it began. A few dads of boys on Beartown's youngest team are still drifting about, telling one another what they'd do if "any of them" dared to show their faces here again, but as usual it isn't the men who talk who you need to be afraid of here. The caretaker throws them out when it's almost time for the A-team's training session, they'll have to go home and act tough to shadows instead. Tails takes a nervous turn around the rink without really knowing what he's looking for, then he sits down at the top of the stands and watches the A-team's training, and thinks, thinks, thinks. The rings under his eyes look like someone's spilled a fizzy drink on a suede jacket, he's normally good at concealing his anxiety but today he's so bad at it that the caretaker suffers an attack of sympathy and goes up and gives him a paper cup full of really bad coffee, and says:

"Cheer up, Bambi! You look like someone stole your butter and rammed your money up your ass. This is hardly the first time there's been a fight in this rink, is it?"

Tails loosens his tie so that his thick neck can settle in more comfortable folds.

"No, no. But it's different now. There's more at risk."

"Oh, so those rumors are true for once? It's a badly kept secret, that one. So the politicians are going to try to merge the two clubs again?"

Tails doesn't even try to deny it, there's no longer any point.

"It isn't a merger of two clubs, it's the closure of one. Either Hed or Beartown."

"Can't be us, surely? When they haven't even got a rink over there?"

"No. More than anything, we have sponsors and a much better team," Tails nods, but without much conviction.

"But . . . ?" the caretaker prompts.

Tails groans.

"But there are politicians involved, and they don't know their ass from their elbow! They used to complain that we didn't have any money, and now that we've GOT money they're moaning about 'hooliganism.' They're worried that if we're allowed to take over all Hed's resources, there'll be trouble between the supporters. So they've employed an advertising agency and have come up with an idea to shut down BOTH clubs and start a NEW club here in Beartown, with a new name!"

The caretaker almost spits out his coffee.

"So . . . no Hed Hockey and no Beartown Hockey? That's the stupidest thing I've ever heard!"

"What do you think I said? I've sat in a million meetings with those numbskulls over in the council building to make them see sense and save this club, and I've PROMISED them that there won't be any more violence! And what do I hear today? That there's a riot going on in here and that Teemu and his bloody peasants' army have been standing in the forest throwing bottles at cars with families in them! How am I supposed to explain that? Well?"

The caretaker says nothing for a long time. Then he exclaims with a laugh:

"Are you expecting ME to answer that?"

No, of course Tails isn't. He's just trying to think, and sometimes that works better if he can talk at the same time, so he raises the cup and says:

"This isn't your headache. Thanks for the coffee. It was terrible, as usual. How's the team looking?"

The caretaker rocks his head from side to side and mutters:

"Without Amat? Well, Zackell better find a replacement for him, or else we'll be glad we've got a good goalie, because he's going to have his work cut out for him!"

Tails glances down at the ice and agrees. If they had a star on this team last season apart from Amat, it had to be the nineteen-year-old between the posts, the guy whose name half the town barely knows because they're so used to calling him "Mumble." If he didn't like the nickname, no one would have known, of course, but he doesn't seem to have anything against it. His silence and talent have helped make it easier for the Beartown fans to like him, which is no mean feat considering that the goalkeeper he replaced was Vidar, who grew up in the standing area of the rink with his brother, Teemu. It's an even bigger achievement when you consider that Mumble is from Hed. He had to swap teams when Vidar died in the car accident, Hed didn't think he was good enough back then, but now they would have swapped half their A-team to have him back. Nothing gives Tails a stronger feeling of schadenfreude than thinking about how badly mistaken they were about that, there are always men who are utterly certain that they can tell which children will grow up to be the best players, but this sport can still shock us when it wants to.

"Yes, any team with him on goal stands a chance. He's got a winner's head!" Tails nods.

The caretaker inserts a portion of chewing tobacco in his cheek so large that it's hard to believe there was enough room for it in the tub.

"Yes, I've seen my fair share of odd guys stand on goal here over the years, but damn me if this one might not take the prize. Never says a word, not even when they win, doesn't even seem happy. It's like he just plays with a great big . . . darkness inside him."

"All the best players have that," Tails replies, as if it was obvious.

"Really?" the caretaker replies.

Tails watches the goalkeeper down on the ice.

"Peter used to get beaten at home if he so much as spilled his milk. Benji didn't dare tell anyone he was gay. Amat is the cleaner's son in the rich kids' sport. All the best players have a darkness inside them, that's why they end up the best, they think the darkness will disappear if they can just win enough times . . ."

The caretaker wonders quietly if Tails is talking about the players or himself with that last remark, but says nothing. He wonders if Tails was about to mention Kevin as well, to illustrate the same point, but says nothing about that either. Instead he just pats Tails on the shoulder and says:

"Chin up, Bambi, you'll think of a way to deal with the politicians. You always do!"

Tails sits there alone with the whole town on his shoulders. He's good at radiating self-confidence but today he's wobbling. There's always been a struggle for resources in this forest, the politicians have talked about closing down one of the hockey clubs for decades, but the idea of shutting them both down and starting a new one is harder to defend against. "Isn't that what you wanted?" one politician asked in surprise earlier today, and Tails almost threw his phone at the wall. "I wanted you to shut Hed down! Not us!" he roared back, only to be told: "What's the problem? I didn't think you were sentimental?" It's a good thing he and Tails weren't in the same room, because then it would have been the politician hitting the wall rather than the phone. Not sentimental? Tails has lived here all his life, has played for the same club, built up the same town. If you don't have feelings for one particular place on the planet, you may as well live anywhere. Sentimental? Everything he's truly proud of achieving in his life is connected one way or another to Beartown Hockey. If they change the name of his club, they erase his whole identity. He can't permit that, he needs to fight with everything he's got, and because he doesn't have time to come up with a brilliant plan, he comes up with a simple one instead.

When the training session is over he goes down to the boards and waits until Mumble comes out, then, with a smile so big that it opens his whole face up into a great big hole, he offers to give the boy a lift back to Hed.

"I just want to know you get home safely!" he assures him.

Mumble says nothing, but he probably already knows that isn't true.

43

Brothers

Johnny and Hannah sit up all night in their kitchen arguing the way only the parents of young children can: really angrily but really quietly.

Hannah is upset that Tobias got into a fight over in the ice rink, of course, but she's just as upset that Johnny isn't as upset with their son as she is. All of his anger is directed toward Beartown instead, he claims Tobias was fighting in self-defense, as if that justified everything. Deep down Hannah is probably most annoyed that she can't help thinking he might be right.

Johnny and the other firemen spent two hours in the garage drinking beer and peering at the engine of the van after they came back from Beartown. They didn't fix anything, of course, but they looked very sternly at the engine as if it could be talked into working properly. Hannah would have laughed at that if she hadn't heard what they were discussing, because she's heard that sort of discussion before. People often joke that firefighters in Hed are recruited straight from the ice rink, but it's only half a joke, most of them used to play together and the fire brigade just became their next locker room. If you argue with one, you argue with all of them. Hannah often teases Johnny about being terrified about any kind of change, and the fact that he wants the same food and the same brand of beer and the same armchair for his whole life, to which he usually mutters that she ought to be seriously fucking happy about that, because people who hate change tend not to change their wives either. That makes her laugh and she can't resist saying "Shall we go down to the Barn and see who gets the most offers?," and that shuts him up. In fact she dislikes change as much as he does, because when things don't need to be changed you know that they work, and she needs to trust her colleagues at the hospital just as much as Johnny needs to trust his. They need to trust their neighbors, because they babysit their children, and they need to trust their childhood friends because that's who they call when life gets messy. If they defend you, then you have to defend them. Hannah isn't an idiot, she's the first to admit that Johnny can sometimes be the stereotype of a backward-looking, conservative, prejudiced old guy, but sometimes he's right. Sometimes he defends the right things.

So this is the worst kind of argument. When they understand each other.

"You need to make sure your friends don't do anything stupid now . . . ," Hannah whispers across the kitchen table.

He snaps back so fast that even she is forced onto the back foot.

"Us? WE'RE the ones who shouldn't do anything stupid? You know that one of the dads on Toby's team called the police when the trouble started today? And you know what they said? That they didn't have the resources to send anyone unless someone had been hurt! It was grown-ups who started this, Hannah. Grown-ups! If there's a single unlicensed hunter in the forest the police can send fifty armed officers, but people can attack our CHILDREN without any kind of punishment?"

She can see that he's having trouble holding his hands steady around his coffee cup. She's always said that ninety percent of his childhood friends are complete idiots, and most of them have kids on the hockey teams. And if those idiots don't trust society to protect their families, they'll do it themselves, and God help anyone on the other side if that happens.

"I understand that you're angry, don't you think I want to go over there and punch every last Beartown mom in the face? But we need to think of the kids!" she retorts.

"That's exactly what I am doing!" he protests.

"Is it? Tobias doesn't do what you say, he does what you do! You're his hero! How are you going to teach him it's wrong to fight if you do the same thing?"

Hannah yelled at Tobias so hard when they got home that the windows rattled, Johnny just sat beside her in silence. Then it doesn't matter how loudly she shouts.

"For God's sake, I can't tell him it's wrong to defend his sister . . ."

"I'm not saying that! But we have to punish him, surely you can see that? We can't let him think it's okay to start fights and get into trouble!"

"We've told him off . . ."

"No. I was the only one who told him off!"

"For God's sake, darling, he's going to be suspended from the hockey team! There's nothing we can do that would be worse than that," Johnny replies, the look on his face getting sadder and sadder, the coffee in his cup getting colder and colder.

They sit in silence for something like twenty minutes. Then Johnny sullenly picks up his phone and lets her listen as he calls his colleagues and the other dads on the team, advising calm. He says they should all think on it. Not start any unnecessary trouble. He hangs up and throws his arms out toward her, as if to say: "Happy now?," and she snorts irritably: "I'm so sick of having FIVE children!," then goes up to bed. He follows half an hour later, she can hear from his footsteps that he's feeling remorseful. It's long past midnight when she falls asleep, a long way from him, but when she wakes up early the next morning his big arm is wrapped around her. She hopes she's managed to teach the kids that, at the very least: we might argue, but we stick together. Tightly, tightly, tightly, we stick together.

———

Amat never shows up for the A-team's training session that evening. Zackell isn't surprised. Bobo is miserable about it, but he still walks home from the rink with easy strides, with his phone in his hand and a text from Tess that he reads one hundred times. Found your number online. It was a shit way to meet today but I'm glad we did. Call me if you want.

He calls. She sits on her bed and talks quietly so she doesn't wake her family. He makes her laugh. It's the best phone call of his life.

———

It's late at night and the house is completely quiet when the door to Tobias's room is gently pushed open. Ted stands there whispering his

brother's name without result, so eventually he pads in and tweaks Tobias's toes until he jerks awake.

"What the . . . ?" Tobias wonders, still half-asleep.

"I just wanted to . . . you know . . . say thank you for what you did,"
Ted whispers.

Tobias yawns and sits up against the wall, making space for his
younger brother on the bed. Ted's body is bigger than his thirteen years
but his eyes are considerably younger. He's just a frightened little kid
inside. Tobias boxes him gently on the shoulder.

"No need, Teddy bear. Now, back to bed with you."

"You didn't have to do that," Ted whispers, looking unhappily at his
brother's black eye.

"Yes, I did," Tobias yawns.

He got a serious telling-off from his mother when he got home, the
sort only she can dish out, but it was worth it. Everyone always assumes
that Tobias starts fights, because it's usually true, but not this time. He
wasn't the one who rushed out of the locker room in a blind rage when
he heard that Tess was in trouble down in the stands, he actually did what
his sister had told him: keep calm and make sure Ture was safe. It was
Ted who lost it and ran out into the corridor, straight into two guys from
Beartown. Tobias yelled at him to leave it, but Ted, sweet, kind, clumsy
Teddy bear, shoved one of the Beartown guys as hard as he could in
the chest, out of pure instinct. Naturally, the guy shoved him back even
harder, and Ted stumbled backward and accidentally kicked over the
candles on the floor beneath that photograph of Ramona. He got to his
feet and even though he can't fight to save his life he still tried to punch
the first Beartown guy in the face. The second one tried to join in at once,
of course, but found himself lying on the floor before he even got started.
Tobias had emerged from the locker room, and unlike his brother, he's
more than happy to fight. He floored the next guy who came running
over as well, fully aware even then that he could forget any hope of trying to explain this to his mom. "Get back in the locker room and lock the
door and take care of Ture! I'll get Tess!" he yelled to Ted.

Ted did as he was told and Tobias began to collect black eyes and cracked knuckles outside. Then everything went the way that it did.

"You didn't have to," Ted says once more beside him on the bed.

"Yes I did, because you'll get suspended from the team if they find out you were the one who threw the first punch," Tobias explains with a yawn.

"But now YOU'RE suspended from YOUR team instead," Ted persists unhappily.

"Never mind. They can manage without me. You're important, you're the best player on your whole team, I'm just . . . I'm like Dad," Tobias says calmly, moving one of his pillows onto the floor as if the matter was closed.

"And I'm not?" Ted whispers, hurt, because he thinks Tobias means that he isn't brave like their dad.

Tobias looks seriously at his younger brother, reaches out one hand, and takes a firm but affectionate grip of his ear.

"What the hell, Ted, I'm just saying I'm like Dad. I'll play hockey for a few more years and then I'll get a normal job. I'll get married to someone around here and become the sort of man who does DIY around the house and fiddles with his car and drinks beer and tells tall stories in the Barn on the weekends. That's enough for me."

"So what will I be, then?" Ted wonders.

Tobias lies down on the floor, letting his younger brother sleep in his bed like he has a thousand times before, and the big brother falls asleep instantly as usual, but just before he drifts off he yawns out the truth:

"You can be what you want, Teddy bear. Whatever you want."

44

Those of us who love sports don't always love sportsmen and women. Our love for them is conditional on them being on our side, playing on our team, competing in our colors. We can admire an opponent but we never love them, not the way we love the ones who represent us, because when ours win, it feels like we win too. They become symbols of everything we ourselves want to be.

The only problem is that sportsmen and women never get to choose if they want that.

Mumble would much rather take the bus home to Hed, but Tails is too important a man in this club for the boy to dare to turn down the offer of a lift from him. They cruise through the center of Beartown, insofar as Beartown can be said to have a center.

"It may look run-down now, but you have to see the potential! I promise you, anyone who invests in property here will be getting a good deal! This is going to be a prime location in a few years!" Tails is explaining brightly, as if Mumble had any money to invest in anything at all.

The nineteen-year-old nods cautiously and hopes that's what's expected of him. Tails interprets that as an indication of great interest and points enthusiastically through the window:

"Over there, near my supermarket, that's where we're going to build Beartown Business Park. Have you heard about that? It's going to be offices, but we're going to build housing as well. I can sort out a really nice apartment for you and your mom, what do you say to that? It's time to move out of Hed, isn't it? You're one of us now!"

Mumble daren't contradict him, so Tails goes on eagerly:

"You know, I use you as an example when I'm trying to convince businesses in Hed to take offices in Beartown instead? 'Everything gets better in Beartown,' I say, 'just look at our goalkeeper!' No one in Hed could see your talent, but with us you've become a superstar. Sometimes you just need a chance, don't you? A bit of self-belief! It's amazing what you can achieve then. Look at Beartown! A few years ago we were on the brink of bankruptcy, but now we have a freshly renovated rink and will soon have one of the biggest office and housing construction projects in this part of the country! One day we'll have an airport and an art gallery too, just you see! Big skiing competitions and a really big hockey academy. People don't believe me, but you know what I say to that? We should have been dead already! We shouldn't exist at all! But we're still here, and you know why? Because only towns with ambition survive!"

Mumble has heard the other players in the team make jokes at their sponsor's expense, but he's also noted that most of them have a certain respect for him. Tails talks a lot of shit, but he also gets a lot of shit done, and that's a quality everyone respects. That he wins.

So perhaps he's right with that stuff about ambition, Mumble thinks. That if you just think about your world differently, it becomes different. Mumble wonders if that works with the past as well, if you can erase it through sheer force of will, he'd quite like to ask Tails but nothing comes out. But much more comes out of Tails:

"Did you hear about the fight in the rink today?"

Mumble nods warily. Tails smiles so hard that his chins wobble.

"That's why I thought it best to drive you home, so we know that our star gets home safe!"

Mumble can't help thinking it would be safer for him to take the bus to Hed rather than turn up there in a car with Beartown Hockey stickers in the rear window.

"Are the players talking about the rumors of the clubs merging?" Tails goes on to ask.

Mumble gives a quick nod, he can't see any reason to lie. Tails's fingers clasp the wheel a bit tighter and he speaks more slowly. Slowly for him, anyway:

"It might be hard for you players to understand, but we might actually be stronger together. Do you understand?"

Mumble nods even though he isn't really sure that he does understand. All he wants is to play hockey. He wishes it wasn't so complicated. Tails hits the steering wheel with the palms of his hands in sudden delight:

"They need to be scared of us, you see! The big clubs in the big cities! In my time, back when I played, we loved the fact that they hated us. They said we were rednecks who couldn't play, so we embraced that. We played uglier and harder than they could even imagine, we used every trick we could think of, when their coaches used to drive along this road through the forest . . . straight into the darkness . . . they were terrified. They felt like they were alone on the planet. That's why we won. And you know what? We're going to get those days back again! Think how good we could be with our best players combined with Hed's best, and the full support of the council! We can be a big club again!"

Mumble nods even though he's actually terrified, because he doesn't even know if there'd be room for him on a team like that. He's already come close to losing hockey once, he knows how small the margins are. He's always been a late developer, the last in his street to learn how to ride a bike, the last in his class to learn to read. It felt like he was the last kid in Hed who learned how to skate, that's why he ended up on goal. Two years ago he was too poor even to warrant a place there, so when Zackell gave him a chance here in Beartown instead, he thought she was teasing him. More than anything, he thought everyone would hate him because he was replacing Vidar. He was so nervous in his first few matches that he let in shots that were barely on target. On one occasion Zackell made a gesture that he took to mean he was being replaced, but when he skated toward the bench she snorted in surprise: "Replace you? When you're playing like this? No, you're going to have to stay out there and feel ashamed!" Maybe that's how she's formed all her best hockey players, Mumble ponders now with the benefit of hindsight, by understanding that in most other clubs people simply don't feel ashamed enough.

The next day Amat was the only player who was at the rink earlier than Mumble in the morning and later than him in the evening, and soon they were training just as much and just as obsessed as each other. Mumble never dared ask if Amat wanted to train together, but Amat himself suggested it. He fired thousands of pucks from every possible angle every morning and evening, and Mumble couldn't have failed to become a good goalkeeper then even if he wanted to. Soon the supporters were chanting his name, first the older ones in the seats, then even the younger crowd in the standing area, where Vidar's brother stood. Zackell offered Mumble the chance to play with Vidar's old number and Mumble refused, and that rumor spread to the Pack, they loved him for that as much as the fact that he keeps getting shutouts. When he turned eighteen last year they gave him a hand-painted mask with the bear on one side and Vidar's initials on the other. Mumble had never received a gift from other men before in his whole life. After that, you couldn't have scored a goal against him with them in the stands behind him even if you'd been armed to the teeth.

"What do you say?" Tails says loudly beside him, and Mumble has no idea how he should reply, so he takes a chance on a nod, and that seems to be the right decision.

"Exactly!" Tails declares.

They drive through the forest and he starts talking about which parts are owned by which people around here. But almost all of it belongs to the state, he points out.

"We don't even own the forest we live in! So who's going to look after us if we don't look after ourselves? Eh? A few miles in that direction the politicians are talking about building a wind farm! Two hundred yards tall! Do you know how noisy those monstrosities are? And do you imagine any of the money earned from the sale of that electricity will stay in this region? Hell, we won't even get the electricity! The government loves green electricity, but do you know where they don't want to build wind turbines? Where they live! That's why we have to develop our own infrastructure here, we need to grow, create jobs and capital so we can oppose decisions like that! People say I'm a capitalist but I'm not, I'm just a realist. You know capitalism's like a wolf?"

Mumble really doesn't know, but that doesn't matter. Tails is self-sustaining now.

"Do you know what the worst myth about wolves is? That they only take what they need. If you believe that, you've never seen what a wolf does when it gets into an enclosure. It doesn't take what it needs, it kills everything it can, and it doesn't stop until someone chases it away. The government doesn't understand that, because they don't realize that wolves aren't our biggest threat—they are! Banning the hunting of predators? Sure, and who takes the hit from that? It sure as hell isn't the big cities. Building wind farms? Sure, and where do they build them? That's what I mean about merging the hockey clubs, together we'd stand a chance! We're a district with bulls on one side and bears on the other, but sure as hell the wolves are everywhere!"

Mumble looks out of the car window, when he used to travel along this road in the bus as a child he used to try to count all the trees. There was something comforting about that, he felt at the time, the fact that there were too many to count. Too many for numbers to deal with. If he'd been better at not keeping his mouth shut, perhaps he would have told Tails what he had really learned from growing up in Hed and playing hockey in Beartown: that for people in Hed, Tails is the wolf. In Hed, Beartown is the big city now.

Tails goes on talking, but he's mostly just repeating himself now, Mumble still doesn't know why the man offered him a lift. He doesn't know that this isn't really about him, Tails just needed an excuse to drive to Hed.

The trees thin out, the forest opens up toward the end of the road, Tails's car rolls into Hed and he actually drives the last bit in silence. For several minutes. That must be a personal best. The streets are dark and deserted, Mumble is relieved about that, he hopes that the wrong people around here won't notice the bear stickers in the car's rear window. Tails slows down outside Mumble's mom's house, but he isn't in any hurry. Instead he turns to Mumble and repeats his offer of arranging a nice big apartment for them over in Beartown.

"Thanks," Mumble says, the first word he's managed to say in the whole conversation.

Tails smiles broadly.

"Now go and get some sleep. Training tomorrow!"

Mumble nods, grabs his bag, and gets out. He can see that several of the neighbors are already peering out at the street from behind their curtains. He hopes that Tails drives off quickly.

Naturally, Tails doesn't hurry at all. Instead he takes a quite extraordinary detour, giving himself little errands to all sorts of different parts of Hed. He stops at a kiosk and buys a newspaper, he stops at a pizzeria and uses the bathroom. He even drives to the home of a businessman he knows and drinks a cup of coffee. They're old friends, have done a lot of business together, and by coincidence the businessman has recently received a very advantageous offer to rent an office over in Beartown, thanks to the help of his good friend. Now Tails needs a favor in return. He parks his car at the end of a dark cul-de-sac a short distance from the businessman's house, they spend a while drinking coffee in his kitchen until they're sure the area is empty and quiet, then they sneak out the back way together and grab a suitable-sized rock. The businessman keeps a lookout and Tails throws it. A short while later Tails calls the police to say that his car has been vandalized. Naturally, the police don't have the time or the resources to drive out, but they file his complaint. It takes an hour for the local paper to find out about it and call him, which is actually forty-five minutes longer than Tails was expecting.

45

Hornets' nests

The night before Ramona's funeral is the first really cold one of the autumn. Not the first when the temperature falls below freezing, nor even the first with snow, just the first one that can't really be described in words, no matter how many years you've experienced it: the first one when you're already accustomed to it, when the cold feels normal rather than the exception. Summer is long dead, but tonight is when we lose our memory of it, the last light slides away and a sack is pulled over the town. Tomorrow suddenly our fingers won't remember life without gloves, our ears can't quite remember the sound of birdsong, and the soles of our feet have forgotten all about puddles that don't crunch when we step on them.

The editor in chief of the local paper has experienced cold in many other places, but somehow it feels more raw here in the forest, it gets under your skin so that you never really thaw out, and if she didn't hate clichés so much she might have said the same about the people. Her former colleagues far to the south thought she was crazy to take this job, and she can't really argue with them. A small operation with nonexistent resources located in the middle of nowhere, and surrounded by a populace who seem to bear an inherited hatred for her entire profession. So why did she do it? Well, why does anyone ever do anything? It was a challenge. It was difficult. When your whole identity is wrapped up in being a journalist, perhaps you naturally reach a point in life when only impossible battles feel worth the trouble.

She puts her phone down. The office is dark and empty, the only person still working apart from her is her dad. He's still sitting where he's been sitting all day, squeezed in on a stool near the window with his heaps of paper and his marker.

"What was that about?" he wonders curiously.

"The police have had a report of a vandalized car in Hed. Apparently it belongs to Tails," she replies.

He doesn't ask how she found out, people talk and rumors spread everywhere, it just happens a bit quicker here.

"The sponsor?"

"Yes."

His sarcastic whistle contorts his cheeks.

"What a HUGE coincidence that HE of all people should be the victim of something like that, today of all days!"

She tilts her head sarcastically.

"Dad! Are you accusing Tails, an honest, law-abiding, tax-paying citizen, of LYING?"

Her dad snorts.

"I don't know about lying, if you were to go around to his house I'd guess that his car really has been vandalized. How it happened is a different matter. But you're not asking me if it's a lie, kid, you're asking me if you ought to publish it?"

She smiles with a sigh, a sound she's mastered better than anyone else he's ever met.

"It's news. We're a newspaper."

"You sound just like me."

She isn't sure if he's saying that with pride or apologetically.

"No, I sound a bit like you."

"Now you sound like your mom."

She smiles and sighs again.

"So you, who taught me that 'the only duty of journalism is to tell the truth,' think I should publish something I'm fairly certain isn't true?"

"Stop being silly and putting words in my mouth! Have you even called this Tails guy?"

"No."

"So call him. Then you won't be publishing something that's happened, you'll be publishing his version of what happened."

She leans back in her chair.

"I really don't know if I should be taking advice on ethics from you, Dad," she says.

Her dad just laughs, and even if she's still angry with him for manipulating Maya Andersson into talking to him on the train, she understands his intentions. When she was little she used to hear about how he had uncovered scandals and ruined powerful men's careers, but also their lives, their families' and their children's lives. It was his job to scrutinize those in power, but he was so good at it that the consequences were momentous even for the innocent, and she often wondered how he could sleep at night. The answer was both simple and complicated: his only loyalty was to the story being told. True ruthlessness always demands a belief in some sort of higher purpose. She honestly doesn't know if she can say the same about herself.

Her mother used to say "You're like your dad!" whenever she wanted to hurt her daughter when she was small, but it became more and more of a compliment as the years passed. "You're the sort who always has to start a fight!" she was told by her teachers, and in time she stopped feeling ashamed of that. Once she was thrown off of her soccer team for starting a fight with a girl on her own team who refused to admit that she'd touched the ball with her hand. Afterward her mother just sighed: "You can't cope with cheating. That's your problem. You refuse to accept that the world is made up of gray areas." There's probably no better description of the girl who one day grew up to become editor in chief of a newspaper.

"Shall I come straight out and ask Tails about the accounts while I've got him on the line? What is it you usually say? 'Give the hornets' nest a bit of a kick'? We probably won't get a better opportunity, will we?" she asks her dad.

They've discussed the ins and outs of the accounts with each other every moment since he arrived. He's read every line of every set of annual accounts for Beartown Hockey, and he just keeps repeating: "There's something missing here, and here, and here . . ." It isn't enough to find minor inconsistencies if you're going to go for a hockey club, you need to be able to prove blatant criminality, so they need to start by working out who is ultimately responsible. The council owns the ice rink, the members own the hockey club, but the sponsors have the money. And the guilt lies somewhere among all of them.

"Do it at the end, let the poor bastard talk all about his vandalized car first!" her dad nods.

She dials Tails's number. He's evidently expecting the call, fully aware of what he set in motion when he reported the vandalism to the police, but he's still surprised to hear her voice.

"The editor herself?"

They've had a few dealings with each other before, Tails isn't exactly the sort of man who holds back from calling the newsroom on a regular basis to "correct" stories he thinks they've "got completely wrong."

"I just wanted to verify the rumor," she replies.

"What rumor?" Tails said, well versed in the art of playing really stupid, but also with a trace of nervousness in his voice that doesn't escape her—he'd been hoping that one of the less experienced reporters would call.

"That your car was vandalized by hooligans in Hed."

Her dad smiles at the leading question, she puts her phone on speaker so he can hear Tails's humble, magnanimous reply:

"Someone . . . well, yes . . . someone threw a stone through the windshield, yes. But I think it would be irresponsible to speculate about who it might have been."

"But you had a Beartown Hockey sticker in the window, and you'd just given a lift home to a Beartown player who lives in Hed," she persists.

Tails pretends to think for a while before he replies:

"Yes, that's right, I was concerned that our player, he's very young, our goalkeeper, might be attacked on the bus otherwise."

"What made you think that?"

"Sadly parts of our ice rink were vandalized when youngsters from Hed were there training, two of the boys on our junior team were actually assaulted!"

She takes some notes. Glances at her dad. Then she asks:

"Are you saying that parents in Beartown should be concerned for their children's safety?"

Tails lowers his voice dramatically:

"I don't want any parent to have to be concerned for their child's safety, no matter where they live. And I don't think any citizen should have to worry that their car might be vandalized because of a sticker in the window. In Beartown we don't believe in violence and threats, we believe in cooperation and solidarity—that goes for both local businesses and sports. I'd like to think that the inhabitants of Hed want the same thing. You can print that!"

The journalist asks the question she knows he's been waiting for:

"There are various rumors that the council wants to close down both Hed Hockey and Beartown Hockey and instead set up an entirely new club. Do you think these attacks have anything to do with those rumors?"

Tails pretends to think for a long time.

"The council can't close down a sporting association. It belongs to the members."

She pretends to ask a critical question that really just gives him a chance to feel important:

"So you're saying that Beartown Hockey, which plays in a rink owned by the council, doesn't need any money from the council? I think a lot of taxpayers will be happy to hear that!"

Tails's voice drops to a tone of affected sorrow:

"You know as well as I do that ice hockey gives far more back to the council than it costs. Just look at our youth program! And our investment in girls' hockey! Is it right for those to be harmed by this? No, all I can say is that I hope that those in positions of power within the council don't let a few violent elements affect their decisions about our sport. There would be more than a hint of the mafia about this if our elected politicians decided to punish Beartown when we're the *victims* of vandalism and threats. I don't think people around here would accept that."

With that, he thinks they're done, he thinks he's got her right where he wants her, but she just takes more notes and glances at her dad again. Her dad nods that it's time.

"Tails, while I've got you on the line, we're sitting here looking through Beartown Hockey's annual accounts for the past few years . . ."

Tails falls so silent that she says, "Hello?" to make sure he hasn't fallen off his chair.

"Well . . . that's . . . what . . . why are you doing that, if I might ask?"

"We're a newspaper. News is our business."

"Yes . . . yes . . . but what do you think you're going to find there? Everything's been done correctly, I can assure you of that!"

So she begins to trap him in his own words.

"Really? How do you know that? You're not on the committee, are you? Sponsors aren't supposed to have any insight into the finances of a club owned by its members, surely? Especially not you, seeing as you were only recently investigated by the Tax Office?"

Tails loses his composure for a moment, which is unusual.

"Listen! Firstly, I haven't been found guilty of a SINGLE tax offense, and secondly, I have NOTHING to do with the club's accounts!"

"So why are you getting so upset?"

"I'm not getting UP . . . I . . . okay, look, I can tell that you're trying to dig up something negative! Why don't you write something positive for a change? Well? About our investment in girls' hockey? Integration! Our new statement of fundamental values!"

"We've written about all that. Every article we've published in recent months has been positive. But now I just want to ask a few questions about the accounts."

Tails is silent for longer than she's ever heard him be silent. Then he snarls:

"I don't know anything about that, I'm just a sponsor, as you pointed out!"

Her voice is mild but uncompromising:

"Perhaps you could find out from the committee who I should be talk-

ing to, then? If the rumors about the council wanting to set up an entirely
new club based on Beartown's position in the league are true, I'm fairly
certain that external auditors will have to conduct a thorough review of
all the club's finan—"

"Yes, yes! I'll check!" Tails yells, but she can hear that he regrets it, his
outburst has revealed plenty of sore points.

She smiles.

"I appreciate that. Sorry to hear about your car. I'll write the article
myself, it'll probably be online early tomorrow morning, so if you think
of anything else you'd like to add, you can always let me know directly."

Tails ends the call with an abrupt "Sure!" She hangs up.

"What an asshole!" her dad grunts.

"Oh, he's not so bad. He has a certain charm. A surprising number of
these hockey guys do, actually, I'm almost a tiny bit fond of them."

"Are you serious?"

"Yes. They remind me of you," she laughs.

That's only partly a joke. She does actually have a degree of respect
for Tails, just as she does for Peter Andersson, they're fighting for something invisible, passionate about their club and their town. She finds it
hard not to feel sympathetic about that. For good and ill, it's always the
other sort of people, the ones who aren't crazy about anything at all, that
she has trouble identifying with.

"Asshole!" her dad repeats.

"So what do you think?" she wonders.

"About which part of it?"

"Should I write about his car?"

"Of course. It's news."

She drums her fingers thoughtfully against her temples.

"So what do you make of Tails?"

Her dad folds his hands on his stomach.

"I think he's in a bind. I don't think he's used to losing. And assholes
like him can turn dangerous then. But you've kicked the hornets' nest
now, so we'll see what comes out . . ."

"You were the one who told me to kick it!"

"What do you listen to me for? I'm crazy!"

She bursts out laughing. So does he.

"How much is missing from the accounts?" she asks.

He pushes his glasses up onto his forehead and gestures to his piles of paper.

"Loads! There's nothing obvious unless you look really closely, they've covered their tracks pretty well, but . . . just from what I've uncovered so far, I'd say that Beartown Hockey has spent several hundred thousand in the past two years whose origins no one can quite explain. The factory signed up as a sponsor, of course, but I've checked their bank transfers and they're much lower than the accounts claim. So the money's coming in, but it's coming from somewhere else. Do you follow?"

"You think it's black market money?"

"Well, I think it's seriously bloody gray! Some of this looks like money laundering, several people on the committee of the council's property company have also been on the committee of Beartown Hockey, and now they're doing business together. There's a consultancy firm over in that pile as well, it's owned by a local construction company that does business with the council, and they've spontaneously transferred money to Beartown Hockey in a way that looks seriously murky. I need to dig deeper into all of that . . . but take a look at this . . . I think this is the REALLY big deal: Have you heard about this 'training facility'?"

"What training facility?"

"Yes, that's what I was wondering! The council bought it from Beartown Hockey a couple of years ago, I've got hold of an email that an official at the council sent to the club about it, but I can't find any other information about the purchase. All the documentation is gone."

The frown on the editor in chief's brow deepens.

"Money laundering . . . corruption . . . if just half of what you're saying is true, the club could be demoted by the hockey federation, it might even face bankruptcy . . ."

Her dad looks at her very seriously.

"Kid, if this is true, people are going to end up in prison. Peter Andersson, first and foremost, because his name is on all the documents. And by some massive bloody coincidence, he just happens to be childhood friends with that Tails? How much smoke do you need before you believe there's a fire? Eh?"

She leans back in her chair and stares up at the ceiling. Then she mutters:

"We need to dig deeper."

Her dad does something very, very unusual at this. He hesitates.

"First I have to ask, kid . . . are you sure you're doing this for the right reasons?"

"YOU'RE asking me that?"

He nods slowly. He hasn't had a drink since he arrived, and sobriety is gnawing away at him, but he's made up his mind that he needs to give her everything he's got, one last time.

"You're not like me. You can't just switch off your conscience. So if you're only doing this because you want to win, let it be. Because if I dig into this, Peter and Tails are first in line to get covered in shit, and I thought you said you like them?"

Her voice cracks so badly that she feels embarrassed, she can hear how she sounds like a young child clenching her fists after a soccer match when she blurts out:

"I do! I . . . do. Sure, they've done a lot of good for sports, for the town . . . but what does sports matter if there's no justice? What's a community? If they've built this club on lies and dodgy deals, then it's all . . . it's . . . it's CHEATING, Dad! And if we let them get away with it, what does that make us?"

46

Servants

There's no justice. None that applies to everyone, anyway, at least not here, Matteo learned that early in life.

He's fourteen now, and his sister always told him that this age was the worst, that people were at their worst then, she said he just had to survive these years. But of course she was the one who didn't do that. She said he could be anything he wanted to be, but he can't now. Because he wants to be happy.

He used to love drawing, so in the past few days he's tried to draw her, but he can no longer remember her inconsistencies, he can only see her as if she were made of porcelain. Hair carved out of wood, eyes like a doll's. He draws her as if someone were describing her to him.

His parents arrive home late in the evening before the funeral, they don't say anything, just come in as if they'd only been to church or the supermarket. His sister is lying in a box on the chest of drawers in the hall. He sneaks out and picks it up carefully, but it's too light, there can't be room for her in there. She was big, with a laugh that could fill hallways, a sense of humor that could lift the roofs off buildings. His mother calls from the kitchen and Matteo almost drops the box.

"Don't you want to call one of your school friends and go out for a bike ride, Matteo?"

Matteo swallows and it feels like he has lumps of ice in his lungs. His sister always used to say that their mother lived in a fantasy world, that she was like one of those funny photographs where you stand behind a board and stick your head through a hole so that your face ends up on a cartoon character of a lion or a fat old lady. "That's what life is like for her, she just sticks our heads onto whatever she dreams that we are," his sister said, and it used to make Matteo so angry. Not at his sister, but at the injustice. He's never had a friend, he's never called a single classmate, his mother has just seen other children riding their bikes out in the street and assumes that's the sort of thing he does too.

"Yes, Mom," he calls.

It's snowing outside, and icy cold in here, because from time to time she gets it into her head that the air is stale and throws all the windows wide open for several days. As if she were airing out everything that's wrong. She's standing in the kitchen baking, the way she always does when she doesn't want to look at anyone, his dad is sitting in another room with his books, because he lives in a different sort of fantasy, one where he can just switch off and not have to feel anything at all. "You say we have to be God's servants, but that's just another word for slaves!" Matteo's sister once yelled at them, and that upset their mother so much that her whole body just shook and she clapped her hands over her ears and screamed. Matteo spent the whole night hugging her and the following morning his sister apologized to him. That night she whispered: "They never speak out about anything to anyone, Matteo. Not their bosses, not people in the church, not God! They just back down and obey and accept that we have to live like this! All the damn rules and prohibitions and never having any money, is that how you want to live? Don't you want more than this?" Matteo didn't know what to say to that, he'd never considered the possibility that there might be alternatives, but he understood why his sister started drinking, because it was a way to escape being here. Not long after that their mother found alcohol and skimpy underwear in her room, and that was the first time Matteo heard the word "whore" inside the house. Their mother prayed for her daughter's soul every night, loudly so she would hear, so her daughter stopped coming home. Matteo was too young to understand everything that happened in those last few months, all the things she was subjected to, but after she disappeared abroad he went and shut himself away in her wardrobe, breathing her in until he fell asleep. When he woke up tucked away in the far corner, he scratched his cheek on something sharp on the floor, the corner of her diary. That was how he found out about everything. That's why he knows that even though she might have died in another country, and the police said it was because of the drugs, that isn't actually true. She was murdered here in Beartown. The people here killed her. Her heart broke into so many splinters that they were spread across the whole world.

Now her parents aren't even going to have her buried in the church they attend, the one that's several hours away, they're going to get it done in the church here in Beartown, the one they've always turned their noses up at. That way they won't have to tell anyone in their own church that their daughter died of an overdose abroad, they can just pretend that she's still alive, traveling around somewhere out there, still sending postcards.

Matteo has hidden her diary in the same place where he hides his computer, behind the broken tumble-dryer in the basement, he's only read it once but he remembers every word, every exclamation mark, every bubble in the paper left by the tears she cried as she was writing it: "*No one believes me, because if you fuck one guy here, you owe them all a fuck! fucking democracy, Beartown style! only virgins can get raped here!! why would the police believe me when even my own mother doesn't??? whore whore whore whore I'm just a whore whore whore to her and all the others so I can't be raped because you can't rape a whore!! not here.*"

It's been two and a half years since she packed her bag and lied about the church she was going to, and just disappeared. She actually left Beartown shortly after Maya Andersson was raped by Kevin Erdahl, but not even when the whole town was suddenly talking about sexual violence every second of every day did Matteo hear his own parents mention a single word about it. For a short while he wondered if they were ashamed, if they regretted not believing their daughter, but that passed when he saw what happened to Maya. She got her justice, her retribution, her revenge, didn't she? It didn't take that much, did it? No. Not much at all. It only took one witness, that Amat, who eventually plucked up the courage to say what had happened in a town where that meant he was immediately beaten up and assaulted by the rapist's friends. It only took the whole Andersson family sticking together when the entire town turned against them. It only took Maya going to the hospital and undergoing all sorts of terrible tests, and her filing a complaint with the police that just led to humiliating speculation that she'd taken drugs, and maybe she'd been sending out ambiguous signals, and did she actually understand that this could actually ruin Kevin's career?! It only took hundreds of anonymous comments online saying that she was obviously lying and just wanted attention and that everyone knew she was the one who fancied Kevin and not the other way around, and that she was too drunk to be raped anyway, and that she was just a whore who deserved to get raped and that someone ought to murder her. That was all it took! It only took Maya's father almost losing his job and the whole hockey club almost going bankrupt. It only took evidence and witnesses and money and powerful friends and a trial. And after all that, after ALL THAT, Kevin still wasn't convicted! His family just moved away and then everyone pretended nothing had happened, and somehow that was supposed to be seen as justice. One tiny little ounce of retribution, that's what Maya had to make do with, and all that took was everything.

Absolutely everything.

So what chance would Matteo's sister have had? None at all. Matteo didn't understand why she left home until he found her diary, now he wishes he'd never found it, that he didn't have to live in her darkness. He had hoped so desperately that she could be free far away, but now he knows that the guys in this town had already created a prison, they left chains inside her that she could never escape. Matteo is only fourteen, but his parents are servants, they will never avenge her, so he'll have to do that now.

He takes a small pen from his schoolbag and draws carefully, carefully, a small butterfly on the box she's lying in. Then he goes out and rides his bicycle in the snow, under the streetlamps, when his mother sees him through the window he waves, and she waves back.

47

Warriors

$\int$unday arrives. Ramona's funeral doesn't honor her memory at all. She expressly told these bastards while she was alive that they could feed the pigs or fertilize the flowers with her when she was done with this earthly life, as long as they didn't make a fuss and invite a load more bastards who would just have to stand there pretending to be sad. No one listened to her, as usual. The whole town attends the funeral.

Benji is woken early by Adri. The dogs get their food first, then the humans, they eat in silence standing at the kitchen counter. Benji barely manages to eat anything, his body isn't used to waking up at dawn, that's usually bedtime. Adri forces coffee into him and lays out his only suit. It barely stretched across his shoulders and chest when he left Beartown two years ago, but now it's too big for him. Adri has polished their father's old smart shoes and left them in the hall, she gives him a white tie that she bought specially, and Benji can't be bothered to protest. A white tie is only for family members at funerals, but Adri doesn't care what Benji thinks about that, or anything else for that matter. He wasn't even asked where he wanted to stay when he arrived home, his sisters just decided for him. He ended up with Adri because Katia only has a small apartment and Gaby doesn't have room now that their mother isn't well and has moved in with her. The idea of Benji living on his own isn't even discussed, he can travel right around the world as many times as he likes, but if you have three older sisters you're never an adult.

When daylight creeps above the treetops Gaby and Katia arrive, with their mother in the backseat, and Adri and Benji squeeze in next to her. Their mother spends the whole journey brushing Benji's hair, against his will, and the sisters laugh so hard that the car rocks. That boy can bear a lot of pain, but horses are usually groomed more gently than he is now.

Time is unreliable when it comes to those we love. When they leave us it feels like a lifetime, as if they've become strangers, but the first morning after they come back it feels like they've never been gone. The problem for Benji is that there are so many people who are about to catch sight of him for the first time now. So many people whose reactions he can't predict.

There are only a few people at the church when he arrives at the churchyard with his mother and sisters. His mother takes a dozen foil-wrapped bowls out of the trunk, because no matter where she's going she always has food with her. She and his sisters walk toward the gates and do what they always do: find something to help with. For a few moments they forget Benji, forget the looks that everyone else gives him, forget what he used to be in this town, and what he became. So he's left standing by the car without really knowing what to do, aware of everyone walking past him sneaking glances and whispering. His sweaty palms search desperately for something to occupy them, but he can barely light a cigarette. He suddenly wishes he'd never come home. Christ, he isn't ready for this. He sees men in black jackets over by the gate, Spider and a few of the others, Teemu's closest men. They're standing there to make sure no one who shouldn't be there attends the funeral, and Benji doesn't know if he's one of them or one of the others, he used to be better at not letting other people see his insecurity, but those pounds aren't the only things he's lost in the years he's been away. The cigarette goes out between his fingers. "Isn't that Benji?" one little kid whispers to another a short distance away. "God, he's so thin, has he got AIDS or something?" the other one whispers back, and they giggle hysterically. A grown-up shushes them angrily and both kids throw their arms out and hiss: "What? He is the gay one, isn't he? YOU said . . ."

Benji doesn't wait to hear the rest, he turns and walks off in the other direction, slipping on the thin covering of snow in his dad's best shoes. He doesn't know where he's going, just someplace where there aren't any people. The words "are you looking for something or running away from something?" echo in his head. A bartender on the other side of the world asked him that early on in his travels, and he didn't know what to say, so he said: "Both." He almost fell in love with that bartender, he almost fell in love with so many men over so many nights, but when the sun went up he always found himself looking for his clothes on the floor, looking for a way out. He met a woman as well, she was a diving instructor who found him asleep on a jetty one morning, he couldn't quite place her faltering English accent but they became good friends. Such good friends that one night, after he had spent a very long time trying to stare holes in the bottom of bottles, she smiled and said, in Swedish: "You're so easy to fall unhappily in love with, because you don't fall in love, you're just unhappy." It was the first time in several months Benji had heard his own language, it turned out that the woman grew up just three hundred miles from Beartown, practically around the corner. "Why didn't you say you were from home?" he asked. "Because then you'd never have talked to me, because you don't want to think about home at all," she replied. It was true. They spent all night talking in the language he had almost forgotten, she joined in with the songs the cover band was playing up on the stage, and Benji was drunk enough to close his eyes and believe he was back in the forest again, not by the sea. It wasn't the first time he felt homesick, just the first time he admitted it. The woman made him promise to stay with her for a while, and Benji promised, but he was soon packing his bag—it got easier and easier every time— and moved on. In another town he met a handsome young man who had a battered old boat, and they lived out on the water for weeks on end, but as soon as the man managed to get Benji to say something about himself Benji was lost to him too. On their last night together Benji lay on his back on the deck under the stars, as high as a kite, and told him how ice hockey felt. How it really felt.

Being one of those men down on the ice. Not one of the power-less men in the stands, the ones who could only shout and hope, but one of the ones who could really change things. Someone who could fight and bleed and win or lose everything. The handsome man lay beside him and gently touched the tattoo of the bear on Benji's arm. "Have you ever seen a real bear?" he asked. Benji rolled over and kissed him. The next morning the man woke up and the boat was empty.

"BENJI!" an angry voice shouts across the parking lot.

Benji carries on walking.

"BENJI!" the voice roars again, and his name feels like gunshot pellets on the back of his neck.

He stops like a rat trapped in a corner, turns around, ready for anything. The men in black jackets have left the gate and are walking straight toward him. He has been loved by them but he's also been hated, the way only someone who has been loved can be, when they found out about all his secrets. Once he symbolized everything they wanted Beartown to be: everyone feared him and he feared no one. He was just a boy then, but he was their man on the ice. Their warrior. Theirs. The roar that can rise up from a stand full of men in black jackets when you're full of adrenaline and throwing yourself at the Plexiglas is something Benji has never felt anywhere else, because it doesn't exist anywhere else. How many times has he wished that he could have stayed there? That the truth had never come out? Warriors are supposed to love other men, not fall in love with them. Benji thought he had experienced every sort of silence on the planet until the first time he walked into a room full of men making jokes about fags and everyone fell silent when they caught sight of him. He thought he had experienced every sort of hate until Hed supporters started throwing dildos onto the ice when he was playing and he could see in the eyes of Beartown's most devoted supporters that he had shamed them. They hated him for that, he doesn't blame them, he understands that they have never been able to forgive him. "You're one of us," that may have been the last thing Teemu said to him two years ago, but what does that mean now? Nothing. Benji was still a hockey player then, they still had some use for him, he was special. Now he's no one at all. He should never have come home.

"BENJI!" Spider bellows, the craziest of all of them, not as a request but as an order to stand still.

Benji doesn't move. He just lets the men approach. The first raises his hands, then the second, it happens so horribly fast and hurts so horribly much when they hug him, because his body is still covered with bruises from when he got beaten up at the airport.

"How the hell ARE you? Damn it's good to have you home! Shit, you're thin, are you anorexic now, you bastard?" Spider exclaims, and the other men deluge him with insults that are actually compliments because that's their only way of communicating, apart from compliments that are actually insults.

Then they talk about the elk hunt. About cars and rifles. The weather. Benji is still half expecting to be hit, but when it doesn't happen his shoulders eventually relax and he says quietly:

"I . . . I'm sorry . . ."

He nods toward the churchyard, but Spider just laughs.

"Are you going to cry now? Do you think Ramona would have let you do that? She'd have beaten your skinny ass to splinters and then lit the fire with them until the whole town stank of ass!"

But there's incalculable loss in his eyes, in all the men's eyes. The skin of their faces is swollen with alcohol, drowned inside to stop them drowning in tears outside. They belonged to Ramona, she belonged to them, most of them were closer to the old bag than their own parents. So even humor isn't a defense now, it's an act of defiance, you're not getting us, bastard grief. One of the men's girlfriends is calling from behind the cars that she needs help carrying chairs, because the church is going to be full, so the men go off at once, still talking to Benji as if it's obvious that he's going with them. So he does. They talk about hockey but no one talks about Benji and hockey, no one asks if he's going to play again, someone mentions that the council wants to try to merge the clubs, and Spider replies that "they're welcome to try, and we won't need any extra chairs at their funerals!" At that, the girlfriend kicks her boyfriend's shin to get him to kick Spider. When Spider exclaims: "What did I say wrong NOW?," the girlfriend hisses: "Just remember who you're talking to, because we're in a goddamn church!" And of course Spider retorts with a grin: "Don't swear in church, Maddy!" Oh, how they laugh, all of them, Benji included. They carry more chairs into the church and discuss girls and snow scooters and none of the men in black jackets probably really know what they're doing, but there and then they give Benji the very finest gift you can give someone who always used to be special: they treat him as if he isn't special at all.

48

Thieves

Early on Sunday morning one fireman phones another fireman to ask for a favor. Bengt is at one end, Johnny at the other, the latter is still upset about the fight at the ice rink but his considerably older boss counsels calm:

"They're cut up about that Ramona's funeral. How would you feel? Let it lie for a few days. There are decent, sensible people over in Beartown too, give them a chance to talk some sense into the worst idiots and we'll see how everything looks before you grab a baseball bat and go over there looking for trouble."

Reluctantly, Johnny promises to do as he says. Then they talk about the elk hunt, almost all the firemen will miss it this year because their work clearing up after the storm doesn't leave room for anyone to take any time off. "Just what we need right now," Bengt laughs. "A load of restless idiots with fresh ammunition and nothing to shoot at!"

"I'll talk to the guys again, calm them down as best I can," Johnny promises.

"Good, good, how are Hannah and the kids taking it all?"

"The kids got home and were angry about everyone in Beartown, but Hannah was mostly angry with me. How it's supposed to be my fault, God only knows, but that's nothing unusual."

Bengt laughs so hard he starts to cough.

"Sounds like my wife. Every morning I wake up and I'm already on minus points with her. If I do everything right all day I might get back to zero, at the very most. And the next morning I wake back on bloody minus points just the same. Speaking about the wife, can I ask you for a favor?"

"Didn't you just ask for one?" Johnny points out.

"Yes, yes, but my leg's in plaster and I can't drive, and the wife's winter tires have arrived. Could you pick them up for me?"

"Sure. Where from?"

"From the trash bandits."

"The trash bandits?" Johnny repeats skeptically. He hasn't been to the scrapyard since the new owner took over, but naturally his colleagues at the station have talked about it a lot. "I wouldn't open my mouth there if I had gold fillings because you'd lose them before your tongue even noticed," was how one of his colleagues summarized his feelings, but Bengt replies calmly:

"Cheap tires. Nothing wrong with that."

"Do you want me to get a receipt?" Johnny smiles.

"Probably best NOT to!" Bengt laughs.

But Johnny promises to pick them up. He drives the van through Hed and stops at the scrapyard below the mountain. It's more a hill than a mountain, to be honest, but once things have been given a label in Hed it's hard to change. He gets out of the van without locking the door, his cell phone's lying on the passenger seat and a fat man in a leather jacket standing a couple of yards away smiles thoughtfully:

"You're not going to lock your car, yes?"

Johnny raises his eyebrows.

"Why should I?"

The man doesn't take his eyes off him, still smiling, almost expectantly.

"Most people lock their cars here. There are rumors that we're thieves, haven't you heard? Maybe someone will take your phone, yes?"

Johnny looks into the car, then looks around the scrapyard, looks back at the man again, and replies calmly:

"Tell one of your guys to try and we'll see what happens."

The man bursts into a long, hearty chuckle and holds out his hand.

"Lev."

"Johnny," Johnny replies, shaking it hard.

Lev nods at the T-shirt under Johnny's jacket, with the badge of the fire brigade on the chest.

"Fireman, yes? Not afraid of fire, not afraid of thieves, what can I do for you?"

"I'm here to pick up some tires for my boss," Johnny replies.

"Bengt, yes? Very good. We'll fetch. How is his leg?"

"Thanks . . . good, he's doing well," Johnny replies, a little surprised. Lev holds the palms of his hands up.

"People talk, yes? We heard about the accident. Hope he . . . how do you say? Gets himself better, yes? Anything else?"

Johnny squirms, takes a deep breath, and gestures toward the van:

"This isn't running the way it should. The wife's complaining. Could you take a look and see if you have any replacement parts?"

He doesn't say he needs help fixing it, he still needs to feel that he can fix something himself, but he might as well buy replacement parts while he's here. Lev appears to evaluate him and the van for a while before he says:

"My mechanic will look. Takes half an hour. You drink coffee, yes?"

Johnny nods. Everyone drinks coffee, surely? Lev leads him away from the scrapyard toward a small house nearby, then goes into the kitchen and switches the coffee machine on. Johnny steps warily in after him, there's hardly any furniture, Lev has been living here for several months but it still looks like it's occupied by someone ready to leave at a moment's notice.

Johnny takes the mug Lev hands him. He feels he should make small talk but doesn't know where to begin. So he does what he usually does, looks around to find something he can use to change the subject, looks out of the window at the little yard at the back and exclaims:

"What happened there?"

There are several sections missing from the fence, and even if a bit of snow has fallen, the yard is clearly covered with muddy tire tracks. Lev puts so many lumps of sugar in his coffee that Johnny can't help thinking it will soon be more of a dessert than a drink, then he replies:

"Teemu Rinnius. 'The Pack.' You know them, yes?"

Johnny nods, suspicious but curious.

"Of course."

"Teemu wanted to give me a message. I don't think he likes telephones. So he left me a . . . what do you call them? A hearse!"

Lev gestures pointedly toward the destruction in the yard. Johnny peers at him.

"A hearse? The Pack did that? What the hell had you done to them?"

Lev shrugs his shoulders in resignation.

"Business with Ramona."

"The woman who died?"

"Yes, yes. She owed me money, yes? So I said I would buy the Bearskin pub in place of the debt. This was Teemu's response."

"Buy the Bearskin? You said that to Teemu?" Johnny laughs, because he would have paid good money to see the look on the idiot's face when that was proposed.

"No, no. I was . . . how do you say. A diplomat, yes? I went to Peter Andersson."

"Oh," Johnny mutters, his tone of voice giving away what he feels about that name.

"You're friends?" Lev wonders with an uncertain smile.

"We used to play hockey against each other when we were younger."

"Yes? Before he played in the NHL?"

Johnny drinks his coffee and licks his lips in an attempt to prevent the bitterness from seeping out, but it doesn't go very well:

"Long before that. We were only teenagers, I was never as good as him. Have you contacted the police about what Teemu did?"

The tip of Lev's nose moves sadly from side to side.

"The police? No, no, police and lawyers, they don't work for people like me. They work for people like Peter Andersson. I went to him, like a man, he and Teemu responded with the hearse."

Johnny looks out through the window, having some difficulty imagining that Peter Andersson, whatever else he might think of him, could be behind something like this. But people change, and these are strange times, in both towns.

"We used to call Peter 'Jesus' when we played Beartown, because everyone there thought he was the savior of the whole world. Always a bit better, a bit fancier than the rest of us. What are you going to do to him and Teemu now, then?"

Johnny regrets everything he's just said, but particularly that last question. Lev puts another sugar lump on his tongue before saying:

"Nothing."

Naturally, Johnny doesn't believe him. They finish their coffee in silence, Lev needs a spoon to get the last of it out of his mug. One of the men from the yard comes and knocks on the door, explains what's wrong with the van without Johnny really understanding, but without him quite being able to admit that.

"Bengt's tires are in the back. And reserve parts for you, yes?" Lev translates.

"What do I owe you?" Johnny wonders.

"For a fireman? Nothing! Not worth mentioning!" Lev replies calmly with a smile, and once again Johnny has no idea if he means that the replacement parts aren't worth mentioning, or if what Johnny now owes him isn't worth mentioning.

"You should call the police," Johnny says, nodding toward the yard, mostly because he doesn't know what else to say.

"No worries. I've lived in a Hed and a Beartown many times, yes?" Lev replies.

Johnny scratches his head.

"How do you mean?"

Lev smiles benevolently and looks for the right words.

"I've lived in towns like yours before. In many countries. People around here seem to believe that all immigrants are born in big cities, yes? But I was born in a Hed. I'm a forest person, like you. There's a Teemu everywhere. A Pack everywhere. They want to say to us: 'We're in charge. You must obey. You must back down.' Yes?"

"And you're going to?" Johnny wonders, sounding more curious than he's really happy about.

Lev tilts his head a little to one side.

"You have a saying here: 'The only time I back away is when I'm taking speed!' Yes?"

"'The only time I back away is when I'm taking aim,'" Johnny corrects with a slight smile.

"Exactly. Exactly!" Lev nods.

He holds out his hand. Johnny shakes it. Lev keeps hold of it a few moments longer than necessary and looks him in the eye.

"If there's a fire, I'll call you, okay?"

"Absolutely, if there's a fire, call me," Johnny laughs.

"And if you need me, you call me, okay? What do you call it? 'Being neighborly,' yes?" Lev goes on, without breaking eye contact.

Johnny ought to be wary, he knows that, but instead he nods emphatically. As he walks away, he finds himself hoping really, really badly that Teemu Rinnius and Peter Andersson and all the other bastards over in Beartown have finally picked a fight with someone more dangerous than they can handle.

He drives the van to Bengt's and unloads the tires, then he goes home and lies to Hannah about where he bought the replacement parts. Otherwise there'd be a hell of a fuss about that as well.

49

Secret smokers

"Marriage."

There ought to be a different word for it once you've been married for enough years. When you've long since passed the point where it stopped feeling like a choice. I no longer choose you every morning, that was a beautiful thing we said on our wedding day, I just can't imagine life without you now. We aren't freshly blooming flowers, we're two trees with intertwined roots, you've grown old within me.

When you're young you believe that love is infatuation, but infatuation is simple, any child can become infatuated, fall in love. But real love? Love is a job for an adult. Love demands a whole person, all the best of you, all the worst. It has nothing to do with romance, because the hard part of a marriage isn't that I have to live seeing all your faults, but that you have to live with me seeing them. That I know everything about you now. Most people aren't brave enough to live without secrets. Everyone dreams about being invisible sometimes, no one dreams of being transparent.

Marriage? There ought to be a different word for it after a while. Because there's no such thing as "eternal infatuation," only love lasts that long, and it's never simple. It requires a whole person, everything you have. The whole lot.

The children are making their own way to the funeral today, so the parents are on their own at home with everything they can't talk about. Kira is standing outside the bedroom door, not daring to breathe, because Peter is sitting on the bed in there trying to knot his black tie and crying. She backs away all the way to the staircase, then pretends she's just come upstairs and calls: "Do you want coffee, darling?" And he has time to wipe his tears and clear his throat and call back: "Yes, thanks, darling, I'll be right down!"

He comes down the stairs, his tie slightly too long, she isn't standing in his way and he walks past her as usual, but suddenly they bump into each other anyway. Her fingers find him and she buttons his jacket to pretend that they're not just looking for intimacy. He stops, almost dizzy, and they look past each other because if they look each other in the eye right now they would probably both crumble. It's been so long since they touched each other that her fingertips are enough, they're like electric shocks to him, she dares not rest the palms of her hands on his chest. Dear Lord, how close you have to be to giving up each other to remember to fight for each other.

She whispers:

"Ramona would have been proud of you."

He whispers back:

"Are you?"

She nods with heavy eyelids. What is she thinking there and then? Perhaps she'll never remember it again, or perhaps she'll always deny it, even to herself. There really ought to be a different word for "marriage," but perhaps also a different word for "divorce." One for when you're only almost there. When you want to whisper that I don't know what I want, I just don't want it to be like this. A word for simply saying that I can't bear it. I can't bear it if all we're going to do with each other is just bear it.

"I . . . Peter, I . . . ," she begins, and all the oxygen goes out of the room.

She says "Peter," not "darling," and she pauses just long enough for him not to let her finish the sentence. So he quickly leans his forehead close to hers and whispers:

"I love you!"

Her smile comes so fast, caught by the intensity in his eyes, his breath so close to hers, and then she says the same thing with such obviousness that they can both pretend she had never come close to saying anything different:

"I love you too."

It's been so long since they said that, but now it's very recent. Above all the other words for love, there ought to be one for this: one that says how many times we've come close to losing each other but turn back and start again. One for the very smallest things, the inches, when we brush past each other in the kitchen instead of only almost doing it. Something that says I can't bear it. I can't bear it if you can't bear me. I can't bear it without you.

They set off for the funeral together and he doesn't let go of her hand the whole way.

Ana's dad is awake, hungover but not yet drunk again. The old guys in his hunting team are standing in the yard, waiting to set off to the church with him. They're also sober for the funeral, but the whole thing is just a countdown to the first beer at the wake afterward.

Ana and Maya are walking ahead of them on their own, Maya with her guitar still on her back. She's been home to change and Ana immediately got annoyed because she'd "dressed up." Maya pointed out that this was normal if you were going to a funeral, and Ana replied: "God I hate the fact that you're attractive, it's the absolute worst thing about you! I need uglier friends!" They cut through the patch of woodland just behind the houses on the edge of the Heights and leave the men's voices behind. Only when they're really close does Maya realize that they're walking along the jogging track, that it was here that she waited for Kevin with the rifle. Ana seems to realize too, she's about to turn off but Maya takes hold of her arm and leads her on. They pass the place where she squeezed the trigger, where Kevin wet himself when the gun clicked and she dropped the cartridge she had never loaded on the ground in front of him. The two young women trample over the memories and two invisible little girls pad after them. Because they're always walking behind us: the children we were before the worst that has happened happened.

"I didn't know I'd feel like this . . . ," Maya says quietly when they're a few hundred yards farther on, when they can slow down and look out toward the lake and see almost the whole town.

"How?"

"That I'd still be this angry."

Ana scrapes her shoe through the thin covering of snow and confesses: "I still dream of killing Kevin."

"I wish you didn't. He isn't worth your dreams," Maya says.

Ana scrapes her shoe harder.

"I dream about Vidar too. But those are better dreams now. Before I just dreamed about him dying, but now he's alive sometimes. He's an idiot, a complete moron, but he . . . well, you know . . . he's alive."

Maya takes her hand, Ana holds it tightly. They walk in silence for at least a quarter of an hour, reaching silent agreement on lengthy detours, but eventually and unavoidably they come close to the first houses. When they see the churchyard in the distance Maya says:

"I miss the light here. The way it changes when the days are at their shortest. It's as if you can see in the air how cold it is."

Ana wrinkles her nose and snorts:

"You sound like a tourist."

"I am."

Ana doesn't even laugh at that, so Maya has to tickle her to get her started. Then she can't stop until they're close to the churchyard and a boy is standing there alone, smoking. He's been carrying chairs all morning and is dressed in just his suit pants and a sweaty vest now, despite the cold. He's much thinner than they remember. Maya and Ana both have to stop themselves insulting each other for being too eager to give him a hug, so in the end Maya just gives him a clumsy half hug, and Benji looks at her like she's crazy. She's missed that look. He's twenty years old now, and has been through a lot, inside and out, but as soon as he smiles he looks just like a teenage boy who climbs the tallest trees and carries the biggest secrets again. Most dangerous on the ice, most alone on the earth.

"You look good," he compliments Maya when she lets go.

"You look like shit," Maya laughs back.

He turns to Ana and she hugs him first like a distant relative and then like the mast of a ship in a storm, there's no in between with her. He grins.

"Are you really walking unarmed through the streets? My sisters tell me you don't do anything but hunt these days, so I thought you'd have your rifle with you. Now who's going to protect me if there's a fight?"

"Don't worry, I can take anyone here if they're stupid toward you," Ana grins back with her fists in the air.

Maya sticks her own fists in her coat pockets. She's trying not to feel worried for her friends, but they're not making it easy for her.

"Where have you been? I mean . . . where did you go?" she asks, nodding toward Benji's suntanned skin without saying anything about all the new scars on it.

"Here and there. And now I'm here," he says carelessly.

"I'm sorry about Ramona," Maya says sadly.

He nods slowly but can't formulate a reply without his voice breaking. So he turns toward the gatepost where his white shirt and jacket are hanging, and fishes out a white tie from the jacket pocket and holds it out to Maya, saying:

"For your dad."

"Are you kidding? He's only just managed to knot his OWN tie!" she smiles.

"He should have this," Benji insists.

"Isn't white tie just for family?" Ana wonders.

"He was family," Benji says.

Maya takes the tie and clutches it so tightly that it ends up crumpled. Then she sees someone farther away, laughs, and exclaims:

"Okay . . . is that my *brother* standing over there smoking in secret?"

Ana peers at the fourteen-year-old boy, who really isn't as well hidden among the bare trees beyond the gravestones as he probably hopes. Then she lets out an impressed whistle, just to scare the shit out of her best friend.

"Is that Leo? You're kidding? He's pretty hot now!"

"Stop it!" Maya exclaims, and Ana bursts out laughing.

"I don't think he's your type, Ana. I'm not so sure about *me*, though . . . ," Benji points out, unconcerned, and Maya hits him on the arm as hard as she can.

It doesn't really hurt, but unfortunately Ana hits his other arm out of solidarity and his knees buckle a couple of inches as he whispers:

"Are you taking steroids now, you psycho?"

"You're the one who's lost all your muscle on some sandy beach somewhere, you ridiculous hippy," Ana grins.

"See you inside, I need to shout at my brother!" Maya declares, and sets off toward the trees.

Ana and Benji stay where they are, and he pretends to be frightened and whimpers:

"No, no, don't hit me again! Not my face!" when she shoves him playfully in his side. She giggles.

"What about you? Aren't you going to wear a tie?"

He purses his lips.

"No. Ties are gay."

Ana laughs so hard that she's practically grunting when she breathes in and blowing snot from her nose when she breathes out, and he laughs so hard at her laughter that he loses his breath.

———

Ruth.

Ruth. Ruth. Ruth.

No one here even knows her name. None of them will see her headstone and remember who she was. Ruth. Ruth. Ruth. Her name was RUTH and Matteo hates everyone who doesn't know that. Who doesn't remember. Every last one of them.

That morning he hides in the closet so his parents won't see his computer. He hooks up to the neighbors' Wi-Fi to watch a video of how to knot a tie. If Ruth had been here she'd have helped him, he's never had anyone to ask but his sister, his dad has disappeared deep inside himself and his mother is living inside postcards no one else can see. They haven't even given him a tie, he helped himself to one of his dad's, they won't notice he's wearing it because that would mean actually looking at him. Or speaking to him. The house was silent before they came home with Ruth but it's even more silent now. The lack of words is worse than loneliness.

Matteo wonders if his parents are so certain of their faith that they believe their daughter is in Hell now. He wonders if they hope they end up there too, so they can see her again. He wonders if they're scared. He wonders if they cried their way silently through last night, like he did.

Ruth used to say that Matteo was too soft, then she would regret it instantly and assure him that that was the most beautiful thing about him. She was a good big sister, she would have followed him to Hell if it was him in the box in the hall. She once said she hated the world because it forced children like him to become hard simply to survive, but then she saw that he got scared and ruffled his hair and said it was probably good to be soft, because then you didn't break when you fell. Like flower petals. Perhaps that's what happened to her, she grew hard, the way a rose that freezes to ice can be shattered with a hammer.

In the car on the way to the churchyard Matteo's mother looks out through the window and the three surviving members of the family have the only conversation they will have all day:

"Look, the flags at the ice rink are flying at half-mast," his mother says, surprised and almost proud, and that cuts Matteo up because of course that was all his sister wanted their mother to be while she was alive.

"It isn't for Ruth. It's for the woman who owned the pub," he therefore blurts out without thinking.

The fear that his mother will get locked into one of her anxiety attacks, shaking and holding her ears, instantly washes over him. But her gaze merely disappears behind the shiny gauze of her fantasies and she says happily:

"I'm sure it's for both of them."

It isn't. They don't even know her name, Matteo thinks. But all he whispers from the backseat is:

"Yes, Mom, I'm sure it's for both of them."

When they reach the churchyard there are already people hurrying about in the parking lot. They're carrying boxes and crates, as if they were preparing for a rock concert rather than a funeral. Matteo recognizes a lot of them, men from the hockey club, they aren't even aware that there are two funerals taking place today, and they couldn't care less. The priest meets them guiltily at the gate and asks Matteo's parents if they would consider holding the ceremony in the chapel rather than the church.

"As you can see, the church is being prepared for a large funeral, and they're carrying chairs in right now, so I thought it would be quieter for us in the chapel, because of course there aren't so many of us here for . . . yes, for . . . for . . ."

Not even the priest remembers.

"Ruth. My sister's name was Ruth," Matteo whispers, but the priest doesn't hear him.

"It doesn't matter. The chapel is fine," his dad replies mildly with his head bowed.

His mother doesn't appear to be listening at all. It all goes rather quickly. The priest reads from the Bible and Matteo doesn't need to open his to follow the text, he knows almost all the passages by heart. The only time his mother shows any emotion at all is when the priest at one point uses a more modern translation of one verse than his mother considers correct. She wrinkles her nose and snorts toward Matteo, and Matteo uses his whole face to let her know that he too thinks this is terrible.

When it's all over his parents stay in the chapel for a short while with the priest and Matteo goes outside into the morning light again.

"I hate you being dead, because I can't talk to anyone else about death except you," he thinks, straight up toward the sky, and only then do the tears come, all at the same time. He sobs so hard he can't breathe, bent double, then he starts to run, stumbling and tripping, away from all the voices. He sinks down behind a tree beyond the gravestones and punches his thighs until they're covered in bruises and he loses the feeling in them. He closes his eyes and cries, and doesn't open them again until he detects the smell of smoke.

A boy the same age as Matteo is standing, badly hidden, a few trees away. He's holding a cigarette like someone who's still working out how to hold it, trying out different grips with his fingers, inhaling the smoke through his mouth and breathing it out through his nose. Matteo recognizes the boy from school but the boy never sees Matteo, their skills at hiding are very different, they haven't spent the same amount of time practicing.

Someone calls "Leo?" from farther away and the boy swears and drops the cigarette without bothering to stub it out. He steps out from among the trees and walks between the graves. A girl a few years older is walking toward him.

"Are you *smoking*, Leo?" she hisses gleefully.

"Shh! Don't be a sneak, Maya, don't say anything to Mom and Dad, okay?"

"It'll cost you two cigarettes, little brother!" she giggles and he swears and passes her the packet. They disappear toward the other end of the churchyard, walking close together, brother and sister. Nudging each other in the side, laughing, irritating.

Behind them among the trees Matteo bends down and picks up the cigarette Leo dropped. It's still alight. No one sees the lonely boy smoke it.

50

Families

Kira notes that the parking lot is full when Peter turns in toward the church. He's just about to put the car in reverse and try to turn around to look for a space out on the road instead when two teenage boys in black jackets whistle and gesticulate in his direction. One of them removes three red cones from a spot right next to the gate and waves to Peter to park there.

"Teemu told us to save the best space for you!" the guys are careful to point out to Peter as he gets out, still surprised.

They don't want a tip, they don't want praise, they just want Teemu to know that they're reliable. Peter reaches for Kira's hand as she comes around the car and it takes a moment for her to take his, he can tell she does it reluctantly.

"Teemu's guys?" she says, an accusation as much as a question.

"It's not . . . like that . . . it's just . . . ," Peter begins, but he really doesn't know who he's trying to convince.

"Dad!"

Maya saves him, she and Leo are walking toward them from the other direction, and she gives him a hug and hands him a white tie.

"From Benji."

"I think white ties are only for family, I . . . ," Peter explains gently.

"You're family," a voice replies from the churchyard gate.

It's Teemu. He's standing beside the priest. "Only in this town," Kira thinks, "only in this bloody town do you see hooligans and priests side by side." But when Peter glances at her she nods and says with feigned encouragement:

"You go ahead, darling! I'm going to see if there's anything I can help with!"

He goes and she stands there watching her husband and the priest and the hooligan, freezing with abandonment. Then she detects the smell of cigarette smoke that's just settled on a jacket nearby, then something warm in her hand. Maya's fingers, closing around hers.

"I've missed you, Mom."

Dear God. Kira almost walks back to the car and sits there instead. Our children have no idea what they do to us.

———

After they finish talking to the priest, Peter and Teemu remain inside the church, surrounded by infernal noise, doors slamming, chairs scraping and clattering as they're set out along all the walls. The echo reminds them of an ice rink.

"What happened with . . . Lev? Have you . . . talked?" Peter asks, as worried that he won't be heard over the noise as he is about being overheard.

Teemu looks at him as if to ask "Do you really want to know?" and of course Peter really doesn't. But he feels he ought to know.

"We left a message," Teemu says.

"Where?" Peter wonders.

Teemu scratches his freshly shaven chin and adjusts a few strands of hair in his perfect, swept-back hairstyle. Even his tie is impeccably knotted, white, like Peter's, they could have been mistaken for father and son.

"In his yard."

Naturally Peter regrets asking. He remembers his anger when he heard what Lev had done to Amat in the NHL draft, he remembers the barely veiled threats when Lev showed up at his house again, but he also remembers what the Pack did to him several years ago when they were unhappy with his work at the club.

When Kira got a phone call from a moving company because their house had been put up for sale without their knowledge, and when Tails called to say that someone had placed an announcement of Peter's death in the paper. There's a difference between forgiving and forgetting. Perhaps Kira could lower herself to accept a truce with someone like Teemu, but what Peter is doing now is very different. He's turned

Teemu into an ally. Sooner or later a person has to ask himself: if the person I used to fear is now my protector, which of us has changed sides?

When the congregation begins to pour into the church Peter feels like a wasp in a beer glass. He's standing next to Teemu and one by one men and women come over and shake his hand, the way they used to when he was general manager, some of them cast nervous glances at the company he's keeping, but plenty of them don't. Some of them shake Teemu by the hand as well. Out of respect for Ramona, perhaps, but also out of an appreciation of the political situation in the town right now. Everyone has heard about the trouble at the rink, and no one imagines that's the end of anything, everyone knows it's only the beginning. In a week's time Beartown's and Hed's A-teams will meet in the first game of the season. There may be times when you might want to mark your distance from men like Teemu, but this isn't one of them.

It takes twenty minutes to fill the church, and twice as long to explain to everyone left outside why they can't come inside. Ramona's funeral is conducted with open doors.

Maya sits next to Ana in the pew behind her mother and younger brother. When they see how slowly Peter walks toward the microphone at the front, they realize that his legs are so unsteady that he's afraid of stumbling. He's played hundreds of hockey games in front of thousands of people, but nothing on the ice could scare the shit out of him as much as having to give a speech. He adjusts his white tie, as uncomfortable as if it were a medal he hadn't deserved. The church falls silent and when he clears his throat it sounds much louder than he expected, it even makes him start, and the ripple of laughter from the congregation and the new silence that immediately follows leave him paralyzed. But then. Eventually, he manages to unfold a crumpled sheet of paper from his pocket and say:

"I . . . I'll keep this short. I . . . I couldn't decide what to say today. I don't want to stand here and pretend that I knew Ramona better than any of you. The truth is that I hardly knew her at all. Even so, I miss her the way you miss . . . well . . . like you miss a parent. I . . . sorry . . ."

He looks down at the sheet of paper, it's shaking so hard that the rustle can be heard all the way to the back row. He breathes in through his mouth, out through his nose, then tries stiffly to remember his speech:

"The only thing we could really talk about without falling out was hockey. One time I said to her that this sport is so strange, we devote all our lives to it and what's the best we can hope for, really? A few moments . . . that's all. A few victories, a few seconds when we feel bigger than we really are, a few isolated occasions when we can convince ourselves that we're immortal."

He pulls himself together and folds the sheet of paper up and presses it into his pocket, because he's shaking so much that he realizes it's becoming a joke. He doesn't know if it's the audience in the church or the one in Heaven that's worse, but he just does what he used to do in the locker room: bites his lip so hard that the pain and the taste of blood force his mind to focus:

"A few moments, I said to her, that's all this sport gives us. And then Ramona poured a large shot of whiskey and laughed at me and said: 'So what the hell is life, then, Peter? More than moments?'"

Teemu is sitting in the front row, his face motionless but with his fists quivering on his knees. Benji is standing alone right at the back of the church, as close to the door as possible, his tears dripping softly onto the stone floor. Peter tries to steady his voice. Three boys without dads. If you want to know who Ramona was and what she really meant to this part of the world, you only have to look at the desolation in their faces. Peter looks up and forces himself to say:

"That's what you left us with, Ramona. Moments. Stories. Anecdotes. No one could tell them like you. You were this town. You WERE this town. The whole of Beartown misses you now. Say hi to Holger. Good . . . good-bye."

He bows to the coffin and tries to walk back to his place without stumbling. He almost succeeds. As he sinks down next to Kira she reaches for his fingers, gently, gently, but just as she almost touches his skin Teemu's mournful grunt breaks the silence:

"Bloody hell! Now the beer in Heaven's going to be REALLY expensive!"

The laughter that explodes then, from hundreds of bodies but just as suddenly as if from a single mouth, is so loud and communal and liberating that it lifts every single person in there. It straightens their backs, drags them back up to the surface, like the intake of breath just before a goal and the roar immediately after. Peter laughs so much that Kira's hand just misses his when he raises it to wipe his tears. She sits there unmoved.

After the funeral, as hundreds of smiles stream out between the tears through the church door, Maya sits on the wall outside with her guitar on her lap, noting down all her feelings on her phone. One day it might become a song, but never one that she can bear to sing.

> *You said life was simpler here*
> *Maybe it is, it isn't clear*
> *If only it wasn't so isolated*
> *If only it wasn't so complicated*
> *Or complicated in the right way*
> *Who can say?*
> *If you love just as hard*
> *And hate just as hard*
> *If you pretend you can bear the load*
> *And secretly live by a different code*
> *Then maybe life is simpler here*
> *Maybe it is. To me, it isn't clear.*

Then she sees her mother come out of the church, alone. Her dad is still in there, surrounded by people who want to shake his hand. And Maya writes:

I'm a romantic who's never been in love, because children become
all the things that they see
I've always believed in everlasting love, which never happens,
yet it happened to you and he
But now, what to do?
Is it still he and you?
Mom, both of you are so weary now
Dad, both of you are so sad now
Such brittle and delicate and fragile dreams
Worn down so the wind can destroy you, it seems
When all that needs saying is:
I'll never get over you
Three small words of salvation:
I need you
I
Need
You

She's interrupted by Ana coming around the corner with a beer in each hand, Maya has no idea where she got them, but if there's anyone who can find alcohol in a churchyard, then obviously it's Ana.

"Who are you writing to? Your best friend?" Ana grins.

"Yes, but your fat head is blocking the signal!" Maya retorts, and slips her phone into her pocket.

Then the two young women sit on the wall and drink beer and insult each other, and on one side of them sit the two invisible girls they used to be. And, almost certainly, on the other side of them sits Ramona.

51

Truths

The concept of "truth" is hard to come to terms with, but for a local newspaper it's all but impossible.

The editor in chief notes with a degree of reluctance that she's thinking more and more about something her dad taught her as a child, the classical philosophical principle: "The simplest explanation is often the truth."

She doesn't attend the funeral, she wouldn't be welcome, journalists are tolerated around here, but no more than that. In Beartown people complain that the paper supports Hed because that's where its offices are. In Hed people complain that all the paper does is fawn over Beartown. There's no neutral ground. You're either for or against these people, there's no way to win, so she reminds herself that it isn't an editor in chief's job to do that.

Her dad suggested that he attend the funeral, because no one knows who he is, and after a lot of hesitation she eventually agreed. "But don't talk to anyone, just take pictures!" she demanded, and he promised a little too readily. She looked at him suspiciously, because he didn't look stressed and angry like he usually does, he was calm, the way he always was when she was growing up and he had made a breakthrough in his investigation into some politician or celebrity and knew that he "had the bastard now." "What have you found?" she wondered curiously, and only then did his face crack into a happy smile as he dropped a bundle of papers on her desk: copies of contracts she's never seen before. Now he's at the funeral and she's sitting here reading them in astonishment, thinking that you could lock the old man up in an empty room and he'd still emerge with state secrets.

At first glance the contracts at the top of the pile look innocent enough: they concern the sale of some land two years ago, the seller was the council, the buyer the local factory. Nothing odd about that, the factory wants to expand and the council wants more jobs, the price was in line with the market value, nothing for anyone to complain about. But beneath that contract her dad has placed copies of other contracts he's found: one concerns the sale of the same piece of land a short time later, this time sold by the factory and bought by Beartown Hockey. The sale price was considerably lower this time, so low in fact that if it was correct, the market must have collapsed in value by over ninety percent. It appears to be a terrible piece of business for the factory until the editor in chief sees the next contract: a couple of days later the factory buys another piece of land, right next to the factory, which everyone knows they've wanted to buy for years. The seller? The council. So that was the condition, the editor in chief concludes: the council couldn't sell the land cheap to the hockey club without someone noticing, so the factory agreed to act as a middleman in exchange for being allowed to buy the piece of land they really wanted.

That's bad enough, but that isn't the end of it: the next contract in the pile shows how, sometime later, the council bought *back* the same piece of land next to the ice rink, the land they sold in the first instance, from Beartown Hockey. But for much more money. Because now the contract doesn't just say "land," but also "building," because this exchange suddenly involves the hockey club's "training facility." The cost is divided into many small amounts over a long period of time, but in total amounts to millions. And that's not all: the next contract in the pile is signed on the same date by the same people, and commits the council to allowing Beartown Hockey to rent back the training facility it had just sold and carry on using it, almost for free.

The editor in chief sighs bitterly, because although she can hardly think of a more obvious way for the council to channel taxpayers' money into the hockey club, she knows it isn't a big enough scandal for anyone to be held to account. It's too complicated for most of her readers to understand, not exciting enough, not enough of a "good story" as her dad usually says. So why did he look so happy when he gave her the pile of papers?

She has to leaf through them all the way to the bottom to find out. There she finds not contracts but a printout of a photograph. It's fuzzy, but she can still see that it shows the parking lot down by the ice rink, her dad has written the day's date at the top and on the back he has written: *"There is no training facility!"*

She just stares at the photograph. Millions of taxpayers' money, but there's nothing there, not a single construction crane or barrier. They haven't even tried to make it look real, so confident were they that they'd never be found out. Because why would they? They've gotten away with everything so easily up to now.

The editor in chief leans back in her chair and tries to deploy all her journalist's training to question herself now. Is she being objective? Is she being fair? Because she can see Peter Andersson's signature all over this chain of documents, but could he really be the brains behind all this? It happened after he resigned as general manager, so why was he even signing these papers? Maybe he signed them without understanding the consequences? Maybe he was tricked into it?

No, she already knows what her dad would say to that: "Fish rot from the head down, kid. This is financial doping and it's been going on for years, and it started at the top. Peter probably resigned as general manager right before the deal with the training facility precisely to cover their tracks. What have I always taught you? If there seems to be several different explanations: choose the simplest."

52

Moments

Everyone needs to feel needed. For some people that's as important as desire and admiration and love. For others, particularly those who have devoted their whole lives to a team sport, it's more important than anything.

"Nice speech!" the old man says, shaking Peter's hand after the funeral.

There's a long line of other old men behind him who want to say the same thing. Everyone wants to shake hands, wants to talk a bit of hockey, several of them want to tell him that they miss him on the management team at Beartown Hockey and hope he can take Ramona's seat on the committee now. Peter doesn't know how to laugh that off, it's such a ridiculous idea, but like all ridiculous ideas it has a tendency to seem less ridiculous the more times you hear it.

"There's only number crunchers and analysts and shit like that everywhere in hockey these days, without people like you and Ramona there won't be any heart left in it! You win hockey on the ice, the way it was in your day, not by looking at data like they do now!" one of the last old men declares, and when Peter is left alone afterward he has trouble stopping himself from longing to get back in.

Not the way you long for the future, for the summer, or for a holiday, but the way you long to get back to yourself. To how it was "in our day," even though that time never really existed except in our filtered memories. You long to be the person you think you were, during some sort of youth when you tell yourself that life was uncomplicated, or the man you imagine you could have been if only you had the chance to do everything again. Not longing for that is difficult for most people, and for some it is all but impossible.

The church is almost empty now. Peter gathers together his few belongings and his many emotions and touches his fingers to Ramona's photograph one last time. It was taken by someone without her knowledge, because no one ever dared to try when she was aware of it, she's young, standing behind the bar with Holger with her arms up in the air, so someone has evidently scored a goal on television. Possibly even Peter.

"Only moments, eh, Ramona? Was that it? I reckon you could have given us a few more. Who am I . . . going to talk hockey with now?"

His voice grows thick and his eyes prick with that last sentence, and shortly afterward his whole face is burning with embarrassment when he turns around and realizes he isn't alone. Elisabeth Zackell is still sitting in her place ten rows back in the church, as if she's waiting her turn. The hockey coach and bar owner may not have shared anything that could be called a friendship, but for Zackell it was probably as close as she got, she used to eat boiled potatoes and drink lukewarm beer in the Bearskin, and insofar as it could be called conversation, she probably shared more conversation with Ramona than anyone else in the town. Ramona, of course, thought Zackell was a "bloody woman, a vegan, a teetotaler, and God knows what else," and even if she did manage to teach her to drink a bit of beer she could never cure her of the rest. But Zackell was good at two things, winning and keeping her mouth shut, and that went a long way. So when the old men in the bar tried to tell her how to train the hockey team, Ramona always snapped: "Do you want to learn about hockey? Really learn something? Then you shouldn't talk to Zackell, because you're too damn stupid to understand anything she knows!" No one knows anything about Zackell's feelings, perhaps because she doesn't have as many as the rest of us, or perhaps because she doesn't see the point in showing them, but when the Bearskin burned down two years ago, she was the one who ran inside to rescue Ramona. She ate her potatoes for free after that, but she still had to pay for her beer. After all, there had to be some sort of limit to charity.

"Sorry . . . I'll leave you two in peace . . . ," Peter says apologetically, and starts to walk down the aisle between the pews.

"Who?" Zackell wonders, genuinely taken aback and looking around her as Peter approaches.

"You and . . . I thought you were waiting to . . . ," Peter begins, but the hockey coach's face is as impassive as the lake.

"A lot of people seemed to like your speech," she says instead, looking as if she's really, really trying to find something to talk to him about, like an adult talking to a child when that adult really, really doesn't like children.

"Thanks," Peter says, then realizes that's the wrong word, because she never said that *she* liked it.

He's never figured out how to talk to her, not even when he worked at the club, but he learned to respect her determination. Ramona once told him that Zackell might not fit in in Beartown, but there probably wasn't anywhere on the whole damn planet where she would fit in better, because where the hell else would you put a coach like her? "On a team in one of those towns where people try to convince themselves that there are more important things in life than hockey?"

"I heard you'd resigned as general manager," Zackell suddenly says.

Peter can't help but burst out with laughter, and it echoes around the church.

"Yes, two years ago."

"Oh?" comes the reply.

"Are you serious? You've only just heard? I was actually your boss, Elisabeth," he smiles.

She replies, completely untroubled:

"I usually notice if someone leaves because they get replaced. But they haven't replaced you. I thought you were on holiday."

Peter's laughter dies quickly and awkwardly away. The club no longer has a general manager, the committee and Zackell herself share his former responsibilities, and considering that Zackell ignored every opinion Peter ever had about her job, he presumes that his absence must have been easy to miss. In an attempt to change the subject, he says:

"I heard you signed an extension to your contract as coach, congratulations!"

"For all the good that'll do. All coaches get fired," Zackell replies, and if she was the sort of person who made jokes, he would have assumed she was joking.

"Interesting reaction to a new contract," Peter smiles.

A few young men in black jackets have started gathering up the chairs at the back of the church, but Zackell shows no sign of moving.

"What's the best job you can imagine as a hockey coach?" she asks, and if she was the sort of person who teased people, he would have assumed she was teasing him.

"Coaching an NHL team," he replies.

"And which team in the NHL is the best?"

"The team that wins the Stanley Cup," he replies, a little more warily.

Zackell nods, showing a degree of patience that's uncharacteristic.

"In the past twenty years, sixteen different coaches have won the Stanley Cup. Of those sixteen, three still had their job five years later. Two left of their own accord, one retired, one got ill. The other nine were fired, five of those within two years. So, out of the best coaches in the world, only three of sixteen managed to hold on to their job for five years after winning the biggest title in the world. Do you know how long I'll have been at Beartown if I stay for the length of the contract I've just signed?"

"Five years?" Peter guesses.

"Five years! So obviously I'm going to get fired. Either we won't win the league this year, and then I'll get fired, or we'll win and get promoted to a higher league and then not win that, and I'll get fired for that instead. There's always a reason to fire the coach. You should know that, you fired Sune so you could employ me just because I am a woman."

"That was . . . hang on a minute . . . that ISN'T what . . . ," Peter starts to protest, but she just shrugs her shoulders.

"That was a mistake. Because the problem with employing a woman because it's politically correct is that it's extremely politically incorrect to fire a woman."

"Fire you? The club hasn't been this successful for years!" Peter groans, starting to understand why Ramona was always so drunk when she talked with Zackell in the Bearskin.

Then Zackell suddenly stands up and gets ready to leave, and says in passing:

"I'm going to look at a player tomorrow. Do you want to come?"

Peter tries to digest all this information at once.

"What? Tomorrow? Haven't you got training with the team tomorrow?"

"They can cope. Coaches are overrated. All teams will win a third of their games and lose a third of their games, it's the team that wins the remaining third that wins the league, and you know which team that is?"

"No?"

"The team with the best players. So I'm going to look at a player. Besides, I'm banned at the moment so I can't attend the training session."

"Sorry? Banned?"

"The committee received a complaint. I've broken one of the rules in that new declaration of values. If the players do that, they have to miss one training session, so I insisted that the same thing should apply to me. Do you want to come tomorrow or not?"

"What . . . hang on a minute . . . what were YOU reported for?"

Zackell sighs wearily:

"A woman contacted me to complain that one of the boys' coaches had said all the players on her son's team were useless, but that that could possibly have been excused if there had been any attractive mothers among the parents, only they were all ugly. And I replied that he definitely shouldn't have said that, because not *all* the players are useless!"

"And she didn't take that the way you intended, I imagine," Peter concludes glumly.

"No. She got very angry. And then she said that the boys' coach had said she was only angry because she hadn't had sex for so long because she was so ugly, so I said maybe that wasn't only because of her appearance but also her personality? So now I'm under 'investigation' by the committee because apparently that contravened the club's 'values.' It would have been different if I was a man, of course."

Peter wishes he had an aspirin.

"Hang on . . . do you mean that you wouldn't be under investigation if you were a man?"

"I mean that if I were a man, I'd already have been fired. They fired the coach of the boys' team instantly."

"I don't know what to say."

"Shall I take that as a yes?"

"To what?"'

"To you coming with me tomorrow to look at that player?"

She looks at the time impatiently, like someone who has to be somewhere.

"Why me? You've got Bobo and . . . ," Peter wonders, and then she says something that would be hard for most people to argue against, and impossible for him:

"I need your help."

———

"If you could choose, would you rather be important or loved?" the psychologist asked Kira not that long ago, and it's still nagging away at her, driving her mad. She's sitting in the car in the church parking lot thinking that she should have replied: "If you could choose, would you rather I paid your invoice or shoved it where the sun doesn't shine?"

Leo is cycling home from the funeral, Maya is walking with Ana, so Kira is sitting here alone waiting for Peter while the whole town wants to talk to him inside the church. It feels like she's stumbled into a wormhole and gone back in time, because now he's someone again and she's the one who just has to wait. She'd forgotten how much she used to hate herself for hating that so much.

She watches the people outside the car, many of them in Beartown Hockey tops as if this were a rally rather than a funeral, and thinks "stupid rednecks." She feels instantly ashamed, even though she doesn't say it out loud, because she knows this is what her mom always called "the worst kind of sickness: jealousy. Incurable!" Kira wishes she could be happy as quickly as these people. Explode with joy because someone manages to poke a puck into a goal in a game where all the rules are made up. She's always wished she loved something so unthinkingly, it looks like such a wonderful little bubble to live in, that belief that you're part of something much bigger than yourself. As if hockey cared. It doesn't give a damn about us, about anyone, it just *is*.

She envies hockey supporters the way she envies deeply religious people: for their blind faith. She will never be as important to anything as these people are to one another every time they're packed together in the stands.

"Kira?"

The man outside the car suddenly calling her name makes her jump so badly that she hits her head on the side window.

"Tails? What the . . . ?" she snaps back, and he takes that as an invitation to squeeze into the passenger seat.

"Hello!" he says, as if this were perfectly normal behavior.

"Hello?" she says as he closes the door and glances warily in the rearview mirror to see if anyone has seen him.

"It's such a shame," he says sadly, and she misunderstands and says solemnly:

"Yes . . . yes, sorry . . . I'm sorry, Tails."

He looks at her in surprise.

"Sorry about what?"

She blinks, feeling a little frustrated.

"I'm sorry . . . about Ramona. I know you were close."

Tails's head wobbles from side to side.

"Oh, I don't know about that, she probably mostly thought I was just a clown who never stopped talking."

Kira can't help smiling.

"We all think that, Tailcoat, but that doesn't mean we aren't close."

He brightens up so much that he could probably replace at least a hundred of those wind turbines the government wants to put up on every little hill around here. No one calls him by his real name, everyone calls him Tails, but very few are allowed to call him Tailcoat. He likes that best of all. As if there's only ever been one guy with a tailcoat.

"Yes, well, I'd like to talk to you!" he goes on in a tone somewhere between all the worries of the world and not a single worry in the world.

"Is it about that new office you offered us? I don't feel like talking about that, Tailcoat, God . . . my partner hates the fact that we don't have an office in a bigger town farther away and Peter hates the fact that we don't have an office in Beartown. Hed was a compromise, and I really . . ."

But Tails is already shaking his head defensively.

"No, no, it isn't about the office. I mean . . . obviously the offer of the office is still open! It's all sorted! But that isn't what I want to talk about. This is about . . . well, it's rather sensitive, you know . . . I don't want to sound cold. But Ramona was on the committee of Beartown Hockey and . . . well. You know."

Kira sighs so deeply that her rib cage never quite seems to settle again. Of course. Of course! It's always about the hockey club, even now. Before Ramona has even been laid to rest, she has to be replaced.

"I see. But if you want Peter to take her place, you shouldn't be talking to me. You'll have to talk to him yourself, I can't . . ."

So many images flit through her mind as she speaks, a thousand photographs of small moments, a whole life together with her husband. *Her* husband. Her *husband*. How much of him is there left to share? If she gives him back to hockey, will there be anything left for her? Can a marriage survive that, one more time? She feels like screaming out loud, venting all her frustration, but Tails merely shakes his head again:

"No. No. It isn't about that. Actually, yes, maybe it is about that, but not in THAT way. Okay: we have a spare place on the committee. But we don't want it to go to Peter. We want you to take it."

At first there's silence. Then the shock hits Kira so strongly that she almost slaps Tails across the face. Then she screams.

"What . . . seriously . . . what the f . . . what are you TALKING about? Why would you put ME on the committee?"

He's desperately trying to hush her, and that rouses her suspicions, which aren't exactly calmed when he says:

"Why not? Who knows this town and this club better than you?"

She stares at him for a long time, feeling confused, until the penny finally drops and she just feels stupid.

"You've done something stupid. You need a lawyer. That's why you've come to me."

Tails's chin swings left and right in agitation as he retorts:

"Don't insult me, and above all don't insult yourself, Kira. A lawyer? Couldn't I get hold of a hundred lawyers if I needed to? But we don't need them. We need the *best* lawyer. And I don't know anyone better than you."

Flattery is harder to withstand than a storm. Kira blushes when, instead of telling him to shut up, she hears herself say:

"Why?"

"The media are poking about in our accounts," he admits quietly, glancing in the rearview mirror again.

"The media? What for?"

"Nothing, nothing! It's just the local paper, that new editor in chief, she's full of big-city attitude, probably thinks she'll get some damn prize or something if she uncovers 'the hockey town's secrets.' You know how it is."

He falls silent and looks embarrassed, just for a moment, but Kira can still hear what he's almost saying. She heard it for years after she moved here with Peter, the way all the old men in the town wanted to know why the local paper "only writes negative stories about hockey?" when it was almost always cheering the team on. "Why is hockey always treated worst?" the old men would still complain, as if they were

a persecuted minority. "Horse riding has fatal accidents, gymnastics
has pedophile scandals, soccer clubs are owned by dictators . . . but in
the eyes of the media, hockey is still always worst!" They're forever
the victims, those old men, always persecuted, always the victims of
conspiracies. As if they themselves didn't make the rules of this game,
everywhere and always. Tails stopped saying things like that two years
ago, or rather he stopped saying them in front of Kira, but he probably
still complains when there are only old men in the room and the members of the club are preventing the sponsors from doing whatever they
want. They'd probably prefer the league table at the end of the season
to be decided by bank transactions. "You have to hit people like that
where it hurts: in their wallet," Ramona always said. That was actually
one of the last things Kira remembers her saying. So it should be easy
for her to despise Tails now. To dismiss him. But then he says:

"Kira, please, a lawyer on the committee would be good for us, that's
all I'm saying. We haven't got problems, but now that the council is
talking about merging the clubs or setting up an entirely new one, those
damn journalists have started digging, and you know what it's like: if
they find the tiniest little lead they'll concoct an entire labyrinth. We just
think it would be good to have a lawyer on the committee. To have you
look through the paperwork, just to be on the safe side. The club can't
employ you directly, that wouldn't look good, but if money's an issue
I've already agreed with the other sponsors that your firm would deal
with all the legal work related to the construction of Beartown Business
Park over the next few years. That's going to be lucrative, I promise! But
perhaps we could meet at yours tomorrow, at your home? That would be
better than your office, me coming to your house, then we'd just be two
friends talking, so to speak. If anyone sees us."

Kira doesn't meet his gaze, because she's too ashamed that she's
actually trying to persuade herself that she's interested in what he's
saying because there might be a lucrative contract for the firm at the
other end of it. Because that isn't true. What gets her interested is what
he says next:

"Obviously, this has to stay between us, Kira. Don't tell anyone. Not even Peter."

Kira is ashamed, of course, but it's a bit intoxicating, the thought of knowing the innermost workings of the hockey club. For once, finding out the town's secrets before everyone else. Perhaps she only wants to enjoy that for a very short while. Is that so wrong? Is she so terrible? She doesn't even want to think about that. So she asks instead:

"'If anyone sees us'? What do you mean by that? Who would see us?"

53

Pictures

The cell phone on the editor in chief's desk vibrates as a message arrives from her dad. She leans forward and sees that he hasn't written anything, just sent three photographs from the funeral. The first shows Peter Andersson going into the church with Beartown Hockey's most notorious hooligan. The second is of Peter Andersson coming out of the church with the coach of Beartown Hockey. The third shows Tails getting out of Kira Andersson's car.

Her dad didn't need to write anything beneath the pictures, because his daughter already knows what he's trying to say: How could the Andersson family claim not to have anything to do with Beartown Hockey now?

The Andersson family is Beartown Hockey.

54

Lies

"Are you going to be at home tomorrow?" Kira asks innocently.

In hindsight she'll think that her and Peter's biggest mistake when they argue is always the same: that they pull away when they ought to be reaching out, they raise their voices instead of lowering their guard, that they hold grudges rather than keep their ears open. But their worst sin, the very cruelest of all, is when they don't tell the whole truth and then convince themselves that this isn't the same as lying.

"How do you mean? Have you got something planned?" Peter asks, just as innocently.

They drove home from the funeral in silence, without holding each other's hands, he kept all ten fingers on the wheel and she made herself busy with her phone. Now she's made herself busy repotting the plants in the living room, and he's baking bread in the kitchen, and if she told her psychologist that, he'd probably have a stroke from the excitement: Peter is obsessed with creating something, Kira is desperately trying to keep something alive. When she comes into the kitchen to get water, they pass each other near the sink, he has flour on his fingers, she has soil on hers, they ask innocent questions and receive innocent replies. That's how easily one lie gets laid upon another:

"No, no, I was just wondering. I thought . . . I thought I'd work from home. So I can drive Leo to school if you're busy!" she says.

"Really? Well, yes, that would be good. I have actually got something to do, I was going to say no, but . . . well, it's so stupid, no big deal . . . but Elisabeth Zackell asked if I'd like to go and look at a player with her . . . ," he says tentatively, glancing at her.

"Really?"

"Yes? Is that stupid?"

"No, no, I didn't mean that at all! I was just surprised, that's all."

Peter strews some more flour across the counter.

"Like I said, it's just nonsense. It isn't even the club asking, just Zack-ell herself, almost as if we were . . . friends."

Kira holds a potted plant under the tap. She's so good at acting non-chalant.

"Well, in that case, I think you should go."

He kneads his dough. Is almost as good at it himself.

"You think?"

"Well, if she needs your help you don't mind doing it, do you?"

"Hmm, yes, maybe. We'll be driving there and back in a day, that's all, so I'd be back again tomorrow evening. Is that okay? Or do you need me in the office?"

He's a bit too eager to get her approval. She's a bit too quick to grant it.

"No, no, we'll manage. Go ahead. No worries."

He nods hesitantly.

"Well, then."

"Well, then," she nods.

Peter convinces himself that he's telling the truth, even though he isn't telling the whole truth, because he hasn't said how much he's hoping that this might be a way back into the club. Hasn't said that he's dreaming of hockey again because this, whatever it is that they have, isn't enough for him. Hasn't admitted that he needs to be needed, that it's important for him to be important. So he bakes his bread in silence and slides the trays into the oven. *Bang, bang, bang*, in they go.

In turn, Kira probably knows that she ought to tell him everything Tails said, that she's been offered the seat on the committee, but she convinces herself that she's a lawyer first and foremost in this instance. Not a wife. So she just looks at the compost being washed down the drain before she picks up another pot, empties it, then refills it once more. Dig-ging. Saying nothing.

55

Howls

Everyone is connected around here, and connected most tightly by the threads we never see. When we remember these days in hindsight we might perhaps note the dark irony in the fact that Ramona, who knew and influenced so many people when she was alive, had, through her funeral, a profound impact on people she never even met. Because everyone in Beartown is there mourning her loss today, so no one is at work, which means that the factory has to call all the employees who live over in Hed to cover the shift. One of them, a young woman who only finished her own shift a few hours earlier, goes in at once. Her mother tells her not to, but the extra money and the Sunday-work supplement are too good to turn down.

"Especially now, when there's so much to buy," the young woman says.

"Just be careful, don't wear yourself out, it's even more important that you look after your body now!" her mother insists, and the young woman rolls her eyes but still promises.

The machine she's in charge of today in the factory is old, the shift before hers reported a fault this morning but no one had time to tell her. She's tired, feels sick, and perhaps her head is a little dizzy. The investigators at the factory will ask thousands of questions about this afterward to try to make it look like it was her own fault. But the truth is that the mechanics couldn't get here because of the storm, and management didn't dare risk disrupting production, so they faked the repair form and let the machine run. There should always be two people operating it, but because they're short of staff today the young woman ends up there on her own. The health and safety officer is already arguing with the factory's management about so many other things that no one had spared any thought for the fact that the emergency stop button is too far away if you're on your own and something gets trapped. No one who hears the howl will ever forget it.

56

Teammates

After the funeral two hockey players who didn't attend it are hanging around on the other side of the road. They both wanted to pay their respects to Ramona somehow, but one is shy and the other ashamed, so neither of them managed to persuade themselves to go inside the church. It isn't until the door opens again and people are coming out that the ashamed player notices the shy player standing twenty yards away and goes over to him.

"Hello!" Amat says.

Mumble nods gently in response. His lips move to form a reply but nothing comes out. They stand next to each other with their hands in their pockets, looking at the church.

"I . . . couldn't bring myself to go in. Everyone just wants to ask if I'm going to play hockey again," Amat says quietly, because with Mumble he suddenly feels he can speak freely.

Mumble just nods slowly, but the look in his eyes shows that he really does understand, so Amat doesn't feel too ashamed to ask:

"Maybe we could train together one day? Like we used to last year? I need to get in shape. I don't know if Zackell will take me back on the team but I need to find somewhere to play. I . . . I *need* to play again, if you get me?"

Mumble nods. Both because he gets it, and because he really would like to train with Amat again. He used to hate those darting wrists and the skates that could change direction in the air, the shots that seemed to come out of nowhere, but now he misses the challenge. Hockey needs to be difficult.

"Maybe we could ask the caretaker if we could use the rink one evening, or we could just play on the lake if it freezes soon?" Amat says.

Mumble's nods are more eager now. That also counts as a language.

Benji takes the back route around the church with his jacket pulled up over his head, like a cat padding as quickly as it dares to avoid being seen, in the hope that no one will stop him and want to talk about hockey. In the middle of the low rumble of hundreds of mourners' subdued conversation it's lucky that he recognizes the sound of size 14 sneakers running, because at least then he has time to brace his knees and dig his heels in to save his back from breaking when Bobo throws himself at him in a hug like a fully grown dog who thinks he's still a puppy.

"BENJI! BENJI!!! SHIT I DIDN'T EVEN KNOW YOU WERE HOME! HOW ARE YOU?" the delighted lummox manages to blurt out before they've even finished hugging.

Benji slips nimbly out of his embrace and hushes him at first, then laughs.

"Seriously, Bobo, have you done anything except eat since I left?"

"Have you been eating at all? Wasn't there any food in Asia or something?" Bobo grins, so happy that he's skipping about on tiptoe until he can no longer resist throwing himself into another hug.

"I've missed you too," Benji sighs. Maybe it sounds sarcastic, but it's true.

There's a special sort of love that you can't get from your mates, only from teammates.

"Amat! Mumble! Look who's here!"

Bobo's voice carries high above the crowd when he catches sight of his two teammates on the other side of the road and immediately starts dragging Benji over there. Benji, Amat, and Mumble unite in directing a shared "Shhh!" at him, seeing as the last thing any of them wants is to attract attention, and the last thing you ought to do if you don't want to attract attention is be in Bobo's company.

"Bloody hell, Bobo, do you want a megaphone? I don't think all the dead heard you!" Benji sighs, and Bobo looks at him the way you do when you don't understand a word of what's being said but are still just as delighted.

"Maybe we could . . . go somewhere else?" Amat suggests when he sees people in the churchyard starting to glance curiously in their direction.

Benji nods quickly, just as keen to get away from there, so they start walking, and it only takes a few hundred yards for everything to feel the same as normal. Four guys of roughly the same age talking about hockey. Benji nods toward Amat's stomach and asks if he's "been training hard lately?" Amat smiles and says, "It's complicated," then asks if Benji has been doing any training, and Benji says: "You know me. I get into shape by resting." All four of them laugh and then Bobo gets a text message and then two more, and when Benji and Amat start teasing him that maybe he's got a girlfriend now, they aren't prepared for the fact that that's exactly what he's gone and done.

Tess texts that her parents aren't home, if Bobo wants to see her. "We need to come up with a plan that keeps my brothers busy," she says, so Bobo turns to Amat, Benji, and Mumble and asks, with the biggest, most naive eyes in the entire forest:

"Can you do me a favor?"

What teammates could say no to that?

When Bobo says he's going to get "some wheels," Benji, Amat, and Mumble are expecting something normal, so when he returns to pick them up they can barely contain themselves.

"What's that? A . . . campervan?" Amat wonders, looking from one end of the ridiculously long vehicle to the other. It looks about a hundred years old.

Bobo nods happily.

"Yes! I got it from Dad! He got it from his hunting team. They all thought it was a write-off, but I've been fixing it up, one bit at a time."

"One bit at a time? You've got quite a lot of 'bits' left, haven't you?" Benji smiles as he gets in.

The campervan is so rusty and buckled that he and Amat entertain themselves for the whole trip finding things that are actually in one piece. For a very short while they think that the door to the glove compartment is intact, but a moment later Benji is sitting with both it and half the dashboard in his lap.

"Your dad didn't have anything a bit more stable to give you? Like a skateboard with three wheels or something?" Benji grins.

"Seriously, Bobo, did you do something bad to your dad? Is he angry with you?" Amat laughs, then tells Benji and Mumble about the time Bobo drank some of Hog's vodka, and had heard that you should top it up with water afterward so it didn't show. It was all fine until Bobo put the bottle back in the freezer where Hog kept it, and the following morning he had to explain to his dad how vodka was able to freeze solid.

Everyone laughs except Bobo, he looks so deep in thought that in the end Benji has to ask something you hardly ever want to know the answer to:

"What are you thinking about, Bobo?"

Bobo gives him an honest reply, because he can't do otherwise:

"I was thinking how crazy freezers are. Just think, if you put a piece of meat with a best-before-date of tomorrow in the freezer, then leave it for a month, then when you take it out it's still okay to eat! It's like you've stopped time! Freezers are time machines!"

Benji's eyebrows disappear beneath his hair.

"Out of all the things you could be thinking about . . . that's the sort of thing you go and pick?"

"Don't you? I don't understand why everyone isn't thinking about things like that the whole time!" Bobo replies, very seriously.

Benji and Amat laugh, Mumble stays quiet, not because he doesn't appreciate the humor, but because he's the only one thinking about where they're going. Bobo is in love, Amat probably hasn't realized how serious the conflict between the towns is, and Benji, of course, is the same as always: not afraid of anyone. But Mumble is weighed down with anxiety, because they're heading straight toward Hed and he knows what's going to happen when these guys show themselves there.

There's going to be trouble.

57

Different hells

Johnny and Hannah are having one of those rare moments when they both finish work at almost the same time. They really ought to buy a lottery ticket every time that happens. He picks her up at the hospital, they kiss in the car like two teenagers, and Hannah laughs out loud at how silly he is when he tries to go further. She tells him to take her home first, like a damn grown-up, but then the van won't start and then it's lucky for him that she loves him so much, because otherwise he'd have heard a few things considerably worse than "silly."

He gets out to check what might be wrong, and only then does he notice that he's got four missed calls on his phone. In just a few minutes? Just as he raises it to his ear to call the station, he hears the car door open and Hannah's voice calling:

"Darling? They've just called me! I have to go back in!"

"Johnny? We need you at work!" a voice yells at the same time from the fireman's phone.

Johnny sighs. As does Hannah. They smile at each other across the hood of the van. At least they got a few minutes together, like silly teenagers. That's something.

Then they run.

The production floor at the factory in Beartown has always been political dynamite. It can determine the outcome of an entire council election. Two years ago one local politician, Richard Theo, ran a campaign based, at least on the surface, on unemployment, but it was really intended to implant the words "Beartown jobs for Beartown people" in people's consciousness. Obviously that was when the factory in Beartown was short of jobs, now there's more like a shortage of workers, but a good slogan is hard to shift. The staff who come from Hed are still prone to suspect favoritism every time a management position or a better shift is given to someone from Beartown rather than one of them. Under those circumstances, it's even easier to interpret what happens to the young woman today as something other than an accident.

The young woman is from Hed, the woman who normally works that machine is from Beartown. She's on maternity leave at the moment, but her replacement is also from Beartown, so he was at Ramona's funeral. So the young woman from Hed was a replacement for a replacement, and the machine has been reported as faulty but cleared by a stressed manager, who by coincidence also happens to come from Beartown.

Richard Theo's words are easy to remember then. Beartown jobs. Beartown people.

When the machine seizes up, the young woman doesn't know why. She calls for help from her workmates to clear the blockage, but none of them has time. She's worried about messing up her own productivity figures in the factory's new digital monitoring system if she waits too long. So she tries to sort it out on her own. The machine splutters, then starts up again when she isn't expecting it, and in one horrible breath she's sucked in under iron and cog wheels and hears bones being crushed. Only then, when her lungs finally find some air, do the screams make their way out of her. It feels like they're never going to stop.

———

Afterward we'll talk more about the trouble than about the accident, more about what the men did afterward than about what happened to the young woman. The fire brigade has to cut her out of the machine, she's almost unconscious with pain but her injuries don't appear to be life-threatening. It isn't until her brothers, who also work at the factory, manage to force their way through the crowd to Johnny that he realizes why Hannah was called back into the hospital again.

"She's pregnant! She's pregnant!" the brothers are howling hysterically.

The ambulance doesn't stop for anything along the way, the fire engine right behind it, followed by the brothers' car, the sirens sweep deafeningly through the forest. When they thunder into Hed the entire community stops.

"Out of the way! OUT OF THE WAY! MAKE SPACE!" Hannah yells as she rushes out of the hospital entrance and clears a path for the paramedics from the ambulance. Johnny has to throw himself out of the fire engine and literally grab hold of the brothers to stop them getting in the way.

When the stretcher bearing the young woman is wheeled in and all the staff rush after it, there's a patch of blood left on the pavement. The brothers are left standing there, staring at it impotently. At roughly the same time two young men roll into the parking lot in a small car. They're hardly more than boys, with naive expressions and facial hair that wouldn't hold up against a decent towel, and they have no idea what's happened. They don't even work at the hospital but on a building site right next to it, but they're playing music that's a bit too happy, and they have a little bear in a green hockey sweater hanging from the rearview mirror. That's enough. The brothers take this as a provocation, they need one desperately, anything at all.

The fight breaks out so quickly that not even Johnny has time to throw himself between them. Before the other firemen get there, the two young construction workers from Beartown are lying on the ground beside their car, battered and terrified. The firemen pick them up and brush them down, but it's too late to calm them down, they jump into their car and drive away from there in panic, and on the way to Beartown they call their friends and tell them what the brothers did. A couple of their friends work at the factory. A short while later, one of the brothers' girlfriends has her car vandalized in the parking lot there. She has a small Hed Hockey sticker in the rear windshield.

Things always happen quickly when everything goes to hell.

———

The world never feels bigger than when you're holding the smallest person. You never feel more incompetent than when you realize that you're suddenly someone's parent and that no one is planning on stopping you. "Me?" you blurt out when the midwife says you can go home: "But I've got no idea what I'm doing! You're going to let me look after a human being?"

If you're a parent, you probably remember how you carried your first child at the start. How carefully you drove home. How incomprehensible everything was when you sat motionless in the dark to make absolutely certain that that tiny, wrinkled creature was still breathing. A minuscule rib cage rising and falling, and every so often a little whimper from the horizon of dreams, or just a whistling sigh that had you performing lonely little pirouettes on tiptoe around the crib. The way your heart reflexively grabbed hold of your lungs when five tiny fingers took hold of one of yours and didn't let go.

Being a midwife is strange, because if you do your job perfectly you have to start again almost immediately, waving off one family and welcoming another at once, without ever getting to know anyone. Perhaps that's the deepest injustice of the job: that the children and mothers who take the longest time and who you really get to know are the tragedies.

What was it Hannah said to Ana in the forest a few days ago? "You have to make the most of the happy endings whenever you get the chance." Hannah hopes that she does this herself, that her soul has bathed in tears of joy and the breaths of newborns enough times, because otherwise she doesn't know how she's going to get through today.

There are two women lying in beds at opposite ends of the hospital. One gave birth in the forest during the storm and will soon be able to take her little son, Vidar, home to their little house in Beartown. The house he'll remember as his childhood home, the lawn he played on, the little roads he learned to ride a bike on. His snowball fights, his hockey games, his first broken heart, and his first great love. His whole life. The other woman will be flown to a larger hospital where she will need operations for several broken bones, and when she does eventually come home to her little house in Hed, it will be without the child she was expecting.

The carriage her partner thought was way too expensive but which she thought she could pay off with the extra money for working a Sunday shift is sitting in the hall of their home and she will crumble in despair. In a few weeks her partner will find the box containing the crib in the storeroom, the one she kept nagging at him to put together, and he'll sob so hard that it feels like his ribs will break. For the rest of their lives they will always walk past the display windows of the sports shop and think that there's one bicycle too many in there. A pair of skates too many. A hundred thousand adventures and trees to climb and puddles to jump in too many. A million uneaten ice creams. They will never be woken too early on holiday mornings, never whisper-shout "Quiet!" when they're talking on the phone, never put small gloves on the radiator. The greatest fear, the tiniest human being, will never be theirs.

The factory will make the mistake of calling the whole incident an "accident" in the paper tomorrow, but everyone in Hed will say that's what it's called over there. In Hed it is called what it was: "the fatal accident." Soon there will be muttering around breakfast tables and in staff-rooms that if it had been the woman from Beartown, the one who should have been standing at the machine, the one who gave birth to a healthy and happy baby and named him after one of Beartown Hockey's worst hooligans . . . then the politicians would have turned the factory upside down in their hunt to find the guilty parties.

Perhaps it isn't true. It's just so easy to agree with.

———

Hannah and Johnny are still at work today, so Tess picks up her youngest brother Ture from his friend's house. At first he runs on nonstop about the differences between various superheroes, then he quickly moves on to the philosophical question "why do people think you're naked if you're only wearing socks but not naked if you're wearing underpants, because you have the same amount of fabric on your body?" She's too distracted by her phone to listen. Tobias and Ted meet up with them along the way and all four siblings start planning dinner. Their dad told Tobias that they could order pizza, which he'll get told off for by their mother seeing as she's already told Tess that they can't, but Tess said that Ted had said that Tobias had said that Dad said that they could, their mother was too tired to argue about second- and third-hand sources, so now it's going to be pizza. Sometimes it's good that there are four of you, because you can use each other in diversionary maneuvers.

"Are you listening, or what?" Tobias wonders, seeing as Tess is writing on her phone but doesn't appear to be taking notes about his extremely specific order for extra cheese and deep-pan base but no olives and only red peppers and definitely no yellow, and so on and so on.

"Mmm," she says, but Ture manages to sneak a look at her screen and exclaims:

"You're sending a text! Who are you texting! Why are you sending love hearts?"

Tobias's and Ted's eyes open wide, as if their sister's lizard-skin had slipped out by mistake from beneath her human disguise.

"Are YOU sending love hearts? Who the hell to?" Ted says.

Tess, who isn't exactly known for sending the most emotional text messages in the family, turns bright red from equal measures of embarrassment and fury.

"If you want a long life you'll mind your own business!"

If Tobias and Ted had dared, they would have tried to snatch the phone from her hand, but even Tobias isn't that careless with his health. Ture, on the other hand, isn't old enough to have understood how angry his big sister can get when she actually gets angry. So he clambers up on her back via her legs and manages to catch a glimpse of the screen and blurts out:

"Bobo! She's sending love hearts to him, BOBO!"

Ted manages to stop his little brother from being thrown into some bushes when Tess shrugs him off her, and Tobias jumps out of the way when it looks like she's about to start kicking out at random. She's hyperventilating and all three brothers back away with their hands in the air.

"Sorry, sorry . . . ," Ture is whispering.

"We were only joking . . . ," Tobias and Ted agree.

Her phone vibrates in her hand. Once, twice, until she looks down and sees what Bobo has written. Even then, despite the fact that she's so angry she could hide snakes in her brothers' underwear drawers, she can't help smiling.

"Can you keep a secret?" she asks them.

Of course they can't. But they promise to try really, really hard. Because somewhere deep beneath all the mischief and misbehavior they love their big sister, and this is the first time they've seen her in love.

58

Shots

Bobo stops the campervan outside Tess's family's house and is so nervous that he manages to blow the horn when he's trying to turn the engine off.

"Nice, Bobo, really discreet!" Benji smiles, and Bobo blushes.

The residential area is unusually quiet for a Sunday. The temperature is too low for anyone to be cutting grass, but no one has pulled out their snowblower yet, most people are indoors preparing for the elk hunt. Even the dogs seem to have taken the day off.

Ted and Tobias are standing in the small yard next to the house, firing pucks on a practice ramp they built with their dad when they were little. Ted is playing as if he's in the final of the World Championship, Tobias as if he's too tired for this shit but can't just let his younger brother win. Ted doesn't even notice the campervan, but his big brother saw it in the distance from the corner of his eye. When Benji is the first to get out Tobias stiffens, stops holding the stick as a tool and starts holding it as a weapon.

"What the hell is *he* doing here?" he splutters, first angry, then scared.

He agreed to let his sister invite Bobo but she didn't mention anyone else, especially not that psycho, Benjamin Ovich. Tobias always stands with the Hed supporters during all the A-team's games, so he knows all too well who he is, he used to be known only as "Number 16" here in Hed, as if he were a genetic experiment. Everyone in Hed was delighted when he abandoned hockey and moved away two years ago, Tobias included, because they hated him the way hockey supporters can only hate psychopaths they'd have loved to have on their own team. The first thing Tobias thinks now is that this is a trap, that Benji is here to beat him to death, as revenge for the fight in Beartown's ice rink yesterday.

Benji is wearing just a T-shirt, he took his white shirt off after the funeral and the only top Bobo had in the car was obviously a green one with a bear on it, so that's the first thing Tobias sees. He's only fifteen and Benji is twenty, but Benji recognizes his body language, and how prepared he is for trouble. For a few moments man and boy evaluate each other, and even if Tobias is tall and muscular for his age, he grips his stick in a way that says he knows perfectly well what little chance he has.

Then Bobo unfolds himself from the driver's seat and Tess lets out a yelp of delight from the kitchen window in a way Tobias has never heard his sister do before. His grip on the stick relaxes slightly. Then Mumble and Amat get out of the side door of the campervan and only then does Ted look up with eyes radiant with giddy admiration.

"Toby! Toby! That's . . . that's . . . do you see? It's . . . he's . . . Amat! It's Amat!" he whispers, just loud enough for absolutely everyone to hear how embarrassing he is.

Tobias breathes out in a long groan toward his brother and feels his heart rate slow down a little, but he doesn't take his eyes off Benji. Benji just looks amused and lights a cigarette.

Bobo pulls a large wicker picnic basket out of the back of the ramshackle campervan, then can't get the door to close. This doesn't appear to bother him. Tess comes out of the house as if she's having to force her feet not to leave the ground and fly off with her. They do try their hardest, their very hardest, not to wrap themselves around each other's necks in front of his friends and her brothers. She invites him into the kitchen and he immediately starts asking thousands of questions, about her and the house and the family. She isn't used to that, she's used to boys only wanting one thing, so in the end she asks what he's got in the basket. He shows her. Pasta and meat and vegetables and stock and cream. She laughs and thinks that she was right after all, boys really do only want one thing.

They want to make dinner.

Of course Amat can see the way Ted is looking at him, like a child who's caught sight of his idol. Usually Amat hates that, not long ago he'd have gone straight back to the car and demanded to be taken home at once, but he isn't a superstar anymore. Arrogance is a luxury.

So instead he asks: "Do you want to play?"

He'll persuade himself it was for the thirteen-year-old's sake, but if he's honest he just wants to play. Sooner that than talk.

Ted can't manage more than a nod, so they play, he and his idol. Mumble silently shows little Ture what to do when he stands on goal, because that's the good thing about seven-year-olds, they don't require any dialogue. Ted tries a wrist flick and Amat gently corrects the way he angles his knee and how to put more force into the shot. When he tries a shot himself, Ted, Ture, and Mumble just stand and stare.

"How do you do that? That's like a bolt of lightning!" Ted gasps.

Amat can't look him in the eye and mutters:

"It's just training. Your shot right now is better than mine was at your age."

Dear Lord, it's a miracle that Ted's chest doesn't explode at that. He's spent so many hours on this practice ramp that once a nosy neighbor on the street threatened to report Johnny to Social Services, because she was annoyed by the noise and because she thought the boy's parents were forcing him to go outside and fire pucks at the wall all one June evening when it was pouring with rain. Hannah had to go around and explain that she WISHED Johnny could force the kid to do something, because then maybe it would force him to come inside and EAT! But Ted's obsession comes from within. And nothing can be done about that.

If that neighbor had looked out of her window now perhaps she would have changed her mind, because one day she'll boast about who her neighbor was. Ted and Amat are laughing loudly as they challenge each other. Amat wins most rounds, but when Ted wins one he races around the yard with his arms in the air and Ture on his back, as if he's won the whole world. Amat gives Ted a high five when he comes back. Maybe one day the two of them will play in the NHL together.

In the kitchen Tess and Bobo are giggling and a love story begins. Out here others begin. None of them are such a bad idea.

While the others are firing off shots on the practice area, Benji leans against the campervan and lights his second cigarette in five minutes.

"Are you going to hit me with that stick, then? Because if you're not, you might as well put it down, or I won't stop worrying that you're going to poke yourself in the eye," he calls across to Tobias in a tone that isn't remotely unfriendly.

The fifteen-year-old realizes he's still holding the stick like a weapon in his hands and quickly lowers it and looks down apologetically.

"Sorry. Sorry. There's just so much trouble with people from Beartown recently. When you got out of the car with that top on I just thought . . . shit, here we go . . ."

"I feel too sick to fight," Benji confesses.

"Hungover?" Tobias wonders tentatively, because Benji is sweating even though he's standing there in just a T-shirt when the temperature is below freezing.

"I don't have a problem fighting when I'm hungover. Only when I'm sober," Benji chuckles. He hasn't had a drink since he got home to Beartown and is starting to feel the whole of his body cry out in protest.

As he says this, Tess's laughter rings out through the kitchen window and Tobias raises his head in surprise like a meerkat emerging from a hole.

"Is my sister LAUGHING?"

"Doesn't she normally do that?" Benji wonders.

"Only when Ted or I hurt ourselves."

When Tess bursts into another fit of giggling Benji smiles:

"I think maybe Bobo has just told her that he spends a lot of time thinking about how freezers are like time machines. You can choose whether to laugh with him or at him, but you can't help laughing."

"Time machines?" Tobias repeats.

Benji shakes his head in resignation.

"Forget it. It's far too complicated. How old's your brother?"

He nods over at Ted.

"Two years younger. Thirteen," Tobias replies.

"THIRTEEN? What do you feed him? Rottweilers? He's the size of a bloody house!"

Tobias nods proudly.

"He's hot shit at hockey. He's gonna be better than Amat."

"Better than his big brother, then?" Benji teases, and is taken aback when Tobias replies instantly:

"He already is. He just doesn't know it yet."

Benji taps the ash from his cigarette and almost looks like he wants to pat the boy on the shoulder.

"You should play for Zackell, our trainer over in Beartown."

"Ted should be playing for her, not me."

"No, you should be. She likes players who know their own limitations."

Tobias realizes this is a compliment, he's just too much of a Beartown-hater and too much of a fifteen-year-old to be able to accept it.

"Shame your team's full of sons of bitches and faggots!" he blurts out from pure instinct, then feels like knocking every last tooth out of his own mouth afterward, assuming Benji doesn't do it for him.

But Benji's expression barely changes as he replies:

"We *aren't* sons of bitches. But you might be right about the rest."

"Sorry . . . I didn't mean that," Tobias mumbles awkwardly.

Two years ago, when everyone in both Beartown and Hed had just found out what Benji was, Tobias was standing among the Hed supporters when the teams met. He remembers what they screamed at Benji. The way they threw dildos onto the ice. It had been so easy for Tobias and all the others to explain it away afterward, that's just what hockey is like, you look for your opponent's weakest point, it's never really personal. Not racist, not sexist, not homophobic. You're just trying to win. But that explanation feels much thinner now that the man he was screaming at is standing in front of him. The fifteen-year-old feels himself shrinking with shame. Benji, however, just grins and replies:

"You're sons of bitches and faggots too. You just don't know it yet."

Tobias laughs in relief, grateful that he still has all his teeth left when he plucks up courage to ask:

"Is it true that you knocked down four players on the other team once?"

"Who told you that?"

"Dad. I think you're the only Beartown player he's ever liked. But he'd never admit it."

Benji lights another cigarette.

"It was probably only three. And none of them knew how to fight on the ice, so it doesn't really count."

"Can you teach me how to do that? How to fight on the ice?"

Benji smokes his cigarette, and for a few moments he hates himself for coming back to the forest where this is all he is. Someone capable of violence. Someone to fear.

"So you think your brother can go as far as Amat? What about you, how far can you go?" he asks, to avoid having to answer Tobias's question.

"Not that far. Hed's A-team, maybe, unless they get promoted, because then there wouldn't be room for me. And if they don't, you know, shut down the whole club."

"Why wouldn't you be able get further than that?"

"Because I'm not like Ted. I'm like you."

"Like me?"

Tobias's neck flushes from the sudden rush of blood.

"Not like . . . gay, I mean, I'm not . . . like *that*. Not that there's anything wrong with that, but I mean . . . as a player. I don't want hockey enough to become as good as it demands. I don't live for it. Not like Ted."

Benji laughs, and the smoke catches in his throat.

"Is that what you think it was like for me?"

Tobias nods, still feeling embarrassed, but with total conviction.

"If it wasn't, then you'd still be playing. No matter what we yelled at you from the stands. If you'd really loved hockey, nothing would have stopped you."

Benji rolls his eyes, stubs his cigarette out, and starts patting his pockets to find more.

"Bloody hell. Zackell *really* would have loved you . . ."

Tobias tries to take this as a compliment, he really does.

In the kitchen Bobo is making dinner and asking questions, because his mother taught him that those are the two best ways of courting a girl: "Because girls aren't used to either of them." Bobo knows he doesn't have much else to offer Tess, so he's hoping it will be enough. It is.

When Tess's laughter reaches across the yard again, Tobias stares at Benji's face for a long time, still slightly wary, then he asks very seriously:

"Is he okay? That Bobo? I know he's your friend. But is he . . . an okay guy?"

Benji has big sisters too, so he understands the question. So he replies:

"You could probably find better, but you could definitely find a hell of a lot who are worse. He's the kindest, most loyal person I know. But seriously? What your *sister* sees in him, God only knows!"

Tobias thinks for a long, long time before he looks down and answers:

"She can probably see that he's friendly."

"Is that good?" Benji asks honestly.

Breathing through his nose, Tobias pokes around his shoelaces with the stick.

"She doesn't want a remarkable life, just a . . . normal one. Our dad's a fireman, our mom's a midwife, we've spent our whole childhoods getting told we're being raised by heroes. The sort of people who run toward fire. But Bobo isn't a hero, and my sister can probably see that. He wouldn't run toward fire, he'd run toward her."

Tobias falls silent with embarrassment when he realizes how silly that might sound. Benji runs his fingers through his long, messy hair and smiles uncomfortably. Neither of them can relax in the lack of words that follows, so Benji looks around and catches sight of a patch of ground on the drive where water has leaked out of a split hosepipe, freezing an area of about one square yard. He goes over, followed by Tobias, and when they get there, out of nowhere Benji grabs hold of Tobias's top and jerks so hard that Tobias loses his balance and falls to the ground. Benji catches him at the last moment and says:

"You need to think about where you place your feet. Then use my own weight against me."

Then Benji teaches him how to fight on the ice. You couldn't find a better teacher.

Over on the practice ramp Ted finally plucks up the courage to ask Amat:

"What was the NHL draft like?"

Mumble is showing Ture how to move if he wants to be a goalkeeper, but glances anxiously at Amat when he hears the question. He's pretty certain no one else has dared to ask straight out like that, like a thirteen-year-old with dreams too big to be contained by his chest. Amat fires off another shot, then replies thoughtfully:

"Everyone was the best. You encounter good players here at home, in the league, at training camps, wherever. But everyone you meet over there is the BEST where they come from. They've been ready for the draft all their lives. It's . . . pressure . . . a hell of a lot of pressure. That's the only way I can describe it. Heavier than I've ever felt. Like being suffocated."

Ted fires a puck. Leans on his stick.

"My dad says pressure is a privilege. If you don't feel pressure, that's just because you've never done anything valuable enough for people to have expectations of you."

"Can I recruit you as my agent if I get to the next draft?" Amat smiles.

"In a few years' time you can be my agent!" Ted blurts out, and never in his entire life has he said anything so cocky to another person.

He feels ridiculously ashamed and Amat can't help admiring that, because he can hear himself in the boy. He remembers the way he used to play hockey before he only played hockey for everyone else's sake. The next shot he fires off whistles through the air and almost tears the net to pieces.

"I'll never be able to shoot that hard, no matter how much I practice," Ted whispers, impressed.

"You don't need to practice more, you just need to think less," Amat replies.

The teammates from Beartown are in a good mood when they leave the house in Hed. Bobo kisses Tess so cautiously on the cheek that Benji mutters:

"I've seen people be more sensual when they seal an envelope, Bobo."

Bobo's face turns dark pink and even Mumble laughs out loud. He's never had a gang of friends, has never experienced a day like this, when you just hang out with each other for hours without really doing anything at all. This lack of expectations is new for him, as is the laughter, which is why he drops his guard enough to nod in agreement when Bobo offers to give him a lift home.

"See you at training tomorrow!" Bobo calls out as they drive off, unfortunately so loudly that the lights go on in every house along the street.

The campervan drives off toward Beartown and Mumble goes inside his house, but it's too late, everyone has already seen who dropped him off. A short while later someone throws a stone through the window of the apartment he shares with his mom. A message from the hockey fans in the area is written on it in red ink, and it is as unimaginative as it is effective:

"Judas! Die!"

59

Youth

A child died in the hospital today. There are always people who claim it isn't a child until it's born, but Hannah has never been able to get her head around that line of reasoning. The grief is the same, and the guilt, if all children are your children, then everything is always your fault.

Late in the evening she's sitting at her kitchen table at home in Hed, exhausted and worn out from crying, until in the end she's just empty. One of her colleagues drove her home from the hospital and they didn't say a word to each other, the only thing Hannah could think about was something Ture asked when he was four or five years old: "Do you get old in Heaven, Mommy?" Hannah didn't understand the question, so her youngest son reformulated it in frustration: "Do you still have birthdays when you're dead?" When Hannah admitted that she didn't know, he whispered disconsolately: "So what happens to the babies who die in their mommies' tummies if they never get big? Aren't they allowed to play? Not even in HEAVEN?"

It was one of those moments that hit her extra hard because everything with Ture was the last time. The last child. She's the mother of four children and that's enough, oh my, it really is more than enough, but still . . . something happens to you when you realize that it isn't a choice anymore. Children never let you forget that you're growing older. Ture is seven now, Tess seventeen, with him everything is things Hannah won't do as a mom again, and with her daughter everything is things she's never done as a mom before. "Small children, small problems, big children, big problems," one of her colleagues said just after Tess was born, but of course that isn't true. It's the mistakes that get bigger. Hannah's own mistakes.

She rests her forehead on the table. She's had such a long day, but sadly that's no excuse, because, as she's always telling the children: "We don't make excuses for our behavior in this family." Our own orders are always the hardest to follow. Several hours have passed since Tess slammed the front door behind her and disappeared, the argument went so fast and it was all Hannah's fault, she knows that. She arrived home exhausted from the hospital, her feet and lungs aching, even her skin hurt, so she was already close to exploding. It started with her finding a piece of rubber trim on the drive that looked like it had fallen off a car. She might not have thought any more about it if one of the neighbors, the nosy cow who's always complaining about Ted practicing his shots, hadn't marched over from her yard to announce that Hannah's children had had a "party" all afternoon. She might have let that go too, because of course Tobias and Ted denied everything, but even if Ture was old enough to know that you don't tell tales, he was still young enough to be bribed with chocolate. By the time Hannah had found out from him precisely who had been here and why, and that Tess now had a boyfriend and that they had been alone in the house while her brothers had been in the yard, she was already on her way up the stairs, blinded by anger and fear and the illusion of betrayal.

A long day, no excuse, but one of the most unfair things about having three younger siblings is that the way you're raised will always be based on expectations. So Tess was punished because she has gotten her parents used to expecting her to be the sensible, reliable one, the one her mother never had to worry about. So Hannah stormed into her room with the very worst of all things a parent can say:

"I expected better from you, Tess!"

That's really just another way of telling a teenager that she ought to make more of an effort to lower expectations for next time. Hannah knows that, deep down, but this was one of those occasions that almost all parents experience at some point, when we start shouting and can't stop. Disappointment with our children is always just disappointment with ourselves, and nothing has a longer braking distance than that. So Hannah yelled at her daughter and was totally unprepared for being yelled at in return:

"You haven't even asked what happened!" her daughter shouted, and instantly regretted not saying what she meant: that her mother hadn't asked how she *felt*.

Because her mother ought to know. Everything the daughter has learned about real love has been learned here at home.

"I shouldn't have to ask! You were supposed to look after your brothers and instead you brought a boy home! And a boy from BEARTOWN, at that! Do you even know what happened today? There was a full-blown fight at the hospital, you could have . . . ," the mother yelled, and the daughter shot back instantly:

"IF TED AND TOBIAS BROUGHT GIRLS HOME YOU'D JUST BE HAPPY, BUT YOU'RE SHOUTING AT *ME*? DO YOU THINK YOU OWN ME OR SOMETHING?"

Hannah will claim that she was too exhausted to back down and apologize then, but sadly the truth is that she was simply too proud. Mothers and daughters know how to wound each other in totally unique ways, possibly because daughters often carry the guilt of their mothers' consciences, until they end up arguing about sins that they haven't even committed.

"Tobias and Ted can't get pregnant!" Hannah snapped. That's how little time it takes to create one of those moments that mothers collect and wake up regretting in the middle of the night.

Children's screams aren't their best weapon. Silence is. The only advantage parents have is that it takes kids years to realize that.

"Do you really have such low expectations of me?" Tess whispered.

Then she strode past her mother and walked downstairs, and her mother is so used to this child being the one she doesn't have to worry about that she didn't even react at first when the front door slammed shut. She didn't comprehend what had just happened. But it didn't open again, her daughter didn't come back, and by the time Hannah rushed downstairs and out onto the drive, she was gone.

So now Hannah is sitting alone in the kitchen with all her regrets. Johnny hasn't come home yet, Ted and Ture daren't even come downstairs, so Tobias ends up doing that. Of course. The child she's always worried about most, has always had the lowest expectations of.

"Have you called Dad and told him Tess has gone?"

With her forehead still pressed to the table, Hannah mutters:

"No, no, are you crazy? If she's at Bobo's he might go over there and . . ."

She stops herself before she says something stupid, but her son knows exactly what she means anyway. He says nothing for a long while, then sighs:

"That Bobo's okay, Mom. He's kind. He adores her."

"THAT isn't what this is about . . . ," his mother says defensively, but the words dry up in her throat when she hears how much she sounds like her own mother.

Tobias doesn't sit down at the kitchen table, he just touches her shoulder with his fingertips and says:

"What's that thing Dad always says about hockey players? That stuff about the leash?"

Hannah bites the inside of her cheek and mutters:

"'You have to trust the best ones and let go of them, because if you resist they'll just chew through their leash and then they're gone forever . . .'"

"That's how it is with Tess," her son says.

Hannah puts her hand over his fingers and makes him squeeze her shoulder tightly before she whispers:

"Is this when I lose my daughter, is that what you're saying?"

Tobias isn't smart enough to know the answer, but he is smart enough not to lie, so the only response his mother gets is silence and his nose pressed against her neck.

———

There's no life like the life of young people. No love like first love.

The campervan rolls into the Hollow and Bobo and Benji drop Amat off outside his apartment. In every locker room they have grown up in, they have been told how important it is to "play your own game" and to "direct the match." Not stand around waiting for something to happen, but do something yourself.

Amat is all too aware that he ought to apply that to his pride now. He stands there in the parking lot, waiting and hoping for Bobo to ask if he'd like to come and train with the team, instead of simply asking himself. It goes too quickly, like the first kiss or the last "sorry" said to who or whatever you are about to lose, and if you don't seize the opportunity perhaps you'll end up spending your whole life wondering what might have been.

But Amat can't get the words out and Bobo is looking at him with eyes that steadily get more nostalgic and less hopeful. They'll soon be grown men, and all they will talk about then as each year passes will be more about memories and less about dreams. This is the end of the age when everything is still possible.

Bobo raises his hand in a sad farewell, Benji touches two fingers to one eyebrow in salute. Amat gives a brief nod. It's been a fun day, a really fun day, one of the last truly carefree days.

The campervan turns and drives away. Some kids are running around the yard playing with sticks and a tennis ball, and as Bobo drives past they wave and call out to him:

"Are you selling ice cream?"

"Get a real car, you loser!"

"Even child molesters don't have cars as ugly as that!"

Bobo just laughs, the kids in the Hollow have always been a bit more loudmouthed than everywhere else, but Benji rolls down the window on his side and sticks his head out, and that shuts the children up at once. He jerks the door handle hard, as if he's about to leap out, making them jump. It takes a moment before their little hearts start beating again, and Benji and Bobo laugh as they drive away. The mouths of the kids behind them start up again at once, all of them arguing with each other, "I wasn't frightened, YOU were frightened!"

"Do you remember when we were that small?" Bobo grins.

"You were never that fucking small!" Benji grins back.

Bobo has to concede that there's a degree of truth in that. When he pulls out onto the main road his phone rings, and even if he tries to hide it, his face lights up so much when he sees the name on the screen that he almost drives into a ditch.

"Hi! Hi! No, nothing! Now? Come to mine? Yes, of course . . . but what about your parents? No, I'm coming, I'm on my way!" he chatters.

Benji sighs when he ends the call.

"If you're going to get Tess, I'm coming with you. You probably shouldn't be in Hed on your own if you're planning to sleep with one of their girls . . ."

"How did you know it was her?" Bobo wonders, and Benji laughs so hard that the whole car rocks.

"It's good to see you in love, Bobo. Really good. You deserve it."

"Seriously?" Bobo whispers uncertainly.

"Seriously," Benji assures him.

They set off along the road between the two towns and pick Tess up, she's waiting where the forest ends and the houses haven't yet started, she couldn't wait to get out of Hed. She just says she's had an argument with her mom and Bobo doesn't ask any questions and she loves him for that, the way he always lets her explain what she wants to explain, no more, no less. Benji drives the campervan back, Bobo sits in the back with Tess's head on his shoulder, his creaking skeleton trying to contain feelings that are far too big for it.

"Is this going too fast for you?" she whispers.

"Everything has always gone too fast for me, I'm not very quick," he whispers.

"Will you forgive me when I get really angry with you?" she asks.

"What have I done?" he asks anxiously.

"Nothing. Yet. But sooner or later you'll do something, if it's going to be you and me now."

She feels his heart pound like a jackhammer beneath her cheek.

"You can get as angry as you like, as long as you don't leave me."

"Deal," she whispers.

Then they head into that very first, best silence of a relationship. When everything is safe. When everything is us. One day they will get married and have kids of their own and Tess will say the same thing to Bobo then that she once heard her mom say to her dad: "If we get divorced, I hope we don't part as friends. I hate it when people say that. If we get divorced as friends, that means we don't love each other enough to be able to hurt each other anymore. So if you love me, really love me, you need to love me so much that it drives you mad." He will never stop.

"Bobo?" Benji asks from the driver's seat as they pass the Beartown town sign.

"Yes?"

"Can I buy this campervan off you?"

"No."

"What? It's completely broken down, but hell, I'm starting to like it, it feels like me!"

Tess laughs. Bobo smiles and replies:

"You can't buy it, Benji. But I can give it to you."

"Seriously?"

"Seriously."

There's no life like youth, no love like first love, no friends like team-mates.

60

Talent

$\mathcal{L}$ackell picks Peter up early on Monday morning. Her Jeep is rusty, his old tracksuit top has grown tight, the whole world has gotten older since he was last on his way to watch hockey.

"What's that?" Zackell asks, nodding at the bag in his hand.

"Bread!"

"Bread?" she says, as if the word were particularly exotic.

He offers her some but she lights a cigar instead. He waits for her to explain where they're going, but evidently she can't see any reason to say. They drive for one and a half cigars until he finally loses patience:

"Seriously, Elisabeth? Do you want me to just sit here without you even telling me which player we're going to look at? If I'm going to be any use, I need to be prepared!"

"Don't worry, you won't be much use," she replies bluntly between two long puffs.

He frowns.

"You said you needed my help?"

"Did I? Maybe I did. But I don't. It's enough for you to be here. You can sleep now, the drive's going to take six hours."

"Six HOURS?"

"One way."

"But I'm in a hurry to get home!" Peter lies, and feels ashamed, because if he was, he wouldn't be here in the first place.

"The papers are in the back, if you feel like having a look," Zackell offers without giving the slightest indication that his opinion will make any difference.

Peter considers trying to pretend that he has enough ego left to ask her to turn the car around, but that would be pointless. So he sighs and reaches for a folder on the backseat, opens it, sees a picture, and raises his eyebrows.

"Hang on, I recognize this guy. I went to look at him a few years ago, he was . . . no, hang on . . . this guy's name is 'Aleksandr,' so it can't be him. The other guy's name was . . ."

"It's the same guy. He's changed his name," Zackell informs him.

Peter leafs through the folder. She's right, it is the same guy. Five years ago, when he was fifteen years old, he was one of the brightest talents in the whole country. He was the same age as Beartown's golden generation, led by Kevin, so Peter kept a close eye on all the competition back then. He and Tails even had a grand plan to try to persuade the kid and his dad to move to Beartown, so they traveled to a tournament to watch him play. That turned out to be a waste of time because the boy never showed up. His team said he was injured, but Peter heard from the general manager of another club that that was a lie: "They left him at home. A God-given talent, strong as an ox, can take any amount of beating! But he can't be coached, that one. Bit of a diva, discipline problems too. Misses training, argues with his coaches, refuses to pass the puck, won't take instruction, can't play on a team. Huge shame, he's going to throw away his entire career." The general manager was proved right, during the years that followed the boy was thrown out of three different junior teams, and he argued and moaned his way out of every opportunity until the phone stopped ringing. He's twenty years old now, and already a has-been. Sadly there are a number of players like that in every generation, Peter knows that from experience, they live off their innate talent until they hit their teens, but as soon as demands start to be made of them they kick back.

"I remember him as . . . something of a troublemaker," Peter says cautiously to Zackell.

"The season starts one week from now. If he wasn't a troublemaker he wouldn't still be available," she replies.

Zackell never builds teams, she builds gangs of bandits. Peter recognizes the headache he's starting to get now, because he had it every day when he was general manager.

"I wouldn't advise you to recruit him, but you won't pay any attention to that, so perhaps you can tell me what you see in him?" he therefore says wearily, expecting Zackell to fire back some sort of pithy retort as usual, so her reply surprises him:

"There's a common misconception that hockey players follow leaders. They don't. They follow winners."

"And this . . . Aleksandr? Is he a winner? Has he even been in a club long enough to win anything? He seems to have been thrown out of every club he's been in, but you think we can change him?"

Peter feels ashamed of saying "we," because he can hear the hopefulness in his own voice.

"No. Players can't change. But there's nothing wrong with Aleksandr, he's just misunderstood," Zackell replies.

"In what way?"

"All his coaches have tried to fool him into thinking that hockey is a team sport."

––––––

Tails takes great care to make sure that all his staff see him arrive at work each morning. He walks through the storeroom, asking questions and making jokes, shaking hands and slapping backs, talking loudly and laughing louder. He may be the boss, but he's never been the sort of man people naturally follow, hockey was merciless when it taught him that lesson, he became the team captain's best friend, but never team captain himself. So he has to fight for his authority, has to be seen and heard and remind everyone who he is, even if some of his employees maybe laugh behind his back when he leaves. What matters is that they know who he is.

He goes to his office and waits an hour. When he finally sets off for his meeting, he sneaks out the back way. The light in his office is still on, his jacket is hanging from its hook, his phone is still on his desk, as if he's just popped out to the bathroom. His car is still in the parking lot, the window still smashed above its Beartown Hockey sticker. He's still hoping, with increasing desperation, that this will provide a topic of conversation for the locals, as well as a distraction for the newspaper. If he can just get everyone talking about Hed's hooligans instead of Beartown's accounts, maybe there's a chance that he can sort out all his problems.

He rolls his shirtsleeves up and sets off on his old bicycle toward the smart houses. The supermarket and warehouse have grown so much in recent years that it takes him several minutes to escape their shadow. He used to take pleasure in that, but for a while now he hasn't been able to see his life's work for what it is, only for what it could become. And, more than anything, how quickly it could be lost. The only business secret he has ever possessed is his optimism, but that's looking pretty shaky right now. One of his contacts in the council has called to tell him which documents the editor in chief's father has gotten hold of. Tails isn't an idiot, he was aware that this might happen, but he wasn't prepared that a local reporter would be so smart. Or so persistent.

Hardly anyone really knows what the word "corruption" means, but Tails has actually looked it up: "Abuse of public influence for private gain." He's often repeated that silently to himself. People often accuse him of not having a conscience, but he can't help thinking that he's nothing but conscience. Sure, maybe he has abused "public influence" and massaged a few rules, but has he gotten any private gain from it? No. Quite the opposite. He loses money every day by sponsoring Beartown Hockey. Everything he does is for the good of the club and the community. His moral disclaimer is as simple and effective as that.

Hardly anyone knows what the word "success" means either. They think it's a mountain summit, but Tails knows better, there's no summit, just a never-ending climb. Either you continue to claw your way upward, or you get dragged or kicked down. If you stop for a moment to enjoy the view, someone stronger and hungrier will appear from below and take your place. That's how the world of business works, that's how communities work, and that's how hockey works. A new match, a new season, a new battle for promotion or relegation. The fight never ends. You always have to find thousands of little ways to stay ahead of everyone else.

So when is it enough? When do you finish? Why do you keep going? Possibly never, possibly not before your own funeral, possibly just because you want your life to have had some meaning, and this is the only thing in the world you have ever felt you could influence.

"Those bastards, they've never loved anything," Ramona once said when they saw the supporters of the big city teams on television, clearly more interested in eating hot dogs and popcorn than in the hockey game down on the ice. "They don't care, they never lose control of themselves because nothing means that much to them, they don't hold anything sacred except their own reflection," she said, and obviously Tails knows that plenty of people in Beartown regard him the same way. Perhaps Ramona did too. Most days he just accepts that, someone has to take on the role of bad guy, just like when he used to play hockey and would scrap by the boards so that Peter and the other stars could shine out on the open ice. But some days, when he feels that all he gets for all his work is ingratitude, he wishes that someone would ask what he personally has risked to save Beartown Hockey. So he could answer: "Everything."

He has the two sets of the hockey club's accounts on the back of his bicycle, the one that was handed in to the Tax Office and the other one, the one that only Tails and a few other people know exists. Now, for the first time, he's going to show it to an outsider, and once she's seen everything she could make all the politicians unemployed, put the club on the brink of bankruptcy, and send powerful men to prison.

Her own husband, first and foremost.

———

"Okay, we've got plenty of time, explain to me why hockey ISN'T a team sport?" Peter chuckles.

Zackell lights another cigar and replies as if she can't believe he doesn't already understand:

"It isn't a team sport until a player is grown-up and plays in an A-team. Because that's when games mean something. But up until then? In the junior team? Who cares who wins those games? The only thing that matters at that age is that the best players become as good as possible. Aleksandr has had coaches who yelled at him not to be selfish, to pass the puck, but what for? So that a mediocre teammate could score a goal? So that a mediocre coach could win some meaningless tournament?"

Peter has to admit to himself that he's never even thought of hockey in that way.

"So you mean, if there's a star on a junior team, the coach and all the other players should only exist to serve him, so that he can become as good as possible? Even if that means they lose games?"

"Of course!"

Peter laughs. He doesn't know how to tell her that she's simultaneously the least empathetic and the most empathetic coach he's ever met.

"Why did the kid change his name to Aleksandr? I didn't even know he was Russian."

"Half-Russian. That means that one of his parents is . . . ," Zackell begins, as if Peter were a very young and very foolish child.

"Thanks! I know what 'half-Russian' means!" Peter sighs.

"First you want me to explain everything, now you don't want me to explain anything . . . ," Zackell mutters in surprise.

Peter rubs his eyebrows.

"So if Aleksandr doesn't want to play for anyone, what makes you think he'll want to play in Beartown?"

"You."

"Me? I thought you said you didn't need my help."

"I didn't say that, did I? I said I didn't need your advice."

Peter groans so loudly that some saliva ends up on the windshield.

"It's as if my mom has been reincarnated as a hockey coach . . ."

"What does that mean?" she wonders.

He rolls his eyes.

"Oh, nothing . . ."

"You speak in riddles sometimes, has anyone ever told you that?" she points out.

"*I* speak in riddles? Bloody hell . . . ! Are you serious? So what were you thinking I might say that would make this guy want to play in Beartown?"

Instead of replying, Zackell merely says:

"Things must be going very badly between you and your wife at home."

"Sorry?"

She nods.

"The fact that you haven't asked that question before now suggests that you were really looking for a reason to get away from home."

Peter loses his temper and snaps:

"Why did you actually ask me to come with you?"

She replies, as if the answer was obvious:

"Because you aren't a winner."

He stares at her for half a cigar.

"So why am I here, then?"

With all the patience she can summon up, Zackell replies:

"I need to recruit a winner, because hockey players follow winners. But do you know what winners do?"

"No?"

"Winners follow leaders. That's why you're here."

———

Kira has compost on her fingers when she opens the terrace door. Peter has gone off with Zackell, Leo is at school, Maya evidently has more days off from college for the funeral seeing as the dean down there appears to think that Beartown is in another country, so she's off somewhere with Ana. The house is empty. Even so, Tails makes his way through the yard instead of coming to the front of the house, and they eat Peter's freshly baked bread in the kitchen with the blinds drawn.

"How are things otherwise? How are the children?" Tails begins, and Kira rolls her eyes.

"Please, Tails, you crept in here like a spy, we've known each other long enough for you not to have to start this conversation by lying that you care about the children."

"Lying? When have I ever lied to you?" he exclaims, horrified.

"Only all the time, nonstop, every time we've met since the very first time I met you around twenty years ago . . ." She smiles, and he starts to laugh.

This is his greatest asset: he laughs easily, loudly, and infectiously, always pushing forward.

"Okay, okay, Kira. No bullshit! Like I said: we need a lawyer on the committee. We've got a few problems with the local paper. I don't know how much they've uncovered so far, but I need . . . well, *you* need . . . we should be prepared for the worst. I need to know how deeply we're in the shit if certain things . . . come to light."

She shakes her head wearily and pours coffee.

"Do you want an honest response, Tails? You don't represent the club, you're not on the committee, you're just a sponsor. You can't commission me on their behalf."

He waves his fingers dismissively, almost knocking his cup over without realizing.

"Let me worry about that. Just take a look at what I want to show you, okay?"

He dumps the accounts down on the table and Kira can't help feeling worried. At the start of the conversation she's angry about how differently she and Tails see the world, but at the end she's going to hate herself because of how little difference there is between them.

61

Smoke

The editor in chief and her father are shivering as they sit on cheap folding chairs on the dirty roof of the building that houses the newspaper's office. It isn't a very tall building, but it's located on a hill so you get an unexpectedly good view of the town. The day is barely halfway through but the daylight is already starting to fade and the cold is determinedly gnawing away at whatever warmth anyone may have absorbed from the sun.

"What are you laughing at?" the editor in chief wonders.

"When you were little and I asked where you wanted to live, you said New York. This isn't exactly New York, kid," her dad replies.

Lights are starting to go on in the buildings, a few cars are rolling through the streets, they can hear chain saws in the forest as a memory of the storm. But nature has started to recover, the people too, and the editor in chief has difficulty suppressing her curiosity at the resilience of both of those. She glances at her dad, he's smoking his pipe, she remembers that smell from when she was young, always a sign that it was a good day. He only smoked his pipe when he wasn't planning to drink.

"Thanks for not drinking, Dad," she says quietly.

The corners of his mouth twitch, not without some effort.

"I can't drink and work at the same time anymore. Not well, anyway. I'm too old to go into a fight drunk, you know."

She smiles.

"I know you think I inherited all my worst characteristics from you . . ."

"That's certainly what your mother thinks," he mutters.

"No. She knows I inherited some of the good ones as well."

He lets out a hoarse laugh.

"You're a damn good editor in chief, kid. I'd never have been any good. You have to care about people to do that job. You've got all that from her."

She closes her eyes and breathes in the pipe smoke. He missed large parts of her childhood. They never understood each other back then, but they do now. As a child she missed her dad, but as an adult she has gained a friend. A comrade. She wonders if she would have exchanged one for the other if she could do it all again.

He shuffles irritably on the folding chair.

"What's making that banging noise? Sounds like a damn gull has gotten caught in an air vent . . . ," he mutters and half stands to see, but the chair is too unsteady and his body too old to allow that sort of nonsense, so he sinks back down again resignedly.

"It's just the kids down in the street firing balls at the garage," his daughter replies, well used to this.

He pricks up his ears and listens, guesses that they're of middle-school age, one of them yells "4–4", and another shouts furiously: "No it's not! You're CHEATING! It's 4–3!!!" The next bang is the sound of them fighting and their small bodies crashing into the garage door.

"This place . . . I don't know if I've ever been anywhere where everyone competes the whole time the way they do here . . . ," he says with a grunt.

His daughter smiles.

"That's what I said. The people around here are like you. You can't live without a fight either."

He coughs to hide a laugh of agreement.

"No idea what you mean. I'm the embodiment of peace and calm."

She reaches over and pats his arm, very briefly, but that means everything to someone who thought he had burned all his chances of being a dad again. Then she gestures toward the community below the building and explains sadly:

"It was you who taught me this, do you remember? To seek out the highest point in a town, because you learn something from seeing the whole place at the same time."

"And what have you learned about Hed?"

She points:

"There's a school over there. I walk past it each morning, it reminds me of the one I went to, do you remember? In the middle of town. Kids from McMansions mixed with children from public housing. Some turn up on ramshackle bicycles, others get dropped off by parents in expensive SUVs."

"Are you trying to say you were poor because you cycled to school? We lived five minutes away from . . ."

"No, no, be quiet! You've got the wrong end of the stick! I'm trying to say that you and mom did a good thing: my friends came from all different parts of society. It's not like that anymore, the rich parents saw to that, now my old school is full of kids in designer clothing who go on skiing holidays. And they're trying to do the same thing here. There's a smart residential area in Beartown called 'the Heights,' with the most expensive houses in the whole area, and the parents up there are trying to set up their own school so their kids won't have to socialize with the poor kids. If they succeed, it won't be long before the same thing happens here in Hed."

"What are you getting at?"

"You asked what I'd learned about Hed. I read recently that the big hockey clubs are trying to make the top league in the country a closed shop, the income from the television rights is huge and they can't risk getting demoted. So they want to stop all the smaller clubs, all the Heds and Beartowns, from getting all the way to the top. The rich want to shut out the poor, same thing everywhere, always. It's no excuse, but . . . well, sometimes I can't help thinking that's why people are the way they are in these towns. They have to fight the whole time. Maybe even cheat. Otherwise they don't stand a chance."

The pipe smoke curls around her dad.

"It's a nice view, but don't let your conscience get in the way of your intellect, kid. When you publish everything we've found out about the training facility in Beartown, someone there will dig up the same sort of crap about Hed. When this is all over you could very well have killed off both clubs. But that's your job."

His daughter doesn't open her eyes. She asks the question even though she doesn't want to hear the answer.

"What makes you think Hed has fiddled with the books as much as Beartown?"

His reply is more sad than cynical:

"Everyone fiddles with the books these days, kid. Have you seen the players' wages now? And the tax rules in this country? If everything was done properly, no one would stand a chance. When a hockey club down south came close to bankruptcy the council bought 'the inventory' of the stadium for several million to prop up the accounts. The inventory of a stadium that the council ALREADY owned. If those politicians had nine backsides each, they still wouldn't have had enough for all the different seats they're trying to sit on. One of the biggest clubs in the whole country calls the local bus company 'the bank' because the club never pays for transport to away games, but the bus company never demands payment because they know that at the end of the year the council will step in and pay for everything so the club doesn't go bankrupt. There are elite clubs whose finances are so weak that they're in bankruptcy, so all the wages are paid by the state's wage guarantee, but they carry on recruiting players by getting a sponsor to pay and sign all the paperwork. And they're allowed to carry on playing games! How is anyone who follows the rules supposed to compete with that?"

She slowly breathes in the last of the smoke from his dying pipe.

"Now it sounds like you're on their side, Dad . . ."

He sighs.

"Damn right I am. I'm old and sentimental and I don't drink anywhere near enough anymore so I'm no longer mean. But YOU can't back down now! We need to tell the truth about Beartown Hockey, even if it crushes everything and everyone out here."

His daughter breathes the way you do when you're getting ready to jump off a cliff:

"Do you think my conscience is making me a bad journalist?"

Her dad struggles up from his chair.

"No. Your conscience is what makes you the best sort of journalist, kid. Okay, let's go inside, it's bloody cold out here and that damn banging is driving me mad! Next time you're going to have to find a hockey club in Hawaii for us to kill off!"

62

Idiots

What's the hardest thing about ice hockey? If you ask a hundred coaches you'll get a hundred different answers, all just as confident, all just as unwilling even to contemplate that they might be wrong. That's because they're all wrong.

Because the hardest thing about hockey, the very hardest of all, is changing your mind.

Tails's expensive white shirt is transparent with sweat and his watch, the size of a teacup, clatters against the edge of the table. His shoes are so expensive that it would have been cheaper to buy the whole alligator. Kira knows that because the only recycling Tails understands is recycling jokes. Every time Peter has had a barbeque in the past twenty years and asks how Tails would like his steak, Tails replies "Just frighten it a bit with your headlights and put it on the plate!," and Peter laughs EVERY time. Could there be a lower threshold for friendship? One of Tails's alligator shoes has no lace, because it got caught in the bicycle chain on the way here, his fingers are black and cut from when he tried to disentangle it, he's always been a real dolt. When Kira was little she always laughed when her mother used that word as an insult, but when she grew up and met Tails she realized exactly what it meant: he's a genuine, pure-blooded dolt.

But he isn't stupid. Unfortunately. So when he's drunk his coffee and Kira asks him to explain why they had to meet in secret, he pulls his laptop from his bag and plays a video. He filmed it himself in the stadium, it shows preschool children being interviewed after their coaching session. Tails's voice comes from offscreen and Kira is reluctantly impressed by how good he is with the children. Adults always think of him as bullish and pushy, but children often interpret those characteristics as straightforward and honest.

"What do you like best about hockey?" he asks a gang of boys, and they offer different versions of the same thing: Scoring goals. Being with your friends. Skating really fast. Winning. But then a girl of around six or seven appears on the screen, her body is slighter than all the others but the look in her eyes is bigger, and when Tails asks her the same thing she looks totally uncomprehending. "What do you mean, like best?" she wonders with her training top hanging around her knees. Tails pauses the video and smiles proudly at Kira:

"That girl's so good that we let her play with the boys, you know, but we had to stop because the parents got so angry that she was destroying their sons. *Destroying* them, Kira. She's a phenomenon. A cherry tree. You know that's what we usually call the brightest talents around here? Like Peter was at her age!"

He presses play once more. His voice asks: "Can you say your name for the camera?" The girl on the ice replies as if she were laying siege to an enemy fortress: "Alicia!" Tails's voice replies: "Okay, Alicia, I'm just wondering what you like best about hockey. It could be anything at all. What do you like best?" The girl stares into the camera for a long, long time before she replies, in a very weak voice and with scorching honesty: "Everything. I like everything best."

Kira doesn't know how the mother of any child could look at that little girl and not want to step through the screen and take her in their arms and promise that everything is going to be okay. Especially when Tails goes on to ask: "So what do you like *least* about hockey?," and the girl replies with sudden tears in her eyes: "When you have to go home."

Tails switches the video off. Kira is rocking on the kitchen chair beside him, and snaps:

"I've got two teenage children and I'm on my goddamn way into menopause, Tails! Don't you think I'm emotional enough as it is?"

Tails mumbles an apology and surprises her by actually sounding completely genuine when he replies:

"Sorry. I just wanted . . . before I show you all the club's problems . . .

to remind us both about what we're fighting for here. What's at risk."

He's a dolt. But he's not stupid.

———

It's a small ice rink next to an empty parking lot. Peter has never been there before, but that doesn't matter, he still feels at home. He recognizes all the sounds, every echo and smell, even the light. But above all he recognizes the feeling of . . . now. In every part of life, out there in reality, he is conscious at every moment of the past and the future, but ice rinks leave no space for that. In here everything is now, now, now.

"Are you ready?" Zackell asks.

"For what?" Peter asks, and soon wishes that he hadn't.

Down on the ice he sees Aleksandr. Built as if someone had designed a hockey player in a laboratory. Tall, broad shoulders, clearly incredibly strong, yet still very supple in his movements. Every muscle moves correctly, his skating technique is perfect, even his wavy shoulder-length hair is annoyingly fault-free. Yet there's still something not quite right. He looks older than twenty, both in his eyes and in the way he moves. He's skating in a figure eight, and every glide is practiced and perfect, yet lacks the keenness of youth, he's like a circus horse running in rings, tied by a rope. His dad is standing in the middle of the ice yelling instructions, Aleksandr hardly seems to hear, when Peter approaches the boards the dad yells louder and more intently, but the twenty-year-old doesn't raise his tempo at all.

"He got nervous when he saw you, you're his idol," Zackell points out.

"Stop that, Elisabeth, that boy isn't old enough to know who I am," Peter smiles modestly.

Her eyelids flutter as if the fact that he's so slow-witted physically hurts her.

"Not him. The father!"

Only then does Peter understand, because he really isn't smarter than that. He isn't here because Zackell needs help persuading Aleksandr to move to Beartown, she needs help persuading the dad. Peter recognizes the man, even if they never met, he's in every ice rink: didn't quite make it as a player himself, but every day he convinces himself that was only because he didn't get the right coaching. So now he's living vicariously through his son, a spoiled and bored talent who has had everything served up to him on a silver platter, but who can't even be bothered to reach out and take it. Aleksandr has probably had private tuition since primary school, his dad probably sponsored his junior team and traveled the length and breadth of the country taking him to expensive training camps and prestigious tournaments, but what happened? The boy didn't have the desire. All teenagers have a window when they have the chance to fulfill their potential, but no one is ever prepared for how quickly that window closes.

"I'm guessing Beartown wasn't their first choice. How many clubs have been here before us?" Peter asks quietly.

"At least ten," Zackell replies blithely.

"And none of them wanted to recruit him? Isn't that a warning sign for you?"

"Who says they didn't want to? Maybe that wasn't what he wanted?"

"Why wouldn't he want it?"

"None of them offered him the chance to play against an NHL pro."

"What?"

Zackell is carrying a bag on her shoulder, and she opens it and pulls out a pair of gloves and skates in Peter's size.

"You're joking?" he says.

"I'm not very fond of jokes," Zackell informs him, and walks toward the boards.

Aleksandr's dad comes over at once, wide-eyed and enthusiastic, but Aleksandr doesn't even bother to say hello.

"Hi! Hello! Big fan, big, big fan!" the dad calls to Peter and Peter nods back, feeling incredibly uncomfortable.

"Peter wants to join in," Zackell announces.

"Wow! What an honor! Did you hear that?" the dad calls back to his son, who could hardly look less honored.

"So maybe you could take a break for a while?" Zackell suggests.

At first the dad doesn't seem to understand, then he looks affronted, then resigned.

"I'm normally always on the ice, I'm . . ."

"But you could make an exception for an old NHL pro," Zackell declares, without a trace of a question mark.

The dad glances sheepishly at Peter, still unwilling to give way. He tries to sound annoyed when he's really just feeling humiliated:

"Of course, of course . . . but my son's PHYSICAL game is his real strength! Have you seen how big and strong he is? He's fantastic in front of goal, no fear at all! And I've taught him to play just like the elite clubs play. I have a whole system for how I set up the cones out here, how will you be able to see that if I'm not there to demonstrate? I think . . ."

Like all dads, he isn't at all prepared for how little Zackell cares about what he thinks.

"A system? I'm not here to look at a system."

The dad opens his mouth to protest, but she's already turned away. In the end he moves very reluctantly toward the stands. In the meantime Peter is just as reluctantly putting on the skates, so slowly that if Zackell hadn't disliked touching other people so much, she'd probably have kicked him onto the ice herself.

"Aleksandr? This is Peter Andersson. He's played in the NHL and is your dad's idol! If you can get past him you can have my car!" she calls to the twenty-year-old.

Peter and the dad just laugh. But Aleksandr turns around for the first time and looks more interested.

"Are you joking?"

"I hardly ever joke," she assures him, and puts the car keys on the top of the boards.

The twenty-year-old has had a hundred coaches. Very rarely does any of them surprise him.

"What happens if I fail?" he wonders suspiciously.

"Why would you fail?" Zackell wonders genuinely.

Aleksandr smiles warily, as if he's forgotten how to do it. His dad is sitting slouched in the stands, looking ten years older than he did on the ice. When their eyes meet, there's no love in the twenty-year-old's, as if the circus horse has just realized that the rope has been cut. Peter sets out hesitantly onto the ice behind him and can already feel that this is going to end with groin strain and a couple of seriously painful visits to the bathroom tomorrow. Aleksandr fetches an extra stick for him. When he sees the older man take a couple of shaky warm-up circuits, as if that was likely to make any difference, he asks:

"How long is it since you played in the NHL?"

It isn't mocking, just genuine curiosity, but the situation alone rouses something inside Peter. Something he isn't proud of. So he snaps back:

"If you get past me, I'll tell you!"

The corners of the twenty-year-old's mouth twitch. Then he turns effortlessly as if he steers his skates by the power of thought alone while Peter hears his own back make a noise like bubble wrap when he leans forward. The old NHL player doesn't look prepared when the twenty-year-old sets off from the center circle, it should only have ended one way, but when he reaches the blue line Peter suddenly bursts into life so quickly that even he is surprised when he knocks the puck away. He may be old and awkward, but some instincts never leave you. Aleksandr stops abruptly in astonishment, his eyes darken, as do Peter's. Aleksandr fetches the puck and sets off again, just as arrogant but considerably angrier now. This time he approaches with such speed and force that he's convinced he's already got past when Peter's stick appears out of nowhere and knocks the puck away again. He starts again, but Peter reads his movements and when he gets close he can feel Aleksandr flinch. The twenty-year-old has all the technique, all the training, but he's afraid of getting hit. When his father's voice roars from the stands, Peter has heard it a thousand times before, in a thousand other ice rinks:

"DON'T FLINCH! STAND YOUR GROUND! TAKE THE TACKLE LIKE A MAN, FOR GOD'S SAKE!"

Aleksandr adjusts his helmet and sets off again, but Peter steps in easily and knocks the puck away. This gets repeated three more times before Zackell calls from the boards:

"Aleksandr! Do you know that you're stupid?"

The twenty-year-old stops abruptly. That gives Peter a chance to catch his breath with his hands on his knees and sweat stinging his eyes, convinced that this is what a heart attack feels like. Aleksandr glides toward Zackell.

"What the fuck did you say?"

"Do you know what a mongoose is?" she asks.

"What the fuck did you call me?"

Zackell sighs as if she had just shown him a library and he was trying to eat the books.

"It's an animal. It hunts cobras. Can you see how stupid that is? The cobra is faster and its venom can kill any animal, but the mongoose still attacks the cobra because it's a complete idiot. And do you know what happens? The mongoose wins. Do you know why?"

"Are you a biology teacher or a hockey coach?" Aleksandr snorts.

"This isn't biology. It's physics," Zackell points out.

Aleksandr adjusts his helmet, fighting to hold on to his arrogance, but it isn't going well. He glances up toward his dad, but Zackell goes on:

"Don't look at your dad, he isn't here. This is our world now, yours and mine."

The twenty-year-old breathes out, it's barely noticeable, but the skin around his jaw relaxes slightly.

"Okay . . . tell me . . . why does the mongoo or whatever it's called win?"

Zackell taps her temple.

"The mongoose wins because it adapts. The snake lunges the same way every time, without thinking, without learning anything, but the mongoose bases its attack on all previous attacks. It tests and evaluates, jumps back, entices the snake to attack farther and farther away. Because when the snake is completely stretched out it's at its slowest and most defenseless. So the mongoose bides its time, feints, then counters the snake's lunge with a single bite right through the snake's brain. It looks like luck, every time, but it ISN'T luck. Do you understand?"

"Well . . . no . . . ," Aleksandr begins, scratching his forehead.

Zackell shapes her fingers and palm into a little snapping mouth in the air.

"You play like a cobra, you're predictable, but all your coaches have made you believe that you're dependable. But no one can depend on you. I wouldn't let you watch my beer, even if there was none left. So there's no point putting you in a 'system' and talking to you about 'position,' because you're far too stupid for that. That's why you fall out with all your coaches and get thrown off of every team. But that's also what makes you brilliant, because you're so stupid that no one can actually imagine what you're capable of. If you play like a cobra Peter will take the puck off you every time. So you need to play like a mongoose. Play like a total idiot."

Aleksandr doesn't look entirely convinced, at times during her explanation he actually looked at her as if she was trying to get him to smell a fart she was particularly proud of. But he goes back out onto the ice, fetches the puck, and skates back to the center circle, more slowly this time, thoughtfully. The hardest thing in hockey is to change your perception. The hardest thing to change your perception about is yourself.

He sets off, Peter is waiting by the blue line, and afterward the former general manager will say it felt like Zackell had brought on a different player. Just as they meet and Peter is prepared for the collision, Aleksandr vanishes into thin air. It looks like he takes the puck with him as he stumbles. It looks like luck.

Peter flails in the air before collapsing onto his backside, yelling at the pain in his groin, and ends up lying in an embarrassing heap for several minutes. When Aleksandr has fired the puck into the goal he turns around and hears a clattering sound on the ice. The car keys. Zackell is already walking toward the door of the ice rink.

For the first time in a very long time, Aleksandr loves something about hockey again.

63

Tails pushes the two sets of accounts across the kitchen table and says, with a degree of uncertainty that he usually tries to hide with stupid jokes:

"I'm trusting you here, Kira. If you're going to sit on the committee . . ."

"You don't appoint the committee, Tails, the club's members do that . . . ," she interrupts.

"Don't worry about the members, I'll take care of that!" he interrupts in turn.

"Is that why you're here, sweaty and scared, because you've taken care of everything so well so far?" she wonders derisively, shaking his self-confidence so much that the ceiling lamp sways in the draft.

"I just need to know that you're a lawyer first and foremost right now. That everything is . . . confidential."

Kira looks at him for a long time.

"Are you worried I'm going to talk about what I see in these files to someone outside this house, or someone inside it?"

"Both."

"Okay. So let me ask as a lawyer: once you've shown me all the problems and I get to work, what do you want to happen then?"

Tails instantly gives a practiced response:

"I want to make Beartown Hockey an elite club again! The most logical way to do that is to get the council to shut down Hed Hockey. Pull their old ice rink down and invest in Beartown instead. We're going to build a state-of-the-art training facility here, as part of Beartown Business Park! Twice the income and half the costs: the council gets one A-team instead of two, one junior team, one administrative team . . ."

Kira nods slowly, and thinks bitterly: "And one general manager instead of two. And one caretaker. And one cleaner." Because that's

typical of men like Tails, they'll exchange anything for growth without sparing a thought for what happens if their dreams come true. Fire
staff if necessary, recruit stars from outside so there's no longer space
on the team for local boys, raise ticket prices so that the most faithful
supporters can't afford to attend games. Without realizing that one day
the club will be so successful that Tails himself will be left out in the
cold.

But she replies like a lawyer:

"And to achieve that, you need to prove to the council that Beartown
is superior, in terms of both sports and finances? That the brand is so
strong that it would be madness to try to start a new club under a new
name?"

Tails grins and exclaims:

"See, didn't I SAY?! I could have gotten other lawyers, but I need the
BEST!"

The compliment passes her by and she leans forward and fixes her
eyes on him.

"What have you done, Tails?"

His grin is working on autopilot:

"Well, I haven't . . . murdered anyone! But you know what journalists
are like, they've done some digging in our accounts, and who has spotless
accounts? I bet not even you do!"

That hurts, even though he doesn't realize it. She hasn't told anyone
about her financial problems with her own business. Not even Peter. Her
eyes waver as she repeats:

"What have you *done*, Tails?"

The grin vanishes. He nods toward the files. She opens the top one and
only has to read a few pages before she looks up and shakes her head, half
in sympathy and half in accusation:

"Dear God . . . is this really right? You're on the brink of collapse?
I mean, I knew things were tough financially while Peter was general
manager, but didn't the factory step in as sponsor and solve all this?"

Tails nods disconsolately.

"Yes, but their money came with conditions. We were supposed to be good for their brand. And do you know how much it costs to run a hockey club? Above all, a hockey club like ours?"

"What does that mean?"

He throws his arms out, working himself up.

"The girls' team, like you saw on the video. The breadth of our investment, and our equal opportunities youth program. Our new declaration of values and the cost of developing those. All our social projects. Everyone only sees the A-team, but we've even got a preschool in the ice rink, Kira! The whole district's kids learn to skate with us! The media who are scrutinizing us now are the same media who pressed us to develop the whole of this politically correct castle in the air, all they write about is how we aren't 'inclusive' enough, but who's going to pay if everyone's going to have access to everything? No one wants to admit that everything we do beyond the A-team is a luxury! And if we're going to be able to afford a girls' team, the A-team needs to win games first. We need to bring in money from sponsors. That's what makes the whole thing work. It's like my dad used to say: everyone wants to eat meat, but no one wants to work in an abattoir."

Kira looks over at the folder closest to Tails.

"What's in that one?"

He clears his throat.

"All the things no one else is allowed to see."

"The abattoir?"

"Yes."

"Show me. Show me everything."

So he does.

———

Peter doesn't see the woman until he's dragging himself off the ice. She's sitting on her own, at the very top of the stands. Aleksandr sees her as well and suddenly smiles a smile that probably only she ever sees.

"Mom?" he mumbles in surprise.

She waves halfheartedly and he waves back as if it's unusual, them waving to each other in this setting. As for his dad, he glares at her with a mixture of shock and anger. Peter has seen this before, the ice rink so easily becomes the preserve of just one parent, the other is at best left to spectate, and at worst ends up as an intruder. It actually takes Peter a little longer than it should to understand that if both the father and Aleksandr are surprised to see his mother here, then there's only one person who could have invited her.

The mother gestures to her son that she'll see him outside. Aleksandr nods and sets off toward the locker room at once. His dad calls after him, but in his eagerness to recapture his authority he ends up shouting the wrong name, his old name, so his son pretends not to hear. His dad shouts louder and starts to follow him, but Peter takes his arm.

"Let me . . . sorry . . . can I speak to him?"

The dad snaps, half in anger and half in despair:

"Sure, sure, you try! But no one can reason with him! No one! Especially not when his mom's here!"

He stomps off toward the stands like an aggrieved child.

"Aleksandr?" Peter calls when they're alone in the players' corridor.

The twenty-year-old turns around with soft, almost fragile movements.

"Yes?"

"Good session," Peter says, holding out his glove.

Aleksandr clenches his fist and taps it to Peter's.

"Thanks. You too."

"I'm too old for this sort of thing, I won't be able to walk for weeks . . ." Peter smiles.

Aleksandr's tongue probes the inside of his cheek nervously.

"I didn't know I was so easy to read. You took the puck so easily."

"Not that last time, I didn't stand a chance!"

Aleksandr looks almost embarrassed.

"I was . . . testing a new thing. Didn't know if it was going to work. My old coach hated it when I tried new things, but that one out there said a load of stuff about a fucking mongoose. I don't even know what that is . . ."

"A bit like a meerkat, I think."

"What the fuck's a meerkat?"

Peter bursts out laughing. He looks back toward the ice and the stands.

"How many clubs have been here to look at you?"

"Fifteen, maybe."

"So why aren't you playing for any of them, then?"

"They don't want me," Aleksandr mumbles awkwardly.

Peter smiles.

"You're being easy to read again now. I think you said no to them. Unless your mom said no."

The twenty-year-old's tongue wanders around his mouth.

"Okay. Honestly? I only do these tryouts because she wanted me to! I wanted to give up hockey! But Dad's decided everything I've ever done in my life and Mom asked me to give her the chance to decide for once . . ."

"And you'd do anything for your mom?"

Aleksandr nods.

"She's done everything for me."

"But she doesn't usually come to the rink?"

The twenty-year-old shakes his head, looking down at the floor.

"No. This is kind of mine and my dad's world. Well, it used to be."

"Is it your mom who's Russian? Is that why you changed your name?"

The answer is defiant but brittle:

"My name was always Aleksandr but Dad only let her give me that as a middle name. He didn't want people to think I was foreign."

Peter leans on his stick, longing to take his skates off.

"What did he do to your mom?" he asks quietly.

"He had an affair!" Aleksandr replies so quickly that it seems to shock even him.

Peter nods sympathetically.

"Then I can understand why you're angry . . ."

"Angry? ANGRY? He was with a crazy bitch who was seven years older than me. She could have been my big sister. He broke Mom's heart!"

Peter nods, more sadly than with any confidence.

"Do you know what, Aleksandr? I think you used to like playing hockey when you were little because it made your dad proud. And I think you enjoyed humiliating me out on the ice today because you were humiliating him at the same time. But I think you should find some other reason to play."

Aleksandr sounds breathless even though they've been standing still for several minutes.

"Should I play for you instead? In Beartown?"

Peter laughs.

"Not for me. I don't even work for Beartown Hockey anymore."

"So why are you here, then?"

Peter replies before he has time to consider how stupid it might sound:

"Because I wanted to mean something, I suppose. Because I wanted to be a good person. Do good things. And hockey is the only thing I know where I can make the world a bit better. That's why I can't let go of it. Maybe your mom can see that you're the same, and maybe that's why she can't quite let you give up."

Aleksandr clutches his stick as if he's briefly considering breaking it against the wall, but instead he takes a deep breath and looks at Peter, and asks in a quiet voice:

"Is she good? That coach?"

"Zackell? She's kind of crazy in every other respect," Peter replies honestly.

Aleksandr starts laughing.

"Damn? Talk about a hard sell!"

"But she'll get the best out of you," Peter says, just as honestly.

The boy's gaze flickers.

"You think?"

Peter nods.

"She's the only coach who's been here who realized that it wasn't your dad who decides where you play. And not you either."

For the first time, Aleksandr looks younger than his twenty years, much younger. He smiles cautiously, almost expectantly.

Outside in the parking lot his mother, who has turned down every other coach who has been here, is shaking hands with Elisabeth Zackell. Not because this coach has promised to make her son a winner like all the others. But because she's promised to set him free.

———

Kira isn't concerned about what the word "corruption" means, that isn't her job, but she is thinking a lot about the word "embezzlement." It's a treacherous concept, just like the people who do it, because it always starts with little things. A few rounded corners become shortcuts, a small loophole becomes grafting, dishonesty becomes criminality. The first of these are often not even illegal, just favors and payback, friends helping friends. The coach of Beartown's junior team, for instance, barely gets any wages, because the club wants to avoid paying tax and national insurance, so instead the coach receives payment in the form of one of the sponsors renovating the coach's son's summer cottage. Is that illegal? Maybe not. But it's a door that's been left ajar. Up in the A-team, the club signs all new players' contracts in April, but they don't officially start until August, so the player can claim unemployment benefits all summer and the club doesn't have to pay their wages. Some of the players drive cars that are never taxed because the local car dealer registers them as "demo models" and just happens to allocate them for "test drives" for the length of the hockey season. Other players live rent-free in apartments owned by the council's housing association, and even if the club officially "pays" the rent, no money is ever transferred. In return, members of the housing association's board get to sit in the best seats at all hockey games. Is that embezzlement? A line that has been crossed? Maybe not. But that door is no longer merely ajar.

At the end of every season the club arranges a dinner for "the friends of Beartown Hockey," where the players and committee celebrate with sponsors and local politicians and their families, their children play on a bouncy castle, and everyone goes home talking about "a sense of local cohesion." Soon afterward the local politicians decide that all local sports associations should be allowed to rent the ice rink at a "zero tariff" next year. This is officially described as a "broad subsidy to promote public health," but by sheer coincidence it turns out that only one association gains from this. The hockey club books all the slots, suddenly discovers that it has "overbooked," and sells the excess slots to local businesses that want to hire the ice rink for "events." In conjunction with these "events" the business also hires "staff" in the form of a caretaker and cleaner from a limited company owned by the club. These "events" hardly ever actually take place, but the invoices look genuine, and the businesses can use income they don't always want to declare to shift money into a hockey club whose accounts no one ever asks any questions about. The same sponsors might occasionally, over a beer in a hunting lodge, suggest that instead of plain sponsorship, "materials" might be bought for the club that the businesses can write off from their own activities. It's a conjuring trick: replacement parts for an industrial business are turned into equipment for a hockey club, red numbers become a gray zone, dirty money becomes clean. None of which is actually illegal, or at least it doesn't *feel* illegal, and in a hockey club full of sensitive individuals, that's all that counts.

But then every decision, every contract, slips closer and closer to being a criminal act: the club has debts and asks the council for more money, but the council is concerned about what voters will think. So instead the club finds a new sponsor, a consultancy firm registered abroad, which for some mysterious reason agrees to pay off all the debts. The consultancy firm is owned by a local construction company in Beartown, whose largest client by far just happens to be the council. During the year that follows the company adds some "unspecified costs" to all its invoices for council construction projects, and in that way the council has suddenly sponsored Beartown Hockey with taxpayers' money without it being visible. The administrator at the council who authorizes payment of all the construction company's invoices without any questions also gets a bonus: because of his "extensive experience of sustainability issues," he has been brought in as an "adviser on environmental matters" to the board of a white goods company whose owner just happens to be the cousin of the owner of the construction company.

Kira looks through line after line of the files, only pausing to rub her eyelids with the palms of her hands.

"Let me guess, Tails. This construction company is the same one that's going to build this 'Beartown Business Park' that you keep going on about? All the crooks in the same boat?"

He clears his throat.

"You know how it is, we're a small town, we need to stick together, it isn't . . ."

She looks up and he falls silent, embarrassed. The worst thing about the files is that Kira can see how ingeniously it has all been constructed: the old guys at the hockey club and the construction company and the council know perfectly well that this could never be entirely hidden, so they haven't even tried. They've just made everything so complicated to explain and so easy to explain away that no one would be bothered to listen if the journalists tried. It isn't a big crime, just thousands of small ones, and as long as everyone can blame everyone else, no one would be punished.

But then Kira turns a page and the angry outburst comes so abruptly that Tails manages to hit the bridge of his nose with his coffee cup.

"Hang on, why is MY company listed as one of the sponsors?"

"Before you get angry . . . ," Tail begins, but of course it's too late.

"Are you mad? We expressly said NO to the invitation to sponsor the club!"

"Yes, yes, but you misunderstand, you don't have to pay anything, it just looks good if you're on the list. You know, that *you* personally are there . . ."

So this is the reason, Kira finally realizes. Tails never needed a lawyer, he just needed a saint to wash the brand clean. Kira is the wife of the former general manager, but above all she's the mother of the daughter who was raped by the hockey star. If *she* can sponsor the club, if *she* can sit on the committee, then how could the journalists accuse the club of being unethical?

"Is this how you see me and my family? As something you can exploit?" she asks, more hurt than she wanted to admit.

Tails is flushed with guilt.

"Your business is respected, a big legal firm, and that attracts other sponsors. And you don't even have to pay anything, just . . ."

"So you're building a pyramid scheme?"

"No . . . no, surely you're going too far now? I wouldn't call it . . ."

She shakes the papers in his face.

"That's EXACTLY what it is! You bring in 'sponsors' with a lot of credibility but who don't pay anything, merely to attract other sponsors who have to pay the full amount. And now you want me on the committee as a figurehead so everyone will think you've sorted everything out, because now you're a politically correct club with 'values' and 'equality'!"

Tails is huddled up on the other side of the table, his fingers scrape unhappily against the porcelain edge of the coffee cup. Then he whispers ominously:

"No. No, it isn't like that. At least, not *only* like that. I . . . I need your help as a lawyer as well. Not only me, but . . . Peter."

"What are you talking about?" Kira snarls.

That's when Tails pulls the last file out of his bag and puts it on the table.

"Here. We're going to build a training facility. Beartown Hockey, together with the council. It's part of the plans for Beartown Business Park. But we had problems with the financing, so we sold it . . ."

"What do you mean, sold it? You haven't even built it?"

"No, that's the point. The council has, so to speak, bought it from the hockey club . . . in advance . . ."

Kira looks through the documents, at first frustrated, then increasingly horrified. She follows every thread of the tangled mess: the council sells the land to the factory, who sell it much cheaper to the hockey club, who then sell it back to the council for millions, only now it's suddenly called a "training facility." At the same time the factory is allowed to buy another patch of land that it has wanted for a long time from the council, without any questions. Favors and counter-favors.

"This is . . . I don't even know what to say . . . I might have been able to save you from everything else you've shown me, but this? Someone's going to end up in prison for this," she manages to say.

Tails smiles stiffly, then gears up as if he's straightening his back and makes one last attempt to be optimistic:

"Yes, but listen to me, Kira: it's only illegal if it gets uncovered *now*! Because we are going to build the training facility, *soon*! Do you remember Alicia in the video I showed you? You know she hasn't been able to train since the storm because we've got so many teams in the rink that there's no room for the youngest teams. So we just need a bit of time! Just hide this from the journalists for a little while! Once the training facility is built, and once Hed Hockey has been closed down and there's only Beartown Hockey left, then no one's going to care about how it happened!"

Most of all, Kira hates him because she knows he's right. But her eyes roam over the documents until they reach the bottom of the page and her heart stops.

"Hang on, why . . . Peter . . . why has Peter signed this?" she splutters.

Tails's smile is so strained now that he has to tug at his collar to breathe.

"He was general manager, so . . ."

Kira's fists clench so quickly and slam down so hard onto the table that he jumps.

"Not when THIS was signed, you bastard! He'd already left by then! What the hell have you DONE?!"

It isn't just sweat running down Tails's cheeks now. He blinks hard.

"Peter signed it because I asked him to. It . . . it needed someone like him. The board of the construction company and that official at the council and the owners of the factory, they all got cold feet when we were preparing to sell the training facility, so they demanded that someone they trusted sign it. And everyone trusts Peter. He'd already started working for you then, but we hadn't appointed another general manager, and I . . . I knew he felt guilty . . . he felt he'd left the club in the lurch. You know what he's like. He wants to save the whole world."

Kira's cheeks are throbbing.

"So you asked him to sign something you knew was illegal and he was so stupid that he did it?"

Tails looks down at his lap.

"He signed it because I asked him to. Because he trusted me."

"So you used him!"

"Please, Kira, I was just trying to do what was best for the town. But if this goes wrong the whole club . . ."

She leans across the table so far that he almost topples off his chair.

"The club? I don't give a damn about the CLUB! Don't you realize that PETER COULD END UP IN PRISON?"

"I . . ." is all Tails manages to say before she grabs hold of his shirt collar, making the seams creak.

"If my husband ends up in prison because of you, I'll end up in prison for murder, you need to be very clear about that!" she hisses.

Then she lets go of his collar and marches out into the hall without waiting for a reply. Shortly after that the front door slams and the house falls silent. Tails doesn't know what to do, so he makes more coffee and waits.

64

Knocks

On Monday Amat spends hours running through the forest on his own. When he gets back to the yard between the apartment blocks early that afternoon the first of the children have gotten back from school, they're already out playing with sticks and tennis balls, just like yesterday. Amat shoves his hands in his jacket pockets and pulls his hood over his head out of habit, to stop them from recognizing him and calling his name. He goes home and closes the door and his hands automatically feel for a bottle in his bag before he realizes something very strange: he doesn't feel anxious. Or at least, not as much as normal. His chest has felt so weighed down for so long that he's almost forgotten how it feels, whatever this is—"calm," perhaps? The moment feels like a broken bone that has been incredibly painful for months, then one morning hurts very slightly less. His breathing feels a little easier. The window is closed but he can still hear the shouting and laughter from down in the yard. It doesn't annoy him the way it usually does. Instead it drowns out some of the voices in his head, extinguishes some of the doubts, instills a little hope. Just a tiny bit. There's no happiness as infectious as the joy of playing hockey.

"Can I join in?" he asks as he emerges from the door with an old stick in his hand.

"With . . . us?" the children stammer.

He nods.

"Sure. Come on. Me and you two against the rest."

The children cheer so loudly that it echoes across the whole of the Hollow, their sticks clatter against the pavement under the thin covering of snow, someone shouts "cheat!," someone else yells "YES!," and palms slap until someone's mother calls from a balcony that it's time to come in and eat. Then one of the children turns to Amat and cries:

"Can we play again tomorrow?"

Amat pulls his hood up, sticks his hands in his pockets, and smiles weakly:

"I hope I won't have time."

They don't understand what he means, they just run home with all their dreams and Amat stands there and lets his old dreams out from deep down inside him.

Then he laces his sneakers extra tight and runs through the town, and doesn't stop until he reaches Zackell's door.

Bang bang bang.

He knocks on the door in time with his heartbeat. But there's no answer. He walks around the house, but there are no lights on and everything is quiet. He runs down to the ice rink but her car isn't in the parking lot. He stands there, out of breath, his thoughts swimming against the current, a hundred voices in his head screaming "give up!" but he doesn't listen this time. Instead he turns and runs in the other direction, home to the only person he can imagine confessing everything to, the only person he can ask for advice now. The only person apart from his mother who has always believed in his potential no matter what he's done.

———

Maya heads home just after lunchtime. Ana is with her because there's no food at her place and she's heard that Maya's dad has started baking bread. Ana loves bread. As they pass the running track on the Heights her friend nods and exclaims:

"Isn't that your mom?"

Maya bursts out laughing.

"MY mom? Are you kidding? She wouldn't bother to run if a volcano erupted!"

But she peers through the trees and it really does look like her mother. Maya rubs her eyes, but the figure has already disappeared. She and Ana carry on walking home, the front door is unlocked, none of the family are home but Tails is sitting on his own in the kitchen drinking coffee.

"Hello!" he says cheerfully.

Maya just nods in resignation and gathers together bread and toppings from the fridge. Ana whispers:

"What . . . what's Tails doing here if there's no one else around?"

Maya sighs with all the depth of a collection of epic poetry.

"I've decided to stop asking questions about what happens in this house. It just gives you a migraine if you try to understand."

―――――

Amat clenches his fist, raises it, gets ready.

Bang bang bang.

Knocks. Heartbeats. Steps inside the house, the door opening, Amat gets ready to confess immediately: "Sorry, Peter, forgive me! I messed up! Help me!" A whole childhood flickers past inside him: the first time he put skates on, his first goal, the first defeat, and always Peter's voice somewhere on the ice or in the stands. A gentle hand on his shoulder, a quick "it'll be okay" or "well done." That's what he needs now. He's been practicing the whole way here.

But as the door handle is pushed down his mouth seizes up, because it isn't Peter who opens the door but Maya.

"Hi Amat!" she exclaims in a mixture of happiness and surprise.

"Hi . . . sorry . . . ," he mutters in a mixture of confusion and desolation.

"It's been ages! How are you?" she chirrups.

"What?" he mumbles distractedly.

He feels ashamed of how shabby and forlorn he must look as she stands there in the doorway looking perfect, as usual.

"Are you okay?" she asks, a little concerned.

He nods slowly several times, repeats the movement more quickly to convince himself, tries to breathe in through his nose and out through his mouth. He pulls himself together again in order to take his whole life back:

"Is . . . is your dad home?"

Maya shakes her head.

"No, he's gone off somewhere with Zackell. They're going to look at a new player, I think!"

Amat just stares at her. His ears are ringing, his temples are throbbing, his heart is beating with giddiness. "A new player." They've already replaced him. He falls straight into the abyss of missed opportunities that only eighteen-year-olds can contain.

"Oh . . . okay. It . . . don't worry . . . it wasn't anything much," he whispers with a sob in his throat.

"Are you sure you're okay? Do you want to come in?" Maya asks.

But Amat has already turned and started to walk home.

65

Big city types

Aleksandr stops his new Jeep at a gas station. As he walks over to the bathroom Peter turns to Zackell in the backseat.

"Can I ask you something?"

"Can I stop you?"

He sighs.

"Have you spoken to Amat?"

She looks surprised.

"Since when?"

"Since . . . the summer. When he didn't get drafted."

"No."

"Why not?"

She shakes her head at the foolishness of the idea.

"He hasn't come to training. How am I supposed to talk to him then?"

"Call him, maybe?"

"Call him? What for?"

"To find out if he's thinking of playing."

"If he wants to play, he'd come to training, wouldn't he?"

Peter's neck creaks with frustration.

"So instead of ASKING Amat, you dragged me all the way here to recruit Aleksandr to replace him?"

Then Zackell tilts her head to one side and really tries her best not to call Peter "a total idiot."

"You're a bit of an idiot. Aleksandr isn't going to replace Amat."

"So what is he going to do, then?"

"He's going to annoy Amat."

Then Zackell lies down on the backseat and falls asleep, and sleeps so deeply all the way to Beartown that Peter can't help wondering if the real reason she gave her car away was so she didn't have to drive home.

Peter and Aleksandr talk hockey all the way. Nothing but hockey. The Jeep rolls into Beartown late that evening. The twenty-year-old was called by one name as a child, chose a different name as a teenager, but in this town he will acquire a third name. Rather unexpectedly, it's actually Peter who comes up with it when Aleksandr suddenly asks:

"Is this place the way you think it is? Typical rural small town?"

"What's a typical rural small town?" Peter wonders.

"You know, the sort where people just hate everything. Hate wolves, hate the authorities, hate outsiders . . ."

Peter realizes then just how incredibly much he really is from here, because he actually takes offense at that, but instead of snapping back he smiles:

"Hmm. You know what people around here hate most of all?"

"No?"

"Cocky bastards from the big city."

The occasions when anyone has ever heard Elisabeth Zackell laugh out loud are easily counted, but this is one of them. After that, no one in Beartown calls Aleksandr anything other than "Big City." Funnily enough, he learns not to be too upset by that.

Zackell jumps out of the Jeep outside her house with a curt:

"Training tomorrow, Big City! Be there on time!"

The twenty-year-old stays in his seat but Peter gets out and walks after her. She looks surprised. Peter looks rather surprised too, as if his feet are moving quicker than his brain.

"Listen . . . Elisabeth . . . I just want to say thank you."

"What for?"

"For taking me with you today. It meant a lot to . . . well, feel like part of the club again."

"In my defense, I didn't actually know that you'd left the club," Zackell points out, and Peter bursts out laughing.

"No, no, of course. But thanks anyway. It's been a fun day. And you were wrong, by the way!"

"About what?"

"About the team with the best players always winning. That isn't enough. They need someone who understands them too. Someone who can see the best in them."

He kicks the snow. She puts her house key in the lock. He's on his way back to the car, and she doesn't even turn around when she says:

"Ramona hardly liked anyone, but she liked you, Peter. I hardly like anyone either."

She's already closed the door behind her when the meaning of those words sinks in to him. It isn't until he's sitting in the Jeep again and Big City asks where he should drive that it occurs to Peter that Zackell might not have given any thought to where the player was going to live.

He needn't have worried about that. Of course Zackell had a plan. Obviously Big City is going to stay with Peter.

———

Kira comes home with a decision. When Tails leaves the Andersson family's house she and he have agreed on two things: Tails should start making phone calls, and Kira will do something terrible. So she goes into her daughter's bedroom, sits down on her bed, and looks at Maya and Ana very seriously.

"I need you both to do something for me."

"What?" the girls ask.

"You mustn't tell anyone that Tails was here today. Not even . . . your dad. I need to tell him myself . . ."

The atmosphere in the room becomes oppressive, to put it mildly. Maya sits in silence for so long that Ana eventually sees it as her duty to say what they're both thinking out loud:

"Sorry Kira, but I have to say, if you're going to have an affair, I think you could do a lot better than Tails. You're pretty damn hot! There are probably loads of men who . . ."

At first Kira doesn't understand, then she understands everything all at once, upon which she stares at Ana with such horror and disgust that Maya laughs more than she can remember having laughed in that house since her little brother was six and managed to shut himself in the fridge.

Peter gets home and stands in the hall. Kira comes out of the kitchen. She'll ask herself many times why she doesn't just tell him the truth there and then, that Tails has been there and that she knows all about the contracts and the training facility, but Peter has a look on his face that she hasn't realized how much she's missed. He looks excited. It's irresistible.

"Darling! Zackell and I have recruited a player! Well, I mean . . . Zackell recruited him, but I . . . we both helped! He's special! Special in a good way, I mean! He could be . . . incredible!"

Kira can hardly believe the noise that comes out of her throat then, but she laughs. Of all the things she could have done. She laughs and laughs and laughs, because he looks so childishly happy and she'd forgotten that it was this boy she fell in love with. So she says nothing about anything that's happened today, she just thinks that she needs to protect her husband, she needs to make sure he doesn't end up in prison because she can't breathe without him.

"Let me guess, he has nowhere to live so he needs to stay here?" she smiles, and Peter's eyes open wide.

"How did you know that?"

"Because that's what always used to happen when you were general manager. I'll go and make up the bed in the guest room."

She heads upstairs to find sheets, but has to stop several times just to catch her breath.

"It'll only be for a few nights!" Peter calls after her.

But then Big City walks in through the front door and stops in the hallway, just as Maya comes out of her room, wondering what all the fuss is about. Big City's and Maya's eyes meet and neither of them says anything, but all the color suddenly drains from Peter's face. He looks from one to the other and realizes that he's made a terrible, terrible mistake. Suddenly Kira hears him call up from the ground floor:

"ONE night, Kira! One night maximum!"

Ana spends the night there too. The last thing she whispers before they fall asleep is:

"That turned out okay! First your mom asked you to keep a secret and then your dad turned into a psycho when he saw you wanted to sleep with that guy. That's, like, the most normal I've seen your parents in ages."

"I don't want to sleep with that guy!" Maya retorts a little too quickly, and Ana rolls her eyes so hard that her head almost spins around like an owl's.

"No, no, of course you don't. Sure. You were just eating him up with your eyes . . ."

"I DID NO SUCH THING!"

Ana snuggles closer, turns her back to Maya, and whispers:

"I'm glad you want to sleep with guys again."

"Screw you . . . ," Maya whispers, and takes Ana's hand and falls asleep with it clutched tightly in hers.

66

Disappointments

Monday is one of the longest days of Hannah's and Johnny's lives. Tess is playing the part of wounded daughter to perfection, she's gone just long enough for them to start to panic but not long enough for them to be able to play the martyr. She spends the night sleeping in Bobo's bed, he sleeps next to her on the floor, his younger siblings sleep in a heap at the end of her bed like puppies. Hog doesn't understand what the hell is going on, there's never been a girlfriend in the house before, so he tentatively asks Tess what she'd like for breakfast, then he makes her promise that if Bobo ever behaves badly toward her, she's to tell Hog so he can kill him. Tess smiles and promises. She sleeps with her hand hanging over the edge of the bed so she can feel Bobo's breath against her skin. The next morning she wakes to the smell of tea, toast, and scrambled eggs.

She takes the bus back to Hed and goes to school as if nothing has happened, because she knows her parents will phone the school to see if she's turned up, which is a much harder punishment for them than if she disappears. Now they'll have to sit and wait impotently until the end of the school day to see if she comes home or not, and there's nothing more cruel that she could do to them.

When it's time for dinner she puts her key in the lock and her parents leap out of their kitchen chairs and stumble into the hall, poised somewhere between giving her a hug and a telling-off, but she doesn't give them time to choose. Bobo is standing next to her with a basket in his hand and he looks at least as uncomfortable as Hannah and Johnny, but perhaps Tess is just testing him. If he does this for her, then he'll do anything.

"Bobo's brought food, he's going to cook dinner! In twenty minutes we're going to sit down and eat it together like a normal family," she says, leaving no room for negotiation.

Said and done. Her brothers are let down from upstairs and the family eats the pasta like it was a hostage situation. Johnny doesn't say a word, but Hannah isn't given that opportunity because Bobo keeps asking her questions. About her job, her upbringing, her house. When they've finished eating, Tobias and Ted rush desperately to their rooms, away from the suffocating awkwardness of the conversation. Johnny in turn pretends he has to go to the bathroom, then comes up with something very important he needs to do in the garage. He's furious, Tess can see that, her dad just doesn't know how to express it, and his daughter doesn't know how to apologize without apologizing. How to explain that she's sorry if she's upsetting him, but not because she's disappointed him. Because the disappointment is his own fault.

Bobo clears the table and washes up without being asked. Ture goes into the kitchen of his own volition and helps. Hannah sits silently at the table, glancing at her daughter and searching for words. In the end she takes the easy way out and talks to Bobo instead:

"Are you the oldest child in your family, Bobo?"

"Yes," he nods as he shows Ture how to load the dishwasher more efficiently.

"You can tell. You're very good with children. Who taught you to make food this well?" Hannah asks.

"Mom," he replies.

"Tell her she's done a very good job. Not just with cooking but with . . . all of you."

Hannah glances at her daughter to get confirmation that her apology has now been delivered, so that she can be forgiven, but instead Tess looks up from the table straight at Bobo with tears in her eyes. The young man in the kitchen smiles sadly and replies:

"My mom's dead. But she was brilliant. Everything I know comes from her."

The house has probably never been more silent, and Hannah has probably never felt more stupid. Her larynx feels like rope and her whole body contracts as if she's already waiting to be told off by her daughter. But nothing happens. Tess just looks equally sad.

"Sorry, Bobo, I should have told Mom . . . ," she whispers.

Her mother's cheeks flush.

"No, no, it's my fault, Bobo! I didn't even think . . ."

But Bobo just shakes his head disarmingly at Hannah, almost unconcerned.

"No, no, don't feel bad. She would have liked you! She'd have been furious with me if I'd made you sad!"

Hannah feels like she needs nine glasses of wine to handle that, but instead she makes her excuses and lies about needing to go to the bathroom. There she rinses her face and swears at herself for ten minutes before she goes out to the garage and swears at her husband instead.

"You're such a damn COWARD, hiding out here when your daughter's sitting in the kitchen with her . . ."

"Don't even say the word!" Johnny grunts in warning, but he's already looking around to see if there's anything he doesn't want her to throw at him.

"BOYFRIEND! He's her BOYFRIEND! And he's a good one! You're just going to have to accept him!" she says, doing her best to sound firm but not succeeding.

Johnny could have picked a thousand different replies, and by some miracle he manages to pick the very worst one:

"An ignorant fatso from Beartown, is that the best Tess can get? And now she wants to bully us into accepting him? I've . . ."

Hannah's back is ramrod straight. That's never a good sign.

"Tess has chosen him. Once upon a time you chose me and not everyone in your family was so damn happy about that either, as you might remember?"

He protests, but more cautiously now:

"They hardly know each other, Hannah . . ."

She snorts:

"How well did we know each other the first time we . . ."

He snaps:

"There's a hell of a difference, I . . . you were . . . that was different!"

"How?"

Johnny makes his very biggest mistake then, he judges a young man's intentions by the very worst of his own youth:

"Have you any idea what sort of guy he is? Don't you think I know what people like him are like? He just wants to sleep with a girl from Hed so he can boast to his friends about having been with a Hed bitch . . ."

Hannah's lips grow thin, her fingers creak as they curl in toward her palms.

"Because that was how you and your friends used to talk about girls from Beartown when you were their age? Has it ever occurred to you that not all boys are the sort of pigs you were?"

Johnny's shoulders slump so far that his collarbones can barely cope with the strain.

"That's not what I meant . . ."

She doesn't let him apologize, just interrupts with quiet fury:

"Do you know what Tess has got? She's got something wonderful. Something I envy her for. Something no one else in this family has got. She's got DECENT JUDGMENT!"

She slams the garage door so hard it echoes through the whole house. In sheer frustration Johnny knocks a jar of keys to the floor, the sort no one knows what they're for and which all dads seem to have hundreds of. Somewhere in the world are all the locks they fit, and perhaps on the other side of those locks are all the answers to how you always end up on minus points with your family no matter what you do.

When Bobo finally leaves the house Tess stays behind. Peace hasn't yet broken out between her and her mother, this is only a truce, but Hannah takes what she can get. Tess goes up to her room but she doesn't slam the door. When Bobo is walking to his car, a rusty little green Peugeot, Johnny steps out onto the drive from the garage. Bobo is one of the very few men in the area who is actually physically larger than Johnny, but he still stops as if he's expecting to get beaten up.

"Is that your car?" Johnny asks at the end of an entire childhood's worth of breaths.

It isn't easy to become a grown-up, but that's nothing compared to how hard it is to let someone else do it.

"Yes . . . yes, Dad gave it to me! Well, he actually gave me a campervan, but I gave that to a friend. We had a customer who wanted to scrap it, but I fixed it. It isn't much to look at, but the inside is okay!" Bobo nods, trying not to sound too enthusiastic, too boastful or too ingratiating.

Johnny scratches his beard and nods toward his van.

"I'm having trouble with the engine in that," he admits, which is pretty much the same to him as waving a white flag.

Bobo nods enthusiastically.

"We had one of those in the workshop! I can probably fix it for you!"

"Do you think I'm going to let you be with my daughter just because you fix my car?" Johnny wonders suspiciously.

Bobo shocks him with his honesty.

"I don't think it's up to you whether she's with me or not. I think that's her decision."

"Good answer," the fireman reluctantly concedes.

"Sorry," Bobo says, because he says that word so often that it sometimes slips out from sheer habit.

Johnny scratches his beard for a long time.

"Do you seriously think you could fix the van?"

Bobo nods.

"Yes. Cars are the only thing I'm good at."

"Was it your dad who taught you? You're Hog's son, right?"

"Yes! Do you know him?"

"I played hockey against him. He broke his nose crashing into me when we were juniors."

Only when Johnny smiles does Bobo allow himself to join in, then he says:

"He probably skated into you by mistake. Dad can only skate in one direction."

Johnny laughs loudly for the first time at that, he hears how rough it sounds, an old man's laugh now. Then he says, weighed down by all the time that passes far too fast:

"Tess is smart, Bobo. Really, really smart. She has the best grades of anyone in her school . . ."

"I know," Bobo mumbles, already beginning to suspect where this is going.

"If she's going to go on with her studies she'll have to move away from here, there aren't any opportunities for her here."

"I get that."

"It's nothing personal, Bobo. I'm sure you're a good guy. But I don't want you to hold her back. If I'm honest, I think her mom is hoping deep down that she's going to stay and have an ordinary life, because Hannah can't live without Tess, but . . . damn it, Bobo. She can be anything she wants. She could be something big, our daughter. Do you understand? She isn't like . . ."

Bobo nods with his back bent. He blinks too hard too many times for it not to show how badly he's falling apart.

"Don't you think I know Tess is too good for me? That she's special and I'm just ordinary? I'm not so smart, but I'm not THAT un-smart! I don't know anything except cars and a bit about hockey, I know I can't GIVE her anything, but I will never . . . never . . . try to hold her back, I . . . I'll never act badly toward her. And maybe I can't study at university like her, but I'm pretty good at fixing things and I'm fairly strong and my friends like me and Tess likes me. I try to be a good man and I think I could be a pretty good dad one day. And I WON'T hold her back. If she wants to move away from here, then I'll go with her. I can live anywhere if I can live with her. There are bad cars to fix everywhere. And if you want to try to get her to stop liking me, go ahead, but I'm not going to give up . . . I can't . . ."

Johnny stands and stares intently at the snow for so long that Bobo eventually stops babbling and can't figure out if the man has been listening or not.

"No. Like you say, I don't make decisions for Tess," Johnny says after an eternity.

He can't help asking himself what he's really angry about, and the answer really isn't flattering. He isn't even angry, just empty. His daughter left home yesterday without talking to him first. Got herself a boyfriend in secret. She has a whole life now that she hasn't told him about, and what sort of dad does that make him?

Bobo's voice is barely audible when he replies:

"She cries when we talk about you, and I don't want her to cry. So either she'll have to stop liking me, or you're going to have to start liking me."

Johnny looks up, exhausted.

"You know something? Cars aren't the only thing you're good at, Bobo."

"No?" Bobo whispers.

Johnny shakes his head. Smiles forlornly.

"No. The food was okay too."

67

Love stories

It snows all night, and on Tuesday morning it's so cold that when Big City goes out with wet hair from the shower to get some things from the car he has to break his hair like Legos when he comes back in. Peter has to lend him a winter jacket seeing as what Big City thought was a winter jacket turned out to be just a jacket.

"It's, like, autumn, how cold does it get in December?" he asks anxiously.

They set off to the ice rink together. Of course Peter ought to go to work, but he pretends he has to show the boy the way instead, anything to get a chance to see the twenty-year-old's first training session. Ana and Leo have to go to school, so Maya decides to go to the ice rink as well, mostly to tease her dad, which really does work splendidly. He walks demonstratively between her and Big City the whole way, so Maya takes extra care to give Big City compliments on how nice his hair is and how good he looks in his new jacket, until her dad dad-grunts uncomfortably the way only dads can. When they reach the rink Big City is collected by the caretaker to go through the list of equipment he needs, and they disappear, but Peter walks around holding the sleeve of Maya's jacket all day as if she was four years old and he was scared she was going to fall in a swimming pool. She lets him. Only when they are sitting alone in the stands does she say:

"I'm glad you're worrying about normal things again, Dad."

He doesn't know what she's talking about, and nothing is more normal for a dad than that. Then they go to the cafeteria and buy chocolate balls.

———

Kira goes to the office, shuts herself away with her colleague, and spends all day going through old cases and new accounts and prepares herself for the worst. "Always hope for peace but always prepare for war" one of Kira's tutors at university told her when she was a student. Those words carry extra weight now. They make her whole body ache.

"Thanks for doing this," she says, exhausted.

"I'd have been insulted if you didn't think it obvious that I would," her colleague replies.

Kira forces herself to smile.

"I know you'd do anything for me, but you're doing this for Peter . . ."

"I'm doing it for you."

"You know what I mean."

Her colleague glances up from behind her fringe and sighs.

"Screw it. You want me to tell the truth? I'm doing this for both of you. I've never thought that Peter deserved you, but you know what? You don't always deserve him either. There have been so many times when I've thought that surely *now* they're going to get divorced, those two, but you really can't. It's impossible for you two to live without each other. So you're not allowed to. I won't allow it. You've been through too much, and if you don't manage to keep your love story going, then the rest of us might as well give up all hope!"

Kira wipes her cheeks on her sleeve.

"You make it sound like a never-ending battle."

"Isn't that what love is? Loving someone is one thing, but who the hell can bear being LOVED for twenty years?"

"I really do love him . . ."

Her colleague smiles.

"I know. Everyone knows. Bloody hell, EVERYONE knows, Kira. You and he are fighters. You always find something, somewhere, and then you fight for it to the death. That's probably why I'm still working for you. You make me feel like I'm on the side of the good guys."

Kira sniffs.

"You don't work for me, you work with me . . ."

Her colleague pats her on the head.

"No. I worship you, I really do, but everyone works for you. Even your husband."

Kira screws her eyes shut so tightly that her temples hurt.

"I . . . I know Peter's naive and credulous, but he . . . he would never do anything illegal on purpose. He'd never expose me and the kids to the risk. Dear God, he won't even park the car too close to a fire hydrant! But even so . . ."

Her colleague squeezes her arm and whispers:

"Seriously, though, Kira, where's the fun in defending someone who's innocent? That isn't even a challenge!"

––––––

All sports are built on minuscule margins. Thousandths, inches, ounces. Behind all of the most famous achievements in sporting history there are thousands of invisible "if only"s and "if that hadn't"s and "so close"s.

Benji is driving the campervan through Beartown, blowing smoke out of the wound-down window. He slows down when he reaches the ice rink. He has to sit there for a long time with weed in his lungs and childhood in his heart merely to check if he wants to go back, but nothing happens. He wonders if he would have gone on loving hockey if he had stayed here two years ago instead of taking off. He finds himself asking more and more often who he might have been if his life hadn't been governed so much by other people's decisions: if his dad hadn't done what he did, if Kevin hadn't done what he did, if all the others hadn't done what they did, and no one had ever found out the truth about Benji . . . what would his life have been like then? If he had a time machine now, would he have used it?

He takes some deep drags and pulls out his phone, calls the same number three times without getting an answer. All sports have minuscule margins, sometimes it's just a friend who doesn't give up hope on you.

He lets the campervan drive on, all the way to the Hollow, drives around the parking lot below the apartment blocks and looks at the time. There are no children outside, days like this are the exception every year, suddenly there's too much snow to take your sticks out and play in the yard, but the ice on the lake isn't thick enough for you to grab your skates and play there. The campervan rolls slowly in front of one of the buildings until it reaches a basement door. Then Benji calls the same number again and hears a phone echoing in the shadows.

Sports and margins: a two-inch-wide goal line can determine how an entire life is remembered. A final can be decided at the last second so that a town far out in the forest more than twenty years later still defines itself with the word "almost." A boy can be born several thousand miles away and still end up being the one who one day makes them feel like something else.

Amat is skulking by the shadow of the wall with his hockey bag on his back. Benji pulls up beside him in a time machine.

"Training starts soon, do you want a lift?"

Amat tries to smile but his jaw is shaking too much with cold and fear.

"I don't know," he admits.

Benji leans against the steering wheel and blows smoke out through his nose.

"How long have you been standing here?"

"I . . . don't know."

His lips are blue and his eyes are exhausted from the fear of disappointing everyone again.

"Why don't you just go to training and talk to Zackell?" Benji asks.

"Because I don't know if I'd be welcomed back," Amat shivers.

Benji smokes and runs a careless hand through his hair, almost burning off his eyebrow in the process. That makes Amat's chest bounce with giggles and probably warms them both up. Benji brushes the sparks from his pants and mutters:

"I'm not going to give you a motivational speech, if that's what you're waiting for . . ."

Amat manages a sarcastic sigh between shivers.

"No? I thought you were going to yell 'pain is just weakness leaving your body' or 'winners don't wish for success, they create it!'"

Benji grins. He rolls a new cigarette between his fingertips, filling it carefully and looking for his lighter.

"No. I'm not here for your sake. I'm here for mine."

Amat stamps in the snow to force the blood through his body.

"Okay?"

Benji nods seriously.

"I've never seen anyone play hockey like you, my friend. I can't bear having to live the rest of my life wondering how good you could have been if you hadn't given up."

Considering it isn't a motivational speech, it's actually a damn good motivational speech. Amat's breath catches. He will never forget how Benji looks just then: inquisitive eyes and messy hair in an old campervan. A gentle heart. An outstretched hand. A little click when he reaches across the passenger seat and opens the door. Amat hesitantly puts his bag in, but doesn't get in himself. Then he says:

"Okay. Take my bag and I'll run. It's going to be hard enough persuading Zackell to take me back as it is, I can't show up stinking like a hash factory . . ."

Benji roars with laughter so hard that the smoke catches in his throat and he coughs until someone yells "shut up" from a balcony. He likes that about the Hollow, you never have to wait long to find out what someone thinks. He pulls the bag onto the seat and turns the campervan around in a wide circle.

Amat is already running along the main road when the campervan catches up and overtakes him. Benji blows the horn cheerily, Amat watches the rear lights as they vanish toward the town. It's one of the first ice-cold days of the year and one of the last truly happy ones. Amat starts playing hockey again this evening, he never gives up, but Benji will never find out how good he can be.

Enemies

Tails is used to complicated transactions, he's built much of what he owns on unusual deals with dubious partners weighed down by hazy loyalties, but this Tuesday is odd even for him. For months he has tried to persuade powerful men to shut down the hockey club in Hed, but now he finds himself trying to save it. He starts a war by trying to find peace. He needs friends, so he calls enemies.

The first call is to a politician, the second to a hockey supporter, they have barely anything in common except that hardly anyone calls them by those words. Most people call Richard Theo and Teemu Rinnius far, far worse things.

"Why are you calling me?" both men ask suspiciously when they find out what Tails wants to talk about.

"Because we want the same thing," Tails tells them both.

"And what's that?" the two men wonder, and Tails replies:

"To win."

Richard Theo is sitting in his office in the council building, laughing loudly.

"I've heard you don't like my politics, Tails, so why would you want to help me?"

"I don't think you like your politics either, Richard, I just think you do whatever it takes to beat your opponents," Tails replies from his own office at the supermarket.

Richard Theo purses his lips.

"If you want a favor, you should ask your friends in the party that actually runs the council. After all, I've heard that my party is just a little protest party on the margins. Perhaps it would be better for you to talk to someone with real power?"

Tails sighs over the line.

"You and I both know that after the next election you'll be running the council."

The politician smiles contentedly at the other end.

"Don't say that! I think it suits me better to be in opposition, because around here people love complaining."

"The other politicians can't do what I need help with," Tails admits.

"Really. You have my attention. What are you after?"

The tone of gentle mockery in his voice hides how intrigued Theo is.

So Tails explains. He says he's changed his mind about the merger of the two hockey clubs. He's suddenly realized that the towns need their own clubs, for the sake of public health, but mostly for the sake of the children.

"Absolutely, absolutely, 'the children,' of course," the politician laughs sarcastically, but Tails pretends not to notice.

"I'm going to set up a pressure group of local businessmen to push for the rebuilding of the ice rink in Hed as part of the same budget as the construction of Beartown Business Park! To demonstrate that the council's investment will benefit the *whole* district!"

Richard Theo thinks for a moment.

"I assume you're soon going to tell me how this helps me?"

Tails takes a deep breath.

"Almost all the politicians in the council have decided that they only want one hockey club, not two . . ."

"Because that's what you and your 'pressure groups' have persuaded them, yes. You're the people who have been pushing to get Hed Hockey closed down because it would save so much taxpayers' money!" The politician chuckles, but he sounds genuinely curious about where this conversation is going.

"If all the politicians are on one side, you can win a lot of votes by standing on the other side," Tails points out enigmatically.

The politician sighs and pretends to be disappointed.

"My whole financial policy is based upon cutting unnecessary expenditure by the council, and now you want me to support a plan which would see millions plowed into the renovation of the ice rink in Hed, and save Hed Hockey? Why would I do that?"

Tails's chest rises and falls so deeply that it creaks before he realizes that there's no point lying to Theo, he's far too smart a snake, so he admits:

"I know that you helped steer the takeover of the factory by foreign owners a few years ago. You got them to sponsor Beartown Hockey and save the club's finances. So you know perfectly well what contacts and capital are worth. But you also know that if the clubs are merged, external auditors will examine all the accounts, and there are things there that would be unsuitable for . . . well . . . 'public consumption,' so to speak."

The politician rocks back and forth on his chair, holding the phone between his shoulder and his chin, and starts tapping at his computer. He hasn't read the local paper as thoroughly as he usually does in recent days, but now he finds the article about Tails's vandalized car. Then he smiles. It isn't the auditors Tails is afraid of, it's the journalists.

"Can I ask something, Tails? It seems as if you've been doing all you can recently to present Hed Hockey as a club on the brink of bankruptcy, full of hooligans who vandalize cars? But now all of a sudden you want to rescue them?"

Tails tries to control his pulse.

"Circumstances change, I suppose. I'd like to think I'm capable of changing my opinion."

Richard Theo taps at his keyboard again.

"Hmm. Let me guess, your change of opinion has something to do with the fact that you need to conceal the evidence of that business about the 'training facility' that the council bought, and which you all think I don't know anything about?"

Tails is breathing heavily at his end of the line.

"There's an awful lot that I hope you don't know anything

about, Richard, but very little that I imagine actually gets past you."

The politician tries to resist the flattery.

"So you want to create a new narrative now? Bury the scandal about Beartown behind the news that the council is investing money in Hed? Because you hope that if enthusiasm about the hockey clubs is strong enough, the reporters might stop digging? That isn't going to work forever, Tails. Sooner or later someone is going to investigate anyway."

Tails loosens his tie, he's sweating so much that he has to keep switching the phone from one ear to the other.

"I don't need forever, I just need a little while. So I have time to get all the paperwork in order. You know how it is: scandals aren't as interesting to anyone in hindsight. Once the training facility has been built, no one's going to care how it came about. And by then the reporters will have moved on to hunt for other scandals. It's like hockey: it's only cheating if you get caught."

Richard Theo doesn't laugh at this last remark, he's never been very keen on sports, but he hears the logic in what Tails is saying. Theo knows that everything and everyone is connected here in the forest, hardly anyone has been better at exploiting that than him, because no one is independent in a small community. Not even journalists.

"So what do you want from me?" he asks.

Tails has evidently rehearsed his reply:

"Let me be honest: I need your political support, but Hed Hockey doesn't just need the council's money, it also needs sponsors. The way Beartown has the factory. It would look far too suspicious if *I* tried to find sponsors for the club I hate, but I think *you* could do it. So . . . well . . . if you help me to save Hed, I can save Beartown."

"And what do I get in return?"

Tails closes his eyes, ashamed of what he says next:

"I'll see to it that everyone knows that it was you who saved both clubs."

Theo snorts.

"That isn't enough, you know that."

Tails breathes in quickly, breathes out slowly.

"What more do you want?"

"I want to be involved in this 'Beartown Business Park' that you're building."

"I didn't think you were interested in making money . . . ," Tails blurts out, making the mistake of sounding hopeful, because suddenly he thinks Theo can be bribed.

The response sounds almost amused:

"No, I've got enough money, Tails. The only capital I'm interested in is political. But this district needs to grow in order to survive, and you have to build to grow. Men like you do the building, but men like me decide where and how you get to do it."

"So you want all the public credit for Beartown Business Park?" Tails guesses.

"No, no, my friend, not ALL the credit. Just a shovelful here and there. A few photographs in the local paper. And in the fullness of time I'll ask for one more condition."

"Which is?"

The politician taps at his computer and says:

"I don't know yet. But I'll get back to you. Now, let me get to work."

———

Teemu has stopped his car a little way into the forest, he's standing in the snow, smoking and listening to Tails's bullshit with extremely limited patience.

". . . so you see, Teemu, you and I want the same thing! What's best for our club! I need . . ."

"It isn't your club. It will never be your club," Teemu corrects with a darkness in his voice that makes Tails gasp for air in his office even though they're separated by several miles.

"Okay. Okay, sorry. I . . . can I be honest, Teemu?"

"Please do."

"I know that the club wouldn't have survived without the supporters in the standing area. But without a few of us in the seats it wouldn't . . ."

"You mean your smarming to the council? I've heard that it was YOUR idea to merge Hed and Beartown! Why have you suddenly changed your mind?"

Tails swallows and chooses his words with great care.

"The politicians in charge of the council don't want to merge the clubs. They want to shut them both down and start a new one. They think that hockey is a 'product,' Teemu. They don't want people like you in the stands, and soon they won't want people like me either, not real supporters. Just consumers. They think they can get rid of us from the stands if they erase our history. No Hed, no Beartown, just some new damn club that some PR company has invented . . ."

"You probably shouldn't make comparisons between you and me," Teemu advises, but he doesn't sound quite so threatening now, so Tails feels bold enough to go on:

"There are journalists digging into Beartown's finances. You know what journalists are like, they go looking for scandals, and scandals always require a scapegoat. And the scapegoat they've chosen is Peter."

All he can hear at the other end of the line for almost a minute is the gentle crackle of Teemu's cigarette. Then he says in a low voice:

"Okay. What do you need?"

Tails breathes out and wipes the sweat from his brow.

"It isn't anything that I want you to do, it's something I want you not to do: you and your guys mustn't start any trouble right now. If there's more violence, the council will see that as another good reason to shut down both clubs. And then everything's over for us. And I really don't want to give those reporters any more reasons to dig into Beartown Hockey . . ."

"What exactly are you worried the reporters will find?"

"No need to worry about that."

Teemu's tone isn't threatening, but it almost is.

"I'm not worried. I'm interested."

So Tails doesn't come straight out and say what he really wants, but he almost does.

"The editor in chief has been poking about in the club's accounts."

"Do you want me to keep an eye on her?"

"What? No, no, don't do anything stupid!"

Teemu understands exactly what they're talking about. Over the years he has become extremely good at hearing when someone can't ask him for precisely what they're asking him for.

"I won't do anything stupid. But I need something from you too, Tails. You've got to help us save the Bearskin."

"The Bearskin? From what?"

"Do you know who Lev is?"

Tails knows, of course. Everything is connected, in the end, tighter and tighter. Teemu explains the story of Ramona's debts and Lev's threats. Tails promises to talk to his political contacts and see what he can do. Before they end the call he says cautiously:

"Thanks, Teemu. I know you'd rather have seen Hed Hockey go bankrupt. I have a feeling you've been dreaming of killing that club off almost as long as I have . . ."

Teemu lets out a short laugh. He sometimes forgets that Tails also possesses hatred, it almost makes him sympathetic.

"Well, what else am I going to do, Tails? If we can't play against Hed, we can't beat the shit out of them. And if they haven't got a hockey club of their own, maybe those little assholes would start supporting ours, and do you think I want them in MY stand? Not on your life!" They end the call. This is how a community's corruption is measured. It isn't cheating if you don't get caught, and it isn't a scandal if it never gets revealed. Until then, there are just secrets. All forests are full of them.

———

That afternoon the editor in chief of the local paper stops to get groceries from the supermarket. She wants to surprise her dad with his favorite dish. While she's looking for the ingredients she can't help noticing two young men several times. They're never right next to her, but they're always near. When she pays they're farther back in the same line, and when she walks across the parking lot she thinks she sees them out of the corner of her eye, but when she turns around they're gone. When she gets in her car another vehicle drives past, a little too close and a little too fast, making her jump. She doesn't have time to see the license plate, but she could swear that the driver was wearing a black jacket.

When she gets home it's started to get dark, and she sees shadows everywhere. That night she wakes up when it sounds like someone is trying the handle of the front door to see if it's locked. The next morning a young man on a moped follows her all the way to work. To start with she thinks she's imagining it. Soon she hopes that she is.

69

Leaders

Zackell is sitting in the stands in the ice rink, the caretaker is sitting beside her, he glances at his watch and grins:

"Getting the A-team to train this late is a good way to wind them up."

She doesn't respond. The caretaker emits something midway between a cough and a snort. After Hed started using the ice rink she changed the schedule so that Beartown's A-team trained last of all the teams. Everyone else interpreted this positively, as if she wanted to set a good example and show that all the teams are of equal value, but the caretaker could see what Zackell was really doing. The same as always. Testing her team.

"Have you decided who's going to be captain this season yet?" he asks, and of course she doesn't answer that either, but he imagines he can see a trace of a smile seeing as he's asked the same question every day of preseason.

There are plenty of big words that get repeated on a hockey team, but perhaps none gets trotted out as much as "leadership." The problem is that it means different things in different places, because not all leaders can lead every team, there are so many different ways to take a group with you, and most leaders only know one. "What's it called when you go out into the forest and other men follow you? Leadership. What's it called if the same man goes out into the forest on his own? A walk." He told Zackell that joke once and she smiled then too, but not as if she thought it was funny. The caretaker could never figure out if it was because she didn't understand the joke, or because she thought he was the one who didn't get it.

"Should I lock the doors?" he wonders. She's wanted him to do that recently to teach the players to arrive on time.

But Zackell shakes her head.

"No. We're waiting for one more."

Then she gets up and goes down to the locker room. The A-team is only half ready, and there's a lot of moaning and whining about the late training session. It's ridiculously easy to unbalance a group of grown men, you just have to disrupt their routines. Zackell has never had any difficulty understanding that all wars are started by men, but if any of them ever managed to win one it was nothing but a miracle.

Bobo yells at the players to shut up when she comes in, and they quiet down just enough for her not to have to raise her voice when she says:

"We're sharing the ice with the juniors today."

"What the . . . ," the players begin, and the cacophony of grown men feeling sorry for themselves starts up.

The team has slowly gotten used to Zackell's peculiar training ideas, or has at least accepted them. All players do that if something works. Winning cures everything. But this business of only training on half the ice is still driving them crazy. Not long ago Zackell read a newspaper article about a small hockey club down in one of the big cities which, despite a lack of time on the ice and a general shortage of resources, year after year nurtured players who got drafted to the NHL. When the chair of the club was asked why he thought that was, he replied that perhaps it wasn't despite the lack of time on the ice, but because of it. Two or three of the youth teams always had to play at the same time, so everyone had to get used to playing on a small area, and it turned out that this made them better players. "Ice hockey isn't really played five against five," the chairman said, and until Zackell showed Bobo the article, Bobo had never thought about hockey that way. There are ten players on the ice during a game, but at any given moment hockey is only played on the square yard where the puck happens to be. Having to train in confined spaces turned out to be an advantage, and that's all hockey is: a series of slight advantages. A margin of a few inches.

So Zackell doesn't listen to the whining, she just leaves the locker room. Bobo lets everyone sigh and groan and swear for a few more minutes before he smiles secretively:

"I know you hate sharing time on the ice. But today we aren't sharing the ice with the juniors to train, because we're going to play . . . A PRACTICE GAME!"

The atmosphere changes in the space of one breath and a deafening cheer breaks out, because some things never change: everyone in here was once a scrawny junior who had to play a practice game against the men on the A-team and got crushed, and the reward for that is that if you train for enough years you will one day be an A-team player yourself and get the chance to crush the next generation.

"Can we play in our old tops?" one player asks eagerly.

Bobo shakes his head apologetically.

"No, sorry. You have to wear the white ones with your names on them," he says, and the players mutter unhappily at that, as usual.

Last winter the sponsors printed new training jerseys for every player, one white and one green, the club had never had names and numbers on training tops before but now all of a sudden it was important. No one understood why until Tails turned up at a training session with a photographer, who stood in the center circle and started taking pictures in the middle of the session. Tails wanted pictures for his advertising brochure and he wanted them taken from the ice in a way he couldn't manage during a game, so this was his solution. The players realized pretty quickly that the photographer was only focusing on one player, so one of them grunted to Tails: "Wouldn't it have been easier to print Amat's name on all the tops, then the photographer could have gotten pictures of any of us?"

Tails didn't even seem to notice the jibe, but that was how he got them all to hate those tops, and that's why Zackell is making them play in them today. She wants them annoyed. Bobo looks at the clock on the wall, goes out into the corridor, goes back in, looks at the clock again, and is about to give up hope when he hears the outside door creak and Amat tumbles in, breathless and flushed. Bobo's heart forgets its rhythm and his feet trip over themselves, and he only just manages to stop himself from running over and hugging his friend. Because that too is a test.

Amat wishes everything was so easy that a hug could resolve things. He walks toward Zackell over by the boards, she pretends she hasn't seen him, he stands there, overweight and pale and can't even summon up the courage to look her in the eye. She says nothing, forcing him to speak first.

"Can I . . . can I train today?" he manages to say.

"We're full," she replies coldly, nodding toward the ice where Aleksandr has just skated out.

Amat looks at him. He's big and strong, at least a head taller than Amat, and he moves with the natural self-confidence and privileged arrogance that Amat has always lacked. "The complete package" as the old guys in town usually call that sort of talent. That was what they used to say about Kevin.

"Okay . . . can I . . . I mean, can I use the gym? If I won't be disturbing anyone?" Amat asks, and notices to his own annoyance that he's fighting back tears.

Zackell doesn't even look at him when she replies:

"We're playing a practice game against the juniors. There's a space on their team if you want to play."

Amat nods down at the floor with a head so heavy it's a miracle he can stand.

"Great. Thanks," he whispers.

"You can pick up your green training top in our locker room and get changed with the juniors," Zackell instructs him blankly.

So first Amat has to go to the A-team locker room, which falls totally silent when he steps in seeing as no one has seen him since the spring, to fetch his green jersey. Then he has to go across the corridor and into the juniors' locker room, which also falls totally silent, but for completely different reasons. The juniors are only a few years younger than him, but that doesn't matter, in this context they're just kids and he's an idol. One of them leaps up and offers him his place on the best bench with the most space, but Amat shakes his head sadly and sits down in the corner right by the bathroom. That's where you always put "the worm," the youngest and worst player on the team. That was where he had to sit the last time he played on the junior team.

"Are you playing with *us?*" one of the other boys eventually plucks up the courage to ask.

Amat nods and a happy murmur spreads around the room. Then they all fall silent again and Amat feels fear cut from his stomach to his throat when he realizes they're all watching him. He doesn't want to take his clothes off, definitely doesn't want to talk, but these guys are evidently expecting him to say something. He suddenly wishes that Benji was here, because he would just have stood up and said "Come on, let's go out and slaughter them!" or something, and they'd all have leapt up and cheered and followed him. But Benji is Benji, and sadly Amat is Amat.

"Sorry!" the player next to him says just as he's thinking this, his fingers slipped as he was tying his boots and he hit Amat's leg.

Amat sees that the boy's hands are shaking.

"Nervous?" he asks quietly.

The boy nods.

"We're playing the fucking A-team! They're going to crush us!"

Amat has no answer so he says nothing. He gets undressed and the silence around him is like insects under his skin. When he picks up his training top he sees that the boy next to him is looking on enviously. The juniors have similar tops, but they don't have their names on the backs, for the A-team those names may have been a PR stunt, but for the juniors they are a status symbol. If you get your name on a training jersey that means the club isn't thinking of dropping you.

"Has anyone got a knife?" Amat asks quietly.

The others look confused.

"A knife?" one of them repeats.

"I've got one," a small boy in the opposite corner says, because you can always rely on the fact that in a Beartown locker room there'll be at least one hunter, and they always have a knife.

It gets passed from hand to hand around the benches and when it reaches Amat he grabs it and starts unpicking his name from his top. Letter by letter until his looks like all the others. Then he stands up, passes the knife back, and says:

"I'm not good at giving speeches and shit like that. And you're right, the A-team is going to crush you today. They're bigger and stronger."

He clears his throat and falls silent, just long enough for someone to say:

"Great pep talk!"

The whole room bursts out laughing, Amat included, and something loosens up inside him. Something that has been there a long time. So he starts talking without knowing where he's going.

"I . . . well, I read about a figure skater. Don't remember her name. But she was in the world championships and she was the big favorite, so her coach told her to remove all the difficult jumps from her opening program, just do the simple things but do them perfectly: that way she'd win. So she went out . . . and fucked everything up. She fell on things she'd never fallen on before. Couldn't do anything. By the time she'd finished she was bottom. Worst moment of her life. So she went into the locker room and sat there on her own and thought . . . 'fuck it,' pretty much. So she went out and did the next round and landed all the most difficult jumps, the ones none of the others could do. She moved from last place to bronze. Do you see? Because . . . well . . . I don't know what the hell I'm trying to say, I'm no good at this sort of thing, but . . ."

The room is silent and everyone is waiting for some sort of point. He hasn't got one. It feels like giving a talk in school and realizing you've misunderstood the whole task. Amat is about to try to sink through the floor when the boy next to him says:

"I read about her too. The figure skater. I think she said afterward something like she can't skate easy programs because then she thinks too much. She's only good when she challenges herself . . ."

One of the other guys exclaims:

"Like my mom always said when I was little and moaned about us playing good teams: 'It's SUPPOSED to be hard!'"

Several of the other players burst out laughing.

"My mom too! Classic Beartown-mom stuff!"

Amat sits back down and joins in the laughter, ties his skates, and gets up again without thinking of the consequences. Then the rest of them get up. When he walks toward the corridor they follow him, and when they storm onto the ice it's a moment every junior behind him will remember and boast about for the rest of their lives: the day we played with Amat.

The letters of his name are left on the bench in the locker room, so that everyone knows that he isn't playing for himself this time.

―――――

Beartown Hockey's A-team didn't exactly start out as Sunday-school preachers, but it's been a long time since they swore this much during a training session. They have to skate themselves sweaty and bloody just to keep up, every junior excels himself in every change of line, they give everything they've got for Amat, who seems to be everywhere. He may be overweight and slower than he has ever been, but still no one on the A-team can keep up with him. So they do the only logical thing: they swipe and hack and tackle him hard. A couple of times he takes such ugly slashes that he's sent flying, but when Bobo looks over to Zackell to see if she wants to call a penalty she just shakes her head. She wants to make him mad, she wants to know what he can do with his anger. A couple of times Amat flies up and looks like he's about to lash out, but he manages to control himself, even when he hears the A-team players laughing and making fun of him. He gets a stick across the back but sees it coming, so he steps aside and pulls free and takes the puck back, flies past two opponents with a frenzy no one has seen in this rink since he was the best here last winter. His top is sitting more tightly around his stomach but the longer the game goes on, the more he starts to look like the old Amat. The unstoppable Amat. The only reason he doesn't score ten goals in the end is that Zackell keeps pairing him against Aleksandr, who might be slower but plays much smarter. No matter what Amat comes up with, Aleksandr manages to reach it with his stick, time after time, knocking the puck out of the way. In the end the two of them are almost only playing against each other, hunting back and forth across the ice like shadows. Several times Aleksandr is left standing with his hands on his knees during breaks in play, gasping for breath, and Amat throws up at least twice in the players' bench. It's a hell of a game, really one hell of a game, Bobo feels sorry for everyone who isn't there to see it. The juniors score four goals, three of them from Amat. Aleksandr only scores two, but the A-team scores six in total and wins the game. It doesn't matter. When Bobo eventually blows his whistle for the end of the game the A-team players stay on the ice and applaud the juniors. Only briefly, hitting their sticks on the ice a few times, but that means the world to the teenagers.

They gather in their respective locker rooms, but Amat can't even drag himself there and slumps to the floor in the corridor. Aleksandr is the last player to walk past, he stops for a moment, prods Amat's skate with his stick, and says:

"I look forward to playing against you when you're in shape."

Amat smiles.

"Me too."

It's a small challenge, they both need it. She's not stupid, Zackell. Aleksandr goes into the A-team locker room and Amat forces himself to his feet to limp to the juniors'. He hears a rumbling laugh behind him and knows who it is without even having to turn around.

"Shut up, Bobo, I know I'm walking like an old woman . . ."

"I haven't even said anything!"

"No, but I know what you were ABOUT to say so I'm saying shut up! And don't touch me, I hurt everywhere already . . ."

Bobo roars with laughter and wraps his huge arms around him mercilessly.

"Didn't I say? You're like those lupines!"

"Thanks, mate," Amat grunts.

It hardly ever strikes him these days, but there and then it occurs to him that most people really never change, but some change entirely. Bobo used to be the biggest bully and tormentor when they played on the junior team, not that anyone would believe that now. Possibly just as little as anyone would believe that Amat used to be an elite sportsman.

"What do you think she'd have said about you today?" Bobo sniggers, nodding toward the photograph of Ramona on the wall.

"She'd probably have said I was a fatso," Amat smiles.

Bobo pats his stomach contentedly.

"She'd have looked at me and said that now the big fatso has shit out a little fatso!"

Amat laughs so hard that his whole body hurts. Then he shuffles toward the sound of jubilant juniors farther along the corridor.

"Wrong way!" Bobo calls out, not as a friend but as the assistant coach.

Amat turns around as if he thinks he's the victim of a cruel joke.

"Really?" he struggled to say.

"Really! Zackell's counting on you for the first game against Hed this weekend! So run, fat boy, run!"

Amat tries to hold back the tears. Bobo has already moved his things into the A-team locker room. No one remains silent when Amat steps in this time, no one even looks up or gets out of the way, they just carry on talking as if everything is the same as usual. As if he belongs there. His old place is free, Aleksandr is sitting in the place where the guy who made the joke about Lev used to sit back in the spring, because that guy doesn't play here anymore. Whether that was because of the joke or because he just wasn't good enough for the A-team is something Amat will never know.

He takes his clothes off, aware of everyone glancing at him, and walks alone to the shower room. No one follows him. He stands alone under the warm water with his sore muscles and even more sore ego.

When he comes out again there's a knife on the bench. His teammates have all picked their own names off their training tops. No one says a word, they just throw the names in the bin and go and shower, one by one, until Amat is left alone with the sound of his own breathing on the bench in the corner. That's how he came to lose a game and win back a locker room.

———

The A-team's training sessions don't usually get much of a crowd, but today the stands are strewn with familiar faces. Maya and Peter are sitting there eating their chocolate balls, the caretaker is keeping them company, and after a while the former coach of the A-team, Sune, appears with his dog. Halfway through the session they hear light steps on the stairs and a whisper:

"Sit in front of me! I don't want him to see me!"

It's Fatima. She's been longing to see Amat train again but is terrified that he'll catch sight of her and feel the pressure. That she might somehow break the magic. Peter and Sune laugh that she's going to end up being one of those superstitious mothers who collect more bizarre rituals they have to perform on game days than their sons.

"Soon you'll be sitting here with incense and talking about driving out evil spirits if he doesn't score enough goals . . ." Sune grins.

He can say whatever he likes, of course, because she's not listening. Her boy is playing hockey down there, nothing else exists then. Maya is sitting in front of her, and when Amat scores Fatima grabs her shoulder so hard that she feels embarrassed. Maya laughs and assures her that it doesn't matter, but then she turns and catches sight of something, and that makes her squeeze Fatima's hand a little too hard instead: the door to the ice rink opens and a lone figure creeps in and sits down in the far corner.

"Speaking of evil spirits . . ." The caretaker smiles when he sees that it's Benji.

Sune and Peter turn around as if their own child has come home. Neither of them manages to say a word, so Sune's dog's enthusiastic barking will have to suffice for them all. Zackell is standing down by the bench and she sees him too, she isn't big on emotions because she isn't big on people, but she still hasn't let anyone play with the number 16 since he left. She'll save that number on every team she ever coaches, because deep down she'll never stop hoping that precisely this will happen: out of nowhere, the door will open and he walks into the ice rink as though nothing's happened. She'll coach far greater talents, quicker and more technically skilled, but she will never have a team where she wouldn't have swapped any of them for that long-haired idiot. He meets her gaze on the other side of the ice and gives a curt nod, she nods back. That's all. Benji is scared that if he goes closer she might ask if he wants to play hockey again, and he can't bear the idea of disappointing her, so he keeps his distance. Zackell isn't big on regretting things, but she'll regret not going over to him at once and saying that she's missed him. Just like she will always regret never saying that to Ramona.

The training session continues, the players on the ice are too busy to see what's going on in the stands, so Benji sits right at the top in the shadows and just listens to the noises. The slice of the skates, the echoes, the panting. *Bang bang bang*. He left Amat's bag outside the rink a good while ago, and made fun of him for being so nervous, but now, of course, it was Benji's turn to stand outside in the cold, shaking so much that it took half the training session before he could bring himself to open the door and step over all the ghosts of his past. One of them gets up now and walks slowly around the ice and sits down next to him without asking for permission, then tucks her arm under his and rests her cheek on his shoulder.

"Maya Andersson at hockey training? That new guy Bobo was talking about must be seriously hot!" Benji exclaims and she hits his arm as hard as she can and laughs.

"You're such a muppet, the whole lot of you are such muppets!"

Benji just grins and nods toward the ice.

"Is that him there?"

Maya snaps:

"Yes. His name's Aleksandr but Zackell just calls him 'Big City' because they're such stupid muppets that I can't stand it!"

Benji frowns.

"He IS pretty damn hot, Maya . . ."

"I knooooow . . . ," she sighs resignedly.

He bursts out laughing. She has chocolate balls in her pocket and he's been smoking weed all day so he devours them, one bite per ball.

"Good to see that you haven't changed entirely, at least." She smiles.

Benji closes his eyes quickly and opens them slowly. He looks up at the roof as if he's trying to see right through it.

"Is it weird for you, coming home? It's been seriously weird for me. Just this rink, it feels cramped now, but when we were young it was . . . enormous."

"Yes. It's all weird. I don't even feel at home in my own house anymore. I don't even say 'going home' when I come here . . . ," she admits.

He says nothing for a long time. Then he asks:

"Do you ever think about what your life would have been like if Kevin hadn't existed?"

She whispers, as shocked by the question as she is by the speed of her reply:

"All the time. Do you?"

His chin moves in the world's smallest nod.

"Do you think you'd still have been living here then?"

After an eternity of reflection she replies:

"Yes. I'd probably have gone on being a naive and happy little girl. I'd have gone to parties and drunk disgusting shots and gossiped at school about who had slept with who. I'd have sat up all night listening to Ana bang on about how sexy that Benji was . . ."

"I'm still sexy!" Benji interrupts firmly.

"Yeah, yeah, you bastard, you are. But you knowing it makes you a bit uglier." She smiles.

He appears to hesitate before he asks:

"Then what? Once you graduated from high school in Beartown? Would you have stayed then? If it hadn't been for Kevin?"

She considers this carefully.

"Yes . . . maybe? Maybe I'd have gotten together with some crazy hockey guy and had a little house with a little yard and two children and a cat called Simba and a dog called Molly . . ."

"I love that you've given names to your future pets but not your future children," Benji grins.

"For the time being I'm far more keen on pets," she grins back.

"Are you happy, then? In that little house?"

"Yes. Yes, I probably am. But I write really bad songs."

He laughs.

"I'd have lived there with you if your husband left you."

"If my husband left me it would probably have been because you'd slept with him, you bastard."

"True," he concedes.

"I'm proud of you," she whispers into his sweater.

"I'm proud of you too," he replies into her hair.

Someone yelps breathlessly a few rows below them.

"What about me? Isn't anyone proud of me? You're shit friends, the pair of you, you're the pits! Can you believe that I had to use the stalker app I installed on your phone to figure out that you were here?"

Ana clambers cheerfully over the seats up toward them. Maya has nine missed calls on her phone, she realizes with embarrassment.

"Hang on . . . you installed a stalker app on my phone? So you can see where I am? What for?" she blurts out in accusation, and Ana throws her arms out in a gesture of complete incomprehension:

"Because of situations exactly like THIS!"

70

Players

Once all the other A-team players have showered and gone home, Amat, Mumble, and Big City are left sitting alone in the locker room. They're almost ready to leave when Amat plucks up the courage to ask:

"Do you want to do some extra training early tomorrow morning, Mumble? Like we used to . . . just come here and practice a few shots . . . I can ask the caretaker to open up for us."

Mumble nods enthusiastically. Big City raises an eyebrow and wonders tentatively:

"Can I join in?"

Amat nods happily. Then he stands beside his bag for a few seconds before summoning up the courage once again to suggest:

"Unless you want to maybe do it . . . now?"

It isn't even a discussion. They take off all their clothes and get changed into their training gear again. Out in the stands the little crowd has started to move toward the door, but when the players show up again they all turn back: the caretaker, Fatima, Sune, Peter, Benji, Maya, and Ana. The ice rink ought to be shut up and dark by this time, but no one is going to suggest that now. Amat takes a turn and fires a puck into the right of Mumble's goal, and the rattle of the net lifts every soul in the rink, and when he laughs and cheers it's the first time Fatima has heard her child happy in months.

"Laughter in an ice rink, so the world hasn't totally gone to hell yet, that it hasn't . . . ," the caretaker mutters, then wanders off to his storeroom to be alone with his feelings.

Sune laughs and his dog licks his face. Peter has never felt like he's come home as much as he does right then. In the stands on the other side of the ice sit Benji, Maya, and Ana. Amat stops below them and calls mockingly to Big City:

"Hey! Have you met Benjamin Ovich? He's a legend in this town! He actually used to be pretty good at hockey! Not as good as YOU, of course, but he was perfectly OKAY . . ."

Benji resists as long as he can. Longer than anyone would believe. But then he curses and stands up, muttering:

"Get me a pair of fucking skates so I can break that idiot's legs . . ."

Maya and Ana laugh so hard that it sings around the ice rink's roof, Amat too, but Big City stands next to him and whispers:

"He meant you, right? He meant he was going to break YOUR legs, right?"

Benji storms into the caretaker's storeroom and comes back out on a pair of skates. The caretaker has spent a lifetime in this rink and has seen more than most people can imagine, but he can't remember a better moment than this. Zackell and Bobo are up in the office to plan the next training session, but when they hear the noise and cheering from down on the ice they go back out into the stands. Bobo sees Benji and looks like a Labrador that's just heard keys jangling in a door, Zackell nods, apparently unmoved, and says:

"I can finish up in the office. You go and play with your friends."

Bobo stumbles euphorically down the stands but Zackell doesn't go back to the office. She stands and watches as Benji chases Amat across the ice and Amat bounces away and laughs and Bobo pulls on a pair of skates and throws himself into the fray and one of the very best things of all happens: almost-adults forgetting that they're adults.

They split into teams: Benji, Bobo, and Mumble on one side, Amat and Big City on the other. That's uneven so they shout up to Peter in the stands and nag him until he goes down to fetch a pair of skates. Maya can hardly believe her eyes, but her dad comes out onto the ice and actually seems to be . . . having fun.

Big City finds Amat with passes where no passes ought to be able to get through. It looks like luck every time. Amat lands the puck in the net and as he skates past Bobo on the way back he pants:

"Did you see that pass? Poor Hed in that first game. Poor, poor Hed. That guy can read my mind . . ."

Big City actually only makes one mistake: he draws the puck away and darts past Benji, and Benji loses his balance and everyone laughs. After that he isn't allowed an inch of ice without Benji being there like some furious badger.

"Did you really have to laugh? He's going to kill me!" Big City whispers to Peter when he stops close to the goal, but Peter just chuckles:

"No, no, don't worry, Benji isn't going to kill you here. Far too many witnesses. You'll just 'disappear' suddenly when we least expect it. There's a lot of forest around here, you know, you can bury anything out there!"

Big City stares at him as if he's really, really trying to figure out if the local sense of humor is that stupid, or if Peter is actually serious. Behind him Benji is chasing Amat from one end of the rink to the other, and by the time they reach the far end they're both red in the face from exertion. Bobo skates over to see if they're okay, but just as he's about to suggest that they take a short break Benji's body folds over and he throws up all the chocolate balls he's eaten across the goal line and Bobo's skates.

"OH MY GOD . . . BLOODY HELL . . . FOR CHRIST'S S— NO! NO! EURGH, I STOOD IN IT!" Bobo yells in panic and tries to jump out of the pool, with the predictable result that he slips and lands with a thump with his ass in the middle of the mess.

No one in the rink can breathe properly for several minutes, the laughter must have reached all the way to Hed. Fatima comes running over with a bucket and some rags but Amat skates over to the boards and stops her, takes the cleaning things from her, and goes out to clean up himself. Benji feels so guilty that he almost hits him.

"I've cleaned up after worse pigs than you," Amat grins.

"Not much worse!" Bobo points out in disgust, and when he sees how the vomit has frozen to the ice he almost throws up too.

"Is it the smell, Bobo, is it upsetting you?" Amat teases, and he and Benji laugh until their throats are hoarse.

Bobo's huge frame is racked with retching and Benji has to crouch down because his ribs are hurting so much from laughing. Bobo, incredibly indignant, is leaning against the boards and swearing blind to Amat that he's going to make Zackell reconsider her team selection and that makes Benji shriek with laughter, begging Bobo to stop talking because he can't take any more.

For Bobo's sake they move across to the other end of the ice, mark out a smaller area with caps and water bottles as goalposts. Then they play again, the way they used to play on the lake when they were younger: at full pelt without rules. Uncomplicated and simple. Us against you.

Amat will remember this evening as the start of something. Bobo as the end of something. For Peter it feels like belonging to something again, for Mumble it feels like belonging to something for the very first time. For Big City it's like getting a second chance to be a little kid and fall head-over-heels in love with hockey again. How it feels for Benji nobody knows, this is the last time they see him play.

One day Maya will write about this evening, her notepad soaked with tears:

> I remember that evening a while ago
> One of the last we knew before the blow
> For one night we finally got to see
> The man we dreamed you'd always be
> Your body a blur
> Your heart at ease
> You were all you wanted to be
> Happy and safe and free
> Where you are now my friend? I cannot know
> But I remember that evening a lifetime ago

71

Murderers

All children are victims of their parents' childhoods, because all adults try to give their kids what they themselves enjoyed or lacked. In the end everything is either a revolt against the adults we encountered or an attempt to copy them. That's why someone who hated their own childhood often has greater empathy than someone who loved theirs. Because someone who had a hard time dreamed of other realities, but someone who had it easy can hardly imagine that things could be any different. We take happiness so easily for granted if we've had it from the start.

Perhaps that's why it's so incredibly hard to explain what hockey is to someone who really doesn't get it. Because hockey is something we've always had, or haven't had at all. If you don't fall in love with it in time, you'll have gotten so big that you imagine that it's a sport. You have to have been a child the first time your body played and your heart relaxed to know that it's just a game. And if you're lucky, really lucky, it never stops being just that.

Snowflakes the size of oven gloves are falling on Beartown and the laughter inside the ice rink can be heard all the way out to the parking lot. It probably sounds either perfectly logical or completely mad, depending on who you are, but in some places a game can save an entire childhood. If you're always in the middle of it you don't feel any anxiety, any fear, because there's no room for those. All the game contains is eager cries and breathless laughter, and when all your friends are teammates you're never really alone. You don't fall asleep at night, you collapse, and your parents have to carefully peel your hockey jersey off you in bed. The next morning you wake up ravenous, you bolt your breakfast down, and you rush outside, because there are already kids playing out in the street. There's always a new game, always one final goal that decides everything. If you love a game, really love it, you remember almost nothing else of your younger years. All your happiest moments were when you had a stick in your hand, shoulder to shoulder with your best friends, a few square yards between two goals were the whole planet and we were the best in the world. The very finest thing you can give a child is somewhere to belong. The biggest thing you can have is being part of something.

That's why it hurts to be a different child. The one whose name no one remembers when they look back at school photographs because that child was never part of anyone else's childhood except their own. It's so cold being outside other people that you freeze to death all by yourself.

Matteo is standing in the darkness among the trees at the edge of the parking lot at the ice rink. He puts one foot down carefully on a frozen puddle and listens to the crack as the ice breaks. He wonders if the lake has started to freeze yet. When it does, it's a bigger day than Christmas for the town's hockey guys. There have been winters when even Matteo is glad when that happens, because then they get so absorbed in their game that they even forget to be bullies for a while. But sadly that never lasts for long.

Ruth always said: "Just get through these years! Just survive this town! Then you'll be free. We'll head out into the world, you and me, okay? Just make yourself invisible at school and stay away from the hockey guys." But that isn't so easy when the town is full of them. At around this time of year three years ago, when Matteo was eleven, he was riding his bike down by the lake when he got caught by some of the older boys from school. At first they tricked him into thinking he could join in, it's always so easy and so cruel, then they persuaded him to go out onto the ice to see if it was strong enough. "Farther out! Farther out!" they yelled, encouraging him at first, but soon threatening instead. "Keep going, or we'll break your legs when you come back!"

Eventually Matteo was so far out that when the ice started to creak he knew that if he started running it would be a death sentence, all his weight concentrated on one foot would send him straight down into the cold and darkness and he'd never get back out again. He's had hundreds of nightmares about that since then: seeing the light but being trapped, his little fists banging against the ice from below, trying in vain to find the hole, slowly drowning. So he did the only thing an eleven-year-old could think of, he lay down on his stomach and tried to spread his weight as evenly as he could. He had planned to crawl back toward land, but didn't dare. So he just lay there and wept.

He doesn't know if the boys on the shore regretted what they'd done then. After all, everything always began as a joke for those bastards, that was the excuse their parents always made afterward. It was a boyish prank. You know what children are like. It was just a bit of fun. Matteo couldn't hear if they were laughing or screaming because he was crying too hard out there with his lips pressed to the ice. It took a roar for him to react:

"WHAT THE HELL ARE YOU DOING?"

Carefully, carefully Matteo raised his trembling chin and looked toward land. Two teenagers his sister's age had stopped their moped up on the road and were now on their way down the slope. The boys ran off in all directions in horror, one of the teenagers was about to chase after them, fists raised, but the other one stopped him and pointed at Matteo. The ice creaked and Matteo screamed for the first time. The teenagers looked around in desperation for something to use as a rope, and when they couldn't find anything they took their jackets and tops off and tied them together. The lighter of them snaked out as close to Matteo as he could, tossed the improvised rope to him, and slowly, slowly pulled the child to safety.

Matteo can hardly remember what they said to him, his teeth were chattering too much, the roaring in his ears was too loud. But they asked where he lived and he managed to point, one of the teenagers rode his bicycle and the other let him ride on the moped. His parents were away doing more of their endless charity work with the church so only Ruth was home. She came rushing out of the house when she saw them and smothered Matteo in hugs before she asked the teenagers what had happened and they told her. Matteo didn't know that the teenagers were from Hed, or that the red jackets they were wearing came from the hockey team there. One of them held his hand out to Ruth and introduced himself.

That was how she met her murderers.

72

Campers

All the grown-ups go home first. They know that the magic in an ice rink full of laughing youngsters can be lost if another generation gets a little too close, like treasure that turns to ash if you open the chest. Maya, Ana, and Bobo are waiting on their own out in the parking lot for Benji, Amat, Mumble, and Big City to get changed and join them. Sune's dog is sniffing around their feet, used to thinking of this as its territory since it was a puppy. Since Sune retired it's actually spent so much time in the rink that it was even allowed to be in the last official A-team photograph. Mumble is playing with it, all animals love him, possibly because they recognize that he can't make himself understood either, despite wanting to.

"Do you want a lift home, then?" Bobo asks, but Mumble shakes his head and walks off to the bus stop.

"Training tomorrow? Early!" Amat calls out.

Mumble nods silently but with a smile that would have made any words redundant. They go their separate ways. Bobo drives Amat's bag to the Hollow, then he drives straight home to call Tess. Amat runs. He'll sleep soundly tonight, and wake up ravenous in the morning.

"How about you? Do you need a lift?" Benji asks nonchalantly, glancing at Big City.

"No . . . no . . . ," Big City replies evasively.

"Do you need anything else? I can help out with all sorts of things!" Benji grins with a shameless wink.

Big City glances at Maya and says, embarrassed:

"I . . . I might need somewhere to live. It doesn't feel like Peter wants to have me living there. I mean, it's great that he offered, but it doesn't really feel right. I think he locked my room from the outside last night . . ."

His cheeks are red. It could be embarrassing to try to discuss this here with Maya standing right next to him. Fortunately Ana is there to guarantee that it's embarrassing:

"He's just worried Maya's going to sneak into your room at night and jump on you!"

"Ana, you are SUCH a . . . ," Maya hisses, and Ana dances away laughing from her attempts to hit her.

"Really? Maya Andersson wants to fight? Has your new best friend taught you how to do that, or what? Come on, then! Hit me as hard as you can!" she teases, with the calm confidence of a martial arts fighter, and of course Maya could have spent ten years trying to hit her without ever getting close.

Big City looks at them, slightly shocked, and Benji looks at him with interest.

"I've got a campervan," he says.

"Sorry?" Big City exclaims.

"A campervan. If you need somewhere to live."

"I mean . . . seriously?"

"I meeean... seeeeriously?" Benji repeats, mimicking his accent.

Big City scrapes the sole of his shoe on the snow and pulls the jacket he borrowed from Peter tighter around him.

"You mean you've got a campervan that people . . . like . . . go camping in?"

Benji laughs so hard that he's shaking.

"I'm going to take a wild guess and say that you've never been camping, then, Big City?"

"ARE YOU GOING CAMPING? WE'LL COME!" Ana calls out quickly from a few yards away, where she is easily fending off a wildly flailing Maya with one hand as if she were a small child.

"It's below freezing," Big City points out.

"And?" Ana asks, not understanding.

"I've got weed and beer too," Benji informs them.

So they go camping.

Benji maneuvers the campervan along barely passable forest tracks, and miraculously manages to drive all the way to the water's edge without toppling the van, even if he came damn close, and parks it so they can see all the way to Maya and Ana's island from there. It used to be Kevin and Benji's, two boys' most secret place in the universe and their haven each summer, but those summers are long since gone and when Kevin moved away, Benji passed the island on to the girls. They're women now. Maya rests the tips of her fingers on Benji's shoulders, very briefly, and whispers:

"It's very romantic here, so I'm going to say straight off that if you bring my future husband here and try to sleep with him, I'll kill you."

Benji roars with laughter. He and Ana try to light a fire together until Ana threatens Benji with a big stick for doing it wrong, so then she does it on her own. There are fallen trees here and there, victims of the storm that passed through like a bandit on the run, but the gashes and wounds in the landscape are slowly being covered by snow and forgetfulness now. By spring, nature will have suppressed the impact of the winds that roared through last week, just like the people will. The youngsters sit huddled up in sleeping bags in front of the flames, drinking beer and smoking weed, looking at the stars and drifting into the fog. It's a good night, one of the very best, the sort you stay awake almost all the way through because you're clinging to a sense of almost calm in your soul. As if you've almost found the answers to almost everything. Tomorrow everything will be gone again, of course, but you know that. That's why you don't want to go to sleep. Eventually though Maya starts yawning and struggles to her feet from her folding chair in her sleeping bag and slurs:

"Bloody hell. It's been a long time since I've been this drunk. I have to see. No I have to SEE. No I have to seeeee . . . SCREW IT YOU KNOW WHAT I MEAN!"

The others laugh so hard their cheeks hurt.

"Go and SLEEP, you drunk, God, your new best friend down there at music college must be really shit at drinking if you've got this little stamina!" Ana giggles.

"What new best friend?" Benji wonders.

"The one Maya has abandoned me for!" Ana nods, so drunk that her pupils are in different zip codes.

"Well, I'm going to sleep with her future husband just for that!" Benji assures her, and he and Ana fail spectacularly to high-five each other.

Maya promises to tell them both to go to hell properly tomorrow morning when she's sober and can say the words. She's asleep before her head hits the pillow inside the campervan. Ana stays outside for a while so she can say that Maya collapsed first, then she tells the boys politely but solemnly to go to hell, and goes in and falls asleep back-to-back with her best friend.

Benji and Big City stay where they are, Benji looks at him and he looks at the sky.

"Are you going to do what all the tourists do now and say that you've never seen so many stars before?" Benji teases.

"We have stars where I come from too," Big City smiles.

Benji sounds almost insulted:

"Not as good as ours. Just like the hockey players."

That's a lie, of course, he noticed Big City's wrist movements and passes today and knows precisely how good he is. Big City looks him in the eye and knows that he knows, so he doesn't need to say anything, and instead asks thoughtfully:

"I looked Peter up online, he was the team captain of Beartown twenty years ago, right? They almost won the championship with him?"

Benji takes some deep drags with his eyes closed.

"That's Beartown, right there. Almost the best, almost all the time."

Big City rubs his fingers as if he were spinning invisible wedding rings on them.

"He said something, Peter, when he and Zackell came down to watch me train. I asked why he was there when he doesn't even work for the club anymore, and he said something like . . . he wanted to be good. That hockey was his way to make the world better."

"He's special," Benji says, and the way he says it contains all the best and worst of a person.

Big City takes a couple of slow drags and replies:

"It must be pretty damn special to . . . you know . . . be part of a team like that. One that shocks everyone. It must be a real brotherhood, you know? The sort that makes everyone better than their best? Like those dynasties in the NHL . . . they never last . . . they're only invincible for a few years before they all get too old and the team gets sold off. I wonder if you actually know how special it is when you're right in the middle of it?"

Benji half opens his eyes and looks at him, lit up by nothing but the dancing fire.

"Is that why you're here? To become special?"

Big City smiles sheepishly.

"Maybe."

Benji looks at him for a long time, then the question comes so fast and so disarmingly that it takes Big City by surprise and he chokes on the smoke.

"How many concussions have you had?"

"Wh-why . . . why are you asking that?" Big City coughs.

Benji shrugs his shoulders calmly.

"When we played today you were brilliant when I went for the puck, I didn't stand a chance. But when I went for your body you shied away every time. I played with a guy once, he was brilliant too, but he got like that for a while when we were fourteen and he'd had a concussion. He jumped away from every collision for several months."

Big City finishes coughing and puts a couple of branches on the fire, burning himself in the process of course, then mumbles:

"Was it that Kevin Erdahl?"

Benji looks surprised, for the first time all evening.

"How did you know that?"

It's Big City's turn to shrug his shoulders:

"Dad used to keep an eye on all the best players in the country when we were that age. He pinned a list on my wall. I actually saw you play once, Dad drove four hours to a game just to show me who I was up against. I remember being insanely jealous of Kevin."

"He was ridiculously good."

"Yes. But that wasn't why. I was jealous because he had you. Nobody dared touch him."

Benji says nothing for several minutes. Then he just repeats:

"How many concussions?"

Big City sighs.

"Six. The first when I was twelve, the most recent one last year. I got cross-checked in the back and flew into the boards. The guy got two minutes, I was out for nine weeks. I spent the first three days doing nothing but throwing up, I couldn't think, I just wanted to kill myself. I couldn't even be outside the house because the sun sort of cut into my head, it's the worst thing I've ever experienced, I lost my memory of that whole weekend. I still get migraines. I have ringing in my ears, it never stops. Sometimes it's just completely dark in here. I saw a guy in a game on TV get a similar blow, and you know what the commentator said? 'That's the recipient's responsibility, he needs to keep his head up!'"

He taps his temple. Benji can see the pain in his eyes and nods.

"Yes. I read about that NHL player whose personality changed, had all sorts of trouble. Permanent brain damage, but no one knew that until he died and they did an autopsy . . ."

Big City closes his eyes.

"When I got back to the team the coach wanted me to play more on the body, in front of goal, it was all 'fighting' this and 'fighting' that. He was obsessed with winning the physical game, you know, 'own the boards' and all that crap . . ."

"'Eat the puck!' 'Chew barbed wire!'" Benji mimics, because he's come across that sort of coach a million times.

"Exactly," Big City laughs bitterly.

"What happened then?"

"I didn't dare. And he saw that. I no longer fit into his system. So he benched me for not having 'a hard head,' and when I got annoyed he went to the club and said I had 'disciplinary problems.'"

"And did you?"

"That was probably the only club where I *didn't* have disciplinary problems. I was pretty immature for years, a cocky little shit, but I really did like that club . . . I wanted it to work. But I can't play the way those coaches want anymore . . ."

"And here?"

Big City breathes slowly through his nose.

"That Zackell seems . . . different."

"That's putting it mildly," Benji smiles.

"So maybe she'll let me play differently?"

"All I can say about her is that she probably already knows crap about you that you don't know yourself yet. Sometimes that's a good thing," Benji declares.

"And when it isn't good?"

"Most people don't want to know the truth about themselves."

Big City takes a while to digest this. Opens one last beer.

"I like Peter. I expected him to be a stuck-up asshole like all the other old pros, but he was . . ."

"Special?"

"This whole town is special. Is it the inbreeding or something?" Big City laughs.

"And the weed," Benji coughs.

The pair of them laugh for a long time, alone beneath the stars. One single really good night.

"How good was he? Peter?" Big City asks after a while.

Benji answers at once:

"He was the best. Seriously, though . . . he was obsessed. The stories about how he used to train are insane. When you're little you think things like that are a myth, you know, but I've seen old recordings and it was like nothing I've ever seen. He looked so damn slow, but no one got past him. No one!"

"As if he could slow down time. I noticed that when Zackell got me to play against him."

Benji nods seriously.

"Everyone thinks it was talent, but it was just practice. And obsession. It was the only thing he had in his life. How good do you think you could have been by now if you'd been like him?"

"What makes you think I'm not?" Big City smiles.

"You've got a game this weekend and you're sitting here smoking weed and drinking beer in a campervan in the forest," Benji points out.

Big City laughs, both relieved and weighed down.

"I couldn't have been as good as Amat, anyway. He's extreme. I don't think I've ever met anyone faster. He can get to the NHL. But me? No. Dad always thought I could be but he doesn't understand what it takes. You need to have something you're truly exceptional at, and I'm just . . . *good*. Dad could see I was the best in my little bubble, you know, there's someone like Amat in every little town. And in the NHL? They play one hundred games a year over there . . . I mean, the sacrifice that takes! Nothing but hockey, all day long, all year round. I don't think I could handle that. Dad's crazy, you know, he'd have chopped off his arm for just one season in the NHL. He had the desire but not the talent, and maybe I've got the talent but not the desire . . ."

"Desire is a talent," Benji says.

Big City's heart almost breaks when he hears that.

"What about you, then? Why did you stop playing?" he whispers.

"I stopped being in love," Benji replies.

Big City says nothing for a long time before he dares to ask:

"Do you think you could be again? In love?"

Benji looks him right in the eye and it's the sort of night when nothing feels impossible, so he replies:

"Maybe."

They go and lie down inside the campervan, facing the other way to Ana and Maya, and it's ridiculously cold but Big City still sleeps the whole night through without waking up once. It's been a long time since that happened. The next morning he wakes up early and steps out into the forest and sits alone and listens to something he hasn't heard before, at least not this completely, this overwhelmingly.

Silence.

73

Scratches

The night has taken Beartown, but it's already been dark for so many hours that it's barely noticeable. A gate creaks at the church and a lone figure steps carefully through the shadows, treading so softly on the snow as if it were glass and he barefoot. A few flickering candles by the graves are all he has to orient himself by, but he still seems to know where he's going.

Churchyards are meant to be final destinations, but for many of us all the gravestones are question marks. Why? Why you? Why so early? Where are you now? Who could you have been if everything had been different? Or if just something very small had been? If you had had different parents, a different name, if you had lived somewhere else?

There's almost no one who will remember her name. They'll say: "Oh yes, her, she was in one of my classes, she was the one who just disappeared a few years ago, wasn't she? I heard she ran away from home. Her parents are religious fanatics or something, right? That weird church, whatever it's called? I heard she was a junkie. That she went abroad and died of an overdose. Goodness, what WAS her name? I don't remember!"

Ruth. Her name was Ruth. It's on the gravestone. Just dates beneath it, nothing else, no poem or brief description of her. But at the top, in one corner of the stone, someone has carefully and tenderly carved a little pattern of scratches. You have to get really close to see that it's a butterfly.

The figure looks around in the darkness. One day his name will be on a gravestone and plenty of people will say: "Who? I don't remember him . . ." Then someone will have to remind them of the name everyone calls him, the one he was given because he hardly ever speaks: "Mumble."

He goes close to Ruth's grave, sinks to his knees, and runs his fingers over the letters. Then, shivering with despair, he repeats the same word over and over again, out into the night:

"Sorry. Sorry sorry sorry."

74

Chances

When Maya and Benji and Mumble and the others were standing outside the ice rink a while ago playing with Sune's dog, as if everything was fine and the world was good, Matteo was standing hidden in the darkness, watching them. He saw Amat and Bobo say good-bye to everyone, Bobo drove Amat's mother home and Amat ran. Benji, Maya, Ana, and that new player whose name Matteo doesn't know walked off toward an old campervan. Mumble walked alone toward the bus stop as if he was going to catch the bus to Hed, but when he thought no one was looking he turned off and went to the churchyard instead. Matteo crept after him. Now he's sitting hidden among the headstones, listening to Mumble sobbing in front of Ruth's grave.

Matteo doesn't know if that makes him hate Mumble more or less. He always thought that the guys who murdered his sister didn't care, didn't grieve for her, didn't even see her as a human being. But this is probably worse, he decides. It's worse that Mumble saw her as a human being, because if she was something else, just an object you could use and dispose of, then at least that made sense. But to do what they did to a human being? A real person? Then you're just evil. Then you deserve nothing but Hell.

If Matteo had had a gun he would have sent Mumble straight to Hell, right there and then. But now he's going to have to wait a few days for his chance.

75

Jam sandwiches

B*ang!*

Bang!

Bang!

When Sune retired there were plenty of people in the town who worried that he was going to spend all day sitting on his own with nothing to do, but now he can't understand how he ever had time to work. He has a dog that doesn't give a damn when he shouts at it to stop biting the furniture, and an almost seven-year-old girl standing in the yard firing hockey pucks at the wall. "They work well together, those two, demolishing the house from either side," Sune often mutters as he stands in the kitchen making liver pâté sandwiches for the hooligan inside and jam sandwiches for the hooligan outside. The last time he saw the doctor he was asked if he felt more tired than usual, and replied: "How should I know?" They didn't get any further than that, because Alicia had been left holding the dog out in the waiting room and they heard a commotion and then Alicia stuck her head into the treatment room to ask if potted plants were expensive. "Grandchild?" the doctor wondered with a smile, and Sune had no idea how to explain that they weren't even related. Once, thirty-five years ago, the same thing happened in the supermarket, only then it was a little boy who was following Sune around impatiently with a hockey stick in his hand, and someone said: "What a handsome son you've got." Sune didn't know what to say then either, the boy's name was Peter Andersson and no one had taught him how to fire decent shots and he'd never eaten a proper jam sandwich, so Sune set about remedying both of those. It became a lifelong friendship. Peter is the most beautiful cherry tree Sune has seen in Beartown, that was how he used to think of the very greatest talents: pink blossoms breaking into flower against all the odds in the middle of a frozen garden.

He never had kids of his own, at the end of his career he was only coaching grown men and never children, he had stopped thinking about cherry trees when Alicia had her first training session as a four-and-a-half-year-old. Youngest in the group, smallest on the ice, clearly the best right from the start. She's almost seven now, and so good that she causes uproar among the parents when the club lets her play with the boys. "Some adults are just stupid," Sune said sadly when she asked why she wasn't allowed to carry on training with them, but he hardly needed to tell her that. She already knew everything about adults. She no longer has as many bruises since Teemu paid a visit to her home and informed all those present about who was now protecting the girl, but she still has the sort of home environment where no one notices if she comes home for dinner, and on many days it's probably appreciated if she doesn't. So after school she goes straight to the ice rink if she has training, and home to Sune's if she doesn't. Other children might have made drawings for him to stick on his fridge, but Alicia isn't keen on drawing, so the puck marks in the plaster of his wall have become much the same thing: small marks in time that say someone you love grew up here.

It started with Sune teaching her how to play hockey but it went on with him teaching her everything else you need to know in life: tying shoelaces and chanting times tables and listening to Elvis Presley. She started following him and the dog out into the forest, and the old man taught her everything he knew about trees and plants, with occasional breaks for a short "take the dog and run on ahead, I'll catch you up" when he felt breathless and his chest hurt. That was happening more and more often these days, so often in fact that that was how he taught the girl to ride a bicycle, he ran behind her out in the street holding on to the parcel rack and when he couldn't run anymore he whispered "you cycle on ahead," and she did.

When she started school she came around to his place on one of the first days and said he needed a packed lunch because he had to go with them on a class trip. When Sune didn't understand what she was talking about she sighed irritably and said he was "an extra grown-up." When Sune still didn't get it, Alicia took her hockey stick and said she didn't have time for this, he'd have to call the teacher himself if he was going to be so slow. So, to the accompaniment of *BANG BANG BANG* from the yard, Sune did precisely that, and the teacher explained that she had told the children in class that they needed "an extra grown-up for the excursion," and Alicia had held her hand up and said that she knew one of those.

So now Sune and his dog go on all class excursions. When Sune heard the girl present it as "Sune's dog" to her classmates he felt obliged to correct her: "It's your dog too." As she stood and fired pucks that afternoon it felt like she needed a longer stick because she'd grown at least four inches.

Today she knocks on Sune's door early, before going to school. It's Wednesday morning, the middle of the week, the middle of the month, there isn't always food at home then. So she and Sune go to the shop to buy milk and bread and jam and liver pâté. Sune walks slowly on the way home. Alicia asks how old you have to be to play on the national team, he replies that it isn't about how old you are but how good you are.

"How old will you be when I'm allowed to play on the national team, do you think?"

Sune smiles.

"How old do you think I am now?"

"A hundred?" Alicia guesses.

"Yes, sometimes it really does feel like it," Sune sighs.

"Can I carry the bag?" she asks.

He pats her head.

"No, no, it's fine, take the dog and run ahead, I'll catch up to you!"

She does as he says. She lets the dog off the leash in the yard then stands and fires pucks at the wall for a while longer before school starts.

Bang. Bang. Bang.

76

Detours

Benji calls his sisters early on Wednesday morning and Adri swears the whole way to the lake. He's been given a campervan, the donkey, and obviously he's driven it down to the shore and gotten stuck in the snow overnight.

"It's a campervan, not an all-terrain vehicle, of course you got stuck here, you donkey!" Adri informs him as she jumps out of her car, but naturally that gets her nowhere with this particular donkey.

"It isn't a campervan anymore, it's a summer cottage now. Genius, if you ask me!" Benji grins.

He and Big City and Maya and Ana squeeze into Adri's car and she has to roll down the windows because they smell so badly of teenagers and hangovers that they could frighten foxes away. When they get back to the kennels Benji's laughter fills the kitchen in a way that his sisters and mother haven't heard in years. If Adri didn't know better, she'd have said he sounded like someone who's fallen in love. She almost can't manage to be angry with him. But only almost.

Ana skips school, Maya evidently doesn't have any plans to get back to college, so they have breakfast then set off into the forest again. They don't know exactly where they're going, but if these are the last days they're going to get when they can pretend to be children and that life is uncomplicated, then goodness knows, they're going to make the most of it.

Adri and Benji drive Big City to the ice rink. When he waves and goes inside Benji watches him and his sister watches Benji.

"You stink," she says affectionately.

"I can shower, what are you going to do about your face?" he retorts just as affectionately, and she hits him in the chest so fast with her fist that all the air goes out of him.

They drive an extra long detour around town, taking their time, listening to music, and talking without really saying much. When their dad took his shotgun and went into the forest Adri, as oldest sister, had to take on many of what she assumed were a father's duties. She taught Benji to fight, perhaps she should have taught him a bit more about how not to fight. She wants to tell him that he can choose not to be violent, but he'll only pretend that he thinks she means not fighting other people. She means that he shouldn't be so violent with himself. But today he's actually laughing in a way that makes her think he might be doing that.

"I love you, you damn donkey," she says, tugging his ear until he's laughing and yelping.

"I love you, sis. Thanks for always coming and getting me when I get stuck," he adds with a smile.

She'll never forget that.

11

Backs

When the editor in chief arrives at the newspaper's offices on Wednesday morning, the whole building seems to squirm uncomfortably. Half of the staff don't even look up from their desks when she walks past. Only when she reaches her own desk and sees who's sitting on the other side of it does she realize why.

"Hello! We've never met, but I've heard a lot about you! My name is Richard Theo!" the politician says as he gets to his feet, with the self-confident awareness of someone who knows that introductions are completely superfluous.

"Are you looking for a job?" she asks sharply.

He's secretly impressed by how quickly she adjusts to the situation, most people only dare to be so condescending toward Richard Theo behind his back. A long, long way behind it.

"I've got one, thanks. But we'll have to see what happens at the next election. Maybe I'll be in touch!" he smiles.

She grants him a smile in return, albeit a small one.

"So I assume you're here to tell us what a great job we're doing here on the local paper?"

"Something like that. Do you know what the meanest thing people say behind my back is?"

"Sorry?" she blurts out, unable to conceal her confusion, which was evidently his intention.

Theo looks almost hurt when he explains:

"They cite the prime minister who said that 'politics is will,' then they say mockingly that my version of that is 'politics is winning.' Naturally, I humbly disagree. For me politics is about doing. About getting things done. Not just empty words. Do you understand what I mean?"

"I doubt it," she says suspiciously, and he smiles broadly as if all he has said has been nothing but spontaneous nonsense, whereas in fact every word had been carefully considered.

"What's the meanest thing people say behind your back, do you think?" he asks inquisitively.

She peers at him, wishing for a moment that her dad was here, but he's still asleep at home after sitting up all night examining Beartown Hockey's accounts. What would he have said about Richard Theo? That there are two types of politician, the editor in chief concludes: the provocateur and the manipulator. One prods and pokes at random to see where the sore points are, whereas the other knows exactly what he's looking for.

"I don't speculate about what people say about me," she replies sharply.

"No? I thought that was the job of you newspaper people, reading public opinion?"

He smiles, she tries to reciprocate, but she's a much worse liar than him. She notes that he has today's newspaper open on his lap. The letters page. The editor in chief is well aware of what it contains, because she made the decision to publish it. The anonymous mother of a young player has written a scathing critique of Beartown Hockey's "macho culture." She had evidently submitted a complaint about one of the coaches of the boys' team and the coach of the A-team. The mother had been promised that the boys' coach would be fired and the A-team coach suspended. Instead she has discovered that the A-team coach missed just one training session and that the boys' coach only had his job "paused" for a month and would soon be taking charge of a new team. The mother writes that this is clear evidence of the hockey club's "patriarchal culture."

"If that's what you want to talk about, the letter was sent anonymously," the editor in chief says.

Richard Theo raises his eyebrows in amusement.

"This? No, no, that's none of my business. It strikes me as a good thing that people feel free to air their opinions about the club these days."

"Anonymously, yes," the editor in chief points out.

The politician holds his hands up.

"The confidentiality of sources is one of the cornerstones of democracy, I've always said that! Isn't the phrase 'patriarchal culture' odd, though? When the A-team coach is a woman?"

The editor in chief sighs the way you do when someone who definitely doesn't know what "confidentiality of sources" means deploys the phrase as a rhetorical accessory, then she says:

"I think 'patriarchal' describes a mentality rather than gender in this instance."

"Really? How modern!" the politician exclaims cheerfully.

"But that isn't why you're here?" the editor in chief asks, with a quiver in her voice that reveals her impatience.

So Richard Theo takes his time making himself comfortable and making small talk about the furnishings and the view before he gets to the point:

"I'm here in my capacity as a concerned citizen. I've heard a lot of rumors in recent days about a tension between Hed and Beartown which is starting to develop into . . . what shall we call it? 'Frustration'? I'd like to talk to you about what you and I can do to stop the situation escalating unnecessarily."

The editor in chief looks at him for a long time without quite being able to determine his agenda. So she decides to play for time by acting stupid:

"Oh? How do you mean?"

Theo understands perfectly well what she's doing, but like most men in positions of power he can't resist the opportunity to lecture a woman, so he says:

"We've had a full-scale fight between the boys' team players over in the ice rink in Beartown. Then one of the sponsors had his car vandalized here in Hed. And then there was the tragic accident at the factory that led to more violence, first in the parking lot at the hospital, then another vandalized car in Beartown. I'm concerned that this might be only the start if we don't do something to pour water on these burning embers."

"And you're here with the water, I presume?" the editor in chief wonders skeptically.

He takes a demonstratively slow breath.

"I've heard that one of your reporters is digging into the accounts of one of the clubs. Your father, I believe? Naturally, he's well known to us politicians. A legend, almost! So I want you to know that I have the utmost respect for the free media's right to hold the powerful to account, in fact I wish you would hold the powerful a bit MORE to account in this district, because there really are one or two stones that could do with being looked under . . ."

"Feel free to get to the point," the editor in chief suggests.

"I just want to reassure myself that you're not starting a witch hunt unnecessarily. Stirring up people's feelings until they do something violent. Because surely even the news media have a degree of social responsibility, don't they?"

The editor in chief leans back in her chair. She would have felt more confident if this conversation had taken place a few days ago, but now she seems to be seeing ghosts in the middle of the day and black jackets everywhere at dusk, and in the end that does something to even the most thick-skinned of people.

"I don't comment on investigations my reporters are working on, but I can assure you that regardless of whether it's my father or anyone else working on them, they will be correct and fair . . ."

The politician almost leaps out of his chair with feigned despair at having been misunderstood.

"Of course! Of course! I wouldn't dream of suggesting what you publish or don't publish! No, never! I'm just here to point out the importance of . . . timing. At a time when so many people are worried about what's going to happen to their hockey clubs, I'm sure neither you nor the newspaper's proprietor would want to risk being perceived as having . . . picked a side?"

She notes the way he stresses "newspaper's proprietor" as a subtle threat, but doesn't remark upon it.

"No matter what we do, someone will think we're taking sides. If we write something positive about Hed we get one hundred angry phone calls from Beartown, and vice versa. But as I said, everything we do will be correct and fair. I don't want to comment further on any possible investigations to a politician, because THAT could definitely be seen as picking a side, couldn't it?"

Richard Theo smiles contentedly, as if he hasn't yet decided if they're going to be best friends or the worst of enemies.

"You're not from around here, are you?"

"No. But you already knew that."

"I actually grew up in Beartown, not that you'd guess? I lost my accent when I lived abroad. I suppose I learned to see things as both an outsider and a native when I came back. May I give you some advice?"

"Can I stop you?" she asks with feigned toughness, even though she is actually a little shaken by how hard his expression is when he says:

"None of us should believe that we can cope with everything on our own. We live close to nature here. In the forest and on the lake, you need friends. Plenty of things can happen that we aren't prepared for. Like recently during the storm, you really wouldn't have wanted to be alone out there then. That would be foolhardy, not to say dangerous."

He stands up before she has time to reply. Holds out his hand so fast that it doesn't occur to her to refuse to shake it.

"Thanks for stopping by!" she says loudly, trying to sound confident.

He squeezes her hand tightly for a long time before nodding toward the letters page in the newspaper in his lap and declaring with a smile:

"That would never have happened when Peter Andersson was general manager of Beartown Hockey, I'm certain of that. He's an honest man. Someone I and many others have the greatest respect for. The *greatest* respect."

The editor in chief hates how obviously perplex this leaves her, and the way he enjoys seeing it in her eyes. She was prepared that news of the investigation into Beartown Hockey would leak out, but she will never know how Richard Theo found out that she was targeting Peter Andersson. It could have been someone at the council who had noticed which documents her dad had requested, but it could just as easily have been someone here in the office who talked, they're all reporters but some of them are, first and foremost, from Beartown. She'll never quite understand how everything and everyone is connected. In that respect, sadly, Richard Theo is right.

You need to be from around here to do that.

78

Team dogs

Adri and Benji stop by Sune's house. Adri wants to pick up an old set of training jerseys that she's going to try on the girls' team. It was never her intention to become a coach, but then very little of life is actually intended. She never planned to breed puppies either, it just turned out that way because she was good at it. Sune got his puppy from her several years ago when he retired, it was Benji who picked it for the old hockey coach, saying: "That one. Because he's a challenge." He really was, so now Adri is training Sune how to train a dog, and he's training her how to train under-seven-year-old hockey girls. The pair of them started up the whole idea of a girls' team, that was how they found Alicia, they went from door to door around the whole town asking if there were any girls who wanted to play. There's never been anyone who wanted to play more than Alicia. Secretly, Adri has never felt prouder of anything.

"Coffee?" Sune asks, as if there was actually any doubt.

"Is it scorched as usual?" Adri wonders.

"Apologies, your majesty, I didn't know that such fine folk would be visiting, or I would obviously have chilled the champagne!" Sune replies.

Adri gives him a hug, and she hardly ever hugs anyone. He has no family left in the world, but he has so much family in this town these days that he almost doesn't have time to shout at them all.

"Have you seen the newspaper?" he asks, nodding toward the open paper on the kitchen table, he and Adri must be two of the last people on the planet who still refuse to read their news on tablets and similar new-fangled nonsense.

"The letters page? Anonymous cowards as usual," Adri snorts.

Yes, of course she's seen it.

"What is it you usually say? 'Just because you're an idiot doesn't mean that you're wrong'?" Sune smiles.

Adri smiles weakly too. Everything the anonymous writer says is actually true: the endless arguments about resources, parents trying to influence team picks, coaches who express themselves like Stone Age men. Adri knows, because she knows what everyone says about the investment in the girls' team, even though no one dares say it in front of her. When she and Sune set up the team there was no question of getting sponsorship for their equipment, they had to fight the rest of the club just to get time on the ice, but when it came to marketing Beartown Hockey, suddenly it suited everyone to have the girls on every glossy publicity brochure. The hypocrisy sickens her, but she still says:

"I don't like the phrase 'patriarchal culture.'"

Because there are plenty of men like Sune, the people who write these letters forget that, they forget whose shoulders clubs like this were built on in the first place.

"Just because you're an old man doesn't mean that you're not an idiot," Sune smiles.

The house is surprisingly quiet, Adri peers into the hall and realizes that's because the dog is outside and Benji has already settled down in an armchair and fallen asleep. There are photographs hanging on all the walls around him, the really old ones of aging hockey guys have had to make way for all the pictures of Alicia and the dog. There's even a framed cutting from the local paper about the "team dog" after it was included in the A-team's photograph.

"Sugar?" Sune calls from the kitchen.

"Nope," she replies.

"Did you hear that Tails's car got vandalized in Hed?"

"Yes. And that fight in the rink too. Players from the boys' teams. I don't know what they expected when they let Hed train here."

"Trouble at the factory after that accident too."

"Yes. Yes."

"And Hed's thirteen-year-olds play Beartown's thirteen-year-olds tomorrow."

"So I heard."

Sune says the next thing as if he's just thought of it, but Adri knows him well enough to realize that the entire exchange has been innocently leading up to this:

"I heard that Teemu's guys might show up. Things are tense between them and the guys in Hed after everything that's happened."

Adri raises her eyebrows above her coffee cup.

"Are those idiots really thinking of bringing their fight to a game between . . . thirteen-year-olds?"

Sune shrugs his shoulders resignedly.

"Same thing as usual, I suppose: young men and their territory. Oh, maybe I'm just an anxious old man. But I just wanted to mention it, in case you can talk some sense into any of them. Or in case you want to . . . keep anyone away from there."

Adri nods firmly. She's known Teemu Rinnius since they were little, no one can talk sense into him. But that isn't who Sune means. He wants her to make sure that Benji doesn't get caught up in the middle of it all. Because he has a tendency to do that, the donkey.

Bang.

Bang?

Bang? Bang?

Sune has always written things down. For many years it was mostly to do with hockey, of course, short phrases mixed with circles and triangles and lines pointing this way and that. Only when he started to get older did he start writing other things down. What he's felt and how he feels. It started with physical things, because his doctor asked him to keep a diary of his aches and pains, but the words grew inward. Recently he has been writing a lot about death. He's reached an age now where that has become unavoidable, not like youth when you can deny it or middle-age when you suppress it. Most of all, Sune writes lists. Instructions for how everything works in the house, which windows stick when the weather is bad and which plug sockets should be avoided if you don't want an unforgettable experience. Which side of the yard floods in spring and which plants on the terrace have recently been repotted. And the dog, of course. Sune has a whole notebook full of nothing but his veterinary history, his favorite brands of liver pâté, and crystal-clear instructions for the day he dies and the dog has to be taken care of. He tried to give it to Adri not so long ago, but she lost her temper. "You're not going to die, you miserable old sod!" she roared, then refused to discuss it for a second longer.

It was a declaration of love, as big as she could give.

Bang?

Sune has never tried to write about love. Perhaps he should have. Something about how much of it you can experience without ever getting married or having children of your own. How much of his own has been wordless, given to others and reciprocated without a single word of acknowledgment. Hockey can't speak, of course, it just is. Dogs can't speak either. They just love you.

Bang?

That damn animal. Unmanageable and impossible, wild and crazy, never gives him a moment's peace, and there's nothing Sune is more grateful for than that. He was never really prepared for the love he would feel for his dog. That's what he says, my dog, even though the entire basis for what he feels when it looks at him is the exact opposite: that he belongs to it. That he is its human. It trusts him so much that it sometimes becomes too much for him, because he doesn't know if he can handle the responsibility. He doesn't know if he can cope with being so needed. So loved. No matter how many mornings he gets woken by those eager paws on the edge of the bed, that rough tongue on his face, he is still taken aback by its acceptance of him. Dogs are like hockey, a fresh chance every morning, everything is constantly beginning again.

"What are you going to call it?" Adri wondered the very first time he held the puppy, and Sune thought for a long time. He had never thought about a name. It suddenly felt like an immense responsibility, and the little scrap of a puppy could hardly tell him what it thought either. So in the end Sune didn't chose a name at all, because all his loves have been wordless. He chose a sound. The one he loves most of all. The sound he has heard in the ice rink all his life, and hears against the wall of his house every afternoon now. The sound that tells him that there's still life, that he's still here, that he's still needed by someone.

"Bang," he said. "I might call him Bang."

Bang?

He goes around the house shouting it now, breathless and with one hand on his chest. He always feels like he's got indigestion these days. But the dog doesn't come. After a while Adri senses that something's wrong and follows him outside, calling as well, so loudly that Benji wakes up and comes running out. Bang may be a stubborn creature, but it's time for food now and the greedy little dog never misses that.

BANG? BANG? BANG?

He's lying deep in the bushes behind his favorite tree. He looks like he's sleeping. But his little ears don't react when Sune steps across the grass, his little paws don't move, his little heart doesn't beat. He doesn't chew his slippers to pieces. He doesn't bark so that Sune can tell him to shut up. He doesn't lick his face. He's no longer there.

79

Tears

The vet sits quietly by Sune's side in the kitchen for more than an hour. Adri washes every plate and glass in the whole house even though there's no need, just to keep her hands occupied so she doesn't break everything in sight. Benji goes out into the forest with dark eyes and comes back with bloody knuckles and a stone large enough for a small grave. One of the neighbors fetches tools so they can carve the dog's name and dates. Beneath them, Sune asks him to carve the only message he can bring himself to say:

You run on ahead.

Adri and Benji are waiting in the schoolyard when Alicia finishes school. She cries for hours, cries so much that it's impossible to believe that so many tears could still be inside that little body, cries until the daylight has gone and she's sitting curled up by Bang's tree in the darkness, refusing to move no matter what anyone says. Cries until she's lying exhausted in the snow and Benji has to go out and get her so she doesn't freeze to death. He knows what death is like for a child, he knows what it's like to be overwhelmed by emptiness, so he says nothing to console her. He makes no promises about Heaven and tells no lies about paradise. He just does the only thing he can do to help. He puts a stick in her hand and whispers:

"Come on. Let's go and play."

They reach the ice rink in the middle of the night. Adri has called ahead so the caretaker can leave a window open for them to climb through. Benji and Alicia play until they can hardly breathe. Then they lie on their backs in the center circle, above the painted image of the bear, and the girl who is almost seven years old asks the boy who is barely twenty:

"Do you hate God?"

"Yes," Benji replies honestly.

"Me too," she whispers.

He considers just how irresponsible it would be to tell the seven-year-old that these feelings will get easier to cope with when she gets old enough to smoke really good weed, but he imagines that Adri would break all his fingers very slowly, so he doesn't. Instead he says:

"It's going to hurt a hell of a lot for a hell of a long time, Alicia. There will be some grown-ups who tell you that time heals all wounds, but it never bloody does. You just get a bit damn tougher. And it only hurts a tiny bit fucking less."

"You swear a lot," she smiles, and that's the first time the corners of her mouth have moved in that direction all day.

"I don't fucking swear much at all, you fucking fucker!" he grins.

Then she laughs so much the sound echoes around the ice rink, and then there's still hope of life. They lie on their backs on the ice and Benji tells her that Adri has a bitch up at the kennels who's just had puppies, but instead of saying that Alicia can have one of them he just asks what she thinks they should be called. So instead of getting angry and screaming that she doesn't want any other dog except Bang, she starts thinking. They come up with a hundred names, sillier and sillier, laughing so hard that they can't breathe. The last fifty all have something to do with "shit," and Alicia's favorite is "Shit sandwich," because that's the most disgusting and cutest thing she's ever heard. Benji's looking forward to the telling-off he's going to get from Adri when the kid yells that at the next training session.

"Were you scared when you used to play a game?" Alicia asks after a while.

"Always," Benji admits.

"I sometimes get so nervous that I throw up," she says.

He reaches one large fist carefully across the bear on the ice and takes hold of her little hand.

"Shall I teach you a trick? The way we're lying now, I used to lie like this when I was little. I used to climb in through that window the night before I was going to play a game, but you mustn't tell the caretaker!"

Alicia nods and promises.

"Then what?" she wonders.

"Then I would lie here and look up at the roof and think, 'Now I'm alone in the world.' I sort of memorized the silence. Because I've never been scared when I'm alone, only among other people."

"Me too."

Benji hates the fact that the child knows exactly how that feels. She's too young for that. But he tells it like it is:

"No one can hurt you when you're alone."

Her fingers clutch his a little tighter now, the bear beneath them, eternity above them. Her thin voice asks, exhausted:

"Then what?"

He replies slowly:

"Then when I played the game and got nervous, I would just look up at the roof and think that I was on my own in the rink again. And then everything went quiet inside my head. I was suddenly able to shut out all other sound. I felt completely alone, and then nothing was dangerous. Everything was fine."

Alicia lies there without saying anything for several minutes. She hurts so much in so many different places inside her, but there and then she doesn't feel anything, because Benji is lying next to her and it's autumn and a new hockey season is about to begin and everything can still be okay. The roof above her is endless and nothing is dangerous. It isn't until Benji feels her fingers relax in his that he realizes she's fallen asleep. He carries her all the way back to Sune's. Puts her to bed on the sofa and falls asleep on the floor next to her.

The next morning Adri tells him that they've found rat poison wrapped in liver pâté all over Sune's yard. Not in any of the neighbors', just here. Neither of the Ovich siblings can put a single word to their darkest thoughts just then, but they don't need any philosophical principles, they only need instinct to know that the simplest explanation is often the truth: Beartown's and Hed's supporters have just embarked on war with each other, everything is vengeance for previous vengeance, and everyone knows that Bang was the mascot for the whole of the green club. His picture was even in the paper, under the headline "the team dog." If you really want to hurt Beartown, and are too cowardly to attack a human being, then this is what you do.

Benji's voice isn't agitated, it isn't threatening, what he says is merely a statement of fact.

"I'm going to kill them. Every last one of them."

On other occasions Adri would have protested, but not now. When the Ovich siblings get in the car to drive home, Sune stands at the kitchen window thinking that someone has just made those two their mortal enemy, and it would be hard to think of a more dangerous decision to take in this forest.

He feels something move by his pant leg and he's about to reach down to pat Bang's head before all the loss and despair hit him and he almost starts crying. Then Alicia tugs his pant leg again and puts her little fist in his big hand and asks:

"Can we make jam sandwiches?"

Of course they can.

As many as she wants.

80

Banging

When Mumble leaves Ruth's grave in the churchyard in Beartown on Tuesday night he takes the bus home to Hed as if nothing has happened. Matteo stays where he is, hidden in the darkness, wishing he could pretend the same thing. He wishes desperately that he could kill Mumble with his bare hands, but Matteo is only fourteen and Mumble is a man. He wouldn't stand a chance. We will say in hindsight that boys like him commit their crimes because they want to feel powerful, but that isn't right, he just wants to stop feeling powerless.

He starts to cycle home through the town but his tires slip on the snow and he falls several times. The chain comes off again and he cuts himself when he tries to put it back on. Blood trickles down the back of his hand but he's so cold and wet that he doesn't even notice at first. He's whimpering with frustration and fury, but what good does that do? He drags his bicycle home, so tired that he doesn't really notice which route he takes. When he reaches the row houses he hears an old man calling his dog. They're out for their evening walk, used to having the streets to themselves, Matteo doesn't bother to hide but they still don't notice him.

"Bang! Come here! Yes, that's right, come here! Good boy! Now let's go home and have some liver pâté!" the old man declares cheerfully.

Matteo knows who he is. His name is Sune, and he used to be the coach of Beartown's A-team. He knows who the dog is too, it's been in the paper, everyone in Beartown loves it.

Matteo doesn't feel powerful, he just wants to stop feeling powerless, just for a single moment. He thinks about the green jacket Mumble was wearing in the churchyard, Sune has one just like it, he'd like to take something from them so that they know how it feels. Because he's sure they'd mourn the dog more than they ever mourned Ruth. In the town of bears, girls are worth less than animals.

Matteo drags his bicycle all the way home, creeps over to the neighboring house with the elderly couple, and thinks about trying to open their gun cabinet again, but drops the idea and instead goes into their storeroom. He doesn't know what he's looking for until he sees the warning signs on two small boxes on a top shelf.

It's early Wednesday morning by the time he heads back toward the row houses and identifies Sune's yard. On the way back he passes Alicia, who bangs on Sune's door and wakes him up because she wants breakfast. They go to the shop and when they come back she hugs Bang with her whole body and lets him off his leash in the yard, and that's the last time she sees the dog.

81

Warnings

Thursday morning arrives in Beartown and Hed and everyone wakes up angry. It's exactly a week since the storm but it feels like months. Two years have passed since the last outbreak of violence between the towns that led to someone's death, but soon we won't be able to say that. We'll have so many excuses, we always do, we'll say that the conflict between the towns is complicated and that nothing is black and white in situations such as this. We'll sigh in a rather patronizing way, explain that the hatred between two communities and two hockey clubs is nothing new, it goes back generations. We'll say it isn't about hockey but differences in culture, differences in traditions, differences in how the towns made their livings right from the outset. We'll talk about the council's priorities and financial resources and which industries the district could actually survive on. We'll mention jobs and how the authorities don't understand that the only thing ordinary people in places like this really want is to be left in peace. To govern themselves, live in freedom, hunt in their own forests, fish in their own lakes, and keep what is produced rather than shipping everything down south. We'll give careful accounts of how many of the local disputes are actually often the result of political decisions made in the big cities, by people who have never set foot in the district. In Beartown it will be said that those bastards at the other end of the main road are jealous and in Hed it will be said that those bastards beyond the trees are self-satisfied hypocrites who think they're better than everyone else. Someone will mention the fight between the boys in the ice rink, someone else will talk about cars being vandalized in Hed, then the accident at the factory will be mentioned, and then even the most sensible voices will be raised beyond the bounds of reason. What starts as a discussion of the working environment and safety at the factory will soon descend into political slogans and when one side claims that they're discriminated against, the other side will cry: "So don't come and work here, then! Go and steal jobs in your own damn town instead!" Everyone knows someone who knows someone who either knows the young woman who got caught in the machinery or the young woman who is on maternity leave and whose shift it originally was. Everyone knows either the brothers who hit the young men in the parking lot at the hospital or the young men who got hit. Everyone in Hed has met a bastard from Beartown at a wedding or a hockey game sometime, and everyone in Beartown has met an asshole from Hed in an ice rink or at work. All the worst things we believe about one another can always be proved with a story we've heard from someone who heard it from someone else.

We'll say that this has long historical roots. Deep cultural causes. That the antagonism has been passed down for generations. That you can't understand it if you're not from here. We'll say it's complicated, oh, so very complicated, but of course it isn't really at all. Because if Ramona had been here she would have said it like it is: "It's not bloody complicated at all. Just stop killing each other, you damn fool idiots!"

But now we no longer know how to stop ourselves.

———

"But it was only a dog."

Of course no one actually says that, but it feels to Sune as if all his neighbors are thinking it. Everyday life just carries on out in the street while he sits in a million pieces in his kitchen. When he collects the mail someone goes past and says "sorry for your loss," but that isn't what he wants them to feel sorry about. He wants them to feel sorry about his life, and the fact that he's going to have to see it out now without that ill-disciplined, unruly little monster. Without paws on the edge of the bed and bite marks on his wrists. How's that going to work? Who's going to eat all the liver pâté in the fridge? He receives a few text messages and phone calls from the committee of the hockey club and a couple of coaches of the youth teams, all very sorry, but not as if it had been a person. They're sad that Sune is sad, of course, but they don't really understand his loss. Because of course it was only a dog. It's so hard to explain that it's more than an animal when you're that animal's human. Perhaps it takes more empathy than most people are capable of. Or more imagination.

For that reason, it's both unexpected but also entirely logical that when the doorbell rings and there's someone standing outside with tears in his eyes, it's Teemu. Behind him stand a dozen men in black jackets. They hand over an enormous wreath of flowers, the sort you put on a coffin, and Teemu says:

"The guys wanted to share their condolences. Is there anything we can do to help?"

"That's very kind. But it was only a dog."

Teemu pats him hard on the shoulder.

"It's never only a dog. It's family. Everyone knows how much you loved him. We loved him too. Damn it, he was Beartown's team dog . . ."

One of the men behind him, with tattoos on his neck and hands and probably on most of the skin in between, says with a tremble in his voice:

"I know I didn't know him that well, but I'm really going to miss him. He felt like part of the club!"

Sune stands there with the floral wreath in his hands and loss on his cheeks and doesn't know what to say. But if anyone can understand the unbridled, unreasonable love you can feel for an animal, it's probably men who have been told all their lives that they love something more than they should: "But it's only hockey."

The Pack feels precisely everything, precisely all the time. They know that the extent of grief isn't measured by what you've lost but by who you are. They have imagination. So much imagination, in fact, that the very thought of losing something they can't live without makes them lethal.

"Coffee," Sune says without a question mark, and leads the way into the house.

The black jackets follow him and they drink coffee. One of the men notes that the tap in the bathroom is dripping, so he fixes it. Another washes the mugs. A third dries them. When they go, Teemu leaves an envelope full of cash on the kitchen counter.

"Not much," he says quietly.

"Keep your money, I . . . ," Sune begins, but Teemu raises his hand disarmingly.

"Not for you. For Alicia. We know he was her dog too."

As he is leaving Sune says:

"Teemu . . . we don't know each other that well, you and I, and I know you're angry . . . you should know that I'm pretty damn angry myself but . . . don't take revenge because of the dog, okay? He wasn't all that keen on people fighting. And I don't want Alicia to be either."

"Revenge? Who from?" Teemu asks, ostensibly not understanding at all.

That's when Sune knows with absolute certainty that someone in Hed is going to pay dearly for this.

————

Back at the kennels Benji and Adri Ovich feed the dogs, then eat their own food in silence standing at the kitchen counter, then they do weight training for the rest of the day in the gym Adri has built in the barn. Benji's weaker than he used to be, his big sister notes, but she also notes other things: when he first came home from his travels last week his eyes were lighter, as if they had gone pale in the sun on sandy beaches, but now they're dark again. He looks stronger, but also harder. Before he had to catch Alicia in the schoolyard yesterday and tell her what had happened to her beloved dog, Benji moved around Adri's house in a way that reminded her of a wounded bird. Today he's moving like a wounded bear. Yesterday he was vulnerable, today he is explosive.

82

Skates

Peter spends the morning baking bread and hoping that his phone's going to ring. He prods it every five minutes to make sure the battery hasn't died, but it remains obstinately silent. Kira doesn't even seem to have noticed that he isn't at the office. That's how important he is to the business. He has trouble finding the words to express how this makes him feel: Hurt? Angry? Inadequate?

He bakes so much bread, damn, such a lot of bread, the whole kitchen counter is covered by the time he's done. Then he goes and grabs his green jacket and walks to the ice rink. He might as well, seeing as no one else needs him, the thirteen-year-olds are going to play a game and he can't think of a more entertaining age for hockey than that. At that age everything is still just raw talent and potential. All dreams remain intact.

It's still early when he reaches the rink, not many people, but a few old guys are wandering about. They look up when he steps in and say:

"Okay, Peter! We heard about that new player . . . Alexander? Is that his name? Is he any good?"

Peter smiles:

"We call him 'Big City.' And yes, he's good. You'll see."

The old guys like that, of course.

"'Big City'? Well, that's easy enough to remember. And Amat is back? Could they make a good pairing?"

Peter nods happily:

"Zackell knows what she's doing."

It feels almost like old times for a short while. The old guys slap him on the back and declare:

"Don't be so damn humble, Peter, everyone heard that you went down with Zackell to recruit the new guy! And if Amat comes back, you're bound to have had something to do with that as well! Everyone wants you back as general manager, you should know that whenever you get tired of making coffee for your wife or whatever it is you do in that law firm over in Hed . . ."

Peter does a really good job of trying to laugh as if that's a funny joke. A really, really good job.

When he sits down in the stands the caretaker comes and sits next to him. That's when Peter finds out about Sune's dog and about the black jackets who are on their way here to watch the game.

"Should probably get ready for trouble," the caretaker mutters anxiously, and then it really does feel like old times again.

A bit too much.

———

Kira and her colleague are sitting in their office beneath teetering heaps of open folders on top of more open folders.

"What do you think?" Kira asks, exhausted.

"I think it works to our advantage that this is so damn complicated that no normal person will understand what Peter has done wrong," her colleague replies in an attempt to be positive, which doesn't really work seeing as Kira understands exactly what Peter has done.

"Looking the other way when a crime is committed can be just as bad as actually committing it," she says.

Her colleague is right, a lot of what the club has done can be dismissed as legal bagatelles by a good lawyer, that's why Kira is so angry with Peter for signing those documents concerning the training facility. They lie there like fingerprints on a murder weapon. Because everyone can understand this: you can't steal millions of taxpayers' money and sell air and let the council buy a building that doesn't exist. That makes you both immoral and a criminal.

"Have you told Peter you know all about this yet?" her colleague wonders.

Kira shakes her head.

"No. He'll just say he didn't understand what he was signing. And I'll believe him. I'll . . . choose to believe him."

Her colleague smiles weakly.

"I'll believe him too. He may be a bit of an idiot, your husband, but he isn't this stupid."

Kira sighs.

"Stupidity is not reading things before you sign them. How smart is that? I don't know if I can argue that he hasn't committed a crime by claiming that he's this naive . . ."

Her colleague slowly nods her head.

"Do you want to know what I think? I don't think the newspaper will dare publish this. People would hit the roof if they tried, they see Peter as some sort of damn saint . . . and IF they publish it, maybe they won't need a scapegoat? Maybe they'll focus all their criticism on the committee and politicians rather than on a specific person . . ."

Without wanting to know the answer, Kira asks:

"But what if they do need a scapegoat?"

Her colleague looks unhappy.

"Then Peter would be perfect. Absolutely perfect."

Kira tries to reply, but there's too much of a sob in her throat. She hopes that Tails will find a way to rescue Hed Hockey, that he can find enough allies to stop the local paper, and she hopes that all this will be enough to conceal what Peter did. Because even she probably isn't going to be able to bury this.

———

A team of very young kids is training down on the ice. The caretaker goes off to replace some lightbulbs and check the windows and emergency exits before the thirteen-year-olds' game, and Peter goes with him to help out. When he was general manager he always took pride in not only knowing all about the team, but all about the ice rink as well, what needed to be maintained and oiled, replaced or repaired. In a small hockey club no one has one job, everyone has at least three.

"Damn . . . ," Peter says when he goes to take off his jacket and the zipper breaks.

"Has that jacket shrunk or has your stomach grown?" the caretaker grins.

"A bit of both," Peter admits.

"I've got some pliers in the storeroom. I'll mend it for you. You can't go around like that, lad," the caretaker grunts, because even if Peter lives to be eighty he'll still be a "lad" to this man.

When they reach the storeroom Amat is standing outside with his skates in his hand. He looks extremely uncomfortable when he catches sight of Peter, and fumbles so much with his hands that he drops one skate.

"Do they need sharpening?" the caretaker wonders with the special happy voice he reserves for the players he likes best of all.

"Only if . . . only if you've got time . . . I don't need . . . ," Amat manages to say, there's so much he wanted to say to Peter when he went around to his house the other day, but when nothing got said it was as if the words took root inside him instead.

"Just need to mend a jacket first," the caretaker informs him.

But Peter bends down and picks the skate up from the floor and says:

"I can sharpen them, Amat. Come in and tell me how you want them."

The three men from different generations stand next to one another amid the spark and spin of the sharpener, squabbling quietly about the angle of the blade. The caretaker points out that they need less sharpening now that Amat has put on twenty pounds, and Peter winks at Amat and says:

"He just pretends to be smart, he doesn't actually know how to change the setting on the machine, he's sharpened every skate exactly the same way for a hundred years."

"You could have run your skates through a fistful of grit, you never skated five yards in an entire game anyway . . ." the caretaker retorts, then goes to look for a better set of pliers.

Peter and Amat are left by the sharpener and over the grinding sound Peter asks:

"Are you going to stay and watch the thirteen-year-olds? It feels like only yesterday you were that age. Well, I mean, I know it's a long time ago but sometimes it just feels like . . ."

Amat is staring fixedly at his skates.

"I know what you mean. Sometimes I feel that way too."

Peter runs his fingertip softly along the blades.

"That's why the whole town likes watching kids play. There's nothing but hope at that age."

Amat's voice cracks when he replies:

"I should have listened to you back in the spring."

Peter shakes his head gently.

"No, no, you were right. You're a grown man now. I had no right to lecture you about what you ought to do . . ."

"If I'd listened to you, I might have been playing in the NHL now," Amat struggles to say.

Peter turns to him, obliging him to make eye contact.

"You're going to play in the NHL one day. Not because of me or anyone else, but because you're a damn good hockey player."

He hands over the skates. Amat takes them and says toward the floor:

"I wouldn't be where I am without you."

"Stop that, you have a God-given talent, you had—" Peter protests, but Amat interrupts him quietly but firmly:

"Talent isn't enough. Or at least it wouldn't have been enough for me. You need someone who believes in you too. Not just me . . . you've done the same for Benji and Bobo, and now you're doing it for Aleksandr as well . . . we aren't your kids, but you've always made us feel like we are. You've always believed in us more than we did ourselves."

The caretaker comes back. The door closes. The sharpener squeals. Amat nods awkwardly and mumbles "thanks," then heads off. Peter stands there, not daring to put his jacket back on now, because there's no way it's going to fit around his chest. The caretaker glances at him irritably and grunts:

"Are you just going to stand there, because I've got twenty pairs of skates that need sharpening . . ."

So Peter stays for several hours. He hasn't felt so useful in a very long time.

The ice rink has already started to fill with people when Amat emerges from the storeroom. The crowd makes him nervous so he doesn't stay to watch the game. In the parking lot he sees Mumble, with his bag over his shoulder and the same tense expression when faced with the crowd. It's started to snow again.

"Mumble! Do you want to go somewhere and play? We can see if the lake's frozen?" Amat calls, and of course Mumble nods.

Matteo stands among the trees some distance away and watches them go.

83

Provocations

It's Thursday afternoon and the house in Hed is vibrating from bodies moving up and down the creaking staircase. Ted is packing his bag because he has a game today against Beartown's thirteen-year-olds. Tobias is still suspended from his team, so for once he's going to go along and watch Ted, because their games have usually clashed for the past few years. Tess is dropping Ture off with the neighbors. Obviously Ture is furious about this, but even if no one knows yet just how bad things are going to be today, this morning Johnny just felt instinctively that their youngest son shouldn't come to the ice rink with them. Johnny and Hannah are both trying to hold back their emotions as well as they can, with varying degrees of success. The accident at the factory hit them hard, they haven't even had time to talk about it properly with each other, maybe they've even been avoiding that. Johnny helped cut the young woman free from the machine and Hannah looked after her at the hospital. Now Hannah is emotional and Johnny is sensitive. She expresses her feelings, he holds his in. She lets off steam, he's likely to explode.

"I'll go and pack the van," he says, even though there's nothing to pack, he just goes out and sits in the driver's seat with Springsteen on low volume.

Hannah lets him go, then heads toward Ted's room. The thirteen-year-old is already wearing his red training jersey, and as usual has been ready to leave earlier than anyone else. Unlike Tobias, the fifteen-year-old, who as usual has only just woken up and is still trying to locate a pair of socks that match. Hannah is helping him, muttering without thinking:

"Are these your socks? They look like Dad's! How big are your feet? It feels like only yesterday that I had to tie your laces every time you were going to skate . . ."

"It's been, like, ten years since you tied our laces, Mom," Tobias and Ted say with a grin at the same time.

"No, it was five minutes ago! Last week, at the very most!" their mother retorts defiantly.

It isn't you who've grown, it's just that the rest of my world has shrunk around you, she thinks, hugging her boys. Now she only has one child left who needs help tying his skates, and even Ture hardly lets her do that anymore. It's a terrible thing to have taken away from you, because that moment when one of your children goes out onto the ice, when they take their very first step during training or in a game, for the whole of their lives that has been one of the very few moments when she has felt like a good mother. Like a mother who knows what's going on. Just for a moment. Now they do everything themselves just like she always wanted when they were little and annoying, and now she wants to have it all back again because now they're big and independent.

Ted and Tobias argue about what music they want to listen to all the way to Beartown. Tess puts Springsteen on just to annoy them, but of course Johnny thinks it's for him and grins smugly until they emerge from the forest and see the line of traffic heading to the ice rink.

"Shit, that's a lot of people! What's happening?" Tobias exclaims.

"Are all these people here to watch OUR game?" Ted gasps.

Johnny and Hannah sit in silence, gazing warily across the parking lot from side to side through the crowd. There are small groups of men in black jackets standing here and there, naturally they don't usually go to the thirteen-year-olds' games but things are different today. The violence that is coming becomes a self-fulfilling prophecy. The Pack has heard all the rumors that men from Hed are coming here to fight, so they think they have to defend their boys in Beartown, so the men in Hed think in turn that now they have to come here to protect their own boys. And then no provocation is needed. This hatred is proceeding of its own volition.

This is never going to end well, Hannah thinks, but says instead:

"It'll be great to have such a good atmosphere for the game, won't it? Look how many people from Hed are here, it'll be almost like a home game!"

"This IS a home game," Johnny grunts unhappily.

It should have been, anyway. It should have been played in Hed's ice rink this weekend if the roof hadn't collapsed. Now it's been moved here, on a Thursday because there was no other slot available, and someone in Beartown has obviously taken care to put Beartown's name first on the list of the day's games outside the entrance. As if this were a home game for *them*.

"Perhaps that isn't so very important, darling," Hannah says pointedly, and he sullenly stops talking.

They follow the other cars past the flagpoles with huge green flags flying at the top. The smart new roof of the ice rink is covered with snow, sparkling in the sunlight. All the parking spaces close to the rink are occupied by expensive SUVs owned by hockey dads who all look the same. They all have Beartown Hockey stickers in the rear windows. Johnny drives the van past them. The chassis clatters, Springsteen is roaring, and a short distance away a gang of teenagers are yelling: "WE ARE THE BEARS! WE ARE THE BEARS! WE ARE THE BEARS! THE BEARS FROM BEEEEARTOWN!" Somewhere else a group of children in Hed respond: "HED! HED! HED!" To which a chorus of boos from all corners of the parking lot is crowned by the teenagers: "HED BITCHES! HED BITCHES! HED BITCHES!"

"Lovely Beartown with their lovely, lovely 'values,'" Johnny rumbles quietly and Hannah can't be bothered to tell him to be quiet.

Tobias and Ted jump out of the car and without a word Tobias takes his younger brother's bag and carries it for him, so he won't get stuck in the crowd with it if there's any trouble. They see Ted's coach and the rest of the team close to the entrance to the rink and head in that direction, with Hannah's words echoing in their ears:

"Concentrate on the hockey now! Don't start any trouble! Do you hear me?"

Tess is standing by her side, glancing a little way past the entrance. Hannah looks at her, looks at the entrance, then sighs:

"Can you see Bobo, then?"

Tess nods happily. "Can I . . . ?"

Her mother nods.

"Okay, okay, you can go. But stay close to him! If there's any trouble, you can at least make sure he's the one who gets hit. He's a big enough target, anyway . . ."

Tess runs off, as carefree as if she were at a fairground, which, to be fair, this almost feels like now. She's laughing so happily that Hannah almost relaxes, because apart from a few overexcited chants she has to admit that people seem to be in a pretty good mood: anticipation in the air, children with heavy bags, open car trunks with bags of pastries and flasks of coffee. The towns have borne such hatred toward each other this past week, but now that they're here it's as if they're all rubbing their hands in the cold and remembering the warmth of the sport instead. They hug old friends they haven't seen since spring, a whole long summer has passed when everyone drifted away to campsites and holiday cottages, but now real life is beginning again. Now everyday life will be governed by drop-offs and pickups once more, and every evening hundreds of families will have something to talk about again, because if all these children didn't play hockey their parents would never have this much space in their lives. How many more years of this will Hannah herself have, at best? Soon it will be over. Soon they'll be grown-up. Mothers have no armor to get them through life because they give every last bit to their children, by the end of their teenage years there isn't even any skin left, so every feeling of loss cuts right into her flesh now.

"I'm going to get a hot dog, are you staying here?" Johnny says, completely untroubled beside her, and she can't help wishing that lightning would strike him just then, not fatally, but almost.

"A hot dog? Now?" Hannah snorts, but she shouldn't be surprised, her husband is a living waste dump, she's spent half her life trying to "hide" cheap chocolate at the top of the drawers where he can find it easily when he's been drinking beer, so that he doesn't carry on his drunken search until he finds the expensive chocolate that she's hidden lower down.

She sees the families of two of Ted's teammates a little way away and walks over to them. Johnny walks over to get a hot dog. That's how quickly the whole family gets split up in the crowd.

84

Lawyers

The entire Andersson family ends up in the ice rink this afternoon, but none of them can really explain why. Maya and Ana stop by the house to eat bread, Big City is there fetching his things, because he's moving permanently into the summer cottage that used to be a campervan. He slept there on his own last night, Benji has moved to his sister's house for reasons Big City hasn't quite understood yet, but Big City himself was so happy there among the trees down by the water that he decided to stay.

"Are you going to watch the game today?" Maya wonders innocently when they bump into each other in the kitchen.

"What game?" Big City asks.

"Hed's thirteen-year-olds are playing Beartown's."

"Thirteen-year-olds? Is that a big thing here?" he wonders in surprise.

"It's Beartown against Hed. That makes everything a big deal here," Maya replies.

"Are . . . you going?" he asks.

"We are NOW!" Ana declares.

They persuade Leo to go too, he pretends he's doing it reluctantly, on the way he shares a cigarette with Maya and Ana and he's never felt more grown-up. When they get to the ice rink Maya sends their mother a text message:

> We're going to watch the game.
> Come along?

Kira is sitting in her office with her colleague buried in documents, and texts back in surprise:

```
        The thirteen-year-olds? Didn't
            think you were interested
                        in that?
```

She receives the reply:

```
    Who cares who's playing, Mom,
    come and hang out.
```

Good luck resisting that if you're the mother of teenagers.

———

Johnny doesn't want a hot dog, he just saw the hot dog stand from the road when he turned into the parking lot and recognized the guy standing behind it. A thin young man with a scrappy beard. Johnny saw him at the scrapyard, he's one of Lev's guys. There are four middle-aged men in green jackets standing around him, one of them far too close to his face, arguing loudly. One of them grabs the hot dog stand angrily, Lev's guy resists but doesn't fight back even if he looks like he could. He's outnumbered and outclassed by the green jackets, even if the men are overweight and have the same desperate hairstyle fighting against rapidly receding hairlines.

Johnny unzips his own jacket as he approaches, then stops a couple of yards away and clears his throat:

"Is there a problem here?"

The men in green jackets turn around in a rage that quickly fades. That's partly because of Johnny's size, of course, but also the T-shirt with the logo of the fire brigade they can see beneath his open jacket. Not that the men respect firemen, these sort of men don't respect anything, but they know that if you fight with one fireman, you fight with all of them. Johnny might be on his own here, but he might as well have been a whole gang.

"Selling hot dogs isn't allowed here!" one of the men eventually exclaims, sounding tougher than he probably is.

"Not allowed? Selling hot dogs? Are you serious?" Johnny laughs.

"The boys' team is selling hot dogs in the cafeteria inside the ice rink! This bastard's standing out here selling them at half the price! How are our lads going to sell anything in there?"

Lev's guy turns to Johnny and says with barely suppressed fury:

"Is this not a free country? A free town?"

"Well it certainly isn't YOUR goddamn town, so maybe you can just piss off back to wherever you came from? Anyway, what sort of meat's in those hot dogs? Rats and bats?" one of the men snarls.

Johnny just looks at him so hard that he shrinks, the way men with big mouths and small fists always do. One of the other men takes his friend by the arm and mutters an apology to Johnny:

"That was . . . sorry . . . let's not allow this to get out of hand now. Our boys in there are just trying to sell hot dogs and earn a bit of money for their team's kitty. The parents are just upset . . ."

Johnny snorts and nods toward Lev's guy.

"Upset about what? Do you think you own this parking lot, then? The council owns this parking lot! He's just as much a part of the local community as you are!"

"Okay, okay, sorry . . . ," the man says, holding his hands up.

"Don't apologize to me, you idiot! Apologize to him!" Johnny snaps, nodding toward Lev's guy again.

The men look at him as if he can't possibly be serious. Then one of them grabs hold of the others and mutters:

"Come on. Let's go inside. The game starts soon. We can sort this out later."

Johnny and Lev's guy stand where they are and watch them go. Johnny feels his pulse racing. None of those men was Peter Andersson, but he realizes now that each of them reminded him of Peter Andersson. And that was evidently enough.

"Thanks!" Lev's guy says.

Johnny turns around and nods curtly.

"Let me know if they bother you again. This isn't their parking lot.

The entire district doesn't belong to Beartown Hockey, even if they think it does."

Lev's guy puts his hand on his heart and gives a short bow of gratitude. Johnny hasn't the faintest idea of what to do in response, so he fumbles with the zip of his jacket and gives a sort of wave that turns into half a salute. Lev's guy prepares a hot dog for him and hands it over. Johnny feels in the back pocket of his jeans for money but is waved away.

"Free for firemen!"

Johnny nods appreciatively. He eats as he walks. It's a damn fine hot dog, he concludes, definitely better than the crap they serve in Beartown's cafeteria.

Ana, Maya, Leo, and Big City are wandering about by the ice rink, drifting from group to group. Ana disappears from sight for a minute at most, then returns with eight cans of beer in a plastic bag.

"How . . . how did you do that?" Leo gasps.

"I just asked a guy," Ana says, as if it was obvious.

"She can find beer anywhere, even at a funeral!" Maya confirms.

"Surely that's the EASIEST place to get hold of beer?" Ana exclaims.

They sit down on some rocks at the far end of the parking lot and drink. Maya lets Leo have one, she drinks two, Ana three. Big City declines, he's got training this evening.

"Are you worried the coach will shout at you?" Ana teases.

"No. I just don't want to disappoint her," he eventually admits when he can't think of a good lie.

Maya pats him on the shoulder encouragingly, then says in her very thickest forest dialect:

"If you don't want to disappoint people, you've come to the wrong town. We're not happy unless we're a bit disappointed here, you know."

Big City smiles awkwardly. Maya has never seen anyone with so little reason to be modest be so shy.

"I'm good at disappointing people. I'm trying to get worse at it."

The beer was stronger than she expected and Maya drank both hers pretty quickly, so she's about to say something extremely inappropriate, but she doesn't have time before Leo mumbles:

"I don't feel well . . ."

"HAVE YOU DRUNK ALL THE BEERS YOU LITTLE SHIT?" Ana roars, turning the empty bag upside down.

Leo's head is spinning too much for him to be able to reply.

For once, Kira is grateful that the temperature is below freezing, it gives her an excuse to hide behind a thick coat with the collar turned up, a woolly hat pulled down over her eyes. She slips unnoticed through the crowd outside the ice rink, texting her daughter to ask where she is, then gets a minor shock when she finds Maya and Ana behind the counter in the cafeteria, where they're selling hot dogs and chocolate balls with a group of players from the boys' teams dressed in green jackets.

"Hi Mom!" Maya exclaims in surprise, as if she's forgotten that she was the one who asked her to come.

"We're trainees!" Ana informs her cheerfully.

Kira leans over the counter and whispers through their breath:

"Have you . . . been drinking?"

"A tiny little bit!" Ana roars in a way that she herself imagines is a whisper.

"Where's Leo?" Kira wonders.

"Bathroom!" Ana giggles with considerable restraint, and Maya starts giggling hysterically. Kira does her best to be angry with them. She *really* does try. But they're too happy and she's too tired and in far too great a need of family members she doesn't have to worry about. So she goes around the counter and makes the girls drink some water, then she ends up standing there herself, selling chocolate balls and hot dogs. Just like old times.

Tess and Bobo come up to the cafeteria, not actually holding hands, but as close to each other as they can manage. So close that their hands and fingers occasionally get tangled up. Quick glances, fleeting smiles, tiny electric shocks everywhere.

Big City is standing in a corner eating chocolate balls, Bobo stops to talk to him, Tess turns around and looks the way her little brother did when he caught sight of Amat the other day.

"Is that . . . is that Kira Andersson? The lawyer?" she hisses to Bobo, tugging at his arm.

"Yes? Kira! HI KIRA!" Bobo yells, waving, and Tess adopts an expression that she will use every time he embarrasses her in public until they grow old together. Kira looks up and waves back, and when she meets Tess's gaze the girl blushes so hard that Bobo thinks she's got something stuck in her throat and is about to perform the Heimlich maneuver before he gets a serious telling-off from his girlfriend, the first but certainly not the last. Kira comes over and hugs Bobo, and holds her hand out:

"Hello, my name's Kira . . ."

"I know, I know, you're the lawyer!" Tess babbles.

"Yes, how did you know that?" Kira laughs, surprised.

"I go past your office when I pick up my little brother from school. I've seen the sign. So . . . I looked you up online . . . ," Tess confesses, blushing hard again.

"Tess wants to be a lawyer too!" Bobo adds, because he hasn't yet learned to keep quiet in situations like this.

He'll get it right eventually. He's going to have plenty of years in which to practice.

"I . . . that isn't settled yet . . . but I do want to study law. But everyone says it's really difficult," Tess says, embarrassed.

"It's supposed to be hard. That's why it's worth doing," Kira smiles amiably, seeing all her own insecurities when she was that age, when she used to wash up in her parents' restaurant in the evening and wonder if she could ever stand a chance among all the rich kids at university.

"Do you think I could do it?" Tess asks, so bluntly that it surprises both her and Kira.

She starts to stammer an apology for asking such a silly question, but Kira takes her arm warmly and replies:

"I'll say to you what my mom said to me: there's only one way to find out."

Tess's eyes are radiant, and she replies without thinking:

"I want to help other girls. Girls who get raped or assaulted or . . . I mean, not that it's ever happened to me! But I know it happened to your daughter! I want to be one of the people who . . . help. Like you!"

Kira didn't exactly go to the cafeteria today prepared to have the wind knocked out of her, so it takes her a moment to catch her breath.

"It can be a tough job at times," she says in a low voice.

"Everyone in my family has a tough job," Tess whispers back.

Kira can see the fire in the girl's eyes and thinks that this must be what it's been like for Peter all these years: this is what a cherry tree in blossom looks like. So she smiles and nods slowly and reaches in her inside pocket for her wallet.

"Here's my card, my cell phone number's on the back. Call me whenever you want. Come to the office whenever you want. If you really want to do this . . . if you *really* want it . . . then I promise to help you."

Tess holds the card as if it were a golden ticket to a chocolate factory. She realizes too late that she sounds like a crazy stalker when she says:

"I heard that your daughter moved to go to college in another town. Did that make you very sad?"

The corners of Kira's mouth tremble.

"Yes. But I'm very proud as well."

The words pour out of Tess as if someone had turned her upside down:

"All the law courses are a really long way away and my mom doesn't want me to move."

"Moms never do," Kira admits.

There a thousand other things Tess wants to ask, but she doesn't get the chance because someone suddenly yells from the stairs leading down to the rink:

"FIGHT! THERE'S A FIGHT!"

Then they hear the shouting from below. Men yelling to their sons in panic, other men yelling at each other in rage. Then the clatter of footsteps as everyone tries to get away from something much worse.

85

Hearts

Hed Hockey's thirteen-year-olds go into the away team's locker room but come out again just as fast, green in the face. It stinks in there, a nauseating, corrosive, disgusting smell that fills their nostrils so fast that their gag reflex doesn't stand a chance. A gang of boys in their early teens in green tops and back-to-front caps are giggling hysterically until the caretaker realizes what's happened and chases them out into the parking lot with a hammer in his hand. Hed's thirteen-year-olds stand there retching. The smell could be butyric acid, or old prawn shells, or rotten meat, it's the oldest trick in the book in Beartown to psych out an opposing team. Lovely, lovely Beartown with their PR brochures about how sponsoring them is the right thing to do, but this is how immaturely they behave. Everyone in Hed is used to it, but this sort of thing is usually done to the adult team. Not thirteen-year-olds. This game is different.

"WE ARE THE BEARS!" the crowd roars from the stands. "WE ARE THE BEARS!" a sea of black jackets repeats, making the walls vibrate down in the corridor where Ted and his teammates are standing. Their coach is trying to give them instructions about where to get changed instead, but he can't make himself heard over the noise. "HED BITCHES HED BITCHES WE'RE GOING TO KILL YOU HED BITCHES!," the crowd roars and Tobias, who is standing alongside, sees the terror in the young players' faces, they're just children, sending them out onto the ice this evening would be like sending them off to war. Tobias catches his younger brother.

"Ted!"

"Yes?"

Tobias grabs hold of his younger brother's arm and yells:

"Think about cake!"

Ted lets out a surprised laugh and his whole body relaxes in his older brother's grip.

"What?"

"You love cake! Think about cake and you'll relax!"

"You're really stupid . . ."

Tobias nods seriously.

"Don't be scared because they're shouting out there, okay? Be grateful! Do you want to play in the NHL? Then you need to be able to play in front of a crazy crowd, and they don't come crazier than this bunch of psychopaths. If you can survive this, you'll be able to cope with anything else in the future. Just go out there and play your game and make the people yelling shut up. Every time they scream, you score a goal. So break them. Take everything they love away from them."

The younger brother leans his head close to his brother's and says:

"Thanks, Toby."

His big brother hisses:

"Don't thank me. Go out there and win. Crush their fucking hearts."

Their eyes meet briefly. The big brother has always been as tough as anything off the ice, but often gave way on the ice, but the younger brother is the opposite. As long as Tobias protects Ted this side of the boards, no one will be able to stop him on the other side. They're fifteen and thirteen years old, but the playing career of one of them is almost over while the other's has only just begun. When Ted follows his team toward the doors leading to the parking lot so they can get changed in their parents' cars, Tobias stays in the corridor with his hands in his pockets. While the younger brother gets ready for the game, the older brother turns and goes and stands among the Hed supporters in the standing area. A few of the older guys recognize him, they used to go to the same school, now they're shouting and waving for him to come and stand with them.

"It was you who hit those Beartown fags here the other day and got suspended from your team, right?" one asks.

Tobias nods, slightly reluctantly. They slap him on the back.

"No way in the world should you have been suspended! You should have gotten a medal!" Tobias knows who they are of course, his dad has always told him to stay away from their sort: "Those idiots are only looking for trouble, Toby, when you get older you'll realize that you're going to have enough trouble in life without going to look for it . . ." But when the guys sing and jump in the stands, it makes Tobias's heart pound. His ears roar, the adrenaline is pumping. So he sings and jumps as well.

When Ted's team steps back into the rink after getting changed, several of their dads follow them, all the way to the players' entrance, furious about the stench in the locker room which forced the boys to get changed in such humiliating circumstances out in the parking lot. They're yelling about "unsportsmanlike behavior," and someone grabs hold of a thirteen-year-old from Beartown who yells something inaudible back, which obviously makes all the dads of the Beartown team rush down to the players' tunnel to defend their boys, and that's how easily it all kicks off. That's how quickly it happens.

Benji and Adri arrive at the ice rink just before the game starts. Sune was too upset to come with them. He's gone out for the same walk he always used to take his dog on, at the same time, and he'll do that for a long while yet. When he gets out of breath and has to stop and clutch his chest, he still whispers "You run on ahead" out of habit.

Benji and Adri go up to the standing area for Beartown fans. The black jackets close ranks around them on all sides without a word. Adri knows that many of them have been off hunting elk this week, they've interrupted the hunt to come home and watch a game between a bunch of thirteen-year-olds, and that isn't a good sign. For anyone.

Teemu is standing closest to her and Benji. "BEARTOWN FAGS," the Hed supporters roar, "HED BITCHES," the Beartown fans respond. It's only words for the time being, but Teemu glances at Benji and Adri to see their reactions. From Benji he gets no reaction at all, just slow breathing and neutral eyes, as if he's either slowing down from something or getting ready for something. From Adri Teemu gets just a short glance and a surprised:

"I can't believe you're so calm."

Teemu nods secretively.

"I've promised that we'll be calm today."

"Promised who?" she wonders.

"The club," he replies.

He hasn't even told his closest associates that he's spoken to Tails. He's just told everyone that they need to stay calm unless he gives a direct signal, and they obey, not out of fear but because they love him. It's a brotherhood no one else in this town understands, he knows that, but if anyone comes close, it's probably Adri. He still has difficulty interpreting the look on her face now, probably because she isn't really sure how she feels, she's torn between feeling proud of Teemu and his guys for not starting any trouble already, and a longing for them to do so. Throughout her life Adri has seen so many people hurt others that she's grown tough, but when someone harms an animal she loses all her inhibitions. Her mind turns black. She understands Teemu more than ever at moments like that.

"BEARTOWN FAGS," one stand is chanting.

"HED BITCHES," echoes back.

The chants roll back and forth across the ice. Normally the stands would be almost empty for a game between thirteen-year-olds, but this hasn't been a normal week. On Saturday the towns' A-teams will meet in the first game of the season, and Adri finds herself wondering what the hell these guys will bring with them then. Tanks?

"MURDER, PLUNDER, RAPE, AND BURN! WE'D HAVE SCREWED YOUR SISTERS IF YOU HADN'T SCREWED THEM FIRST!" some of the Hed supporters are chanting.

"IF YOU WANT IT, COME AND GET IT! NO ONE FROM HED DARES TO FIGHT!" Teemu's guys are shouting around Adri.

The number of red fans over in Hed's stand can't match the number of green fans, largely because they aren't as well organized, when they sing they're a hundred separate voices, but when Teemu's guys raise their voices they do it as one man. A single, terrible man capable of anything. Everyone over in Hed's stand knows this, of course, they know they're in the minority, so they do what all supporters do in those circumstances: they seek out their opponents' weakest point. Anything that can be yelled to get at them, hurt them, wound their pride. They hit upon the easiest and worst thing possible.

As Ted and the other thirteen-year-olds are elbowing their way past the shoving match their dads have started down in the players' tunnel and step out onto the ice to warm up, a rumor starts circulating through Hed's stand: something about Sune, the former A-team coach. Something about a dog that was in Beartown's team photograph. Something about how even the most feared members of the Pack are mourning the animal's loss.

What happens next is simple and effective, spontaneous and obvious, incredibly stupid and instantly destructive: a young guy off to one side behind Tobias starts to bark.

"*Woof woof woof*," and at first some of the other guys around him just laugh.

Then someone else does it louder:

"*Woof! Woof! Woof!*"

Suddenly the whole stand is barking. It starts as a joke, but quickly becomes threatening. Salt in open wounds. A direct provocation. Beartown's supporters don't respond by singing, nor by chanting, they do something much worse: they fall totally silent. And then everything else falls silent too.

It's hard to explain how a packed ice rink sounds if you've never experienced it, but even ordinary popcorn eating children and hot dog munching pensioners have an ability to shut out the wall of sound after a while. Especially in Beartown. Everyone is so used to the fact that the fans in the two standing areas chant "BITCH" and "FAG" at each other that they may as well have been doing it in a foreign language, the popcorn eaters and hot dog enthusiasts don't even hear them, they sit back in their seats and chat about mortgages and grandchildren and the weather. Perhaps they're also a bit complacent, because it's been more than two years since there was a real fight in here. Everyone has forgotten how it sounds when the Pack makes a charge, everyone feels safe, like children with their noses pressed against the glass of the lion enclosure. The black jackets' yelling is like a whirring extractor fan in a kitchen that you don't even notice until someone switches it off.

But now, in the total silence that suddenly falls on everyone when it happens, there is nothing but terror and fear. It used to be more than two years since that last happened, but now it's very recent indeed.

"*WOOF!*" a solitary guy says somewhere in the Hed stand, too pumped on adrenaline to notice that everyone else has their mouths closed. Someone hisses "Shut up," someone else starts singing something else, but it's too late.

"What do you want to do?" one of the guys below Teemu asks.

Teemu is standing with his gaze fixed on the Hed stand at the other end of the rink. There's nothing in his eyes. No empathy, no forgiveness, no mercy. Perhaps he's thinking of the promise he made to Tails not to start any trouble this week, but he wasn't actually the one who started this. The men from Hed have come to his rink, his home, to boast about killing Sune's dog, and he's not allowed to do anything about that? Like hell. His voice is cold:

"Fuck it. Break the neck of every last one of them."

The black jackets jump over the barrier and start to run as a single organism. The whole of the seating area seems to hold its breath, families with children and pensioners trip over each other in their rush to get out of the way. The black jackets surge forward like a single wave of darkness, trampling hot dogs and popcorn everywhere.

Adri grabs Teemu's arm and yells:

"DIDN'T YOU SAY YOU PROMISED THE CLUB YOU'D STAY CALM?"

Teemu stares at her, not with any regret, but perhaps with sympathy:

"The club? We are the club."

Then he runs too, with Benji beside him. Adri tries to stop her brother but she doesn't stand a chance. The barking from the other stand has already been swallowed up in an agitated roar, but Adri's palms can still feel the weight of the little animal as she lifted it into its grave. She might not want violence, but she can no longer criticize the people who do.

The dads down in the players' tunnel recognize the danger the way you hear the rumble of an approaching flood wave, they yell to the thirteen-year-olds on the ice to get off, panic breaks out and chaos takes over the entire rink in an instant.

Tobias sees the black jackets approaching from the other end of the rink, and sees his own stand divide into two groups: those who start to back away and those who rush forward to meet the threat. Tobias has two parents who have always taught him to run toward fire, so he doesn't even think, he just jumps over a barrier and drops several yards, landing on concrete, then he runs as fast as he can straight for the ice. All he can think is that he has to get his younger brother away from here.

Hannah and Johnny come running down the stand, consumed by the same thought, but the crowd is too dense and the chaos too overwhelming. They are swept along with the flow toward the corner of the rink closest to the locker rooms, which is where Bobo manages to reach out a hand and grab Johnny's shoulder. Johnny spins around and falls apart inside in every possible way when he hears Bobo yell:

"TESS IS WITH ME! DON'T WORRY! GET TOBY AND TED AND MEET US IN THE PARKING LOT!"

In the other direction Hannah loses her grip of Johnny's fingers for a single moment and it's as if they're torn apart by merciless undercurrents, in the flash of an eye they're ten yards apart. Tobias and Ted appear out of nowhere, Ted still with his skates and all his hockey gear on, Tobias flailing wildly to clear their path. Behind them Teemu and the first of the black jackets reach Hed's stand, some of the men in red who have stayed behind to defend it have torn bits of wood from the floor of the stand and are swinging these makeshift weapons wildly toward the black jackets as they try to clamber upward. Noses get broken, jaws cracked, but the black jackets just keep moving forward. Someone's going to get killed, Johnny has time to think, but Hannah pulls herself through the crowd and grabs hold of him before he has time to finish the thought.

"THE BOYS! GET THE BOYS OUT!"

The father of one of the boys on Ted's team is having a full-blown fight with two of the dads from the Beartown team behind her, an elbow hits her on the temple and she almost loses her balance, Johnny sees what happens and throws every single person between them into the air. Just as he reaches her, Tobias gets to her from the other direction. Johnny hardly recognizes him, the fifteen-year-old looks like a grown man, entirely without fear. He's pulling Ted along behind him, and helps his mother up with the other hand. A small gap opens up in the crowd and the whole family sees it at the same time and pushes toward the exit. The boys first, then Hannah, and Johnny at the back, and he makes the mistake of casting a glance over his shoulder as they run. He never sees the man who comes running around the corner from the storeroom beyond the locker rooms, they crash heads by mistake at full force and for a few seconds everything in Johnny's head goes completely silent. Then he feels his forehead getting sticky but without feeling any pain. He blinks confusedly through water-filled eyes and sees the man in front of him sink to his knees with blood gushing from a split eyebrow. It's Peter Andersson.

86

Blood

The cafeteria quickly fills with panic-stricken families with children fleeing the violence. Kira doesn't have to think about what the right thing to do is, she just stands, legs wide apart, in the doorway. She assumes she has some sort of naive idea of guarding it in case the men down at the ice decide to storm the cafeteria, even though she's already thinking: "So how, Kira? HOW are you going to stop them?"

Then she feels someone brush past her left side, then someone else on her right. Maya and Ana. Maya is there to protect her mother, Ana is there to protect the whole world. Only once do two young men come running up the stairs, Kira doesn't even have time to see if they're Hed or Beartown, but they're clutching lengths of metal piping in their hands and that's enough for Ana to wait until the first one is close enough to get a kick to the chest that he'll never forget. He flies backward and his friend stops midstride with his eyes staring wildly. Then he makes the best decision of his life and flees.

"SHIT!" Ana yells, jumping back on one leg, because it feels like she's just broken her damn foot again, why the hell do guys have to be so damn HARD when you kick them?

Kira pulls her and Maya back into the cafeteria again and closes the door behind her. A few minutes pass, then it's as if the inferno outside suddenly stops, like someone pulling the plug from a loudspeaker. When they open the door again the ice rink is almost empty.

Peter is on his knees whimpering with pain as blood trickles into his eyes. Johnny is bending over him, not to hit him but to help him, but that isn't how it looks. Teemu sees them from up in the stands. And then everything goes to hell.

Adri still hasn't moved from the Beartown stand. It doesn't even occur to her to run off in any direction. She doesn't want to fight, but she doesn't want to run away either. She isn't full of hatred, nor full of fear, she just feels empty. Only when she hears someone calling her name does she get dragged back to reality and turns around. It's Benji. He's holding Alicia in his arms. How he managed to get hold of her Adri will never understand, but somewhere between the Beartown stand and Hed's Benji heard the child's voice, and, while all the black jackets carried on running forward, he veered off.

"What are you even doing HERE, you crazy kid?" he yelled.

"I wanted to watch the game but Sune didn't want to, so I came ON MY OWN!" Alicia snapped back, trying to sound angry even though she was actually terrified.

Benji reached down and lifted her out of the chaos, and is now carrying her as if she was his little girl. She has her arms wrapped around him like she's always been his, clinging on like seaweed to a body that's just stepped out of the sea. Adri's fury vanishes instantly, leaving nothing but exhaustion. She straightens her back as if she needs to get the feeling back into all her limbs, then quickly guides her brother and the little girl toward one of the emergency exits. When they emerge into the parking lot all the tension disperses and Alicia starts to cry and the Ovich siblings don't even stop to glance back toward the chaos in the ice rink, they just keep going toward the trees. They walk the whole way back to Sune's, turning away from the crap instead of running into it, taking care of someone instead of taking everything out on someone else. Alicia doesn't let go of Benji the whole way home. She sleeps next to Adri on the sofa that night. They might never be counted as a family by the authorities, but one day, many years from now, the girl will play her first game with the national team. When she's asked what name she wants on the back of her jersey, she'll give their name.

Peter looks up and blinks through the blood, he sees Johnny's outstretched hand and he sees Teemu jump down from the stands with some sort of metal pipe in his hand, but with all his strength Peter can barely manage to utter a feeble, faltering:

"Look out!" Not to Teemu but to Johnny. The fireman spots the danger and knocks the metal pipe aside at the last moment. Teemu loses his footing and stumbles straight into Peter, which buys Johnny a few seconds to back away, and by the time Teemu finds his footing and is about to rush at him, someone else is standing in the way. He's short and fat, but the zip of his jacket is pulled down and Teemu sees the pistol tucked into his belt long before he sees Lev's face a little higher up.

"Come!" Lev says tersely, shepherding Johnny behind him.

He has the pistol in his hand now, holding it half-hidden in the palm of his hand, pointing at the floor, but his eyes are fixed on Teemu.

Hannah, Tobias, and Ted are standing a few yards away. They back away behind Lev, and Teemu stands so still that everything around him also seems to slow down. Perhaps it's a direct chain reaction when a few members of the Pack see what's happening to their leader and stop instantly, then a few more, and a few more, and when enough black jackets stop fighting, everyone else does as well. The crowd is still dense, but it becomes less aggressive. People tumble out into the parking lot, less panic-stricken now. The last of them almost stroll out as if they were walking out of a cinema. Hardly anyone except those closest to Lev even saw the pistol. It all happened so quickly, and out of nowhere it's over.

"Community spirit, yes?" Lev says to Johnny with a smile almost of amusement as they step out into the snow.

Johnny is too shocked to answer, so blinded by fear that something could have happened to his children, and so grateful that Lev managed to get them out that he isn't even thinking about the pistol, which disappears into the man's belt again. They part with a curt nod, and Lev seems to vanish into thin air among the vehicles in the parking lot.

Teemu doesn't look frightened, mostly just surprised. Almost fascinated, in fact. As soon as Lev disappears he seeks to shake it all off, as if it were just a children's game where this was what you should expect. He bends down and asks:

"Are you okay?"

"Don't know," Peter replies honestly.

"PETER!!!" a voice yells, cutting into his ears.

"Oh fuck, now you're going to get it," Teemu grins.

Peter will never stop being surprised at how calm he is. He seems to have developed an immunity to adrenaline.

"DAD!" Maya cries out, running beside her mother, and behind them stumbles Leo, who looks like he's been sick but that's too long a story for any of them to feel like explaining to Peter right now.

"WHAT HAPPENED?" Kira cries so wildly that even Teemu bounces out of the way, but he still can't stop himself blurting out:

"Oh, you know, just hooligan behavior, typical of Peter to start fighting! We tried to stop him, but you know how he gets when he's angry . . ."

He's seriously pretty certain Kira would have killed him there and then if Peter hadn't thrown himself between them. The lies come so easily to Peter that he surprises himself:

"I ran into a post, that's all, darling. It was nothing but a stupid accident."

87

Profits

Out of all the men in the ice rink today, only two are dressed in a suit and tie. They're sitting a long way from each other, possibly unaware of each other's presence. One is Tails, the other is Richard Theo, the supermarket owner and the politician who each have such a bad reputation in their respective fields for their competitors to believe that they don't follow the rules. They themselves claim that that's precisely what they do, they just play the game better than everyone else. They've come to the rink for different reasons. Tails hopes to be able to steer events, Theo merely hopes to analyze them. Tails watches the thirteen-year-olds on the ice, Theo just watches the crowd. One looks at players, the other looks at voters.

Tails has spent all day hoping desperately that he's going to be able to instigate a truce between Beartown and Hed long enough to save both clubs, but when he sees the size of the crowd and hears the first *"woof!"* from the Hed stand, he knows it's all over. It doesn't matter that Teemu has promised to stay calm. No one stands a chance.

But Richard Theo sits there, apparently untroubled, watching as the trouble breaks out. The supermarket owner runs toward the ice like a man possessed, trying to stop everyone from killing each other, but the politician is thinking that perhaps this is exactly what's needed: what saves the two clubs might not be peace, but war. He just needs to figure out how to use that to his advantage.

It's Peter Andersson who turns out to be the answer, as he so often is in this town, one way or another, Theo thinks with a little smile. He's sitting so high up in the stands that in the end he's the only person who has a complete overview of the chaos down below. He usually says that his political successes have come about because when everyone else runs in one direction, he runs the other way, but this time he just has to sit still.

He sees Peter Andersson rush out of the storeroom and crash into a large man the same age wearing a fire brigade top. He sees Peter's eyebrow split in a fountain of blood, but he also sees how Teemu reacts instantly as if it's his duty to protect Peter and throws himself toward him, then he sees how Lev appears to defend the fireman. The alliances might be unexpected, but they aren't illogical, at least not to a politician who has built his whole career out of unusual friendships.

When everything suddenly calms down right after that, when the trouble is over and the ice rink drains of people like water from a basin, Tails is drenched in sweat but Theo is cool. One is only thinking of all he could lose now, the other already has a strategy for how he can get everything he wants.

While Tails is wandering around the parking lot to see if anyone is seriously hurt, Richard Theo walks calmly to his office. It's a beautiful evening, the stars are bright and snow is falling, the ice is in his nostrils and crunching beneath his shoes. He loves this place, no one would believe that if they heard it, of course, but he's traveled all around half the world and still hasn't seen anywhere like this. The forest and the lake, the wilderness and snow, it's unbeatable.

He isn't surprised that this town drives people to violence, it could have driven him to violence too if he thought someone was trying to take it away from him. That's the insight that's going to help him solve everyone's problems. That's how he's going to win.

88

Hooligans

Bobo and Tess are waiting beside the van. Johnny and Hannah leave their sons with them and turn back to see if anyone is injured or needs help. Surprisingly, they don't. The thirteen-year-olds who were supposed to be playing are unharmed, of course, because they were wearing full hockey gear the whole time, and among the parents and other people in the crowd there are just a few bruises and scrapes that happened in the crush rather than from any fighting. The men in the standing areas were only after each other. Johnny knows that some of the younger firemen usually call it "Honor among hooligans." Several of them have tattoos of the red bull, much bigger than his own. They're firemen, but first and foremost they're from Hed, and they're different from him. Angrier. Unless Johnny has just gotten older. Sometimes he thinks that boys who grow up in his hometown now have fewer ways to identify themselves than he had in his day. Every individual needs to feel important, is looking for something to belong to, but there are fewer and fewer things to cling on to in Hed. "We only fight the Pack, we never touch civilians," one of them once said, and Johnny can't help thinking that that's the problem, that they use the word "civilians" as if they were soldiers.

Car engines are starting up everywhere and the parking lot quickly empties. In other towns and among other people the panic would probably have been greater, but here people seem to get over it in a matter of minutes. Almost all of them have seen a fight between hooligans before, as soon as the drama is over everything goes back to normal, tomorrow most of it will be forgotten.

Johnny realizes that the only thing that might feel different this time is that it has been so long since it last happened. Two years since the last really big fight, which ended with a gang from Hed setting fire to the Bearskin and the Pack from Beartown hunting them through the forest, cars crashing and a teenage boy from Beartown getting killed. After that it was as if everyone realized that things had gone too far, and that if the conflict continued it would have led to all-out war. Even the worst of the men from Hed pulled themselves together enough to stand up and join in the singing of Beartown's song in the next match: "We are the bears." That was a white flag, and Teemu and his guys accepted it. Everyone backed down. For two years. But now? Even if today's trouble is soon over, Johnny knows that this is either the end of a small conflict or the start of one that's much, much larger.

Sirens can be heard from the road, here and there is the sound of children crying, but also relaxed conversation and even the occasional laugh. Johnny walks back to the van ahead of Hannah, Tobias doesn't see them so he turns to his siblings and blurts out excitedly:

"Did you see the pistol? Did you see the looks on all the Beartown bastards' faces then? Did you see how they shat themselves? Now they know they can't fuck with us!"

But Tess is standing a yard away, next to Bobo, and she just shakes her head sadly and whispers:

"No. Now they just think that they have to get pistols too."

Hannah doesn't hear that. Johnny pretends he hasn't heard it. But he hopes that Tess is wrong. Dear God, how he hopes.

89

Truths

It's late Thursday evening and all the black jackets from Beartown are sitting in the emergency room at the hospital in Hed. Teemu broke two fingers on someone's jaw, and a couple of his guys have broken noses from someone's fist or elbow. They're in a ridiculously good mood, despite or perhaps precisely because of that, joking and singing inappropriate songs. Above all, they're teasing Peter, seeing as the former general manager had to come here with his split eyebrow, and the nurses quickly decided to put everyone from Beartown in a separate room so that there wouldn't be any more trouble with anyone from Hed. Every time a nurse comes to call someone in, all the members of the Pack beg her to "take the boss first!" Then they nod toward Peter, wide-eyed, and whisper: "Please, don't take us foot soldiers first, help the Godfather! He's the one who gives the orders!" Peter pleads with Teemu to shut them up, but Teemu is laughing too much to be able to stop them.

"You lot don't take anything seriously, you really don't take anything in life seriously . . . ," Peter mutters.

"Well, we're not the ones who pick fights with firemen and get threatened with pistols, so maybe you should try taking life a bit less seriously?" Teemu grins back at him.

It isn't easy for Peter to argue against that, it really isn't. One of the men in the Pack receives a phone call, nods to Teemu, who immediately gets up and walks off into a corner with him, where they talk quietly. Perhaps it's about the men in the Hed stand, perhaps it's about Lev, Peter will never know because that's when his name is called by a nurse and he gets led away to have his eyebrow patched up. The doctor asks what happened to him and Peter says he "ran into a post." Considering how solid that fireman was, it doesn't altogether feel like a lie. The doctor sends him home without any ceremony when he's finished, there's a long queue this evening and no time for small talk.

When Peter returns to the waiting room Teemu grins:

"Welcome back, Godfather! How does it feel?"

"Like I've run into a post," Peter smiles.

Teemu puts his hand on his shoulder and asks quietly:

"Listen . . . I'd like to open the Bearskin for the guys tonight. Just my closest guys. Have a few beers and . . . well, you know . . . like old times. Is that okay with you? I promise we'll clean up after!"

"You've got the keys to the Bearskin, haven't you?" Peter wonders, not really understanding, and not sure how to respond to what Teemu's saying.

"I know. But I don't want to do it if you're not okay with it. There's . . . there's no one else I can ask for permission."

So Peter nods. Teemu nods back, slowly. Then one of the guys behind him hands over a bouquet of flowers and Teemu passes it on to Peter.

"For me? Wow. You didn't have to . . . ," Peter begins, but Teemu stops him making a fool of himself by quickly whispering:

"Not for you. For your wife."

"For . . . Kira?"

Teemu nods.

"The guys heard that she's helping the club as a lawyer now. That there's a bit of fuss with some reporters and Kira's agreed to help. The guys wanted to say thank you."

Peter blinks uncomprehendingly.

"Kira? Helping the club? Where did you hear that?"

He didn't need to ask, of course, because the answer is so obvious:

"You know. People talk."

Kira is sitting in the car in the parking lot outside the hospital, waiting for Peter. They dropped Maya, Ana, and Leo off at home in Beartown first, partly because Leo was sick in the car, and partly because Ana gave Peter so much advice about what he ought to do "next time he gets in a fight" that it would have been unbearable to have her in the car all the way to Hed. Kira's glad about that now, because young men in black jackets have parked their cars around hers as protection against any rush from Hed supporters, and she's happy she doesn't have to explain that to the children. The Pack that used to threaten Peter's life when he was general manager, and whose black jackets Kira managed to tear Leo away from wanting to be a part of with her fingernails bleeding, they're now her protectors? She can't even explain that to herself. But these are strange times. Terrible times.

Her phone rings and she answers, almost relieved when she sees her colleague's name.

"I heard about the fight! Were you in the rink? Are you okay?" exclaims her colleague, who sounds like she's drunk something like a dozen glasses of wine.

"Yes, fine, Peter split his eyebrow so we're at the hospital."

"Split his eyebrow?"

"He says he ran into a post."

Her colleague says nothing for a few moments.

"An awful lot of shit seems to happen to you."

Kira sighs.

"Don't even start. How are you?"

"Fine! I'm at home! Quite drunk! I've found something we can use if Peter gets charged!"

Kira sits bolt upright in her seat.

"What?"

"We say someone forged his signature! Seriously, have you seen your husband's signature? It looks like a small child's."

She's right. Before Peter went off to the NHL he had to sign so many autographs that he learned to write it really simply so he could do it quickly. Anyone could probably imitate it after a few minutes' practice.

"You're a genius!"

Her colleague sighs:

"I am, aren't I? But . . . well . . . you know, it would be seriously against the law to lie about that, of course. You and I could both end up in prison if we tried. But it's . . . a last resort. If everything else goes wrong."

Kira nods, with tears in her eyes.

"Thanks."

"Anything for you, you know that."

Kira takes a sudden, shaky breath.

"Do you think I'm doing the wrong thing? In purely moral terms? Defending Peter like this?"

Her colleague breathes softly over the line, not as if she's hesitating but as if she's trying to find the right words.

"You know, Kira, all my thoughts about morals and ethics boil down to one single thing: not if it concerns your family. You can have a thousand principles, but not if it concerns your family. That's what you protect first and foremost, above morals, even above the law. Family first. You're loads of things, but you're a mother first. A wife first."

Kira leans her head against the steering wheel.

"Thanks. Again. I know I've said thanks before, but thanks again."

Her colleague sounds almost insulted.

"You're my family too."

Peter walks dizzily out of the hospital, and goes past Kira's car twice before he recognizes it. Then he tries to get into the driver's seat and Kira just chuckles:

"There's no way I'm letting you drive! You've got more bandages than a mummy!"

So he lumbers around to the other side and gets in the passenger seat. Kira is furious, of course, but that's as it should be. She gets angry when she's scared. She's the sort of person who shouts at her children when they get hurt, that's how they know she loves them.

"It was a damn hard post," Peter tries to joke, putting one hand to his eyebrow.

Kira glances at him without starting the car. Her tone is gentle but the words cut straight through his skin:

"It's okay with me if you don't always tell me the truth. But don't try to lie. You're a bad liar, because you haven't had much practice, and I love that about you. That's why you're the only person on the planet I can trust."

The whole of Peter's face hurts when he screws his eyes shut.

"It was . . . an accident. I ran straight into a guy from Hed, I didn't want to say anything because I didn't want you to misinterpret it . . ."

Her anger appears out of nowhere, as if it's been carbonated:

"MISINTERPRET it? Look around you! Are THESE our friends now?"

She gestures toward the black jackets in the cars to the right and left of them. To be honest, the question is directed at herself as much as him. She's hated the hooligans for so long but right now she's glad they're at Peter's side, because that might just scare off the reporters, and how is a lawyer supposed to reconcile herself to that?

Peter looks simultaneously embarrassed and focused. As he hands over the flowers, he says with a mixture of accusation and apology:

"I got these from Teemu and his guys. They said you're working as a lawyer to help Beartown Hockey now, and they wanted to thank you. Do you maybe feel like telling me what that's all about?"

Only then does Kira realize. The men in the black jackets aren't there to protect Peter, they're there to protect her.

"I . . . ," she begins, fully prepared to launch into an excuse, because if there's one thing about herself that she's ashamed of, it's the fact that she's such a good liar.

But then she looks her husband in the eye and he looks the way he did the first time he walked into her parents' restaurant more than twenty years ago, after losing a stupid hockey game that was the biggest of his life. She remembers everything she fell in love with: a boy looking for something, a good father, a decent man. So she tells the truth. Everything. All in one go.

"Tails came to the house the other day, when you went with Zackell to look at Aleksandr. I think maybe that was his idea all along. He needed you out of the way so he could talk to me . . ."

Then she takes such a deep breath that it makes her giddy, and then she tells him about being offered a seat on the committee. About the work her firm would get regarding Beartown Business Park, how that's a way for Tails and the other sponsors to bribe her and bind her closer to the club. Make her as dependent on the town's interwoven network of favors and counterfavors as everyone else, so that she'd have to save the club at the same time as saving Peter.

"Saving . . . me?" Peter whispers, barely audible, sounding so pathetic and shocked that his larynx can hardly say the words.

Kira tells him calmly and factually about all the contracts she's seen, all the gaps in the accounts, the training facility that doesn't exist, and all the documents concerning it that have Peter's signature at the bottom.

"What you've all been doing at that club in the past few years, darling, it's . . . I don't even know which words to use . . . it's basically money laundering. Corruption. In legal terms, it definitely counts as accounting crimes and 'disloyalty to principal.' The local paper has brought in a reporter from outside to dig into the whole thing, and sooner or later he's going to find all the things you've hidden. Considering how much council money is involved . . . bloody hell, darling . . . you could end up in prison!"

She runs out of air before she runs out of words. Her fingers are vibrating against the steering wheel even though the engine's switched off. Peter sits beside her, deathly pale, falling thousands of miles straight into a black hole. His whole identity crumbles. He's sweating, hyperventilating, wants to open the window but is scared all the secrets inside the car would just fly out. In the end he feels so ill that he leans his head against the glove compartment. A few minutes pass before he manages to say:

"The training facility? I . . . I didn't know what I was signing, darling, I know it sounds like a lie now, but if I'd known it was illegal I'd never . . . never! I thought I was just doing Tails a favor . . . I signed hundreds of documents when I was working for the club, and when he called after I'd left I felt guilty and thought . . . oh God, darling, I didn't think at all. I'm such an idiot. I'm such an IDIOT! He said it was all okay with the council, that they just needed a 'big name.' I just trusted that he . . ."

"I know," Kira whispers, but he isn't listening, he's too busy questioning every decision he's ever made.

She's thinking that the most incomprehensible thing about both him and Tails is actually how surprised they are that reporters are even looking into this: as if they were little children in the middle of a game who turn around in shock to find that someone's been standing watching them the whole time. Who do they think they are? What do they think reporters do? Did no one at the club have a plan for what to do if everything was uncovered?

Peter gasps:

"I can't believe I'm such an idiot. I can't BELIEVE it. I just . . . I mean, I knew that some aspects of the players' contracts were a bit of a gray area. That the board and the sponsors might be fiddling things. But I always pretended not to know. I told myself that I knew nothing about finance, I should just focus on the hockey. But darling, I . . . I would NEVER do anything illegal, not on—"

"I know! I know! I know you're innocent!" Kira interrupts, suddenly harder.

His voice become little more than a gasp:

"How? How do you know that? Even I don't know that!"

Her eyes are exhausted, her cheeks wet, her lips dry.

"Because I know you. I have so many secrets from you, but you have hardly any from me. I've started seeing a psychologist again, I haven't told you because I thought I could just sort everything out myself. A while back the psychologist asked me how I feel, and I said it was as if I was drowning, and he asked what was stopping me, and I said 'my husband.' I said . . . you. Because I see land in you, darling. I get air from you. And you're the worst liar I know. That's how I know you haven't committed any crimes on purpose."

"I love you, you're the only . . . you and the children . . . you're the only . . ."

"I know."

They can hardly see each other now, no matter how hard they blink.

"What are we going to do? I have to go to the police and confess everything, I have to . . . ," he begins desperately, but she shakes her head.

"No. I've spoken to Tails. He's talking to all his contacts right now, all the sponsors and politicians. We're going to sort this."

"How?" Peter sobs.

The look in her eyes may be broken, but her voice doesn't waver at all when she replies:

"I don't know yet, but you need to trust me, I'll find a way."

"You can't stop the reporters if they . . . ," he whispers.

Kira looks out through the window, at the men in black jackets, and wonders silently what she's capable of. How far she's prepared to go. Then she hears herself say:

"We're going to persuade the newspaper not to write about this. Or we create a situation where they no longer want to."

"The newspaper OUGHT to write about this, I made mistakes . . . I mean, they're RIGHT . . . ," Peter replies.

"This isn't about being right," Kira says.

"What is it about, then?" he sniffs.

She doesn't even have an answer to that. Because what is it about? Being on the right side? Convincing yourself that you're fighting for the right things? Or is it just about survival? When all is said and done, is that all we're capable of? Trying to win at any cost? She doesn't know, she'll be wondering about that for the rest of her life, but for now she just says:

"Protecting our family. Above everything else. You and me and the children. That's the only thing that matters now. I'm going to find a way to fix this, you have to trust me."

"I trust you," he whispers.

She moves her hand incredibly slowly, as if the movement might break her arm, reaching out her fingers until they find his. She smiles a smile that's as brittle as it is defiant, a small sign of resistance against the chaos:

"And when this is over, darling . . . then I sure as hell want a bloody holiday. I want just one morning when no one asks me for help, okay? I want a hotel breakfast and those silly little glasses of fruit juice and croissants. Damn it, I want CROISSANTS, darling. Okay?"

He manages to smile, just about, but promises with all his heart. She drives them back to Beartown, keeping hold of his hand the whole way.

90

Inheritance

The caravan of vehicles full of Hed supporters arrives home through the forest. Families from the seated part of the stands turn off toward their residential areas, but the young men from the standing area turn off the other way, toward the Barn. They have a few bruises and broken noses that will have to be patched up at the hospital, but most of the damage is superficial enough to be drunk away. The pub they know only as the Barn survived the storm surprisingly well compared with the roof of Hed's ice rink, as if God had to choose between letting his people watch hockey or get drunk afterward. If you forced the clientele there to make the same choice this evening, they wouldn't have found it so damn easy either.

Hannah no longer drinks at the Barn, she's a grown-up now, she drinks at home in the kitchen. Johnny is sitting opposite her. She has wine in her coffee cup, he has whiskey in a glass that she can't bring herself to tell him is actually a tea light holder. Tess went upstairs to put Ture to bed, and fell asleep next to him. Tobias went out like a light in his room with all his clothes on, as if his body sleeps better the more stress it's been subjected to. It's starting to get late, it's pitch-black outside the windows, yet they can still hear the sound of banging from the yard. Ted is out there, firing pucks in the light of all the flashlights he could find. The neighbors for miles around must be able to hear, but even the least tolerant of them doesn't show up to complain this evening. Perhaps they have more important things to worry about, perhaps they're just taking pity on a thirteen-year-old whose match was called off and who now has to get rid of the adrenaline some other way.

"I should have seen it coming. We should never have gone to the game in the first place," Johnny chastises himself.

"No one could have known it was going to get out of control like that," Hannah says tersely, but he can hear her teeth grinding, like the little hiss when a fuse is lit.

"I don't know Lev, if that's what you're about to ask. I picked up Bengt's tires there and we had a chat, that's all. Teemu has been threatening him about some debt, that's why Lev came to our defense."

"Defense? Is that how you see it?" she counters.

"How do you see it?" he asks sullenly, even though he can tell it's a trap.

"He made everything worse! It was a hockey game between kids, and he had a pistol on him! Where do you think we live? Some war zone?"

Johnny sighs. Spins his glass. He's realized now that it's a tea light holder but she can drop any idea that he's going to admit that. It's cheap whiskey anyway and a bit of wax is hardly going make much difference.

"I can talk to him . . ."

"The person you need to talk to is Tobias! Did you see his eyes? He looked like . . . ," Hannah splutters, stopping herself before she says "like you."

Because that's the truth about their eldest son. He looks like his father when he gets angry. Johnny stares down into his glass and lets the whiskey roll from one side to the other.

"He handled himself well. The first thing he did was go and get his little brother. Isn't that what we've taught him?"

Hannah sighs into her wine. Yes, it is. It's exactly what they've taught him. So what's she so angry about? Does she even know? Exhausted and resigned, it slips out of her, as if she's merely testing the thought out loud:

"I've hated the idea of Tess choosing to move to another town to study for so long. Today is the first time I hope she does. That she moves a long way from all this. I want her world to be . . . bigger."

"There's plenty of violence out in the world too. There are idiots who fight everywhere," Johnny snorts.

"Yes. But out there at least she'd escape the sort of violence that gets passed down the generations," Hannah replies, and at that Johnny raises his chin and whispers, hurt:

"Because I'm the sort of person who wants to beat people to death?"

Hannah shakes her head.

"No. Because there have been moments in the past week when I've wanted to."

The silence shrinks the kitchen, swallowing all the oxygen. Johnny contemplates making a lame joke, saying that Tess couldn't possibly inherit any tendency to violence from her mother because Hannah is so useless at fighting, but now isn't the time for that. He understands what she means. He drinks his whiskey, kisses his wife's head, goes upstairs and tucks Tess and Ture in, then goes and sits on the floor beside Tobias's bed. His son is snoring loudly but his heart is beating slowly. There's fresh snow on the window and Johnny feels ancient. Like all parents, he just dreams of his children having things a bit better than him, a bit easier, but there's no way to protect them against the world. We can't even protect them from themselves. So he closes his eyes and thinks that if Hannah is right, if the boy in this bed really is going to turn out like his dad, then there's only one thing for Johnny to do.

To become better.

Ted fires puck after puck, harder and harder, and somewhere inside he's so surprised that no one has come out and yelled at him to stop, that when he sees his mother out of the corner of his eye, he lets go of his stick without even arguing. He's drenched with sweat even though the night is ridiculously cold. His mother is wearing Tobias's jacket and Tess's woolly hat, and Ted's fairly sure the shoes are his old ones. He's about to say he'll stop and go inside and go to bed when she blinks hard at him and asks:

"Can I join in?"

He lets her.

91

Traces

When we tell this story afterward, it will probably be obvious that it's a slow chain reaction where everything happens one thing at a time. But for some of the people involved it will always feel as if almost all the important things happened at once, out of nowhere, within the space of a few hours.

The night is extremely cold, and when Friday morning comes the editor in chief is out before the snowplows. She pads to the office in the dark. She looks over her shoulder at first, still a little paranoid about thinking she's seen black jackets everywhere in recent days, but she's alone on the streets. No one except journalists are awake. It's the day after the trouble at the ice rink and she knows that two of her reporters are already in the office writing articles about it. When she took the job here and met them for the first time, they both introduced themselves as sports reporters, but one of them turned out to work on the news desk and other is responsible for the family pages, but the joke at her expense was pretty simple: here everyone works on sports, so you may as well get used to it. She probably hasn't, not quite yet.

When she got out of bed this morning her dad still hadn't gone to bed. They relieved each other like two factory workers. He sat up all night, hunched over her kitchen table, surrounded by papers and files, most of which she had never even seen before.

"What's this? I thought you were going to try to work out the details of the trouble at the game yesterday?" she wondered, but her dad just waved her away as if she were a little girl again.

"This is more important. Look at this! All these documents show how taxpayers' money has been paid out in fake grants and illegal loans in connection to various council construction projects in the past ten years.

Do you remember when the council here got delusions of grandeur and applied to host the skiing world championship? Look at all these payments wealthy businessmen in the area made to this construction company. I think these are bribes to politicians. Above all, to this politician, the woman who leads the biggest party on the council! And look here, who do you think works for the construction company? Her husband and her brother!"

The editor in chief made coffee and tried to make sense of her dad's papers.

"Dad . . . you may be right, perhaps this is a big scandal . . . but what does this have to do with our investigation into the training facility and Beartown Hockey?"

"This is much more important than Beartown Hockey! That investigation is NOTHING compared to this!"

She stared at him in surprise.

"Can I ask where you got these documents from?"

"I did my job, found a source, don't worry about that . . ."

His eyes crossed with tiredness. It was impossible to get any more sense out of him. So she told him to go and get some sleep.

Now she's padding through the snow, unable to stop worrying about something he said: "This is much more important than Beartown Hockey." They've spent all week digging into the club and Peter Andersson, but now he's suddenly changed track in the course of one night? She's worrying so much that it makes her distracted and she's just staring down at the ground ahead of her instead of looking up. When she reaches the offices of the newspaper she doesn't see the men standing in front of her until she's too close to run. She turns and tries anyway, almost instinctively, until she sees that they're not wearing black jackets. They're wearing red ones.

"Hi!" one of them says, holding out a large fist, and she catches a glimpse of the tattoo of a bull on his lower arm beneath the sleeve of his jacket.

She doesn't shake his hand, but she doesn't knock it aside either. One of the other men smiles amiably. He has a big black eye, presumably a souvenir from the fight in the ice rink.

"We're just here to keep an eye out! We heard that those bastards in the Pack over in Beartown have been threatening you and your staff. Don't worry, there's no need to be concerned, we're here to take care of things now."

The editor in chief looks from one to the other in confusion, then exclaims:

"I don't know what you're talking about. What threats?"

The first man winks at her as if they're sharing a big secret.

"We get that you can't say anything. But we got a tip-off that you're investigating Beartown Hockey, and that the crazies in the Pack are trying to stop you. Don't let them! Everyone knows they're all crooks, the whole lot of them, I hope you really stick it to them! We're going to have guys here to make sure nothing happens to you."

The editor in chief doesn't know what to say. For heaven's sake, she's barely even awake yet, so how much weirder can today get before the sun has even risen? Quite a lot, it turns out.

"You've got to be kidding . . . ," she mumbles as she walks into the office and sees who's sitting at her desk, leaning back comfortably.

"Good morning!" Richard Theo says cheerfully.

The editor in chief sighs.

"Okay. Did you change your mind about looking for a job? Perhaps I could employ you as a cartoonist?"

Theo smiles, rather impressed by her immediate instinct for conflict. Plenty of people are like that the first time they meet him, but they tend to be more cautious the second time.

"I won't take up much of your time, I promise. I'm sure you have a lot to do after the incident yesterday."

She smiles.

"The 'incident'? Interesting choice of words. It was hooligans rioting."

He looks surprised.

"Oh no, I wouldn't describe it like that at all. I was there. I was never concerned for my own or anyone else's safety. A few young men on both sides just let their frustrations get the better of them, that's all, the sort of thing that happens everywhere. Even in the big cities, I believe?"

This last remark is so pointed that the editor in chief softens slightly.

"The last time you were here, you said you were worried about violence between the two clubs' supporters. Now you're saying they're all good friends?"

Theo holds his arms out apologetically.

"I just don't want things to be misinterpreted. For people to read something in the paper that they misunderstand. Because that could LEAD to violence, don't you think?"

"We're going to report what happened . . . ," she begins.

"Peter Andersson had his eyebrow split yesterday, did you hear that?" he interrupts quickly.

"No . . . no, I didn't know that," she admits.

"It was purely by accident, I can assure you! He collided with another man in the commotion. But naturally there are people in Beartown who would prefer to see it as him being attacked. You know how popular Peter Andersson is in Beartown. There are lots of people who want to protect him. Yes . . . speaking of that . . . there are evidently lots of people who want to protect you as well? I saw your friends outside!"

He adjusts his tie over his perfectly ironed shirt. The editor in chief is irritated by how sharp he looks so early in the morning.

"If you're referring to the men by the door, I don't actually know . . . ," she begins.

"Of course not. But they seem to be under the impression that you need protection. I wouldn't want that to be misinterpreted either." He nods.

The editor in chief feels a chill creep down her spine when she starts to realize what's going on. Who has been spreading the rumors that got the men at the door to show up.

"What are you trying to say?" she hisses, hating his relaxed smile.

"If you write about Peter Andersson straight after he has, according to some rumors, been attacked and assaulted by Hed supporters, the same Hed supporters who are now standing guard at your door, don't you think it might look like you've . . . chosen a side?"

"Don't threaten me, Richard. I'm a journalist. That's a bad idea."

"Threaten you? That isn't my intention! Oh, you'll have to forgive me!" he exclaims with such an expression of extreme despair that it looks almost genuine.

He stands up. She tilts her head to one side.

"Was that all? You came here so early in the day just to say that?"

He pretends to think, as if he's forgotten something, then slaps his forehead gently and theatrically, and adds:

"Now that you come to mention it: I've actually got a tip-off for you! Have you heard that Hed Hockey has got a new sponsor? Perhaps you're familiar with the fact that the owners of the factory sponsor Beartown Hockey? Now another proprietor has put money into Hed!"

The editor in chief's curiosity gets the better of her caution.

"Proprietor of what?"

"Your proprietor."

He's so pleased when he says this, like a dad cleaning out the bank in a game of Monopoly. He says the name of the company, and of course the editor in chief knows perfectly well what it is. They own the company that owns her newspaper.

"Why would they want to sponsor a hockey club all the way out here?" she asks, uncomfortably adjusting her clothes to hide her cold shudder.

"An old friend of mine from my student days is on the board. I called and told him that Hed Hockey is having financial trouble and that it would be a good deed if the owner of the local paper sponsored them. Because that's what we do around here. We help each other. Don't we?"

She replies through tightly clenched teeth:

"Does your friend know that half the newspaper's subscribers live in Beartown?"

Theo shakes his head.

"No, no, he doesn't know anything about hockey. He thinks it's just a sport."

Her lips disappear beneath each other in a mixture of anger and resignation.

"So you think I won't dare to investigate Beartown Hockey now, because it will look like I'm only doing it because the newspaper is sponsoring Hed?"

His self-assurance is repugnant:

"No, no, you misunderstand. I think you won't investigate Beartown Hockey because you've just been given a far better story to publish instead."

"What's that?"

Theo pulls his elegant coat onto his shoulders and raises an eyebrow.

"Hasn't your dad told you?"

He walks out through the door and disappears before she has time to reply. The men with bull tattoos are still there when she runs home. By the time her dad wakes up she has already been through the whole argument with him in her head so many times that she can't be bothered to do it in real life.

"So you sold out our investigation of Peter Andersson for another story?" she merely says disconsolately.

"A much . . . better story," he retorts, still not properly awake, but she can see that he feels ashamed.

"I didn't think this of you, Dad. I didn't think you'd back away from a fight."

Her dad looks at her for a long, long time. She sees tears begin to well up and is so shocked that she has to sit down. He says:

"I picked a fight we can win, kid. I called an old colleague of Richard Theo's and . . . he's dangerous. Properly dangerous. He's crushed people's careers just for the fun of it. I don't scare easily but, damn it, what happens to you when I leave here and a man like him is now your enemy? He isn't like the other men here. He's smarter. He's got a completely different set of contacts. He won't send hooligans to frighten you, he'll send lawyers who will wreck your entire life. People like him come after you with everything they've got, and they don't stop until they've taken everything and everyone you love away from you . . ."

"When I was little, you always said that a journalist without enemies is a journalist who isn't doing his job, Dad." Her voice is shaking with disappointment, and he'll never quite get over that.

"But you're too young for enemies, kid. Too young for enemies like THIS. You have too much ahead of you. And I . . . damn . . . I'm too old for fighting. At least with men like Richard Theo. The documents he sent me, kid, they're not small fry. He gets what he wants, everywhere. Do you know how much money he's already rustled up for Hed Hockey by barely so much as snapping his fingers? Think about what he could do to you . . . don't let your career die out here in the middle of nowhere because of pride. Please. Don't be like me, don't try to fight the whole world at once. Wait until you're in a bigger newsroom with more backup, and go for him then if you want to. But I came here to help you, and this is the best way I can do that. So do you want my advice? Take the story he's offering you. It's a better story than the one about Peter Andersson. He's just one man, without much power at all, but what Richard Theo has given us concerns extensive corruption all the way up to the very top of the council . . ."

"And if that turns out to be nothing but lies?"

"Then we carry on digging into Beartown Hockey, we can . . ."

His daughter hides her face with her hands.

"No. No, we can't, Dad. They'll have covered all their tracks by then. It's already too late."

All the energy drains out of her. She slumps down across the table. This is what it feels like to lose.

92

Islands

Darkness falls and Friday starts to draw to a close. Benji barely leaves any footprints in the snow as he moves between the trees. That always used to surprise people who encountered him on the ice, the combination of agility and strength. Adri always says it's incredible that someone so agile can be so bad at dancing, and he always replies that it's incredible that someone can be so bad at cooking as she is yet still be so fat. Then she hits him really hard, and perhaps that's what she'll miss most of all. She and Alicia and Sune are up at the kennels now looking at the new puppies, Benji set out from home with no real idea of where he was going, so he's heading down toward the lake. He has no real dreams he's longing to fulfill, so he makes do with seeking out company. Big City is sitting on a folding chair outside the campervan, wrapped in a sleeping bag, he's learned how to make a fire and is happy when Benji appears because: that he has someone to show that off to.

"You do it the way Ana did it," Benji notes sulkily.

"Her way worked, unlike yours." Big City smiles.

He doesn't look at all surprised that Benji is here. That's what their relationship is like now: they have a sense of what the other is going to do. If they had ever played hockey together they would have been unbeatable. Benji sinks down onto the flimsier of the folding chairs without bothering about a sleeping bag and gives an impressed nod:

"I didn't think you'd survive one night on your own out here. But you're forest folk now."

"I'd never really seen a forest in my whole life until a couple of days ago," Big City says.

"Whether you're forest folk or not has nothing to do with the forest," Benji replies.

They look up at the evening sky. Benji thinks of something Ramona once said: "Men are scared of telescopes, you can't look at the stars without shitting your pants because you can't think about how big the universe is without seeing how small you are in comparison. Nothing scares a man more than the thought that everything he does might lack all meaning." The lake is freezing, the island that lies a short way out is isolated by the winter that's on its way, it doesn't look like much from here, but all Benji's happiest summers were spent there, when he and Kevin would set off as soon as hockey training finished and live there like castaways for weeks. Out there everything was unspoken but nothing secret. Benji has never experienced that with anyone else.

Big City looks up at the stars for a long time before saying:

"You were right. Your stars are better than the ones where I come from. Less air pollution here."

Benji nods slowly.

"But more wind turbines. They're fucking shit as well. Frighten the game away."

Big City laughs and mocks his accent.

"The 'game'? Is that hunting talk?"

Benji smiles that smile of his, as if he can see straight through everything and everyone.

"I prefer fishing, to be honest."

"When do you have a chance to fish here? Quarter of an hour in August?" Big City wonders, nodding out toward the water, which has already turned to ice even though it's only early autumn in Big City's world.

"All year round. In summer you sit in a boat and tell lies for nine hours and get zero fish. In winter you drill a hole in the ice out there and sit on a chair and tell lies for nine hours and get zero fish."

"That's a lot of lying," Big City notes.

"You have no idea. Sometimes it gets so painful that we have to tell the truth," Benji replies.

He gets some beer from the campervan and offers one to Big City, who shakes his head.

"Game tomorrow."

Benji nods, and if Big City didn't know better he'd almost say he looks a bit envious.

"Against Hed, right? You don't know what that means here. That's good. Play like it doesn't mean a thing."

Big City runs the back of his hand over his stubble, he normally shaves every morning as part of a rigorous routine of habits and details that have shaped his entire life, but out here he doesn't care. He turns toward Benji and asks, not in a patronizing way, just curious:

"I heard that Hed chant 'Beartown fags' at games. Does that bother you?"

"Where did you hear that?"

Big City clears his throat.

"I heard one of the guys on the team say something in the locker room."

Benji nods slowly.

"Why would it bother me?"

Big City searches for words deep inside himself. They come out hoarse and strained.

"I just wondered what you do to cope with being . . . different."

Benji smokes in silence for so long that Big City is convinced he didn't hear the question, but then he says:

"Personally, I usually get high and knock people's teeth out. But I'm sure there are other ways. Meditation, maybe? I've heard a lot of good things about meditation, but it's fucking hard to smoke at the same time . . ."

Big City smiles past the sarcasm.

"Was it easier or harder to be yourself when you were traveling?"

Benji sniggers.

"It's easier to be anything if no one knows who you are. And it's easier to be from Beartown the farther away from here you are."

Big City leans back in his chair, he'd like to ask more but doesn't dare, so he slowly lets the subject drop and admits:

"You're tricky people. But I have to admit that you can do sunsets. I've never seen sunsets like the ones here."

"That's because you've never seen a sun that sets right after lunch before."

"True. Very true," Big City laughs.

Benji suddenly says, quietly but clearly:

"You're going to fit in here. Better than you think."

That means more to Big City than he lets on. He's never fit in anywhere.

"What else am I going to do? Keep going north until I find people even crazier than you lot?"

"The only person north of us who's even crazier is Santa."

They roar with laughter. Benji drinks his beer and smokes his weed, and Big City closes his eyes and listens to absolutely nothing.

"How long is it since you played hockey?" he asks after a while.

"Just over two years," Benji replies.

"What have you been doing instead?"

"Traveling. Smoking. Dancing."

"Where?"

"Asia, mostly."

"Why there in particular?"

"Hardly anyone knows what hockey is there."

"Did you find what you were looking for?"

"What do you mean by that?"

Big City's voice is gentle but firm:

"No one travels that far unless they're looking for something."

Benji blows smoke through his nose.

"If I'd found it I probably wouldn't have bothered coming home. Have you found what you were looking for?"

"Where?"

"Here."

The confidence vanishes from Big City's voice.

"I don't know what that would be, to be honest."

Benji opens another beer.

"That's the whole point of looking, isn't it?"

Big City says nothing for a long time. Then he whispers:

"I . . . I'd like to pay rent for living in the campervan."

"Forget it. That would make me your landlord."

"What are you now?"

Benji turns to look at him.

"Your friend."

He recognizes the look of someone who has never had a friend. Big City has spent such a large part of his life lying that it hurts right now, and he accidentally blurts out the truth:

"If I liked guys, I could really fucking fall for you. You know that, right?"

Of course he knows. But Benji still grins, that damn smile that's as much a bird's as a bear's. Then he says:

"You're already in love with me. You just haven't realized it yet."

Big City laughs. Benji too. Their laughter sings across the forest, over the lake, all the way to the island.

93

Tails is sitting in his office at the supermarket. He answers the phone before the first ring has died away.

"I've solved your problem," Richard Theo informs him curtly.

"What . . . already? How . . . ," Tails begins, and when the politician explains he is left both impressed and slightly scared.

The new sponsor of Hed Hockey is such a simple solution. Liberating for Tails, devastating for the local paper.

"Those journalists won't be a problem anymore. But the council still has to be convinced to keep both hockey clubs. So we're going to need another favor from your friend Kira Andersson," the politician goes on.

"Kira? What do you want her to do?" Tails wonders with an ominous lump in his stomach.

"What I've heard she's best at: persuading people. You just need to persuade her first."

"About what?"

"A torch-lit procession."

Tails is about to start asking stupid questions, but the politician has neither the time nor the patience, so for once he simply explains his plan. When he's finished Tails exclaims:

"That's . . . smart. It could work. But if Kira does that in Beartown, presumably someone else has to do it in Hed?"

"I've got a name and an address for you, write this down . . . ," the politician replies.

"Okay, okay, what number house did you say?" Tails mutters as he makes a note on his arm with a pen.

"And, as you might remember, I had one more condition for doing all this," Theo points out when he's finished.

"What do you want?" Tails says anxiously.

"A different investigation is going to be published in the paper before long, about a different sort of corruption, and every good story needs a few scapegoats."

Tails tries to swallow but his mouth is too dry.

"Oh?"

"I want to choose the scapegoats. And you're going to help me."

———

When Kira arrives at her office Tails is already sitting on the bench outside. His tie is loose, the top button of his shirt undone under his coat.

"The newspaper is dropping the investigation into Peter and Beartown Hockey," he says without any preamble.

She just stares at him. His words make her feel dizzy. Can this possibly be true? She doesn't know if she should jump for joy or throw herself down on the ground and make snow angels, and for a moment she even wants to hug him, but thankfully that passes very quickly.

"Tails! Oh, Tailcoat, are you serious? We're . . . I'm . . . what on earth did you do?" she gasps.

"Called in a lot of favors. And offered a lot of favors in return," Tails confesses, without any pride.

Relieved, she plonks herself down beside him on the bench.

"But are you sure that Peter's . . . safe? That nothing's going to happen to him now?"

Tails nods.

"Completely sure. But I need to ask you for a favor."

"Anything!"

"Don't say that until I've asked."

She squints at him.

"Is it illegal?"

He starts to laugh. A rattling, hearty laugh that starts somewhere deep in his stomach and rumbles across the whole parking lot.

"No, no, no, but I don't know if you wouldn't rather it was something illegal when you hear what it is . . ."

He tells her what he needs. What Richard Theo has asked from him. She blanches.

"A torch-lit procession? That's your grand plan to save both hockey clubs? A *torch-lit procession?*"

Tails shakes his head slowly. He holds his index finger and middle finger up toward her.

"Two. Not one torch-lit procession. Two."

Then he passes her a piece of paper.

"Who's this?"

"Someone you have to persuade to be on our side if this is going to work."

———

"You're a hopelessly simple but horribly complicated person," the psychologist once said to Kira. It was a quote from a book he had read, and was followed by a long explanation about some theory about the functions of the brain that he liked a lot, but Kira never heard any of that. She got stuck on those words: simply complicated. Complicatedly simple. Is there any other sort of person?

After her meeting with Tails she drives straight home from the office. She sits opposite Peter with the whole kitchen table covered with their fingers reaching for one another. She tells him everything Tails said, and Peter takes the longest breath she has ever heard him take. They don't realize until that moment how tired they are. How shattered. When they finally relax, their muscles start to ache, and as the stress eases tears well up behind their eyelids.

Neither of them says anything, but they're both thinking about Isak. How they learned to cry inwardly when he died. Silently, silently, silently they taught themselves to cry for years so their other children wouldn't hear. They think about everything they fight so hard not to think about normally, when the very air itself hurts: how they wanted to lie down with their cheeks to the ground and whisper into the grass to him down there. How they wanted to throw themselves into his grave, go with him wherever he was going. He was so small, so very small, how could anyone leave someone so defenseless to journey alone into darkness? He wasn't even big enough to be left on his own in the kitchen, but suddenly everyone expected them to leave him in the churchyard? Overnight? Who was he going to call out to if he had nightmares? Whose bed would he crawl into? Whose shoulder would he fall asleep lying on? They hated themselves so much, his parents, because they couldn't die with him. Because they went on living.

How much of everything they've done since then has just been their attempts to do something important, something big, something worth being late for? So that they could whisper "Mommy and Daddy just had to save the world" when they eventually saw him again in Heaven? Almost everything.

Would he be proud of them now? Have they lived worthy lives? Have they been good enough people?

They cry inwardly. Silently, silently. Then Peter gets up and washes his hands and turns the oven on and starts to make croissants. Kira kisses her husband and picks up her jacket and goes out to the car and drives to Hed.

They're simple, complicated people. "You always find something, somewhere, and then you fight for it to the death," her colleague said to her. And that's what Kira does now.

Women

Hannah is shoveling snow from the drive and clearing the yard. Johnny is at work, the children are at school, and their things are everywhere. It's usually Johnny who goes around muttering as he tidies up, of course, he's a natural pedant, but today she's doing it herself. What you miss most when you have a family is the feeling of being bored. You're never bored again. Recently Hannah heard some younger nurses at the hospital talking about a colleague who'd had an affair, and all she could think was: Who the hell has time for that? Don't people ever sleep?

She picks hockey pucks out of the flower beds and hangs lost gloves up to dry and gathers all the hockey sticks together and leans them up against the house. She sees the car out of the corner of her eye in the distance, it's a bit more expensive than the ones people on this road drive, the sort you have to really think you're something to believe you belong behind the wheel of. The woman driving stops and gets out, checks an address on a piece of paper and looks at the houses, then meets Hannah's gaze across the low fence and suddenly looks uncertain.

"Sorry . . . but are you Hannah?"

Hannah is still holding a Hed Hockey stick in her hand as she approaches the boundary of the property. She knows who Kira Andersson is, but Kira doesn't know that yet, so Hannah decides to act stupid.

"Who's asking?"

Kira almost smiles. Even the women in Hed speak as if they're ready to start fighting at any moment.

"My name's Kira. I'm married to Peter Andersson. I believe he and your husband crashed into each other at the ice rink yesterday, Peter split his eyebrow . . ."

"It was an accident!" Hannah replies so sharply that Kira stops.

"I know, I know! Sorry, I didn't phrase that very well. I know it was an accident, That's not why I'm here. Well, it IS why I'm here, but . . . it's a long story. Can I . . . can I start again?"

She smiles awkwardly, rubs her sweaty palms together. Hannah leans on her son's hockey stick with an expression as if Kira were there to persuade her to change her religion.

"By all means."

Kira takes several thoughtful breaths and makes a fresh attempt:

"Okay. So, my husband and yours ran into each other yesterday . . . so, first of all I'd like to ask if your husband's alright?"

Hannah can't help smiling.

"Alright in the head? There was nothing right about his head to start with. How's yours?"

Kira returns Hannah's tentative smile.

"Peter? When he played hockey his coach used to say it was his thick head that protected his helmet, not the other way around. So I think he'll be okay."

"Good. I've got some things to do, so if you'll excuse me . . . ," Hannah says, clearing her throat.

Kira nods understandingly and looks over at Ted's hockey ramp.

"Yes, yes, of course. I can see. How many kids have you got?"

"Four. You've already met one of them," Hannah says, slightly irritably, because she's starting to think that Kira is making fun of her now.

"I don't understand . . . ," Kira manages to say.

Hannah tilts her head to one side.

"Why are you here? What do you want from me?"

"I . . . sorry . . . maybe there's some sort of misunderstanding. Which one of your children have I . . . met?"

"My daughter. I found your business card in her jacket this morning."

Hannah regrets saying that, she doesn't want to sound like the sort of mother who looks through her daughter's pockets, but Kira doesn't look like she's judging her.

"Tess? Is she your daughter? I didn't know. I'm so sorry. She was just asking me about my work. I . . ."

"And today you're here to talk about my husband?"

Kira puts her hands in her coat pockets and nods.

"I understand that it must look like a strange coincidence."

Hannah looks at her for a long time to see if there's anything there she can't trust. She doesn't find much. So she says:

"My daughter wants to study law. She doesn't know anyone who's done that. I assume that's why she was asking you."

Kira can hear the pang of jealousy in the mother's voice. She recognizes it, she sounds the same every time Maya mentions one of her teachers at music college. She knows how it feels to have a child who lives in a world you don't understand.

"She just wanted some advice about courses, I . . ."

"I'm a midwife. We have to study for our job too," Hannah points out.

Kira blushes.

"I know. I didn't mean it like that, Tess is extremely smart and well-brought-up. I appreciate that that comes from you."

Hannah snorts.

"You don't have to flatter me. I was angry when I found your business card, but Johnny says I need to let go of the kids. So I'm trying. You have an office in Hed, right? If Tess goes away to study, can she come back and work for your company then?"

The question comes so abruptly that Kira is taken aback. This wasn't exactly how she had imagined this conversation going.

"Of course. Of course . . . I mean, if she's good enough."

Hannah replies like someone who knows nothing about law, but everything about her daughter:

"She'll be the best."

Kira lets out a short laugh. Lord, grant me the self-confidence of a mother from Hed, she thinks, but deep down she knows she's just the same. She and Hannah have very little in common, yet somehow still almost everything.

"She's welcome to come by the office whenever she likes if she has more questions."

Hannah nods, jealous but grateful. Then she says, without sounding impolite but certainly not the opposite either:

"Do you want coffee or are you going to get to the point? Why are you here?"

Kira is on the brink of asking for coffee, but doesn't want to risk being unnecessarily provocative. So she explains everything as simply as she can:

"Some friends of mine saw our husbands collide in the ice rink yesterday. It made them . . . anxious. Peter is something of a symbol for hockey in Beartown and I think your husband is the same here. My friends are worried that people will think they were fighting. That could trigger even more trouble. But then one of them had the idea that our husbands might actually prefer to promote . . . peace. I'm sure you've heard the rumors that the council wants to close down both hockey clubs?"

Hannah drives her son's hockey stick into the snow as if she was trying to plant it.

"All I've heard is that the council wants to shut down Hed Hockey. That they don't want to pay to rebuild the ice rink here."

"My friends are pretty sure the real plan is to shut down both Beartown and Hed and start a whole new sports club. We want to try to get the politicians to change their minds. So that we can save both clubs."

Hannah lets slip a doubtful snort.

"Why would you want to save Hed?"

Kira sighs so deeply that she leans forward and puts her hands on her knees, not even looking at Hannah.

"Can I be honest? I don't even want to save Beartown! But it is what it is. I'm just trying to keep everyone happy here, damn it!"

She doesn't mean to come across as angry, she's just very, very tired. Hannah smiles, because she's never heard anyone sound more like a mother.

"Are you from down south?" she asks.

"Mmm," Kira replies distantly with her hands on her knees and her eyes focused on the snow.

"You can only tell when you get angry, otherwise you sound like one of us," Hannah says.

It's a big compliment. Very big. Kira glances up at her.

"Be careful. One day your daughter will come home from university with a different accent."

"As long as she doesn't show up in one of those silly cars I think it'll be okay," Hannah replies, nodding scornfully toward Kira's car.

"Next time I'll smash the window before I arrive so I fit in," Kira replies.

Hannah laughs loudly and disarmingly. She leans against the fence. Hesitates a long time before she can bring herself to ask:

"Do you know a young girl over in Beartown by the name of Ana?"

Kira starts to laugh.

"Are you kidding? She's my daughter's best friend!"

Hannah's eyes look glossy as she tries not to reveal the extent of her emotions.

"I was the midwife she helped deliver a baby in the forest during the storm. I'd just like to thank her again."

"What baby?" Kira wonders.

"She hasn't . . . she hasn't mentioned it?"

"No, no, but that's actually exactly the sort of thing I'd expect from Ana." Kira smiles.

"That she helps mothers give birth in the forest, or that she doesn't bother to mention it?"

"Both."

The women laugh quietly. Kira straightens up, and her back lets her know how old she is. Hannah looks down at her fingers.

"Ana's welcome to come down to the hospital whenever she likes. If she has any questions about . . . my job."

Kira nods appreciatively.

"I promise I'll tell her. She'd make a wonderful midwife. And she . . . needs strong female role models. As many as possible."

The two women's eyes meet in a truce, at last.

"Okay. So what do you want my husband to do to help you?" Hannah asks.

"It isn't our husbands who are needed right now. It's you and me," Kira replies.

95

Songs

The fire next to the campervan bounces up into the darkness, as stubborn as a three-year-old refusing to go to bed. Benji's phone buzzes and he lifts it up. It's Ana and Maya. They're bored. Want to know where he is. He says he's at the campervan and they reply simply: "On our way!" Even if Benji would rather be alone with Big City for a while longer, if he has to accept more company, there were certainly worse options. He's missed those two goofballs, they're like two crazy squirrels darting through the world, they seem to live every moment and he hopes they never stop. Never stop laughing as they embrace, never stop sleeping back-to-back. They drive down in Ana's dad's pickup, with Ana swearing the whole time because he's left his rifle in there again when he was drunk. Maya has called Amat and Bobo and ordered them to come as well, and they evidently don't disobey in spite of the game tomorrow. So Bobo parks his car up at the road and lumbers down through the trees with Amat and Mumble following him, because they weren't going to let Mumble escape if they couldn't, so they picked him up from Hed first. They get one last evening, the whole gang. They laugh so much, they'll be grateful for that in hindsight, that every time they look back they'll start laughing like Benji and Ana when the grass really got to them, when they started making really atrocious puns. Later on Benji and Amat go off to pee and as they stand there leaning against their respective trees, Benji says to his friend:

"Listen, never forget that you're from the Hollow."

"You're drunk and high, I'm not listening to you," Amat laughs, but Benji grabs him by the shoulder, almost making him fall in the snow.

"I said, never forget that you're from the Hollow. Because those bastards in this town have never let you forget it, so don't let them forget it now. When you're playing in the NHL and someone asks where you're from, say, 'I'm from the fucking Hollow!' Okay? That will mean everything to those scruffy little kids playing hockey out of the yard behind your apartment."

Amat promises. They hug each other beside the tree one of them just peed against. Amat will never break his promise. As he walks back to the campervan Benji stands back and looks out across the lake. After a while Bobo wanders over to pee, and Benji pees once more to keep him company.

"If you could manage not to turn Aleksandr into an alcoholic out here, that would be great, Zackell and I are going to need him this season!" Bobo says, as sternly as he can manage.

"I can't promise anything. Who knows, maybe drink will save him from the sport?" Benji replies.

Bobo laughs his deep rumble of a laugh, and if, against all odds, there was any game left in these forests, there wasn't after that.

"I've missed you so much, mate. I hope you're going to stay here now. You know, one day you and I and Amat will be like Peter and Tails and the guys from the old team twenty years ago. We'll be sitting in the Bearskin and will be fat and rich and we'll own the whole town and talk about old times."

Benji coughs out some smoke.

"Time is relative, Bobo. This is now, but it's old times . . . NOW! What you just said: already old."

Confused, Bobo scratches his head.

"How much did you say you'd smoked?"

"Just enough!" Benji declares.

"Just stick around this time, promise?" Bobo repeats.

Benji shakes his head.

"No, no, I'm not going to do that. But I'll try not to forget to come back home."

"I fucking love you," Bobo whispers, and the best thing about him is that he makes no attempt at all to laugh it off with a "but not like *that*." He's more than capable of just loving someone, the gentle giant.

Benji smiles.

"I love you too. But not like *that*, so don't go getting any ideas."

Bobo rumbles with laughter again. They walk back to the campervan. Benji grabs a beer, Bobo takes one too, there have to be some advantages now that he's a coach and not a player. They drink a toast and look into each other's eyes. Everything is perfect.

Ana gets it into her head to go down to the lake "to see if the ice will hold." Restless, as usual. The others go with her, of course, because what else are they going to do? Benji and Maya hang back, sharing a cigarette. She tucks her arm under his.

"You look happy. That makes me happy."

"You too," he says.

She takes some deep breaths with her eyes closed, trusting him not to let her fall.

"Do you think we'll be able to make peace with this town in the end? Just come back and live here as if nothing happened?"

"Maybe," he says.

"I don't know where I belong."

He kisses her hair tenderly.

"You belong on a big stage in front of a hundred thousand people, all around the world."

She holds his arm as if she's scared it's the last time.

"You can do whatever you want to, as long as you never hurt yourself. Promise me that."

His heart is beating slower now, his blood is calm, as if it might actually be possible: to make peace with everything.

"If I fancied girls I might have fallen in love with you," he says.

"If I fancied donkeys I might have fallen in love with you!" Maya retorts, and his body bubbles with laughter.

"When are you going back to college?" he asks a few moments later. She sighs.

"I don't know. I pretty much fell out with everyone before I left."

"Great!" Benji declares.

"Great?"

"Yes. You write better songs when you're angry and alone."

"Worst compliment ever!"

"You know I'm right. Sing something for me," he asks.

"I haven't got my guitar here."

"I'm not sure you know what a 'song' is," he points out, and she hits him in the ribs.

"Stop being such a muppet! You know what I mean! I can't sing if I don't play at the same time. It doesn't work. It's . . . unnatural."

"All of you is unnatural."

"Hmm. Says the most normal person in the universe, obviously."

He smiles that smile. Free from cares, they walk down to the shore. Ana and the guys are competing to see who dares walk farthest out on the ice. She wins, of course, by a mile. Maya leans her head against Benji's shoulder and promises:

"I'll sing for you tomorrow."

She'll sing for him every night from now on.

———

In the darkness farther away a lone boy is standing far out on the ice. He hears the laughter from Ana and the others as they dare each other to go farther out, one step at a time. When Mumble slips and starts to laugh, it's obvious how happy he is. Matteo stands alone and lets his anger course through him. He almost enjoys it. When the youths in the distance go back up toward the campervan, Matteo walks so far out on the ice that in the end it feels like he's walking on baking parchment. He stops there, both feet firmly on the ice. Makes himself as heavy as he can. Thinks calmly to himself: "If the ice breaks, I die. If the ice holds, you die."

It holds.

He walks back home and climbs through his neighbors' window. The house is dark and empty tonight, perhaps the elderly couple have gone away somewhere, so Matteo walks all around their house, looking at their lives. Imagines who he might have been if he had had people like this. On a chest of drawers in their bedroom there's a row of photographs of their only grandchild, a blond boy, apparently always so happy he could almost burst. The most recent picture shows him in ice hockey gear, his green top is a little too large, the look in his eyes euphoric. The oldest picture is from when he had just been born. The date is engraved on the frame. Matteo looks at it for a long time. Memorizes it. Then he goes down into the basement and enters the code on the lock, and the gun cabinet opens.

96

Torches

Richard Theo's idea is simple, but not simplistic. Kira and Hannah shake hands over the fence, the lawyer and the midwife, one from each town. Then Kira goes home and Hannah goes to see her neighbors. She starts with the ones who are the worst gossips, says nothing about whose idea it is, that way it will soon come to seem spontaneous.

Cell phones start buzzing in Hed. When Kira gets home and goes around to her neighbors, the same thing happens there. The words that start it all are so simple, but there's nothing simplistic about them:

The council wants to shut down both our hockey clubs. Whether you like hockey or not, you have to resist. Because these clubs are just the first step, then the politicians will come for everything else. They'll start by pulling down the ice rink in Hed and replacing it with houses that no one who grew up here can afford to live in, but before long they'll have built on the whole forest, because then we won't notice when our towns merge together. In the end there won't even be a Beartown or a Hed anymore—first they'll create a new hockey club, then they'll create a new town. If we let the politicians decide how we watch hockey, they'll soon decide how we live our lives too. They have no respect for us or our history, they just want to turn this whole area into their personal cash machine. Don't let them get away with it!

No one remembers if it's Hannah who says it first, or Kira, or someone else entirely. But the message gets repeated until everyone has heard it. Richard Theo sits in his office and waits. All the other politicians have gone home for the day, but he knows they'll soon come running back in panic. It will be too late by then, they will have missed their chance. It would have been enough if the people who set out had numbered in the dozens, but many more join in. It's one of those rare occasions when the combination of events in the past week, every little part of the chain reaction, has affected everyone, one way or another.

Tails raises the flags outside Beartown ice rink and the caravan of cars sets off along the road through the trees. Row after row of workmates, teammates, childhood friends, and families. In the space of just a few hours the message seems to have reached everyone, the oldest are pensioners, the youngest still in their strollers. Even Teemu and his guys show up, it's the first time anyone has seen them in jackets that aren't black. They could be anyone in the crowd now. Hockey supporters. Citizens. Voters. At the edge of the forest the cars stop and everyone gets out and stands in a line. It took a few hours to get hold of all the torches, the last ones are homemade, fashioned from twigs and chicken wire. Then the forest burns.

The editor in chief sees it from the roof of the newspaper building with her dad. Richard Theo is standing alone in the window of his office. He will never be asked exactly how he managed to fit all the pieces of the puzzle together, but if he were he would have answered: "In my experience, most people can only cope with having one enemy at a time." So instead of letting the towns fight with each other, he gave them a shared opponent. Politicians. "Because everyone hates politicians, even politicians," he would have said if anyone asked. But no one will, because all of this looks so spontaneous. Like a popular movement. Grassroots. All those words that make it sound as if change just grows naturally.

The torch-lit procession from Beartown heads toward the council building like a never-ending flaming snake. The second procession, with just as many families and neighbors and hockey supporters from Hed, is standing waiting a few hundred yards away. They meet just below Richard Theo's window, he's the only politician who is still at work, so he's the first one who can go out and meet them.

"I understand your frustrations. Believe me, I share them!" he promises the people at the front before they have even presented their demands. Most of them never even realize that they haven't really formulated any demands, but that doesn't matter. Richard Theo has already done it for them. He climbs up onto a wall and gives a speech. Simple words:

"I hear you! And I promise that all the other politicians soon will as well! They want one team, one town, in the end just one party as well. They want everyone to think the same about everything. But I support your demand for two hockey clubs in two towns, not because I love hockey, but because I love democracy. It's a human right to be able to choose who you love, but it's also a human right to choose who you hate! People can be browbeaten and cowed and even imprisoned, but no one can ever force us to love something. We have the right to our hatred of people who aren't like us. We have the right to define ourselves. So our feelings and our boundaries are not for sale. These are our towns, and this is our way of life. And these are . . . our hockey clubs."

He says these last words slowly, as if he has just thought of them. When he says "hockey clubs," a lone voice calls out from a long way back in the Beartown ranks, it's too dark for anyone to see who it is, but it shouts:

"DO YOU WANT US? COME AND GET US!"

Soon even the Hed crowd are shouting the same thing. It's a classic war cry between the towns, but it's being aimed in another direction now. Because people can only cope with one enemy at a time. Naturally, the rest of the council has belatedly realized the seriousness of the torch-lit procession, but it's too late now, some of them haven't even shown up, and some have made the mistake of mixing with people in the crowd in an attempt to look like ordinary people. Instead it makes them look like nobodies. This is the end of their power and the beginning of Richard Theo's. He has the whole of his speech written on a sheet of paper in his pocket, and now he crumples it up, he didn't even need the whole thing. He was planning to say that each hockey club was like a ship of Theseus, from the Greek myth, where each plank was replaced when it rotted, until in the end nothing remained of the original, prompting philosophers to ask: "Is it still the same ship?" Ice rinks are also replaced, plank by plank, until everything is new, sponsors disappear, coaches get fired, all the players grow older and are replaced by younger names. Everything changes. The only thing that really is unchanging in a hockey club is its supporters. "You're the ship," Richard Theo had been thinking of ending his speech, but then someone started shouting "Do you want us?," and of course that was much better. Much, much better. In the end two towns are standing there in two torch-lit processions, chanting the same thing about how much they hate each other, demonstrating complete unanimity for the right to complete fragmentation. Not even a politician could have conjured up that solution.

———

In the newsroom of the local paper the editor in chief and her dad are drinking beer. They're planning to publish their revelations about corruption between the politicians and businessmen in the council district in a couple of days. About the leader of the largest party, who happens to be Richard Theo's biggest opponent, and how both her husband and brother work for a construction company that's engaged in dodgy practices. The paper will write about suspicions of widespread corruption in connection to the application to host the skiing world championship, and the proposed construction of a conference hotel that has been under discussion for years. But not a word will be mentioned about the training facility. Powerful people will suddenly find themselves powerless, some will end up in prison, just not the people the editor in chief originally had in mind.

But the whole series of articles will be delayed. Neither she nor her father nor anyone else knows that yet. There will be other news to write about first.

———

A cell phone buzzes somewhere in the forest near the campervan.

"Is that yours?" Maya wonders.

"I shut it off when you and Ana got here," Benji says, because who the hell was he going get a message from who was more fun than them?

It buzzes again and Maya laughs:

"Well it isn't mine! Everyone I know is here!"

"A 'torch-lit procession'?" they hear Bobo exclaim a short distance away.

Ana leans over to look at his phone, then bursts out laughing:

"Have any of you heard anything about a fucking torch-lit procession? I mean, you get out of town for ONE night and suddenly something HAPPENS?"

Amat's phone buzzes too, a text from his mother. Then Maya's, from Leo: `Mom's lost her mind and pretty much organized a huge demonstration out here. Everyone's got, like, torches? Come home??`

So Maya and Ana set off in Ana's dad's pickup. Maya has to hold his rifle. Bobo follows, with Benji, Amat, Big City, and Mumble squeezed in around him. Beartown is empty when they arrive, but they reach Hed just in time to join the procession. At first they don't understand a thing about what's going on, but then they see, in the light of hundreds of torches, banners with the hastily written slogans: "Two towns, two teams!" They see green jerseys everywhere, then they see the red procession in the distance. Maya walks among her childhood friends and it feels like not having to be grown-up for a little while longer. A few last minutes. For a single night she feels completely at home again. She knows that hardly any of her classmates at music college would understand this, but for the people in this procession, a town isn't just a place where you live, it's a place where you belong. A hockey club isn't a hockey club, it's everyone you know. It's your grandparents' club, your mom and dad's club, there's a pub in town that used to be owned by a crazy old woman and a nice old man and it was their club too. It belongs to your neighbors and friends and the girl at the supermarket checkout and the mechanic who mends your car and the teacher who educates your children. It belongs to lawyers and general managers and firemen and midwives. A hockey club is the girl you played with in the forest and slept back-to-back with throughout your childhood, even though she doesn't even like hockey. It's the most handsome, wildest boy with a smile that's big enough for him to be able to contain all that is darkest and most beautiful inside him. The hockey club doesn't play for itself, it plays for us. If you come here and play against Beartown, you won't be facing a goalkeeper and five players out on the ice, you'll be facing the entire town. That's why there are so many torches. Everyone is here.

When they reach the council building some old politician gives a loud speech about the right to hate each other, but toward the end of the night the atmosphere is almost jolly instead. Ana finds some beer somewhere so Amat has to drive her dad's pickup so she can drink in peace and quiet. When he tries to explain that he doesn't have a driver's license she snaps: "So do you need a damn police badge to eat soured milk too? There are three pedals and one steering wheel! I know you're a GUY but how hard can it be?" Beer doesn't bring out her most diplomatic side, it really doesn't, but Amat does as he's told. Bobo follows them with the rest of the gang, they drop Mumble off outside his house and almost yell "BEARTOWN FOREVER!" across the entire neighborhood just for the hell of it, but Maya manages to stop them. She's had stones thrown through her bedroom window too, she knows what that does to a person. Mumble gets out onto the pavement and looks at her and his eyes are suddenly full of a sorrow she doesn't understand, it might even have been shame.

"Are you okay?" Maya asks him.

Mumble nods shyly down into the snow. Maya has her dad's green woolly hat pulled down over her ears, her eyes are sparkling as she holds her hand out through the window.

"Don't let any goals in tomorrow, okay? Not a single one, you got that?"

He nods again. She smiles. Then the cars turn and drive home and Mumble stands and watches, without saying a single word of all the things he wants to say.

———

When all the cars are driving back to Beartown after the procession Kira turns to Peter in the passenger seat and says:

"You should open the Bearskin tonight, you and Teemu. Open it up for everyone. People need it."

So they do. A long queue snakes out along the pavement. Even Kira turns up to have a beer, just one, next to Tails. Peter drinks scorched coffee and Teemu dances on the table with his shirt off, a green scarf tied around his head. The Ovich siblings are all behind the bar. Benji washes glasses and passes them back to his sister Katia, who's spent so many years working in the Barn in Hed that she's been serving drunks since she was barely old enough to get drunk herself. Their sister Gaby takes the money while her little children play games on her phone on the floor, and Adri walks around the pub doing what she does best: telling men to shut their mouths before she does it for them.

Toward the end of the night Tails is sitting alone at the end of the bar. He has one promise left to keep, the one he gave Teemu. Kira has given him the documents he needs, and he's sold all his expensive wristwatches and has the money in an envelope. He waits until all the others have gone home and Benji has finished the dishes and has gone outside to smoke, before he goes over to the three sisters and says:

"I have a business proposal for you."

The scrapyard in Hed may be isolated, but it has plenty of eyes and ears. Faint light is shining behind the curtains of some of the trailers, and a solitary black-and-white dog pads from the gate toward the little house a short distance away, but it's so old that it seems to get lost halfway and has to pad back and start again. A car stops outside the house and Adri gets out and knocks on the door until Lev opens it.

"Yes?"

"Are you Lev?"

He's wearing sweatpants and a flannel shirt that's buttoned wrong. He looks like he's just woken up, but is curious nonetheless.

"Yes?"

"I'm here to pay Ramona's debt," Adri says, handing him the envelope of cash that Tails gave her.

Never would she have believed that she would end up being the business partner of that snob in a suit, or that she would be buying the scruffiest pub south of the North Pole with him, but life never stops being a surprise. Ramona left no will, but with Kira's help Tails has managed to sort out all the legal issues surrounding her estate, with her landlord as well as the bank. The only thing they need now is an agreement with Lev. Unfortunately he isn't interested.

"I don't want money, yes? I want a pub."

Adri looks him in the eye. She looks crazy. Lev likes that a lot, she reminds him of his nieces, they're also psychopaths, every last one of them.

"If you want our pub, you don't actually want a pub, you just want problems," she says.

The tip of Lev's chin moves thoughtfully from side to side like an old metronome. He appears to consider her threat very carefully before he hoists his sweatpants a little higher up his stomach and says:

"Drink, yes?"

She holds his gaze for several long, wary moments. She's unarmed, and she knows that he isn't. But she still goes into the house with him. He pours drinks from bottles with no labels. She looks at him and asks:

"You haven't got any bigger glasses?"

He likes her at once. A lot, an awful lot. Crazy women.

"Coffee cups, yes?"

"Sure. Anything apart from these egg cups," Adri mutters toward the shot glasses.

They drink. They drink a lot. Exchange small talk, tiptoeing around the real topic of conversation, like two champion fighters testing each other's limits. Lev asks about the forest and about the town and Adri asks about the scrapyard and about the machinery in it. They talk about the criminal gangs that pass through here at regular intervals, stealing everything from fuel and tools to entire work sheds that they ship out on trucks in the middle of the night. They have a lot in common, they both hate thieves but have been called that plenty of times themselves. They aren't black-and-white people, everything is gray to them, they've accepted their nature. Lev asks if she hunts, and Adri looks like he asked "Do you eat food?". Of course she hunts. Lev laughs and says he's hunted all over the world except in this country.

"Only rules here, yes? Can only hunt at these times, only these animals, only this gun, rules, rules, rules . . ."

Adri laughs bitterly. The bureaucracy surrounding gun licenses is enough to drive anyone crazy, but crazy it the last thing you should be, because then you won't get a gun license.

"You know how it is. Every time the gangs in the big cities shoot each other some politician decides it's time to ban hunting rifles. As if those gangs are running around with our rifles. They use smuggled pistols, for God's sake . . . ," she sighs.

The man on the other side of the table smiles indulgently at this.

"The hunter is the most dangerous gangster in this country, yes?"

He pours more drink. She leans back in her chair.

"If you ask the authorities, it looks that way. They complain that the police don't have the resources when seventeen-years-olds are playing at war in their own cities, but when people up here go out in their free time and leave salt licks for the elk, armed police storm our hunting cabins just to make sure we haven't left a gun cabinet unlocked, or, God forbid, have infringed a wolf's rights . . ."

He laughs hoarsely. She stops talking and empties her glass, putting it down with a bang and a look that indicates that the small talk is over. He accepts that. And says:

"Ramona owed me. This is my debt, yes? I want the pub."

Adri looks down into her empty glass, balancing between diplomacy and an angry outburst. Closer to the latter. But just as she looks up the black-and-white dog comes in through the terrace door, creeps over and lays its head in Lev's lap. He pats it tenderly. Adri has heard all the rumors about him, about the drugs and guns that are supposed to be hidden in the scrapyard, but the man is now treating the dog as if it were the last lily of the valley on the planet.

"What sort is she?" she wonders.

"She's a, how do you say? A 'pure-breed mongrel'!" Lev chuckles.

The dog appears to fall asleep with its head in his palms.

"Do you treat it well?" Adri asks.

"Better than people. You're the same, yes?"

"Yes."

He pats the dog gently.

"She was a good watchdog. In her youth. But now? Almost blind. Almost deaf. Just kind. But what can you do? Never had a friend so good. You understand?"

Adri nods. She understands.

"I have a good watchdog. The best you'll find. She's just had puppies. I'll bring two of them over here. I can train them for you too. But you take the money and leave our pub the hell alone, and then we're even. Understood?"

Lev smiles as he contemplates this for a long time.

"And Teemu?" he eventually asks.

"Teemu won't do a thing against you if I tell him not to," she replies.

Lev laughs. They drink some more. Shake hands. Then the Bearskin pub belongs to the Ovich sisters, and the first thing Adri does is go over there and raise the price of beer. If Ramona is watching her from Heaven, the old bag will be up on her feet dancing.

97

Perpetrators

The stories of Beartown and Hed could have ended here, but stories about towns never really end. The only stories that end are the ones about people.

Two and a half years have passed since Maya was raped by Kevin. Two years since she left Beartown. It was her story that started all this, which changed the hockey clubs and influenced politics and shook a whole town and half a forest to its very foundations. Maya had no butterfly tattoo on her shoulder, but she could just as well have, because she could just as easily have been Ruth. They were so alike, in so many ways.

The only thing that separated them was everything.

Ruth is dead, Maya is alive. Ruth left Beartown six months before Maya did. Ruth fled, Maya moved away. Ruth will never play guitar in front of thousands of people or sleep back-to-back with her best friend in a campervan or laugh so it echoes through the trees at dawn on one of the first winter days of the year. Ruth is forgotten, as if she never existed, as if what she was subjected to doesn't matter.

"There are always two of everything, one we see and one we don't see," Ramona used to say. She never knew who Ruth was, hardly anyone did. Her story wasn't the start of anything. But it will be the end of something.

Because one of the very worst things we will ever do in this forest is to try to tell our daughters that girls like Ruth are the exception. That isn't true, of course. It's Maya who is the exception. That's why those who do that, those who get the slightest bit of retribution or an ounce of justice, call themselves "survivors." Because they know the truth about all the girls like Ruth.

Many years ago two little boys grew up in Hed, they became each other's only friend, because they never had anything else to compare with. One was fairly big and the other rather small, one wasn't scared of anything and the other was scared of everything. The smaller one was bullied by other boys on his street because he was the last to learn to ride a bicycle, the last one to learn to skate. The big one chased them away, not because he was strongest or most dangerous, but because he was unpredictable. The boys in the street called the small one "mongo," but they called the big one "psycho." He had no limits, everyone knew that even then.

The boys started playing in the forest together during the day, and in the evenings they would watch films in the smaller boy's home. He lived alone with his mother and the bigger boy liked that, because he had four brothers and two angry parents, so in his house you could never hear the television. The smaller boy wished he had four brothers and two parents. Envy is the lot of almost every child.

The first time they met, the bigger boy held out his hand and said: "My name's Rodri." The smaller one took his hand but didn't know what else was expected of him, because no other child had ever asked what his name was. Rodri grinned: "I'm going to call you Mumble, because you always mumble! That doesn't matter! I like talking!"

It was Rodri who taught Mumble to skate. They attended their first hockey training session together in Hed, and it was Rodri who suggested that Mumble should go on goal: "You don't need to be good at skating for that, and you never need to worry about getting beaten up, because no one can touch the goalkeeper, and the whole team will defend you! It's sort of a secret rule, even if they think you're a mongo, on the ice you're just the goalkeeper!" That's the nicest thing anyone has ever given Mumble, the chance to hide behind padding and a helmet and just be allowed to join in. They played together for several years, Rodri had big dreams but not much talent, but for Mumble it was the other way around.

They met up every day after school. During the summer holidays they spent all their time together. It was always Rodri who came up with what they should do. He dreamed of being a hero, he could spend hours conjuring up scenarios in which he rescued children from a burning house or defenseless women from bloodthirsty murderers. They often sat in Mumble's basement and looked at the school yearbook and discussed which girls he would like to rescue most and how they should demonstrate their gratitude afterward. Naturally, the girls didn't even know who Rodri and Mumble were, but soon they would realize what they had missed out on, Rodri was convinced of that.

If Rodri had been better at hockey, perhaps the sport might have made him a hero, but he felt the coach never gave him a chance to show what he could do. There was always one of the rich, popular, good-looking boys who was allowed to play instead. It was an intolerable injustice that Rodri could never accept: that the boys all the girls already wanted to sleep with were also the ones who were best at hockey. So in one training session Rodri got into a fight with one of his teammates, and when the coach stepped in Rodri hit him so hard he fractured his jaw. "That boy has no limits, he never has, he's always been a little psycho!" declared one of the other coaches who lived on the same street as Rodri, and so Rodri was thrown out of the club. Mumble was left there. He was so quiet and took up so little room that it was as if no one really reflected on the fact that he was still best friends with the psycho. Mumble was the goalkeeper, after all, and you can't touch the goalkeeper.

Rodri still came around to Mumble's each evening. Waited for him outside the ice rink after training. Mumble got better and better at hockey, but there was hardly anyone who noticed. Rodri got more and more dangerous, but no one noticed that either. They became teenagers and one day Rodri arrived at the ice rink on a moped. He said one of his brothers had gotten it for him. He had cigarettes too. Soon he taught Mumble all about drugs, without Mumble ever taking any himself, Rodri used to sit on his bed and talk manically for hours about things he had seen online: politics, conspiracy theories, porn, guns, chemistry. He dreamed of producing his own methamphetamine. It would make him rich and you didn't need much equipment to make it, he said. They could make it in Mumble's house. Rodri's house was no good because his brothers would just use whatever they made. Then he would talk about girls, the way he always had, ever since the boys were in primary school. Rodri still hadn't slept with anyone, but he would soon, he swore. The words he used about girls changed so slowly and gradually that it was hardly noticeable. "That pretty one" became "that hot one," then "that sexy one," and "the one with nice eyes" became "the one with big tits," and "the mean one" became "that fucking little whore." Soon he was sitting in Mumble's room pointing out the worst whores in the school yearbook, one after the other. He said exactly which ones had slept with who at all the parties he and Mumble never got invited to. The worst whores were obviously the hockey whores, according to Rodri, because they only slept with hockey players. Which was unfair. Because they were already the biggest and strongest and most popular. They already had everything. One evening he lectured from Mumble's bed: "Feminism has fucked everything up for men! It's biological, did you know that? That women should stay at home and have babies and look after the home, and men should build society and protect the family! Women say they want equality, but they actually want tyranny, you understand that, right? They never want guys like us. Because we're losers. They only want the meanest guys. Because they say they want freedom but biologically they want to be dominated. It's in their nature. They want a man to force them up against a wall. Do you know how many girls have fantasies about burglars? A masked man attacking them? They don't dream about heroes. That's just in films. Heroes never get the girls in real life!"

Mumble didn't take it seriously. Or else he didn't understand. He just tried to nod and make his friend happy. When the drugs faded from Rodri's body he would start to sweat, then he would freeze, then he would borrow one of Mumble's red training tops from the hockey team. His friend fell asleep on the floor next to Mumble's bed. He slept there the next night because his brother had fallen out with some other guys in town and there could be trouble at home, Rodri said. Before he fell asleep the second night he related a new fantasy he had, about how he and Mumble could stop those guys and kill them and become heroes.

The next day they became heroes for real.

———

Ruth left the country exactly two and a half years ago, just after what happened with Maya and Kevin became public knowledge. Maya had gone to the police and the whole town had turned against her. Everything was going to change in time, but no one knew that then. Ruth didn't stay to find out what happened. She had been through all that herself a few months earlier, she knew what this forest did to girls like her and Maya.

Shoot. Dig. Silence.

During the last two and a half years of her life, far away from here, Ruth hated herself most for two reasons: that she left her little brother, Matteo, alone in that terrible house with their terrible parents, and that she had forgotten to take her diary. She didn't dare contact Matteo because she was worried her parents might find out where she was. She wrote in her diary right up to the day she left, and the moment she left it was too late to go back for it. She wondered if anyone would find it, and hoped that it wouldn't be her little brother. She wished him a real childhood, cycling and playing computer games and only encountering evil in comic books. Every day she counted the weeks and months before Matteo turned eighteen, so she could go back and get him. She didn't have time. The six-year age gap was too great. And maybe he wouldn't even have wanted to go with her if he could?

The sister and brother loved each other even as little kids, but they never had much in common. Besides, Matteo had something Ruth lacked: their mother's love. She always went where he did, and because Ruth couldn't stand her she kept her distance as much as she could. Their

mother and all her neuroses. Her phobia of stale smells that made her
air the whole apartment until it was freezing, her conviction that the
neighbors were spying on them, her fear that the dogs in the area were
the Devil in animal form. There was no end to it. Their dad just sat in
a different room with his books, physically present but more and more
distant mentally. As if he was conjuring up mental illness as a means of
escape. Ruth both hated and envied him that ability.

Every weekend they went to their church, full of other families that
were different in the same way as Ruth's. That had just as many rules,
just as many prohibitions, where everyone just talked to their children
about fearing God but never mentioned love. One day Ruth yelled at her
mother: "You say we have to be God's servants, but that's just another
word for slaves!" Her mother had one of her hysterical breakdowns. Several years later Ruth still couldn't say for sure if they were real or if her
mother was just pretending. Ruth didn't regret it though, she just hated
herself for how upset it made Matteo.

She stormed out of the house, slamming the door behind her, but
was forced to go back home again that evening. She had no one to flee
to then. She had no friends at school, all the girls there were perfect
little dolls with perfect clothes and perfect parents and perfect lives.
They giggled and talked behind Ruth's back, saying "she's in a religious cult" and that "her family is crazy." In the end it became so
normal that it didn't even hurt anymore. Ruth became good at staying out of the way, making herself invisible, all she thought about was
surviving school until she was eighteen and could go somewhere far
away and choose a different life. At least she did until one day she
found her first real friend and everything changed. Ironically enough,
it happened in church. A family that had just moved to Hed appeared,
and their daughter was the same age as Ruth. Her name was Beatrice.
They became best friends instantly. They shared the same hatred of
the rules and prohibitions, they both had a sense that they were living
on the wrong planet, as soon as Ruth got the chance she started taking
the bus to Hed and when Beatrice's parents were away they listened to

music and wore makeup and watched films they would never normally be allowed to watch. That was the best time in Ruth's life. You never get the same kind of friends again like you have when you're a teenager. Not even if you keep them your whole life. It will never be the same as it was then.

When they were sixteen Beatrice managed to get them invitations to a party in Hed. They drank and smoked like all the other youngsters and for the first time Ruth felt almost normal. She even kissed a boy, and ended up on a sofa in a dark room with him, where he tried to have sex with her but he couldn't manage to get up what he needed to get up. Ruth laughed nervously at him and he became furious. He rushed out and ran home. The next day Ruth heard from Beatrice that he had told everyone in school that they had had sex and that she was useless in bed. That was how Ruth learned that the truth doesn't matter to guys. The rumor that she had been at a party in Hed spread to the school in Beartown and for a while the perfect girls couldn't decide whether to call her "Hed whore" or "cult slut." When she turned seventeen, Beatrice gave her a pair of good headphones so she wouldn't have to hear them. That evening they drank hooch alone in the forest and Beatrice hissed happily in her ear: "Damn, I love being drunk! Shit, now I need to pee! I'm going to pee like a camel!" Ruth laughed so hard she was rolling around on the ground. She never had another friend like Beatrice, no one ever gets that.

The text came so suddenly the next day, when Ruth was on her way home from school, so drenched in panic that it froze her blood: My parents have found my hiding place!! They've called your parents!!!!!! Ruth ran the last bit of the way but it was too late. Her mother had turned her room upside down and found everything. The thongs, cigarettes, birth control pills, she had no idea what her mother would think was the most damning. But for Beatrice it was even worse, because her dad found her phone and all the messages from boys. Within a week Beatrice had moved away from Hed, she was sent to an even smaller town over six hundred miles away to live with a relative. Ruth couldn't help thinking that the girls at school were right: they really were dealing with a fucking cult.

————

It was Rodri's idea, as usual. "Let's get the moped and go to Beartown! Find some Beartown whores! You know that all the girls in Beartown fancy guys from Hed, right? That's because Beartown guys have such small cocks. It's genetic!"

Mumble didn't want to go, but he didn't want to say no either. He didn't want to disappoint his friend when he was in such a good mood. So they put their red jackets on, so the girls would know straightaway that they were from Hed, and set off. They didn't find any girls, of course, it was far too cold, so they just stopped by the side of the road in the forest near the lake and Rodri drank beer and talked about things he had read. He was interested in religion at the time, he talked and talked and much later Mumble would wonder if that was the worst thing of all about Rodri: that he was so intelligent. That he could do the terrible things he was about to do in spite of that.

It was starting to get late, and with the darkness came an even rawer cold, they were about to turn the moped around and head back to Hed when Mumble peered down toward the lake and saw the child on the ice. He wasn't standing up, he was just lying there with his body spread out in panic, to make himself as light as possible. On the shore stood several older children shouting and mocking him. Mumble began to run, at first Rodri didn't understand why, but when he did he saw his chance to become a hero:

"WHAT THE FUCK ARE YOU DOING?" he yelled, and when the kids on the shore ran off he wanted to run after them and kill them but Mumble stopped him, pointing to the child out on the ice.

It was Rodri's idea to take their jackets and tops off and tie them together to form a rope. Mumble was the lighter of the two, so he crawled out on his stomach close enough to throw it to the boy. Then they pulled Matteo to safety. He was so cold and scared that he could hardly say a word through his chattering teeth, but they managed to get a name and which direction his home was in. Mumble rode the boy's bicycle and Rodri followed slowly on the moped with boy sitting behind him.

Matteo's sister was the only person at home. She came running out and hugged her brother so hard that he couldn't breathe. Then she thanked the guys in the red jackets from the bottom of her heart.

"Ruth!" she said, holding her hand out in introduction.

"Rodri!" Rodri smiled.

Three years later she dies in a country thousands of miles away. He's never even been there. But Matteo knows he's still the one who kills her.

98

Stones

Every community has places that have strange names whose origins everyone has forgotten. Beartown has "the Hollow" and "the Heights," which at first were presumably just nicknames based on the geography, but which at some point became proper names used on road signs. In the end no one can really remember how that happened. Or whose idea it was.

Early on Saturday morning there's a knock on the door of the Andersson family's home, hard but not aggressive. The clenched fist hitting the wood belongs to someone who has lost, someone who almost won, but she's still proud enough to stand with her back straight.

Peter opens the door, the smell of freshly baked croissants hits the editor in chief, she's holding a cardboard box in her arms and looks as surprised by the smell as he is to see her.

"Hello . . . I . . . ," Peter begins.

They've never met before, but obviously he knows who she is. The forest isn't that big.

"I wanted to give you this," she says ceremoniously, nudging him in the chest with the box.

It's lighter than he expects. He looks down between the flaps and sees that it's full of documents.

"I don't understand . . ."

She breathes slowly to stop herself from screaming.

"You have good friends, Peter. Powerful friends. I hate the corruption in these godforsaken towns, but now I suppose I'm part of it. Richard Theo wanted me to give you this so you could be confident that we won't write any articles about you. This is everything we managed to unearth about you and Beartown Hockey."

He looks down into the box. She's expecting him to play dumb, or perhaps get angry, she's almost hoping for the latter, it would have been good for her self-image. But instead he blinks, moist-eyed, and asks:

"So this is all my fault?"

The editor in chief shuffles involuntarily on the steps.

"Yes . . . yes, that's one way of looking at it. For what it's worth, in a way I'm glad I didn't have to ruin your life. I know your daughter has been through hell. You seem to be a good dad, so I assume you've been through hell too. I've heard that you do a lot of good things for young-sters in this town. Perhaps that . . . balances things out."

He can see in her eyes that that isn't true. She still wishes she could have nailed him. Sent him to prison. He cheated, and she's the sort of person who can never quite live with that. She turns and is walking back to her car when he suddenly calls out:

"Can I ask . . . do you think it's possible to atone for a crime without serving out your sentence?"

She looks back over her shoulder.

"How do you mean?"

Peter clears his throat, clearly upset.

"I know what my crime was. I looked the other way. I didn't ask ques-tions. I pretended I couldn't feel that something was wrong. I didn't get involved. I . . . kept quiet."

The editor in chief takes a deep, cold breath and feels almost calm. It feels almost like justice, that confession, maybe she can live with this victory.

"What is it you say in that club of yours? 'High ceilings and thick walls'?" she asks.

"Yes. Is that how I can make amends? By making the walls thinner?" he asks genuinely.

The editor in chief never expected the conversation to go this way. She has to fumble for thoughts and arguments, and eventually comes up with:

"My dad loves history. Medieval, most of all. Whenever we went on vacation when I was little we had to go around looking at churches, and he would talk about every stone in them. I remember him saying that when a rich man had committed terrible sins, the priests would say he could get God's forgiveness if he built a cathedral. Obviously that was just a way for the priests to trick someone into paying for their ridiculously flashy building projects, not altogether unlike the way hockey clubs exploit councils to build ice rinks these days, but when I was little it was . . . well . . . I don't know . . . I still thought there was something nice about that. That powerful men at the end of their lives had to humble themselves by turning their money into stone."

Peter stands there looking down into the box, his tears dripping slowly onto the contents.

"Thank you."

The editor in chief bites her lip. Then she whispers:

"Earn it."

She drives away with angry tears in her eyes and a bag of freshly baked croissants on the passenger seat.

99

Victims

After Beatrice disappeared Ruth was left alone again. It was worse this time because now she knew how the alternative felt. Her parents were so ashamed that they didn't even force her to go to church, possibly because they wanted to pretend that they too had sent their daughter away, because that was evidently what you were supposed to do. Whenever they went to any of the church's charitable events they also left Matteo at home, because people would come to those from churches in other towns and the parents were worried he might tell someone the truth about his sister. On one of those days when they were on their own at home, Ruth borrowed the computer her little brother kept hidden to send a message to Beatrice. Matteo was only eleven, but he'd hooked the computer up to the neighbors' Wi-Fi, Ruth was amazed that he had managed to figure out their password, but he just shrugged his shoulders and said that almost everyone uses the names of their children or grandchildren, so he looked up the neighbors' names online and tested all the combinations he could think of until one of them worked. "You're a genius!" Ruth said, making him blush. Then he went off on his bicycle so she could talk to Beatrice in peace. He thought that was what she wanted, he always assumed that he was just in the way, and she didn't even notice him leave.

When, several hours later, she saw him come back, sitting frozen and terrified on the back of a strange guy's moped, she rushed out of the house in panic and hugged him to pieces. The guys in the red jackets told her what had happened. They seemed kind but a bit weird, one of them talked all the time and the other one didn't speak at all. One said his name was Rodri and that his friend was called Mumble because he never said anything.

"Are you hockey guys?" Ruth said, nodding toward their jackets.

"Yes!" Rodri said, quick as a flash.

"Shame. I'm so sick of hockey guys." Ruth smiled. Rodri immediately became obsessed with her.

In the days that followed he drove over from Hed to ride past her house, he had heard that her parents were some sort of religious lunatics so he didn't dare knock on the door, but he rode up and down the road, hoping that she was at home and would see him. One day she stopped pretending she hadn't seen him and crept out to meet him. He gave her a ride to part of the forest just outside Hed, where he and Mumble had found an abandoned shack that they had turned into a den. Mumble read comic books and Rodri introduced Ruth to drugs she had never tried. When she threw up he and Mumble took care of her. "You're just having a whitey, don't worry, it'll soon pass," Rodri whispered, holding her hair back gently so she wouldn't be sick on it. Afterward he drove her home and when she jumped off the moped he tried to kiss her, and when she resisted he grabbed her wrist so hard that she let out a scream. "You're playing hard to get, I like that," he said. She didn't know what to say, she felt so disgusted by everything and her head was still so giddy that she just went into the house and fell asleep.

He started texting her, sometimes fifty times in a single day, and she didn't know what to do. She wrote to Beatrice and asked, but Beatrice merely replied that guys were just like that sometimes. A bit too horny. It wasn't that strange, was it? And he seemed nice, so perhaps he just didn't know how to behave with girls?

Ruth wasn't sure. A couple of days later it was so cold when she left school that she went to the bus stop instead of walking home. Some of the perfect girls were there, and started giggling when they saw her. "Nice clothes, is that the cult's uniform?" one of them said, and the others burst out laughing. "They dress like that because their dads don't want other guys to be tempted, so their dads can sleep with them themselves!" another one declared, and they giggled more quietly but more hysterically. Ruth wanted the earth to swallow her up and wanted to smash their faces into the glass of the bus stop at the same time. Then someone in the road called out, and when she looked up she saw it was Rodri. He had swapped his moped for a cross motorbike, at least that's what Ruth thought they were called. He said he'd gotten it from one of his brothers. "Do you want to come to a party in Hed?" he asked. Ruth looked at the perfect girls and saw how scared they were, how dangerous they thought Rodri looked, so, just so she could see the stupid looks on their faces, she jumped on the motorbike and he roared off.

He hadn't been invited to the party, but everyone on Hed's hockey team was invited, and because Mumble was with them no one questioned them when they showed up. The party was being hosted by a rich kid in a big house, which was so crowded with people who were so drunk that once you were inside no one cared who you were. Rodri kept giving Ruth drinks and she never saw what he put in the cups. She started to feel funny. He whispered in her ear that she was lovely. That he was in love with her. That he wanted to make her feel good. She didn't even know how they ended up in that room, or if they were even still in the same house at the same party, he started to take her clothes off and she yelled no. She yelled at him to stop. But the music was so loud and he was so heavy. She passed out, she didn't know for how long, and when she woke up she was naked. Her eyes kept flaring. She felt so terrible, but when she tried to crawl away from him he got her in a stranglehold and hissed that he would kill her and her little brother. She was so terrified that she froze to ice. For her the rape went on forever but for him it never even started. For the rest of his life he could never understand that he was a rapist. He thought he was a hero.

When he eventually breathed out and groaned and relaxed, she saw her chance, tensed her whole body and kicked him away, then flew up, but she was still so drugged that she could hardly stand. She stumbled toward the door as she tried to button her blouse and pull up her panties. She could hear him behind her, she wasn't sure if he was laughing or something else. Afterward she couldn't describe the room, or how long she was in there, but she never forgot that when she emerged into the narrow passageway near the stairs, Mumble was standing there. She could see the horror and shame so clearly in his eyes. He had heard her scream, she was sure of that, but hadn't dared do anything. He had just frozen to ice out here, the way she did in there while Rodri did what he wanted.

Ruth just ran. Her head was spinning and her heart was pounding, her legs could hardly carry her. When she got downstairs the party was still going on, someone whistled at her, someone else called out: "Freshly fucked? Sweet! Do you want another round?" She elbowed her way desperately through the crowd of drunk teenagers, and it wasn't until she got outside that she realized she was half-naked, but the cold was almost liberating. It muffled her. She couldn't even cry because her teeth were chattering so hard on the way home.

In her diary Ruth wrote:

When girls start primary school and the boys hit us and pull our hair during breaks and we go to an adult and ask for help, the adults say: The boys are only doing that because they like you!! That's how you teach boys that they have rights over us. Then we get bigger and then they rape us but we're just stupid little whores because we don't take it as a COMPLIMENT? They beat us and kill us but it's only because they like us. Why don't we understand that?

On the next page it says:

didn't even fuck that other guy in Hed but he told everyone I did and that meant I was already a whore. And whores can't get raped.

On one of the last pages she wrote:

I've got no chance if even my own parents don't believe me. Why would the police believe me then? Why would anyone? You aren't going to believe me until Rodri kills me.

On the very last page, in shaky handwriting, she wrote:

*Parents always think they have to talk to their daughters about guys.
We shouldn't wear short skirts and shouldn't go out alone and shouldn't
get drunk and shouldn't let guys like us too much. But you don't have to
talk to us about guys because we already know all that, for fuck's sake,
because we're the ones they rape!! Talk to your damn sons instead!!!
Teach them to talk to one another and teach them to stop one another.
Raise just one fucking boy somewhere who can become a head teacher who
understands that when boys pull girls by the hair, it's the fucking boys
there's something wrong with. Tell your sons that if they have to THINK
about whether or not they've had sex with a girl who didn't want it, then
they HAVE!!! If you can't understand if the girl you're having sex with
wants it or not, then you've never had fucking sex with a girl who wants
it. Stop telling your daughters. We already know it all.*

The next morning Ruth was so sick she thought she was going to die.
She almost hoped she would. She wished she could pour corrosive acid
into her brain and get rid of all her memories from the night before. His
breath, his hands everywhere, him inside her. "I love you," he had whispered. "Don't play hard to get! I know you want it! I know you've fucked
other guys!" he hissed. After that came the threats to kill her and Matteo.
Then she just lay still. Just trying to survive.

Right before lunch the next day she received the first text: Thanks
for yesterday gorgeous!! he wrote. She didn't understand. Was
he making fun of her? Was he threatening her? The next text said: Love
you. See you this evening? Kiss!! This went on for several hours
until Ruth picked up her phone and wrote, still dizzy and hungover: I
didn't want to. I was drunk. I didn't fucking want to.
He wrote back: Stop it!! Of course you wanted to! Didn't I
show you a good time? I can practice!!! Come to the shack
and we'll do it again!!! She wrote: Forget it you fucking
creep. I'm going to report you to the police.

Her phone was silent for several minutes. Then came a photograph.

Then another one. She was wearing clothes in them, but she knew she wasn't wearing clothes just after they were taken. A minute after the photographs arrived, Rodri phoned. At first she didn't dare answer, but he kept calling until in the end she didn't dare not to. His voice was totally devoid of emotion, like one of those automated computer voices: "Then I'll post all the naked pictures of you online so everyone can see what a little whore you are." That was what the flashes she had seen when she woke up in that bed had been. He had taken pictures of her while she was unconscious.

She couldn't breathe. Couldn't think. She switched her phone off and hid it under her bed, as if that would help. She didn't dare leave the house in case he was out there waiting for her. She couldn't sleep. Couldn't eat. She just lay on the floor, crying and crying and crying.

That night he started sending more text messages. He demanded that she meet him. `You can have the pictures, I'm not going to show them to anyone, just come over here!!` he wrote. She didn't dare say no. They met in the shack in the forest outside Hed and the worst thing of all was how gentle he suddenly was. Almost afraid. He whispered that he was sorry and that he loved her and that he hadn't realized she didn't want to. He was drunk too, he said. He didn't know what he was doing, he said by way of excuse. But it was pretty much her fault as well, he went on to point out. Because why did she go to the party with him if she didn't want him? Was she just using him? Did she really just want to fuck someone else there? Why wasn't he good enough? What was wrong with him?

He touched her cheek and she shook with fear and he interpreted that as love. "We can have a nice time. I'll make it nice. I promise," he said, and started kissing her neck. "I just want those pictures back," she whispered. So he promised. He promised and promised and promised. If she just had sex with him one more time, voluntarily, then he would delete all the pictures. He'd let her watch while he did it on his phone.

So she had sex with him. He deleted some of the pictures. But not all of them. Over the following days he sent her text messages at night and she had to do it all over and over again. He had drugs and she took them, so that she could bear it and forget and run straight home afterward. He interpreted that as love.

In the end he fell apart and wept in front of her, saying it wasn't his fault that he was doing this. She had forced him into it. It was her fault. When he took hold of her wrist she knocked his hand away and ran. He hunted her through the forest but she was quicker. When she got home Matteo was lying asleep in his bed, and all she could think was that it didn't matter if the pictures ended up online, she just had to get Rodri away from here, she had to protect her brother. So the following morning she went to the police.

She sat in a small room with a glass of water that she couldn't drink because her hands were shaking too much. She was seventeen years old. The police suggested she call her parents. She didn't want to. The police talked and talked, and different people kept coming in and out of the room. Ruth felt as if she was floating about in a vacuum. Someone asked her if she had taken drugs. They told her that if she told the truth, she would get help, nothing bad would happen. She made the mistake of believing them. She admitted that she had taken drugs. She admitted that she had slept with Rodri several times. She even admitted that she had almost slept with another guy at another party but that he hadn't been able to get it up. She showed them Rodri's text messages, showed them the pictures he had sent, but all the police saw was a seventeen-year-old with clothes on, who looked drunk and happy. As if she wanted it. Nothing Rodri had written indicated that he was threatening her. He seemed almost regretful? As if there had been some misunderstanding?

Ruth protested and protested, but she no longer knew how to explain. After all, she couldn't even remember all of it! She didn't even know what he had put in her drink! The police asked why she hadn't reported this before. She had no answer to that, other than that she had been afraid. The police said that they understood and then they persuaded her to call her parents after all. They promised that they would talk to them. That everything would be alright. She made the mistake of believing them again.

She remembers the look on her mother's face in that room. Wounded. As if Ruth had hurt her. She remembers her dad, uncomfortable and anxious, as if he just wanted to get out of there at any cost. "We're not saying that you're lying, young lady, but surely you can see how this looks?" a voice said, and it took Ruth several minutes to understand that it was her mother. Obviously she knew that her mom hated her, but this much? Her voice grew thick as tears began to fall. "He raped me, Mom!" Her mother sighed at the police with a pointed expression. "Sadly I think we're going to have to talk to our daughter at home. Perhaps we can come back tomorrow? She's something of a fantasist. And a junkie, as you've realized. She has a whole drawer full of thongs and birth control pills, so this is hardly the first boy! Perhaps he didn't want to go out with her afterward and then she regretted it and made this all up? You know how girls can be at this age!"

Ruth's mind spun out of control. She ended up throwing up on the floor. She remembers one of the police officers, a young man who seemed to understand that something wasn't right, placing a cool hand on her forehead and giving her some water and saying: "Perhaps you can come back tomorrow when you're feeling better, and try to tell us what happened again? It all sounds very complicated. But perhaps we'll be able to make more sense of it tomorrow, when you're a little more . . . together?"

Ruth didn't remember how she got out of the police station. She didn't remember much of the drive home either. All she can remember afterward is her dad saying, as they turned onto their road: "You need to bear in mind that this boy could sue you for defamation. What you're doing is dangerous. You could ruin his whole life." When they got out of the car, Ruth's mother did something she had hardly ever done: she took hold of her daughter's hand, gently and tenderly, almost like a proper parent. "Come on, young lady, let's go in and have something to eat. We'll pray to God for guidance for you. God will help us. Then we'll forget this. This weekend you can come to church with us again, I think. Then everything will feel better."

Ruth never went back to the police. The young man at the station waited. Perhaps he hated himself afterward for not doing more. Perhaps he managed to suppress it. Everyone like him is just trying to do their job. They all say they're just following the law. It's just that laws aren't written for girls like Ruth. They're written against her.

In the weeks that followed Ruth made herself smaller and smaller when she was among other people. She harmed herself more when she was alone. Bizarrely, her mother seemed kinder toward her than usual, as if her love was a bribe, if her daughter could only stay quiet about all that silliness, perhaps they can be a perfect family again? As if they had ever been that. Ruth's dad hardly spoke to her at all, except to say: "We'll just have to hope the police don't contact the boy. Otherwise he'll probably sue us. How would we afford that?"

If they had had any relatives they would have sent her away like Beatrice, but they had broken off all contact with the rest of their families when they joined the church. Now they were imprisoned by each other. At night Rodri would send more text messages. Always about how he loved her. Missed her. After a while he started writing about how nice it had been in the "cottage," as he had begun to call the shack in the forest, and Ruth began to realize that he had fantasized a whole parallel universe where everything that had happened was a love story. One evening she saw him in the street outside her house. Another time he drove past her school. She started to get messages from anonymous accounts on social media saying that she was "a conceited little whore who thinks she's better than everyone else." She knew it was him, of course, but how could she prove that? Who would believe her?

A few months later a rumor started to spread around the school about what Kevin had done to Maya. Or rather, what Maya had done to Kevin. Ruth heard it in the cafeteria, everyone was talking about it. Maya was a few years younger and Ruth didn't know her, but she had reported Kevin to the police after a party, and Kevin hadn't been allowed to play in a crucial hockey game with his team as a result. Everyone went completely crazy.

Ruth didn't dare look around because she was so frightened someone would be able to tell what she had been through. She had turned the accusations of the police and her parents that she was nothing but a liar over and over in her mind so many times that she was starting to think they might be true. Perhaps it hadn't been so bad? Perhaps it was all her own fault?

That night she read all the comments online about Maya. Everyone was saying she was a whore. That she was lying. That they hoped someone would kill her.

Ruth would be turning eighteen that spring, and it struck her that she had to disappear far, far away from here as soon as she possibly could. So she did.

100

Juice glasses

It's Saturday morning. Kira has gone to her office so she can sit and look out of the window, so Maya almost frightens the life out of her when she suddenly calls from reception. When Kira comes running out, her daughter exclaims irritably:

"How big an office do you actually need? Talk about hubris. You could hold rock concerts in here!"

Kira is so pleased to be surprised and then declared an idiot by her daughter, today of all days, that she gives her an awkward hug, with the result that Maya gets annoyed because she almost drops the whole picnic. Ana had to drive her here so she could bring the flask of coffee, the freshly baked croissants from Peter, and most important of all: tiny glasses to drink orange juice from. She sits on the floor with her legs crossed and eats with her mom, the way she did when she was little and Kira agreed to go camping indoors because she felt guilty about working too much and Maya knew exactly how to exploit that.

"I have to go home after this weekend. Well . . . I mean . . . I need to get back to college," Maya says, hating the fact that she accidentally said "home."

Her mother just smiles understandingly.

"Does it feel tough?"

Maya nods a little pathetically, the way you only do in front of your mother.

"Yes. It feels like shit. I kind of burned all my bridges with everyone before I came up here. But I should probably go back and just fight. Maybe Benji was right: my songs are worse when I'm happy all the time."

"I'm sorry it's so tough, darling," Kira whispers.

"It's supposed to be hard, Mom," Maya smiles.

"I know, I know, but I . . . I just want you to be happy all the time!"

"Don't worry."

"I'm your mother, you can't stop me!"

Maya smiles in such a way that it's impossible to know if she's about to make a joke or start crying.

"I'm sorry that what Kevin did to me almost broke you and Dad."

Now it's Kira's turn to look like she's about to cry.

"Darling, it didn't do . . ."

Maya nods, so grown-up and so strong, so honest and vulnerable.

"Yes, Mom. It did. Your love was like organ donation. You and Dad and Leo gave me pieces of your hearts and lungs and skeletons so I could put myself back together again. And now you hardly have the strength to stand up and keep breathing yourselves. I think about that so often, and I think about all the girls who don't have you. I feel like I only just managed to survive this. How the hell does everyone who doesn't have you as their mom even stand a chance?"

Good luck having a daughter and not going to pieces when you hear that.

101

Graves

Mumble heard everything. Remembered everything. He had stood outside the bedroom at that party while Ruth screamed no and begged Rodri to stop, but Mumble didn't rush in. The last thing Rodri did before it happened was ask Mumble if he wanted to join in. "Come on! We can share her!" he declared exultantly, but Mumble shook his head in panic and Rodri could see in his eyes that he was on the brink of running off. So his eyes darkened in the space of a second, his fingers shot out and grabbed Mumble by the neck, and he snarled: "Stay and keep watch. If you leave I'll kill you."

Mumble just stood there and said nothing, but he heard everything. When Ruth came running out he stepped aside and she ran past and out and away. When Rodri came after her he stopped so close to Mumble that their foreheads touched, and he swore: "If you breathe a word of this to anyone, I'll say you were part of it!"

Mumble's life continued in something of a daze for the following few months. He trained so hard that he collapsed with exhaustion each night, it was the only way to stop himself thinking, the only way he could sleep. Every time he woke up he hated the light. Hated all the images that came back to him. Hated his weak larynx and his feeble heart.

Rodri called and sent text messages all the time, when Mumble didn't respond Rodri sent him all the pictures he had taken of Ruth. Mumble deleted them all, but he knew what it meant. It was Rodri's way of making him his accomplice.

Sometimes Mumble went down to the lake at night and hoped the ice would break beneath him. He almost hanged himself twice but didn't have the courage. The only thing that helped him forget was hockey, so that became the only thing he did, that was how he got so good at it.

When everything happened between Kevin Erdahl and Maya Andersson, obviously he heard the rumors, like everyone else. The way Kevin got suspended and the whole of Beartown protested. Mumble was a few years younger, his team in Hed was supposed to play a game against the Beartown boys the same age, but it got canceled because the coaches were worried there'd be trouble. Everyone just forgot to tell Mumble, as usual, so he was standing alone at the bus stop to go back home to Hed when Ruth came walking along the other side of the street. They were both equally shocked. Neither of them could breathe.

Ruth had been to the mailbox in the center of town. She had found a church online that took in "young people with problems," and needed to mail an application to go and stay there. She was walking past the ice rink and when she reached the bus stop she just froze, just like the night of the party. She hadn't seen Mumble since then. She didn't know what she wanted to say to him. She didn't know if he even thought Rodri had done anything wrong. Maybe Mumble thought she deserved to be raped, like everyone else?

So she plucked up all her courage and shouted across the street: "Can you tell Rodri to leave me alone? He won! No one believed me! Can he just leave me alone?"

Mumble didn't answer. He just disintegrated inside. Ruth went home and locked herself away, and two days later a woman called from the church. Ruth recited such a magnificent series of lies about her "problems" that the woman started to cry. It was all made up, because they would never have believed the truth.

So Ruth left town, but of course never arrived at that church. By the time everyone realized she had gone abroad, all she had to do was stay away until her eighteenth birthday, then she was free. She had stolen all her parents' cash before she left home, that was one advantage of having a mother who thought banks were a conspiracy dreamed up by atheists and Devil worshippers, it wasn't much but it was enough for train and ferry tickets and her first few stumbling steps out into the world. Ruth arrived in a different country, the first few nights were chaotic but she managed to make new friends, it turned out that she wasn't so peculiar here as she was at home. Unless she was just peculiar in the right way now. She wished she could contact Matteo and tell him, but she didn't dare, she just counted the months until he too was eighteen and she could go and get him. She met two girls who worked in a café and she borrowed their computer and plucked up the courage to go online once, and found that she had a message from Beatrice. Her old friend said she had made peace with her family but had left the church, met a guy, and got engaged. They were going to buy a little house. She had emerged from the other side of the darkness and was now happy, and Ruth thought then that perhaps it had all been worth it. If one of them was happy. She switched the computer off and never turned it on again. The girls at the café took her to a party. They danced. She had fun, undemanding, shameless fun, for the first time in ages. The world opened up. Everything was possible. For two and half years she actually laughed an awful lot, replacing every rotten little piece of herself like some mythical ship until she had become a new person. Her universe became so large that her childhood started to feel invented. She thought about writing to her little brother a million times but never did. She went to parties and danced, and one night the drugs took her. It happened so fast, in the middle of everything, her heart just stopped beneath the lights on the dance floor. She was dead before she hit the ground. The paramedics told her friends that it happened so fast that it probably didn't even hurt.

Matteo will never think of it as his sister dying. Only as her being killed. When he found her diary and realized what had driven her away, realized the pain she was numbing with drugs and what had led to her overdose, he had already made up his mind. He once heard a woman in his parents' church say: "If you're planning revenge, prepare two graves." Matteo's mom told her off, that woman, because she thought the quote was from the Bible, but it wasn't. Perhaps that's why Matteo remembers it.

He's not planning for two graves now. He's planning for three. One for Rodri, for his crimes. One for Mumble, for not helping Ruth even though he could have. And one for himself.

Maya's story could easily have ended the same way as Ruth's story. The things that took everything in a completely different direction were so small. A mom who fought, a dad who loved, a brother who was there, a best friend who took on the whole damn world. An old-witch who owned a pub, who went into a meeting at the hockey club and spoke in Maya's defense. And, last of all, a witness who had seen everything and eventually dared to say so out loud.

That was all. No more than that.

Amat said what he had seen, and even if Kevin was never convicted or imprisoned for his crimes, the town could no longer close its eyes.

But every time we tell the story now we commit new sins, because we pretend that what Amat did is normal. It isn't, of course. Hardly anyone does what he did. Mumble is the normal one. He's the one who's like the rest of us.

One morning there was a knock on his door in Hed. It was Rodri. There was nothing but recklessness in his eyes as he held a knife to Mumble's throat and whispered:

"If you tell anyone what happened, I'll come here and kill you and your mom! Understand?"

Mumble nodded, not even daring to breathe. His mother was doing the crossword in the next room. Rodri's eyes fluttered for a few moments, then he ran off toward a motorbike out in the street and rode off. The next time Mumble heard anything about him was when someone said Rodri's brother had ended up in prison and Rodri had moved away. He'd moved to a town several hours away to live in his brother's apartment.

The last text message he sent Mumble said: Think about what happened to Kevin. No one will believe you. You're just as

guilty as me. We'd both end up in prison, and you'll
never play hockey again.

The following season Mumble got the chance to change clubs, from
Hed to Beartown, when Beartown's goalkeeper, Vidar, died. The first
training session with Zackell as coach was the best time of the life Mumble had barely felt he was living. Zackell seemed to understand him. She
saw what he could be rather than what he was. Mumble didn't even know
he had any real talent but she turned him into a star. He started to arrive
at the ice rink first in the morning, and was last to leave it each night. He
trained and he trained. He got real friends for the first time in his life. He
got a complete life.

Does he deserve that? If he can't be forgiven, can he be . . . given this?
The chance to live a life? Play hockey. Laugh. Maybe even be happy, if
only for a few moments. Can he be spared? Is that fair? Is that right?

He doesn't know. He'll never know.

————

During the night between Friday and Saturday, once the torch-lit
processions are over and everyone has gone home and the towns are
asleep, Matteo finds three hunting rifles in his neighbors' gun cabinet.
He searches everywhere for cartridges but can't find any. So he closes the
cabinet, climbs out through the window, and runs home, where he wraps
the rifles in his sister's old sweaters and hides them in his wardrobe. Then
he looks online to see how he can get hold of ammunition. Instead he
manages to find a forum where someone else has asked the question he's
wondering about: "Can you kill someone with a hunting rifle?" One of
the quickest responses comes from an anonymous account: "Of course
you can, if you're an extremely good shot. But much better to get hold of
a pistol, any idiot can kill someone with a pistol. Much more effective if
you're going to shoot yourself afterward too. If that's what you want?"
Matteo doesn't know. He really doesn't know. Is that what he wants?

After a lot of hesitation he creeps out of the house with his sweater-wrapped treasure under his arm and cycles through the forest, all the way to Hed, slipping over a hundred times but managing not to swear. He doesn't feel pain anymore. He isn't even angry. Emptiness consumes him now and that's a blessing.

His legs are exhausted by the time he reaches Hed, but there are burned-out torches here and there on the ground and the snow has been compacted so much that he can cycle without falling over the whole time, and everything becomes a little easier. As he approaches the scrapyard he sees there are still lights on in the trailers, so he goes ahead and knocks. A bearded man in his twenties comes to the gate, but doesn't have time to say anything before a voice behind Matteo says:

"We're closed, yes?"

Matteo spins around and looks Lev in the eye. The man has a black-and-white dog beside him, which squints at Matteo and sniffs the air. Matteo forces his voice to stay steady and says:

"I have three hunting rifles. I'd like to know if you'd take them in exchange for a pistol."

Lev's eyebrows sink closer together, his lips narrow, his jaw tightens.

"Pistol? No pistols here."

Matteo stands his ground with a child's inability to realize the danger he's in.

"I was at the game! I saw you in the ice rink! I saw that you had one! I just want . . . I want to buy one too! Come on! They're good hunting rifles!"

Lev adjusts the gold chain around his neck and looks very thoughtful.

"And you want the pistol for . . . what? Hurting someone, yes? Bad idea, my friend. Very bad, little child, okay? Cycle home instead. Sleep. Go to school. Live good life."

Matteo loses his temper so fast:

"I'M NOT A GODDAMN LITTLE KID! DO YOU WANT TO DO BUSINESS OR NOT?"

Lev stands in front of him perfectly calm, but the look in his eyes makes the fourteen-year-old stumble backward and fall over his bicycle.

"No business. We're closed, yes?" Lev repeats, and gestures firmly toward the gate behind him, then he holds the palm of his hand in the air as if the next warning would be a slap.

Matteo is whimpering in despair. He yanks his bicycle out of the snow and hurries out through the gate, but slips on a patch of ice and drops all the rifles, and only just manages to stop himself from screaming and crying out loud. He's thinking that if he didn't already have a mission he'd have killed Lev too. Because he isn't some fucking little kid. Everyone will see. Then he hears a different voice, younger than Lev's, from farther along the fence.

"Psst. Friend? Come here."

Lev might refuse to sell a pistol to a fourteen-year-old, but not all his employees have the same scruples. Matteo has to go home to Beartown again and fetch all his parents' cash and his computer, then he exchanges them and the three old hunting rifles for a pistol that he can probably use to shoot his way in and out with.

Early on Saturday morning he finds a moped in the yard of a big detached house that some spoiled teenager couldn't be bothered to put in the garage like his parents had made him promise to do. Matteo breaks in through a basement window, sneaks up to the hall, and finds the key on a hook. He drives far beyond Hed to the next town, slipping on the ice in the darkness and almost crashing several times. He comes so close to dying.

It's dawn by the time he rides into the outskirts of a larger town. He waits outside a gray apartment block until he loses the feeling in his fingers and almost can't feel the trigger. When Rodri comes out, sleepy and with bed-hair, Matteo waits until he's sitting in his car. For a moment he thinks about holding back and following him, just to see where he's going. Does he have a job? Friends? Does he have anyone in his life who loves him? Matteo will never know. He rubs his fingers together like crazy to get the circulation back in them, then he walks across the parking lot and waits until Rodri sees him through the windshield. Matteo wants to be sure that his sister's killer recognizes him. Then he fires three shots through the windshield. He waits until Rodri slumps down and he's sure that he's dead. Then Matteo gets back on the moped and drives home to Beartown. It breaks down halfway. He stands at the side of the road waving at passing cars for help, but those who see him don't stop, and those who might have stopped don't see him. One of the vehicles that drives past in the other direction is a police car. How differently this story might have ended if it hadn't just driven past on its way, because the police were hurrying to get to a reported gunfire incident at a parking lot in town. Then Rodri would have been the only person who died.

A truck slows down, flashes its headlights a little way off and Matteo runs over. The driver is so shocked that the boy is only fourteen and alone out here that he makes a long detour out of his way to take the boy where he wants to go out of the goodness of his heart. He drives him almost all the way to Beartown. He never knows what he has been the cause of.

Matteo gets home just before the start of the game. He fetches his sister's diary and cycles through the town. He stops at the Andersson family's house. He stands there for a long time, spending ages thinking about leaving the diary in their letterbox. He knows what happened to Maya, he knows her mom's a lawyer, maybe they could tell Ruth's story. She would get some sort of justice. But Matteo doesn't dare, he's too scared that someone will find the diary too soon and figure out what he's about to do and try to stop him.

Besides, he realizes in despair, he can't do that to his mother. Once she's lost both her children she's going to need to create some extreme fantasies just to survive. He can't deny her that by forcing her to know what really happened.

So he finds an unlocked shed in a yard farther along the street, steals a hacksaw, and cycles down to the lake. There he makes a hole in the ice and drops the diary through it. When he gets back to the built-up part of town he leaves his bicycle and just follows the stream of people, walking toward the ice rink with thousands of others, just one of the crowd. Invisible.

———

Saturday morning, the first game day of the season. The towns have waited so long and the forest seems oddly upbeat. There's no violence in the air, no one's shoulders are raised, because after the torch-lit processions there's peace once more. It may be a fragile peace, but it's still a brief pause for everyone. Today we're all on the same side, somehow. Today is just about hockey.

Amat sets out from home with his bag over his shoulder. His mother kisses him on his head. He crosses the parking lot and starts walking from the Hollow to the ice rink in town, like he's done a million times before. How many steps in total? How many miles? Will he be able to measure the distance to a dream when he eventually reaches it?

He hears the voice calling his name, but is so surprised that at first he can't place it. He spins around and the weight of his bag almost pulls him over.

"Hello? What are you doing here?" he blurts out to Peter.

Peter is standing with his hands in his pockets, gazing off toward the horizon.

"Waiting for you. Have you got time to look at something?"

"Now? I need to get to the game . . ."

"I know. I'm sorry. But I can give you a lift? It won't take long! We'll still be in time!"

Something about the bright, unadorned enthusiasm on his face makes Amat curious. The former general manager leads him away from the apartment blocks, toward the forest at the edge of the old quarry, and doesn't stop until they reach a large, open space where there was once talk of building a supermarket. Then they said it might be a medical center. At one point someone even dreamed of a small business center. None of it ever came to be, of course, because this isn't the part of Beartown where things get built. The town may be getting bigger, but nothing grows in the Hollow.

"There!" Peter says, pointing at absolutely nothing.

"I . . . I don't understand . . . ," Amat says, seeing nothing but snow and gravel.

Peter sees something else. He sees redemption.

"I've been thinking a lot about how hard it was for you to make it all the way to the A-team, Amat. Almost impossible. You should never have managed it, but you're . . . unique. The motor inside you, your heart, I've never seen anything like it. I just don't want every kid who comes after you to have to be like you to have a chance. I want the next kid from the Hollow to have things . . . a bit easier. Just a bit easier."

"What does that have to do with gravel?" Amat asks, touched but confused.

Peter smiles.

"I want to build an ice rink there. Not a big one, just somewhere to train, a place to . . . hang out. Somewhere we can have a skating school, a kids' team, somewhere people can do extra training if they want to. The council's going to build a fancy modern training facility over by the ice rink, but I think we can build something here as well. Much smaller, of course, just a classic . . . ice box. But I'll make sure all the paperwork is correct this time. I'll ask all my friends for help. I reckon you have a lot of a friends as well. Plenty of workmen live in these blocks, don't they? I know a few as well. I think they'll come if we ask them. I think we can get this done, you and me and a few others. I don't know, maybe one day the Hollow can have its own team? Maybe we can dream? Is that stupid? Does it sound . . . ridiculous?"

Amat's chest rises and falls at least twenty times before he takes his phone out and aims it at the gravel.

"No. It doesn't sound ridiculous."

"What are you doing?"

"Taking a picture. So I can show all the spoiled, snotty-nosed kids in my 'hood where I come from when they have their own ice rink here in a few years and are taking it all for granted . . ."

Amat looks so tall, suddenly, as if he's grown taller than Peter overnight. Peter laughs. Everything is only a dream so far. He doesn't know if he dares actually believe he can get this done. But Beartown is a special place. What a fucking town. There are so many places and things here that have strange names whose origins everyone has forgotten.

In a few years hardly anyone will remember why the ice rink beyond the apartment blocks and gravel pit in the poorest part of town is always called "the Cathedral." But the man who dreamed it up knows, and the boy who one day scores his first goal in the NHL knows. He'll be interviewed on television afterward:

"Do you want to say something to everyone watching in your hometown? How do you pronounce it? You're from Beartown, aren't you?" the reporter on the other side of the Atlantic will ask.

Amat will look directly into the camera and say: "No. I'm from the Hollow."

102

Best friends

Kira and Maya's office picnic is wonderful, full of stupid jokes and uncomplicated laughter, until it is suddenly interrupted by the sound of something shattering on the floor down by the entrance, followed by someone swearing loud enough for it to echo through the building. They leap up and rush in that direction, Kira's colleague has stumbled in through the door and is now standing in an expanding red puddle, muttering:

"That was my BEST wine! Why are the doorsills so tricky?"

Kira's voice is a mixture of concern and confusion:

"What are you doing here? We're not supposed to be working today, are we?"

Her colleague proudly holds up her bag containing three bottles of wine that are still intact.

"I'm not going to work. I usually come here to get a bit of me-time."

"Don't you live . . . alone?" Maya wonders tentatively.

"That doesn't mean you can't have me-time!" the colleague declares.

Maya laughs.

"Can I have some wine, then?"

She can. Kira doesn't get any because she's driving, serves her right, says her colleague. When she and Maya have finished the bottle Kira asks them quietly:

"Can I ask something? I've been . . . thinking."

They look at her with half-a-bottle eyes and say:

"Hmm?"

Kira speaks slowly, as if the words are trying to slip their leash:

"I was talking to a young girl. A couple of years younger than you, Maya. Her name is Tess. She wants to study law, her mother asked if she could come and work here with us once she's finished. I said of course she could, but of course that's a lie. Because Tess wants to help women who have been assaulted and raped. She wants to defend them when no one else will help. She wants to fight for . . . for . . ."

Maya reaches out and touches her arm and completes the sentence:

"For the next girl like me."

Kira nods, looking down at her daughter's hand.

"And that isn't what we do here. Not anymore. We work for money now. For big business and entrepreneurs. I . . . don't want to do that anymore."

"What are you talking about?" her colleague exclaims, suddenly horrified.

Kira looks her in the eye.

"I love you. I don't know how I'd ever be able to come to work every day without you. But I need to do something . . . different. You can have the business, I'll sign my share over to you, Tails has just given us all the legal work concerning the construction of Beartown Business Park . . . that's . . . you won't have any financial problems. I promise."

"So what are YOU going to do?" her colleague wonders, aghast.

Kira blurts everything out:

"Set up a smaller law firm. Where people like Tess can come and work, to fight for the next Maya. So that everyone doesn't act as if Maya was . . . the last one. So that all those old men can't act as if they've fixed everything, throwing together a new 'declaration of values,' a few molestation accusations, and PR brochures and fancy statements in the press, as if that was enough? I want girls like Tess to come here and fight so that the old guys never forget that this job is ongoing. It doesn't end. I want someone to stand here and yell: 'What justice? Whose justice?' when they declare that 'justice must run its course' in order to protect their sons. I want someone to shout: 'How far? HOW far can this go?' when they say 'We need to protect boys too, this mustn't go too far the other way either.' I don't want them to . . . damn . . . someone has to stand here and remind them that girls aren't the problem! That this isn't the last time! Kevin wasn't the last man!"

Maya and her mom's colleague just nod, and Kira can't for the life of her understand why they don't look surprised.

"Okay. I'm with you," her colleague says curtly.

Kira shakes her head in frustration.

"No, no, you don't understand. I won't make any money. You can have the whole company, the contracts for Beartown Business Park will mean . . ."

Her colleague looks happily bemused.

"What am I supposed to do? Stay here and get rich? I don't even like expensive wine. I'm going with you. Wherever you go."

Maya sits there and watches the two middle-aged women hug, and thinks that when she gets old, really, really, really old, she hopes she's just as crazy as they are. Kira starts drinking wine without thinking about the consequences, until in the end Maya has to call Ana to get her to come and pick up all three of them. Ana comes at once, without asking any questions. None of the four women likes hockey but they decide to go and watch a hockey game anyway.

Kira locks the office. In a few months' time she will surrender those keys and hand the whole business over to some of the employees, and she will sell her expensive car. The new law firm's first office will be her kitchen. One day women throughout the country will know who they are. That too is a sort of cathedral.

———

In Hed Johnny is cleaning the van. He can never figure out who makes more mess inside it, the kids or Hannah. Every morning with them is like waking up in a garbage dump after a tornado. But Hannah comes out and pinches his backside when he's leaning over with the little vacuum cleaner and whispers in his ear:

"Be careful today. Don't get into any trouble and don't get hurt, because when you get home and the kids are asleep, I'm going to have sex with you, and the only person who gets to hurt you is your wife! Do you hear?"

He laughs. She's a crazily beautiful woman. A beautiful, crazy woman.

She dances off teasingly into the house to get the children ready, they are going to watch the game with him, Hannah has to go and work at the hospital. When Tess walks out of the house her mother stops her and hands her Kira Andersson's business card:

"You . . . dropped this. It fell out of your jacket."

Tess smiles, forgiving her mother for the lie.

"Hmm, 'fell out.'"

Hannah breathes through clenched teeth.

"It's . . . it's hard for me to admit that you look up to other women rather than me now. It's . . . really damn hard. But Kira said you can come by her office. One day maybe you could work there. I . . ."

She doesn't get any further, because it's hard to talk when you're being hugged so tightly you're suffocating.

———

Adri drives through the forest and stops on the slope above the campervan. She has Alicia with her, the girl rushes down through the trees and throws herself into Benji's arms.

"Hi best friend," Benji whispers.

"Hi best friend," she giggles back.

They go to the game together. Big City gets a lift, but almost regrets it when Alicia asks half a million questions before they've even left the forest tracks. "Are you good? How good? How hard do you shoot? Are you quicker than a cat? A normal cat, I mean, not a superhero cat, just an ordinary cat! How quick are you? Benji, how quick is a cat? Can we train together one day? Today, maybe? How old are you? Fifty? Benji, is Hed any good? Are we going to beat them? By how much? What do you mean, 'don't know,' just say a GUESS!!!" It never stops. Big City has a headache by the time they arrive. Benji laughs and says to Alicia:

"Do you want to come into the locker room and say hello to Amat and the others?"

Alicia stares at him with her mouth open, as if he's just asked if she wants to go and say hello to Spider-Man and Wonder Woman. Benji holds her hand as they walk into the ice rink. She's cocky at first, but the stands are already full of people and the noise sounds like a roar to her young ears, and just outside the A-team's locker room Alicia's nerves get the better of her and she whispers:

"No let's not I don't want to it doesn't matter!"

Benji holds her hand a little tighter. And says calmly:

"Look up at the roof. Only you and me on the planet. We're alone. No one's going to hurt us."

They stand there until she can't hear the crowd anymore. Everything is quiet. There's nothing to be scared of. She's still holding Benji's hand when they go into the locker room, tightly, as if it's the last time.

Zackell is sitting in her office making the last preparations before the game. There's a soft tap on the door, Big City is standing there and she looks up:

"Yes?"

He fumbles for words.

"I just wanted to say . . . thank you. Thank you for believing in me and giving me a chance out here, I . . . well, I guess I never thought I'd be happy in a place like this. But it already almost feels more like home than . . . home."

"Yes?" Zackell repeats, with her usual perfect ear for expressions of emotion.

Big City clears his throat.

"Is there any particular way you want me to play this evening? In terms of tactics?"

She seems to think for a while. Then she says:

"Surprise me."

She will never tell him, because she doesn't do that sort of thing, but there will be few players over the years who give her as much joy as him. Few players who do the unexpected so often. Who are so different.

Big City goes to the locker room. Everything is still unfamiliar so far, but he will stay in this town for many years. He will buy a small house not far from where Benji's campervan is now, and he will spend a lot of time sitting in a boat catching zero fish. He will learn to tell lies properly, but never about himself anymore. His mother will eventually move up here. Well, maybe not move, but she will come to visit and never go home. She's forest folk too, it turns out. You don't always know that until you have a forest to be folk in.

Bobo is standing in the corridor outside the locker room. Tess gives him a quick kiss before she leaves him to get on with his job. She will move and study in a town far away, but she will come back when she's finished and work with Kira. Hannah is right, she's going to be the best. Bobo will run the car-repair workshop with his dad. He carries on as Zackell's assistant coach for a few more years, but when he and Tess get married and have their first child Bobo stops coaching the A-team and starts coaching the little kids' team instead, because they train earlier and he can always be home in time to have dinner ready for his wife when she gets home from work. One day he will coach his own kids, all of them.

In the stands Hog takes his seat, as proud as anything. He's sitting on the Beartown side of the rink, but a man from Hed still makes his way over there. Johnny holds out his big hand, Hog shakes it after a moment's hesitation.

"He's a good lad, your Bobo," Johnny says.

Hog nods, initially surprised, then grateful.

"He still doesn't deserve Tess."

Johnny grins weakly.

"No. He doesn't. But none of us deserve our women."

Hog moves over, the two men are both so big that three seats are barely enough for them. Half a lifetime ago they did their best to kill each other out on the ice but now they're going to be family and have to become friends somehow. It can be useful to have a bit of help with things like that. Fortunately Ana and Maya are sitting a couple of seats away, so Hog leans toward them and asks if Ana has any beer. She does.

Obviously you aren't allowed to bring beer into the ice rink, but if Ana wasn't allowed to do things she shouldn't, she'd never leave the house. She'd never be allowed to be in her own house either, come to think of that. Hog and Johnny drink surreptitiously from paper cups, not because Johnny is afraid of security but because he's afraid of Hannah.

"You'll all have to come around for a family meal," he declares through clenched teeth.

"Bobo would like that," Hog replies curtly.

"I hope so, because he'll be doing the cooking," Johnny grins.

Hog bursts out laughing. They drink a toast. They sit next to each other and actually talk about hockey for ten minutes without falling out. One day they will both be grandfathers to the same kids. Good luck to those grandchildren if they dare to pick a favorite team.

Down in the corridor outside the locker room Amat is walking along with his bag over his shoulder. He stops when he reaches Bobo and they give each other a long hug.

"This is our last season together, then you're going to be a pro," Bobo says, his voice thick.

"You're going to be saying that every season," Amat smiles.

But Bobo is actually right. The rest of the team is already in the locker room, Amat sits down between Big City and Mumble, and as they get changed Amat asks them:

"Do you want to do some extra training tomorrow?"

They nod. Then Big City asks:

"How about tonight? Are you busy after the game?"

They aren't. Out in the stands a thousand voices are roaring as one: "DO YOU WANT US? COME AND GET US!" Both standing areas are chanting the same thing, the whole forest is in uproar. Mumble's face is impassive but his knees are bouncing nonstop.

"Nervous?" Big City asks.

Mumble nods, embarrassed.

"Don't be. We aren't even going to let Hed borrow the puck," Big

City grins, as if the hubris of the forest folk has already started to rub off on him.

"FIGHT US! FIGHT US! NONE OF YOU DARE FIGHT US!" the standing areas are chanting outside, to politicians and those in positions of power, and to the whole world, all at once. ·

"I'd forgotten how much they yell," Amat says.

"I've never heard anything like this," Big City admits.

"Wait till we go out. It's like a hurricane," Amat declares.

"Any tips on how to handle it?" Big City asks.

And Mumble surprises everyone, not least himself, by suddenly grinning and replying:

"By winning."

They roar with laughter. And just then Benji comes into the locker room holding Alicia by the hand. She has questions.

Many, many questions.

Zackell comes down from the office and walks back and forth outside the locker room. She's nervous, which doesn't often happen. So she smokes more cigars than normal. The caretaker swears and goes and opens the emergency exit so that the fire alarm doesn't go off. He forgets to shut it.

Ana's dad is sitting in the row below his daughter. He's sober. She called the guys on his hunting team and they told her he didn't drink anything yesterday because he knew he was going to the game with his daughter today. "Let's hope he has a drink before the next hunt, anyway, because he's the best hunter in Beartown when he's sober, and that's unfair to the rest of us," the old men grumbled. Ana leans forward and asks:

"Dad, did you bring the pickup?"

He nods quickly but assures her eagerly:

"Yes, yes, but I haven't been drinking! I swear!"

He's so afraid of embarrassing her, so horrified that she'll be ashamed of him. But she smiles, and then he smiles too, the smile he keeps just for her. Then she asks thoughtfully:

"Dad. Did you remember not to leave the rifle in the truck?"

His eyes open wide.

"It wasn't . . . I wasn't drunk . . . I was just stressed!"

She shakes her head wearily.

"Did you at least lock the truck?"

He gets up at once and pushes his way along the row to rush out into the parking lot and check. She calls after him. When he turns around, ready for her to start shouting at him about something else as well, she yells so that the whole stand can hear:

"I love you, Dad!"

He isn't perfect, her old man. But he's hers. And she's never ashamed of that.

103

The game is about to start, but it will never be played. Instead, now everything that we will never stop regretting starts. Every single person in the ice rink will go over and over these minutes for the rest of their lives, asking silently: "Could I have done anything different? Something small, something microscopic, anything at all? Could I have stopped him?"

We're on our way into a night when we question everything we have ever done, all that we are, and the entire society that we've built. Because what is it? The whole lot of it? Only the sum of all our choices. Only the result of us. Can we cope with the way it turned out?

This hockey game will never be played, and for many of us it will feel as if we never really emerge from the ice rink. We will be stuck in the nightmare forever. We are a people who tell stories, who try to use stories to put what we have experienced into some sort of context, to explain what we have been fighting about in the hope that it will excuse what we have done. But stories reveal both the very best of us and the very worst, and can one ever outweigh the other? Are our triumphs greater than our mistakes? What are we responsible for? What are we guilty of? Can we look ourselves in the mirror tomorrow? Can we look each other in the eye?

No.

Not after this.

104

Regrets

Lev is sitting on the terrace outside his little house next to the scrapyard in Hed. The black-and-white dog is resting by his feet. The evening is cold, the air fresh, his chest aches with loneliness. He's so good at never revealing this to the guys he employs, because otherwise they would be uncontrollable. He has always been amazed by grown men who show that they are scared, that's such a luxury, like a rabbit that knows nothing about predators because it's never seen one. Where Lev grew up, a man didn't show his fear even if his heart broke. That was why he picked Hed. He's lived in many places but he chose to settle down in this forest because the people here are also survivors, and not that much less dangerous than he is. He thought that perhaps here he isn't quite as different as he was in the places he has been chased away from, perhaps here they would let him live a peaceful life among them. Perhaps here he would have time to build up something.

He is a violent man, but if you ask him why he will reply that it's because he hates violence. He has a pistol so he doesn't have to kill anyone. He frightens people away rather than take the risk of letting anyone get too close. That is how he has survived, but it has also left him lonely. He doesn't often let himself feel that, but that woman, Adri, who was here and bought the Bearskin from him, she set off something inside him, kicked a door in somewhere inside his rib cage. She made him remember his nieces. It's for their sakes that he wants to build something. For their children's sakes. Lev never had children of his own, almost his entire family died in a war the rest of the world didn't even call a war. He has seen good people capable of great evil, but also terrible people capable of great goodness. It's the same everywhere: almost everyone loves too much, hates too easily, forgives too little.

But most people want the same as him: to live in peace, to let your heart beat a little more slowly when night comes, to earn a bit of money to support the ones you love.

He built up the business at the scrapyard so he could send money to his nieces and their children. One day perhaps he will build a big house here that they can all come and live in. Is he a good man? No. He knows that. He has done many things he ought to regret, but he regrets hardly any of them, and isn't that the definition of evil? A man can do a lot of bad things to protect his family, might be prepared to defend all he has built up with violence if he built it for their sakes. One day perhaps Lev's nieces' own daughters and sons can become lawyers and bosses, he hopes so. One day perhaps they can belong to a place as obviously as Peter Andersson does, without having to apologize or say thank you the whole time, without either stealing or begging for charity. But until then? Until then Lev will do what he has to.

Regret? Yes, there's one thing he regrets. The boy. Amat. Everything that happened with the NHL draft. Amat reminded Lev of his younger brother as a small child, in another forest in another time, they played hockey the same way. So no matter what Peter Andersson and other men might say, it wasn't greed that drove Lev to help Amat. At least, no more greed than was driving Peter Andersson himself. Lev helped him because he saw someone he loved in that boy, and now he regrets not seeing him as just that: a boy. Where Lev grew up, there were no boys of Amat's age, they were already regarded as men, because in a violent place childhood is over in the blink of an eye. If that. Lev isn't a man who finds it easy to admit his mistakes, but he knows now that he should have asked Amat which he wanted more: acclaim or money. It was so obvious to Lev that only people who are already rich care about acclaim, but it might have been different for the boy. Perhaps he wanted something that Lev can't even understand.

Regrets? Yes, Lev probably does have a few, in spite of everything. He regrets not listening. He regrets not being at the game now. He would have liked to see Amat one more time. Flying forward, just like Lev's brother once did. It's a miraculous game. A wonderful game.

He closes his eyes. Hears footsteps on the gravel outside. Heavy breathing.

One of the men who works at the scrapyard comes out of one of the trailers, wild-eyed. He runs as fast as he can out through the gate and along the road to Lev's house. He bangs madly on the door until Lev opens it angrily with a small glass of strong liquor in his hand.

That's how he finds out what another of his employees has done. What he sold to that fourteen-year-old who was here wanting to get a pistol. One of the other men at the scrapyard saw Matteo in Beartown earlier today, they were on their way to sell hot dogs outside the rink and saw the boy walking to the game. "He looked like darkness," the man says. There probably isn't anyone who has driven his car through the forest as fast as Lev does, either before or since.

The parking lot is empty when Ana's dad gets out to his pickup. The game is about to start inside, somewhere up by the road an old American car is driving far too fast, presumably in a hurry to make it to the start of the game. Ana's dad tries the door of his own truck and crumples with shame when he discovers that it's unlocked. The rifle is there, of course, he had forgotten it just as Ana predicted, not because of drink but because of age. That's worse.

Just as he's about to hide it under the seat and lock the truck before going back into the ice rink, he sees a lone figure pad along the side of the building. At first it's just a movement in the corner of his eye, like when he sees something in the forest and doesn't immediately know if it's an animal or a person, but he can always rely on his instincts. He knows when something is wrong, when something is moving in an unnatural way. A whole life in the forest has taught him what fear looks like, what flight looks like, and what hunting looks like.

He takes a few steps between the cars and sees the figure, a young boy, peer in through all the windows and try all the doors. Then he sees one that's open, an emergency exit at the end of the corridor by the locker rooms, it ought to be closed, it can only be opened from the inside, but the caretaker left it open to air out the cigar smoke.

The boy suddenly runs toward the door and that's when Ana's dad sees the pistol in his hand. He doesn't have time to shout and warn anyone before the boy has slipped inside. It happens so fast, so incredibly remorselessly horribly fast.

The American car swerves into the parking lot. Ana's dad grabs his rifle and runs toward the ice rink.

Mumble is sitting on the bench in the locker room. Matteo walks in. To begin with no one sees the pistol, but then it's as if everyone sees it at the same time. At first someone thinks it's a joke, it looks so unnatural at the end of a fourteen-year-old's arm, but then they see his eyes. There's nothing there. If there was ever a human being in there, he's gone now. Then comes the first shot.

BANG

The second and third.

BANG BANG

And everyone screams. Runs. Flees toward the shower room and bathrooms. Anywhere. They crouch down beneath basins and behind doors. No one who is there will forget how it feels when you stop believing that you're going to die and start knowing that it's happening right now. Now it's over. So many people say that your life passes before your eyes, but for most of us we only have time to think about such small things: a single person. A small hand in ours. A giggle. Breath against the palm of our hand.

BANG

Mumble knows he's going to die. He's the one Matteo is aiming at. Mumble realizes that it's all over the moment the boy walks in so he just sits still and screws his eyes shut and hopes it will be quick. That it won't hurt too much. It doesn't hurt at all. He waits for his chest to explode and for his body to slump to the ground, but nothing happens. When he opens his eyes there's blood everywhere and there are two bodies lying on the floor.

Alicia is moving around the locker room like a small but persistent fart. Questions, questions, questions. A top she wants signed, a sort of skate she wants to know more about, a way of binding a hockey stick that she wants to know the secret behind. She gets a hug from Amat and looks like she might faint. Benji is sitting on a bench on the other side of the locker room, He's relaxed, leaning back, almost on the point of dozing off. He doesn't notice Matteo walk in. He doesn't see Alicia standing in the middle of the floor. Right in front of Mumble.

BANG

Hannah is at the hospital. She doesn't hear the cries in the corridor, doesn't know that the alarm has come from the ice rink, where her family is, doesn't hear something breaking in her colleagues' voices. A splinter of glass in the soul of every nurse and doctor who passes the information on. Hannah doesn't even know it's happening, because she's in here doing her job. Twice, in fact.

It's like a cruel joke, as if God wants to point out that He can do what He likes with us. Unless this is the opposite: His penance.

As two cherished lives end over in the ice rink, the twins' hearts start to beat in Hannah's arms. Two childhoods begin. Beep-bo. Tickles and helpless giggling. Climbing trees. Puddles and boots that are too big. Ice on the lake. A million ice creams. Whisper-shouts from parents on the phone when you're playing with a ball indoors. Swings. Best friends. First love.

This day brings incomprehensible violence and incredible mercy. The greatest fear, the smallest people. Everything belongs to us.

How are we to talk about Alicia?

All our stories are about her, of course. All the ones that end here, all the ones that begin here, she has been the reason for all of them.

BANG

Matteo stands in the doorway and she doesn't understand what he's holding in his hand. She just sees the darkness, it comes like smoke and envelops her, she just hears the sound of screaming and noise of things crashing over. All the men around her run.

BANG BANG

The first shot goes too high. The recoil is too sharp and Matteo's hands are shaking too much, so he lowers the weapon and squeezes the trigger again. The second and third shots hit home. Right in the chest. The body is dead before it hits the ground.

BANG

All the men in the locker room run. Some toward the bathrooms, some toward the shower room, some try to crawl out through the window. All except Benji. Because he's the sort of person who runs toward fire.

He always has been.

Ana's dad rushes across the parking lot toward the emergency exit and peers breathlessly into the gloom. He sees Matteo fire his first shot into the locker room, sees him walk into the room to fire again, but then someone flies into him from inside the room with all his strength. Matteo tumbles back out into the corridor again with a much larger body on top of him.

BANG BANG

Those are the two shots that take Benji's life. Both to the heart. What else could they have hit in there? He was all heart. Matteo heaves his body aside and jumps up to his feet again, aiming wildly around him to carry on killing.

We will say it couldn't possibly have happened the way the police and the media describe. We will say that no one could possibly have hit at that distance, under those circumstances, not even the most exceptional marksman could have done that. Not even the very best hunter in the whole of Beartown, we will swear. That isn't true.

Ana is on her feet in the stands and hears the first shot. Like everyone else, she thinks it's kids letting off firecrackers. Then she hears the screaming and from the angle she has when she stands on her seat, she can just make out the corridor down by the boards, and the door to the locker room. She sees when Benji throws himself straight out through it, right at the pistol, and tackles Matteo to the ground. The following two shots go right through his heart, right through his body, right through the ceiling. When Matteo gets to his feet again the next shot hits him in the head. Ana doesn't even need to see who fired to know. No one else could have done that.

She runs straight toward the emergency exit where she knows her dad is standing with his rifle in his hands. Matteo is dead before his body hits the floor.

But so is Benji.

Everyone who knew Benjamin Ovich, particularly those of us who knew him well enough to call him Benji, would have wished him a really long story. A secure life. A happy ending. We hoped, oh, how we hoped, but deep down we probably knew that he wasn't the sort who would get that. Because he was always the sort of person who stood in the way, the sort who protected, the sort who ran. He always thought he was the bad guy in all stories, the real heroes always do, that's why stories about boys like him never end with them growing old. Stories about boys like him only end with us no longer dreaming of time machines, because if one was ever invented in the distant future, it would already have been used to travel back here by someone who loved him.

There are so many of us.

We can't fight against evil. That's the most unbearable thing about the world we have built. Evil can't be eradicated, can't be locked up, the more violence we use against it, the stronger it becomes when it seeps out under doors and through keyholes. It can never disappear because it grows inside us, sometimes even in the best of us, sometimes even in fourteen-year-olds. We have no weapons against it. We have only been given love as a gift in order to cope with it.

Everyone is running in different directions, trying to find a way out. But Ana and Maya stumble down the stands and force their way through the crowd, when Maya's foot gets caught and she screams, Ana throws everything and everyone around her out of the way until she's free, then they rush toward the locker room. The first people they see in the corridor are Amat and Bobo, covered in Benji's blood. Bobo is holding his friend in his arms and rocking him as if he were merely sleeping. But he's gone. He no longer exists.

There are thousands of things Maya's instincts are yelling at her to do just then, but all she hears is the scream. Not her own, but a little girl's. She's standing three yards behind Benji's body and just screaming and screaming and screaming. No one seems to hear. Everyone is so paralyzed, they're just staring at the blood and the bodies, no one sees the child. Perhaps Maya sees herself in Alicia. Perhaps this is the moment when she becomes an adult, she doesn't know. But instead of kneeling beside Benji like everyone else, she picks Alicia up out of the chaos and runs, out through the emergency exit, past Ana's dad, out into the parking lot and on into the forest. She sits there keeping the girl hidden in her embrace so she can cry and scream without having to see what's happening in the ice rink. Maya just wants to protect her from the blood and the images and the memories, that's all she's thinking, she doesn't even let her own brain absorb the fact that Benji is dead. It's impossible. "Protect the child, protect the child" is all she's thinking. Perhaps there are more men with guns in there, perhaps there will be more shots, so protect the child protect the child protect the child. People come rushing out into the parking lot. Screams and sirens pierce the last streaks of daylight. Maya wishes she could stop shaking, she wishes she could hold the girl tighter, that she could hug away all the shock and despair and all the terrible darkness that will never leave either of them now. But she doesn't know how, she isn't big enough, isn't strong enough. She can't breathe, she's gasping for air, trying to think away the blood and death on the floor in there and she needs to be strong for the child's sake. But how do you do that? Where do you find the strength? She doesn't have it. She's certain she's going to collapse on the ground in the snow when she feels two arms around her own shoulders. It's her mother. Kira didn't run toward the fire, she ran after the children. Behind her comes Tess and soon other women will come, from all directions, in red and green jackets, some even in black. They wrap their arms around each other, in circles, ring after ring, forming a wall around Alicia.

Nothing that happens to the girl in the rest of her life will ever be worse than this. But in the very worst moment, in the midst of the greatest terror, mothers and big sisters from the whole forest ran here to protect her.

No one can fight against evil. But if it wants to take Alicia, it's going to have to go through every last one of them first.

Almost everyone runs as if they don't understand what's happening. Adri Ovich runs as if she already knows.

Words? There are no words for this.

Everything is just shock.
Everything is just darkness.
Everything is just empty.

We have gotten used to so many types of violence, but we could never foresee this one. This one we will never understand. This one we will never get over. Adri picks up her brother and he feels so small in her arms. She carries him out of the ice rink and the whole town stops breathing. A hole in every heart.

How will the sun rise tomorrow? How can daylight still exist? What is the point?

Lev is out of his car before it's even stopped moving. Ana's dad is standing on his own by the emergency exit with his rifle in his hands. Everyone is screaming inside. It doesn't take Lev many seconds to understand what has happened when he sees the blood and the bodies on the floor. He sees the pistol, he could rush over and snatch it up because it's the only thing that could be traced back to the scrapyard and him. But he has too much to regret now, too many sleepless nights ahead of him with Matteo's face in the darkness. Good people can be capable of great evil, and evil people can be capable of great good. So instead of thinking about saving himself Lev turns around and saves someone else. He sees Ana come running over, so he grabs hold of the hunter beside him and asks:

"Your daughter?"

Ana's dad nods, confused, as if he's lost consciousness but his body hasn't realized it yet. Lev waves hysterically to get her to come over to them, and Ana runs, jumping over the blood. She will never forget that, never forgive herself for that. Even if Benji is dead, even if she did it to protect the living, even if it's what he would have wanted her to do.

Neither she nor her dad really know who Lev is. They've heard the rumors, like everyone else, but that's all. He doesn't seem to be in shock, perhaps the only person who isn't, he's seen too much in other forests.

"YOUR CAR? WHICH ONE IS YOUR CAR, YES?" he yells.

Only then does Ana understand what he's thinking, what she needs to do to help, and how badly this could end for her dad if she doesn't. She grabs her dad and drags him like an overgrown child across the parking lot, he's already crying but she can't allow herself that luxury. She drives, he sits beside her, Lev follows them. They stop in the forest, down by the lake where no one can see them from the road, Ana fetches tools from the back of the truck and they work together to make holes in the ice. A lot of holes, all spread out. Then they dismantle the rifle and scatter the pieces in different parts of the lake.

Then they drive to Ana's dad's house, where Lev goes straight into the kitchen without asking permission. The dogs sniff curiously but don't stop him. He searches the cupboards and finds hidden bottles of drink that Ana's dad had hoped his daughter wouldn't pour away so that he has enough ammunition for a relapse.

"Drink, yes?" Lev says, and starts pouring three glasses.

"Are you totally fucking mad? Are you going to start DRINKING now when it's too fu . . . ," Ana snaps, but Lev just hands her the glass and replies:

"What do the police call it? 'Alibi,' yes? Alibi. We were never at the ice rink. We were here, yes? We were drunk. Your dad can't shoot anyone drunk, yes? Alibi."

Ana and her dad breathe out in a single long sigh of melancholy as they accept his reasoning. They have no other choice. Then they empty their glasses. Lev pours more alibi. They say nothing at all, and are soon drinking alone: Lev sits on the floor in the hall, her dad sits in his chair by the fire, Ana in the kitchen. She cries and cries and cries, and this is the last time she gets drunk.

She has never had any idea what job she wants to do, but now she will spend her life trying to save others people's. She doesn't know that yet, but this is where it starts, because she couldn't save Benji's. So she can't afford to drink from now on. She loves her dad, but she can't risk turning into the sort of person who falls asleep in a chair in front of the fire the next time someone bangs on the door in the middle of a storm. The next time someone cries for help. The next time she might be able to save the world.

———

"What an incredible place this is, in spite of everything," Maya's mom once said. Her dad replied: "What's incredible is that it's still here. That there are still people here."

Maya will remember how incomprehensible it was that the sun even rose on the day after Benji's death. That she was still alive. That she kept going. But she understands her parents, for the first time, really understands them. How they learned to cry inwardly when Isak died. Silently, silently they cried for years so that Maya and Leo wouldn't hear. How the very air must have hurt their skin. How they must have wanted to lie down with their cheeks to the ground and whisper into the grass to the child beneath it. How they must have hated themselves for not being able to die with him.

How many of all the things they have done since then have been their attempts to achieve something important, something grand, something worth getting to Heaven late for? Almost everything.

It's unbearable that the sun rises again, that Maya is here and not Benji, for the rest of her life she will stop almost daily and think: "Would he be proud of me? Have I lived a worthy life? Been a good enough person?" Because of course that's all she is, all everyone she grew up with in Beartown is: hopelessly simple but horribly complicated. Ordinary, unusual people. Unusually ordinary people. We try to just live our lives, live with each other, live with ourselves. Accepting joy when we find it, bearing grief when it finds us, and being amazed at our children's happiness without falling apart when we think that we can never really protect them.

Maya has never felt that she belonged here, but this place finally belongs to her more than anyone else. The little town in the big forest. She will talk about the people here with her back straight, her voice steady, will say that most of us don't want anything remarkable: a job, a home, good schools. Long walks with the dog. The elk hunt. A cup of coffee at the start of the day and a cold beer at the end of it. A good laugh. Nice neighbors. Safe streets to cycle on. A lake where you can learn to skate in winter and sit in a boat for nine hours and catch zero fish in the summer. Snowball fights. Trees to climb. A new hockey season. All that. That's all we demand.

She will say that people around her love a simple game, even those of us who don't love it at all. A stick each, two goals, us against you. *Bang bang bang*. She will say that we're just trying to live, damn it. Live in spite of each other. Live for each other.

Live on.

Soon millions of people will know Maya's name, but every night she will only be singing for Benji. Not all her songs will be about him, but they will all be his, somehow, even the ones that are Ana's. One evening, several years from now, Maya will be so famous that she'll be performing in one of the biggest arenas in the whole country. It will be sold out. The first time she steps out into it she will realize what it is used for when concerts aren't being held there. It's an ice rink. It's the biggest moment in her career, and she cries her way through every song.

105

Trees

When Benji is buried, it isn't in a church with open doors but under the bare sky. Two entire towns turn up. The notification in the newspaper is superfluous, everyone knows the time and the place already, even the factory closes, but beneath Benji's name is printed what everyone is feeling:

This hurts too much to touch with words.

It was the man at the undertakers' who showed the quotation to the Ovich sisters. "My favorite poet, Bodil Malmsten," the man said, a little embarrassed at his own declaration of love. Now she's the Ovich sisters' favorite poet too.

Their brother is laid to rest beside their father, not far from Ramona and Vidar. Around here we usually say that we bury our children under our most beautiful trees, but not even the best among us can find a tree beautiful enough to watch over Benjamin Ovich. So we grow new ones, all around the stone bearing his name, we let Alicia and other children plant them in the soil so that they grow up around him. Until he is no longer sleeping in a churchyard, but where he was always safest and happiest. In a forest.

Words?

This hurts too much.

Alicia comes to the funeral hand-in-hand with Adri and Sune. When she sees Maya she lets go of them and runs, not for her own sake but for Maya's.

"Are you scared?" the girl asks.

"Very scared. And very sad," Maya replies with her eyes buried in the girl's hair.

"Is Benji scared, do you think? Will it be dark and cold down there in the ground?" Alicia asks.

"No, no, Benji isn't scared. He isn't even here," Maya replies.

"Isn't he?" Alicia wonders, with her first smile in thousands of breaths.

Maya blinks a million times.

"He's on the ice somewhere laughing now. He's playing hockey with his best friends. He's lying on his back looking at the stars. He isn't scared. In a hundred years you'll see him again, and tell him about all the things you've done. All about your fantastic life. All your adventures. He'll look forward to that."

When Alicia runs back to Adri, Maya sits in a corner of the church and writes on her arm with a pen. She fills her skin. Then she asks Benji's mom and sisters if she can sing at the funeral. She stands on the church steps. The forest has never been as silent as it is then. Slowly, slowly, everything she wants to say to him leaves her:

Are you scared? Someone who loves you wanted to know.
I said: Oh no—he's in a different form though
Because the grave's only a place for memory
The earth around his coffin isn't where he'll be.
Where you are now I cannot say
You're not here, you've gone away.
There's a folding chair by the water and there
I think you sit and laugh and feel a love so rare.
There's ice around your island, you've got your skates,
There goes a boy whose beauty never fades.
You're playing a game, don't even feel cold,
There plays a boy who'll never grow old.
You're everything you wanted to be
You're safe and happy, wild and free.

I don't know where you are now my friend
But in a hundred years we'll meet again.

———

There are many types of leadership. The one we find easiest to admire is, of course, always the one that involves having the courage to lead your followers out into the unknown, bravely going where no one else has gone, upward, forward. But what helps, more than anything, to take Beartown back to mornings where we can breathe again at all after all that has happened is something far less conspicuous. Bobo and Amat lead all the players on the A-team out into the town and they gather the children together. They play and they play and they play. In the ice rink, on the lake, in yards between apartment blocks. They play and they play and they play. It's the only cure they know, the only way they know how to make the world a little better.

Big City goes with them, silent at first but soon something else, something new for him: he becomes the sort of person who talks. Puts a hand on a shoulder, picks up someone who's fallen, carries someone who's gotten hurt. As time goes on he starts to realize that when he sets off the others follow, rather than the other way around. In other teams he was always notorious for being complicated and peculiar and disloyal. Here he becomes the opposite.

One evening when they are playing with the children the parents stay and watch. The following evening one dad asks if he can join in. Soon everyone is playing, everywhere.

It's that sort of town, where everything can change and the people can be transformed. Where we find the strength to play even though our lungs are screaming. Possibly because we're used to withstanding the darkness, both inside and outside. Possibly because we live close to wilderness. But perhaps most of all because, just like everyone else in every other place: If we don't have tomorrow, what's the alternative?

There are many types of leadership, the sort Big City, Amat, and Bobo demonstrate this year isn't the sort that goes forward, but rather goes backward. Back to everything we are. Sometimes the greatest leadership is knowing the way home.

———

A few months from now, Hannah will be holding a newborn baby again. It is a good day, it's incredible that days like this will ever happen again, but they do. She goes home and packs a picnic together with Tess. Johnny is repairing the van down at the fire station with Lev's spare parts and Bobo's help. When they're done they go out into the yard in front of the fire station with all the other firemen and have a snowball fight with their children and younger brothers and sisters.

Tobias is there, he already looks like a fireman, he's going to be exactly like his dad, so his dad is trying to be as good as he can possibly be. Tess will move away from here in a few years' time, but she'll come home again in the end. She's too much forest folk for other places, but she doesn't know that until she sees the world.

One evening Ted's coach calls to tell Johnny and Hannah that he's started to get calls from coaches from bigger clubs, men from hockey academies and even a few agents, to ask questions about Ted. The coach says his parents "should be prepared for the lad's life to change." Ted is one of the brightest talents Hed has seen. One day he will be the best.

Johnny spends hours in the kitchen after that, looking at the whiskey in a glass that's really a tea light holder. He doesn't touch it. Instead he gets in his car and drives to Beartown. Knocks on a door. Eats croissants in Peter's kitchen and confesses in a low voice:

"People are saying my boy could go a long way. Maybe all the way. I was just wondering if you have any . . . advice."

Peter shakes his head apologetically.

"I don't think I can give you any advice about his career. I don't know anything about money and contracts and all that. But I can give you the phone numbers of some old friends of mine, they can . . ."

The fireman on the other side of the table looks up, his eyes glossy with uncertainty. He sounds very small when he whispers:

"No . . . no . . . I don't mean like that. I didn't mean advice for him. I mean for me. I need to know what I have to do to be a good dad. I want to know what you wish you could have had back when you were his age, when your phone started to ring . . ."

Peter is silent for a long time. Then he talks more about his childhood than he has done with any other man. A few years later Ted becomes the youngest team captain in Hed's history. A few years after that he becomes a team captain in the NHL. When he is asked by a reporter where he thinks he got his leadership qualities from, he will reply simply:

"From home."

———

Teemu and other black jackets are going to the hockey games again. Are singing again. Always with slightly heavier voices and a greater sense of loss now, always with a beer in their hands after the game when they walk all the way to the churchyard. Then they sit there and talk to Vidar and Benji and Ramona and Holger and all the others who couldn't come, so they know how it went. Every detail. Every shot. Every goal and every wrong decision by the referee. The beer in Heaven is expensive and the whining is the same as always, hardly anything changes, but one day Teemu brings his newborn son here and introduces him.

His son will grow up and decide that he doesn't like hockey, he likes soccer, and there's a hell of a lot of laughter in Heaven then. Oh, so much laughter.

Elisabeth Zackell becomes a famous coach. She wins hundreds of games. She wins leagues, titles, and trophies. The only thing she never really wins back is that first, uncomplicated joy. Hockey never really becomes a game for her again. But one day in many years' time she will coach a national team, the one Alicia plays on, and then Zackell will make an exception to her strictest rule.

She lets someone play with the number 16 again. For one single game. Alicia gets up from the bench in the locker room and leads her team out and storms the ice, and Zackell watches her and for a single moment forgets that it isn't him.

———

Leo spends several days sitting in his room after Benji's funeral, with his headphones on, inside his game. He plays and plays and waits the way he has done, night after night, for a particular name to appear on the screen. For a player he has never met in real life but encountered here so many times in recent months that it now feels as if they know each other. That stranger has killed Leo every time, almost as if he sought him out every day and hunted him down. Leo can't let go of the desire get him back. If he's just a bit quicker, a bit more focused, he's sure he can get the bastard. Whoever he is.

But his opponent never shows up. Never again. Leo will never know why, but for years, long after he has stopped playing this game, he will log on from time to time just to look for that particular username. If he had looked it up online perhaps he would have found a page in a foreign language that explained that the username is the literal meaning of the name "Matteo." But he never does.

There's a knock on the door to his room. Maya is standing there with her guitar in her hand.

"Can I come in?" she asks quietly, the way he always did when he crept to her room when he was younger after he had a nightmare.

He nods, of course. She sits down on his bed and plays her guitar and he sits in front of his computer and plays his game. It's the last night before she goes back to music college. She will be alone down there for a while, she will be angry and she will write some of the best songs she has ever written.

"I'm proud of you," she whispers to her brother.

"I'm proud of you too," he whispers back.

Leo will do great things in life, he will go far and give her every reason to really be proud of him. She's just being proud in advance. That's the job of big sisters.

When the two Andersson siblings have families and children of their own, one night they will sit in a house much like this one, a Christmas Eve when the generations above and below them have all gone to bed, and they will talk about the people they might have become if their circumstances had been worse. Just a little worse. If they had been born a little poorer. Been hit a little harder, a little earlier, by how violent people can be. If they hadn't had a mom and a dad who would fight anyone for their sake, who would rush through the forest and take on hooligans, the whole town if they had to. Who never gave up, who only backed away when they were getting ready to attack, who knew no limits when it came to what they were prepared to do to protect their children. Even when they knew it wasn't really possible.

Leo will smile and pat his sister's hair gently.

"Without Mom and Dad? You'd have been fine. You're a survivor. But me? I wouldn't have stood a chance."

———

The police never find the rifle that killed Matteo. No one manages to prove where the pistol that killed Benji came from either. The police go door-to-door from one end of Beartown to the far side of Hed, but no one says anything. There will be one or two people around here who will be happy to point out to the authorities after the event that they put more effort into tracking down that rifle than anything else. As if the man who killed a murderer with a hunting rifle was a bigger criminal than the man who gave the murderer an illegal smuggled pistol in the first place.

The trouble between us and those who aren't from around here never really stops. We're that sort of town too.

———

Lev carries on living in Hed. Running his scrapyard. Every winter he travels to another forest far away, with his cases full of toys and cuddly animals. There he drinks strong liquor out of small glasses with his nieces, and plays hockey with their children.

All the things people say about him are true. This part as well. That's why he fits in so well in the towns deep among the trees. They're also capable of being both their best and their worst at the same time.

Perhaps it is grief that brings Tails down. Or perhaps his conscience finally catches up with him. Richard Theo goes to see him a week after the funeral and tells him about a series of articles that the local paper is about to publish. It will uncover a corruption scandal that will crush Theo's political opponents but spare the hockey clubs and Peter Andersson. Theo has built an alliance of businessmen who find him useful and politicians who are scared of him. He's untouchable. But sadly, he explains with what appears to be genuine sympathy, not all of his political allies accept that the hockey clubs should get away entirely scot-free. Everyone needs a small victory, he says. Everyone needs to feel that they've won something. So Theo suggests the simplest solution: give them a few of the contracts Peter signed. Not the ones concerning the training facility, not the very worst ones, just the basic graft so they can feel that they're uncovering something. But then, of course, a scapegoat will be required, and if it isn't going to be Peter, then the story needs to be told in such a way that someone is revealed as having deceived him. Theo holds his arms out amiably:

"I suggest Ramona. She's already gone now anyway. And from what I've heard of her, I can't imagine she'd have anything against being used to save Peter Andersson. If we pin the blame on her, the whole scandal will be forgotten in a couple of weeks and everyone can carry on as if nothing happened."

Tails sits at his desk and looks at his hands for a long time. Then he whispers:

"Peter was my best friend all through my childhood, did you know that? He was so good even before he went to the NHL that opposing players who came here for games would sometimes ask for his autograph for their younger siblings. So I learned to imitate his signature, so I could sell 'signed' photographs without him knowing about it. I can still do an almost perfect imitation of his handwriting."

Theo sits with his eyebrows raised and a look of confusion that's extremely unusual for him.

"What are you saying?"

Tails replies calmly:

"I'm saying that we do as you suggest. We give the paper and your political allies a small victory. We give them some of the contracts and say Peter was tricked. But not by Ramona. I'm going to say it was me who signed those contracts in his name."

Richard Theo looks both appalled and impressed. By the time the story reaches the local paper it has already been leaked to the police. Tails is convicted of fraud. He is sentenced to a few months in prison. He doesn't let anyone take even a fraction of the blame. When he gets out he goes straight home to Beartown and starts building, but not Beartown Business Park or a fancy training facility next to the ice rink, as he had planned. Instead he helps his best friend from childhood build a cathedral. Tails pays for the roof with his own money, he works on it with his own two hands, and afterward he and Peter drink beer sitting right at the top while a hundred kids play down below. It's a simple little ice box, not a luxurious rink, it's reminiscent of the one the factory workers built in Beartown three-quarters of a century ago when they founded the club. When there was nothing but storms and longing around here, love and dreams, hope and struggle. The Cathedral isn't much to look at, it really isn't, but it's the start of something.

It wouldn't have been completed without Tails's help, but no one apart from Peter knows how great his contribution was. Tails never tells anyone. That's his atonement.

———

The editor in chief and her dad go away on holiday. She takes him with her to the sun. They eat good food and take long walks, look at churches, and fall asleep on shaded terraces. It's their last trip together. Her dad passes away not long after that. The editor in chief returns to Beartown and Hed, but soon moves on to work for larger papers in bigger places. She gets more power. It takes a while, longer than she would have liked, but one day she gets the chance to take on Richard Theo. She grabs it.

He too is living in a larger town by then, sitting on higher pedestals, which makes the fall all the harder. In the end she digs up so many scandals about him that she destroys his whole career and ruins him.

She doesn't do it for justice. Nor even for the satisfaction. She does it because she can. She does it because people like him shouldn't always be allowed to win.

———

Amat makes it to the NHL in the end. The night when he scores his first goal the whole of Beartown is awake, despite the time difference. In fact the whole of Hed is probably awake too. And if they aren't, they probably get woken up when Amat scores and the whole damn Hollow explodes.

———

A few years from now, far away from here, a young man will be sitting on a sofa at a party. Everyone around him will be dancing and drinking but his eyes will be glued to the television. It's just a short clip from a concert by one of the country's most famous female performers right now. Her name is Maya Andersson, and the young man has always loved that name. How ordinary it sounds. He's never thought about her accent, has never reflected upon why it sounds so familiar to him. But now he sees her on television and she's singing a song about someone she loved, because it's his birthday, and on the huge screen behind her a photograph of him flashes up for a moment. She knows no one will really see it, a thousand more images flash past right after it, she just included that particular photograph for her own sake.

But the man on the sofa recognizes it. Because he remembers fingertips and glances. Beer bottles on a worn bar counter and smoke in a silent forest. The way the snow feels as it falls on your skin while a boy with sad eyes and a wild heart teaches you to skate.

The man on the sofa packs almost nothing. He takes just a light bag and the case containing his bass guitar and travels to the next town on Maya's tour. He elbows his way past her security guard and almost gets knocked to the floor, and he calls out:

"I knew him! I knew Benji! I loved him too!"

Maya stops mid-stride. They look each other in the eye and see only him, the boy in the forest, sad and wild.

"Do you play?" Maya asks.

"I'm a bass player," he says.

From then on he is her bass player. No one plays her songs like he does. No one else cries as much each night.

———

Mumble plays hockey. That's all anyone will ever really remember him doing. He's either at the ice rink or at home with his mother. He never tells anyone who Matteo's bullets were really meant for. How could he explain? Who would let him say all he needed to? He's too scared. Too small. So he says nothing, upsets no one, lives his life quietly and tries to save every puck each time Beartown Hockey puts him on goal. The crowd loves him, the people in the seats as well as those in the standing area, and in many ways he becomes one of the club's true legends. He never plays for any other club, only here, he becomes more bear than anyone else. He was born in Hed, but Beartown becomes his place on earth. When he eventually has to stop playing hockey as a result of an injury he is a little over thirty, and half a lifetime has passed since the event he has spent every day trying to forget happened. He has played every minute as if he is trying to be forgiven. As if he could just be good enough and valuable enough, and possibly even a little loved, to somehow be able to live a life without always feeling that he doesn't deserve it. He plays as if the ice is a time machine. It never is. The club hoists his jersey up into the roof of the rink and thanks him with a grand ceremony after his final game. The following day he climbs on board a bus with a large hockey bag over his shoulder. He travels many miles to another town, walks through it until he reaches a small cemetery, then moves through the gravestones until he reaches a small, ignored memorial tucked away in a corner. It's positioned beneath a beautiful tree, the sort that gives protection in winter and shade in the summer. Mumble clears the weeds from around it, and lays flowers beneath the name "Matteo." No surname, because his parents were too scared that the people who can never stop hating him would come and vandalize the grave even though it's a long way from Beartown. Mumble traces the letters with his fingers and whispers:

"Forgive me. You should have lived my life. Forgive me . . ."

Then he opens his hockey bag and loads the rifle that's inside it. He wipes the tears, picks up the rifle, and goes into the forest.

Is that punishment enough? No one can answer that. No one will know.

———

What is life, other than moments? What is laughter, other than a small victory over sorrow? A single moment, just one, when everything inside us isn't broken.

There's a tentative knock on the door of the house where Ruth and Matteo grew up. When their parents open the door, the old couple from next door are standing there. The woman is holding an apple pie, the man a flask. He says quietly, perhaps embarrassed about how little he knows about the people who live only one fence away:

"You can talk if you'd like to. We can sit quietly if you'd rather. But we thought it might be good not to be alone."

They sit in the little living room.

"So many beautiful books," the old woman from next door says.

"I'm better at reading than living," Ruth and Matteo's dad whispers.

A little later there's another knock on the door. Outside stands the priest who buried their daughter. They didn't dare bury Matteo in the same churchyard. The priest comes anyway. That's a special kind of job, but also a special sort of person. They sit in the living room and the priest's eyes wander slowly over the spines of the books.

"I see a Bible there. May I read something from it?"

Ruth and Matteo's mother stands up and takes it out and hands it over, her whole body shaking. The priest holds her hand and reads from the fifth chapter of Matthew's gospel:

Blessed are they that mourn, for they shall be comforted.
Blessed are the meek, for they shall inherit the earth.
Blessed are the merciful, for they shall obtain mercy.

From further down the same page, the priest reads:

A city that is set on a hill cannot be hid.
Neither do men light a candle and put it under a bushel,
But on a candlestick;
And it giveth light unto all that are in the house.
Let your light so shine before men,
That they may see your good works.

Ruth and Matteo's parents devote the rest of their lives to charitable work. They move to the other side of the world, work hard in poor villages, and build things for others. The largest of all is a children's home. Every morning they wake up and think they can hear their own children laughing. Just for a moment.

The little house where Ruth and Matteo grew up stands empty for several years. But in the fullness of time it fills with people again. A young couple renovate it, plank by plank, until almost everything is new. Their twins play in the yard. The neighbors make small talk over the fence. Hockey pucks get fired at the wall.

———

Benji's mom's life goes on, arduous but uncompromising. It has to, the days don't wait for us. She has grandchildren, that saves her, grandchildren don't wait either. Birthdays and summer holidays and Christmas Eves and scrapes and gnat bites and giggling. Ice creams to be eaten; skates to be skated on; wonderful, magical adventures to be experienced. And eventually enough time has passed for it to hurt only almost all the time. She has endured. She can miss him without screaming every time. Hug without crying all the time. Laugh without always feeling guilty.

Life goes on. It doesn't give us any other choice.

———

Alicia has a bed she sleeps in, a place where she lives, but she's hardly ever there. She is either at Sune's or Adri's. She grows up in three homes, one very bad one but two really great ones. Besides, she has the ice rink, people who love her, and a sport that worships her. Benji's mom and sisters hug out all their grief for him until it becomes merely whispers of love for her. Like small diamonds made from coal.

Alicia comes home to Sune one day with a puppy Adri has given her. The girl explains very firmly that it's her dog, no one else's, but that it has to live at Sune's.

"I have to go to school and I have to train! And I can't leave the dog all on its own then! So you're just going to have to help!" she declares.

"I see. Yes, I see. Well, I suppose that's what will have to happen," the old man nods.

"Can I have jam sandwiches?" Alicia asks.

Of course she can. As many as she wants.

———

The Ovich sisters visit Benji's grave every day. If he had been there, he would have said that they talk to him more now than they did when he was alive. Whenever they think that, they want to hit him, and that's when they miss him most of all.

They carry on running the Bearskin pub, even if everyone just calls it "Benji's" these days. There's no sign outside. There's no need. They honor Ramona's tradition of simple beer and bad food, at least to start with, then the food gradually gets better because Katia, unlike Ramona, knows how to use a cookbook. Gaby's children do their homework in the bar, she worries about being a terrible mother half the time, but when they grow up they will tell her that they wouldn't swap the way they were raised for anything. Their aunt Adri is mostly responsible for threatening to punch men in the face or actually punching men in the face, depending on the time of day. Teemu and a few of the other black jackets come in one day and offer the sisters a new billiard table that "fell off the back of a truck." They carry it in and some of the biggest idiots in the Pack try to play a couple of times, but naturally they're so hopeless that Adri contemplates burning the thing just to put an end to their torment. But then, early one afternoon when she's on her own cleaning up in the bar, there's a knock on the door. A group of young boys are standing outside, eager and naive, asking if they can play billiards for a while. She lets them in. They don't go home until she drags them out. They come back the moment she opens the next day. She heats up microwave pizza for them and they play and play and get better and better. She wouldn't be surprised if one of them ends up being world champion one day.

This is that sort of town, it really is.

———

It's Ana's birthday. She's not expecting anyone to remember, but her dad is sober and has been up all night decorating the whole ground floor with balloons. The dogs have popped every single one. Ana has never felt so loved.

The doorbell rings and Hannah is standing outside. Tess is waiting shyly a little way behind her. The van is parked by the fence.

"This is for you," Hannah says, with eyes she has to blink the tenderness out of.

It's a voucher for driving lessons. Ana laughs for a long time. Then Hannah asks if Ana and her dad would like to go on a "research trip," so they do. Her dad hasn't even forgotten to take his rifle out of the pickup. They drive several hours to a larger town. Far enough for there to be a college, but close enough for Ana, if she gets a driver's license, to be able to live at home and commute to college. Hannah clears her throat and says:

"This is . . . well . . . it's a small college. Possibly not what everyone dreams of. Tess didn't want to come here because the law course isn't good enough, but maybe for you . . . well . . . I just mean: they have a course in *midwifery* here. You need to become a nurse first. But I can help you. I can . . . I *want* to help you. If you'd like that."

Tess stands beside them rolling her eyes at her mother. Ana doesn't quite know what to say. She isn't like Maya, she doesn't know how to use words to get them to say what she wants. So she goes to the car and fetches a large envelope and hands it awkwardly to Hannah, looking everywhere except into her eyes.

"It's just a stupid thing. I made a Mother's Day card every year at school after Mom died because all the other kids did, but I never had anyone to give mine to. But I thought, you help all mothers, so . . . fuck. Does that sound stupid or weird?"

Hannah can't get a single word out, so Tess has to step over and say:

"No, Ana. It isn't stupid. It's lovely. You're lovely!"

Ana looks in one direction and Hannah looks in the other, and neither of them knows what to do with all the stuff you just carry around all your life without anyone seeing. There's a hospital a stone's throw from the college, and they're both very relieved when someone over at the entrance suddenly starts shouting:

"This needs to move! It's blocking the ambulances!"

It's a nurse, not altogether unlike Hannah, angry as a whole hive of bees. Right in front of the entrance is a truck and trailer, it turns out that the man who drove it there had acute appendicitis the whole way. Getting a taxi was out of the question, of course, did they think he was made of money? But he wasn't able to park the truck properly when he arrived and tumbled out of the cab, exhausted and in severe pain. So it's been left there. The nurse is yelling at a security guard, who replies:

"You think I can drive a truck? Are you mad? Who the hell can do that?"

So Ana steps forward and says:

"I can."

The guard, a man in his best years with his life's worst hairline, turns around scornfully:

"YOU can? A truck and trailer? YOU can drive that?"

Ana merely shrugs her shoulders but her dad replies firmly behind her:

"My daughter can drive anything, Give her the keys."

The guard just scratches his chin at first, then his jaw drops. Hannah and Tess stand and watch, neither of them has ever seen anyone reverse-park a truck and trailer before. When Ana jumps out the guard calls out a compliment that no one hears because his voice is drowned out by a roaring sound. A hacking, thunderous, whirring sound that fills the air and sends shock waves across the grass. Ana tilts her head back and looks up, then she runs over to Hannah and tugs at her arm and yells:

"Hannah? What do I need to study to be able to drive one of THOSE?"

Hannah looks up at the sky and smiles as her eyes follow the helicopter ambulance. It flies to those who need it, those who are injured and those who are crying for help, and those no one else can reach. It flies where no one else dare go. Right into fire, if necessary.

———

Maya sings for thousands of people in hundreds of arenas over the years when she's grown up, but mostly she sings for herself and the best friends she had as a child. One day Ana takes her up in the helicopter, rising straight up into the sky. They take the girls with them, the girls they used to be, two laughing kids they wish they could go back in time and protect. They pick them up off the ground in the forest and hide them inside their jackets and the rotor blades spin and they fly far above the earth. High and free.

Just one single time, ten years after the rape, Maya sees Kevin again. She's just getting out of her tour bus in an arena parking lot, he's just been shopping in a mall nearby with his wife. He's reversing a rusty little car, and when he turns around he catches sight of Maya through the windshield. He's put weight on, looks different now, softer, more uncertain. His wife is pregnant. She has her hand on his, and looks happy. He's built a whole new life. Can he be allowed to do that?

Maya fixes him with her gaze. He is so shocked that he stops the car abruptly. For Maya the incident only lasts a few seconds, but for him it never ends. Then she turns away and walks toward the arena she's going to be singing in that evening. The bass player is waiting a short distance away.

"Who was that?" he will ask.

"No one," she will reply, and mean it.

She doesn't forgive, doesn't forget, but she doesn't use violence just because she can. She doesn't destroy Kevin's life even though he deserves it. She spares him.

But Kevin's wife will ask him who that woman was. Kevin takes a series of terror-filled breaths, but eventually he is too weighed down to carry the lies, so he whispers the truth. Everything. The whole of the reality he has constructed since that night in Beartown collapses around him inside that car. He loses everything.

Can he be forgiven? Can he be spared? Allowed to have a life?

That's something for other people to argue about now. Maya is already flying high above it all.

————

Spring comes, and summer. It's almost unbearable. But then autumn arrives, as brief as the blink of an eye, before winter finally hits us again. Life doesn't go on, it starts again, everything is possible once more. Anything can happen, all the best and all the most beautiful and all the biggest adventures in the world.

Early, early in the morning the caretaker opens the door to the ice rink and turns the lights on. Alicia looks so lonely and small as she skates out onto the ice, but she isn't, she's bigger than everyone and never alone again. She lies down in the center circle and looks up at the roof. When she closes her eyes and reaches out her fingers she hurts in so many places inside, but there and then she doesn't feel anything, because Benji is lying beside her and soon a new hockey season will begin and everything can still be okay. Throughout the whole of her long career, in every ice rink and in every national game, she will do the same thing every time she gets scared or nervous: look up at the roof, reach out her hand, feel that he is there. Because Benjamin Ovich isn't in a grave. Benjamin Ovich is at the game with his best friend.

In the stands sit the caretaker and Sune and Adri, and the whole rink smells of cherry blossom. It's easy to love hockey then, because hockey isn't the past, it isn't yesterday, it's always next. The next change of line, the next game, the next season, the next generation, the next magical moment when something we didn't think was possible becomes a miracle. The next chance to fly up from your seat and yell with joy. Next.

One day Alicia will be the best in the world. She comes from a town with grief in its heart and violence in the air, and she has "Ovich" on her back, she doesn't skate onto the ice, she takes it by storm. Good luck trying to stop her.

Every time she scores, all the people who have loved her leave the ground, and for a few blessed moments it feels like all the sacrifices were worthwhile. This is life. One day she will come back here and teach other kids how to skate. One day she will be the one who is Spider-Man and Wonder Woman.

Her hundred years will be our very best, most loved, most told story. And that says a hell of a lot, because we're a hockey town. We have nothing but stories here. But all our stories have really only been about one thing: ever since the very first, about a boy who made it all the way from here to the NHL and came back with his family, about his daughter who found the best friend in the world, about a terrible crime and love that was like organ donation. About tears and struggle, about hugs and laughter, about a stage and a guitar and thousands of people in the audience. About a boy who was born in a place that had never seen ice but who one day could move faster on skates than anyone else, about other children who became the best in other ways, about the boy who became a coach and the ones who became parents and the girl who flies a helicopter to save the whole world. About a young man who could never see himself as a hero but who died like one, who ran toward fire to save a child. About families and friends. About climbing trees and adventures. About a vast forest and two small towns and all the people here who are just trying to live their lives. Sit in a boat. Tell lies. Catch zero fish.

All of this has been about the same thing: Alicia. Every person we have talked about, every story we've been told, every single one leads to her. This is where all the others end. This is where hers begins.

One day she will make us feel like winners again.

Because she's the bear.

The bear from Beartown.